Islands

Islands

Dan Sleigh

Translated from the Afrikaans by
André Brink

Secker & Warburg
LONDON

Published by Secker and Warburg 2004

First published in South Africa by Tafelberg as *Eilande* in 2002

2 4 6 8 10 9 7 5 3 1

Copyright © Dan Sleigh 2002

English translation © André Brink 2004

Endpapers: Kraal and Castle by A. Bogaert, from *Historische Reize
in d'Oosterche deelenvan Azia* (E2751). Cape Town Archives Repository

First published in Great Britain in 2004 by
Secker & Warburg
Random House, 20 Vauxhall Bridge Road,
London SW1V 2SA

Random House Australia (Pty) Limited
20 Alfred Street, Milsons Point, Sydney,
New South Wales 2061, Australia

Random House New Zealand Limited
18 Poland Road, Glenfield,
Auckland 10, New Zealand

Random House (Pty) Limited
Endulini, 5A Jubilee Road, Parktown 2193, South Africa

The Random House Group Limited Reg. No. 954009
http://www.randomhouse.co.uk

A CIP catalogue record for this book is available from the British Library

ISBN 0 436 20620 X (hardback)
0 436 20632 3 (trade paperback)

Papers used by Random House are natural, recyclable products made from wood grown in
sustainable forests; the manufacturing processes conform to the environmental
regulations of the country of origin

Typeset by Palimpsest Book Production Limited,
Polmont, Stirlingshire
Printed and bound in Great Britain by
Clays Ltd, St Ives plc

For Michel and Peggy Espitalier-Noël

Contents

Voices from the Sea

. . . darkness was upon the face of the deep

SEVEN OF US, or at least seven, carried in our hearts the same woman, from before her birth until after her death. Loved her? About that I cannot say. I know the word exists, and the heart will doubtlessly have a name for it, but its interpretation remains an uncharted bay every man must fathom for himself. Most of us sail in, hoping for good bottom where we can rest and refresh ourselves, then discovering that there are strange and unexpected currents, that the tides change from moon to moon, and the inhabitants are not always friendly. That much we know. Others, like Daniel Zaaijman, who will produce his own story, may be able to say with more certainty. Or perhaps not. Loved! Which of us would admit as much, if it were so? We were soldiers, a herds-man, sailors, a clerk, people with little emotion in our speech and very, very little emotion in our lives, apart from fear and rage.

The seven I know were her father, Peter Havgard, and after him Hans Michiel, the soldier in front of whom she grew up. Then Bart, the fisherman, her stepfather. Then Advocate Deneyn, more learned than most, but the one whose sounding of the uncharted anchorage I trust least. After him the cooper Daniel, who married her till death. Most certainly Jan Vos too, like a slave bent over his labour, and possibly Sven Telleson, of lowly birth and ruined by drink. And I, the clerk, who cannot explain how I feel about her. Impossible? I never met her; it is a yearning only, but yearning is a sentiment, a dream, and cannot be love. How can one like me be sure? I find myself in front of the image of a woman, and ask, Who are you? I go on a journey and find another image of the same person, painted by someone else, and ask again, And you? Ahead of me lies another road, another bridge, another inn with a chapel, once more the same image, again the question.

It is men I tell about. I chose those who carried her in their hearts, from before her birth until after her end. They helped to keep the small raft afloat. Until after her death, and the obligation became mine, since people only really die when they are no longer remembered.

And at last the sea, the green womb-water in which we drift, and drifted once. Deep inside it lives the worm Leviathan, and on it, or cast up beside it, people like foam. They call from the sea, and it is her name I hear: mother of many, friend of sinners and stranded souls, our daughter, friend. Autshumao too calls from the sea. It is those I tell about.

1

THE REMAKING OF CHIEF HARRY

ONE RED DAWN, ten or twelve years before the Dutchman started building this place, Autshumao became leader of the Goringhaicona. He
walked across the dunes to the sea, as if he'd never known the dead
or the living behind him. He was covered in blood, robbed, humiliated, as he walked in the half-dawn from the smouldering stubble of
burnt grass beside a vlei, under the bitter smoke of charred matting
and cattle hides, followed by five children, five women and two old
men. Behind them in the smoking rubble were their dead, ahead of
them was the sea. They were leaving with empty hands. There was no
mat or pot or digging stick to take, no ox or sheep, no milk-bag or
throwing stick or dog. The others, the old men and the women, dragged
bodies into a cold ditch and covered them with branches. Because they
were scared of abandoning this place, the old people burrowed in ashes
and rubble, saying a few words, and later followed Autshumao across
the low dunes to the sea. The sea was open, and its openness was a
kind of security. But he was the first to leave from there, to get away
from where he had lost everything.

On the beach he stopped for the woman who was carrying his sister's
child, and continued with the child on his back. He called her his sister's
child; her name was Krotoa. He owed it to her to carry her; a child
should rely on help from her mother's brother. He took her and carried
her, that girl, but he did not ask anyone to go with him. When they
came near the sea the child was crying inconsolably, and a woman took
her to her dry breast. Autshumao did not take the girl back. Looking
over the twelve people he thought of how he'd never asked them to

follow him or threatened them to obey him. He hadn't promised them anything. They had simply followed him and he had become the leader of the Goringhaicona.

There were few of them, and with sea-stuff and food from the veld they could manage for a while. In the hollows among the front dunes, that very day, they chopped *harubis* with stone, tearing the reeds with nails and teeth, and tied it into mats with rope from rolled grass, and the mats into houses, and set up the houses in a circle among the dunes, surrounded by a kraal of berry-thorn branches.

The thirteen of them, the last of the Goringhaicona, lived apart from the rest of the Koina, between the dunes and the sea, poverty-stricken and mostly ravaged with hunger. The sea gave them its fish and meat, the plain behind the dunes, its meagre wild fruits. Autshumao carried in his heart his longing for cattle and sheep, but he was wary of acquiring cattle. Cattle were clothes and food, and medicine, that was what cattle were, but he had to do without. He was man-alone, it was safer not to own anything. Never again could he put fat and cream on the fire to go up in smoke to Heitsi-Eib'. In order to have peace around him he had to live without Heitsi-Eib'.

At the end of that winter the Goringhaiqua brought their herds of cattle from the Sand Veld to graze in the water pastures along the rivers. Autshumao climbed a hill to check on how many animals his enemies had gained, because without fail so many head of cattle pushed war out ahead of them. From the smoke of his enemies' transition fires, heavy and reeking with cream and fat, he could smell that they were prospering. It was good to see their mottled white-and-brown cattle standing in the shiny water, and the young herders playing on the grass. Cattle meant power; you could rise up and hit out as you wish, against whomever you wish. He tried to discover his own animals among the strange herds, but couldn't see them.

Still, at the sea there occasionally was a touch of luck for Autshumao and the Goringhaicona. In a sandy bay near the watering place, white sailors would drag out their boats from time to time. English sailors, their language and their red-striped flag told him. Autshumao received clothes and bread as payment for accepting a letter in safekeeping, and in exchange offered them honey, a tortoise, some ostrich feathers in friendship. Sometimes they were given tobacco. That was why Autshumao chose those low dunes as a place to live, because it was near the watering place and opposite the deep where the ships came to lie. That was the roadstead.

Autshumao and those with him would argue fiercely among themselves about the odds and ends of clothing and ship's food that came their way, but the brandy was for him only. He had himself rowed on board to eat and drink, and if a turning tide or a change in the wind made it necessary for him to return to shore, he made sure that his hands were empty before he reached his people. Where there is hunger, poverty is generally peaceful.

He was no longer a young man. Once, his stomach filled with bread and brandy, he had been sitting on deck in the winter sun talking to the sailors, and then grew sleepy from the gentle rolling and the hollow booming of the sea against the hull, and on that day the ship *London* had left with him, off to the Orient. All the skipper said was, 'Sorry, old chap. Didn't you notice the weather changing? I have to use this breeze to get off a lee shore. But in a few months' time I'll bring you home again.'

It had been a big ship, not as big as some he'd seen under the Dutch flag, but decorated with red and a touch of gold on the transom and along the railings, and around the gallery windows. Below deck two rows of black cannon lay like sleeping dogs behind closed red gates. On that voyage Autshumao had contracted the seamen's diseases, learned their language, and became Chief Harry. You might hunt him anywhere, Autshumao was no longer there, the ship had carried him to the Orient. Only his heart had turned back early, and went home alone. On that voyage he'd also lost his respect for iron and copper, since it was so cheap and plentiful that the English threw it away. He himself would never accept iron as barter again – his enemies could covet iron, his own time for iron was past. Cattle were money, cattle were food, medicine, beasts of burden, a herd of young hunters, a host of armed warriors. Even Heitsi-Eib' had to wait.

In the Orient he'd seen, when sometimes the ship had been moored to a quay in a river mouth, how dark men with gowns and long hair would stretch their necks like gannets on a rock to talk up to the ship. Their air was dusty since early morning, their seawater tepid, the food strongly spiced, the stars alien. Thunderclouds would come up every day, and disperse again before dark after heavy rain. Dun-coloured cattle with drooping ears would wander among the people, mainly dried cows and heifers, disconsolate animals without a bull, and lean oxen pulling carts. And there'd be beggars stretching their hands towards him, but because the land folk drove them away from the quay with stones he would shake his head at them. So poverty existed on both sides of the big sea; he was not alone. He'd seen the English trading with the people of the land. Money changed hands, never drink or tobacco.

Behind each quay lay a town, behind each town a green jungle like a wall, behind the jungle there would sometimes be mountain peaks, and behind the mountains the thunder. He stopped looking at it. What was there to see? Those were not the dunes and clumps of reeds of his home. Sometimes shouted threats were exchanged between ship and quay. Then once again the sea. The drinking water was insipid, it caused his stomach to run for days and nights, with blood and pain. He became listless, sitting on deck, smoking and yearning for drink. He felt no inclination to go ashore, but remained restlessly on board, listening to the grinding of the ship against the quay and the anxious creaking of the masts, like old skeletons complaining below ground. Then they would sail on again, and at first there would be sea, blue and deep for days on end, and then there would be land.

Autshumao's thoughts were with the people he had left behind, with his sister's child. The world over things were changing. People he had known were dead. Would Gogosoa, the fat murderer, be thinking that from now on his cattle would graze alone in the water pastures? He hadn't seen yet how the white people's ships were approaching from all sides, and how they were building stone houses wherever they came ashore. Strange nations would come to live on Gogosoa's grazing; it was their children who would occupy his land. He could see that in future times it might be better for the Koina to remain friends with the whites, at first to help tend the enemy's animals and children. Better that way, because the white man would rule and his livestock would fill these parts, from the Cape all the way up the coast as far as the Cochoqua, the Grigriqua, and, in the opposite direction, over the mountain towards the sun: the Chainouqua, the Hessequa and the Attaqua, and across the green hills to the Gouri and the Inqua of the forest. Everywhere the white man's livestock would be grazing. For the favour of keeping a few cattle of their own, and a chance to build up their strength, the Koina had to keep the peace with them. That way it would be better for the Koina, who had to greet the new rulers without guns and horses.

Such were Autshumao's thoughts, even before a single Hollander had stuck a spade into Cape soil. Only, he was expecting that it would be the English who would be doing it, not the Dutch; for the ships of the English were criss-crossing the seas, they would meet each other by appointment, at places in the middle of the ocean where there was no sign of which one could say: At such-and-such a place we shall meet on such-and-such a day. And he could hear the English talking about the food and water and firewood of the Cape: 'My dear fellow, a simple takeover. No trouble at all.' One simply pushed away the stinkers, and took over land, water, trees and grass. 'The natives are harmless. Like children, really.'

The colour of the sea turned green again. Autshumao, *Chief Harry*, spent the last days of his months at sea through the steaming tropics on his back, his body pressed against the gunwale so that the sailors wouldn't step on him, and his face turned away from the gaping hatch in the deck. When he opened his eyes he could see red paint on English oak; when he closed them, there was his niece, and behind her a pale yellow mat of thin reeds in the curve of a *harubis* house. In his long dream, going on for days and nights, he could smell dry reeds, and cold ashes among the stones, and cow dung.

At night, like most sailors in the tropics, he remained on deck, until near the end of their journey the evening air turned cool and dew was shimmering on the deck and rigging in the false dawn. At night the golden stars hung in a dense weave over them. The thin black fingers of the masts were probing tentatively among them, moved them from one spot to the next, gathering golden stars from the deep blue night, removing others, shifting, shifting, until one night the new sky was complete. He gazed in wonder at the frothing Milky Way. For the first time he knew without any doubt where he was, in which season of the year – that was how far the moon had already wandered across the sky – and which wild fruits would be ripe by now, and how green the pastures, and where the Koina's camps and flocks would be by this time.

The sailors of the watch looked how Chief Harry got up from under his blanket, and clambered up the shrouds until he found a foothold in the crosstrees of the mainmast. Below him the ship went on digging its face into the flickering water before swinging it out and up like a drinking bull, but Chief Harry climbed higher up the rigging, until he could step on to the maintop yard. With his arms around the mast and his face to the night wind he examined the darkness ahead. He could see nothing but the teeming stars and the slight flickering of phosphorescence far in front of the bows, hear nothing but the groaning of wood and the creaking of new cordage stretching across blocks, and the hissing and churning of seawater along the length of the ship, smell nothing but a cool sea wind reeking of tar and linseed oil as it swept across the deck. With a sigh he recognised in the shimmering field of stars the southern cross, only half risen above the horizon, and he knew for sure that the Cape dunes stretched fresh and fragrant with herbs and shrubs ahead in the glittering night. *Heitse!*

When he arrived home, there was nothing to be slaughtered. Some of his women had left of their own free will to go to the Goringhaiqua. The two old men were dead, or had been left somewhere for dead, but other old people had joined the group, men and women who had grown thin after the loss of their close relatives. He told them that his new name was Chief Harry, but they wouldn't believe him. For all his stories, about people riding on elephants, and all his English, he might just as well have said, Listen, an earwig crawled into my head while I was asleep, and I'm seeing and speaking crazy things before I die. So they didn't ask him any questions. It wasn't necessary.

His sister's child was scared of him, and the deaf woman who looked after her kept the child away from him. It annoyed him and he brought the child sweet things, but they made her ill and the deaf woman loudly blamed him. He also started talking about moving camp, and pulled up sticks and rolled up mats until the others did the same, and then he would move a hundred yards this way or that way and plant his sticks in the ground again. The old men and the women patiently followed him over those little distances. He knew they would get up and go when he asked.

Their meagre food was gathered from icy rock pools at low tide. Sometimes there was a seal on the beach, dead for days, covered with sand lice and deeply corroded by crabs and gulls. But in his camp Chief Harry spoke of cattle and saw in their faces the yearning appear for sour milk, butter, meat, and the dark, heavy smoke for Heitsi-Eib'. He spoke of sheep until their eyes shone with expectation, and of cattle: the hides for shoes and caps, a skin-bag, the tuft of the tail for a fly-switch. Blood, pots filled with blood, he mentioned. By the nodding of his handful of indigents Chief Harry knew that he had won their hearts. Memories of good times invariably revolved round cattle: young heifers, cows with huge udders, or a black bull with a heavy chest and narrow hips, or thirty, forty red fighting oxen with wide horns like the open pincers of scorpions. Autshumao's dream caused old people to see their sons and daughters again, remember huts beside shining vleis where they once lived, pots filled with sour milk. Only the deaf woman didn't hear him, and the two of them stared away together at the endless movement of the sea. They spoke of cattle, but the cattle stayed away; some of his people died in that expectation. Old age and cold moved in among the group. No children were born. Only his sister's child was left now.

In late summer and late winter, when the seasons changed and the wind came from a different direction, there were ships. Then they would bring their bundles of firewood, or a skin-bag filled with honey, to the watering place and receive ship's bread and tobacco in exchange. Chief Harry used his English and would be rowed to the ship. Usually there would be a letter. 'Give it safely to the first Englishman that comes here. I wrote in here that he must pay you.' But the stingy Dutch hid their letters under rocks and left a message on the rock, and then Chief Harry would remove the letters and personally hand them over to the next Hollander. He had to make a living.

More new ships arrived in the bay, new flags and new tongues. Swaggering, the white people walked among the bushes and smelled and plucked and tasted. They did not ask Chief Harry about the wood or the mountain. Six or seven men with guns and a glass would go up the mountain to study the land. From up the slope there would be the sound of their axes where they were chopping wood for masts, three or four trees at a time. They also went right past him to discuss animals for slaughtering with the Goringhaiqua at the vleis, and for that they gave his enemies brandy and tobacco. He knew the sailors would want to lie with women, but all he had with him was old women and his sister's child. Yet he was surprised to see among his people new beads or clothes he didn't know about.

A strange thing happened: some of Gogosoa's people forgot about cattle and came to live with Chief Harry. They would have to live sparingly, but they were willing to do that, provided they could be close when the boats were rowed ashore. For them drink was the new way of remaking, but for him it was a new cause of concern, these vultures descending on a bit of tobacco and drink. He himself coveted it. His people already had to walk for half a day to collect firewood, and soon enough Gogosoa's whole horde would descend on these low dunes to kill them, and chase them off from this place too, just for the taste of tobacco and brandy. Chief Harry heard rumours that Gogosoa's women offered their bodies in exchange for drink. This was a new thing that was beginning. What was to become of him?

He made no attempt to rule over the growing, unruly crowd who had come to plant their sticks for homes among the dunes next to his Goringhaicona. He didn't want them. All he had left to barter was his English. He could feel his dream of many cattle fade away; even his desire for them was fading. If the English came to build stone houses at the watering place, he would be the first to pull up sticks to go and live with them.

He had his niece with him, but there was nothing he could do for her. When the time came for her transition feast, he would take her to her father's people across the mountain, so that they could do the slaughtering her age required. After him, they were her closest relatives. Or if they would not acknowledge her, then on to her sister, old Oedasoa's wife. And perhaps, should she choose to remain here with the English, when she was big enough to look after infants, she could go into their homes to look after their children, instead of staying among the dunes like the others, yearning after little beads.

As a man without cattle or sons, Autshumao knew that the Koina looked down on him. The deaf woman regarded him as a castrated dog without a home. She, who had lost everything, had undergone the rites of transition no fewer than four times: at her birth, when she became a woman, when she got married, when she had her first child. And every time animals had been slaughtered for her. He knew of others like him, for whom nothing had ever been slaughtered, and who now had to stick together so that the wild dogs would not find them alone, all old people with empty stomachs and empty, hopeless hearts.

Among the English he had seen that one could compare life with the steep shrouds of a ship. Each was a step to the next: one climbed for some distance along the foreshroud, then you reached the foreyard where you would rest; then you went higher up the foretopshroud and you reached the foretopyard; and once again you climbed until you arrived high on the foretopgallant under the truck of the mast. From there you can only look up to the sky, or down to minute figures trapped on a ship in the limitless ocean. He, with his grey hair, had only climbed the first two steps of life. And perhaps this was the new way of doing, that youngsters also abandon their leader and forget about cattle, living without any rites of transition.

Then a miraculous thing happened, as if a new sun had risen over the land. He knew how the sun could dry out, scorch, burn and consume the world, but what came into his mind on that late autumn day was a bright happiness, like a light shining in the night. They stood up to their knees in the low tide, among the glistening wet rocks covered with seaweed and smallish black mussels, shivering with cold. Behind them a strong southerly wind was driving the endless low grey cloud over the mountain, and its cold shadow spread across the bay and the dunes and the scrubland. Then they saw two ships from the East moving into the bay.

They came up from the windward side of the island, and were loaded deep. Ivory, pepper and cinnamon, blue-painted pottery and sweet aniseed arrack, that Chief Harry knew, all tightly packed and sealed in the hold. The wind pushed the ships deep, deep into the bay, and fast, so that they'd reached the opposite shore before they let go their sails. There they turned to come up to the anchoring place, but one ship was pushed back by the wind, as if a man had placed his hand in a child's face and shoved it away. The ship tried to turn its head this way and that to get loose, but the wind had it in its grip, holding it, and forcing it backwards, a bowshot inside the breaking surf, against a sand-bank. One could see the smoke of cannon shots jumping from the sides of the ship as they tried to break loose from the sand. The other ship heard it, turned back and started running anxiously to and fro, like a guinea fowl in front of its wounded mate. Chief Harry stood up to his hips in cold water, staring, and thinking: the wind will carry the sound of the shots far to the north across the scrubland, all the way to where at this time of the year, before the rains, the Goringhaiqua would be moving slowly towards their winter pastures, and if they were to turn back because of the sound it would be like a swarm of locusts descending on that small stretch of beach, to scavenge whatever the sea would wash out.

They boiled the black mussels and ate the white ones uncooked, and left some of the women and children empty-handed at the huts, so that Gogosoa's people wouldn't find anything there, as in the early dusk they hurriedly and expectantly started moving up along the beach. Ahead of them, the ship was clearly stuck, toppled over on its side against the shore. Waves were breaking over its hull causing clouds of white water to fly over it like gusts of rain. The other ship lay on three anchors far beyond the breakers. There were boats in the water around both ships, rowers pulling ferociously at the oars. When the Goringhaicona kindled their night fire they could see on the beach in front of them the bright orange sun of another huge fire, the sign of invaders cooking their first meal in a strange land.

The next day they discovered that it was a Dutch ship. They wanted to go closer, but armed sailors moved in between them and the wreck. The beach was littered with stuff washed out. Chief Harry called out to them in English that he would show them where to draw water. A Hollander replied: Yes, water, but also meat and wood. Chief Harry would trek up the coast to try and get meat from his old enemies, the Cochoqua, but first he wanted to find out what the Dutch were prepared to offer. They were generous: they would give him arrack, rice and copper. If Herrie — no Chief Harry to the Dutch — would provide them with firewood every day, and a sheep once a week, they could eat and drink. The ship's cargo had to be salvaged, they said. They would be settling here to guard their cargo until help arrived. Herrie had to keep his womenfolk away from here; his men, the man said, would be severely punished if they lay with Herrie's women.

Chief Harry asked the man in English, 'Are all the women in your land whores then?' All of this just because the man had talked about women, for he wasn't sure where this might lead to in future. He considered giving the man a sheep filled with poison, or mussels harvested in a red tide; he also had in mind taking his people away from here, and inciting the Grigriqua or the Obiqua, who didn't distinguish between hunting and murdering, to attack these sailors at night and kill them all. Chief Harry turned his thoughts over in his mind while the Dutchman was shouting at his men to hurry up with the salvaging, for there was a spring tide coming and a fortune in pepper on board. Then he replied politely in English: That is fine, if the Dutchman kept his men in check the women wouldn't give any trouble. What was more, they could give a hand carrying the stuff washed out while the Hollanders put up their homes. He pointed around him, to hundreds of wet-brown pieces of flotsam littering the beach to the high-water mark at the foot of the dunes, and how more of it came riding out on every wave.

And so it happened; when Chief Harry and his handful of men went back to the low dunes to dismantle their homes and fetch their women, in order to move to where the ship *Nieuwe Haerlem* sat stuck in the sand like a dead whale, they found new beads in brightly coloured strings for necks and arms, and an empty wine flask among the cooking things. Yes, that was one thing about the Dutch, they were there now and needed water and wood, and for that they brought beads. The wine was for having shown the Dutch where to draw water.

At the Hollanders' camp this was the rule: first work, then eat. Because everything was new to the Goringhaicona, they enjoyed gathering in front of the store tent to see what would be unpacked next from the chests, or otherwise they would hold on to the flaps of the cooking tent like a child on its mother's dress. The cook's cleaver, his knives, his food raw and cooked, disappeared in this way. Which was why the rule was made about first working, then eating. These people and those had to gather firewood, those and those had to find green provisions for the pot, and cut bedding-shrub to sleep on, those and those had to lug wreckage from the beach to the pepper tent among the dunes. Chief Harry showed them a sluggish spring, and the Dutch dug there and discovered good water, and he showed them the Reed Vlei and all of them together dragged a net through the water and caught a multitude of fish. The Goringhaicona ate well in that place, and picked up weight, each of them was sporting one or two items of Dutch clothing, and tobacco was no longer scarce. Those times were among the best his people had ever known, and they feared the day the Dutch would sail away. When other Koina with sheep turned up near the camp, the Goringhaicona would retreat in among the Dutch. In that way the Hollanders could tell when strange Koina were coming.

They learned each other's language. The Dutch couldn't distinguish between the many clicks or imitate them, but they could memorise a few names, and most of the Goringhaicona picked up Dutch words. The one who learned the most was little Krotoa. She was six years old, and like other children picked up a new language with ease. She would spend all day with the cook. She helped to scour the pots with handfuls of wet sand, and when they were alone one could hear her prattling non-stop, but when the leader of the Dutch were to ask her to translate a message to her uncle, she was too shy. The cook made her stand, with a spoon in her hand, beside a large pot which she had to stir, and fed her with the choicest morsels and spoiled her with sweets meant for the officers. Perhaps he was the one who gave her the name of Eva, because she generally went about naked. What is certain, is that he was the first of all the white men in her life with whom she became friends. There was no need for him ever to doubt her love, the child's eyes were shining with happiness. Regrettably, it was also the cook who prepared veld fruits for her, boiled up with sweet ginger, and who let her taste sweetbread with a syrup of aniseed arrack. From the goodness of his heart, there is no doubt about that either, but since then there was a yearning in her for the cosy kitchens of white people, and the sweetmeats they prepared. And it is difficult to believe that all she cared for were a spoonful of sugar, a gulp of beer, or the bread and cheese she might expect.

After eleven months ships came from the East to pick up the Hollanders and their stowed spices. The Dutchman told Chief Harry: 'Well, Herrie, the time has come for us to go. I shall tell my superiors that you helped to look after the Company's possessions, and that this is a good place for ships. I will suggest to them to come and set up a place here to supply our ships with fuel and water. Then there will always be Hollanders here.'

'Won't the English come again?'

'They will. But I want us to be the first to build here. We shall hoist our flag, then it becomes our place. And if the English need something, they'll have to buy it from us.'

Chief Harry looked about him in silence. Always Hollanders here? Then they'd start getting the wood and water ready for their ships themselves. The whole world would be made different. What would become of him and the child?

After that the world became different. A flag was planted, and from one full moon to the next the ships got their wood and water. Boats with food, salvaged goods and barrels of water moved to and fro over the sea. The sailors were on land with hatchets, saws and water barrels. Some had permission to wash themselves below the watering place, where they combed lice from bodies and beards, and there Chief Harry showed them how to spread their clothes on an anthill, so that the ants could catch the lice. On the even patch behind the watering place officers took measurements. They planted a stick with a white cloth and paced in one direction, piled up rocks, then returned to the stick and started pacing in the opposite direction. A man with a book and a pencil followed. In the end there were many cairns among the shrubs and flattened molehills. Chief Harry could discover no shape or pattern in it. He couldn't understand what the officers were saying. And he felt he ought to be doing something with his English. If the Dutch were coming to settle here, he'd be worth less to them than his sister's child.

The Goringhaiqua arrived there like a swarm of locusts driven by the wind, with a lot of noise and a small number of cattle for tobacco. Already they were walking with empty bone-pipes in their mouths, hissing through them like lynxes. When they noticed the Goringhaicona among the Hollanders, they started stirring up trouble and throwing stones, and the women fled in behind the soldiers from where they provoked the Goringhaiqua with gestures. Chief Harry took the child by the hand and stood back, towards the beach, towards open space. His people withdrew after him. The Dutch couldn't understand why there should be ill feelings between the two small groups of Hottentots, but for the future shipping service it was of no consequence.

When Krotoa was about ten or eleven, something else happened to change the world. A few shiploads of Hollanders with wide breeches made their appearance and threw down planks and spars and bolts of canvas on the grass at the watering place, and carried ashore barrels and boxes and baskets with saplings, and pigs and dogs and poultry in cages. So that was to become the shop. Chief Harry strolled among the foreigners and their piles of baggage. He would like to meet the chief of the Hollanders. But his dog attempted to mate with a bitch belonging to the white people, and when a soldier took aim with a gun at his red dog, Chief Harry, out of pure fright, brought down his stick on the man's hand. Only his age saved him from receiving a few blows, because the soldier's curses and vociferous threats and his grip on the old man's kaross showed that he'd really been hurt.

A short dark-skinned man wearing a blue cloak touched the soldier's arm with his cane, and said to Chief Harry, 'Go away.' But he followed Chief Harry all the way to the beach. They looked at each other and introduced themselves.

'Chief Harry.' He spoke English only.

'I am Chief van Riebeeck. I have heard of you. You are *Strandlopers*, Beachrangers.'

'Goringhaicona. Watermen, in English.'

'First work, then eat. That was *Haerlem*'s rule. Right?'

'Yes.'

'Come and show me where the people from *Haerlem* stacked their beacons, the cairns.'

They were all overgrown with dogweed and stinkweed, except for one to which the Koina had from time added more stones until it was now three or four times its original size. Van Riebeeck walked around the cairn. What could be the meaning of it? With the eye he measured distances in four directions, then walked over there and kicked the small beacons from under the bushes. Then he called a man with a spade and had pegs driven in and ropes strung between them, and he had the luggage transported from the dunes to the large cairn. Then he took Chief Harry aside, as if to discuss affairs of state with him.

'Could you find us cattle and sheep?'

'Sheep, yes. Cattle, no. The Koina keep their cattle for themselves.'

'I'll need oxen to pull our wagons. What is that big cairn for?'

When he couldn't get an answer, van Riebeeck asked, with an eye on the group of Koina women, 'That little girl there, can she look after children?'

'Yes.'

'Her wages: tobacco and arrack and bread?'

'Yes.'

'You will have to get your dog fixed, you hear? Or leave him at home. Do you think you can find us cattle?'

'This is my dog's home,' Chief Harry said. And in his mind he could hear the Dutchman reply: We shall see.

'Your people over there, would they be willing to work? Tobacco and brandy?'

That day, the first day of the new world, they helped to carry the mountains of baggage the boats had brought on shore. In the afternoon the Hollanders sat down to eat the food that had been brought from the ships in baskets. The Koina were not invited. Was it thrift? Chief Harry was wondering whether he would ever gain something from these foreigners. But after the meal the Hollanders were liberal in their distribution of wine. On their empty stomachs the Goringhaicona found that it went straight to their heads, encouraging them into a shuffling dance. Then the Dutchman blew a whistle. Their people went back to work: digging foundations, carrying up baggage, hammering together tent frames and covering them with canvas. The Goringhaicona noticed that the tide was ebbing and it was time to gather food for their evening meal. Chief Harry went to van Riebeeck to ask for their wages. It was just enough to assuage the first desire for tobacco and stir up the next.

The Goringhaicona among the dunes on the far side of the bay must have seen the ships and the smoke of many fires near the sea, because one morning at first light they turned up with cattle. One could hear them coming a long way off. From the dune Chief Harry could see dust over the bushes. The approaching cattle had already passed the vleis. Then he spied the movement of backs and horns in the distance. There were fewer than thirty of them, accompanied by eight or ten men walking alongside, whistling and swinging sticks and *kieries*. That was what Chief Harry heard as he turned his ear to the morning. And here were the cattle van Riebeeck had been waiting for. It was dumb of old Gogosoa to let his cattle go, for cattle could buy anything. Why did the murderer let his cattle go, unless he was so rich that cattle had become like firewood to him? Cattle! Without cattle a man was nothing. He had to get hold of cattle, for the world was changing rapidly and here he still was with empty hands. When he died one day, there would have to be a slaughtering to celebrate his last transition, and a hide in which to wrap him and put him away. But if he were killed today, he would be as naked as his dog.

He remained standing upright, allowing the young men to come past with the cattle, all of them young oxen. The boys, impatient, with cold bone-pipes in their mouths in anticipation of tobacco, were driving the animals too fast. The oxen voided a green stream of excrement on their heels. Yes, that was what the white man's drink and tobacco were doing. No Koina, driving cattle away from drought, or herding them against lions and wild dogs at night, would subject his animals to that. It was the white man's cursed tobacco and beads that caused the young to disregard their cattle.

Autshumao stood upright beside his enemies to make sure he would be seen. He felt like shouting something, an admonition or a warning, but he didn't. And the boys were blowing a hissing sound through their empty pipes and rattled their sticks and *kieries* like men going to war, and driving the panting cattle past with a slapping of horns, but they didn't give him a second look. They were past warning.

Chief Harry avoided the workplace; he didn't want to be there when those youngsters returned, drunk, on the way back. He was thinking that the boys – not quite men yet – would be willing to work for the Dutch all day, breaking firewood, packing a kraal of branches, carrying baggage, or doing any other jobs in exchange for drink. But all they really did there was barter, from hand to hand, without discussion, and turned back with their treasure in their knapsacks and walked away from there without looking back at their precious cattle. The smoke of their tobacco was already twirling up, skyward. That same morning the first ox was brought down in the Dutch camp and butchered without joy. He walked up the side of the mountain and watched the Hollanders abandoning other work so that they could first stack a kraal of branches. They were cattle owners now. In the eyes of the world they were people of note. They could make thongs, slaughter, produce smoke for Heitsi-Eib', barter, eat, go through the rituals of transition, tan hides, prepare medicine, they could talk about the grass and the water, and cause others to make way if the grazing here became too cramped or too bad.

In the beginning the Dutch used canvas and wood for their building, and while living in that shelter they made excavations for the foundations of a large fortress which slowly rose from the sand and clay where the cairn of the Koina used to stand. A deep and wide trench was dug around it. That first winter of the new world it rained every day, the trench was filled with water and broke through to the sea, and the young turnips and cauliflower were washed from the vegetable beds by that same stream.

Van Riebeeck spared no one, he made them dig, throw up mounds and dykes to stop the water, trenches to carry off the streams, trenches to keep out the wild buck, until his vegetable garden was stronger than the winter itself. All that time Chief Harry and his people sat in misery around smoking fires of green wood in their reed homes along the dunes. Van Riebeeck refused to give them food. 'First work, then eat. That's the law of *Haerlem*.' His own people were ill and he tried to employ the Koina in the garden, but failed. He tried with tobacco, but no, the people couldn't handle a spade.

It was a bad winter for the Goringhaicona. Firewood had become scarce. The sea was too rough for venturing out on the rocks, and it was too early in the season for wild bulbs and roots. Some of the older people died there of cold and hunger, and were laid away among the dunes, unaccompanied by any slaughtering. It wasn't even possible for the survivors to move away from that place according to their custom.

Their fire remained cold. There was nothing but smoke, barely the flicker of a flame down on the stones among the green wood. Chief Harry inhaled the bitter smoke and believed that this would warm him, but his mind was running away from him, and sometimes he had to wake himself, jerking his neck and shoulders to avoid falling over in his cold sleep. The deaf woman lived between two other people, deep in her kaross. Behind the veils of smoke only a bundle of old skins was visible. Close to death, she sat rocking backwards and forwards; if she were to fall asleep, she would tumble into eternity.

Chief Harry touched her with his fly-whisk, and pulled her kaross when she wouldn't wake up. An old tortoise face appeared between her forearms, and he gestured with his hands: 'The child, Krotoa.'

The slits of her eyes were fixed on his mouth. 'What about the child?'

'She can find work with the Hollanders.'

Her face disappeared backwards through the fold of her kaross. 'That's your thirst speaking, Autshumao,' she whispered faintly from the dark slit.

There had never been such a cold winter, without meat, without a piece of fish. He put out an arm and lifted the reed mat to look out: through the grey rain he could see the black mass of the Fort crouched behind the dunes. Inside, there were fires, and there were cattle and sheep in their stables. Who could be the enemies of the Dutch? If some of the English were to come back he would show them where the Hollanders' cattle were grazing. Biding your time, it would be possible to take these people's cattle. *Haerlem*'s law, said the Dutch: work first, then eat. The world was blanked out by the rain; later it would become a green year, with cattle grazing up to their knees in clover. He looked around him. He was cold to his very marrow.

The child, dazed with smoke, was lying with half-open eyes on bedding-shrub against the wall. Chief Harry thought: The best one could hope for, was to die in your sleep. Shut your door, light a green-wood fire, wait, wait, wait, then go without pain. Smoke is the blessing of the poor. He touched the child with his wet hand. Her breath was feeble in the front of her mouth. Slowly he brought her back, but she was unwilling. He pulled up her limp body by an arm, to make her sit. Chief Harry called out loudly at the child. Three old women were squatting hunched up around the fire, rocking dreamily, one of them waking up with a start, an eye gleaming in the black slit of her kaross.

'What are you doing with the child?' she groaned, dismayed.

'We have to eat.'

'You can go and work for them.'

'Their cattle are kept in a stable. There are soldiers keeping watch. Do you want me to go and look after infants in the Fort?' He helped Krotoa to her feet, and hung her kaross around her, with the hair inside.

'Come, Krotoa. We're going to the Hollanders. There's a good fire in their house, and they'll give you sweetmeats to eat every day. Do you remember their white bread with fig syrup, and sweet tea? That's what the big captain will give you in a blue basin.'

The circle of old vultures around the fire woke up, whining in a thin chorus: 'What are you doing with the child?'

'Must she die here? There's food with the Dutch.'

'To what calamity are you dragging her? And who will tend the fire in here?'

'You can tend your own fire.'

The child started crying in fear, and he pushed her through the door opening. Outside he clutched her hand in his fist. 'Now stop your crying. You can't appear before the Dutchman covered in snot.'

He led her across the dunes, through waterlogged trenches, and over the plains where wet grass swept against their bare legs. Drops clung to the greasy outside of their karosses and slid down their legs to the ground. From a waterhole lined with skeins of fresh frogs' eggs along the edge Chief Harry scooped up a handful of rainwater and washed Krotoa's face. The cold took her breath away, and he dragged her along, gasping and crying, in the direction of a black smudge in the heavy rain.

'Krotoa, stop crying. From now on things will get better. Before midsummer we shall have cattle. That means milk and butter.'

'I don't want to go.'

'It's better like this. The Hollander's house is full of food. Bread. Rice. Beads. Have you seen the way their women dress? Beads and combs in their hair?'

The beach was flooded, the north wind swept the rain together with a foaming high tide up against the sandbank, all the way to the trembling brushwood of the front dunes. Two rowing boats lay upended on the dunes, out of harm's way. Around the Fort was the broad trench brimming with churning muddy water, and on the other side of a little wooden bridge a fishing net, bundled up by the wind, flapped on a frame, dripping water. The gateway was between two fish-houses. He pushed the child in under the shelter and struck three blows with his heavy *kierie* on the door. Behind the door somebody shouted: 'Two blacks at the door.' And from the far side of the courtyard another voice replied: 'With or without cattle?' Then again the watchman: 'It's old Herrie and the child, corporal.'

Chief Harry asked Krotoa, 'What are they saying?'

'He wants to know if we have cattle.'

There was no word from behind the door. The Dutch had a habit of keeping one waiting; it made one humble. But the English did that too. Above their heads the flag was plastered against its pole like a wet rag. The rain came softly sifting down against the earthen walls of the Fort, eroding the sides in thin furrows. A wet wind was stroking across the tops of the little bushes. The child was shivering with cold. He'd promised her, 'Inside it will be warm.'

Then she looked up at him. Their eyes were locked together in mutual support. Below the pointed hat the small face was triangular, with two large black eyes, sunken into their sockets above the high cheekbones. Her two thin legs below the kaross were like twigs. She was wasted away. If only the Dutch could get some flesh on her. 'Your mother always had a shining face, shining arms and legs, hair shining with fat. I have neither hoof nor horn to give you, child of my sister, but inside this place it will be warm.'

'I don't want to go. I'm scared.'

'You're so clever. You needn't be scared of them. Do you remember the ship *Haerlem*? And your people aren't far away.' He pointed through the darkness and the rain. 'Just over there, at the dunes.'

Then they waited in silence again.

The heavy bolts were drawn back, one down below near the ground, the other above their heads. When the gate swung open it was van Riebeeck himself standing there, wrapped in his black oilskin like a wet bat. Behind him were two soldiers with pieces of canvas around the shoulders and wearing rusty iron hats. Water dripped from the thatched roofs surrounding the courtyard.

'Come in.' He led the way to his large stone house against the back wall. The gate was swung shut behind them, with a gust of wind and a clanging sound, and bolted. And then at last they were out of the rain. But with the slamming of the house door, once again aided by a gust of wind, fear jumped up in Chief Harry. Caught. *Heitse!* Then he looked round: there were wooden floors, windows high in the walls, guns and pikes against the wall. Doors to the left and right, the small white bitch on a rope mat in front of a dancing fire.

In front of the hearth were two low benches. Van Riebeeck moved one into position for Chief Harry. Krotoa kneeled on the mat with her hands to the flames, and the dog looked up and softly patted her tail on the mat. Van Riebeeck asked, 'Is this the little one who speaks Dutch? I've heard about you.' From a blue bowl on the hearth rack he took a cube of brown beet sugar and put it in her mouth, smiling at the joy on her face. Then he asked in English: 'Well, Herrie, what is going to become of us?'

'That I cannot tell.'

'You people are hungry. Is that why you came here? You're hungry, all of you. You brought the child so we can give her something to eat.'

'Yes.'

'We are hungry too, Herrie. Don't you believe that? Early this morning in this weather I sent out a boat to the island to find penguin eggs. They're not back yet. Yesterday my men brought a baboon, three or four days dead, from the mountain so we could eat. I don't have food for my own people.'

'How do you eat then?'

'We catch fish, we eat seals and penguins.'

'Yes, you can give us some of that.'

'No. *Haerlem*'s law: work first, then eat. A child will be fed, and a woman can be helped, but a man must work. Is it like that with you too?'

'We're hungry all of us. Gogosoa took our cattle. What is it to us if you have to eat baboon? We must make do with locusts, mice, crows, all the filth of the veld.'

'But this winter you'll have to work.'

Krotoa remembered a word, and said out loud: 'Sugar.' Van Riebeeck listened as if it was a request, but when she didn't look up at him he placed another cube in her hand.

'What is your name?'

She dropped her chin on her chest, and he asked Chief Harry: 'Little Eva?'

'Krotoa.'

'What kind of food did you get from *Nieuwe Haerlem*?'

'Bread and rice. Meat. Arrack. Tobacco.'

'What work did the child do there?'

'She helped with the cooking and with the pots.'

'That's what I heard.' Van Riebeeck went to the door to speak to someone in the next room, and Eva heard the words and cried, 'Bread and cheese!' so that van Riebeeck looked round.

'You have sharp ears, little Eva. Wouldn't you like to come and live with us?' And to Chief Harry: 'You will have to learn Dutch. There's no need for English here. The English won't be coming, it's all over for them.' The child took a third sugar cube from his hand. Then he took his pipe from the shelf above the hearth, filled it from a barrel on the table, while he kept an eye on Chief Harry. With his back against the warm hearth wall he placed an ember on the tobacco, leisurely inhaled until it glowed, and allowed the smoke to twirl from his mouth. 'English tobacco, from the new colonies in America. Deliciously sweet. Not as pungent as the black Turkish grass they try to fob off on us here. Tastes more like charcoal.'

'I know English tobacco. Virginia.'

'Precisely. I suppose it's a while since you last smoked? The custom is for us to offer tobacco in exchange for meat. It doesn't make much difference to me, but we need sheep for meat and I need cattle for my transport wagons. Pack oxen and draught oxen. But you say you don't have sheep or cattle?'

The sweet smell of tobacco hung in the room. Chief Harry didn't want to beg yet. Their custom of tobacco for meat wasn't his, it was their ships that brought the custom here. The bad thing was that apart from his English he had nothing to barter. So he remained silent.

'Things are going badly with us at the moment, Chief Harry, but we shall recover. A flock of sheep, teams of working oxen, wagons, that's what you are going to see here. I shall see to it, with the help of God. Cereal, gardens, tobacco fields. The bay filled with ships. Many soldiers, you'll see.'

A cook brought in a tray with bread and cheese, and two mugs of warm mulled wine. Krotoa came to stand against the table.

'Put it down first,' van Riebeeck told the cook. 'I want to finish talking.' Then he counted it off on his fingers: 'First, an interpreter. If little Eva wishes, she can come and live here with us. She will eat at our table. All I'm asking in return is for her to help my wife with the children, the laundry, that kind of thing. Second: odd tasks like carrying water, scouring pots, firewood. The old women from your place can do that. Third, the most important. I must have sheep and cattle, to provide for the ships, food for our garrison, but above all for my transport wagons. Even if I have to go and get it myself. Even if I have to kill for it.'

In response to Chief Harry's soundless nod van Riebeeck pointed the stem of his pipe at him like a pistol.

'It's your job to find me the cattle.'

'Me?'

'Yes, you see to it. Make sure I get enough sheep and cattle, then you and your women and this child will get food. Food and tobacco, and brandy. What do you say?'

That evening Chief Harry went to the deaf woman with a small tortoiseshell of snuff, and told her with many signs that Krotoa was at the Fort, but would regularly come over with bread and tobacco. He hooked his bow and quiver over his shoulder, and then walked out in the rain to the Cochoqua, where there were more of Krotoa's relatives. He was sleepy from the afternoon's eating and drinking, but as long as it was raining his tracks were safe. In the north-west the sky was already dark, and between sunset and daylight he wanted to cross the tract of veld where the Grigriqua's cattle were grazing. That was yet another nation that spelled trouble for him.

The next evening he reached the Cochoqua, with two fat female tortoises in his knapsack. Oedasoa agreed that he'd been right to act with such caution. Only a few nights earlier the Grigriqua had tried to burn down their homes. The reed mats were too wet to catch fire, but they did get away with three or four head of cattle. And that was about all Oedasoa said, for this chief of one-half of the Cochoqua was a silent man. Chief Harry spent two days there, talking to Oedasoa and his wife, but the answers and questions came only from the woman. She wanted to know about her little sister, Krotoa. She invited him to bring the child to her. The child was growing up, and there was a wedding gift waiting for her here in Oedasoa's camp. Later she understood that Autshumao would not part with that child while there was food and drink for the Watermen in the kitchen of the Hollanders.

Oedasoa's wife was glad that the child was out of the cold now. Yes, it was better for her there than to catch klipfish in the rain. *Heitse*, the white people had an easier life than the Koina. But was it a married man in whose house Kroton was living? Was there a woman who could take care of the child? And all the while Oedasoa sat listening in silence, rolling thin thongs between his palms. His eyes were cast down as Chief Harry spoke. When the woman spoke his eyes were on her. A big wedding gift, yes, he said, but then Krotoa would have to come and live here, marry a man from this camp, and their children would have to be Cochoqua. A hundred cattle, five hundred sheep, would be her portion. Her livestock would remain part of the Cochoqua herd. As for the girl's rites of transition, he would discuss that with his wife later.

'Suppose she wants to stay with the Dutch?' she asked.

'What do you give to a daughter who does not want to be yours?'

'Give sheep to the Hollanders, then I'll bring you rice and tobacco,' Chief Harry interrupted. 'One skin-bag of rice means food for seven, eight days. You needn't sit here waiting for wild bulbs all the time.'

'How many sheep does the Hollander want?'

'It's mainly for breeding, but also for food. Once he has a breeding flock he will leave us in peace.'

'Then we can help him in that way.'

'And some cattle, especially oxen for riding and carrying.'

'*Heitse!* We can never let our cattle go.'

'Just for a while. Let me have two oxen and seven sheep.'

'But what will they give to Krotoa? What will she be getting there, from the Dutch?'

'They eat well. He said he'd give her clothes like those his women wear. Everyone eats well with the Dutch.' He thought of his own voyage to the East. 'Perhaps he takes her on a ship to his country.'

'Will he ever give her back? They're building houses of stone. That means they will not be going away again.'

'Ships are always coming and going.'

Oedasoa's wife glanced uneasily at her husband. She waited until he raised his face to her, and was frightened by the helplessness she saw there. Then his eyes were cast down again to the slender thongs under his fingertips. She quietly watched how the strips that once were tough springbok hide, that once were living buck, became softer and rounder as they were rubbed together, rounder and softer as Oedasoa stroked the wild buck out of them.

'Get your young men to drive the cattle and sheep past the Grigriqua, Oedasoa,' Autshumao explained. 'A few at full moon, a few at new moon, until the Hollanders have enough. In due course everyone from your camp, including your women, will want to barter with the Dutch. They give tobacco for run-down cattle too. Then you will have to stop the Dutch from getting too many.'

Oedasoa was wondering about this Autshumao on whom he'd always looked down. There were enough cattle and sheep here to provide for their own needs for ever. After these winter rains they could expect a good increase. They could easily spare some animals for rice and tobacco. Autshumao had said that if the young men drove the cattle past the Grigriqua, they would return with rice and tobacco. But the Grigriqua would ambush and rob them. At the moment they were only a small group of angry fellows, but there were hotheads joining their ranks, impoverished deserters and runaways ready to prefer robbery to tending sheep and cattle. Where would this matter lead to? His young men who accompanied the livestock would have to be rewarded on their return, with some of the rice, the tobacco. What would they become afterwards? Smokers, drinkers.

After Autshumao stopped speaking, staring into his face like a dog waiting for a bone, Oedasoa nodded. First he would send some of his own animals, then those of other men of his age who might be agreeable.

Chief Harry stayed with Oedasoa for another day, and spoke to the woman about her little sister, how clever the child was with the language. The arrival of these Hollanders might well turn out to be a good thing, he told Oedasoa's wife. The Dutch also promised work for the old women who would go to live there with them.

And Chief Harry's eyes travelled across Oedasoa's cattle and sheep when they went out to graze in the early dawn, and again when at sunset they were driven inside the circle of huts. Then he would be there among the other men, and his eyes were counting with theirs, groups of ten, two full hands at a time. They were beautiful animals, going out to graze in the wet winter grass every day. He studied the young herdsmen too. Good condition, but were they taking bows and arrows with them to the veld, or only a throwing stick? Did they come home with a buck on the shoulders, or only with ostrich eggs or a tortoise for the older members of the family? How far into the land did this silent Oedasoa's voice reach? And had his fighting oxen been trained to lead a herd?

Yes, the boys had a few guinea fowl and a hare, which was not good enough for the young herdsmen of such a big camp. What were they doing all day behind the cattle? Making themselves stiff all the time? The boy carrying the hare was welcomed, and praised as a hunter. Chief Harry, at the rear of the circle, watched in silence; it was an honour he had never known. When Oedasoa looked round from the front row, those were his thoughts as he looked at Chief Harry.

The rain stopped and he went back to the dunes. The huts of his people were empty. He tried to find tracks, but could discover only the traces of the rain. The fire-hole in the big hut was cold, the wood half burned and then suddenly doused. Their calabash, brimful with fresh rainwater, hung from its stick behind the hut. The reed baskets were missing from the dome of the roof. At the outside cooking place the mound of shells was as he'd last seen it: flattened, cold and spattered with wet sand. Nothing had been added to it in his absence. On the open sea near the island a deeply laden boat went past under small sail. From the height of the dune he could see people working on the earthen walls of the Fort; wheelbarrows were pushed along planks, up to the top. Others were carrying round sea boulders from a boat on the beach.

Uneasy, he went on to the Fort. When he arrived at the gate, his dog was lying against the wall, its belly round with food. The dog looked at him, yawned, and closed its eyes. A soldier with a pike and a rusty iron hat came from the guardhouse carrying two pieces of fresh, smoking pot-bread in his hand, dripping with butter. With a full mouth he gestured at the ground. He wanted Chief Harry to put down his bow, his quiver of arrows, his assegai and his *kierie*. This was the Fort, with its cannon, its pikes and guns, all its soldiers. They were not scared of him, but to them he was like a child, he might do something irresponsible. He had to wait there for van Riebeeck. Beside him, where the guardroom door stood open, he could see how thick the Fort's walls were: two full arm-lengths, pure stone, clay, broad wooden beams. On top lay rafters for the roof, heavy young trees over the full width of the room, from one wall to the other. He tried to imagine how they would chop down a tree like that, how the blows of their axes would sound in the deep forest under the mountain cliffs, how the soldiers would struggle to drag it up the slope from the forest, how their boots would slide in the black mud, how they would swear at their god. They needed oxen. That was their weakness. They were helpless without draught oxen.

When van Riebeeck arrived, Chief Harry told him: 'You're going to need a lot of oxen to do all your work.'

'Yes, that's what I told you.'

'What will become of us Koina once you have taken all our animals?'

'Now you're exaggerating. What did you hear from Oedasoa, will he let us have sheep and cattle?'

Chief Harry thought: What does this man understand of the Koina's needs? It's not like his tea-and-bread. Our cattle is everything, everything. He said, 'I see my dog lies at your gate. The women have gone from the homes.'

'They came to ask for work.'

'And Krotoa?' Chief Harry could not keep the alarm from his voice.

'What does Oedasoa say? Is he willing to supply us?'

'Sheep and cattle for rice and tobacco, every new moon. But how many? he wants to know. And how much rice and tobacco?'

'He will get enough, as much as the animals are worth.'

'An ox does not have a price. You can never pay enough.'

'Everything has its price. Every man has his price, Chief Harry. But we won't cheat anyone. No one will leave here with empty hands.'

But already he had seen the cattle going up in smoke even before the young men turned to go home after the bartering. And he saw them standing against a bush, letting the white man's precious drink run from their bladders into the ground. Finished. Such bartering turned cattle into nothing.

'Now where does Krotoa sleep? Oedasoa wants to know.'

'Eva sleeps with our children in their room. Do you want to see her? Come.'

They went inside, and van Riebeeck ordered his cook to bring food and drink for Chief Harry.

The child, when she came, was like a little Dutch girl in black and white, with wooden shoes for the winter and a starched cap with earflaps. Her face was somewhat fuller, her eyes filled with laughter. She smelled like a Dutch woman. She was happy. At a distance from Chief Harry she remained standing, looking at the Hollander as if waiting for his permission. Van Riebeeck noticed it, flapped his cloak over his shoulder and went outside so that the labourers could see him among them in this weather; it urged them on. Now that he knew there would be cattle, he could plan further. First, he would have a branding iron forged.

Inside the big room Chief Harry asked Krotoa, 'If they carry firewood for the Dutch all day, who will be looking after our homes?'

Krotoa answered gravely: 'They're not going back to the dunes. They are staying here now.'

'And the food the Hollander promised?'

'They get it. They eat in the fish-house at the gate.'

Chief Harry slowly drew his hands down his face, from forehead to chin, as if his fingertips were stripping off the skin. His Goringhaicona were disappearing in the Hollander's work. The homes among the dunes would remain empty, decay in the wind and be blown away in the next dry season. He would be there alone in the winter, without the dog, gathering his meagre food and fuel. There were three empty huts, for the hyenas, for him, for the hei-nun. And if the Sonqua came in the night, sliding on their stomachs through his door, there would not be a dog to bark or a watchful ox to low.

'You must remember, Autshumao, my name is Eva now.'

Chief Harry nodded. It was going to be very different from before. The cook came in. There was a bowl of milk-and-bread and a mug of Spanish wine. Chief Harry drank deeply, and ate of the warm milk-and-bread.

'And my master said you may bring the huts here. You can put them up against the back wall.'

'Your master,' he said. 'Are you talking about the man with the wide breeches? Is he now telling me where to sleep?'

She patiently remained silent under his threatening eyes. Now that he was standing alone, the one who had no food, now he wanted to play the master. After he had slurped up his wine, she told him that she had to go and tend the children.

Chief Harry turned round outside the gate to look after van Riebeeck. Staring at van Riebeeck's back he thought he knew what was in the man's thoughts. There he was walking along the length of wall that had caved in from the rain, where soldiers were working on scaffolding to brace the wall with sods and stones. The Dutchman was worried about his length of earthen wall. From the sea it looked some days as if his Fort had been razed by heavy artillery fire. Should the natives so wish, they might run up that incline like children up a sand dune. So far they had been too peaceful and fragmented to think of murder, but if they were to stand together there would be trouble for van Riebeeck. Or would the Koina lack the courage? The much-needed draught oxen had to come from the Koina, who else could supply them? A fence of poles, tall and heavy enough to keep out lions and thieves, was what was needed to protect his draught oxen. He would need hundreds of tree trunks to expand the cattle kraal, of the yellow-wood behind the Table Mountain; there were no other trees tall and heavy enough growing in the vicinity. Many trees would be needed, and many, many oxen to drag the wood from the forest to the wagon road. After that, a second team of oxen to take a wagon with a full load of tree trunks to the Fort. Then the trunks had to be cut into beams and boards. This was what the Hollander was thinking, as he walked on in the rain.

When the first new moon came, Chief Harry went to the ford in the Brakke River to wait for the Cochoqua. It was the old halting place of the Cochoqua from the north and of the Chainouqua from the east side of the mountain. The river was running strong and the ford was deep after the rains. He usually tasted the water here, to find out whether the sea had entered the mouth, but now in the heart of winter the stream was coming down too strong, and there was little chance of sea fish in the vleis further down. Did van Riebeeck know that twice a day the sea pushed right up here to the ford, that he could easily catch enough fat mullet here to feed all his people? He would keep his mouth shut about it. Here, among the bushes, there was also a cairn raised for Heitsi-Eib'. Chief Harry flung a piece of limestone on the long, low mound, and departed holding his hand to the back of his head. In a dense patch of shrubs on a rise near the ford, he dropped his bundle and made himself a place to sleep.

Before daybreak the animals were there on the opposite bank: two men driving a herd of six sheep and a cow before them. Chief Harry stretched his cold limbs, waited on hands and knees for a while to listen to their talk, and then rose. They were glad to see him; it was the first time they had come here; they were unsure about the ford and would rather try higher up. But Chief Harry calmed them: they could carry the sheep, the cow could get through on foot. Once the small herd was on the Cape side, he showed them the way to the Fort. 'And listen, there they're blowing the horn.' From a distance they could hear the notes of a trumpet. It was a strange sound in this land, and the herdsmen stopped in their tracks for it. All three were thinking of the sound with which an elephant frightens off its enemy, and in all three of them a feeling of awe rose for the Company. Then Chief Harry led them along the cattle road to the Fort.

His companions were silent, uneasy. It was the first time they'd come to the Fort, and seen white people, and caught their first sight of a chair, a tin plate, flint and steel. They squatted on either side of Autshumao's low bench. From the beginning of the discussion Chief Harry felt sure he had van Riebeeck in his hand. He would speak English only. Van Riebeeck still thought of calling in his little Eva, but Chief

Harry told him, 'I speak for them, and you can understand me.' And he explained to the Cochoqua that the child was working for the Dutch and that they were conspiring against him to rob the Koina. Van Riebeeck filled three small bowls with brandy and water, on second thoughts crumbled a cube of sugar into each, filled three pipes with tobacco and placed them in their hands. Then he sat down at his clavichord and started playing hymns. Chief Harry raised his bowl to the visitors. 'Cheer, ho,' he said, and drank.

Van Riebeeck's first question was: 'What can I do with one cow, Herrie? I need hundreds.'

'The people won't part with their cattle. The cattle are everything to them. Almost like . . .' He looked around. Like what? What was precious to the Dutchman? On the English ship there was a wooden cross with the figure of a man nailed to it, and you could beat an Englishman to death, but he wouldn't go past there without touching his hat, otherwise he'd be lost like a dog who couldn't find his way home. 'If we don't have cattle, we must become robbers, or hunters in the mountains, or take food from the cold seawater. That means hunger and times of suffering.'

'I believe,' van Riebeeck said, 'that in the end they will sell or barter. They *will*; the first cow is already in my kraal.' He looked satisfied, watching them as they sucked on their pipes. The first pipe turns a man into a smoker. 'Now, Harry, ask them how many cattle Oedasoa has.'

'Forty.'

'I want to hear it from them. Ask them. I want to know the truth.'

'I know Oedasoa. He has forty cattle.'

'I don't believe it.'

Then Chief Harry turned to the Cochoqua and asked them, 'How many cattle does Oedasoa have?' And he translated the answer: 'Oedasoa has forty cattle.'

Van Riebeeck wouldn't accept it. If the Koina were so poor, this service station the Lords Seventeen had entrusted to him would never get going. Scores of cattle, hundreds, were necessary for breeding stock, draught oxen, pack oxen, for slaughtering, for milking, but most

important of all was transport. Everything that had to be taken overland had to be carried by oxen. So it was a matter of oxen or, by God,
he would turn these people into slaves. He would proceed calmly and
with patience. Either they or their cattle would bear this burden, but
the service station would succeed.

He poured neat brandy into their bowls. 'Why do the Cochoqua
have so few cattle?'

'The Goringhaiqua stole from them, the Grigriqua also stole,' said
Chief Harry.

'No, I want to hear it from them.' He remained suspicious, but Chief
Harry put the question and gave the answer: this was how it was, it
wasn't otherwise.

In the early afternoon the two men departed with their rice in two
small canvas bags and their tobacco wrapped in coarse sacking. They
were chewing black tobacco as they went. Chief Harry looked at their
tracks from the morning, covering sheep and cattle tracks of the day
before. His head was tired of the tug o' war with the Hollanders, but
he was satisfied that he'd got what he wanted. Now Oedasoa would
know never to send too many cattle at a time, and van Riebeeck would
know he'd have to pay for what he wanted. And his own plans were
going nicely. The year would still turn out green for him and the child.

They were discussing weapons as they walked. He tried to explain
how the cannon and rifles of the Hollanders worked. All he could say
for sure was that there was no magic involved. Anyone could make it
work, even a child could do it. Only on rainy days it was no use. In
India he'd seen many black soldiers carrying guns, but his thoughts ran
ahead too fast on that business, and took fright and had to scamper
back to the cattle path, to the tracks of cattle leading to the Fort. Yes,
little Krotoa had better stay at the Fort for now. When she was old
enough for her transition feast, and afterwards when she was old enough
to choose a man, he would take her away to the Cochoqua, or to old
Sousoa on the east side of the mountain. That still lay ahead, the child
was just twelve. But he had to keep the peace with the Dutch, to make
sure he himself would first find his feet.

On the bank of the river, at the ford, they placed three stones on

Heitsi-Eib's cairn. Then Chief Harry took out his knife, a good English knife, and cut the string of the tobacco pouch. The roll of black tobacco, deliciously soaked in brandy, gleamed invitingly as he undid the small pegs, rolled off two palm-lengths, and cut through it with a single stroke of the blade. Then he pushed the pegs back in, thrust the roll into the pouch, tied the string and gave it to them.

'The Hollander gives me this piece because I talk on his behalf with Oedasoa. If Oedasoa wants to learn Dutch, he will save me the trouble. The Hollander says Oedasoa must now hear from his people if they want to send sheep and cattle again. They may just as well. You saw for yourselves what the Hollander is prepared to pay for it. And this quantity of dry rice, you will see, becomes much more inside a pot. Tell that to Oedasoa. Two double handfuls are enough for four or five people. And you may tell all the Cochoqua: if they come to the Fort, they will be given brandy and they become friends of the Company. But they must bring sheep and cattle.'

Once – a great day – Oedasoa and Ngonnemoa, the two chiefs of the Cochoqua, personally came with some of their elders to meet the Hollanders and look at the building of the Fort. They handed over the livestock and underwent the transition rites of the Company. With the child present all the time Chief Harry had to take care to convey the Koina's words very faithfully to van Riebeeck, and van Riebeeck's in turn to Oedasoa and Ngonnemoa.

Oedasoa wanted to speak to Krotoa away from the others. He was upset when he saw the child in a blue dress, he couldn't tell why. He handed over his little present of wild bulbs and powdered buchu, and asked, 'Your mother's sister wants to know how you are.'

'It's good. I like it here.'

'What shall I tell her from you?'

'The woman has two little boys. Every day they have to wash their faces and I feed them and put on their clothes.'

'Well, that's good. I can see their clothes are difficult to put on.' Krotoa sounded strangely simple, young and empty to him. Were white people's daughters like this? She was a good child, innocent, having grown up among old women. 'Look, child. This brandy they have, you mustn't drink it. It's not for young people. Young people fall down on the ground when they drink it, and they throw up.' She promised, and then she went to stand with van Riebeeck at the other end of the room, where she laughed and talked as if he were her father. Perhaps she'd already become a child of the Company. Oedasoa wondered whether she had been through the remaking of the Dutch. With nothing at all but that friendly nature of hers she succeeded, without the need for any slaughtering. He would tell his wife that the child was safe, though he knew in his heart that her small feet were wandering away into pitch darkness, ahead of all of them.

Chief Harry accompanied them as far as the ford when the two chiefs of the Cochoqua headed into their different directions. He added his stone to the cairn, smoked his tobacco, and watched contentedly as they disappeared into the veld. Those two, Oedasoa and Ngonnemoa, who usually looked down on him, had now seen that he was the white man's mouth.

Like Sonqua when they're out hunting, he put up a flimsy shelter against the wind, and waited to see what was going to happen next. First the Grigriqua came to the ford with five good cattle. Chief Harry waited for them, took them, brought them back. His reward of tobacco he wrapped in the scrotum of an eland and hid it under the bushes. The news must have spread rapidly, because that same new moon the Goringhaiqua sent cattle. Cattle, not sheep. Did they want to die, then? This time it wasn't the noisy, light-headed youngsters who blew through bone-pipes, but polite men, cautious about what they might experience at the Fort. They told him that they'd been expecting to find him there, he who was now the Company's mouth, and they wanted to ask him to lead them and their cattle to the Fort. He took the cattle path with them, round the back of the Fort, to the kraal of yellow-wood beams where the Company's cattle were secured at night. The animals had already gone to pasture, and from their tracks he could see what an unexpected number of livestock the Company had already accumulated. Almost equal numbers of cattle and sheep, he reckoned, about fifty of each, as far as he could estimate.

Van Riebeeck came to join them there. They were resting their forearms on the top beam and their feet among the cowpats in the grass that had been grazed short. 'We're going to make it now, Herrie. I'm getting more and more hopeful. If the Koina continue to bring livestock the way they have been doing, we'll get it done. The vegetables are also coming on very well.'

'Are you satisfied?'

Van Riebeeck divined that much depended on his answer, and weighed his words. 'It's too soon to say. There are still too few cattle and they're coming in very slowly, but the prospect seems reasonable. And you, are you satisfied?'

'Yes.'

'Your prospects good?'

'What do you mean?'

'Is it going well with you? Are you getting what you need? What do you think of the future?'

'No. I have to gather firewood myself, find food, everything. My people are now eating from your pot.'

'I've heard tell,' said van Riebeeck, 'that you're keeping watch at the ford, then you lead the people here. Surely they can find their own way here?' He was unsure whether Chief Harry had any influence on the trade, but it would prevent loss if he could eliminate him at an early stage. 'Look, if you wish, you can come and live at the Fort, with the rest of your people. You can eat at my table. Let the old women carry firewood for their food. What more do you need?'

'You will expect me to look after your cattle for you. I'm not a child. And I cannot dig or chop.'

'No. You will be my mouth. All you have to do is talk to the Koina. I shall give you food and clothes, and drink and tobacco as you may need. You can put up your homes in the dunes again, then you can walk here to the Fort in the morning and go home at night.'

What he hadn't said, thought Chief Harry, was that if I take on his work, it will be the end of my waiting at the ford for the barterers, and the end of my English. At his dining table all he wants to hear is Dutch, with the child always present to hear what is being said between the Hollander and the Koina.

'I shall work for you,' he told van Riebeeck, 'and then your soldiers can keep guard over me.'

In the months that Chief Harry ate at the commander's table, he spoke no Dutch. It was clear that he understood it well, but he kept to his limited ship's English, the way a drowning man clung to a rope, and for the rest made do with sailor's curses. Van Riebeeck's wife suggested other expressions, hoping that Herrie would use them. She told him about the religion which Eva was learning. She invited him to church, which he refused, and then prayed for him with Eva. Chief Harry, uncomprehending and frowning heavily at Eva, listened in silence to her small sermons.

Commander van Riebeeck saw greater value in keeping the man's pipe smoking and his glass filled. He learned from Chief Harry. He discovered that Oedasoa had forty head of cattle of his own, but that his Cochoqua owned more than a hundred times as many. He learned how the Goringhaicona had become Beachrangers. And about Eva's relationship with the Chainouqua from the other side of the mountain, through an aunt who was the chief's wife. Eva herself was surprised to hear it. He also discovered that the Koina ate very little. They liked fish and bread, and cooked rice, and milk-and-bread, but used meat only in small quantities as if they had an aversion to it. Sweet desserts, so popular with Dutch women, were not touched by them, although the children liked sweets just as much as Herrie enjoyed his Spanish wine. Eva and Herrie often exchanged words in the Koina language at table. Van Riebeeck didn't feel like forbidding it; he did not want to do anything that might estrange Herrie. As long as the cattle herd in the kraal was growing, he was satisfied. Already there were a few pregnant ewes and heifers, the beginnings of his stud.

Chief Harry also watched the Company's herd growing. He was always there with the counting out in the morning and the counting in at night. From behind the palisade he whistled like a herdsman; he enjoyed the way the cattle would turn their heads towards him. But the sailor who worked as the dairy farmer did not like his whistling. He said: 'One captain. These cattle have one captain, not two.'

The dairyman had personally branded the cattle with the new iron of the VOC; he was proud of the animals in his care. In the daytime the cattle were taken to pasture by the same dairyman and a boy, an orphan of thirteen who had been left behind, ill, in the hospital, by a homeward-bound ship. In the early spring the boy and he would drive the cattle to the vleis behind the dunes, where white and yellow daisies grew luxuriant and sweet, and where they could spend their days under the blue sky beside the sea, where they could see ships coming in and going out, the *orang lama* this side of the island, the *orang baharu* around the other side of the island. Their muskets were never far from the hand, for there were lions on the slopes of the Lion Mountain.

In the evening Chief Harry would be there again for the milking. In English and Koina he proffered advice on how to let the cows yield, how to make the calves drink. It irritated the dairyman, because he was an experienced dairyman. His father had been one, his grandfather too. The Koina cattle, scared of him, had to be managed with a hobble and a halter. There wasn't much milk, the cows were dry and hard and didn't like the milker's hand, so that he had to coax the milk out of them with patient cajoling and their mangers filled with young grass. He did not want Chief Harry near his kraal, because the man's whistling upset the cows.

At dusk one day the dairyman and the boy had tied the cows with their head-thongs to the beam above the manger, hobbled the first two and washed the udders with warm water, Chief Harry standing at the gate, his pipe in his mouth, making scornful comments about this nonsense. The milkers had moved in under the cows on their stools, pails between their knees, when Chief Harry's dog started kicking up a racket and dashed through the kraal, barking his head off. The cows snorted, tugged at their halters, rolled their eyes towards the dog, staggering about with their tethered knees, and immediately drew up their milk. The two milkers quickly jumped out of the way, because the cows, unable to move their feet, were staggering dangerously. They had to start cajoling all over, stroking the flanks of the animals and trying patiently to approach again with pail and stool. The sun was setting and there was a whole herd to calm down and coax into milking. They were worried about the dark because they had only one torch.

But the two cows refused to let their milk down again. The dairyman thought of fetching a calf, so that the cow would give milk to her young, but he was still squatting on his haunches cosseting the animal when Chief Harry approached her from behind, cupping his hands around her vulva and blowing a long shuddering breath into it. The cow staggered forward, kicked the bucket from between the milker's knees, trod heavily on his foot, and stumbled sideways against the next cow, causing the orphan boy to disappear with stool and bucket under the animals. The dairyman snatched up his pail, a half-barrel with brass hoops, by the rope handle, swung it in a wide, vicious curve through the air and banged Chief Harry against the head, knocking him back-wards into the mud and wet manure.

From that day Chief Harry stayed away from the Fort. Some members of the household were relieved about it. Eva was concerned, and told van Riebeeck that the old women were saying Autshumao had taken himself off to Ngonnemoa. Ngonnemoa was the Black Captain, who was grazing with the other half of the Cochoqua north-east of the Cape along the big rivers. Van Riebeeck questioned her about the Black Captain to test her knowledge, because he already knew something about the man, who'd been to the Fort once. Lots of cattle, said Eva. Many people and a lot of followers who were neither herdsmen nor hunters, but freebooters who would one day rise up against Ngonnemoa, kill as many people as was necessary, and drive off as many cattle as they wanted.

'Where do you hear that?'

'That's what Autshumao says.'

'And are the two of them friends? Are they related? Or what keeps him there?'

'No,' she said. As far as she knew, Autshumao had no blood relatives in that camp. She didn't know what he was doing at Ngonnemoa's.

Van Riebeeck called in the dairyman and asked him to recommend someone who could take over the care of the Company's cattle from him. Chief Harry was aggrieved, and it would be a good idea to make some gesture to give him the impression that the Company had his interests at heart. He hoped the dairyman would understand how much

his services were appreciated, and why he was now asking this sacrifice of him, but the time was right for it. He would be rewarded with
a good post as soon as something became available.

A week later, maybe a few days more, Chief Harry was at the front
gate with a small flock of sheep. He'd brought it from Ngonnemoa and
wanted the proper bartering price. The tobacco and rice he received
he divided among the old women that evening. This news Eva also
conveyed to van Riebeeck, and she was surprised, because her uncle
had never been a generous man; he could never afford to be one. Very
early the next morning there was a loud argument among the dunes
when Chief Harry drove the five ancient women from the dilapidated
houses into the veld with his *kierie*. And just after the morning prayer
he came to explain it personally to van Riebeeck.

'They were too lazy to go out to work. I asked them: What about
the Hollander's firewood, and his water barrels that must be filled?
What about the dirty pots in his kitchen? I gave them a good hiding.'

'Are they your dogs then, or dumb children that you should beat
them?'

'Don't your officers go about day and night with their canes? I shall
never touch a child, but these were too lazy to get up after I'd given
them food only once. Why must I be the only one who works?'

'Are you their master?'

'Yes, that's what I am. I've been too soft with them for too long'

Van Riebeeck pondered this. It was the first time he'd seen Chief
Harry as a difficult tribal captain, one who disciplined his people, even
if it was in a crude manner. And wasn't Herrie promoting the
Company's interests in this way? Therefore he couldn't forbid the man
to approach the Company's kraal either. Let him show his interest, and
organise his womenfolk at home in a manner befitting a local chief.
But was that Herrie's honest intention?

He asked Eva: 'What is going on with Herrie? Do you think he's
forgotten his grudge?'

'He will never-ever forget that. My master must never-ever trust
him. He's just pretending to be my master's friend.'

At milking time on a summer's evening Harry took up his seat on the top beam of the cattle enclosure again to watch the milking. He'd been told to stay out of the kraal. The new dairyman and the orphan boy were working in silence, their heads leaned against the flanks of the cows, rising only to empty their pails into the large vat. After the winter the cows were in good condition, their coats smooth and shiny; they were clean, with no excrement on the shins or mud in the loins. They were good cattle, cows chewing with half-closed eyes at the mangers. He liked the quiet, smooth flow of the work, watching how they lightly hobbled the animals, fed them green fodder in the manger, talking softly to them.

Opposite, on the wall of the Fort, van Riebeeck was standing with a soldier, also watching the milking. Now there was a man, thought Chief Harry, who'd arrived in this land without cattle, and look at him today. How does that lordly man feel in his black coat? He orders the trumpet to be blown, sends soldiers hither and thither, has the trumpet blown again, commands his sailors to row to the island, has houses built and trees planted, and looks out on kraals filled with fat cattle and even fatter sheep. Yes, a real great captain, this man who'd stepped out of a boat only the other day. Chief Harry envied the man.

He could smell the fresh milk that splashed, foaming, into the barrel. He'd heard that those cows were giving much more milk these days than before, their udders were larger and fuller. By now he'd come to know Dawid Jansz, the orphan boy. He'd been thrown off a ship. The child knew very little about the world. His father had been a sailor, his mother was from Java, one could see that in the child. His work was to cut green fodder from the vleis. He slept in the sheep stable and fetched his breakfast from the hatch of the cookhouse. The dairyman shouted at him in the same voice one would use to shout at a dog. But the boy wasn't timid either and would talk back in the same voice in that mixed-up language, not allowing the dairyman to boss him around. He knew the child, Chief Harry thought. He wasn't worth much.

He saw Krotoa walking with the Hollander's wife along the top of the wall towards her husband. He knew her too, he thought. She was an attractive woman, barely twenty, thin and soft-spoken. She carried her unborn child as if to boast to the whole kraal of cattle with the child she was expecting. But where were her two sons? Somewhere in the house they would be alone now.

Chief Harry turned his head away when he noticed van Riebeeck's wife gesturing towards him, and watched from a corner of his eye. Then she spoke to the Hollander again, and he beckoned to the soldier walking on the wall. After a few words the soldier came hurrying down the wooden staircase to the ground. What now? Chief Harry kept his eyes fixed on the cattle, counting all the dairy cows, afterwards the dry cows, the calves, the young oxen, then the sheep: rams, young ewes, old ewes, lambs.

The world below the Fort wall became silent, oppressive when the wind died down. The dairyman once again emptied his pail in the large barrel, then loosened the cow's hobbling thong, undid the head-thong, chased out the cow, quickly and nimbly hobbling the next cow. The pail came nearly full, it was a good young animal. The soldier walking on the wall approached with a parcel in his hand. 'For Chief Harry, from His Honour's housewife. Put it on for supper. Commander's order.' He kept his voice low. 'You'll have to wash your feet.' In the parcel were wide white canvas trousers, a blue sailor's shirt, and a leather waistcoat. Chief Harry shook open the clothes and inspected them. They were good clothes; he would like to wear them against the cold nights. From up on the wall van Riebeeck and his spies were watching him. He nodded his thanks to the Dutchman, took the bundle, and left.

On a beautiful, quiet evening when the moon was full and no bartering stock were expected at the ford, Chief Harry put on the new clothes, took a full roll of tobacco from his hiding place, and went to see Oedasoa. His knapsack was filled with canna and buchu. He offered it to Oedasoa's wife and explained his story to her: 'Your sister's child is doing well. Our homes are with the Hollander's. He is looking after us. I am a man again, and I need a woman in my house. I have no cattle. I want you to tell that to Oedasoa.'

'What do you want from him?'

'I want Oedasoa to give me some of Krotoa's wedding cattle, to find me a wife.'

'He won't do that. He won't even give those cattle to Kroton. Look, Autshumao, it is a good thing that you want to take a wife, but what do you have to give her? Must she pick mussels for a living?'

He did not look into her eyes, and said firmly: 'No. Those things are finished now. We're going to have cattle. Only a few to start with, but later we will get stronger.'

The strange excitement was back on his face. For the first time since Autshumao had lost his cattle, he seemed ready to laugh again, and it made her happy.

Calmly she looked him in the eye. 'Have you spoken to a woman about getting married?'

'No. I don't know anyone around here.'

She undertook to speak on his behalf, and he thanked her with a piece of tobacco. For the woman of his choice he also cut tobacco and passed it on. The next day she told him what Oedasoa had decided: he would not give any cattle to this man for a remaking, he was too old to be piggybacked by others. But she was willing to help him. From her own herd she would give him some. Chief Harry pressed the rest of the tobacco into her hands.

When she brought a woman she remained to help with the talking. 'Autshumao is chief of the Goringhaicona. He works for the Hollander, and they give him tobacco and rice and beads for it. He is the Hollander's mouth. He knows their language. He is also offering two cows to the woman he marries, and one to her father. Then he also offers two sheep to be slaughtered for the transition feast.'

One day she came to tell him that there was one woman she wished to recommend. She wasn't young, but she was healthy, sturdily built, with a full square face like a Hollander. She had two sons and a daughter, all three married by now. Her cattle were kept with those of her sons.

He went to her house. It was clean, the ground had been swept. There were calabashes filled with curdled milk and with honey beer, rolls of new *harubis* mats, and earthen pots decorated with patterns like the spoor of buck, as if a herd of steenbuck had stood around the edge to drink. They spoke without an intermediary. She was willing to go and live at the Fort. He felt like a young man when he took her Yes to Oedasoa.

The silent man invited him in, made him sit on a mat, offered him sour milk. Chief Harry handed the small tortoiseshell of snuff-tobacco to Oedasoa to open the conversation. Oedasoa took a pinch, drank the sour milk, and said to Chief Harry: 'It's a bad thing which is happening here now. You must stop it, Autshumao. Go and find cattle first. If you don't have cattle, you should not take a wife. You went to ask my wife for cattle for the transition feast after I refused. It's her business, but it was done the wrong way. You did wrong by giving my wife's little sister Krotoa to the Hollander.'

'She works for the Hollander. She gets food, drink, tobacco. They eat three times a day, and every time there is wine on the table. It is hard to die of cold.'

'Is she a smoker then?'

'She earns it for me. The tobacco she gets is for me, and I use it for all my people. The rice and bread are mine. She gets her share at the Hollander's table. The drink is mine too.'

'What does that child get for her trouble?'

'I told you she gets food and clothes and she sleeps in a strong house. She did not have that before the Dutch came. She gets more in that place than any of your wives.'

Oedasoa remained patient and moved his curds closer to Chief Harry. His people were living well. They were a strong group. As far as he could tell, they were content with their life. His thoughts remained with the matter of his wife's cattle. 'You sent my wife's sister after the white man's sweets. She doesn't need it. Once you have smoked her tobacco and drunk her wine, there will be nothing left for that child. You're lying to her. She can come and work here with the others of her age, to earn a share in the Cochoqua's wealth.' He was breathing with greater difficulty, he pressed his hands down on his thighs and pushed up his chest to catch his breath, but kept on staring Chief Harry in the face. 'If she stays there, she will not get any transition feast from me. The matter is simple. I hope you understand.'

'You're right,' said Chief Harry. 'But it was winter then and there was nothing to eat.' He didn't mention that the child had another name, and was wearing Dutch clothes, and that he was convinced Eva would never again rub sheep fat into her body.

Oedasoa nodded in silence. He felt that enough had been uncovered in this conversation; he could now broach the matter of the cattle: 'You're helping the Hollander to cattle, Autshumao. What will happen when one day he needs all the grazing for himself? He will send soldiers to drive the Koina from the pasture. First the Cochoqua, the Gorachoqua, the Goringhaiqua, the Grigriqua. After that they will need Ngonnemoa's land, and take it. Then Ankaisoa's, all the way to the mountain. And then the Hollander will cross the mountain and chase the Chainouqua and the Hessequa from their pastures, so that his own animals can graze there. Where will the Koina graze?'

'It will be a long time before they're so strong.'

'But you, Autshumao, you're helping them to prosper. You're not a Dutchman, why must you work against your own people? And now I want to tell you about my wife's cattle. It is wrong for her to help a man who is trying to harm his own people. She won't help you as long as you're living with the Dutch, that you must know. And bring the child here, before some harm befalls her.'

Chief Harry knew what he meant. The child was growing up, and she was good-looking. At the Fort she found herself among more than a hundred Dutchmen, none of whom has a wife of his own. One could see the way they looked at the slave women, at the handful of white women, most of whom were already married, at the Koina women who did not cover their bodies as the Dutch ones did. What was to become of a poor girl in a strange house?

So there was no ill feeling between them, but from that day no more cattle from Oedasoa turned up at the Fort, and Chief Harry felt as if Oedasoa had kicked him off his property like a dog without a name. He had tried to ask, and was given nothing. The rich did as they wished, and the poor had to suffer whatever came their way. What could a man do if he had no cattle?

And at the Fort van Riebeeck was worrying about transport for his settlement. His small herd was the cornerstone of his planning. A cow was taken to the bull once a year, it took an ox three years to come to the yoke. It might take too long. If more oxen did not turn up for the Company's work, he would place the yoke on the Koina. They would have to learn to shoulder a burden. In China people were the beasts of burden, people carrying baskets on their heads. In South America the Spaniards and the Portuguese used slaves on a massive scale. He was not in favour of slavery, at best it was a necessary evil. But he had to do the same if more cattle could not be found to do the Company's work.

Chief Harry led people who came to barter to the Fort, also to let them see the Dutchman's house of stone. The two sons of the woman who'd been willing to marry him came to see. Van Riebeeck acquainted them with the taste of tobacco very soon, and then imposed *Haerlem*'s law about working first, then eating. The soldiers on the wall kept watch on them: how they walked round the Fort, studied the cannon on the wall, touching the sturdy kraal for livestock behind the Fort, stole a pair of hinges from the smith's workbench. Van Riebeeck said: Let them have their way. That afternoon they stood at the kraal gate and watched the livestock being counted in; and whispered among themselves: *Heitse!* Van Riebeeck had more cattle than Oedasoa himself.

He pointed out the two herdsmen: Dawid and Hendrik, shuffling wordless over the dried manure, clutching their sticks, coat and food bag over the shoulder, patches of sweat between the shoulder blades. They closed the large gate and secured it with lock and chain, before fetching the milking things and boiling water from the kitchen. Chief Harry laughed: Would the animals ever be safe in the care of such as those? These two wouldn't lift a finger to protect the livestock.

Then, one day, Chief Harry heard from his old women among the dunes that van Riebeeck's wife was expecting her child at the next dark moon. It was news he'd been hoping to hear for a long time. This was the opportunity for the greatest remaking of his life. It would change the lives of everybody he knew, and also of the unborn. He would change the whole world. With the wife in labour and the husband, as he'd come to know him, unwilling to go far from her in her confinement, he could do what he'd been planning for so long. For the time being he still kept the matter to himself; only when it was right at hand he'd explain it to others.

He wanted to see the woman's condition for himself, so that he could better estimate the day in advance, but she no longer ventured outside. That didn't matter, his plan was so simple it could be put into motion at any time between the evening and the morning star. And one day the old women were talking among themselves: no more than five days now, it could even happen a day or two earlier.

It was October, at the height of the flowering season. The winter grass was a carpet of green, tangled clover, young stinkweed and sorrel stems. Yellow sorrel and *ramnas* grew in a dense mingling along the dunes and up towards the mountain. The bees clambered drunk and heavy across the pale yellow flowertops, across the white flowers, tumbling down from time to time among the juicy stems to suck lower down from the sticky brown crowns of orange and white marigolds. The green juice dripped from the mouths of the Hollander's cattle grazing up to their knees in the luxuriant growth. Their udders were of a size Chief Harry had not seen in his life. And all of it belonged to van Riebeeck, the one who now would wander to the milking place to see the foam rising deep and yellow in the pails. This summer the Hollanders would stuff themselves with butter, strain their stomachs with buttermilk, curdled milk, cream. And such cattle: placid cows, fat, gentle, with shiny coats. *Heitse*, this man in the wide breeches was a lucky man! His vats were crammed with butter. What was to become in this land of a man who had no cattle?

A few times he walked out to the pasture with the herd, very early, just after sunrise and as soon as the milking was done, past the dunes, out of sight of the Fort, to the large vlei at the Green Point, where the sea almost surrounded the herd. There the herd drank, their muzzles blowing into the deep, fresh rainwater. Among the reeds waterfowl were nesting. All of this was now the Hollander's pasture, unchallenged by anyone. It was a joy to let that herd graze in the marigolds. Here they spent the whole day, and when in the heat of noon the cattle lay down, the orphan boy had to go to the Fort to fetch their lunch. On his return a fire was already burning, and they would place the earthen pot in it to warm. Hot food was indispensable for the Dutch at noon, even in this warm month.

He spoke to his people. They knew how the Hollander goes to church twice every seventh day: once before noon, the second time in the late afternoon. And in between there was a huge meal, and then they had to lie down, like their livestock. It was invariably a quiet day. All the work stopped. Everybody had to be in church, with the exception of only three men. The Hollander had it set down on paper and nailed the paper to the bell post, so that no one could say they didn't know. Everybody in the Fort had to be in church, except for those three. They were flogged if they didn't go, or their pay was taken away, or they would be kept in prison on bread and water. So that everybody could stop working, and wash themselves and get dressed, the bell was rung. Later it rang again. Still later it rang for a third time. Then everybody took their places in the church, except for three men. Chief Harry had told them to hold themselves ready for the third ringing of the bell in the Fort. When the Dutch went into the church, it was time for the transition rites.

The previous day they had to eat well in the kitchen, and ensure that there was an abundance of firewood on the Dutchman's hearth, enough water in his vats, so that he wouldn't become uneasy. The old women would be at home in the morning, as it was a quiet day in the Fort. They had to pull up sticks, roll up mats, make bundles, everything ready to be lifted on to the head. Not a word was to be spoken by anyone about this matter, particularly in front of Krotoa who had become a spy for the enemy. If here among the dunes they heard the bell going for the third time, the women had to put everything on their heads and take to the road towards the big vlei. Walking, not running. If the soldier on the wall noticed them, they shouldn't become hurried, but laugh and wave to him.

That day Ngonnemoa sent eight sheep. Both Chief Harry and Eva were there to advise when copper wire and beads were handed over and the thanks of tobacco and arrack was distributed. In the night van Riebeeck's third son was born.

When they heard of the child's birth, Chief Harry said: Tomorrow it is church again, it's the day that has been set aside for us. When the bell was rung for the first time that morning, he warned them to stay indoors and prepare themselves. When it rang for the second time, he told them to make a start. The soldier on the wall of the Fort came over to their side and watched their packing without a word, turning round from time to time to look down the other side at the congregation clothed in black, crossing the courtyard to the commander's front door. Last of all, the thin sick-comforter went up the stairs, carrying his books under his arm. For a moment van Riebeeck appeared at the door to greet him, looked up at the soldier on the wall and the flag above the gate. Then the sick-comforter rang the bell for the third time, and pulled the front door to after him.

The soldier folded his hands over the barrel of his gun, bowed his head in the direction of the commander's house and recited the Lord's Prayer out loud. When he turned round the Goringhaicona, with their bundles on their heads, were already a hundred yards or more away from the dunes, trekking with all their possessions, children and dogs.

At the second bell Chief Harry crossed the courtyard with the churchgoers, and waited on the stairs to the stoep for the officials with their black overcoats and white cravats like penguins, and with their silver buckles and small walking sticks. Some of them he barely recognised in their Sunday clothes; equally strange were their shiny shaved faces and soft voices. One or two walked beside a woman clothed high and dark in a dress which was taken from the chest once every seven days. Chief Harry politely nodded at those he recognised, and with a cynical grin held out his cupped hands to a few of the most respected. He watched askance as they went up the stairs with raised heads, how each upon entering bowed to van Riebeeck and shook his hand, and how the sick-comforter upon entering first put his hand around the doorframe for a last hard pull at the bell rope.

He entered on the heels of the sick-comforter, but instead of following the congregation to the front room, turned left to the living quarters. Krotoa's place was in the nursery. He walked through the dining room, emptied the blue tobacco jar on the shelf into his knapsack, and pushed open the door to the nursery. The room around her was simple, bare, assembled from rough wood. She was on a low bench in front of a looking glass, thrusting small combs into her hair. Before his eyes her back went rigid with fright. He remained at the door.

'Where's the woman with the child?' he whispered.

'In their bedroom.' She pointed at the room next to them.

'The other children?'

'One is having his food in the kitchen. The other one is asleep in that box.'

'Come with me.'

Krotoa laid the combs in a neat row on the table, and went to him. Her small black shoes flashed forward in turn, her Sunday dress swung on the floor on either side as she walked. Chief Harry looked appreciatively at the straight-backed child with the embroidered collar on her shoulders. He remembered the rainy day he brought her here. She had learned a lot from the Hollander. He took her hand firmly in his own. 'We must get out of here. You can come back another day.' When she drew back towards the child, he put his hand on her mouth, tugged her into the dining room and dragged her after him. 'There's big trouble coming; and we're moving away before the Dutch come out of the church.'

She started whining, in tears. 'The child. Little Lambert can be smothered in his cushion.'

'Little Lambert? Who is looking after *us*? When we go out through the front door, Krotoa, you must walk next to me without a sound. Don't look up at the soldier. We're going through the gate to the dunes. You will see our people moving on before us, and when they see us they will stop to wait for us.'

The soldier on the wall shifted his attention from the group of decamping Beachrangers to the two who had just emerged from the front door. Their hands were empty. The girl was presumably entitled to the dress she was wearing. There was nothing to report. From the council chamber came the sound of a hymn being sung, accompanied by a clavichord and a good strong tenor. It was a glorious spring day. The flag hung motionless from its post. The soldier softly took up the hymn.

Chief Harry and the child caught up with the Goringhaicona halfway to the vlei, where they were sitting in the long grass with their bundles. Far ahead of them the cattle were lying, chewing peacefully, but the flock of sheep was still moving about, plucking at the grass.

'We're waiting here. It won't be long now.'

Shortly before noon Hendrik Willers, the dairyman, took the short cut across the ridge to the Fort, his *kierie* in his hand. On Sundays it was his turn to fetch the food, for there would be a *muts* of brandy distributed after the service. Once the dairyman was well out of sight, Chief Harry gave two shrill whistles between his thumb and index finger, motioning at his people to move on. The boy Dawid got up from the grass, a gun in his hand, and clambered on a granite boulder some distance beyond the sheep to see what was going on. The Goringhaicona were approaching in a long line. The men were rattling their *kieries*; they were prancing, whistling, shouting. The women with the bundles on their heads followed at a trot. The Company's cattle got up, bundled together, then moved away from the clamouring, whistling Koina.

It was wonderful to be walking behind cattle again, wonderful to see the heavy, swinging bodies trotting along, to hear the dull shoving of shoulder against shoulder and the clash and clatter of horns. The Koina almost had the cattle in full stampede when the boy levelled his firearm at Chief Harry at arm's length. Autshumao, tried to ward off the shot with his *kierie* and hurled his assegai forward with all his might. Not without pleasure he saw it sink deeply below the boy's breastbone, saw him drop the gun and sink on his knees into the grass with a startled face and a long groan. Two men clubbed him down into the luxuriant flowers with their *kieries*. Ahead of them the sheep were scattering in all directions, but the cattle were nearly surrounded. They started beating the cattle and chased them to work up speed. All of them, even the children, made a noise, threw stones, beat left and right with sticks. Krotoa was trying to keep up, sobbing. Chief Harry pulled off her blue dress and her shoes and hurled them away.

'Come on, come on. If the Dutchman gets you he'll beat you to death.'

She shrieked in protest against the lie, scuttling through the bushes in her long petticoat, in the wake of the men and the old women. Chief Harry turned back, dragged her by the arm, pleaded with her, threatened her to keep up with them. She was sobbing with fear and yearning for the silent front room where she used to eat sugar and jam from porcelain bowls.

Ahead of her the people were jubilating over what they had done. Chief Harry was dancing with his *kierie* and his throwing stick above his head. *Heitse*, to have here before him once more the bearers of all that was good in life, to smell their grassy breath, to hear their voices, to see their tail-switches flicking over their heels. Heitse, how dead he'd been these years, without livestock. But today he'd had a triple remaking. Once he was a Beachranger, then a Sonqua, now a Hottentot, the way the Dutch saw it – all of it, all of it in one forenoon. And he had a tribe of his own, the Goringhaicona, who could send smoke up to Heitsi-Eib'. Now he could build a circle of new *harubis* homes. Already he could picture it: the smoke of their morning fires hung blue in front of his eyes, and it was time to milk and take the cattle to pasture, and no one had the right to tell him where to graze.

But Krotoa's crying made him turn around.

'What are you howling for? Can't you shut up?'

She cried more loudly. Almost paralysed with sadness she forced out the words: 'Why have you done this, Autshumao?'

He grabbed her firmly by the upper arm. 'For you. There's your remaking. Can't you see how happy our people are?'

She moaned, 'They're not.' And he had to shout very loudly at the cattle to drown out the sound of her crying.

'Forty-two fat cattle, a whole lot of cows with big udders, yes, for you and for me and for our people. Now we can do it just as it is done at Oedasoa's and at the Fat Captain's, the way it ought to be.'

She didn't believe him, and hoped he would notice it from her grief. But this was the day of his remaking and he didn't care what she or the whole world might want of him. One day the Dutch would discover that in this land no one could be without cattle for long. Then they would load their belongings back on their ships and go away from here, and he would let his cattle graze on the plains below the mountain. All of it was his doing, it was his day, and his spirit was proud and relieved. The thought came to him that he was really much smarter than he'd ever realised.

2

PETER HAVGARD

Ho, ho, come forth from the land of the north, saith the Lord:
for I have spread you abroad as the four winds of heaven.
                                    – Zachariah II:vi

'I WAS PLANNING to learn their language from her; that was why I took
her into my house,' said van Riebeeck. 'And I mastered some words,
but the sounds are too much for me. She herself made wonderful
progress with Dutch, and a lot of Portuguese she picked up from our
slaves, and can you believe it, I even heard Malay and English words
from her mouth. That she would have learned from the young clerks.
They like showing off to her. Some days it is here as if one is walking
about in Malacca or Batavia. And when she crosses the courtyard in her
sarong and *badjoe*, everything jerks to a standstill from the kitchen all
the way to the back of the hospital. The East, it's pure East. And very
intelligent, I tell you. I questioned her about the inland peoples, the
strength of a particular group, at what distance from here, how many
cattle. All the usual questions, you might say everything we'd wanted
to know about her people from the time of the Portuguese, but without
a way of finding out. She told me stories. I think she genuinely meant
it, she was always very honest, but of course she could not be sure
herself, and I believe she just wanted to keep me happy. And here and
there she heard something from her old uncle Herrie, or from other
people. I just wrote it all down, as if I believed every word. And whatever our Directors think of it, I was the one who had to act. Look, I

was here, the skipper in the storm. No one could decide on my behalf, you understand? And of course I wanted to trust our little Eva.'

Like two farmers at a cattle market van Riebeeck and Peter Havgard stood, their elbows on the top beam of the kraal, short-stemmed pipe in mouth, their eyes trained more on the people passing in the background than on the livestock in front of them. Van Riebeeck liked the young man, hand-picked by him. Like himself, in his youth, Peter was a surgeon by trade, and he was pleasant company, a man who encouraged one with questions, as if he was really interested in what he heard. They'd started by talking about the problem of land transport. There were no roads here, no canals of any description for conveyance. They were in agreement: only hundreds of oxen, thousands over the years, could solve the problem for the Company. Then they started talking about the cattle and the livestock trade. But it was Eva the young man wanted to hear about.

'So you took her back after what they'd done to the Company?'

'She was innocent of it all, a mere child. After more than a year the old man began sending messages through go-betweens: how it had been the fault of Gogosoa's Goringhaiqua, how he'd fled for fear that he would be accused of the deed. I sometimes thought of such a possibility myself, because some of the same cattle, bearing the Company's mark, were later brought back here to be bartered again. I had to pay for them a second time with the usual bartering goods, and something extra in the form of drink and tobacco. It's like when your hat is blown away, and a week later you see someone else wearing it. If you want it, you've got to buy it back. I was stronger than they and could reclaim my property, but this wasn't about a hat, you understand? I wanted as many of them as possible to acquire the taste of tobacco and brandy. If you asked Gogosoa's people they'd say that they'd taken those animals from Herrie. Traditional enemies of his, apparently, for generations.'

'And did you get back all you'd lost?'

'No. He'd left here with forty-two. We kept an ox, and about sixty sheep. Then we also had four calves in the stable, and after a week one's mother came back to it, a beautiful big-udder cow. Well, it was in October of '53, and as you can see, we've built the stock up again.

Sometimes Oedasoa's men bring a few, Ngonnemoa sends too.' Once again he gestured at the small herd of calves in the kraal before them.

'And Eva? Was she on the run with them all the time? Never longed to be back home?'

'She did, and we missed her too. Not I so much, but my wife and children. Lambert went on asking for her for a long time. And you must remember this: she's one of a family. A daughter only leaves her family when she marries. After all, Herrie is her guardian, and among them a mother's brother has almost more authority over the children than their own father. And with those cattle he suddenly gained status. Yes, he was even strong enough to keep her loyalty for the three years they wandered among the False Bay dunes. I respect the old man, I admit that. He truly had the better of me.'

'Respect for a thief and murderer. In Amsterdam they hang them.'

'While others walk free. Imagine how I felt that Sunday, Pieter, when he robbed us of everything and killed the little herdsman. He fled to the west with the cattle, to the sea. Should I have followed him with one-half of my soldiers? Certainly not, because then I'd have exposed the Fort to an attack from the bushes. You can see for yourself, the whole valley lies open to that side. It was a scheme, I suspected, a common ruse, to divert our attention in one direction and then throw the main force in against us from the opposite side. I thought: We're all going to die here today. And there were my wife and little Abraham, born the day before. So I put every man who could carry arms on the walls to protect the Fort. And old Herrie got away with the greatest of ease. He'd read my thoughts all along.'

From the kraal gate they went around the back of the Fort to the gardens. The paths among the beds were covered with crushed seashells, the beds were green and tidy, the soil dark with kraal manure, the irrigation furrows gleaming with water. Among the turnips and cabbages the slaves stood watching as the masters came past. At the embankment a Hollander was leaning on his spade. 'Good farmer,' van Riebeeck said. 'A good harvest, if the rain keeps on like this.' His eyes moved across his garden from one side to the other. What was he noticing? wondered the surgeon. What did he ignore?

'Our life is a bit easier again, but, you won't believe in what poverty that incident landed us. I had my reputation to think about. My good name was at stake. I could not have them say of me one day that they'd sent that van Riebeeck to get the whole business going and he failed. I had to succeed.' He gestured vaguely at the blue bay. 'We were forced to eat penguins, seal meat, fish, green gulls' eggs. Right here on land, on land, I tell you, people died of scurvy. But we're Hollanders, aren't we, our salvation lies in the sea. I sent out boats, all I had, as small as a galliot, halfway round the world, to St Helena, to Mauritius, for food, and they usually came back empty. But this station had to survive. Fort Good Hope. And what about my reputation? This Herrie had become an important man in the land. At the time I tried to think the way he was thinking, among those dunes with our herd, and the wonderful novelty it must have been to him. His wretched beachranging all ended in one swoop.'

With a smile van Riebeeck shook his head, as if unable to believe it. 'Within a few hours, the duration of a single sermon. Remarkable. I hope he dies in poverty.'

'The girl Eva?' asked Havgard.

'Yes.' As if he returned to reality. 'Pretty child.'

'How old would she be now?'

'I guess about seventeen, eighteen. I don't know when she was born, but when we salvaged the cargo of *Nieuwe Haerlem* in '48, she was about six.'

'Did you see her then, yourself?'

'Yes. And famished, like all the rest. Since then she's always been skinny and small, as if she had been stunted. It's only nowadays that she's been putting on weight.'

'How long has she been living among Christians?'

'Hollanders? A year with *Nieuwe Haerlem,* then a year in the Fort, and now for another four years since she came back.'

Havgard wanted to know more, but he would not ask. 'But a child, a mere child,' van Riebeeck resumed. 'And this I can tell you, as a married man who is well looked after in that respect, and let's keep it between us: every man in this hamlet, from the barracks, from the huts, from the ships, from the slave lodge, goes about every day staring after her. The women are aware of it. They feel jealous, or envy her, or feel threatened in some way. Heaven knows what will become of Eva the day I leave. My wife says . . . Yes, my wife never lets her out of her sight. Still too young, she says. And she knows the child.'

'Among her own people she would quite likely have been married by now.'

'Most probably. But married respectably, and probably to a rich man, for she's a choice girl. But the problem is this, Pieter: Who are her people today? Could it be Maria and I, or Herrie's people, or Oedasoa's, or the people of her late father beyond the mountain? There have been changes here at the Cape which have altered her fate four or five times. I have misgivings about her future.'

Havgard looked around him. Changes? Steep mountains, the distant plains, peasant hovels, the dunes with their cluster of huts of the Goringhaicona and their latest hangers-on, a Fort with flag and cannon, open sea, a few Dutch ships temporarily anchored between the North and the East. And Eva. And he.

It was at van Riebeeck's table that he'd met her. He, after three months as a soldier on *Princes Rojael*, and another three in the Cape garrison, had applied for the vacancy when he'd heard that a surgeon was needed, in the hope that it would mean a post as ship's doctor, off to the East. Yes, the commander had assured him, there were regularly vacancies on the ships, but the East had to wait. 'I know you want to go there, everybody does. I too, but this has to stay between us, old chap. The Orient? Ancient, miraculous, sensual, mysterious, fragrant, foreign, and the place where you will make a fortune, not so? That's the way we all feel. No, Pieter, make a start with your career first. The Company has thousands of soldiers, but few surgeons. The vacancy is here in the Fort. From this day your wages are doubled to twenty guilders. I make you deputy surgeon, and at the first opportunity you'll become surgeon, and then you'll go to the East. If you survive, you may become chief surgeon of that huge hospital in Batavia. Your fortune.'

It was at van Riebeeck's table that he'd met her. Van Riebeeck's wife had personally invited him. The company was small, but convivial: three women, four men. He was the newcomer and was introduced, his name transliterated into Dutch from the Danish Peter Havgard. She was 'Eva, a friend of our family', and he was 'Master Pieter van Meerhof from Copenhagen'. When he protested against the 'master', van Riebeeck calmed him. 'That comes from the ships. On the whalers we call the ship's cook "doctor".' Eva, seated next to him, was opposite Mrs van Riebeeck. He could see her imitating the hostess, with the small napkin to her lips. Eating with the fingertips, small dab of butter on the potatoes, making small talk to her left and right, with her voice low and her eyes cast down.

They did not have much opportunity to talk. Her voice had the same intonation as that of the hostess, with the same pronunciation that reminded him of French. A ship's captain with a tattooed hand and an officer with an orange sash over a bright blue uniform kept him busy. It was as if a Dutch flag was being waved over the table. The one wanted to discuss the tides in the Skagerrak, the other the fortifications at Elsinore. He knew Elsinore personally. His father had been in the garrison there, but he'd seen the ugly fortress only from the plain. The place was haunted, people said. But he didn't want to be burdened with the young ensign. With the skipper he spoke about the Western Sea, while the latter kept to the North Sea, to see whether the sailor would become annoyed. He did not, only tasted another glass and expounded seriously on the speed of the current in the waterway. Van Meerhof's heart warmed to the captain. There was a lot of wine on the table, a good Spanish wine, red and off-dry with a good, ripe bouquet. Van Riebeeck leaned over the table to keep the glasses filled. That set the orange-and-blue ensign talking again.

Eva was quiet. She hardly spoke all night when she wasn't mentioned by name, and from the movements of her hands she seemed impatient to get away from there. This, then, was her stock of conversation; she'd follow the hostess's example and imitate her speech. And if she were untied from her leash one day and left to stand on her own feet, what would she be like? A shallow puddle which would dry up to mud and later to clay, from which nothing further would grow.

After that the commander, or his wife, invited him back to their table time and time again. He would sit next to Eva with other guests and join in conversations about Goringhaiqua and Goringhaicona, Grigriqua and Chainouqua, about ships' provisions and draught oxen, about seasonal migration and the condition of the summer grazing. And around them a world was disintegrating. This thought interested him, without imagining that he himself was in a maelstrom from which escape was impossible and a hideous death his way out. Van Riebeeck regarded this general change in the Cape society as a commercial transaction. Eva's explanation of the events to him was vague, cast in a general glorification of van Riebeeck as a person, which she'd probably borrowed just like that from his wife's mouth.

One evening after dinner they went to walk on the beach, in the direction of the Dunes. 'Not too far in the dark, only last week there were lions around,' Mrs van Riebeeck warned. There was a teeming, shimmering, pulsing night sky overhead and small stars of phosphorus under their feet in the wet sand. Behind them was the flaming brazier of the Fort, and far on the seam of the bay was the lantern of Fort Uitkijk, like a single star above the black sea. Peter was questioning Eva, encouraging her to talk. He himself couldn't offer very much, as she hardly knew anything at all of a world beyond this watering place.

'Lonely,' he said. 'What do people in Africa do when the sun goes down?'

'There are the outposts. They keep guard over the people.'

'Are they far inland?' He already knew the answer.

'No, just along the Liesbeeck, where the free burghers have their farms. Over there you see Uitkijk, and Keert-de-Koe is where the trek road goes through the river, and then Coornhoop in the fields, and Ruijterwacht. And right up against the mountain where the river begins is Houdt-den-Bul. In each of them are a few men with their dog.'

'So have you been to them?'

'Yes.'

'And what are they for, those outposts?'

'You've been here long enough, Pieter. You know that for yourself.'

'I want to hear what you think about it.'

'The Koina want to raid our cattle. We don't want them to succeed.

They say if we get cattle, we shall get strong and keep all the pasture for ourselves.' This was van Riebeeck talking, and 'we' was the Company.

'Yet there is lots grazing here.'

'Yes, but we are going to get too strong.' He stopped to find out what she meant. She walked on without understanding. The evening wind was cold across the beach. What do people in Africa do after sundown? He took her hand. Her grip was warm and strong. 'Eva, the Dutch will never go away from here. You'd better tell that well in time to Oedasoa and Herrie.'

'That's good,' she whispered, and then pulled back her hand. 'I think they know it. I think there will be war.'

'War against whom?' He laughed. 'Surely not against these natives?'

'Why do you laugh, Pieter? They won't win, but they will fight. It is their only hope. All the Koina are crying. They can see this is the end.'

'Are you crying?'

'Some days. Most days I think I am a Hollander.' He himself had seen it written, in van Riebeeck's handwriting, in the Fort's journal: *Krotoa said she has a Dutch heart*. At the time when the Goringhaiqua sheltered a couple of runaway slaves, it had been her proposal that two of Gogosoa's sons should be kept as hostages on Robben Island until the slaves had been handed back. And it was done. Van Riebeeck, in his pride, had also caught Herrie and sent him to the island. And there it was written now: *Krotoa said she has a Dutch heart*. There the three resentful natives were trapped on a barren island with a brackish well, with nothing to see but the distant smoke in the interior where the herdsmen were shifting their herds and families from one pasture to the next.

'Does that not rage inside you, Krotoa, the Koina heart with which you were born?'

On the Fort wall a drummer played a prolonged roll, the sign that the gate was going to be closed. 'Not much. The commander is my father. Life is easier for me, and I can grow old peacefully one day. Come, we must turn back. Do you know what our people do with old ones who will not die?'

He walked back reluctantly. 'It's a very good reason you're mentioning. But if war breaks out, will you help the Hollanders to annihilate your people and occupy all the grazing and water?'

'No.' He could hear her crying. He tried to put his arms around her, but she pulled away from him in alarm, and walked away, rapidly, sobbing. And somewhat annoyed he followed her to the gate. She neither said goodbye nor looked round and crossed the courtyard in the dusk, going straight to van Riebeeck's house. The door above the stairs opened and closed with a flash of golden light.

For weeks he didn't see her. His work, between the hospital and the ships, kept him occupied. The outward-bound fleet arrived at the roadstead. At this time of the year the ships were badly undermanned, because in Germany the farmhands were making hay and refused to go to sea. And those who came were decimated by maladies they'd brought aboard themselves: rat-bite fever, dysentery, syphilis, influenza.

At first light every day he was called from the hospital's waiting room, and followed, case in hand, a slave with a lantern to the quay, where sailors with their oars across their knees held the service boat for him against the scaffolding. He went down the ladder, slipping on slimy seaweed down into the boat, to the bench at the rear, beside the quartermaster, where his medicine chest was put down for him.

In the dark, wet winter mornings it took the service boat three-quarters of an hour, beating into the waves with its bows against the north-westerly weather and with gusts of green spray over the bow, soaking everybody, to the nearest heaving, straining ship. There, with his case fastened across his shoulder with a canvas strap, he had to struggle up a rope ladder, then the ship would roll its gunports under and submerge him waist-deep in the sea. On board he would go to the cabin, where at six o'clock the passengers were seated at breakfast, among the watch officers' dirty pans and dishes which still cluttered the table. In the midst of all this he made room for his writing case. The smell of cooking fat and tobacco smoke in the closed cabin made him nauseous. The journal of the ship's surgeon would be brought for his inspection.

What an existence. For this he'd exchanged a soldier's nine guilders for the twenty of a medical quack. His soul, for a few guilders more. But at least he could afford to buy brandy and need not steal it from the apothecary's chest. The surgeon's journal was brought, with reports on his patients, their symptoms, his prescriptions and his successes or failures. Sometimes it was described in the journal like a game of chess: I prescribed this, then that happened to him; I prescribed that, something else happened. Move and counter-move in a game against the Creator.

If there was an entry about provisions, the cheese, bread, bacon or water, he would have a barrel brought and opened. Meat covered with a light foam and a greenish sheen he had rinsed in vinegar and pepper, but if there were worms in it he had it sent ashore to be replaced. Ship's biscuit was rapped on the table to check for weevils. If weevils crawled out, the cook could crumble the biscuits in the mortar and bake it in lard. Afterwards he, Master Pieter, had to follow the ship's surgeon below to inspect the patients. Between decks, on every single ship, hung a repulsive smell of rotting excrement of dysentery patients who had relieved themselves among the cannon on the dark orlop, of bodies unwashed for four months or more, of stale tobacco smoke, stale food, stale breaths and the disgusting winds emitted by scurvy patients. They lay on the deck, and died on the deck, in the forecastle.

The work repelled him. The poor stinking sick, helplessly sprawling in the mouldy dark, veiled by the bitter smoke of a swinging oil lamp, stretched out hands to him, mumbled, showed their black gums, occasionally vomited on his feet. He distributed his medicine there, offered the second opinion when it was asked for, started compiling a new list of patients in the second degree, those who could still be cured, whom the captain had to send ashore with bedding and blanket, and preferably on a plank, so that they could be carried.

He did not stay for that process, but was the first to climb over the side into the boat dancing below, and urged on his quartermaster to the next ship. In this way a morning passed. Towards noon he would arrive ashore with lice in his stockings, drink a glass of brandy and sleep until he was called for the afternoon shift in the hospital. He did not want to be a surgeon. He regretted having accepted the post. Certainly, the early dream of the golden Orient was still strong in him, sat the broken, festering Europeans with dreams of an East dying in their eyes, filled him with despair. All of them, young and old, wanted to go East, but here their new wrecks lay stranded. And he felt stranded himself, because the East was a distant, tantalising morning star, and the backward Cape far too firmly attached to faceless Africa, and the situation on shore just a fraction better than on the ships. Ashore, at least one could open a hatch for fresh air.

Most likely it was Peter's age which yearned for the bloom and the fruit of life, for he was no longer a youngster; deeply depressed, he was the prisoner of a petrified system. He was the one who did not believe in scurvy, and to placate him van Riebeeck occasionally suggested that he might be right. Scurvy, van Riebeeck had been told by experts who revealed it to him in a proud tone as if the knowledge was a personal achievement, was both the cause and the reason for the existence of the Cape refreshment station. Not the only one, his informers told him, but undoubtedly the first and the worst.

'You must be new to the trade, Master Pieter. Scurvy is the name of the disease.'

'Not in every language, my dear sir. In your tongue it is *scheurbuijk*, a torn stomach, and you see no sign of that here. What you're really trying to say is *scorbut*, which is Latin for scabs or scabbiness. But then I don't see any scabs here either, colleague.'

From ship's quack to skipper and from skipper to commander he was mentioned as quarrelsome, and someone who didn't know much about his work either. But what Peter had seen, and what he believed in, was that skippers very rarely got scurvy, officers less rarely, and common sailors most of the time. Why? The difference was only the better wages with which to purchase food and lodging. Something else he'd noticed in the surgeon's manuals that passed through his hands, was that few of the scurvy sufferers showed similar symptoms. Peter wanted Lords Seventeen to be informed of his conclusion. Apart from the false name, which he could readily understand as it had been coined by common sailors, and which should be corrected, he also proposed to van Riebeeck that all ship's surgeons should send their report books to head office to be examined and compared.

The fellow was setting about it in the wrong manner, if he hoped to succeed, van Riebeeck thought. An older man would handle it differently. He shouldn't accuse, but cajole; not stir up doubt, but harmony; not question, but congratulate, offer a pat on the shoulder, another mug of beer, and gradually, gradually persuade his opponents. But that was not what this fellow with the strong vital urge and slightly more advanced education wanted. With a cold eye he despised ignorance, stubbornness and the burden of authority, in other words, the whole existing administrative structure of his employer, the laudable Company. Havgard had become cynical and apathetic to his patients, colleagues and authorities, including his commander. Van Riebeeck discussed it with him, for it would be a pity to lose his cooperation.

'If you don't believe in scurvy, Pieter, you will have to come up with a different diagnosis for these cases.'

'I don't have enough experience to do that.'

'Then why do you differ from those who do know?'

'They guess. I obey my conscience. What is this scurvy? All the journals are full of it, but what does it look like?'

'Black faeces, stinking breath, weakness, mouth ulcers, loose teeth. Don't let the name worry you, Pieter. It's only a generic one.'

'For several diseases. Explain this to me: There are two ships, they go to sea on the same day, let's say from Texel. They travel together all the way here, and anchor on the same tide in front of this Fort. That is possible, isn't it?'

'More than that. It happens often.'

'Now tell me, how does it happen that on one ship sixty may die of this scurvy and eighty more are suffering from it, and on the other ship only two, or even none?'

'Coincidence?'

'No coincidence. I'm looking for the cause.'

'True, too often for coincidence. But I can't tell why.'

'You must agree that those ships were provisioned from the same warehouse, and that the sailors were recruited in the same cheap holes in Amsterdam. What I say is this: one ship is supplied with rotten meat, or one man carries a disease on board, which turns into an epidemic on the journey. That is my theory. Let the Company take a look at how its chandlers prepare their salted meat, and from which brothels its people are recruited. The experiment can save the expense of this entire refreshment station.'

Disheartened, van Riebeeck changed the subject, returning to his house as soon as he could. He didn't know much about scurvy, but he enjoyed gardening and farming and would continue to use the name scurvy, since his greens were a popular remedy for whatever it was that afflicted his employer's seafaring folk.

Because Peter could find nothing else to do after sundown in Africa and the aimless small talk around the barracks table bored him profoundly, he returned to van Riebeeck. He knew that the man liked to spend his evenings with his family and suspected that the wife didn't trust him with her little Eva. What else was there to do in Africa after sundown?

Van Riebeeck laughingly, not without satisfaction, told him about the early days here in the Cape dunes. Some of those things the world wouldn't believe, but fortunately every word of it had been written down. It was all to be found in the journals. There was much information about the vegetables, and how they cured scurvy. If Pieter felt so inclined he could read the records. All the while, Mrs van Riebeeck studied him pensively, as if she were examining a dress in a tailor's shop for quality, appearance and durability. He looked past her at the inside door. Would Eva be home? He felt unwelcome in their front room, and uncomfortable on their couch that had been built as a church pew. Perhaps he was boring them.

'I'd like to read them,' he said.

When van Riebeeck left to fetch the books, his wife immediately said, 'The children are so restless, I'm going to look,' and left with her husband. In the room next door he could hear two people whispering. What could it be? Then van Riebeeck entered with four heavy volumes. 'Here you can read about old Herrie. I have just about his whole life story here. Curious old soul, quite proud, in a kind of English way, but last month he sat here shaking like a little lapdog, before I had him put on the island. He's no longer what he used to be.'

'And Eva's story?'

'Yes, hers too. Why don't you take the books with you? You should find them interesting.'

Because it sounded like an invitation to withdraw, he went to light his lamp and two candles in the small waiting room of the duty surgeon. First he looked at dates. He wanted to read the entries for yesterday and the day before, but found that the latest volume had not been given to him. Thereupon he poured himself half a glass of brandy, lit his pipe, opened the oldest volume at the beginning, and lost himself in the past. The year was 1651. On Christmas Day, in his imagination, he set out with the first settlers from the harbour of Texel. He calculated that Eva was nine years old at the time.

In the book he discovered a country in which van Riebeeck did not exist. There was a wide weather-tossed bay, a half-circle of pale sand dunes with arid, colourless salt scrub, behind them, a sky-high, angular mountain folded like a brown cupped hand around the back of the bay, a fresh breeze sweeping endlessly under a bright blue sky, and on the north-western horizon a low dun-coloured island behind black boulders, like a stripped shipwreck in a mist of sea spray, reeking of white bird droppings. What else? Inland stood the brown autumn hills curiously stained black and yellow like a leopard, and then a tall mountain range running north and south without any sign of passage. Behind that, probably the celebrated kingdoms of Africa, as rich as those of the East, but unknown and practically undiscovered, because they'd been shrouded by so many myths and dangers. The thought of Africa repelled him, conjuring up images of cannibals, misshapen people, relentless cruelty, dark ignorance.

That night he read about their struggle to provide food and shelter to those who had come to create something out of nothing, to plant where no spade had yet turned the soil, to build houses from stone where nature had intended them to be made of reeds. The first two winters had washed away whatever they had planted, and the summers had withered what was left. Sent to feed the ships, they could not find food for themselves, and had to be fed by the ships. Sailing boats had to go off to islands, months away, for provisions. The walls of the Fort had to be rebuilt again and again. They met natives from various tribes, who gathered their food in different ways. Why? There was one small group who lived by the seaside and ate seafoods, they were Watermen or Beachrangers. Others, who lived from hunting and scavenging, were called Sonqua. The book called them Bosjesmans, Bushmen. Herrie and Eva provided the commander with these names.

Here and there in the book he came across references to Eva. Her intelligence was praised, and her affection for the white people. How old would she have been then? On Sunday, 19 October 1653, between ten o'clock and eleven o'clock, Herrie moved through three levels of Cape existence, starting as a Beachranger, then killing and robbing and driving off cattle like a Sonqua, and ending his day as a Hottentot, a herdsman. That affair had nearly ruined the settlement, but they struggled on, struggled against nature, against famine, against the natives, and mainly against despair. The labourers stole, absconded, died in accidents. So many died: young men with red cheeks from the North came to fill a hole in the Cape dunes, often two or three or four to one hole.

The next day Peter returned the journals he had finished. In the afternoon, after he'd returned from the ships, he did not go to lunch but poured his brandy and resumed reading. What had most plagued the settlers? What had been their most urgent needs? He found a pencil, and wrote on the inside of the back flyleaf of the third volume of the journal the ten words: *fertility, rainfall, river, floods, wind, grazing, timber, fuel, transport, defence*. He thought that he was beginning to understand the situation. And the scene, as on the stage of a theatre, shifted from the Table Valley round the eastern side of the mountain to the valley of the Liesbeeck. There were houses along the Liesbeeck. Ripe wheat billowed in the wind. Sleek cows were grazing in lush clover. And there was a semicircle of armed redoubts all along the river, from the sea to high on the mountain slopes. Why? To force the fruits from Africa. The Fort, here where he found himself, was becoming something like a general's tent, far behind the front line of a war. Then he read about Eva again.

29 October 1658.

Today we bartered an ox and 35 sheep from the Cochoqua. The female interpreter came back to the Fort with us. She told us that shortly after her departure from here the Goringhaiqua attacked her and robbed her of all her possessions. Her mother, who lives with the Goringhaiqua, refused to help her to recover them. Thereupon she went to her sister, the wife of Oedasoa who is one of the two chiefs of the Cochoqua. They had last seen her as an infant, and received her with great joy. She told them about our nation, that she had been brought up by the commander's wife and learned our language and something about our religion, and about our desire to live in friendship with them. To show his willingness, Oedasoa sent us an ox and sheep. He had tried to send us livestock before, but his messengers had been turned back by the Gorachoqua and the Goringhaiqua. He would have liked to pay us a personal visit, but was also prevented by others. The commander asked her whether we could send people with gifts to Oedasoa, and proposed a gift of cinnamon and pepper, and some of the very strongest brandy and tobacco, and a musician who could play the violin. She said that she had wanted to come back sooner, but that both she and her sister had been ill. She had taught her sister to pray, who then wanted to know what else she had learned from the Hollanders. But the Goringhaiqua and Gorachoqua were mightily angry and wanted to kill her.

What disease? wondered Peter. Two people in one home ill at the same time probably meant something contagious.

The next entry reported an expedition to take gifts to Oedasoa, and to escort him to the Fort so that van Riebeeck could seal an agreement with him. Sergeant van Harwaerden left the same day with fifteen Hollanders, the four sheep which the Cochoqua had brought, and Eva. On pack oxen they took beads, copper, beer, brandy (lots of brandy), spices, ship's rusks and brown sugar with them. Van Harwaerden returned with an incredible report: there were huts up to forty or fifty feet in diameter, oxen so big one could hardly see over their backs, so

many sheep that it took three hours to turn them out of the kraal. Two
thoughts occurred to Peter, namely: What disease? And: It should be
possible to accompany an expedition like that.

He read on. Eva had not come back with van Harwaerden. When
they'd last seen her, she was trekking deeper inland with the Cochoqua.
She rode on an ox, like the head woman of the tribe. She'd sent a
message to the commander not to be worried, she would return and
not forget that she had a Dutch heart in her. Next to this inscription
in his journal van Riebeeck noted that he could remember the sister
having in mind a rich young man for Eva. After that Peter scanned the
next few pages. Like a spy running ahead to peep through windows,
he quickly checked every page for her name. He wanted to know where
she had been, who'd been with her, what they had done. In his mind
he accompanied her on that dusty trek into the interior with a few
thousand cattle and twenty thousand sheep, and the short, tawny people
followng at a placid pace. Some of the women were carrying children
on their backs, others walked with rolled mats or earthenware pots
on their heads. The men, with their two or three assegais and a throwing stick, walked on either side of the herd. Some of the oldest and
youngest had been placed on oxen, and among them, like a princess
whose feet should not touch the ground, rode Eva on a giant ox. Ahead
of them stretched a yellow grassy plain, behind it loomed mountains,
and along the foot of the mountains ran a dark line of trees. It indicated a river.

After that Peter read once again about ships coming and going, the
sick dying in the Fort, and of the new farmers along the Liesbeeck,
how they'd harvested grain that summer and threshed the sheaves with
flails. On the very last day of the year Eva arrived at the head of a
small band of children, and she had much to tell. The men had gone
hunting and Oedasoa had been attacked by a lion. They'd tackled the
lion with their bare hands, killed it and dragged it off him, but poor
Oedasoa's shoulder had been nearly torn off his body. For a month he'd
lain, feverish and delirious, and asking her to summon van Riebeeck,
he wanted so much to meet him and his wife before he died. She herself
wanted to stay at the Fort now, she said. She'd taught these nine children

to say grace before eating, and a prayer before going to bed, and Oedasoa had asked that van Riebeeck educate them further in religion. She would appreciate it if van Riebeeck would give each of them a cube of brown sugar on the palm, to taste. That concluded the volume for 1658.

These things had happened before he, a surgeon with a Danish infantry regiment, had heeded the voices from the sea that swept through Europe, calling farmers from their lands, clerks from their desks and bakers from their ovens. Come to the sea on the west coast, the voices lured them, come and man the ships sailing to the East. *Orang lama, orang baharu*, fair East India, those were sweetly flavoured words, sounds to conjure with. Children knew them; at twelve they were tempted to find if it was true what they had been promised. The East, the East, the East, said the voices, it was the sound of breakers on a beach, of wind through rushes, of footsteps on a sandy track, of rustling palms, of the tumultuous young blood in your veins. The East was where every morning the sun displayed its gold, where the Magi had come from. The East was the Holy Land. Why was Peter Havgard still biding at home?

He was not the first from that regiment to go to sea. They'd had four years of war against the Germans and against the four worst winters in years. The rainy season was endlessly wet and dark. Perhaps the bad weather had caused more casualties than the enemy, for the snow, sleet and icy wind, biting cold, the frozen feet and hands, the gangrene and amputations in mud and snow, had killed young and old in both camps.

Because he wished to live, Peter unharnessed the wagon with which he'd carted wounded to the town, in the king's field before the gate, and walked down the road, his coat collar turned against the rain, without looking back or resting, away from the blood-streaked wagon which he'd had to clean every night with a spade and buckets of snow water; away from the army camp and his skimpy bundle of clothes and books, away from the small box with the paltry tools of his trade on the wagon.

The road to the East went west, he discovered. He had to become a soldier first to reach the ships. There was room for farmers, bakers and clerks in the Company's service, but all had to be soldiers first. That morning in the courtyard of East India House in Enkhuijzen a moist sea wind had driven the dry brown plane-tree leaves across the wet paving, from one corner to the other, churning them round and round. There were more than thirty shivering men ahead of him in the queue. They had to appear one at a time, in front of a one-eyed woman with a hump she'd tied up in a black cloth like a child on her back. Each man had to pass her. Some of them she turned back.

She slid open a hatch, and peered into his face. 'What do you want?'

'Become a soldier.'

'Served the Company before?'

'No.' She stared into his eyes, nodded several times with a sour grimace, opened for him, mumbling something like '*mal donder*' – 'crazy fool' in the Dutch language – as he went through. The witch at this door was the one who looked, and chose.

Or was it *madonna*? What Peter heard, hundreds before and after him also heard. Some said it had been up in Hoorn, others said down in Rotterdam. They said she saw omens, and could foretell the future. All her forecasts were written down, and kept in a small box at her house. Twenty years after Peter, a clerk who was to remember the old woman well, tried to enter the East through that same gate. Perhaps he could understand her better, at least his own shoulders were already hunched, his own eyes weak from reading in half-light, and his Latin passable. What he heard there was *mater omnis*, or was it *mater orbis*? Mother of all, or mother of the earth. Could it possibly have been *madonna salvate*? But he, too, had no idea what she was talking about and he wondered why he had been accepted and others denied. What did she have to do with the Holy Virgin? Perhaps it was '*mal donder*' after all.

Peter Havgard had to queue up again at a table in the corner of the front lobby. He could lie if he wished, for no papers were asked. He expected that the Company was looking for people with two legs, two arms, that was all. Those who had been waiting in the queue in front of him, told that in Amsterdam all they asked was, 'Do you see that door?' And if you said yes, you were accepted, because you could hear, see and talk.

Name? He translated his name into Dutch: Pieter van Meerhof. Place of birth? Copenhagen. Age? Twenty-three years. Next of kin? His father in the garrison of Elsinore Castle. Military experience? Four years in the army. Wife, children, other dependants? None. Other obligations? Like what? Well, you may be an apprentice trying to abscond from a contract, or you may be a runaway from Prince Hendrik's army, or a man with accumulated debts. Do you want to hear more examples? None of those, no. Catholic? No.

He was sent to the shop with an advance on his wages, and the next day he and fifteen other fortunates were taken on board at the Peperhuis quay. The chest with his clothes, dry provisions and the few odds and ends of surgeon's equipment he could afford and assemble were sent ahead to Texel by lighter. So he entered the Company's service with eyes shut, in the hope of opening them after a sea voyage and finding that his dream of the East had come true.

At the Cape they were sent ashore. For the while they all had to forget about the East. Here was a wilderness to be tamed, and more hands were needed. When the work was done one day they could resume the journey to wonderful, golden Golconda or Samarkand, or wherever they had been dreaming of. And one day, when it seemed there was a chance of escaping from the Cape as a ship's doctor, van Riebeeck persuaded him, and so he stayed on. Perhaps Samarkand would turn out to be here after all, and just behind the next hill Ophir, Golconda, Eldorado, or the other golden cities of the world. But perhaps, Pieter, the Orient lurks in your heart, van Riebeeck had said. But van Riebeeck was an optimist; his Orient was where his wife was, and his only horizon the Liesbeeck. He himself was a cynical fellow.

'You want to be a ship's surgeon, Pieter? May I ask, what do you know of the trade? For example, how would you drain water from a patient suffering from dropsy?'

'I wouldn't do it, Commander. That's a doctor's work. A surgeon heals above the skin, the doctor below it.'

'Right, right, but in an emergency.'

'Only if the captain orders me.' He groped in his memory. '*Anasarca*. The withdrawal from the lower abdomen should be from the colon.

Administer opium for pain, the powder stirred in milk or brandy. I cut through the upper layer and the bottom layer of skin, then through the peritoneum, find the colon, fill an enema syringe, unscrew the handle, turn it upside down and hold a flagon under the tube.'

'What about a broken lower jaw?'

'A single fracture is easy, especially below the ear. Complex fractures are more difficult. Usually the jaw is so swollen that you cannot find the fracture. You palpate with your fingertips. Probe with a lancet for bits of lead or bone splinters, remove loose teeth, wash the wound and cover with ointment externally. Fit the parts as well as you can, splints on both sides, bandage, first downward and then horizontally around the face, put two long stitches through nose and lower lip, knot and pull tight.'

'And half a glass of brandy.'

'Yes, please.'

'Pieter, you say you put stitches through the whole nose, not just through the septum. From that I deduce that you practised on a battlefield. Tell me: are you a doctor or a surgeon?'

'I attended doctors.'

'Will you accept work in our hospital? I need you here. From today your wages go up from nine to twenty guilders.'

Of shipboard diseases he soon had enough. Worst of all was the filthy condition of the patients and their living quarters. Suffering was no excuse for filth. Some diseases were familiar, and knife wounds were just smaller versions of the black, oozing holes a dagger, a halfpike or a peasant's hayfork could make in a soldier's backside. Knife wounds? One-third of a bottle of brandy in the wound, one-third in the patient's throat, one-third for the doctor. Then for the incision, feeling with the point of the scalpel and two fingers for shards of bone, wood or metal, then rinsing with vinegar, cross-stitches in the intradermis, tacking stitches in the dermis, a light bandage. All that he knew. What he didn't know, and couldn't bear, was dirty people, the awful stench of scurvy breaths, a filthy ship, rotten food. Everything was dirtier and more putrid than in the army camps, where at least the amputees' tents could be pitched below the wind, and soldiers in barracks do not foul their bedding. Most Danish regiments marched and fought in white breeches. Why? For the sole reason of promoting tidiness. All he did here at the Cape was to complain, drink more brandy, and plead for a place on a ship going East. But this attitude made him unwelcome company, and he was convinced that van Riebeeck would not set him free, as the need of that gentleman's beloved Cape was much too great.

What did Eva mean, in his wretched life chained to this rock they called Africa? Was it ordained for her to keep him contented here, so that he would never see the East, nor ever again Denmark? Could this be so? The day he returned the last of the bound journals, he told van Riebeeck that he would like to accompany an expedition in the interior, if the commander could spare him from the ship's duties. For the moment the call of Africa was stronger than that of the Orient, he said. He was interested in this land and its peoples. He did not mention Eva.

Sometimes he encountered the aged remains of Herrie's little group inside or outside the Fort, and if he asked where Eva might be, the answer was: 'Gone to wear a hide skirt.' That was all. Why should she, with her Dutch ways, exchange the sarong and *badjoe* for a piece of animal skin? From what need, from what unnecessary and unappreciated loyalty to her nation, did she persist with it? In her Indian clothes she was slender, erect, well developed, just like a young girl should be. The boniness of her hungry days was gone. How would she look in the hip-skirts of the Koina, with nothing on top? Beautiful, he knew. Something to come home to.

Van Riebeeck in reply said: 'You know how much we need you here, Pieter, and yet I'm glad that you want to go on a journey overland. Who knows what miraculous medicines may be growing here? The Hottentots have told me of aloe juice and buchu. What do we know about their Bushman poison, and what remedy do we have against the Cape puff adder, the scorpion and the button spider? The Company can use your services, old chap. I'll look for someone else for our hospital, but for the time being it remains your responsibility. I'd like to go inland myself, especially now that there are flowers appearing everywhere, but it really is impossible. When we send out another expedition, you will go with it.'

Peter went on those journeys. At first without Eva, later with her. Before Mrs van Riebeeck's eyes their friendship went its unavoidable course. At first there were planned and approved meetings without much emotion, together with five or six others in van Riebeeck's front room. They were seldom alone; it had been arranged by a hand behind the scenes that their twilight strolls on rare windless summer's evenings became group walks. Everybody had to go out on the beach together. There were two of the commander's nieces (two dull, plain girls), a number of young clerks, a young ensign, and about no one else. The pleasure with which Eva greeted him in the evening was noticed, and when he saw that the nieces were treating Eva as a friend, he relaxed. At first Peter tried not to give offence through his frustration, later he no longer cared. They were wary of him. His cool politeness, cautious remarks and questions when answers were expected, might not have made him popular, but did make him acceptable, at best.

About a year after his arrival war broke out between his people and hers. It had become unavoidable. There were two claimants to one food source and the weaker had to make way for the stronger. Who were the stronger, the Koina or the Dutch, now had to be decided.

One day van Riebeeck gathered his people around a table and said: 'Look, you can see how things are going. It was not the intention of the Lords Directors that their ships would provide us with food, but indeed the other way round. Soon I will have to submit a report again, and it won't take much for them to shut down this place and recall us all. You know exactly how the matter stands. The Hottentots keep us thin, the hares and buck ruin our vegetables, and the people are rebellious from hunger. I used to believe that we could succeed here, between the sea and the mountain, but we shall have to expand. Only yesterday I had another look behind the mountain, particularly along the Liesbeeck where old Gogosoa is now lying with his Goringhaiqua.' Van Riebeeck drew his breath and counted on his fingers: 'On that side there is water throughout the year, and probably twice the annual rainfall we have on this side of the mountain. Open, even ground for farmlands, and pitch black with fruitfulness. Firewood in abundance all over the plains. Lovely clover pastures on either side of the river for grazing.

First-class wood for carpentry and ships' timber below the mountain, because there is no wind and the trees grow straight and tall. Therefore I'd like to use the Liesbeeck valley in the interests of the Company from now on. We won't move away from here, we simply found a new colony and raise our flag over there tomorrow. Well, how does it strike you? Either we expand or we take down our signboard and close up shop. In other words, either the end of the Company and the Dutch at the Cape, or success in this place for the next two or three generations. What do you think?'

Eva told Peter that no one in the meeting had asked what was to become of the Koina who had been farming in the valley for generations. The sick-comforter had said that it had been ordained for man to cultivate the earth, which was without form, and void. Peter thought: perhaps van Riebeeck had put him up to choose that verse. He said to her that perhaps they were thinking: that's the way of the world. In early times, apparently, it had been Herrie's pasture, but then Gogosoa had uprooted him, and now the Dutch were going to uproot Gogosoa. That's the way it goes.

After that, van Riebeeck moved quickly. At first farms were measured out in the best spots along the river, for servants of the Company who were encouraged with licences and a gift of livestock and seed grain to become free burghers. In four places along the river he had redoubts of stone and indigenous wood built. Kijkuit, on a dune near the mouth, Keert-de-Koe at the Koina's cattle path through the river, Coornhoop in the midst of the lands, and Houdt-den-Bul along the upper courses of the Liesbeeck. Perfect. And two government farms in the best spots on the mountain slope: Rustenburg, a vineyard and fruit farm, and De Schuur, a wheat farm with a large wooden *schuur* or shed where it was possible to thresh wheat under cover. Now there was a visible eastern frontier, fully delimited with a fence of poles and thorn branches, and the steep banks of the Liesbeeck River itself. Perfect.

From the outset Peter had followed the events with great attention: even from before the first reaction, the first stock theft, the first incident of arson, the first murder, until the entire eastern frontier went up in flames and smoke and the farmers had to flee to the redoubts with their children. He and Eva were deeply involved in it from the beginning.

It was just at the time when van Riebeeck began to congratulate himself on his plan to occupy the whole Liesbeeck valley, when there were fresh eggs and milk on the table daily and stews of fat mutton and cabbage, that the Goringhaiqua began to demonstrate their discontent. Now they understood clearly which way the wind was blowing. The enemy was prospering too much, he was building stone houses and enclosures of timber, and when you build like that you plan to stay. When they heard axes ringing in the forest every day, and saw the big trunks falling with a tearing and splintering crash, when blue smoke rose from the chimneys of farmhouses along the river and Dutch voices urged on the ploughing oxen, resounding far in the still mountain air, the deeply worried Koina said: 'This Hollander wants to lay his eggs in our nest. How come that they are building their houses everywhere and digging up the earth? They've moved in here, right among us behind the mountain. They are taking the ground that is our own.' For them it was a strange experience to watch the water pastures being drained, how whole forests were felled, how fields of sweet tubers were ploughed up. White children were herding cattle beside the river, playing in the vleis, plundering wild ducks' nests.

Relations on either side of the river turned bad. The Dutch wanted the Goringhaiqua's red oxen in front of their ploughs, and the Goringhaiqua were bitter because strangers had come to settle here beside their water pastures. It's Eva, they said, she was to blame; it was she who persuaded Oedasoa to make friends with the Dutch. She was the one who lived in two homes, spoke two languages, wore two kinds of clothes. It was her fault. They hurled threats and stones at her when they saw her.

Half-grown boys shouted vociferous challenges at each other across the river. There was one autumn day, cool, windless, the sky as blue as Indian washing-blue, and the vleis smooth and shimmering. Steven Botma's shiny white ducks were paddling among the reeds and two brown children tossed bits of red locusts on the water to lure the ducks to their side. Botma's son, who was irrigating higher up, saw it and fired a shot into the water to scare the ducks, but some of the buckshot hit the children in the arms and legs. Since that unfortunate day Botma's house, his animals and his family were the targets of stones thrown from the bushes; soon they couldn't risk it outside any more. Then he set fire to the bushes on the opposite side of the river so that there was no more place for a snake to hide in. One morning he saw his dog swimming through the river to the black patch where fresh white molehills had been pushed up, and later that day he saw the dog lying there in the clearing with three arrows in its stiff body. That could happen to his children too. He gave his eldest son a gun and sent him off to sort things out with the Koina: Do unto others as you would have them do to you. The boy had been born abroad, but had already been told that this tract of land would be his. He took the gun in his hand and set off at a trot.

The man who, after Chief Harry's detention on the island, had lorded it over the Goringhaicona, went to complain to the commander. His name was Trosoa. He was a man who'd left the Gorachoqua to beg at the entrance to the Fort. He had a deep voice with something of a growl and a bark in it. Van Riebeeck called Eva to interpret. As she came in she snarled something at the man, but van Riebeeck silenced her. 'Hear what he wants to say.' But they resumed their quarrel, reinforced with gestures. Once again van Riebeeck silenced her.

'What does he say?'

'A white boy shot his dog.'

'What, here at the Fort?'

'No, at the dunes.'

'How did it happen? Ask him if he knows any names.'

She didn't ask, but pointed an accusing finger at Trosoa. 'It's his own fault. He and the Gorachoqua. And the Goringhaiqua and Ankaisoa's people, they're looking for trouble with us.'

Trosoa answered her accusing tone with a deep bark. Van Riebeeck shook her arm. 'What's he saying? Come on.'

'He says the white man is looking for trouble everywhere, but it's a lie. They are the ones who look for trouble everywhere.'

'Wait, Eva. How did I teach you? Just give me the words he says.'

'Botma's son shot his dog.'

Van Riebeeck poured brandy, took out tobacco and pipes, but the man turned it down with a gesture, and glared at Eva with yellow eyes, his breath coming in brief gasps.

'Tell him I shall examine the matter. But he is not permitted to cross the river with his people.'

Once again Trosoa shouted at her, emphasising his words with blows of his fist in his palm.

'He says the Dutchman is a liar. He wants to destroy the Koina. He gobbles up the veld. The white people must get on their ship and go away. It is not their land. The grazing belongs to us.'

'Tell him, I say it is not his either. It is like the sea and the rain, it belongs to all. We use what we need and we don't have to ask permission.'

Eva translated van Riebeeck's reply in a triumphant tone of voice, and Trosoa responded with silence. Then he left.

'Well, what do you think about it, Eva?' asked van Riebeeck, handing her a small glass of sweet wine.

She was scared. 'There will be war. Then the white people and I must die together. I shall have to go to Oedasoa.'

'That's not necessary. You are safe here. They can't do anything to you.'

That afternoon she went to the dunes to ask for help. She said: Oedasoa would reward those who led her safely to his place. But Trosoa prevented them.

'She's a servant to this Dutchman. Look at her betraying her own people. There's nothing we can say or do any more without her telling it to van Riebeeck. She has already sold our pastures, it's all done. Now she wants to crawl in under Oedasoa's kaross.'

In her distress Eva shrilly interrupted him, and he jumped up in rage and hit her with his *kierie*, a blow that sent her reeling back. Dark blood trickled from her hair over her eyebrow ridge, and she took off her blue cap with the ear flaps to press it against her face. Then she returned to the Fort.

Peter Havgard and his oarsmen were on their way back from the quay, and when he saw her crying, he took her arm. She did not want to show her face; he had to put down his case to pull away her hands from her face.

'Who did this, Eva?' But she wouldn't tell him. Together they went to the hospital room. Her face was in his mind, tear-stained, bruised and sorrowful like that of a child who doesn't understand why it has been beaten. The friendly smile she always had, was gone. Innocent and trusting she sat on his bed, the girlish body bent over, in blood-spattered clothes. He mixed some brandy and water in a glass for her, and saw to it that his bedroom door remained wide open while he cleaned and bandaged her wound. He knew the alcohol would cause her to go on bleeding for longer, but it would also help her to relax. He had nothing else to give her. She stopped crying. The gentle move-ments of his hands over her face made her smile.

'Come, now Mrs van Riebeeck will help you. I have to go on duty.' With his overcoat round her bloodstained shoulders they crossed the courtyard. The lookout on the wall shouted over their heads at the gate guard: 'The Strandlopers are moving away! Tell the commander.' On the stoep, just before he knocked, Peter kissed her on the forehead.

War broke out between the Koina and the Dutch. The Koina's complaint was known to van Riebeeck: the foreigners were now taking the fat of the land where the Koina had lived for hundreds of years; they were putting up fences around it and drove the Koina out to the brackish marshes and to sandy plains without veld food, where their cattle suffered from thirst and want of nourishment. But the Dutchman listened to their complaint and said to his Council: It may be so, but this service station must work. The interest of the Company comes first. And it's either them or us. Perhaps there were feelings of guilt towards the Koina in the Hollanders' conscience, which they wanted to erase by removing the Koina from their sight, but there were also resentment and contempt. They bartered the ivory bracelets from the people's arms for wine, they took tortoises and starchy tubers from the people's bags, while the sailors were after the women, to play around with them. It was a very close thing or the burgher Henk Boom caused the death of a native he'd strung up from a beam in his stable.

So there were many places now where the Koina no longer had the right to go. And where could they turn to, if the Hollanders always got more cattle and must have more grazing? One Sunday in May the Goringhaiqua and Gorachoqua removed seven of the Company's draught oxen from the new lands behind the mountain, and sent them running with loud shouting and blows from their sticks. The soldier behind the cattle jumped out of the way when his herd was turned back on him. He saw the Hottentots running crouched alongside the oxen, and fired a quick shot through the cattle. Then the enemy took their bows from their shoulders and let fly a volley of arrows at him, so that he had to fall on the ground among the bushes. Two men on horseback, a free burgher and a soldier, heard the noise from the river, and set off in pursuit of the robbers. The Company's herdsman could hear their shouting and shooting for quite a while, then they came riding back. He went to show them the man he'd shot. They turned him over on his back by foot: the bullet had entered by one ear and left through the other. They cut off the head and he took it back with him as evidence.

Van Riebeeck sent a sergeant and four soldiers to bury the body and then search along the river as far as the Bosheuwel, to track down the oxen. Peter Havgard accompanied the patrol, with the head in a canvas bag tied to his saddle. They stopped at the woodcutters' post, but couldn't find out anything there, and so continued along the road over the rise to the kloof pass. At the entrance to the kloof sat more than two hundred Koina on a sloping ridge, as if they were waiting for the Hollanders. The sergeant rode a few steps forward to speak to them, but they shouted down his first words, and threw stones and *kieries* at him. He took the bag from Peter and hurled it far forward. Then he turned his horse round. 'Retire. There are too many of them.'

Two or three days later van Riebeeck's farmhouse and outbuildings at Bosheuwel were burned down, and although it had been a cook's carelessness that had set the chimney alight, the shock spread all the way down the river that afternoon. At the farmsteads a child was put on every rooftop to keep watch, and every firearm in the houses was loaded. The farmers drew up a petition which was handed to the commander. They wanted the Koina removed from the valley, because they could no longer get to their sowing and ploughing. The fire at Bosheuwel might well give the Koina new ideas, and if the commander agreed, they would like to go to battle against the Koina. But van Riebeeck refused, and instructed them to go and guard their properties. There was no need for him to fire the first shot.

That month of May was the time that would stand out, later, like a beacon in Peter's life. The war moved from one side to the other. One misty morning a small group of Koina rose up among the reeds of the Liesbeeck, stalked the farmhand guarding the cattle of the burghers Visagie and van Roon in the vleis, and hurled a stick at him from a distance of at least fifteen paces. It hit him on the back of the head. Then two of them beat him to death with *kieries*, while the others noisily drove his cattle through the water at speed, to the reeds and bushes on the other side.

The nearest farmers took up arms; they knew that it was a bad day for shooting: one couldn't see a thing and the gunpowder lay damp and useless in the pan. Children, each with a musket in hand, had to run with the message, some upstream, others downstream. Four neighbours arrived on horseback, others came on foot. They followed the trail of fresh cow dung through the wet grass until the tracks divided, then divided again, and again. There they fired shots into the air to gather the people. They were right, it was a bad day for shooting; they had to scrape out powder and dry the pan and load again, and pray. Visagie and van Roon had lost sixteen draught oxen and dairy cows as well as their hired hand that morning. Visagie was left with only one heifer, and he was finished, he could not plough any more, and he walked to the Fort to ask van Riebeeck for a post in the Company's service.

Two days later four cattle were cut out from a large herd and driven away. Three of them belonged to Brinkman, the fourth was Visagie's heifer. That closed down two farms. From then on a soldier was billeted in every farmhouse along the river. Herdsmen, including children, were armed. Peter had to cancel his early visits to the ships, because at dawn he had to ride along the whole frontier, accompanied by a soldier, to visit every house and find out how the people were doing. It was cold work, that winter, with a cotton cap and a small tarpaulin dripping with water, and the wet bushes brushing against his hose, but it was better than Denmark, and better still than the forecastles of disease-ridden ships. It was Eva who first heard that the Koina had kept their war for the wet season. She came to tell that the Koina were no longer scared of the Dutch. They no longer cared what was going to happen to them; they were angry and as bitter as green bile.

It also came about that just after Peter and the sergeant had ridden off in the rain from the sixth and seventh houses, they heard far behind them the furious shouting of fighting people. They hurried back, right into the clucking and whistling of Koina driving cattle and the dull drumming of their *kieries* on the bodies of the animals. Then another eighty or ninety cattle came bursting from the bushes in front of them. The ones in front jostled each other in the narrow paths, those behind tried to force their way past, their horned heads held high. Jubilant shouting could be heard in the rain right ahead of them, but no Koina could be seen yet. They swerved to the left to avoid the stampede and urged the horses on through the bushes, when the sergeant barely missed a young native running beside the cattle. The man jerked up his assegai, but with the broad tip of his boot the sergeant managed to kick him deep in the armpit, so that he tumbled out of the path. Only then did they draw their pistols, tied scarves round the locks, and turned back to follow the cattle; and only when the sergeant aimed his pistol right into the throng and fired a shot did Peter see the five or six men lying flat on the wet animals and driving them on with their heels and blows of their *kieries*. After that the pistols were useless. They pulled the triggers time and again until the flints turned blunt against the steel, but the powder was hopelessly wet. Then a last batch of cattle approached from behind, followed by four Koina.

'Sabres!' shouted the sergeant, and they drew them, brought the horses jumping from the bushes, and they hacked madly at arms, heads and the *kieries* swung at them. The rain and wind tugged at their wet cloaks, their horses could barely turn in the narrow path, and Peter had to grab his saddle tightly and hold on with one hand. As, one by one, the Koina began to leave the fight, he and the sergeant reined their horses in, breathing heavily, wiped the blood-streaked sabres on the wet bushes and dried them on the lining of their cloaks.

At Brinkman's farmyard his kraal of poles and branches had been torn open and trampled. Farmers and soldiers gathered inside the small house around a bed.

'This is Simon, he's dead,' said Brinkman. Peter examined the muddy corpse, unbuttoned the coarse shirt to inspect the wounds, pressed the eyes shut. On his chest and stomach the black charcoal lines of fire-hardened assegai points ended in four black spots of congealed blood, around which the cold skin was puckered and swollen purplish-blue. There was one leaking hole in the lower abdomen, two more in the corpse's side. The sergeant spoke to Brinkman about the cleansing of the corpse. He would send a wagon from the Fort to collect it. 'Master Pieter, you go and tell the commander. The rest of you must saddle up and start the pursuit.'

Van Riebeeck summoned Eva. He sounded upset and suspicious when he spoke to her. 'You can tell them,' he promised with a raised fore-finger, 'from now on we're going to kill. Overwhelm them. Club them down. Destroy them. If we take prisoners it will be for the yoke of slavery. My patience has run out. Four farms have now been destroyed. It is your people who first drew the sword, Eva. Four farms have been destroyed, two men are dead, and now I'm going to avenge them.'

Van Riebeeck wanted Eva to spread his message, and she did. In the rain Trosoa and the Goringhaicona snatched their huts from the dunes once again and fled in the direction of the Kloof Nek. All of them, even the old woman who tended the hearth in the hospital kitchen, streamed up the hillside in single file with their bundles on their backs. That evening the Council confirmed van Riebeeck's threat. In future all the Company's livestock had to be brought inside the Fort overnight. The burghers had to remain at home, and they had the right to shoot on sight any Koina carrying arms. At the supper table van Riebeeck told them about it. Peter watched Eva. What would she do? And what would Oedasoa, the peacemaker, think of this? Eva wanted to be alone, and asked Mrs van Riebeeck with a curtsy to be excused. The tears came readily. Was she sick? No, she wanted to be alone and pray. She offered no greeting and did not look back as she went out.

In the silence Peter said: 'You are asking her to announce a declaration of war, sir. That is the work of an ambassador.'

'She can do it. What I say here in my dining room is known all over the Cape by the morning anyway.'

'But her credentials, and an official notice to the enemy?'

Van Riebeeck looked at him with a smile. The smile said: You are in Africa now. 'A wonderful child,' he said. 'I'll write this in the journal. The Directors must know that there are good ones among them too.'

At daybreak Jan Reijnders clamoured at the gate that his cattle had been stolen. He stood with his bald head uncovered in the rain, his thin clothes plastered to his body, his empty hands raised. He was brought in, given a dry shirt and a place at the fire. His wife and child were with a neighbour, he said. Hopefully they were safe, but he, the free burgher whose farm lay closest to the Fort, had been stripped bare. His dogs had been stabbed to death at his gate. He and his family hid in the bushes while the fury of the raid moved through his house. When they could go inside again and light a candle, his wife had a seizure. She writhed on the floor screaming like a madwoman, the neighbours came to carry her away in the rain.

Van Riebeeck offered a hundred guilders from his own pocket for anyone who could bring in the leader of the raiders, a man named Doman. Fifty for his severed head. For other Hottentots the reward was ten guilders per head. Women and children were to be spared. Sergeant Everard set out with Peter and eight soldiers along the woodcutters' path to the commander's farm. There they turned and started working their way back, down the river to the sea. Along the way they came across six woodcutters, with their saws and axes in canvas on their shoulders and their guns muzzle down on their backs. The forest was unsafe, they were on their way to the Fort. But the sergeant ordered them back, with an insult, to go and cut their wood. Were they now running away from the enemy? Turn about, he said, he wanted to see what their breeches looked like behind.

At Bosheuwel's farmyard the commander's ancient hired hand called at them from the blackened ruin, where he had boarded up a corner with ship's canvas and a few planks. 'You can go. I chased the bastards away.' Twenty of them, not one less, but he'd sent them packing all right. He fetched assegais to show the sergeant. One had nearly gone through him. But his powder was dry and he put the barrel of his musket through the sleeve of his jacket. Every shot he fired went down the full length of the sleeve, of which only charred tatters were now left.

The armed group slowly rode back against the driving rain, leaving one soldier at every farmhouse to strengthen the Company's hold on its eastern frontier. In front of the houses the flooded Liesbeeck came roaring past. On the way back, all along the swirling, beer-brown river, Peter was wondering how a single man could fight off twenty of this country's hunters. Were they leaderless? The old would lack knowledge, the younger ones wouldn't be trusted. European warfare was undoubtedly new to them. The man called Doman would have his work cut out to keep his tiny army of herdsmen in the field against a force of determined Europeans. How would Doman explain to badly armed people that, unless they attacked resolutely and man to man, they would lose this green valley, and everything else besides?

And a settler could never say: Look, there's bad weather coming, we should expect an attack. One had to be ready day and night. Some of the farmers had herded their remaining livestock together into the Company's kraal and left for the Fort with their families. Henk Boom, with his large wife and large children, still refused to give up his tract of land. Their house was sturdy, spacious, clean and built near water. Their vegetables were in full leaf, their grain taller and more lush than anyone else's. Why should he abandon it because a handful of barbarians were unhappy? His neighbours, Cloete and de Wacht, had already fled with all their possessions.

Van Riebeeck gave Boom two more soldiers. He also released the Company's slaves from their chains, armed them with half-pikes, and sent them by wagon to the evacuated farms to transport the furniture and all firewood from the homesteads to the Fort. Next to his own hearth, van Riebeeck had dry fuel for only two more weeks, and that year it was raining every day. Large marshes had formed on the level patches along the river, covering the young wheat crop. Everything was drenched, but there was nothing to be done about that.

Peter doubted whether they would win the war, but van Riebeeck never wavered. He explained to Pieter: If the Koina were the only ones with cattle, they would be the only ones who could claim the Liesbeeck valley. It was imperative for Master Peter to understand this very well, that owning livestock meant more to those people than food and clothing, more than ritual, status or privilege. Cattle meant power, absolute power. That right, the right of power, was now his. In the disputed valley he had built a grain shed and a cattle kraal with the very best yellow-wood from the kloofs of the back mountains; that was the cornerstone of his new plan. The Company would become a frontier farmer in its own right. The few peasants on smallholdings along the river would no longer bear the brunt of the war on the Company's behalf. He would erect a fence to keep marauders out, and a fort for armed horsemen, and the whole area would be guarded with cannon. Wagon roads to vineyards, and wine cellars, orchards, wheat fields and vegetable gardens, would be established there where his enemy tried to stop him. He would put all his might into the project, and turn the entire Liesbeeck valley into one huge fortified farm, to show the brown herdsmen that it would never be recovered.

For the sake of this plan they lived gun in hand that winter and spring. Those free burghers settled in front of the mountain had to parade with the Company's troops, tradesmen and clerks in the Fort's courtyard, but Peter and Sergeant Everard spent their Sundays at Coornhoop, at the frontier. First there was a church service in the redoubt, followed by a long drill with musket or pike outside on the river bank, followed by a large rummer of brandy for every man. The farmers faithfully came with their hired hands, grown sons and soldiers stationed with them, to drill. The Boom family, hefty, tall, red-cheeked people, filled the two front benches in the storehouse of the redoubt, staring gravely into the sick-comforter's face, as if his duties were those of an officer of the guard who had to ensure their safety.

The three daughters peered at Peter from under their bonnets. He was a doctor, he knew what a body looked like inside. Why was he going about alone with the brown girl? He was not like the other Company's men who enjoyed visiting the farmhouses, laughing with young people and drinking with the older ones. How do you meet him? Disheartened, they stared at him.

That Sunday, between the sermon and the drink, they heard the rattle of musket shots, followed by their rolling echoes from the cliffs of the Bosberg. It had to be the woodcutters at Leendertsbos. The shooting continued unbroken, not salvos but brief rattling bursts and loose shots. The sergeant shouted: 'Saddle up,' glasses were hastily filled and emptied down throats, saddles thrown over and buckled to. Messages were given to the womenfolk. Those who had no horses ran with muskets in their hands from the wooden palisade along the footpaths to their little homes scattered like small white islands of peace in the thickets marking the course of the contested river.

Fourteen horsemen rode from the redoubt up the mountain slope to reach the woodcutters' path. It was no more than a wagon trail, two grooves like old wounds in the red earth, running straight across the ridge to Leendertsbos. Peter saw Eva beside the road and reined in his horse, but the sergeant on his left forced him ahead with an open-handed slap between the shoulders, then drew his sabre and struck the horse with the flat of the blade on the croup. 'Go on!' And with a threatening thrust of the sabre he shouted in Eva's face: 'Get out of it! Go away!'

Peter looked back once, but behind the bucking and swerving mass of men and horses he could not see her. Then they rode along the wagon trail following the sounds of war, and immediately after the ridge they descended into the yellow-wood forest. With sabres and pistols in hand they charged screaming in among the trees. There were many Koina, behind tree trunks, or fleeing like buck among the horses. The riders were forced to dodge and duck, thrust and cut, and jerk the horses back to follow the enemy, this or that, that had jumped up right in front of them. Rounds clattered, bullets were flattened against the trees or ricocheted away with whining sounds, leaving white scars in the bark. Then the forest fell quiet. The horses were still alarmed, the men gasping with their heated sabres in their hands. There were no wounded, little blood on the weapons, no enemy dead to be seen. First, reload! They called out to the woodcutters, and then rode in line towards their hut. Outside, the ground was littered with assegais. There were five men inside, all wounded. Leendert Cornelisz had a bleeding slash on the neck. 'That was close,' he said. 'They caught us sleeping. It is the Sabbath, we thought we could lie in a bit.'

Sergeant Everard examined their hut, put out two pickets and ordered his detachment to off-saddle. Together with the woodcutter he measured off a semicircle in front of the hut for a palisade with loopholes at head-height. The wood for it was selected from the pile, and carried to the spot. Then they all began to build together. Peter cauterised arrow wounds and put stitches in the cuts, but while he was tending the wounded his mind was filled with longing. He wanted to go to Eva.

Towards noon they built a fire, picked up assegais and arrows and threw them on it, then brought out food and drink and had a meal around the fire. They felt no respect for their enemy. How many men did they have, and yet, they were too ignorant to attack this simple hut effectively. The sergeant told them, as an example, how, after a battle in France one summer, he and a companion roasted part of a horse in the sticky black grease from a wagon's hub, in the cuirass of a vanquished enemy. There, one felt like a king eating from a golden plate, for you had fought hard and won, and you had vast respect for the enemy. But here you felt worse every day; it was like fighting against bloody common sheep. He looked at Peter. 'I have no respect for them, master. Not on the battlefield, nor in the street. I don't regard them as worthy.'

Until late afternoon they planted poles, joined them with cross-beams and covered them with planks. There were loopholes for twelve muskets and a neat shelf at chest-height. It was the kind of rampart, the sergeant said disdainfully, which would dare young men to try and surround, or charge, as it looked so simple to overrun. But in this land it was totally safe.

When in the late afternoon the shadow of the mountain fell over them, they rode back to the Fort. Peter went to knock on van Riebeeck's door to tell him that he'd found Eva, not far from the place of the fighting. Van Riebeeck had already heard the news. Eva had said that she'd gone to pray, and he was inclined to believe her. There was one of their Hottentot cairns up there, apparently where some holy man lay buried.

'She really prays to our God, Pieter, even though she calls him by another name, because there is only one God. You must believe that if you accept the commandments and the articles of our faith.' Did he perhaps wish to talk to her? A while later, van Riebeeck returned and told him that Eva was washing the children, he should wait. While Peter's imagination was filled with pictures of the young girl washing and drying two small blond boys and wrapping them in nightshirts, van Riebeeck told him about his great project: to cordon off the entire fertile valley with a fence of poles and a hedge of fast-growing shrubs, the four redoubts armed with cannon, a stable for twelve horses, including barracks for the horsemen above. One long, unbroken farm, of grain and vineyards and vegetables and grazing for a thousand head of cattle. Not an inch of land should remain for the natives. They had to remove from under the shadow of Table Mountain.

'What will become of them, sir?'

'Those who want to, can find employment with the Company. Any form of employment, all the trades and crafts. All we require of them is to learn our language and attend church, nothing more.'

Eva stood in the door listening, until van Riebeeck noticed her, then she approached to sit next to Peter on the hard church pew. 'What is it, Pieter?'

'I wanted to ask you, if I may, why you went to the Koina this morning?'

'They are my people, aren't they?'

'But they are our enemies.'

'Still, I will pray for them. One must pray for one's enemies too.'

Van Riebeeck chuckled aloud. 'You too, honourable sir,' Eva said. 'All of us Christians must think of one another.'

'You're right. But wait,' he stopped her. 'First tell Master Pieter where you went. He would like to know.'

'I went to the place where Heitsi-Eib' lies. I asked for lasting peace to come between white people and brown people.'

'You see, Pieter, she prays to heathen idols and then preaches to Christians.'

She did not understand van Riebeeck, but turned to Peter. 'What would you do if you were me?'

'Hopefully the same, if I had the courage.' He pressed her hand, and released it again.

'Did that Heitsi-Eib' answer you?' asked van Riebeeck.

'No. They never do. Perhaps they're no longer there. You white people go and squat behind his cairns and lower your breeches. Who would stay in a place like that?'

'Quite true,' said the commander. 'The Dutch don't want to listen. No respect for the native people.'

But she was speaking to Peter only. 'I did not go to your enemies, Pieter. I did not even see them.'

'And you, Master Pieter, how did you fare?'

'Did the sergeant report?'

'Yes. What do you think, will we win this war?'

'I think so.' He saw Eva's face go pale. 'It may mean the end of the Koina. There are not many of them.'

'We shall totally destroy them, Master Pieter. The sooner they surrender and stop troubling us about grazing, the better. And everybody must come under one authority, there isn't enough grazing and water and fuel and food, unless all parties serve the same cause.'

Eva got up quietly, nodded at van Riebeeck, and went out without saying goodbye to Peter.

'It must be hard on her, Master Pieter,' said the commander. Then he turned to look at the large standing clock behind him.

Peter got up. 'I was wondering whether she went to tell the Koina something. To betray us. That we were all attending church again. Something like that. Perhaps she did.'

'I don't think so. She is a full-blooded Hollander. But watch out,

Pieter, that we do not wake the pride in her, then she'll begin to love us less. She wouldn't like to be seen as a traitor to either side, you understand.'

That night, an hour before the moon went down, the alarm was sounded. There was a man on foot with news that some thirty Koina had surrounded the governor's house at Bosheuwel, and that lions were roaring not far from Coornhoop. Van Riebeeck himself was at the stables. He had braziers lit at all four corners of the Fort so that the whole square was illuminated, he threatened the soldiers, urged on the sergeant, shouted at the cook to get breakfast ready so that more patrols could leave. Peter went out through the gate with the first detachment. It was bitterly cold. The wind was against them, the night air was sharp as glass. The first flagon of wine was handed round very soon, among the horsemen bundled together behind their guide in the sandy road. An old moon, dark as overripe cheese, gleamed low over the sea. The morning star sat large and bright above the black mountains in the east.

Peter lifted his musket from its holster and hooked the band round his shoulder, swinging the gun on to his back. Were the Koina really looking for war, he wondered, or did they simply try to demoralise the Hollander into giving up farming? It made no difference to him. War was what they would get, so that the Dutch, and he, and Eva, could rest. He agreed with van Riebeeck at the Council meeting. This was the time for strong action, and it was their only hope for lasting rest. To hell with this lot, he thought with bitterness. To hell with the Koina. This had to be stopped soon. The sooner they were defeated, the sooner this awful business would end.

In some moments of silence they heard lions roaring near the river, and as they looked in that direction, a small bright yellow dot appeared in the dark as if a candle had been lit there. They rode on, and it became larger, brighter, divided into two, then three, and each flame turned into a fire sending up towering orange tongues into the dark.

'Henk Boom's place,' said the guide. 'We must divide.' The smaller group led their horses with difficulty down the dark slope, through ditches and clusters of bushes, because the only torch had been given to light the way to Bosheuwel. They called out each other's names to keep contact, cursed the dark and the branches, cursed the Hottentots and Henk Boom and the Company, and after nearly an hour they reached the river bank between Coornhoop and Boom's farm. At the redoubt they found only two soldiers, the rest had gone out to help with the fire. The red glow stained a cloud of mixed smoke and cold river mist hanging over the vleis. Boom's spacious, whitewashed stone house with its thatched roof, stable, large kraal of wood and branches and his shed filled with unthreshed wheat, had all been burned down. The doorposts of the stable, made of greenwood, lay on the ground, hissing and blowing out smoke and steam. Some neighbours were still bringing pails of water from the river, but there was nothing left to be saved. Their furniture and clothes had all been turned to ashes. The soldiers walked around the glowing heap of embers from which black beams protruded, to see if there was anything to be salvaged. The family was safe, they had to be removed to the redoubt. The women were crying dumbly, Boom was cursing and swearing that he'd had enough of farming, enough of this goddamned land; all their labour turned to ashes.

It was daylight by the time they could make beds for the family in the redoubt, and pile up all the loose stuff from the farm. Peter offered his laudanum in milk to the women and children. The neighbours would come to help with the rest, but after Boom had spoken to the commander about his future.

When Peter reached van Riebeeck that morning, together with the dismayed Boom and his son, Sergeant Everard stood on the mat of coiled ship's rope in front of his desk. 'A hell of a battle, up at Bosheuwel, sir. No less than two hundred of them, possibly three hundred. The moon had just gone down and everything was as dark as hell. Only inside the house there was light, a little lantern with a candle. The old man there was shooting left and right. And we shot wherever we saw anything moving. They must have thought we were no longer coming, for they could have ambushed us there. We charged the stable, all on foot, you understand, and did what we could. They'd already turned most of the cattle out, then we charged the stable and fired as we ran. Hard to load if you can't see your hands in front of your eyes, you understand. The man who reached the gate first got two assegai wounds, one right through the calf, one in the thigh, but we managed to close the gate so they couldn't drive out any more. And a few of the bastards we'd cornered inside. The next moment they came breaking out through the roof. We shot one of them right there, on the roof. And then we went after your cattle, sir, across the yard, down the hill, branches breaking all over. And we couldn't shoot, for they have a habit of hiding behind the cattle, and we couldn't go closer either, because they threw assegais wherever they heard us. We had to go on foot, to prevent the horses falling in the dark. But I swear they are able to see at night, because they got right away from us. There were only six of us, and one had to stay with the horses. If they wanted to, they could have killed us there, by leaving a few men behind to ambush us again. Easy.'

'Why didn't they do it, do you think?'

'Too scared, I reckon. Or there's no one left among them who can think and lead in battle. It's only that Doman, and I don't know whether he was there tonight. Doesn't look like it. And look, they had the whole farm surrounded, their eyes were used to the dark, and they could see there was a messenger going to the Fort. They knew we would be coming, and by what time we'd be there. They only had to be patient. When we came up the hill on foot, sir, that was the moment to jump us, not so? After that there would be lots of time to drive out your cattle. But sometimes they don't want to fight, they only want to steal.'

Van Riebeeck sat behind the table, his hands folded, motionless. 'The damage?'

'We left early. It was still half dark.'

'Tell me.'

'Well, there were the cattle. They took eleven of the twenty-six. And the vineyard on the northern slope, that's all down. The old man still lives in the little shack he cornered off inside the ruin. He says I must tell the commander not to give up.'

'Is that so? So that he won't be without food in his old age.'

'Sir,' said the sergeant, 'we can destroy the bastards, but let us for heaven's sake hit first for a change. Every time they hit first, and get away.'

'All right. There's no need to curse them. Control yourself. Rather go and see to your animals and your people.'

The sergeant remained standing. No word of thanks for all his effort? Then he looked at Peter, frowned, raised his chin, and left. Peter nudged Boom forward.

'What damage, Henk?'

'I lost house and food and clothing, Your Honour. Last night.'

'You were told to take your grain and furniture to safety, but you wouldn't. I sent slaves to do it for you. But you were full of clever stories. Now look at you.'

'Your Honour.'

'Are your people safe? And the soldiers I sent you?'

'Yes.'

'I also lost everything, but I still get a salary. What about you? Do you want to join the Company again? We can give you a roof over your head and bread on your table. And a gun in your hand, so that you can help us fight.'

Then he gestured towards Peter. 'Did you see anything of this Doman?'

'We were too late. They'd already gone.'

Van Riebeeck placed a few bits of wood and dried grass on the table. 'Somebody found this in Henk's farmyard. They use this to make fire.' Peter had seen it before: apparently they bore the hard wood into the soft wood until it got hot, then they added the dry grass and blew up a spark. To Peter it remained wood and dried grass; he wouldn't even think of going to such trouble on a misty night. 'Well, you may now go and give a hand in the hospital. Take a look at the fellow with the spear wounds, they may be poisoned. I'd start with bread poultices on the skin. I want to know what happens to his wounds, you hear. Now, Henk, come and sit here in the pew, my lad. What about a spot of brandy? Then we can talk.'

For several days Peter did not see Eva, as if Mrs van Riebeeck had locked her up. The poor child; the Dutch despised her because she was brown, and the Koina because she lived with the Dutch. Both of them call her, and point her out, a traitor. There was one sentence in the journal that Peter could remember clearly, word for word: *But you, Eva, you're pleading with the commander*. The word the speaker used was *soebat*. An Oriental word which meant: to curry favour. You're prostrating yourself before the commander, Eva. Those had been Doman's words, when he'd still been one of the wood carriers for kitchen scraps. '*But you, Eva . . .*' Now in wartime the accusation had become a threat, a death sentence temporarily suspended, until Doman could lay hands on her.

The vigilance was not relaxed, the tension became worse. Peter watched as cannon, beside their red mountings, were taken out through the gate on ox wagons. Two five-pounders to Coornhoop, two more to the Groote Schuur, one to the commander's house at Bosheuwel. Boom, who since his childhood had disliked carrying arms, understood that the Koina should never discover what large breaches they had made in the frontier. Even his neighbours should not realise or discuss it among themselves. It was bad for one's confidence to see river farms lying abandoned, land won back by the enemy. The rain-drenched black earth along the vleis still lured Boom. The commander offered him three soldiers to help guard his oxen, should he decide to try again, and seed grain should he want to put a plough to the soil. He would plough again. He rented draught animals from the Company, on extended credit. His wife and children dug up the soggy ruins of his house and salvaged stones, hinges and nails. They sorted the stones and carried away rubble to expose the foundations. From a Monday to a Wednesday afternoon Boom ploughed and then sent the soldiers back to the Groote Schuur with the rented oxen. He wanted to stop early that day, because there was rain in the air and it became dark early. The next day he wanted fresh oxen.

In the afternoon Peter set out with a horse cart and a guard of six men to collect Boom's three soldiers, who, according to the report they'd received, were lying dead in the road above his farm. The first one was in the woodcutters' road, near the place where he'd once met Eva on her way back from Heitse's grave. The soldier lay on his face, and Peter rolled him over. It was a young Swiss, well known to him.

His face, chest and stomach were one clotted mess of bloody earth, and over his mouth the rust-red blood formed a lid. The second had bled himself pale, seated with his back against a rock, his hand clutching clumps of grass on either side. A broken spear protruded between the collarbone and the neck artery. The shoulder was swollen and black blood had coagulated around the stick. The man was scared that somebody might try to pull at it, scared of pain, and scared to die.

The third man Peter couldn't see, but the soldiers called from a deep erosion ditch that they had found him. He mixed opium with brandy and iron drops in a small mug and gave it to his patient, waiting until he was numbed, and then pulled him forward to feel whether the shaft was protruding behind his shoulder. It did so, more than a finger-length. It had to be removed. He couldn't feel loose splinters. He had to be ready to close the vein in case it ruptured. With bandages tightly wound round the assegai, front and back, he first pulled lightly at the stick, and when it moved, plucked it out in one jerk from the swollen joint. Blood and water gushed from the gap together. With his fore-finger he felt in the hole, and was satisfied that no wood had remained behind inside the wound, except for the usual dirt. Fresh blood immediately began to dam against his bandages, and he forced the wet rags with his index finger into the two gaping holes. More bandages around the patient's neck and below the arm, and that was that for the present. He had to look at the other man as well. He laid the patient down on his own overcoat, gulped down a third of a bottle of brandy in large mouthfuls and spat some of it out over the palms of his hands. Then with his medicine chest on the strap round his shoulder, he climbed down into the ditch.

The soldiers there had already figured out the whole story: this was where the fellow had been struck down, that was the way he'd crawled, there he'd fallen into the ditch, from there he'd come to here. He was now on hands and knees in the mud, whispering in muddled German. On the back of his head was a bump as big as a fist, and his hair and neck were caked with blood. Peter tried to bring him to from his brandy flask, but the man refused to drink.

He asked the corporal of the guard: 'Any weapons?'

'No. Powder flasks, bullet cases, all lost.'

'Come, we must get them away from here.'

The wounded man was bleeding. His face was as white as paper, his nails were blue, his hands cold, his pulse slow and faint. Could he have torn an artery? If he put in stitches, the artery would only bleed to the inside. There was nothing else he could do, except to shove more linen into the wounds, and cover up the fellow with everything the soldiers were prepared to contribute. Those who carried the bodies to the wagon told one another what they would do to the devils and their women when they had the chance.

Two days later, when in the early dusk the draught oxen of the Company and the burghers were approaching the Schuur through slanting rain, Doman and fifty or sixty of his men rose from the wet grass in front of the cattle, less than a pistol shot from the Schuur, and came charging and screaming at the oxen. With *kierie* blows on the heads and horns they brought the front ones to a standstill and forced them round, and then drove the whole herd back to the veld with shouts, a stabbing of assegais, blows with the *kieries* and their fists. A few young men jumped on the oxen from behind, and drove them on, kicking them in the flanks. The Company's herdsmen jumped out of the way, tried to fire, and then looked on as the livestock was stolen right out of their hands. Behind the palisade surrounding the Schuur, soldiers had started saddling their horses, while others came running out, shouting, sabres in their hands. They could barely believe that they were losing the Company's precious herd in front of their eyes, and their firearms useless. The tracks and the noise led them obliquely up the slope against the rain and wind. One soldier warded off a blow from a *kierie* with his forearm; the bone snapped with the sound of a pistol shot. A horse, brought down with its rider, was stabbed with an assegai just behind the girth. From time to time an ox that had broken loose from the herd appeared out of the rain, sometimes bleeding from spear wounds.

When the horsemen began to gain on them, the Koina moved in between the animals and the pursuers, shouting defiantly and hurling spears at them. At first the soldiers fell back, regrouped to see what was going to happen, and looked on as the Koina swung their course downhill, to cross the river at the ford near Jacob Cloete's. That gave them a chance to cut round the front, and by shouting and waving their hats they managed to slow the herd down and then to scatter them. In the end the Koina got away across the river with a fraction of their booty. On the opposite bank they turned round and challenged the soldiers to come closer. But one couldn't risk it into the water with a horse, without a gun.

Afterwards they gathered the exhausted cattle and took them up river, stopping many times to rest. The Company's horsemen were drenched; the guns slung muzzle down over their backs were dripping with water. In the pitch dark they reached Coornhoop and there herded the Company's cattle into the kraal.

The next morning, when it was still raining, van Riebeeck sent people to every house and every cattle kraal to gather all the sheep and cattle in the colony and take them to the Schuur. There he doubled the guard. And in the treacherous weather he wanted to send a boat across to Robben Island to fetch Herrie. The quartermaster asked for a postponement, he was expecting the wind to turn south-west in the forenoon, but van Riebeeck refused. He summoned Peter.

'I want you to go with them to the island. Soften up the old man. Warm him up properly and tell him how much we want peace. You must win his trust, so that he can persuade his nation to lay down their weapons. There's only he, or Eva, who can do it. But we stand a greater chance of success with Herrie. Take medicine with you, just in case.'

The quartermaster could not hoist more than a foresail, as the wind already had the boat on its side. With one gunwale largely submerged under green froth, and every wave like a waterfall over the bow, they spent much of the morning tacking about against the north wind. The first tack brought them close to the beach at Janbiesieskraal, the second was aimed directly at the island. Around them the sea and sky were a uniform dark grey, and their progress was slow. Peter had to keep bailing, to keep the sea out of that boat. He swallowed bitter brine, his face and hands were numb with cold, and he could not distinguish any island. From one wave top to the next the boat fell with dull thudding blows that made his whole body shudder. Next to his legs a half-drowned sailor sat in the water with the foresail rope wound around his blue hand. Water streamed from his hair, his head jerked from the thumping of the boat. With burning red eyes they stared at the weather, and bailed, and cursed, and bailed. They cursed everything: the commander, the sea, the savages, the boat, the Company, the weather, the island, everything that lived on it, everything dead. They tried to curse to death the wind and sea, pain and cold. Hour after hour they shouted their frustration against the wind and cursed the rain, and then once again the damned barbarians who wouldn't stop.

It was midday before Peter had to jump up to his neck into the sea, to steady the head of their boat against the breakers, and it was also the first time he'd set foot on Robben Island. After him followed the sailor with the head-rope, to help hold the head until their anchor went overboard.

Then a gang of convicts appeared from the rain to help them. In one solid mass they appeared over the dune, a rough horde shuffling in a tight huddle, a single shapeless grey block like a heavy, sea-worn baulk of wood with human faces chiselled into it. A score of bare feet caused the block to move; just above the sand their single chain alternately jerked and tautened. A short fellow with a shining pate followed behind, pointing a cane in the direction of the boat. A few German words were shouted. They shuffled into the sea, grabbed the boat by the gunwales, moved back to the land and lowered it on the shell-strewn beach.

Then, following a command, they turned round and moved away across the wet sand towards a footpath overgrown with hard young thorns. Their guard suddenly dashed forward, repeatedly beating his cane into the wet grey mass, poked his arm into it and took out Peter's medicine chest.

'*Hundegebrut! Hundegezucht!*' More blows rained on the bundle.

That night they slept in the posthouse. Outside the rain came down steadily. The postkeeper had no food for them. ('How can His Honour send you here without rations? Here every man's food is weighed out. Weeks go by before I see a provision boat. But I know why: it's because he expects to see you back home tonight.') The postkeeper boiled a stockfish, brown, hard and straight as a plank, together with two ship's biscuits, stirred the contents together and slurped it from the pot with a spoon, while his cold guests huddled in the hearth to dry themselves, and shivered.

'What does His Honour want with Herrie?'

'Don't know.'

'Set him free?'

The quartermaster began to talk hopefully. Perhaps, with a great effort, he could make a cosy evening of it. 'No use, postkeeper. The old man always makes a nuisance of himself.'

'He's no use here either.'

'How come?'

'Won't work, just wants to gobble his food and gulp down his wine. You may have him. When do you want to set sail?'

'At first light tomorrow, I hope. I have a feeling the weather is going to change.'

Later the postkeeper went outside with a lantern to lock the prisoners away and set out guards for the night. When he returned and hung his dripping overcoat behind the door, the young sailor pleaded: 'Uncle, don't you happen to have a rusk for us or a drop to drink?'

He gave the boy a look of indignation. 'What? At this post every penguin egg is accounted for. There's water in the barrel, if you've got the stomach for it.' Then he removed a large piece of panelling like a cabin wall from his bunk, and climbed into the open hole beside the hearth. 'I'm off to sleep.'

A smoking wick with a tiny flame floated in a bowl of grease on their table. They remained sitting there, close to the hearth, in the dusk. The only heat now came from the glowing embers and small blue flames of buring sea-wrack. When Peter heard the postkeeper snoring, he shared the Company's brandy from his medicine chest with his comrades, and with his arms around the chest sat longing for Eva's warmth.

They were already awake from the cold when the postkeeper emerged from his bunk, stacked kindling on the hearth and blew it into a flame, before frugally extinguishing the spluttering wick of the night light between thumb and forefinger. They all stepped outside together to urinate against the wall. An icy wind was sweeping across the island. The black night sky was cloudless.

'Look at the stars,' said the quartermaster, his head bent far backwards. It was something remarkable: thousands of flickering stars were teeming overhead, big and small, of all colours, and all crystal clear. 'That's something you seldom see in the fatherland.'

Herrie sat in a low hut like a large kennel at the post's woodpile. The postkeeper opened the door to nudge the man with his foot. Peter could hear leg-irons clinking in the straw, and a voice said in English, 'Damned Dutchman.'

He was short, thin and gnarled with suffering. Peter held the lantern over his face. So this was Herrie. Must be sixty, his hair grey, his face wasted, his eyes veiled behind folds of skin. His legs were somewhat bandy at the knees. That would be from age, not from rachitis. Round his leg was a ring and a chain. He pulled an old kaross over his shoulders and clasped it high in front of his chest.

'Did you bring tobacco?' asked Herrie, once again in English.

'Shut up until you're spoken to.' The postkeeper pushed him forward. 'Go inside.'

At the kitchen table Peter attempted to speak to the old man. He explained van Riebeeck's need. There was war, the Koina and the Dutch were destroying one another, and it was all quite unnecessary. War wasn't good for anybody, and the Koina were doing themselves a grave disservice. But it could be brought to an end without delay. Herrie was needed, because he could help to make peace here. Van Riebeeck would set him free if he persuaded the alliance of tribes to stop their raids.

But Herrie refused to speak. He insisted on having his breakfast, which had been sent to him from the mainland. The postkeeper had gone to collect it. Ship's bread, a dried stockfish and a basin of water. Herrie soaked the bread and fish, drank the water and gnawed at his food. He let Peter do the talking. Peter found that the old man, generally speaking, looked quite well for his years. His teeth were clearly blunt, but there were no symptoms of illness. He pleaded again. He didn't mention Eva's name, in case either Herrie or van Riebeeck hit on the idea of using her as a trump card. He told Herrie that there

was no other person that the alliance would listen to, no other hope
for peace at this time. Perhaps he would be willing to act as a go-
between? In which case van Riebeeck would work out a deal with
him.

'That damned van Riebeeck,' said Herrie. 'Do you know, young man,
that for many years my people and I made a living out of the shipping
service? And then the Company came, and took the food from our
people's mouths.'

The postkeeper warned: 'I'm not going to unlock him, master. You
mustn't trust this vermin. I'll wait until the last moment.'

'All right. Do you have any sick people here, postkeeper?'

'No bedridden ones, thank God.'

'I shall report to that effect.'

They left with the lantern for the long house where the prisoners
were kept. It had clearly been a sheep pen or a stable. The postkeeper
carried his torch along the enclosure, beating his stick against the
wooden walls, and shouting: 'Another day, another day, praise the Lord!'

Two guards approached from the beach. 'All in order at the boats,
sergeant,' one reported, saluting vaguely.

'Good. Take them to work.' The two soldiers waited on either side
of the entrance while the postkeeper unlocked and went inside. Peter
followed; in the torchlight he could see the prisoners standing beside
their bunks, the soldiers squatting among them in the dusk, picking up
one chain after the other at the men's feet and locking them on to the
long stretch chain. Then the postkeeper called: 'Come on.' Like oxen
they approached in pairs, following the two guards. Steaming in the
sharp night air, mumbling curses, distorted from hard work and cold,
shuffling across the salt scrub, crunching across the broken shells and
the wet beach, they moved towards the sea. Behind the dune they were
shouted to a halt to relieve their bladders. A low layer of vapour formed
there around their ankles.

'Come, master. The political prisoner.'

The boat was already afloat when they reached the bay with Herrie.
The sailors were stepping the masts and rigging them. With a tinkling
of their chain over pebbles the convicts crossed the beach in the starlit

dawn. Carrying his kaross across his arm Herrie walked in knee-deep, and clambered clumsily into the rocking boat. The postkeeper put a basket with penguin eggs and a large wind-dried mullet in the back of the boat.

'For His Honour's table. Three full dozen.'

The quartermaster called: 'That's a lie, uncle. There's only thirty-five.'

'Do you want me to count them in front of you?'

'Just joking, uncle. Haven't you got a couple of eggs for us, then? We haven't had anything to eat since yesterday.'

'What? Are you begging me in front of this black man?'

'He is just as hungry, uncle. He won't report you.'

'And here is my letter to His Honour. The fish is written down in it.'

The young sailor pushed the boat deeper into the water, climbed aboard and upon a command of the quartermaster jerked up the two sails and secured them. The morning star was fast fading in the east. The raw dawn wind was icy cold.

Van Riebeeck kept on urging Herrie for a long time to lead him to the enemy, and plead with them for peace. He invited him to eat and drink, and to smoke and drink, but Herrie refused to plead for peace, and returned to the cell below the Fort after every session. Van Riebeeck summoned Eva to talk to Herrie. He and Peter waited outside the door, as the voices inside grew louder and sharper. Herrie refused to listen, and tried to silence her by shouting. She came out alone.

'What does he say?'

'He says I'm a white man's bitch.'

Peter stepped inside. 'Listen, old man. You're insulting an honourable girl.' The old man mumbled, 'Go to hell!' in English, and waited for van Riebeeck to return.

Inside the door Eva took Peter by the arm. 'Maybe he'll talk later. He's complaining of pain in his hips.'

Van Riebeeck discovered that English gin with a few drops of angostura made Herrie more accessible. There were still some reservations, but while under that influence he was prepared to communicate. And he insisted on speaking the Koina language, so it had to be translated by Eva. Translating is not interpreting. She was too young for that, van Riebeeck thought, too emotional, too inexperienced, and too involved in what was happening. As a translator she could be useful.

Herrie was careful not to be talked into an awkward position. He made it clear that he would not lead the Company's troops against his people.

'You told me that the Gorachoqua were your enemies.'

'They are. They're also Oedasoa's enemies. If you are patient, Oedasoa will hand over Doman to you.'

'You will be helping your friend Oedasoa if you tell me where the Gorachoqua can be found, and what their movements and plans are.'

'His trackers can very easily find that out themselves.'

Van Riebeeck smoked his pipe in silence. It wasn't necessary to discuss Oedasoa. The Company's enemies were not just the alliance of tribes in the peninsula that claimed the Liesbeeck valley, but all the natives who moved down to the green marshlands in summer, including Oedasoa, Ankaisoa, and even this indigent prisoner with his Beachrangers who had only vague ties with the alliance. In reality, the war was against all and every one of them.

'Since when is there enmity between Oedasoa and Gogosoa?'

'It was long before you people came here.'

'After Eva's birth?'

'Krotoa. Yes, they gave her that name.' Then Herrie added something which immediately led to a heated argument. Van Riebeeck had to ask Eva to stop it and concentrate on translating.

'He said once again that I'm a bitch running after a white dog.'

'Why?'

'He's had too much to drink.'

'Then forgive him. But I must hear every word he says. When he says things like that, don't talk back, just translate every word for me. I don't want him to bear a grudge.'

'But why must *I* take it? What would Your Honour do if he said such things about Mrs van Riebeeck?'

'Eva, he understands every word. The Company needs him, and you, and me. So let us discuss it calmly. You know you are a daughter in my house, and I'm satisfied with your behaviour. Ask him again why there is enmity between Oedasoa and Gogosoa.'

Herrie wanted more gin and bitters, and to fill another pipe, while he was talking to Eva. Van Riebeeck passed him the tobacco, but refused the drink. 'First tell us.'

Eva relayed a strange story. 'The Cochoqua and the Gorachoqua used to be one tribe with the same name, Cochoqua. Oedasoa's father was the chief, an elegant man, as his son still is. And people as many as trees, rich in cattle, and a host of sheep, all the way from here up to the mountain. In those days Gogosoa was young, and greedy, and often disrespectful. It was clear to everybody that he wanted to be a chief, but it wasn't in his family. He had friends of his own age, and he persuaded them and made attractive promises: how they would never have to herd their parents' cattle, only their own. When Oedasoa's father had enough of Gogosoa's envy he chased him away. Just like that, with empty hands. And Gogosoa and his few followers went into the mountains where they got together with the Sonqua. And the time came when they stalked the old man's huts at night, when they were all asleep, and they set fire to everything, and killed, and took away cattle, and cut open Oedasoa's pregnant wives and threw the unborn into the fire. It was before the people woke up that they were suddenly overcome by the blood and the crying and the flames, and Gogosoa got away with sheep and cattle, and those Sonqua dogs of Gogosoa's then came to live here with the stock, and they were the ones who brought the name Gorachoqua with them.'

Herrie listened attentively to every word. 'What more do you want, Herrie? Let us help Oedasoa. The Company will give you bread and cheese and brandy. Perhaps gin too, but that is expensive. And Oedasoa will be grateful to you if this war can end.'

'Now what will be easier: for me to help you destroy the Gorachoqua, or for you all to go away? Then the war will end. Leave us to graze our cattle and to hunt and to kill one another.'

'Without tobacco, Herrie? And without brandy, like this?'

'Without it. Everything the way it was before. Here where your Fort now stands, cattle will graze again.'

'All right,' said van Riebeeck. 'I can wait.' And after Herrie had been taken away, Eva complained: 'Your Honour mustn't allow him to talk like that. You're not his child.'

Van Riebeeck laughed. 'He wants me to reward him with cattle. Cattle are everything to him. But even if I had them, I wouldn't give him, because he overestimates his importance to the Company.' He poured a tot of the bright, fragrant gin into Herrie's glass and offered it to Eva, and she breathed in the wild, sweet berry flavour. 'You just keep your wits together, my child. Where this Fort is standing now, will be a big town one day.'

At the mouth of the Salt River was a fisherman's cottage, and that was where the Company's luck began to change. Bart Borms, who had gone to check his lines in the early morning, caught a half-grown Beachranger boy who had already stolen a number of fish from the lines when a hook caught him in the palm. He was naked, as he'd come out of the water. He had bitten off the line and was struggling with the barbs of the hook when the fisherman grabbed him. In the Fort van Riebeeck fed him and promised that he'd have the hook removed if he would tell them where the Gorachoqua were to be found. It was as easy as that. Peter cut off the shaft of the hook with pliers, pulled out the point and cauterised the wound, for the hook was rusty and encrusted with old bait. Then the boy was locked up in an empty room, that was far enough away from Herrie's cell.

As luck would have it, there were three ships at the anchorage. Sixty of the Fort's soldiers, eighty men from the ships and twenty free burghers constituted a force that warranted an expedition. The captains were willing; that would be something to recount and boast about once they were back in Holland – about their bravery against the savage African. The prisoner was tied to the ensign's horse with a thong round his neck. He led them across the parched plains, in the direction of the Tygerberg. At the ford on the trek road through the Brak River he asked permission to cast a stone on Heitsi-Eib's grave, but the ensign didn't understand what he wanted and drove him on with blows across the shoulders. The expedition searching for the Gorachoqua kept due east, on and on. For two days the boy kept a distant mountain peak in the eye and pointed towards it whenever he was jerked by his halter. By that time some of the sailors had already fallen by the roadside, or tried to hide some of the Company's precious possessions in the bushes beside the road. The officers conferred, and decided to turn back. Van Riebeeck sent Herrie back to the island, and kept the young prisoner, who was yet to keep his promise, in his cell.

The next attack on the farms was so close to the Fort that van Riebeeck knew that the guide had tried to mislead them. A soldier from the Schuur had collected two borrowed draught oxen from a farm to return them to the kraal, when five Koina appeared from the reeds near Steven Botma's farm and herded the oxen into the river. The horsemen at Coornhoop saw it happen. They were quick to mount and pursue. Spread out through the bushes they charged on, until one of them spotted the Koina and fired a shot from the saddle. That brought the four horsemen together, but as they drove forward the Koina abandoned the oxen, disappeared among the bushes and from their hiding places shot arrows at the soldiers. After that, there was always one at hand to chase the oxen further, disappear, shoot an arrow or hurl an assegai, disappear.

The pursuit took them further and further away from the river, deeper into the wild and rough terrain. The soldiers tried to keep the two oxen together, because if the animals were parted they too would have to divide and then it was a different story altogether. The enemy kept on their attack from different sides, one could now see them daringly standing openly among the bushes, but there was no hope of loading a musket on a turning horse.

The only answer was, sabre in hand, looking about, scare them if possible by aiming an unloaded pistol, hoping their arrows wouldn't hit you. In this way the soldiers managed to get to the front of the oxen and turn them, then the enemy would once again come darting from the bushes immediately ahead of them and drive the cattle back, forcing the horsemen to turn again and attempt to go round the front of the oxen once more. The battle went on milling around the oxen, this way and that, the horses were turned on their hind legs, branches were breaking, blood flowed. All four of the soldiers were wounded, arrow stood solidly planted into a horseman's thigh. Gasping for breath, urged on by the sight of their enemies' blood, the Koina moved right up against the horses and leaped up to grab at the reins. Then the pistols cracked. The first shot went into the open mouth of an attacker, the next, at arm's length, entered through the left breast of a man and tore a big hole out through the shoulder blade. As he fell, the surviving Koina, shouting at one another, ducked out of the battle. One more received a bullet in the back of the head. For some time the soldiers kept up the pursuit, searching this way and that, but it was fruitless, and when they returned to the flattened spot among the bushes the one who had been shot in the chest was gone. There were the two dead, and a lot of blood on the ground, and their two draught oxen, bewildered and difficult to herd. With the oxen back in the big kraal of the Schuur, they sent word that a surgeon was needed, and that they wanted the usual reward for an enemy's head.

Success. Van Riebeeck was delighted. But when he went to look for Peter, he found him and Eva together in the doctor's small waiting room. They sat side by side on the bed. Peter, holding her hand between both of his, was gently caressing it.

'What are you doing here?' he asked angrily. 'No women in the men's quarters. Go home.' And to Peter: 'You ought to know better. Keep her out of here.' As if challenging him, he looked Peter straight in the eye.

'There are two of the enemy dead in the bushes across the river. Go cut off the heads and bring them in. Get salt from the cook and a canvas bag from the quartermaster. But first go to Coornhoop and check our fellows' wounds. There are four with assegai wounds, and one has an arrowhead in the thigh. And rather use salt water to sterilise, you're using too much brandy. It looks to me as if somebody is drinking the stuff.'

Six head of cattle assigned to Pieter Visagie for ploughing his lands were stolen that same afternoon and driven away across the river. And throughout that night they lay listening to the natives singing, high, repetitive and sad, like singing at a funeral. The free burghers in their homes along the Liesbeeck raised their heads uneasily to listen. Only four of the farmsteads from the first settlement along the river now remained.

The youth caught at the fishing lines – van Riebeeck called him Fishman, but his name was Heib'oa – boasted to Eva one morning that it was Goringhaicona, and no one else, stealing the government's livestock. He was glad to be alone with her, because she was beautiful to him, this young girl standing so straight and slim in her foreign clothes, and he hoped she might take a liking to him. There was no other man of his age in this Fort she could look at.

'The Goringhaicona? Those few old people who eat mussels?'

'Look at me,' he said. 'Do I look like old?'

'You are Gorachoqua. You know that yourself.'

'I'm a Goringhaicona now. Waterman.'

'Never,' she stopped him. 'You become a Goringhaicona by birth. Did Autshumao ask you to come and spy on us here?'

'He can't, he's stuck on the island. Trosoa is in his place.'

'But he's Gorachoqua too. You are flies on the milk, that's what the two of you are. You came here to be labourers, for drink and crusts of bread. You'll never be Goringhaicona in your life. Just go and tell the commander it's Strandlopers that stole his cattle. He'll die laughing.'

'Will he?' asked the young man with the inflamed and bandaged hand. 'I'll tell him, and it's the truth.'

'Go tell him,' she challenged. 'Tell him. I shall bring him here.'

'Bring him,' the young man retorted.

When Eva told it to the commander, he laughed. 'That gang of flotsam? I don't believe it. Does he say he was there with them?'

'That's what he says. But he's just boasting.'

A soldier brought the youth from the prison. Eva was to question him.

'Eva will put your words into Dutch.'

'He says it is all right.'

'You told Eva it was Goringhaicona who stole our cattle. Is that right?'

'He says yes.'

'But that's a lie.'

'He says no.'

'We believe it's Doman and the Gorachoqua.'

'He says Doman is with the Goringhaicona now.'

'Why? Ask him how many people are with the Goringhaicona.'

'He says about a hundred.'

'Tell him he's a bold-faced liar. Ask him if he's seen what the skin on a liar's back looks like when we're done with him.'

'What does Your Honour mean?'

'Ask him what I asked you. The way I taught you.'

'He says it's the truth. He says they only come out when it rains. It is true, Your Honour.'

'Control yourself, Eva. Ask him where they graze the stolen cattle.'

'He says in Hout Bay, in the valley among the mountains.'

'How many of their one hundred carry assegais?'

'He says about thirty.'

'Ask him how many Hollanders he has killed.'

In the ensuing conversation Eva lifted four fingers, went on talking, then turned to van Riebeeck. 'He wants to know: he himself, or all the Goringhaicona?'

'What was it you showed him? Why did you show him four fingers?'

She shook her head. 'I was just talking. I raised my hand. I didn't show anything.'

'You're in league with him, Eva. Leave it. I don't want to be lied to any further. Go to your room.' To the soldier at the door he motioned: 'Lock him away. Then call Corporal Giers and Master Pieter.'

Corporal Giers was ready to shoot, and Peter, when he was let in, recognised the grin on Giers's face and van Riebeeck's mood as identical. There had to be an expedition.

'I asked that little sardine Bart caught for us, how many white people he'd killed, to see if he would let slip a confession, but I missed it. I got the feeling that Eva wanted to protect him.'

'Him personally, or all the Watermen?'

'Him, in the first place, that was my impression. But see what you can find out from her about the matter, Master Pieter, when you chat again. I'm expecting good weather tomorrow. I'll ride upriver with the surveyor to see how we must place our palisades. You two go to Hout Bay with the men, and bring back that Trosoa who is now the chief in Herrie's place.'

He would help, Peter decided. Not under false pretences. He was not prepared to spy on Eva. She knew why he wanted to make an end to the war, and how he tried to do it, for whose favour and in whose interest.

They rode out before daybreak, lightly equipped. They crossed the Kloof Nek and swerved round behind the Gable Mountains. When they entered the open valley before Hout Bay towards noon, dogs were barking in the distance. The sound came from the direction of the river, where thin smoke appeared above the trees. Giers ordered them to dismount to prepare their weapons. They formed a circle, faces turned outward, ramming down charges of guns and pistols, shaking powder into the pans, clicking the pan covers shut. Of the enemy there was no sign as yet. Where were the hundred people and the stolen cattle? They proceeded on foot. When the barking of the dogs became urgent, they left one man with the horses, and advanced from one bush to the next. There were only three huts in the shelter behind the dunes close to the river mouth, no more. Giers motioned at them, showing them three fingers, how they had to attack, three men to each hut. They were to fire, and reload, and fire again.

Aiming from the hip they fired four shots into each hut. The ringing silence that followed was broken by screams, then naked people came tumbling from the low doors. The next volley was fired right in among the fleeing natives. Children crawled about, crying. The enemies lay bleeding on the white sand. An old man turned round at the foot of the dune, dark against the brilliant-white sand, raising a hand as if in greeting. A few weak words hung suspended from his open mouth. A woman, her kaross spread over her arm like a wing, called out: 'Don't shoot. We're the Water People.' Soldiers ran after their fugitive targets through the clearings, all firing independently. A man emerging in a crouched position from a hut staggered backwards into the open door, shot through the breastbone.

No one was running any more. Children clung screaming to the adults. Some wimpered, terrified in front of the soldiers, sinking to their knees, making themselves small in front of the muskets. All faces were distorted, tears ran down the dusty cheeks. And some of the soldiers looked surprised: Why were they crying? Who were these people? What had happened here?

'We are Watermen. The commander knows us. He knows us. Watermen. Watermen.' Peter started recognising faces: a kitchen help, the old woman who scoured the pots, here a hewer of wood, one who'd once washed the floor in the hospital. Some dead under the sun, others standing.

'We haven't done wrong. Spare us.'

'Shut your flytraps,' shouted Giers. 'Trosoa, where's Trosoa?'

A middle-aged man with a grey head struggled to his feet in the loose sand, and broke away from clinging children. 'I.'

'You're the thief, you bastard. You murdered our people and stole their cattle.'

'No.'

'Yes, you swine. You're coming to the Fort.'

'No.'

'Good God, are you saying no? Jan van Riebeeck says yes and you say no?'

'No.'

'Come here. I'm bloody well not going to carry you to the Cape.'

Trosoa looked once in the direction of the sea, rose up, and raised his hand towards that strange slanted mountain that rose steeply from the foaming sea on his left. Giers's bullet below the chin flung him backwards, throwing him sprawling against the dune. A moaning rose. In the background a young man dived into the bushes.

'Mount,' ordered Giers. 'Two men stand guard here. Search huts. Master Pieter, with me.'

They spotted the fleeing man without difficulty. Their horses struggled updune as he emerged from the bushes and scrambled over the large boulders at the foot of the mountain, between the slope and overhang on one side and the foaming waves that crashed thundering among the rocks. Nimbly he climbed higher, on hands and feet, only glancing round from time to time before turning his face to the mountain peak again. Giers gave the order to dismount, the muskets were rested across the saddles, and at fifty paces he ordered to fire. Bullet after bullet ricocheted from the rocks around the man and sped away whining out over the sea. At eighty paces someone hit him; they could see him loosening his grip on the rock, losing his balance, staggering back, grabbing at rock edges. Then he came to his feet again, and struggled on slowly, higher, hugging the rock face, from rock to bush, bush to rock.

Peter was the first to follow, his doctor's chest over his shoulder. Then Giers, and two or three others caught up with him. The wounded man looked round. He rested his face against the side of the mountain. Higher up there was only a hollow in the cliff, extending far above his head and curving outward over the churning waves below. He couldn't go any higher. The soldiers took aim again, resting their arms on granite boulders. Bullets smacked against the rock to the left and right of him. He turned, took one step and leaped out over the sea. They could see his body hit the rocks, and be washed off immediately by the next soughing of the sea, and disappear among swaying brown kelp.

'Bastard! There goes twenty guilders.'

The prisoners were ready, lined up, kneeling on the sand in front of their homes. There were two men, twelve women, six children. The corporal had the dead bodies dragged side by side. Everything in the huts was thrown outside. Some spears, beautiful tanned hides of springbok, bows, arrows, quivers, mats, earthen pots were thrown through the doorways and set alight in a single pile in front of the houses. Then Giers brought a flaming brand from the fire and drew it over the huts, one after the other. He called to Peter, and pointed at the corpses.

'Just cut off upper lips, otherwise we have to carry the whole bloody head. It makes three times twenty, to divide among twelve. Perhaps I should shoot two or three more.'

'Don't be crazy. Will you murder for money?'

'You bring the lips. We can testify for one another.'

That night they had to report in a full session of the Council. Van Riebeeck began by outlining his plan for the fortified frontier. A high palisade as at a stock market was needed, through which no ox could be stolen. The only trees with timber of the required length were the yellow-wood in the valleys behind Table Mountain. Their fence had to run from Uitkijk Island, across the river, then along its far bank as far as Rosendaal's house. From there, a growing, living hedge of wild almond trees would be planted, up to the Bosheuwel. Wild almond was a fast and densely growing plant. The only gate or entrance in the entire hedge would be at the shallow ford in the Brak River. That was where everybody, white and brown, had to enter and leave. The redoubt there was named Keert-de-Koe. Suitable name, eh? Stop-the-Cow. The redoubt at Bosheuwel was Houdt-den-Bul, Keep-the-Bull. They nodded, satisfied: bull and cow, that was exactly as it should be, of course.

Afterwards Giers and Peter were called, to report on their expedition. Giers sat with the three upper lips on a white kerchief in front of him. He couldn't speak. Peter had to report. The six councillors listened in silence. At the end the commander asked: 'Was Doman with them?'

'No, sir.'

'How many dead?'

'Four. One was carried off by the sea.'

'And there were no cattle with them? Is it possible they could have passed them on to someone else?'

'I saw no tracks. That might have been due to all the rain, but I don't think that little group was strong enough to undertake anything.'

'They could have assisted.'

'They might.'

'What happened to the rest?'

'They followed us as far as the Kloof Nek up here, rolled down stones at us and shouted at us as far as we came. But they're wiped out. They do not have a skin left among them.'

'You may ask for your sixty guilders from the cashier tomorrow. I'll sign the warrant. Those of you who still owe money on the book must first pay it off; the rest can have it in cash or drink. And for the present, it will be better not to let Eva hear about it, although she will find out soon enough. Those were her people, the Goringhaicona, who used to live here among the dunes. Perhaps there were relatives among them.'

The first time Peter saw her again, when she visited him in his room in the hospital, he told her. She was shocked, and brought her hands to her mouth. 'But the boy was only boasting.' She began to sob, he put his arms around her, and let her cry on his shoulder, before he made her lie down beside him on his bed, until her crying stopped.

The next morning Eva went away to Oedasoa. In her Dutch clothes she walked as far as the ford in the Brak River. There soldiers, stripped to the waist, were digging holes for the posts of the new fence. They called at her, but she passed without looking back, deeper among the shoulder-high bushes, to place a white stone on Heitsi-Eib's grave, and there she took off her Dutch clothes, folded them and put them in her knapsack. Then she wrapped a skin skirt and her kaross around her, put on her bracelets and went on with a stick in her hand. She kept away from the Fort until after the end of the flowering season, and for the first time Oedasoa's Cochoqua did not come down to the Liesbeeck valley that summer.

Once a month the commander rode along the entire new hedge, stopping at farmhouses to inspect the farms and make small talk, to remain on good terms with the new settlers. On these occasions Peter had to accompany him, to examine the ill and the wounded, for without horses or oxen the people had no way of going to the Fort. At the ford in the Brak River the new redoubt of Keert-de-Koe stood finished, built from yellow-wood on stone foundations, and a large tract of land around it had been burnt away to allow the watchmen a clear field of fire. The stones for the foundation came from a handy cairn in the adjacent veld; the last ones were packed into a hole to support the gatepost in the fence. Next to the redoubt was the gate, a single beam suspended from a chain like a ship's hoist. It could be swung forward and back, and raised with a pulley. 'The gateway to Africa,' van Riebeeck joked to the young postkeeper. The yellow-wood beams for the palisade lay piled up there, the ends chopped into sharp points, charred, and ready to go into the ground.

As they rode, van Riebeeck discussed the war with Peter and the sergeant. 'The enemy has been quiet for too long, I think. Why are they so quiet, I ask myself? Is it because the rainy season is over and they won't risk attacking us in good weather? Or is it because those Strandlopers have been behind the war all along? Under Herrie's leadership, or not? Where was Doman? Couldn't they tell? This hedge must be finished soon, and all the redoubts manned and armed. I have to send my annual report with the return fleet.'

One day the remaining Strandlopers arrived from Hout Bay at the entrance to the Fort, emaciated, clothed in tatters, with not even a dog on their heels. Now the old ones wanted to come and live here beside the Fort again, to carry water for the cook and fuel for the hearth. They were still the commander's friends, they had never looked for any trouble. Most of the children had died in the winter at the seaside. There was no more food in the sea.

'Yes,' said the commander, 'I shall see. Put up your houses in the dunes again. I'll think of a plan later.'

Sergeant Giers said to Peter: 'There's one tribe you can cancel off the books now, Master Pieter. The Goringhaicona belong to the past, like the Philistines. They're in the bag.'

Not many days later, after a night in which the south wind boomed over Fort and bay, so that in the morning the dust hung over the sea like a fog bank, they could hear from the cannon shots from Robben Island that there was trouble. An uprising among the convicts? A ship on the rocks? Peter was dispatched with a sergeant and six men. It was more likely that someone was dying, he thought, putting an extra flask of brandy into his box. He also ordered the sergeant to make sure that they had ration bags, in case the weather turned nasty.

The island's postkeeper was nervous. No, fortunately it was no illness, he said, when he saw the medicine chest. But he wanted to invite the visitors inside and offer them something to drink which a friend had sent from the East. It was real *tuac*. Were they *orang lama*, did they know it? Illegal, yes, everybody knew that. So much trouble, and just for him. He had a terrible problem. He'd only been in his post for a few months, and now an unfortunate thing had happened. There had not yet been such a case on the island during his tenure. What the commander might say, or do to him, was anybody's guess. It was that old blackguard, Herrie, again. He had absconded.

'How?' asked the sergeant, since it was in his hands now. 'He can't fly, can he? He must be hiding somewhere here.'

'In our boat.'

'The order was for boats to be chained at night. And for oars to be locked up inside. That is the order for the whole, entire Cape.'

'But the little boat was all broken, it would sink. Since the end of last year we haven't been able to use it ourselves.'

'You mean he swam away?'

'No. He left with the boat and with our only two oars. We're stranded here. Marooned.'

As if he was taking down a statement in a notebook, the sergeant summarised the matter: 'Rowed. In the Honourable Company's only boat. And that in last night's gale.' But his eyes were outside the open door, on the sea. 'A doddering old man, full of aches and pains, rowing in the dark of night in a leaking boat. Where to?'

Downwind, across the banks of crushed shells and dry scrub in front of the posthouse, across a purple-blue sea, they could see the white line of waves breaking against the far-off solid coast. But it was many, many miles away. Blaauwberg, there, seemed barely three fingers high.

'And are there sharks in the water here, quartermaster?'

'Yes.'

'I take off my hat to him,' said Peter. 'What chance does he have of making the shore?'

'None. He couldn't do it, if you ask me. Even if the boat was sturdier than we'd been told. What does he know about boats?'

The sergeant suggested: 'Possibly drowned.'

'Maybe, but then we must arrange a search for the body,' said Peter. 'I must have a body, the law demands it. I think it will be truly a miracle if the old fellow is found alive. But suppose he reaches land and gets back to his people, then the war will flare up all over again.'

The sergeant agreed. 'The commander is not going to like this, I warrant you. It's been such a pleasantly quiet time, recently.'

'Herrie was the commander's trump card. But come on, postkeeper,

I want to take a look at your prison. The last time we were in too much of a hurry, but now we have time. Any sick men in the house?'

'There's a few. The others are working down in the stone quarry today.'

'The sick first. Then we'll go to the quarry.'

'You better hurry up then, master. The wind may change,' the quartermaster called after him, sucking in another sip of the fiery *tuac*.

When they reached the Fort that night and reported the news, van Riebeeck vented his temper on the Goringhaicona outside the gate. They understood enough Dutch now, and the commander's voice had to effect the persuasion. He called them together in the courtyard and threatened that if Herrie was to show up here they had to hand him over as an enemy of the Company, and if they didn't the Company would deal with them as it had with Trosoa. They shouldn't listen to Herrie, it was all over with Herrie. They should never follow leaders again. There were no Goringhaicona any longer. Anyone who said there were Goringhaicona was an enemy of the Company.

Van Riebeeck waited until the third day for the corpse to surface, and then sent a search party along the beach. They discovered the little boat far beyond the Blaauwberg. It had been dragged up high on the beach and left at the foot of the dunes, the two oars neatly pushed in under the thwart. All tracks had already been washed away. The oars were all they carried back with them, except for the bad news that Herrie was free. One could well expect the alliance to resume the war about the Liesbeeck valley more vigorously now.

That winter Peter had less work to do. There was his routine in the hospital and a few ships to visit, but he was expectantly looking forward to Eva's return. He visited the farmers he had met during the war, and approved of the increase in fencing and harvests and children he observed on the frontier. It was spring, and there was a force of youth at work, a fresh life breaking out in many forms. He envied them their family life: the wife, the own hearth, the children. He himself could readily become a free burgher on the river bank; perhaps an existence as a free surgeon might become a possibility later. Eva was often in his thoughts. She would thrive here.

When he was alone in his room he longed for a better life. He was thirty years old, and he'd spent by far the greater part of his life in barracks. That life was beginning to bore him. He had few friends, and apart from the commander and his wife he hardly knew anyone whose company he would look up. The Cape was still too much manned by raw pioneers material, peasants from the barracks and the labouring class who would rather deal with a horse than a book. The commander had a clavichord on which he and his wife played, and the garrison's trumpeter had his tunes, but it was mediocre playing, and apart from that he never heard any music. He wanted a home, a place for his clothes, space for his books, a place to write. The need for a wife had been with him for years, but by now it had become a desire for a better way of life rather than the burning urge all the young men in the barracks were suffering. If he were to ask for his discharge and perhaps became a farmer or a free surgeon, his cares would increase. By the sweat of his brow, from dawn to dusk, for himself and a growing family, for a lifetime. It was much easier to have his meals provided at the Company's mess table, to have his clothes and bedding laundered by slaves every week, and receive the balance of his wages counted out in his hand in cash at the end of a month.

As for Eva, it wasn't as if there were no other young girls at the Cape, but they were scarce and seldom to be seen. The commander did not allow anybody outside after tattoo, and if someone were to slip out to the farmhouses in the dark, he might be caught by a lion, a leopard or a savage before the commander laid hands on him. Eva, pretty enough, with her gay laugh was pleasant company. Here in the Fort she was a child, a simple, laughing young girl who only wanted to be everybody's favourite and at peace with the world. But the burden the commander had placed on her worried Peter. It was an injustice. It was too heavy.

She returned at the height of summer. With her were two men herding a small flock of sheep. It was Oedasoa's gift to Mrs van Riebeeck. She also carried a small tortoiseshell of dried buchu for Mrs van Riebeeck, and a basket of sour figs and wild onions. For Peter she had brought three little strings of red, black and yellow tree seeds.

'There's a message in the colours,' she said when she handed them to him.

'And what do they say?'

But she wouldn't tell. 'Wear them round your neck.'

The two men squatted on the floor in front of van Riebeeck's large table. They didn't want to sit on the pew. That was considerate of them, as their bodies had been oiled for the visit. Oedasoa had sent them with a long message. This was the message: He asked that there should be peace. Enough blood had been spilled into the ground. Was the Hollander prepared to help him so that the killing could end?

'Yes, certainly. For the sake of peace. But we have no quarrel with Oedasoa.'

'He spoke to the Gorachoqua and the Goringhaicona. Gogosoa will return all the cattle that have been taken from you. The cattle are now with Oedasoa.'

'Eva, have you seen the animals?'

'Yes, commander.'

'Do you know where Herrie is?'

'He is there.' She spoke quietly to the two messengers. 'There are many wounded too. Doman's arm is broken and it will not mend.'

'Does he want peace?'

'No. But he cannot fight, a man with only one hand.'

Van Riebeeck considered. 'Now look, we are eager to have peace, you can tell Oedasoa that. But from now on I want to know who I am talking to. They must come here themselves. They will be protected. They will be safe here.'

'Doman won't come. That is what worries Oedasoa.'

'Then he cannot discuss peace with us. Then there is no peace yet between us and him, or between us and all those who follow him.'

'That is what worries Oedasoa.'

'Now look, we thank Oedasa for his gifts, which please us. We should like to talk to him and Gogosoa about peace. But Gogosoa must understand: if I take his hand to greet him and his dog bites me, I shall smash that dog's head. He must keep his dog tied up now.'

'And what about Herrie?'

'If we make peace with Gogosoa, I'll have peace with Herrie. He can come back and live here among the dunes, or go wherever he wants to, as long as he doesn't bother the Company or the free farmers.'

The envoys were entertained and rewarded, and given presents for Oedasoa and his wife, and for Gogosoa. Eva told Peter about Doman, of sabre wounds on his cheekbone and his back, of a bullet wound in his chest and a festering hole behind his shoulder. His arm was tied to his body with thongs. He was suffering badly and used herbs, but it was the poison in his heart against the Hollander which kept his arm from healing.

Once more in the course of that war did Peter ride out in the night with a patrol, to inspect fires seen on the other side of the Liesbeeck. They went through the ford in the Brak River, where the soldiers of Keert-de-Koe opened the gate for them. The fires were in a wide clearing among the dark bushes, high, leaping flames shooting up red stars into the cold black sky. They suspected an ambush. There was only a circle of new huts, no livestock, no people, no voices, no dogs. They waited, and doused the fires, and went home. There were no Koina.

A second overture from Oedasoa was brought from the Bay by the Saldanha sailors. The Bay – that was what free fishermen called Saldanha Bay, as if Table Bay did not count. Together with the message they brought fish, penguin eggs and four mattress covers filled with down. It was an oral message, rather difficult to memorise. Oedasoa had come to them in the Bay and called them ashore. The interpreter was that Herrie, whom they thought was still incarcerated on the island. This was the message: Oedasoa wanted it known that the people desired peace. They had taken the draught oxen so that the Dutch would stop ploughing in the Liesbeeck valley, for where a Dutchman ploughed he planted his heart in the earth. They killed where herdsmen had clung to their cattle for too long. Let Boom account for how he'd hanged a man from a beam. Were they not justified to feel aggrieved? Now they longed to return to their own land, with its abundance of clean water and grass. They wanted to be where Heitsi-Eib's cairns stood. Saldanha Bay was parched and brackish everywhere and their livestock kept on grazing upwind to start their trek south. If van Riebeeck was agreeable, he could write his name on a paper, one for Gogosoa, one for Herrie, one for Doman, so that all three of them could enter through the new gate with livestock and people.

Van Riebeeck had a flagon of arrack brought to offer the Saldanha sailors for their trouble, and wrote three notes (*Let pass bearer . . .*). At the first fair weather they went to sea with his answer. He was satisfied; he could have sent tobacco, but it would have been like sending cheese to a rat already caught in the trap.

Only a month later, when the air was turning cool again and the afternoon shadows began to stretch out long along the ground, did Doman and Herrie go to the Fort. They were in the midst of forty or fifty spear carriers, who moved nervously, suspiciously, half crouched behind a screen of fourteen fighting oxen. There was no light talk among them, they were seething to kill. There the Fort stood in front of them, with its wall of sods and stone that could be scaled so easily; there was the flag of red, white and blue slapping out right and left; there were the soldiers who only recently had danced blood-red in front of their speartips on rainy days. *Heitse*, they could do it again, right here, now, today.

Their arrival was seen from far off, the guard was doubled. Van Riebeeck put his work aside, loaded a pistol and pushed it into the belt of his breeches under his coat, and called Eva into the front room. 'I'm going to treat them coldly. Don't make any loving talk. I have only one answer to all their questions and that is *no*. I'm not glad at all that they're coming here with cattle, and I have a good mind to allow only one of the leaders inside, and give the order for the guard to shoot the retinue. You just translate my words and their words and don't add any of your own. Keep your voice down. Look into their eyes. Blood may flow if we're not careful. Right at the end, after I've sent them away, I shall propose that Master Pieter look at Doman's arm. You must say it only once, don't insist.'

The men with the spears squatted out of the wind behind the eastern bastion while they waited for Doman and Herrie. The fourteen mottled oxen grazed in the scrub in front of them; when they strayed too far, they were whistled back. Dusk crept up the mountainside.

With van Riebeeck behind the table were the sergeant and a

secretary. Eva was seated almost midway between the two groups. Herrie was tired, his hands were trembling on his *kierie*. He was thinner than ever. Doman's face was decrepit, his eyes were yellow and deep in his head, his skin looked ashen, his cheeks hollow, his lips taut over his teeth like those of a sun-dried corpse. He was clearly feeling cold; he clutched his kaross in front of his chest with the hand holding the *kierie*. There was no sign of gifts. Without any welcome van Riebeeck moved on to business.

'My cattle you were supposed to bring back?'

'There is nothing left.'

'Are you asking for peace with lies today?'

'You Hollanders took the land on which our people lived for years. If we go to Holland, will we be allowed to do the same there? Will it be allowed? And you do not remain at your Fort, you trek through the land and take the best without asking whether it suits us.'

'Eva,' van Riebeeck asked softly. 'Have you added some of your own words?'

'No. They were all Autshumao's.'

'Ask him why he doesn't speak himself. He speaks Dutch well enough when he gets thirsty.'

'Must I say that, honourable sir?'

'He heard me himself. Why doesn't he let Doman speak?'

'He says Doman is sick. But I can see that Doman is very bitter.'

'Now tell Herrie he's wasting time with his accusations. I want to know why they are here. Who sent them?'

Herrie refused to speak directly to him. Eva had to say it: 'We want our cattle to graze by the river again.'

'No. There is not enough pasture for you and us.'

'Then were we not right in stopping you from getting livestock? Because the more you get the more you drive us away. Who must by rights withdraw, the occupant or the invader?'

'Tell him this belongs to the past.'

'We used to live off the bitter almonds and wild tubers behind your hedge.'

'We need the land for ourselves. You must realise: we are going to keep the valley, and you have lost it for ever, just as we lost a hundred and forty cattle.'

'And your people, with the wide breeches . . .'

'Who are you talking about, Eva?'

'It is Autshumao's words.'

'Tell him I don't like the tone of his remarks.'

'Your farmers take our sheep, our bracelets; they pull off our earrings and give them to your slaves. They kick and beat us like children.'

'I shall punish the culprits myself.' The irritation was mounting in him, and he knew he should suppress it, but couldn't. 'And look, if you're not happy with this, you can try to take revenge. Just you try. Attack this Fort.'

While Eva was translating, he looked them in the eyes. They listened in silence. Was their placidity a mask to cover their hatred, or had they still not realised that a way of life had come to an end and that their future had been made different? 'You have now heard my last words on the matter. Go back to your chiefs, discuss it with them, and come and tell me what you have decided. Take your cattle away from here. You have spilled Dutch blood. That cannot be paid with cattle.'

The two natives rose up from the pew and moved to the door. 'Commander,' whispered the sergeant, 'let us take them now. They owe us blood.'

'No. Let them go.' But where? Van Riebeeck remembered the day when he'd measured out the first farms along the river. Herrie had been there, he'd asked, 'And where shall we go to?' Where to, indeed? 'Let them go. I want to explore their minds more deeply.'

The sergeant did not understand what he meant.

'Ask Doman about his arm.'

Lightly, Eva followed the two men to the door. She pushed in ahead of Doman, and spoke seriously to him. From the way his head jerked he seemed to be spitting at her.

'What does he say?'

'He's saying bad things.'

'What, precisely?'

'He says Master Pieter's arm . . . He says if Master Pieter wants to help, he must start with his own arm.'

Van Riebeeck wasn't sure that he'd understood the answer correctly, but that evening when she told Peter what had happened, he insisted until she had explained it all.

At the end of the week there was a message that the Koina would arrive the following day to make peace. Van Riebeeck marked on his calendar that it fell on Ascension Day. That was good, he could make them wait and tell them he had to go to church first. He would warn the sick-comforter. Then, if the discussion went well, he could offer the most important ones a little celebration after the service.

They had sent a few cattle as an opening gift ahead of them, and arrived just before the service. From the wall above the entrance van Riebeeck quickly counted: thirteen oxen. Then there was the knot of leaders. He recognised them from their decorations, walking at the head of at least a hundred spearmen. In the rear followed twenty or thirty women. Why so many? He let them gather in front of the gate, while the congregation was entering church through his front door. He sent a message to the minister to keep it short; in an hour he wanted to receive the leaders in this same front room. Eva he instructed to go and talk to them at the entrance. He had a half-barrel brought out to the courtyard, ordered it to be filled, half with arrack and half with brandy, and tied a drinking cup to the barrel with a short cod line. He had white bread brought from the kitchen and placed it in two bowls beside the barrel. He was damned if he'd be caught on his knees twice. Behind him the last churchgoers were entering. The sick-comforter stood waiting for him on the stoep, the bell rope ready in his hand.

'Today you're going to see the rarest entertainment in the world,' he told the guard officer, and gave the sign for the big gate to be opened.

There were the leaders of the Alliance. Peter recognised Doman from his face twisted with pain, but the man was unarmed and was supported on both sides by two others. Then there were Herrie of the Goringhaicona, Gogosoa of the Goringhaiqua, Choro of the Gorachoqua and Ankaisoa from the plain at the Klapmuts Berg. Behind them was a wall of karosses, shoulder to shoulder, above which were jackal-skin caps covering faces shiny with oil, and above those a forest of assegais. Behind them were women singing, clapping their hands, stamping their feet, forcing the whole procession forward. Van Riebeeck greeted the oldest man first with the hand, but Gogosoa embraced him and hugged him to his body, then Choro, then Ankaisoa. He shook hands, laughed, welcomed, embraced. His white lace collar, his starched cuffs, his over-coat were smudged, his black Sunday suit covered in shiny grime, even his stockings were stained with mutton grease.

Only Doman, wrapped in his grey long kaross like a shroud, did not come to greet him. He remained standing between his helpers, chin on his chest. When he raised his head, his warm yellow eyes moved over the Fort's battlements where a double guard were walking with their pikes, and over the bastions, with their cannon which had been turned around the day before to fire inward.

'Come inside,' van Riebeeck invited them with a gesture. 'Eva, tell them they are welcome to eat and drink. It is wine and bread from the Company. I must go to church first, it will not take long.' He wiped his hands on his overcoat, and went to jerk the bell rope himself to announce the beginning of the service.

Peter was glad to find Eva in the crowd. 'Were you ordered to be here?'

'Yes, I was given work to do.'

The people were already ladling and drinking. Those who had a horn cup in the skin-bag, helped themselves, drank, handed back to others, drank. With his hands behind his back Peter waited inside the gate, as he had been ordered. He had to keep an eye, and talk to those who wished to talk. When anyone became rowdy he had to have the person removed. When the barrel got empty, he had to have it refilled, the bread bowl likewise. Already they were crowding and shoving to get to the barrel, grabbing for the cup; it could turn into a stampede. The leaders and the elders stood apart. They were expectant, resentful, their work still lay ahead. What was there to celebrate so urgently? Between two doors in a wall Doman sank down on his haunches, it was noticed by some of the chiefs. Herrie was the first to touch the arm of the man next to him and point at Peter, he pulled Doman to his feet and brought him to the surgeon.

'This is Doman,' he said in English.

'We have met.'

'He says this war will not end.'

'He can tell it to the commander, when he can stand on his two feet again.'

'He needs your help.'

'What does he want?'

Then Eva turned up. She entered into the conversation as if she was part of it. First she spoke to Herrie, then with him. 'Pieter, Doman is in a very bad way. It's his arm. Autshumao wants to know if the Company will look at his arm.'

'I can do it, if the patient is willing.'

'He is so sick that he cannot speak. Must we ask the commander?'

'It is not necessary yet. I'll examine him, then we'll know what to do.'

She turned to Herrie again. Peter could barely hear her voice in the hubbub of the courtyard, where some of the women were now seated with legs outstretched on the ground close to the barrel, and singing shrilly. Bread was passed around, a decorated eggshell was filled from the barrel. Some of the men danced in a circle with shuffling feet, their hands almost dragging on the ground, sending up a cloud of pale dust from the crushed seashells. Others crowded noisily around the barrel, pushing and arguing loudly. The sergeant of the guard came to speak to Peter, a worried man.

'What are we going to do? They're having a church service inside.'

'Nothing. Just let them go on, until the service is over.'

'Pieter,' said Eva, 'Autshumao is willing to let us take Doman to the hospital.'

The patient was helped from the crowd, and in the little hospital placed on the examination table. Herrie, two young men and Eva were present. 'Ask them to hold him down. I will first clean his wound.' In the hospital kitchen he called for hot water and soap, fetched his medicine chest from his room, and when the water came, washed his hands.

Without clothes, Doman's body was like that of a dog strangled on its leash. Was this the warrior who would never ask for peace? He was emaciated, filthy, stinking of putrefaction. It was almost three months since the battle at the river, where presumably he had been wounded. His right arm had been strapped to his chest with thongs. The wound high up on his right breast had healed, but had probably been tampered with, as the lump of scar tissue was rough and irregular, a brownish-grey knot clinging to the wound like the coarse growth from old axe wounds on tree trunks. It might be a bullet hole, and it wasn't an ordinary entrance, the scar was far too big for a bullet. The shot probably came from a gun in a horseman's hand, as it had been fired from above.

He cut the patient's thongs and threw them away, examined the bulging, swollen arm, tried to flex the wrist and the elbow, forcing a terrible scream from Doman when he tried to lift the arm sideways. There were no external symptoms of fractured bones or joints. This arm still had life in it, the nerve was probably healthy and blood circulation possibly normal. The problem was located in the shoulder, purplish-brown and heavily swollen, in the bones of the shoulder girdle, the *scapula*, *clavicula* and the head of the *humerus*. Behind the shoulder, where the bullet had left, the *scapula* was raised like a tent, and from a festering wound in its centre oozed blood, water and pus. It all bore the smell of putrefaction. With warm water and soap he washed away the slime and dirt. Under his hands Doman twisted, thrashed, groaned; the dirty suds streaked down his back and flanks on to the sheepskin, until he lay in a warm, stinking puddle. The young Koina stared into the wound. When Peter looked up, Eva's eyes were on his face. He asked her: 'Come and stand next to me. I want to tell you what I do.' Layer upon layer of sweat and dust he washed from Doman's shoulder, sheep's fat, old scabs, slimy rotting tissue, bits of herbs, small dead insects, a green mess that might be cow dung. He showed it to her on his sponge and explained what he saw. Once the blood was flowing freely, he handed her a length of clean linen from his box and asked her to help with the cleansing. She herself prised the first bone-splinter from the inflamed flesh and pointed it out to him. He extracted it with tweezers.

'Good heavens, what have you found here? It doesn't come from the shoulder blade. Look, it is covered with cartilage, can you see the shiny edge? I believe it's from the head of the collarbone.' Then he probed inside the wound with his tweezers and pulled out a thick wad of sheep's wool. More bone fragments, thin slivers of the *scapula*, bits of the collarbone's spongy head, then a piece of lead.

'This kind of dirt prevents the flesh from healing. The patient needs a big operation, but for now I'm only doing the most necessary. I'll have to make an incision. Stand by with your bandages to swab up when I say so. Tell the others to hold him down.'

'Doman is sleeping.'

His incision right across the wound, through skin and muscle, was the length of his middle finger. He forced it open, and moved the tweezers around until he could feel the jagged bullet hole in the shoulder blade.

'Ask Herrie to hold the candle here at my hands.'

There was much damage to the *scapula*: jagged ends, loose shards of bone, more fragments of lead. He knew the *scapula* well. With eyes closed he called up the shape of the bone and the location of every muscle from his memory. When he'd prepared for his examination at the university long ago, he'd lain on his back on his bed and with eyes shut took a human bone from a box full of samples on the floor, identifying it from the form, left or right side, estimated age, male or female if possible; examined it with his fingertips, inspecting every hollow, protuberance, roughness or curve to which muscles were attached, and naming the function of each, keeping his eyes closed all the time. All medical students prepared in that way. The problem with Doman's wound was that the bullet had never gone out completely. It had entered from the front, at a downward angle, possibly ricocheted from the top rib, and disintegrated. Some of the shards splintered the head of the collarbone and burst backwards through the shoulder blade. Somewhere inside the man, possibly in the lung, a small swarm of bone splinters wandered about. He had to go still deeper, turn the patient over on his back and make an incision from the front. But no, not on a bloodied sheepskin and accompanied by the irritating howls of drunken savages. Still, he'd seen difficult days: once he'd performed a double amputation in a muddy backyard during a bombardment, by the light of a burning brothel.

He could not concentrate any longer; van Riebeeck needed him and Eva in the courtyard. Doman, the enemy, the man who would never make peace, might just as well die, and the Company would be grateful for it. Peace then, for the land, for all the people, for him and Eva, today.

'I want to try something difficult now, Eva. Get some linen from the box. Swab this clean.' He lowered the ends of the tweezers through his incision in the muscle and through the bullet hole, fishing for lead in the tissue below, but touched nothing but the shattered head of the collarbone. He took out the loose shards. Then back into the hole, through the protuberance of the *acromion* which curved forward, searching there in the space between the protuberance and the collarbone, where the shoulder muscles were joined. Then he lowered the scalpel next to the tweezers, all the way down; carefully, and with tiny movements of the point, as if working through a keyhole, he detached the remaining tendons from the bone. This, this was the way in which peace had to come. Doman would never raise his arm again.

'Eva, I've finished here. I still have to cleanse it and stitch it up. We have to be outside in the courtyard, and it is time for the church to come out. I think the commander will need you in the council chamber. Please go and wash your hands, and look, your clothes are stained with blood.'

He sutured the incisions, covered the wound with ointment, bandaged it, washed his instruments and packed them away. Herrie was there beside him, curious about what he'd done to Doman. 'I want this man to remain here in our hospital until he regains consciousness. After that you can do with him what you wish. And don't put your cowdung poultices on the wound. Keep it clean and come and get ointment from me. He will not be able to raise his arm again, but he'll survive.'

Herrie had no answer. Would this ever lead to peace? Peter

summoned the hospital's slaves to put his patient to bed, do away with the filthy kaross and bandages, scrub the table and the floor. Then he washed himself in his room, dressed, and drank some brandy from his flask. Outside the courtyard was filled with dancers, along all the walls, between doors and windows. The circle around the wine barrel became larger as more men jumped into the shuffling line, then shrank again where they slipped away to refill a mug. Along the walls others looked on without interest, women with children, others who wanted no more to drink. On the walls above the soldiers were patrolling from east to west, and from west to east. Peter joined the sergeant of the guard.

How long before the church came out? Sometimes it lasted longer than expected. They walked with their hands behind their backs, imagining that they were relaxed, but knowing that the sounds of Koina singing always caused unrest. The sergeant signalled to the corporal on the opposite battlement. Peter was relieved to see van Riebeeck emerging on the stoep, looking up, and beckoning to them.

'Call the guard down, I want a passage to be cleared for the churchgoers.'

It was difficult. Soldiers, churchgoers in black, and dazed Koina churned in a crazy whorl around the wine vat. He helped to escort the burghers and a few of their women who had come to church with their children, to the gateway. The dancing circle formed and shrank, the dust hung above the courtyard. Eva found him in the throng.

'The commander wants you in the council chamber. All the chiefs enter over there.' She laughed as if something funny was happening. 'The sergeant must stay here.'

The chiefs were calm, cool. They sat on the church pew. The table with the minister's books, the plate and chalice of a rare Communion were still standing between the commander and them. Van Riebeeck was flanked by his interpreter, three councillors and a witness of what had happened in the war. A cool north wind brought the smell of seaweed from the icy pools of the ebbtide into the chamber, together with the high voices of the women chanting in the courtyard.

The commander introduced the people at his side, then Herrie pointed out the Koina with a finger and named them.

'Doman not here?'

'I examined his wounds, commander. He is resting in the hospital.'

Van Riebeeck offered wine and bread, but they did not want to eat. Ankaisoa said something which Eva had to translate.

'He says they have enough food. They just came to talk about the grazing beside the river.'

'Yes. What have they decided about the proposals I made to their emissaries last week? Do they have an answer?'

'They say it is the only grazing in the vicinity that remains green all year. The Goringhaiqua's cattle were always fatter than others, people recognised them by that. But they also want to come and dig wild bulbs, pick buchu, eat berries, and hunt the game that come to drink at the river, and the wild geese in the reeds.'

'Wait, Eva. I know all that already. What is their answer to last week's proposals?'

But she insisted on transmitting her message first. 'They want the Hollanders to go away from the river. Since the beginning of the world they have been eating from that valley.'

'I said it was impossible. We cannot plough on this side of the mountain. It rains too little here. The soil is brackish. There is no wood left. There is too much wind.'

'Go back to Holland.'

'Get them to stop harping on that. Tell them: You attacked and killed our people. You wanted war. Then you were beaten. Now accept it.'

The chiefs leaned towards one another and conferred loudly. It was Gogosoa, short, squat and dark as a mortar, who wanted to put a question. Eva gestured with her hands. 'They want to cross the river, my lord, for wild roots and bitter almonds.'

'No.'

They were silent again. Some of them were staring ahead, frowning; others grinned dumbly like Dutch peasants when a court case was decided against them on a point of law.

'It is already decided. You are not allowed to come near our farms on any pretext whatsoever.'

'Is that just?' asked Choro. 'Is it your river and your grass?'

'It is ours.'

'Everything else is ours?'

'Everything on the far side of the river.' Then van Riebeeck had second thoughts. 'We'll discuss that later. I want to hear about the cattle and sheep now. Master Pieter here knows about every cow and ox and sheep you stole from us.'

They shook their heads in silence. No.

'I shall forget about the livestock. But then you must forget about the valley. That is how the matter stands. It will be written on paper, and even if a hundred years pass it will not change. Come back tomorrow, then we can raise our glasses in friendship.'

Then van Riebeeck got up. The meeting was over.

Choro asked again: 'Is this just? Is this your river? Your trees? And your land? And your sea? And your island?'

'Yes.'

Choro shook his head in disbelief. 'Yours? People without cattle?'

At the door they picked up their weapons in silence, and walked out into the white light. The carousing was far gone. There was no sign from the drinkers and dancers around the barrel that they recognised chiefs. Drunks were lying against the walls, others were staggering between the dance and the barrel, occasionally falling into the dust, rising to their feet, crawling away. Those who couldn't get up were helped to the wall, to sleep in the midday sun. Gogosoa was talking to Ankaisoa. Peter remained standing in the doorway behind Eva.

'What's he saying?'

'Today it is the death of the Koina. That's what he says.'

'Yes.'

'This is where the Hollander is fighting the hardest, even though he talks about peace. He's referring to the drinking.'

'I know, Eva.' There was another soldier on his way with a bucket to fill the wine barrel. The garrison on the wall were laughing and pointing. 'Come, let us escort the guests through the gate.'

'Do you think they want to drink something?'

'No. We'll take them to the gate and say goodbye to them there. Then we go down to the beach. I think the commander will not need his interpreter again today.' Outside the gate among the bushes too, drunken people lay about.

'How is Doman?'

'I don't know.'

'In there the chiefs were talking among themselves, saying they'd fight for the river. I think they are waiting for Doman to get well again. You helped him just now.'

'Was that what they said? I didn't hear it.'

'I didn't want to say it. The commander is always ready to fight. Will we have peace now, Pieter?'

'Perhaps, by the grace of God.'

'Today was Ascension Day, and Communion, and a real pastor. And you and I were not in church. What will become of us?'

'Go to church?' he asked. 'Put on nice clothes?'

'No. For the love of it.'

He wasn't sure that he understood what she had said, but he would interpret it according to his own need. He was reasonably certain in his belief that the war would end.

When they were alone on the beach, he took her by the arm. 'Come here, then I can show you exactly how I treated Doman's bones.'

Afterwards Peter would often think of how the Company had been the only winner. It got what it wanted. That same spring the wheat stood green in the new fields, the small herds of cattle and sheep grazed peacefully, and the Liesbeeck spread its water into shiny vleis towards the vegetable gardens of the farmers. The only Koina to be seen came to the houses in the daytime with bundles of wood, or honey, or a few ostrich eggs. From time to time people with sheep turned up at the gate of Keert-de-Koe from the large kraals, on their way to the Fort. Everybody obediently went through the gate and walked along the old trekking road, and as they left some of the older ones would try to find a cairn among the bushes and then cast their stones where they thought it might have been.

Van Riebeeck could now attend to his other ambition. He wanted to make contact with the emperor of Monomotapa. Gold would bring a glint to the eyes of the Lords Seventeen. In a letter they recommended that he promise double wages to volunteers for such an expedition. He, too, would benefit. There were numerous applicants, and he chose twelve. He appointed his second sergeant as the leader, and Pieter van Meerhof as scribe and surgeon.

For van Riebeeck it was a double relief to send Peter away, because over the past month his wife had been uneasy and full of warnings because Peter had been seeing too much of Eva.

He told her, 'Sooner or later Eva will have to choose a husband, and much rather Pieter than any of the others I see around here.'

The Council drew up a worksheet for them, entitled *Instructie*, which Sergeant Danckaert and Peter had to sign. It bore the names of nations and kings they were to visit, rivers they had to cross, cities along the road, everything with the distances between them marked in miles. The cities Cortado, Davagul, Belugaris, Mogar and Agraselle, the countries Betua and Monomotapa, the rivers St Lucia and Spirito Sancto. They were given samples of spices, gold, silver, silk and cotton for which they had to search, and tobacco, arrack and beads they could promise to the kings. Their weapons, provisions and writing materials were loaded on a few oxen. A compass was pressed into Danckaert's hand. Peter was given responsibility for their journal. He looked forward eagerly to the journey.

They followed the old trunk road to the Brak River and passed through the new barrier at Keert-de-Koe before daylight on 12 November 1660. Their oxen were untrained, the days hot, the road heavy with sand underfoot. The talk dried up; they divided into four small groups, of which those in the rear shouted at those in front to go more slowly, and eventually lost contact with them.

Their first camp was at the marshlands of the Tygerberg, and from there they trekked to Klapmuts Mountain, where Ankaisoa had his summer pastures. Danckaert tried to persuade Ankaisoa to sell them a pack ox, but couldn't succeed. The man insulted him and told him to turn back and remain behind his Liesbeeck. Two of the travellers, unfit for an overland expedition, kept complaining until Danckaert sent them away; he was better off without them. After that they followed the Berg River downstream, towards the distant blue peaks in the

North, across innumerable small streams and a hilly landscape dotted with molehills, into which they often sank up to their knees at every step. With great effort they reached the foot of that mountain. Exhausted from walking and meagre rations, they stank of sweat and all of them were already convinced that there were no cities with beautiful names on this road. Peter looked up at the grey cliffs like his companions, dejected, but still curious about what still lay ahead. They helped one another to hump their loads on their backs, and then climbed up through the rocks, leading the oxen.

Once or twice they saw hunters in those kloofs, people shorter than the Cape Koina, and armed only with bows and arrows. They were wary of the Hollanders and wouldn't come close. Peter lit a pipe of tobacco and placed it on a rock where they could see it. They came down and picked it up and turned it in their hands, sniffed at it, but did not know what to do with it.

After fourteen days of struggling through tall bushes and over cliffs and kloofs, they reached the Olifants River. Danckaert was confident: a Dutch expedition had been there before and named this river. Privately, he thought this was far enough, and tried to persuade the others to turn back. Most of them were relieved; from the mountain tops they could already see that there were no cities in this godforsaken land. Peter remained possessed by curiosity and some excitement. He wanted to go further, to see more strange birds and game and to smell the fragrance of the scrub on the mountain air. Perhaps there were wonders, world-miracles, undiscovered among these kloofs. He was sad to leave that wilderness, but like the others he was exhausted, and willing to return. The men wanted to discard some of the heaviest baggage. Against Danckaert's instructions and threats, the eighteen fathom coil of rope, the cooking pot and the pickaxe were flung down, and cursing and bitter they all descended into the kloofs on the homeward journey.

The one thing they had enjoyed together on that journey was the roasting of meat and the drinking around the evening campfire. On the return journey there was less bickering. The brandy and arrack they had brought along for the kings of Monomotapa were used up in toasts drunk at the fire. 'To Davagul!' and 'To Cortado!' Chunks of venison were roasted on spits, rough voices sang nostalgic songs of the Northern Sea, and they were sublimely happy under the shimmering sky on the black mountain. But every morning after, the sergeant had to use dire threats to get them marching again.

On the day before Christmas they were back at the Fort. Peter and the expedition leader had to report to the commander, answer questions, account for their failure, as if it had been their fault that Monomotapa was not on that particular road. Danckaert blamed the weak discipline among his men, and mentioned some names. In the end he was the only one to receive the promised double wages. The rest had to pay for lost implements and the drink consumed in excess of their rations. Peter sought comfort in Eva's arms, and she welcomed him with a wholesome and happy heart.

Soon afterwards a new service roster was drawn up for the hospital, and again he was on night shift. But within fourteen days of their return he was sent out on a second expedition. He volunteered for it, as he had come to enjoy the freedom of the wilderness. At least it was something good from Africa. Their commission was simpler, but not easier, than before: they had to resume the previous journey and proceed at least as far as the Namaqua. Corporal Cruijthoff would be the leader, receiving double wages from the start. The rest would receive it if they were successful. Of the thirteen men six had been on the previous journey; they were good, solid companions. Peter, as surgeon and scribe, was second in command. Their route had been plotted: Keert-Klapmuts, Berg River. On the second day Peter shot an antelope which they roasted on the coals in the evening. On the fourth day, when as was now his habit, he walked some distance ahead of the group to catch a first glimpse of the game before they fled from the noise of people, a big black-maned lion came from the bushes and stood, growling, in the game track in front of him. He knew it would be fatal to run away, and raised his musket. It was barely twenty paces, and he took a step or two forward. The lion jumped into the bush, and was out of sight immediately. Later that night they camped at a steep, solitary mountain, where they pitched their tents. Peter persuaded the corporal to call it Riebeeck's Castle; that should please the commander. The next morning they had barely set out when a lion charged the man directly behind him. Peter ran back and fired a shot at the animal, and again the lion suddenly turned away, and leaped into the bushes.

He really enjoyed the journey. Fatigue no longer troubled him. His stamina improved, and he was wearing better boots than the previous time. He felt like a prince in an endless hunting ground, where everything belonged to him. His comrades were wonderful fellows. When they camped close to a river they could hear hippopotamuses grazing on the banks at night, and the sounds of jackals and lions near by or far away in the dark. The days were sunny, the veld was covered with flowers and alive with birds, animals, insects. They passed through valleys with running streams, over fertile slopes. Corporal Cruijthoff was a quiet man who preferred bringing up the rear, so that Peter was free to lead, take first aim at buck, and write down the day's events from memory in the journal in the evening. As a result his own name often featured in his account. He was happy. This was real freedom. A Sonqua spied them on their way, followed them for some time, and approached when Peter put a mug of wine on a rock for him. He and the man used their hands to talk. With his fingers Peter formed horns beside his head, making the sound of an ox. He imitated the sound of a sheep, pointing north, said 'Namaqua'. The man understood immediately. Peter took him by the arm, pulled him forward, pointing in the direction they were going. The man said 'Namaqua,' pointed north and beckoned to them to follow. Peter was proud of what he had achieved. He was beginning to enjoy Africa.

On the eleventh day of their journey he named a mountain he had been eyeing for miles after himself, Meerhof's Kasteel. At the foot of the mountain were five or six sweet-water fountains, and barely a gunshot away they found an easy spot to cross over to the Olifants River. That was what his Sonqua guide and his own skills meant to the Honourable Company. With a few comrades he went down to the river, and together with the Sonqua they sat there on rocks smoking tobacco pipes, while the soldiers cornered large bass in the river pools with their hands and brought them out. The group stayed there for a few days to rest the oxen, swim in the cool water, catch fish, and roast the fish and venison on their campfire. During those rests Peter often thought of Eva, and of his few relatives in Denmark. Would his family still be alive? Already their faces had become vague, like a soft, misty landscape with the branches of wintry spruce trees, or like bird tracks in the snow. What would his father say if he knew that his only son lay with a heathen woman? If comrades from the Danish army corps were to meet him today, bearded, stronger and healthier than he'd ever been in his life, tanned like a labourer, would they recognise him? Would they envy him, and say: Why haven't I done this too?

At that resting place a strange thing happened to him. He could never explain it, but he felt he should dutifully write it down in his journal for all to know. He was alone, he was walking with his gun along the river and sat on a boulder for a long time to enjoy the landscape. He was staring across the water. His thoughts were very far away. Then a living monster raised the front part of its body from the water. It had three heads like cat's heads, and behind it three long tails were stretched out in the water. He jumped up in fright, and immediately the monster vanished. With his gun aimed at the smoothly running stream, Peter went up and down the bank to search for tracks or other signs, but saw nothing. A flock of turtle doves came to sit on the sand where he'd seen the monster, and drank from the shallows. Not one of the group wanted to believe him, and he promptly stopped talking about it. But that evening he entered a full account of it in the journal.

A few days later they were among the Namaqua. Where his guide saw cattle tracks, they called at the echoing mountain through cupped hands, set out tobacco, waited patiently, picked up the tobacco, and went on. The Namaqua were scared, but were watching them, the guide pointed them out. On the nineteenth day all the signs were right. Peter asked the group to stay in camp that morning. Towards ten o'clock the Namaqua started calling at them from the rocky outcrops. Peter filled half a dozen pipes with tobacco and lit them from the cooking fire, and went to meet them. A few watchful men came downhill through the bushes, and took the pipes he offered them. He showed them how he smoked, how he sucked, inhaling deeply, and allowed the smoke to slide out through his nose.

By noon the camp was full of visitors, so that Cruijthoff ordered their possessions to be carried into a tent and posted a guard over it. Peter distributed rolled tobacco, showed them how to carve it up on a piece of wood, how to fill a pipe, how to pick a coal from the fire with the fingertips, roll it on the palm, inhale, and tamp the tobacco down with the thumb. He taught them to make pipes from marrow-bones, with a tuft of grass at the sucking end. Whoever wanted to, could smoke from the pipes passed from hand to hand. He was proud of the day's work. He was convinced that this group had been turned into smokers and it was he, Peter Havgard, who had discovered them and won them over for the Company.

The following days were a joy. They visited the homes of the Namaqua, where they were treated to mutton and sour milk. Then the Namaqua would come to visit the Hollanders in turn, smoking and drinking, accepting gifts of beads and sheet-copper, and dancing around the camp-fires until late. They were big, well-built people, taller and more slender than those at the Cape. Some of the soldiers felt like playing with the young girls who went about with bare breasts in this warm climate, and soon discovered the names of some of them, but there were three old women watching over the girls with *kieries* in the hand. The best they could do was to gawk at the girls in the dance. Peter noticed that the Koina's singing always sounded mournful. Why would that be? It made him feel vaguely troubled, but he did not know why.

He also had an opportunity to practise his trade. He put a bread poultice on a festering sore, sewed on an ear almost ripped from the head, cut out an ingrowing toenail, pulled a tooth. In exchange they offered him sheep, a beautiful kaross, ostrich feathers, a softly tanned springbok skin. He hung the kaross over his shoulders and stuck the feathers in his hat. The skin was for Eva. He felt like a rich man, satis-fied and proud like a prince. The sheep were for the whole group, his good companions. On the way back they would slaughter them and eat them.

He was still feeling like a king when they reached the Fort six weeks later. The commander wanted to know what chance there was for those Namaqua to supply him with cattle on a regular basis. Would they be willing to come all the way to the Cape for tobacco? Would they risk trekking through the Grigriqua and Cochoqua pastures? Herrie had said that those groups were traditional enemies, but Herrie was capable of inventing any lie to thwart his attempts at obtaining livestock. Perhaps they should test it, by bringing the two groups together. Van Riebeeck was more interested in their journal than in the travellers' welfare. He was truly happy that they had found the Namaqua, but dissatisfied with most of the journal.

'Meerhof's Kasteel, and Riebeeck's Kasteel? Thank you for thinking of me, Pieter. But I doubt if the Directors would like it. Will there be enough mountains in Africa to honour all the Company's servants? And what about Cruijthoff, your leader, and your companions? There were ten, twelve of you together, why do I read so little about them? What about these lions that ran away from you, what about your river monster? You're writing for the Directors, old boy, remember, not for your grandchildren. Just give facts, and don't let Africa confuse you. But I'm glad to see you're making progress with the language. That is important to us.'

Peter wondered whether van Riebeeck would say anything about Eva. He went to his room. She wasn't there, but she came back in the afternoon, and told him she was expecting a child.

Three days after his arrival Peter had still not recovered from the effects of the expedition. All he did was to make sure, with Cruijthoff, that their equipment were returned to the warehouses, and then sleep, wash and repair his clothes, and do hospital rounds. He had scarcely had another chance of being alone with Eva, but his mind remained busy with the wild and trackless hinterland. There was also the desire for promotion, to be made leader of the next overland expedition. He proposed to van Riebeeck that longer breeches be made of stronger material for the members of the expedition, and taller boots. More pack oxen, perhaps a wagon, less salted meat, more ship's bread.

Van Riebeeck asked him to lead another short mission. He had heard that Oedasoa was in the Groenkloof, two or three days north of the Cape, with a thousand people and three thousand cattle. This was a good opportunity to make friends and discuss the question of thorough-fare for the Namaqua. Van Riebeeck called him an ambassador, and by far the best man for the task. The homeward-bound fleet was expected soon, and he needed to gather a good herd of livestock, to show to the commissioners.

Oedasoa's huts stood in two circles on a clover carpet along a shiny vlei. His livestock were spread out across valleys and hills. He had Peter brought to him, to a rocky stretch at the top of a small kloof that carried a strong smell of buchu and leopards. Table Mountain was still clearly visible in the south, two days away. Oedasoa was herding cattle; he had a few men with him, and a visitor from the Goringhaiqua who was fluent in Dutch. Peter could see other groups of herdsmen and lookouts on the hilltops, forming a large circle around the livestock. He greeted the old man and enquired after his well-being, but Oedasoa was curt.

'Why do you keep on trekking through the land like this? Why don't you stay at the other side of your river? That was what you wanted.'

'I bring Oedasoa the greetings of the commander.'

'I can do without that, and also without this how-are-you business.'

Peter unpacked the presents on the slab of granite next to the old man. 'The commander sends tobacco. Beads of different colours. Strong drink.'

'What do you want from me?'

'He wants permission for the Namaqua to pass without hindrance or refusal this way to the Fort.'

'Must these Namaqua of yours take away my people's honey, graze their pastures, scare off their game, dig up their tubers, make fire as far as they go? What will be left to us for winter food? That is why our fathers agreed long ago where each would live.' His voice became graver still. 'But you Hollanders, you move up and down with your guns without asking on whose pasture you want to live. Locusts. You scare off game all around, and then you ask, "How are you?"'

'The commander wants peace between you and the Namaqua.'

'I have nothing against the Namaqua. They go up that way, we go here by the sea. If they give you cattle, then it becomes our business straight away, because the more cattle you get, the more land we must give up to you. I have people to look after, tell that to your master. And as for your peace, tell him it's a matter between the Namaqua and us. They have big bodies and they carry a shield on the arm, but there are many more of us. *Heitse!* If we have to make war, it won't be in small measures. The Gorachoqua is here now, and the Goringhaiqua are half a day that way – look, you can see their smoke – and opposite them, against the sea, is Ngonnemoa with three, four thousand men. So if the Namaqua want to try our grazing, there's no need for us to talk about peace so soon. We have enough men.'

Peter filled a pipe with tobacco, and held out the little tanned skin-bag for Oedasoa, who emptied it in the hollow of his hand and handed it back. Might that mean: 'Tell your van Riebeeck I'll make a tobacco pouch from his scrotum'?

'Yes. Peace with the Namaqua. Ask your chief, then we'll graze here with the Namaqua, and we'll migrate with them, and soon we'll move away together for the Company. The white man, all over the place.' As he spoke, Oedasoa divided the presents among his young men, a pinch of tobacco, a mouthful of arrack, a few strings of beads, and put the rest in his knapsack. 'Tell your chief I do not want to see the tracks of your Namaqua, nor will I make peace, because already I can see how you are planning to lord it over these pastures.'

Peter closed and tied up his baggage, and lifted his load on his back.

'Wait,' said Oedasoa. 'I still have to talk to you. I know who you are. You said your name, and this man also knows who you are. You are Master Pieter.'

'Yes.'

'I'm talking to you now, not to your *souri* van Riebeeck.'

Peter let his bundle slide to the ground. What could this be?

'It is the matter of Krotoa. You're not behaving towards her as a young man ought to do.'

Peter immediately interrupted him: 'What is it to you?'

'In life I am her father. My wife is her mother. You treat her like someone who has no father or mother. These men are her brothers, her cousins, her uncles. She has many relatives.'

'She has no one. If we do not look after her, she will be poor. Catching fish.'

'No. She will be rich. The cattle that belong to her are grazing over there; they have been set aside for her. But if a young man wants her, he will have to show her parents what he has, show that he can look after her, that she can prosper under his hand. Now she gets nothing, nothing from you, and nothing from the white people. If you want to make her white, then she is no longer one of us, then she gets nothing from us either. You are using my child for your pleasure. Your bull is topping our heifer, and she gets nothing from it. In the end no honourable man will want her. Tell her she is a shame on her people the way she's going on. She will grow old poor.'

'What shame has she caused?'

'She had herself slept with.'

'And is that a shame?'

'Is it not a shame where you come from? Did you grow up among whores then? Tell her there is bitterness ahead if she tries to be white.'

Peter picked up his bundle, cursed the interpreter in Danish, and went downhill to where the soldiers were sitting on the grass smoking.

At the Fort his next expedition was already arranged. Once again it was to the Namaqua, and he would be the leader because of his experience, and because he got along so well with the natives and with his men. But he suspected that it was Mrs van Riebeeck's arrangement, he was being sent away from Eva. On the eve of their departure, and that a mere ten days after he'd returned from his last journey to Namaqualand, van Riebeeck invited him for supper. Eva was not there, she had been sent to Oedasoa.

'To try and make peace,' the commander said. 'The old man seems to be angry with us for some reason or other.'

Peter could barely believe his ears. Eva was being sent to repair his failure. How would she manage that? The Company's work was too hard for her, and if she tried to do it she would get hurt. He had already experienced the insults awaiting her. And he would not see her before he set out on another journey for the Company.

He was given lists to study, of golden jewels, silver chains, copper beads, iron spoons, clay pipes, black tobacco, knives. Here was a list of his men, all volunteers. For chief Akembie of the Namaqua, his three sons and three captains, there was a separate parcel with wonderful things for each. The group's provisions, implements and gunpowder would be carried by three pack oxen. Once again the feeling of happiness, freedom and expectation came over him. It was something he felt when he stood in front of the gateway to Africa, but never in the hospital or in the forecastle of a ship. It wasn't only the climate or the scenery, it was the unknown, like a new book to be read. He went to bed early and lay awake for a long time. Van Riebeeck and his wife had kept Eva from him, had hidden her, had sent her away to keep them from one another. Why, now that she was expecting his child?

When they set their feet on the dusty Koina road at the Keert-de-Koe ford before daybreak, he hurled a limestone into the darkness, in the direction of Heitsi-Eib's grave. This was the road to Africa. Here you left your cares, perhaps even your clothes, behind, and started to peel your eyes for snakes, scorpions, lions. And the pride of his own command caused him to stride on happily, forcefully, his knapsack on his shoulders, and his gun under his arm. The compass was in his bag, but he knew this route already.

Near Riebeeck Kasteel, on the fourth day, a large pride of lions surrounded them. Peter took the lead ropes of the pack oxen in short and tied them together, and ordered the soldiers to form a circle around them. They could see the lions showing their heads above the yellow grass; it meant that one or two of the females had already moved downwind to stalk them.

'Keep them there, don't give them a chance to get closer. Shoot the hell out of them, boys.' The noise of the gunshots caused the lions to go away. Peter distributed a strong ration of brandy. They laughed at one another and cheered, but they couldn't relax. There was no way of knowing whether the lions were following them. It would keep him awake at night.

Two days later they heard from some Koina that the Namaqua they were looking for had trekked away to the north-east. The information was a disappointment. He wanted to be successful on his first command. He decided to follow them. Beyond Meerhof's Kasteel they went down the mountain again towards the Olifants River. From the summit, with the telescope, Table Mountain was visible, far, small and shrouded in cloud, to the south. That was where Eva was, and the Company they worked for, but so remote, as if he and his men belonged to another world.

At the Olifants River they encountered Sonqua. The news stayed the same: Akembie's Namaqua had gone north with their livestock and would remain there until after the flowering time, as long as the veld up there smelled of honey. They were shown the way along which thousands of cattle had recently moved. The tracks were fourteen days old, perhaps less. The cattle dung had not completely dried everywhere, dung beetles were still at work in it. They followed the tracks to the north, from one camp or stopover to the next. Around them the veld opened up wider. Where there used to be mountains before, there now stood rocky ridges and stone koppies; the earth all around was dry and sandy, reddish. It was the landscape of his imagination, with Koina migrating into the unknown, Eva among them. Here was her native land. Of this dust and water she was made. To this only did his Eva belong, and never to him.

After six days they had to turn back. Their rations were almost depleted, and who could tell what might be waiting on the way home? So this was the turning point he had feared all along. He had failed, their hands were empty. At the Fort he would learn what that might mean for his future; whether it would open or close his way to the East.

But there was no major consequence. He received double rations, and the men the drink rations that had accumulated during their absence from the Fort. What Eva had told him upon his previous return from Namaqualand, now showed clearly in her body. His child would be born towards the end of the year. The knowledge of his impending fatherhood made him smile. A son or a daughter? What would the child look like? As for the colour, the matter of its descent, that did not cause him any concern. There were other children at the Cape, born to parents of different races, as there were in Batavia. It was no longer unusual. People knew the cause, and understood the need. 'In the dark all pussycats are grey,' they laughed. 'Otherwise, just keep your eyes closed.' An English captain quoted a proverb: 'Necessity is the mother of invention, and the father of the half-breed.'

Eva no longer interpreted in the Council chamber. For that function Herrie, now wholly dependent on the Company's alcohol, paid them a daily visit from the dunes. There were others too who spoke Dutch, like Doman who had led the war for the river, with his wasted body and withered arm, who now had no other way of earning food. Eva still looked after the van Riebeecks' children – there were now two little girls as well – but she was more like a servant and less like a friend of the family. Apart from her, there were now also a Bengalese slave woman and two Negro male slaves in the household.

In these circumstances Peter was worried about Eva. Outwardly she had become a village woman in a Dutch home, but she was lonely. She spoke a language which only she in that house knew, she alone was from the Cape veld, she alone knew the true meaning of cattle. In the company at table she was quiet, because she didn't know what they laughed about, or where Zaanse Schans was, or who the remarkable Leeuwenhoek was. 'Leeuwenhoek saw human sperm alive under his microscope,' van Riebeeck told the visiting pastor. 'We're living in godless times, brother. May he be forgiven for it,' replied the *dominee*. Peter laughed out loud, which annoyed Eva. She was lonely in this busy, boisterous, growing Dutch fort, and Peter could see her happy face fading. Or was it his imagination, and women just were like that when they were pregnant?

He could see how Eva was also drawing away from van Riebeeck and his wife, their fastidiousness, the polite language of the big house, and the religion she had learned there. She was drinking more, and sometimes swore in Dutch. That she had learned from him. Sometimes she wanted to speak only the Koina language, to him and all the others. He suspected that she had fallen out of favour with the van Riebeecks, and was friendless among strangers. The Dutch women avoided her because she had transgressed the first rule of moral conduct, and had to suffer their cold reprobation. The Koina, her only people, stayed away from her because she had helped the Dutch in the war, and latterly because she had a white man who showed her no respect in the matter of transition rites.

He, Peter, could go about and laugh with friends, talk pipe in hand about places they had visited or heard of, and drink at a campfire, but she had very little to be happy about. So he had new clothes made for her, Dutch clothes; he had to try and earn higher wages to pay for such things. He earned double wages with overland expeditions, but what if he was away from home for six, seven months on end? Oedasoa's words, that there were cattle in his herd which were due to Eva, meant nothing to him. He could never tell her about it, he couldn't ask Oedasoa even for a handful of grass. He was worried about this woman that life had given him, and vaguely believed that one day, one day he would take her with him to the East, that much-desired land, where there was no more misfortune.

In the summer, sometimes, there were the double wages of expeditions to look forward to, and in winter he could earn a few guilders from the free burghers with bloodletting, purges and sprains Apart from that there was only his salary to exist on. They were actually very poor. Eva came to live with him in his small room in the hospital. Van Riebeeck said nothing, he probably agreed that it was better that way. Eva struggled to keep their clothes mended and clean at first, but as her pregnancy progressed, she seemed to shrug off housekeeping. Perhaps there was something more important on her mind, but she didn't mention it. Peter could see it daily, but imagined it was from loneliness as she had no mother or sisters to discuss her pregnancy with. For she was an orphan, an animal strayed from a herd. Occasionally, idly, he noticed the brandy flask in his chest becoming emptier, and ascribed it to her irregular appetite.

She told him when he had to book the midwife, and when he had to go and fetch her, and when he should leave them alone. In the cold October night he walked away, along the beach. He was used to death, but scared of birth. The wind was icy. He thought of his father, old August, a soldier since his youth in a pale landscape, and of his own childhood. And always the sea was there, the green high road between countries, for merchant, clerk, for cook, cannoneer. Now he might never reach the East, for this was where the sea had washed him up, and where he died on the beach.

When he returned home, the midwife was sleeping with a gaping mouth, her head thrown back against the wall. A short candle was burning beside their bed. There was his wife, with the child. Both were asleep. He would not wake them. He touched the midwife's shoulder, and took her outside.

'Did it go well?'

'Yes, the child looks healthy.'

'Boy?'

'Another girl, Master Pieter. A *meid* for the pleasure and comfort of the man. I can only trust that Our Lord knows what He is doing.'

'What do I owe you?'

'I shall look in again tomorrow, then we can discuss it. Sometimes I need help with a difficult case.'

'I have little experience myself. I used to be a military surgeon.'

'It's the same blood, God knows. Wait till your child is grown one day, Master Pieter. Then you will feel that I'm speaking the truth. See that she feeds the child at her breast, and she mustn't wash it too much. That is playing with death.'

He showed her a place in the hospital where she could spend the night. From that hour his life was not his any more.

In the morning he and Eva talked about a name for the child. Both had hoped for a boy, and his name would be Pieter, now it just became Pieternella. Eva was satisfied.

When he saw that the commander's door was open, he went in to announce and register the birth.

'You will want to have her baptised, of course.'

'Yes, she must be baptised.'

'And Eva? Also still to be baptised.'

'I'll discuss it.'

'There is one more thing, Pieter. Once your wife has been baptised you two should get married too. I know you want to go away, to the East. So do I, but I tend to think more about the future of this place, and I believe that one day a doctor should be able to make a living here. Not yet, because the burghers can pay only with pumpkins and eggs. Better to remain a salaried man; your family cannot live on pumpkin. But the day will come when you can hang out your shingle as a free burgher, and then the community will want to know that you are respectably married, otherwise they won't come to you. Discuss it with Eva. And think about your child, who knows what will become of her one day? Maria and I would like to visit and look at your baby, when she is ready for us.'

One day, old Autshumao brought a pot of mussels for Krotoa and the child's making-different, and he mentioned vaguely a gift of cattle that Oedasoa's wife had promised. This child of hers was now his only family. By rights he should look after her, but he has become too poor. Krotoa had to bring up the child properly, so that one day she could go to the Cochoqua and claim the making-different she had been promised. He, Autshumao, would help her with this baby. She just had to tell him if the child needed anything. He would see to it.

In November the veld was many-hued, gloriously sweet with flowers; it was time for the next expedition to Namaqualand. This time Sergeant Everard would lead, once again Peter was second in command, and a young clerk from Culemborg, Cornelis de Cretser, was third. De Cretser would keep the journal, and eight of the ten others were comrades from the previous expedition. Peter felt his pride swell into a boyish pleasure. He could understand that the commander hadn't trusted his journal, but he was more than happy to go on another journey. The plan was not, as Peter suspected, merely to keep the Namaqua in tobacco; Lords Seventeen still wanted them to trek beyond the Namaqua to find Monomotapa, rich in gold, jewels, ivory. That was what the Lords Seventeen expected of him and his dozen companions.

The spring weather was sunny and warm, the sky brilliantly blue. Peter relished mauve mountains, white masses of cloud, herds of antelope grazing in yellow grass and barely looking up as they passed,

brown anthills, swarms of red weaver birds. His eyes were fixed on
ridges, mountain tops, hills, distant horizons, and every day was an
encouraging, enriching experience which made it easier to forget what
lay behind. He was free from the cares of leadership and keeping a
journal, he could hunt to his heart's content, laugh with his companions, and tell stories about ghosts and strange animals. At night, under
the stars, black bats came flitting past, this way and that, in pursuit
of their prey under the dense, pulsing sky, and far away there was the
howling of jackals and rumbling of lions. This was the only freedom.
Sometimes he wondered how he could persuade van Riebeeck to
release him from the hospital altogether. Release, from the commander
as well. He would ask for other work, something outdoors. To the
sea, perhaps, to reach the East after all, if everything else failed. Often
his thoughts were with his child in the Cape, but his desire was further
forward, towards new yellow, summery plains, brown mountain land-
scapes in which no human figures moved.

As on the last journey there were once again Sonqua and Grigriqua,
but no Namaqua, no cattle, no sheep, no Monomotapa. Sergeant
Everard led them further and further north. Late one afternoon they
saw flocks of red flamingos trampling about in a cold lagoon behind
dunes. It was the mouth of the Olifants River. The tide was out, withdrawn far behind a wide, cold grey beach. Behind the chalky dunes
they pitched camp and watched the sunset; huddled in thick overcoats
around their cooking fire they drank and assured one another that the
Cape was the only place for them, and the devil take whoever might
wish for any other place to live.

Empty-handed once again, they turned about there and trekked south
across the meagre and arid sandy veld, near the coast, heading for a
Table Mountain which slowly grew in their eyes and changed colour
from mauve to blue to dun to brown. Then they arrived at a spot where
elephants blocked their way. They tried to pass below the wind, trying
to reach a clump of trees in an erosion ditch, along which they could
move on unseen. When they approached, an elephant bull emerged
from the trees, his ears turned forward and his trunk raised high. 'Stand
fast,' said Sergeant Everard. 'Close in. Close in. A full volley in the

forehead. Wait for my command. Then each man on his own, fast as you can.'

He wanted concentrated fire, but the men closest to the front abandoned the oxen and broke for shelter. Third, fourth from the front was steady Piet Roman, who saw the shield split in front of him and then fired one, two rounds on his own at the elephant's chest, sending white dust flying up from the skin. And every time he reloaded, the elephant was ten paces closer. He dropped another fistful of powder down the barrel before the long trunk jerked him from his feet and dashed him to pieces against the large yellow crescents of the tusks. The oxen were dancing in a frenzy under their burdens, the men turned in flight, and left their Piet to be trampled into the red clods of earth.

Peter ran to the foot of a rocky hill and there fell down behind some shelter. Here and there before him he could see some of his companions hiding behind bushes and ridges. He held his breath while Piet Roman was broken, he lay there trembling while the elephant was trampling the body, blowing dust over his own bleeding wounds, then lifting Piet up again and hurling him about. Another five or six elephants approached, blowing dust, trumpeting, spending a long time smelling the ragged soldier on the ground, shuffling the body around. The men did not move. It was a cold, red sunset by the time the elephants left downwind. Far away there were lions roaring. This was Africa: a brutal place where death and life were neighbours. In Africa man had enemies the Danes did not dream of. Peter was first to get up, to start looking for the oxen.

When he arrived home, Eva was ill. An old woman of the Goringhaicona was looking after her and the child. He knew the old deaf and half-blind crone. Cold potions stood on the small bench at Eva's bedside, and outside on the ash heap were the husks of three weeks' wild bulbs. Pieter went to look at his daughter. Dirty and smelly she lay in her sleeping box, restlessly lifted her hands, and opened her eyes wide for him. That blue she had from him and old August Ede. He picked her up and rocked her, and carried her to Eva's *katil*. Weary and wet with perspiration, his wife shifted groaning on the mattress stuffed with bedding-bush.

'What is wrong?'

The old woman uttered sounds through her toothless mouth. Eva placed her hand on her belly.

'I think it's another baby.'

'That's good.' He pulled up the child's clothes and looked at her thin, pale brown body. There were purple marks of lice and a red, watery rash on her buttocks. 'Eva, I'm going to put away my things, then I'll come and look at both of you. The child must be washed.'

Wan and listless, she said: 'The old mother will rub her in with fat.'

'No. Do you have food to eat?'

'Mrs van Riebeeck sends us some. And Autshumao. But it won't stay in.'

He handed the water bucket to the old woman, and showed a piece of wood from the wood box. 'Firewood and water please, grandma.'

'Pieter, Mrs van Riebeeck says we're living in sin. We must now marry.'

'We can do that later. How are you feeling now?'

'I'm sick.'

'I'll mix you some medicine. You'll be well soon, Eva. I'm staying here and looking after you from now on.'

He removed the window shutters and made the old woman sweep the floor. He built a fire on the hearth, and hung over a pot of soup made of flour and salt and a strip of bacon he'd saved from his rations. Then he warmed a pot of water, washed his child with soap, rubbed her in with sweet oil, and dressed her in clean clothes. From coarse ration flour and water with salt and sugar he made porridge for the child, and put her on his lap to feed her with a spoon. Then he soothed her, talked to her, draped her over his shoulder so that she could break wind and sang to her, and saw a smile appear on her face. He laughed with her. This child was more to him than the gold of Monomotapa. Then Piet Roman came back in his thoughts.

Eva watched him from the bed. 'I've been thinking a lot about you, Pieter.'

'And I of you,' he said without thinking, because he knew how she needed it. The child was warm against his chest, her right hand closed tightly around his thumb. 'I'm going to watch your health, so that you can get back on your feet. And I'm making us soup, and when you have something in your stomach I shall give you medicine. I'm going to stay home for a long time now, then we can have some fun.'

He hung the covers outside in the sun, stripped all the linen from the beds and put it in the laundry vat with his own washing, so that he could tread it later. He had to make a vegetable garden for his family, and perhaps a chicken run, so that they could have healthy food. Perhaps Eva would show interest in it, but he wasn't sure if he should look after a grown woman as if she were a child because she'd grown away from the commander's big house, or see to it that she was happy, that she should mind their child, or make sure that she kept the house and her child and herself clean. No, he wasn't sure at all.

The making-different came sooner than he'd expected. The ships brought letters from the fatherland which caused rejoicing in the commander's house. It was promotion for van Riebeeck, the deeply cherished transfer to the East, with new opportunities for preferment, improvement of salary, private trade, all the recognition he'd long been waiting for. To Peter the news first caused envy, and then, to his surprise, concern. He had got along reasonably well with van Riebeeck, who was someone who cared for Eva. Who would be sent here to replace him? The commander could go aboard and depart within days, while he still required favours from him, for the sake of his wife and child. He could no longer postpone the discussion with Eva.

'You were brought up in the Christian faith, Eva. Would you consider getting yourself baptised?'

'I'm scared I'm not as good as the Church expects of me.'

'You're as good as I am.'

'I don't know, I'm afraid I may be doing wrong.'

She agreed to talk to a pastor. When would a pastor be coming here again? When one did come, Peter invited him to his home. It was so that his wife and child could be baptised, he explained. Eva listened to the pastor in silence. Peter put the questions and explained the answers to her. The pastor wanted to know: Was she sincere and honest in wanting to put away her sins, accept the faith, be baptised and receive the sacraments?

'She is entitled to all that, isn't she?' Peter asked hesitantly.

'In the love of Jesus, yes.'

'Will you baptise her, *dominee*? If she does that thing? She is eager to do it, but she is timid, she doesn't know what it all means.'

'Look, I must first find out what the synod in Amsterdam says. I am no more than a servant myself, and perhaps they will blame me. I'm only here for a while.'

'If you do something good?'

'They can dismiss me. Then I'm left without any income.'

Peter grabbed the pastor by the sleeve. 'What if the commander approves it? Can they interfere?'

'They can. I, you and he all work for the Company, and the Church is not above the Company. We are not above orders.'

Eva said what Peter couldn't. 'What is wrong then, *dominee*? People are being baptised here all the time, they get married all the time. What is different this time?'

'You are not married.'

'Then marry us first.'

'You're not . . .' He fell silent. This was no joke.

'What is it? Is it because your Church is not for the Koina? I go to church every Sunday. Since long before you came here. As long as my lord has been here.' Then, for some reason, she pointed at the row of calabashes on her pot shelf, where she kept her sour milk. 'Tell me the Koina cannot go to heaven, because we don't have souls.'

'Wait, Eva,' Peter warned. 'This is not the way.'

'It's all right, Master Pieter. Look, I don't know what to tell you. All I know is that none of the indigenous people here have been baptised or married in our church before. Without the approval of the synod it cannot be done. I'm going to ask the commander to help me with it.'

'Perhaps I must ask Oedasoa if Heitsi-Eib' will be dissatisfied.'

The pastor was aggrieved. 'That is not what I said. Your soul is not in the hands of the commander. What concerns me is the authority of the Church.'

Peter was surprised by Eva's reaction. What was this then, this rebel-liousness against authority? If the Church were to turn against her because of this, and the commander too, she would be harming her and their child's cause.

But it fell out differently. The pastor came to knock on their door again. The commander had asked him to baptise the woman, marry them, and then baptise the child as well. It should be done first, and afterwards he would forward the papers to Amsterdam. Then they would indeed hear what the Church had to say, but it would take at least a year. There was something else Dutch law required from all people, and that was that their banns should be read on three consec-utive Sundays to the congregation. If Peter and Eva were willing, he would like to help them with the preparation. These were grave matters, the various promises they were required to make. And Commander and Mrs van Riebeeck wanted to see it concluded before they departed. They still wanted to offer them their blessing.

Eva was unwilling. It was now the wish of the commander, or of the commander's wife, and they wanted to bind her to Peter according to their law, and she had to put her hand to their paper. They wanted to drive her into the Dutch camp. She was reluctant to do this, as it meant taking her leave of her own people for ever, just as she would soon have to take her leave of van Riebeeck for ever. She did not want to be chased down a road like an animal. And if something were to happen to Peter, she would become a stray dog among these people. Where would she belong then, and why had the pastor now become silent about his authorities?

Peter tried to persuade her. He took trouble to convince her. If they were married, they would be making a contract to protect her rights before the law. He himself would have a new will drawn up, so that she would inherit in case he met with an accident somewhere. They had to get the law properly on their side. What would become of her and him and their child if van Riebeeck went away? A man with different convictions might come here.

Her objection, she said, was not against the Church, but against the way their government made laws and then broke them again as it suited them. What were their vows worth? It was worth less than cow dung, one couldn't even spread a floor with it.

Two days later she told him that she was willing now.

Van Riebeeck went to listen in the classroom where on three afternoons a week the sick-comforter instructed Eva. He paid the church for a nurse, so that the child wouldn't hang on her when it was time for instruction. He knew she was intelligent, and he wanted to see her happy. Before he left, he would still like to do this for her: place her feet on a Christian path so that his conscience could be at ease about her and her offspring.

Eva was glad. She'd always enjoyed doing what he wanted of her. She could readily repeat the passages from the Bible which they recited to her. She'd known parts of it since childhood. About matters like original sin, and about Eve and the serpent, to which she often listened in amazement, she didn't question them. She wanted them to think that she understood.

The sick-comforter announced that he was satisfied, the pastor could be called, provided he'd bear in mind that Eva couldn't do the impossible. Van Riebeeck knew it too. In those days he sometimes regretted that he had removed her from her natural place. He believed that he could see her way into the future before him, and there was much on that road to be concerned about. He had to prepare her for a wedding, not necessarily above her standing, but outside the world of her origins, and against the day he himself would no longer be there.

'Look, my child, you must know that married people reach an age where sometimes a husband leaves his wife for a younger one. He loses his desire for you, but there may be various reasons for this. We call it young ewe lambs, or greener grass; you will hear that when the neighbours are gossiping. It happens to many, but how will you avoid it, Eva, so that it won't destroy you? Avoid reproaches, never tell lies, forgive viciousness. The devil will try to humiliate you, but be prepared for that. Keep your voice low; if you raise it, you will be lost. Restrain yourself, particularly in front of your children, so that evil is not spread into the world. Be light of heart, and happy, and smile a lot. Curses and temper are for fishwives, make sure that you are not cast out in your old age for that. Don't think that your cooking will win your husband's affection, Eva. Similarly, scrubbing floors will be in vain, and sewing, and all other exertions. All that matters is your company. Refreshing company makes a marriage. Every day. Yes, and never wash your wine glasses with the other pots and pans.'

They were both ashamed about what he was doing, because it was too late; his experience in all this was meaningless. Poor little Eva. What hope was there for a life as a Dutch housewife at the Cape?

To encourage her, he went to listen to her lessons. He sat on the school bench with her and reminded her of her upbringing under his supervision, and showed her a text at the beginning of the Book of Proverbs which said: *Forsake ye not my law*. After he had left for the East, she was to remember it.

Now he was worried, but what could he do about it? If only she'd been with her father's people behind the mountains, that day when *Haerlem* was wrecked, this cup would have been spared her. He needed an interpreter at the time, his wife a nurse, and their eyes had fallen on her. Her natural kindness and the education he'd given her might become her anchors, but what was she to do against the resentment of the Koina and of the haughty Cape ladies, and Peter who enjoyed wandering about so much and was always first to volunteer when there was a journey announced? What would become of Eva when Peter was away? And what, if he never came back?

The day of Eva's baptism, Peter sat in the front pew in church. It was an extraordinary experience. Beside him in the pew were the commander, four councillors, three ship's captains. Once he briefly glanced over his shoulder. Behind them were the people of the Cape, a white congregation clothed in black. Peter recognised some of his companions from the trekking road; they were staring fixedly ahead. Eva was alone at the table with the books and the small bowl of water. Behind her, on chairs on the women's side, were the commander's wife, her nieces, the wives of councillors, then the rest, all passengers in transit between North and East. Peter thought: Are they wondering what kind of person that uncouth Dane is? Will the pastor reprimand him in public for morality's sake? He stared at the wall of the commander's front room. There was a zebra skin, and a lion skin, both belonging to Piet Roman. He'd received six guilders for it. A wonderful shot with the harquebus Piet had been.

His thoughts returned to Eva. If these Cape people were not going to accept her as his wife, she would become depressed. For their child, too, it would be bad. If people made life hard for them here, he would take his family away. And now there was another one on the way, hopefully a son this time. Turning his head slightly, he could see Mrs van Riebeeck examining and measuring Eva with her eyes. Could she see that Eva was pregnant again? Was Eva dressed neatly enough?

Peter shifted his attention to the formulary, as the pastor had moved round the table to talk to Eva alone. He was speaking slowly and emphatically, putting his questions confidentially; these were matters for her alone, and nobody else. And she responded quietly and simply. Her head was slightly bowed, her voice soft. Would she understand what she heard, or believe what she vowed? At the end of the formulary the pastor touched her forehead with water. 'Eva, I baptise you in the name of the Father, the Son and the Holy Ghost. May your name be found in the book of the quick when we are called to bear witness on the Day of Judgement, for the salvation of your immortal soul.'

Eva, or perhaps Krotoa, thought Peter, your name has now been entered, you will never die. I hope this remaking brings you happiness.

The expected homeward-bound fleet would bring van Riebeeck's successor from the East. One could calculate quite closely the day of that gentleman's arrival, as the first group of return ships was dispatched from Batavia the day before Christmas, so that there would be no labour, no bustling or drunken seamen in the streets the next. The second group would set sail from Ceylon a month later. With the most favourable trade winds they would then arrive together at the Cape between mid-February and mid-March. That year it happened so again, but of the seven Batavia ships only three arrived, and van Riebeeck's successor was not on one of them. They told that north-east of Mauritius their fleet had been struck by a hellish hurricane, and that the other four ships had not been seen again. They had hoped, of course, that the missing four would reach the Cape before them, but as was plain to all, it had been in vain. And their admiral had been among them. Lost with all hands: *Wapen van Holland*, *Prins Willem*, *Gecroonde Leeuw*, *Aernhem*.

The passengers brought stories of that hellish hurricane ashore. There had never been such a hurricane. The force and noise of the wind, the pitch-thick blackness of the night, the height of the waves, the damage to ships, the terrible loss of life, was far worse than any East India vessel had ever experienced. Peter heard about it from patients carried ashore with broken arms, legs, ribs. The shock still shuddered in the tones with which they spoke of the terrifying wind which had snapped off masts and rolled over ships, an entire duty watch with all its officers washed from the deck and from the rigging, by a wave that stripped the ship from end to end. Mauritius? That was a new name. For Peter and some of the others it was the first mention they had heard of the island. Where was this Mauritius, where did it fit into the *orang lama*'s knowledge of the Honourable Company's sea route between cold, grey Europe and the golden miraculous East?

For Peter there were other important questions. He was one of those who wanted to know whether the Ceylon ships had been seen after the storm, because the new commander had been on them. It was just possible that van Riebeeck might now stay on for a few months longer. When the Ceylon ships arrived, terribly damaged, the appointed successor was on board, he had to accept and the the certainty of van Riebeeck's departure.

The new commander was a German yeoman, somewhat aged and stiff, but he had a strong face and his eyes were bright. Van Riebeeck took him and the vice-admiral to see his young colony. On horseback they followed the old cattle road, from the Fort to Keert-de-Koe at the ford in the Brak River, and from there along the palisade to Ruijterwacht, where the saplings of the planned almond hedge stood sparse and barely a finger's length above ground. From that height they could see the farmyards, and the grazing livestock in the glittering water meadows of the Liesbeeck. Behind the young trees and the white farmhouses, Coornhoop's battlements with the two cannon protruded, and higher up on the slope were the orchards and vineyards of Rustenburg, and the fallow fields surrounding the high wooden walls of De Schuur. The two visitors congratulated van Riebeeck on what he had achieved. It was a tremendous improvement. The earth was no longer void and without form as before.

It also pleased van Riebeeck to take his guests out riding to his own farm, and the farthest point of the frontier. A bright blue sky stretched high above his colony, and from the sea a fresh northerly breeze blew towards the Steenberg. Autumn was well advanced, but at the end of a sunny day the veld was still warm. Along the way van Riebeeck told them about the war against the natives three years earlier, about the stock losses of his burghers, and the agreement made with the natives. This was his great success, this story. Van Riebeeck turned his tanned and bearded face to the sky to thank God that everything they had seen was in prime order. He also told his successor that there was a wedding pending, an exceptional case that demanded his favour and attention.

A few days after Eva's baptism van Riebeeck left the Cape. She, three months pregnant, cried for a long time and went on quietly sorrowing over him for months. She no longer spoke about getting married, and Peter, apart from his work, also had little Pieternella crying after him at home. The child wouldn't let him out of her sight. He noticed how Eva's face, in spite of her pregnancy, became thinner, and tighter. She now felt van Riebeeck's departure as if she were an orphan, he thought, because she'd never known a father. He could not help her with that, he could never be a father to an adult woman. He would indeed have loved to get away a bit, to the veld, away from the hospital and everybody who looked to him for help there. The hospital and the ships stank of sick people, his own house was constantly cold and dirty. The fresh veld beyond the Olifants River, where there were no houses or people to be seen, was his desire.

Another wet winter settled over the Cape, and Eva's second pregnancy progressed to its fifth and sixth month. There was more and more children's washing dripping in front of the hearth in Peter's house, and it had a musty smell. There wasn't money for a fire to keep the house warm all day; he could barely afford fuel to boil a pot. He and Eva could draw a little heat from a *sopie* brandy, but it was different for his daughter. He had to provide porridge and milk for her.

Sometimes he could get some sago from a friend in the warehouse, or a bit of sugar to make the child happy.

While Eva became withdrawn in her second pregnancy, Peter had only his daughter to play with, when she was healthy. He also spent nights sitting beside her bed, to pick her up when she cried, or clean her when she soiled herself. He stared at her little face in the candle-light, trying to find traces of him or Eva, but saw no resemblance. She was quite unique: small, her skin a pale brown, the hair reddish-brown with fine curls, the eyes bright blue in the daylight, the nose well shaped, but tiny. What was there to be seen in her of him, a Scandinavian? Nothing, except for the eyes. Was it his child?

Later in winter his little garden yielded vegetables: turnips and cabbage, endives and leeks, peas and onions. Peter, in shirtsleeves, enjoyed digging and making beds, rinsing a bunch of parsnips in his water furrow to take home for cooking. He made a vegetable soup which he gave to his wife and daughter with white bread. Eva couldn't survive on that. Eva wanted meat, but unlike in the hunting veld, meat here was scarce and expensive, except if you knew a frontier farmer for whom you could sometimes do a favour in return. Fuel was also difficult to come by; all around the veld had been stripped bare. The sea dunes, originally densely overgrown, were now dead, shifting drift sand, and one had to go deep into the veld to find good solid wood. He couldn't expect Eva to do that. He'd already thought of buying a slave for the fuel and water, but it was beyond his means. Perhaps one day his children would be rich enough to afford slaves, but as a poor surgeon he was obliged to do a small task here or there for a wagon driver, cut his hair, purge him or burn a wart for a small bundle of fuel, carried from the veld on the Company's wagon. And that had to be kept secret. There were Strandlopers who brought fuel for sale from door to door, but he had nothing to give them. He could just about keep a pot boiling on his salary, and they needed the double wages of an expedition for something more.

Peter got along well with the new commander. His name was Wagner; the Dutch called him Wagenaer. His nickname, *Donnerman* – 'Thunder Man' – arrived with him from the East. The gentleman had set patterns of behaviour, with a strict, sharp tongue and a supply of German oaths. Friday mornings he inspected the hospital. Once he stopped next to Peter while he was excising the black stubs of teeth from the putrid gums of a scurvy patient, but said nothing before Peter had rinsed the man's wounds with brandy and removed the wad of cloth from between the jaws.

'So. Where did you study?'

'In Copenhagen, sir.'

'University?'

'For a while. I was in the army for longer.'

'So. You are the surgeon who accompanies the expeditions?'

'Yes, sir.'

'So. What worth do you see in such expeditions? Do you believe in the City of Gold, or what the bloody devil they may call it in these parts?'

Peter spoke while he was making the patient comfortable and cleaning his instruments. The value was in the exploration, he said. They gathered information about the interior, what there was and what not, the way of life and the wealth of the inhabitants, distances, rainfall, wild animals, plants, grazing for oxen and food resources for soldiers campaigning in the interior.

'Is someone making sketches of the plants and animals, for the universities?'

'No. We don't have a draughtsman.'

'So. The most important man in the group is bloody well missing. One drawing is worth a thousand words. The whole civilised world wants to know what is growing and walking and flying and crawling and swimming about here. Bad, you hear me? Bad.' The commander went on between the rows of beds to look at the sick, and left through the back door to the kitchen.

Late in October Peter heard from his old travel companions in the garrison that Wagenaer was considering an overland expedition. The destination was the great river that flowed to the sea north of Namaqualand. Their main purpose was to deliver tobacco to the natives between here and there. There were double wages to be earned, with rations accumulating until their return. Piet Cruijthoff, now a sergeant, would again be the leader. Peter went to register, prepared his clothes and boots, bought brandy on account, corked it in flasks and wrapped these in his clothes. His medicine chest was unpacked, and filled with new flagons, linen and instruments.

The arrangements at home were more complicated. Eva was unhappy, for their second child was due in November, when he would be in the north. She complained about everything and called him a vagabond. But he was not one for shouting and let her have her way without reproach, and when she became too vociferous he left the house to go to the hospital, or to a friend in the barracks, or sometimes with the child on his arm up the long stretch of beach north of the Fort, between the dunes and the sea, with the icy air and grey cloud of spray over Robben Island on the horizon ahead of them.

There were two weddings at the Fort to which they were invited. He had hoped that the festivities would give Eva some pleasure, but she wasn't interested. The two young brides had been washed out here by the unpredictable sea. First there was the wedding of Trijn Ustinghs and Hans Ras, which ended in a drunken brawl among the farmers, and he was called to the reception even before it had begun, to sew up the bridegroom's knife wounds. After that Fiscal Lacus was married to young Lydia de Pape, a beautiful child and the apple of her father's eye. The father was a pastor of the Company and they were on their way to the East, but the gates of the Orient slammed shut before little Lydia in this place.

Peter was satisfied that his wife and child would be well provided for while he was on march in the interior. The government's midwife had promised to look in daily during the last week of November. A Koina woman of her acquaintance would stay with Eva and look after little Pieternella. He gave strict instructions to the woman, knowing that the child would notice his absence and miss him, as he would miss her.

In their free time during the last days before the expedition he and his leader discussed arrangements about courses and destinations along the route, the distribution and packaging of baggage, their duty roster as livestock manager, cook, baggage manager, wood carriers, et cetera. On 21 October the commander waved goodbye to them in the court-yard, and at daylight they left in their ox wagon through the gate, heading east along the sandy track to the gate at Keert-de-Koe. There Peter enquired after the cairn that used to stand beside the road, but the soldier at the gate didn't know what he was talking about.

The wagon made their journey easier and faster. They walked along-side at the same pace as the oxen, with the guns under their arms, and the needs of the animals imposed short laps. Each evening, before the lions started hunting at sunset, they had to set up a strong kraal of branches near drinking water. On 5 November Cruijthoff sent a letter home by two Grigriqua from the Olifants River. His animals and people were still in good health, and they were now trekking north along the Olifants River to the edge of the Sandveld. There they would rest the animals, and prepare for the dry trek through the desert. Where the oxen could not go any further, they would halt and continue the search for the river on foot.

Two weeks later Cruijthoff sent Peter and three others forward with provisions for ten days, to try and reach the great river in the north. There was food for only three days left when they found the kraals of the Namaqua. Peter explained what their aim was, and asked for a guide to the great river. But Akembie refused; he would provide a guide to take them back to the south, but not further north. On the contrary, he would forbid that.

Peter distributed as much tobacco as he could spare, and accepted to be guided back to Cruijthoff's camp. The sergeant was disgruntled; he wouldn't be thwarted by natives a few days from his destination. He was determined to trek north and find that river, whether the local natives approved or not. The whole group set out on the route to Akembie's settlement, and arrived there when their drinking water had already run out. Akembie still refused to provide a guide to the Garieb. His people gave them food and milk, requested them to turn back, and promised a guide for the return journey. The Dutch camp was some distance from that of the Namaqua, and against Akembie's counsel they made preparations and set out in the night for the north. One morning, a few days later, Akembie's runners caught up with them, weapons in hand.

'Akembie says: Return.'

Peter spoke: 'We can't. We have been travelling for months to see that river.'

'Turn back. If you don't turn back, we must kill you here. That is Akembie's message.'

'The *souri* in the Cape sent us to look at the great river. We can travel without help.'

'It is not his land. Now you want our river, as you did in the Cape. If you like our river, your farmers will come and live here. That was what you did with the Goringhaiqua.'

With tobacco and drink Peter tried to keep the peace. Cruijthoff knew what was said, and wanted to shoot, although they were badly outnumbered. Peter pleaded: they were hundreds of miles from home; let them rather return. Two days later they and their escort were back at Akembie's kraal. He refused to talk to them, and forbade his people to offer them meat or milk. Their gifts of beads and brandy were returned. That evening Peter lured a few of the Sonqua who hunted for the Namaqua to his fire with tobacco. He promised them a reward. The plan of the Dutch was to trek in the direction of the Cape at sunrise as if to return home, and then to turn round after a few hours and follow a roundabout route past the Namaqua to the great river. All the details were worked out. Half a day's journey to the south there was a rocky outcrop with a pointed peak. That was where the Sonqua would wait for them. He entertained them lavishly, sealing the promise with a gift of tobacco. The same evening he and Cruijthoff went to ask permission to take their leave of Akembie, as they wanted to set out early, back home. Akembie sent a message: Get off our land.

In the light of dawn they left their camp and by noon they met the guides at the outcrop in the south. After that they slowly continued on the road home until sunset, and outspanned for the night at an old kraal. At first light they turned directly towards the morning star, turned north an hour later, and then reckoned that they were on course again for finding the great river. The Sonqua assured them: two days at this rate, and they would be there. They were in high spirits because of outwitting Akembie. The next afternoon the Sonqua pointed out the dust of approaching runners. They would go and do the talking themselves, the Hollanders had to wait there. Then all the Koina came back together. There was one of Akembie's household among them, a man with feathers in his hair, and he stood before Cruijthoff.

'Your life now belongs to Chief Akembie. He grants it to you for four days on the way back. If we find you after that time, you will be dead.'

Cruijthoff asked Peter to summon Jan Dorhagen. This formed their war council. The others had to place their guns in readiness on the wagon, and remain behind it. The council gathered in front of the oxen, chewing tobacco and brushing the flies from their faces.

'What shall we do?'

'I say: go back. We've truly tried our best.'

'All right.'

They went on chewing, waving at flies. 'Blast open a path?'

'No, we'll die first.'

'We are too far from home.'

'All right then.'

Cruijthoff still proposed: 'We can offer all our bartering stuff to this lot, for two more days north.'

'They don't seem to be in a mood for bartering. If they kill us, they'll take everything anyway.'

'All right.'

'Four days from here will bring us right opposite Akembie's kraal.'

'All right.'

There they turned back for the last time. The guides followed behind, with Akembie's Namaqua. The oxen were exhausted and thin from the sparse grazing, and the procession proceeded very slowly, so that after three days they were nowhere near Akembie's huts yet. Peter wanted them to leave the wagon and oxen there, proceeding on foot to make faster progress, but Cruijthoff wouldn't. The next evening after supper they were still talking around the fire about Christmas, whether they should spend the day resting and allow their animals to rest too, when their sentry jumped in among them with a scream. The thin reed of an arrow hung from his mouth, another arrow was stuck in his thigh. Peter grabbed him, tried to keep his head still so that he could grasp the arrow, and gave a jerk that broke the reed. More arrows came flying over the fire, some of them overhead, others clattering into the tent and the wagon hood. Pelagius Weckerlein was hit full in the chest, Hans Rootkop received an arrow between the ribs, Dirk Wessels one in the forearm. Shaken with fear, Peter thought of his child. Tonight it was his turn to face sudden death. Hands grabbed guns from the pile and fired into the dark. Cruijthoff dragged Lourens Hoffman into the tent by the feet. The others sank down on their knees, loaded, fell on their stomachs, waited. The oxen were milling about in the kraal, bellowing. Cruijthoff took Peter's musket from his hands: 'Go help Lourens.'

Hoffman was calm, but his body was caught in a fit of cold shivering; on his bare arms the hair stood up. With a slight pull the arrow came from his thigh. The point was rough, but without barbs. Peter held it up to the lantern to see if it was poisoned, but couldn't make out anything. Then he looked into the man's mouth. The small poisoned tip was dangling from the palate at the back. He rolled his handkerchief and pressed it in between the jaws to wedge them open.

'Lourens, come and stand with your back against the tent pole. Head back, and hold up this lantern with both hands. Bend your knees, move down a bit, so that I can look inside.' Outside a volley of shots sounded. 'I'm going to count to three, then I'll pull the arrow. Count with me, and force your head back.' He thrust his thumb and forefinger deep into the back of the mouth, took a firm hold, counted, pulled. Hoffman vomited mutton stew over his hand, but the arrow was out. 'Now you must do what the Koina do for snakebite. Suck and spit. Lourens, that's all we can do. Suck at the back of your palate, and spit it out. And from your leg too. Lourens, you must remember, there's nothing more I can do for you.' He looked out through the gap in the tent. He could see most of the men hiding out of the firelight behind stones and stumps. Only one was lying on his back; it was Pelagius beside the fire, with his hands clutching the arrow shaft and his eyes peering up at the sky. It had been the fifth expedition for the two of them together.

Peter went to him on hands and knees. The arrow was stuck between the breastbone and the lowest rib on the right. Pelagius's lips were blue, pressed tightly together in pain, his breath coarse and shallow against Peter's palm. He detached Pelagius's hands and slightly wiggled the arrow. Then he got up, put one foot on the man's breastbone, grabbed the arrow in both hands and gradually wrenched it up from the cartilage. Pelagius tried to grab the slender shaft, so that Peter had to step on his arm, holding it against the ground. He could pull the arrow straight up and loosen it without breaking it. A large purple-brown drop, like a ripe olive, emerged from the wound. It came from the liver.

'Can you hear me?'

'Yes.'

'Are you Catholic?'

'No.'

'I'm going to cauterise your wound.' He knew there couldn't be an answer. In the tent Lourens was still sucking and spitting. Peter dropped opium into brandy, stirred it, took his iron rod and linen from the chest and ran back to Pelagius, bending low. He pushed the rod with its wooden handle in among the coals.

'Drink this, Pelagius. It's for shock. I'm going to look at the others.'

'Are there more of us wounded?'

'Fortunately not.'

Dirk Wessels had already pulled the arrowhead from his arm with his pocket-knife and rubbed tobacco juice into the wound. A sleeve was torn from his shirt for a bandage. Hans Rootkop's wound was high up on his side, so Peter had to make an incision. Hans was the first to ask whether it was poisoned. Then he returned to Pelagius, to cauterise his wound. The cattle were quiet. Cruijthoff called at his men to get up. The enemy had left. Jackals were wailing around them again. Wood was put on the fire. Gradually Peter relaxed in the knowledge that the arrows had not been poisoned, otherwise he would have had four corpses by now.

'What do we do with them, Pieter?' asked the sergeant.

'In the tent overnight. Tomorrow they must ride on the wagon if they cannot walk.'

Throughout the night the fire was kept blazing. The oxen were calm. The guards put on two overcoats and two pairs of breeches each as protection against arrows. If the Koina want to kill us, why don't they attack? wondered Peter. We can only fight until our powder is finished. How come that the people of this country are so cowardly? There are hundreds more of them than us. Too peaceful, perhaps, too confident of the white man's innate goodness. That was how he knew Eva too. She would almost never resist, but she lost heart easily, then became depressed, then bitter, and there was nothing one could do for her. There was no fighting spirit, no sense of imposing her will. One could do anything to her.

They slept little. The wounded were feverish. Lourens was better off than the others; his wounds had been sucked clean. The injuries of the others were swollen and purple. Peter crushed a few ship's rusks in the mortar, chewed it to pulp with gulps of tepid water and bound the warm bread poultices on their wounds. Before daybreak they loaded the sick on the wagon and left for the south. Cruijthoff was cursing bitterly. It surprised them, as they'd come to know him as a quiet man. When they rested the oxen, Peter tried his best with zinc ointment on new warm bread poultices, and with bloodletting. Once the swellings subsided, the fever was gone. Wessels and Rootkop were back on their feet, but Pelagius grew weaker and for long periods lay sweating and in a coma. The zinc ointment and bread poultices drew black blood from his chest. He had no bowel movement, nor did he pass water. When he was awake, Peter fed him buchu infusions. An enema was what he needed, but the man was too weak for it. Pelagius lay on the hard, jolting wagon for days, past Meerhof's Kasteel, and then zigzagging across the rocky bed of the Olifants River. And one day in January, on top of the last mountain, from where they'd hoped to catch a first glimpse of Table Mountain, they came upon a shelter of a few Koina against a cliff.

There were four women and seven children. Cruijthoff entered the shelter, cursing. He threw out skins and karosses and calabashes of water, and pushed the women against the cliffside with the barrel of his gun. The children hid crying against their mothers.

'Dorhagen, Meyer, Wessels, de Smit, fall in for execution!' Cruijthoff shouted at his men. 'The rest of you, take up guard around them; face outward. Rootkop, put the brake under the wheel and hold the leading pair.'

Peter prevented it. He remained between the guns and the thin line of Sonqua. Dorhagen, Wessels and the others protested. Why spill innocent blood? Cruijthoff pointed at Weckerlein's wasted body under the stained canvas. 'What do you see there? These people must be taught a lesson their children will remember.' Peter pleaded with the sergeant. The two of them had always been friends. To the women he said: 'Get away from here. Take your children.' Wailing, they fled from the cliff. Cruijthoff fired a shot over them. To Peter he said: 'It would be you, wouldn't it? With your Hottentot woman.'

Without waiting for an order Hans Rootkop led the oxen down the mountain. Cruijthoff followed him, still cursing. The disappointment kept smouldering in Peter as he followed the wagon.

After they had handed over the wagon and oxen and their supplies at the Fort, Cruijthoff went in to see the commander. It was nearly sunset when Peter was free to go home. Eva was busy at the hearth. She was young again, as shapely as he'd remembered her from long ago. He sank down on a bench at the kitchen table, dizzy with fatigue, and held out his hands to her. She came to sit beside him, her arms around him.

'Good day, Eva.'

'Good day, Pieter.'

'I must be stinking something awful.'

'You smell of the veld. Cattle. Do you want me to heat some water to wash?'

It was good to be home.

'I brought you an ostrich egg.'

She took him to the front room, to show him his son. The little face had a greyish brown colour, wrinkled with sleep. He had reddish-brown hair. Peter laughed when he saw it. Who could the child take after? He felt rich and satisfied.

'Where is little Pieternel?'

'With my sister.'

'Where?'

'With Oedasoa. They're grazing behind the white dunes. I'll have her fetched in the next week. I cannot look after her and the baby too. She enjoys it there.'

He was disappointed, but thought: That is how it happens among the Koina, where the aunts and grandmothers help one another. Eva had no one else. Yet he would have liked to see Pieternella, for many times on the expedition he had thought of her and of his homecoming together. While the water was getting warm, he told Eva what had happened, and how in the end the journey had come to nothing. And now Cruijthoff was reporting back on his own. It was not as it had been under van Riebeeck; the new commander wanted to listen only to his sergeant. Later Peter undressed in front of the hearth and scrubbed his body with soap and a coarse cloth. The next day he would boil his clothes to kill the lice and ticks.

Eva sent word with some Koina who came to the Fort with feathers and honey, and so Pieternella was brought home. She had been rubbed with lard all over, even between her toes. Her hair was teeming with lice, but otherwise she was healthy. He saw teeth in her mouth, and suspected that she recognised him. He kissed her in her kaross and pressed her close in his arms until she began to cry. Then he put his two children side by side to look at them. Where would Eva get such children? They didn't resemble one another at all.

For some time he quietly lived at home, working on the ships and in the hospital, rocking his children to sleep in the evening, reading by lamplight and candlelight at night. Ships arrived, sending in their sick, shipping provisions and fuel, emptied the hospital of convalescents, turned their sails to the wind again and sailed off into the great expanse. Fatherland and Orient had now become strange, distant places to Peter, more remote than Monomotapa and Davagul, where he'd gone off to so often.

In March 1663 an English ship arrived, *George and Martha* from Cuba, over St Helena on its way to Madagascar to buy slaves. Among the services Wagenaer offered its captain, was that of his surgeon.

Commander Wagenaer invited the officers to dinner. The English were fellows who could eat and drink well, and Englishmen coming from Cuba were bound to bring cigars to his table. They did not disappoint him. After dinner the captain felt uneasy, and was reclining on a couch with a glass of brandy in his hand when Peter was called to examine him. Around him the host and his guests had drawn their chairs into a half-circle, smoking and drinking. Wagenaer was seated on the captain's right, with the carafe and cigar box between them. Peter suggested bloodletting. The captain put down his glass, took off his coat, rolled up a sleeve and told him to go ahead. Wagenaer moved slightly to one side to make room for Peter's instruments, and continued questioning him: What had they heard on Cuba? What, at St Helena?

On St Helena they had heard that some months earlier a Dutch pirate had come there, a large man with an English dog. The pirate was on his way home from the Red Sea, over Mauritius, and on Mauritius he'd found forty Dutch castaways whom he'd taken off. At St Helena he offloaded four he did not want on his ship. All the others had joined him and become pirates. Originally, they heard, there had been 140 Dutch castaways on Mauritius, who had lived in different bands on the island, and had been salvaged in groups. For example, Captain Swanley had brought twenty-two to St Helena on the *Truro*. And then two boatloads of them had gone from Mauritius across to Madagascar, where they'd asked for help from the French settlement. Apparently only seven wild fellows now remained on Mauritius, who refused to leave. When a ship arrived, they fled into the bushes. The island was paradise, they said.

'Just as well there is no Eve,' said Wagenaer. 'We sent a ship from here to look for them, on the orders of our Directors. But they didn't discover a single soul. Must be living on venison and palm wine. They will soon go mad.'

Mauritius? Peter knew it lay far off the Company's routes, in the torrid tropics. What would that paradise look like? Robben Island was cold, sandy and windy, but what would it be like in that paradise, with his Eva? Palm wine and deer. He had drawn two small beakers of blood when the captain told him he was feeling better, thank you. Would the doctor care to put a few cigars in his pocket? Excellent cigars. Peter took two. The next day he exchanged both for milk from the Company's dairyman.

When he heard that an expedition to the Chainouqua across the mountains to the east was being arranged, he presented himself, only partly for the money. He was curious, he wanted to see the land behind the high Hottentots-Holland Mountain. Eva had told him that she was related to the important Chainouqua chief Sousoa. He laughed and said that he would there see whom his children took after. But the commander didn't accept him for the expedition. 'Unnecessary,' he said. 'It's a short journey, only four or five days.'

Peter found it strange when those travellers returned with the news that the Chainouqua had only twenty huts and owned no more than fifteen hundred cattle. How was that possible? Long ago Herrie had told van Riebeeck that they had hundreds of houses, thousands of spear carriers, ten thousand cattle. Whence that lie? Now the commander had the impression that all he needed to do was to teach these Chainouqua to smoke like the rest, and the Company's transport problems would be solved.

When the flowering season came round again, Wagenaer summoned him. 'It's time for Namaqualand, master. Do you want to go?'

'Yes, gladly.'

'So. The Council wants Sergeant de la Guerre to lead. I'm asking for volunteers from the garrison today, and then I want you to help us to select the best dozen or so. I asked Amsterdam to send us a draughtsman.'

Of his old companions only the Wessels brothers and Jan Dorhagen, the long-time friend who had still not been promoted, were left. It could be a pleasant group of comrades. He told Eva about the double wages they'd be receiving, the endless flower-covered plains of Namaqualand, the heards of grazing springbok.

'I wish I could go too.' He sensed real longing in her voice.

'I shall ask the commander. I don't know why it cannot happen, except that we have two children. Who will teach them to talk, who will care for their health?'

'There's my sister.'

'They're not her children. If a child falls ill, she will say she couldn't help it.'

A week later they were assembled in the courtyard of the Fort in front of the Kat. The entire population stood behind them while the commander addressed them from the stoep. A few rummers of wine were sent round, three hurrahs were shouted. When the travellers left through the gate following the wagon, with feathers in their hats, Eva and little Pieternella waved to Peter from the back row.

Three months and ten days later they returned through the entrance on foot. They were lean, deeply tanned, tired, laughing. Their provisions were finished. Their pack oxen were worn out. What had they achieved in this time? At the Olifants River Mountain they had taken the wagon apart and buried it. With the provisions and trade goods loaded on pack oxen, they'd set off once again in search of that great river Garieb, the true Vigiti Magna, but the arid plains and heat of Namaqualand had forced them back once more. When they came to where they'd left the wagon, they found it dug out and burned, the ashes were already weeks old. By whom? They had not encountered any Koina or Sonqua anywhere along the way. Where had the Grigriqua and Akembie's Namaqua gone to? What had they achieved? Perhaps there was nothing to be achieved in Africa at all.

Eva was in mourning when he came back. Herrie had died, and Doman. Herrie had been her uncle, and her guardian, who had sometimes brought tubers and honey for her first child. He'd come round to see the girl, often, when Peter wasn't there. He'd assured her that there were cattle with Oedasoa for the child's making-different. The chief's wife had kept them there for her.

'How did he die?'

She didn't know.

'What is the matter then?'

She felt like an orphan. 'Autshumao was my only family. He was the last of the Goringhaicona. The very last. And no one slaughtered for him.'

When he said: 'Herrie was no longer a Koina anyway, he wore a white man's clothes,' it made her cry more.

He understood why she'd cried when he asked the clerk in charge of the journal what had happened while they'd been in the north. There he learned that Eva had taken his two children to Oedasoa, and that Herrie had been ill. That was all the journal knew, but in the hospital there were friends who could tell frankly. When Eva had heard that Autshumao was ill, she'd thrown off the children's clothes and draped karosses over them. One she'd tied to her back and one to her breast, and then had taken to the road with her bag over her shoulder, on the way to Keert-de-Koe. There she'd placed a stone on the new cairn for Heitsi-Eib'. It lay out in the open now, the bushes surrounding it were chopped away. Early in the morning she went through the gate on the old road to the north. The postkeeper reminded her to be back before sundown.

'She cursed me,' the soldier told Peter. 'All of us, all the whites. I've become used to cursing females, Master Pieter, but a man has his pride. Still, I warned her against the lions. There were your children to consider.'

She must have thought that the postkeeper was mocking her, with his pole and chain and lock across the old Koina road. She went off into the bushes all alone. The Cochoqua were grazing days away beyond the Koeberg. And there at the gate she was seen again for the first time, days later. She was so tired that from noon until evening she slept in a corner on the posthouse floor. All three of their heads had been shaved and black stripes had been made on their faces with soot and fat. The two children appeared ill to the postkeeper; both had upset stomachs. He gave her some food, and sent one of his people with them to the Fort.

'What have you done, Eva?' Peter asked. 'What happened to you?'

She said she couldn't remember. Perhaps she just did not want to talk about it. He pleaded, and she told him, and he later realised that she hadn't told him the full story. All she said was that she'd heard about her uncle's illness; it was going to cause his death, they'd said. She wanted to take her leave of the old man, and took the children with her. She cast a stone, a plea to Heitsi-Eib' for a safe journey.

'You're a Christian, Eva.'

'The whites will forgive me.'

When she reached Oedasoa's kraal he had her summoned. He was bent, shrunk, shrivelled as a sour fig. Her sister wasn't there. The two children cried for food. He didn't offer her anything to drink.

'You're coming for cattle,' he said.

'I've come to see my uncle.'

'I shall look after him.'

'I want to speak to him.'

'He doesn't speak.'

She was glad to have seen an abundance of young grass around the camp. The Koina easily trekked away from an old person.

'Then where is my sister? I'd like to see her.'

'She's looking after Autshumao.'

Her voice was too sharp when she said, 'What is it, Oedasoa? I'm tired. I've come a long way to see my people.'

'You came to see the cattle when you heard Autshumao was dying. He will die. You go back to your people with the wide breeches.'

She remained sitting there on the small mat in front of him, putting the two children to her breast to drink. She knew there was nothing to wait for, but she was too tired to get up again. When he didn't want to listen to the children's crying any more, he went to call his wife. They quarrelled loudly outside the door. Her sister helped to clean the children, and brought them food and mats and karosses on which to sleep. Autshumao did not have many days left, she said. He was bleeding to death and ate nothing. And her husband Oedasoa had gone off his head. He'd been like that ever since the white people came, he did not know what to do about them. He no longer slept at night and all he talked about was the Hollanders. He told her to see to it that Krotoa would go home in the morning. Her sister had shaved their hair and blackened their faces, because their uncle was dying. That was all Eva was prepared to tell, but it wasn't all she cried about. There was much to cry about, she said.

Peter didn't know how to comfort her, but he promised never to leave her alone again for so long. Doman had also died, and she barely mentioned it. That was how peace had come about, because Doman could never again lift a spear above his head. That was the end of January 1664.

Two weeks later Wagenaer sent Peter with six others over the mountain to barter cattle from the Chainouqua. Once again he had to offer excuses to Eva. It was additional income for them, he said, and on a journey like that he always saved some of his provisions. At any rate, it was something all Dutch women got used to: that their husbands would be away at sea for months. Moreover, this time he wouldn't stay away for so long.

Eva didn't know what to do to keep him home. When he returned a fortnight later, it was with only three scrawny old beasts. They hadn't been able to find the Chainouqua's kraals.

After Herrie and Doman died, Eva was sometimes called to the Fort to interpret. She was given a few guilders for it, but what she enjoyed was once again to sit in the council chamber between the commander and the visitors, as in her youth. It was like a new life. She became interested in her clothes again. She also evoked the attention of the church council.

A *dominee* of the fleet turned up on a visit one evening. Peter welcomed him. Eva was shy and wouldn't come in. With his daughter on his lap Peter spoke to the man. The minister read from the scriptures and said a prayer, and Peter thanked him for it. It was a long time since prayers had been said in his home, he remarked. He himself wasn't quite sure how to do it. On overland expeditions it was the duty of the leader, but when it was his turn he used quite simply to ask someone to volunteer. There were first-class fellows in his group. There was no reason for the *dominee* to think of him as a sinner.

'Perhaps this is an occasion that may be to your advantage, Master Pieter. The commander believes that a young man with your experience should have made more progress in life by now. I agree. There are still matters that stand in the way.'

'Yes.'

'The Council is concerned that you are not married to the woman you live with. You have now begotten children who are not yet baptised. The Council believes that it militates against morality. Do you personally have any objection against holy baptism or a legitimate marriage?'

'No.'

'Is the children's mother against it?'

'No.'

'Is she here? May I talk to her?'

'She is shy. She doesn't want to come in.'

'Do discuss it with her, brother. You have the same responsibilities as other subjects of the Company.'

'What is required, *dominee*?'

'Have your banns read, get married, then arrange the baptism. If you wish to draw up a marriage contract, there is a notary available. It will cost a few guilders.'

He discussed it with Eva. How would it affect the children? she wanted to know. Would they bury her in a Christian cemetery? Her questions sounded strange. What would it do to her happiness in the final reckoning?

Their marriage vows were taken on 26 April 1664 by Wagenaer personally, in the presence of their two children and other witnesses. It was the first time, he said, that a European would marry a Cape native according to the Christian formulary. He wished them prosperity and gave them his blessing. Afterwards their banns were read on three successive Sundays, and on 2 June their marriage was solemnised, just after the church service.

The commander stood in for Eva's father; and he brought her to the altar. Flushed with pleasure, he beamed at the congregation. After the service, the solemn oath in public, and the blessing hands of the pastor, they went to the commander's living room where a small festive meal had been set out for invited guests. There were still ripe sheaves of wheat at De Schuur, and two of those had been hung cross-shaped on the wall behind the bride's chair. There were cold meats, tarts and pies, fine white bread, fruit, wine and beer on the long tables.

'A gift from the Company,' called the commander. 'Now tell me, to what important guest has the Company offered a wedding feast in this place before? To my knowledge it has never happened. Come and be seated, friends.' Then he raised a finger to his servant watching from the kitchen door: Bring it on. In the late afternoon, holding a tall, ornate beer mug high, he called a German blessing over his guests.

'I was against this marriage at first. Thirty goddamned devils, who thought any different? Entirely inappropriate, they are not of the same blood. Then our *dominee* came to me. Your Honour, he said, let them have their way; in the time of peace even the lion will lie with the lamb. Yes, *dominee*, I said, but there's lying and lying.'

Then he offered them a wedding gift. He clinked a purse in front of Peter's nose, but placed it in Eva's hand.

'A few pieces of silver, my child. From the Company.' There was stamping of feet and applause, hands were flapped on the table, everybody drank. Then he raised his tankard: 'A toast to the bride and bridegroom. A cow in the stable, a rooster on the beam, bacon and beans in the pot, children round the table.' Once again there was stomping, applause, drinking. Eva laughed happily.

'What are you thinking of?' Peter asked her.

'I wish I could tell it all to Mister van Riebeeck.'

'He will hear about it. He will be glad.'

In the early evening the commander and his wife came to take their leave, and excused themselves. Other people of high rank followed, to congratulate them and withdraw. A flute and a fiddle invited the guests to dance. It was a Company feast, and there were no freemen, except for the two burgher councillors and their wives. In friendly mood, and already somewhat relaxed in the first fruit of peace, Burgher Councillor Mostert came to shake hands with the bridegroom: 'As long as that rooster doesn't mess on your head, Master Pieter.'

The dancers moved in straight lines or in solemn circles, men and women stepping towards each other and away from each other, and weaving through and around each other. The ladies lifted their skirts from the floor, the men pranced hand on hip and with the tips of their shoes pointed outward. Others were sitting with dour faces, purely as witnesses, without eating or talking, as if they'd been summoned to an execution.

Peter took Eva's third mug of Spanish wine from her hand and put it aside, and led her to the dance floor. She tried to copy the others, then gave up and compromised by circling around him, confused and shuffling. She clapped her hands softly and started moving away in a bigger circle around him, swaying and stamping. She found pace and rhythm, she sang with her head thrown back, in a high and piercing voice. Stamping and shuffling, her eyes shut as if moving in her sleep, she sent the guests retreating before her swaying body and her shrill song. Peter shuffled dumbly in a tight circle, bowing politely left and right, grimacing in embarrassment at the Dutch faces, round as fresh cheeses, staring at him. And slightly drunk and light-headed, he heard the laughter thinning out around him and even the music held its breath. Apart from the dour band of the curious, the hall was almost empty. Eva alone was dancing. At the tables the chairs were deserted, abandoned in disorder. The two musicians raised wine glasses towards Peter in a voiceless toast.

There was something in the air again. Peter visited the ship *Waterhoen* on the anchorage. There were many sick. He examined them, divided them into groups, and spoke to the captain about transporting them to the hospital. From him he heard that the ship was headed for Mauritius, which was now to be colonised. The leader of the expedition was on board, as well as artisans and soldiers and sailors destined for the infant settlement. Among them were a few survivors of *Aernhem's sinking*, who knew the island intimately after their long sojourn, and who were to form the backbone of the new colony. Some of those fellows had to go into the hospital here. The captain told him in confidence that there was no surgeon in his group, and if Peter would like to consider the matter, he might mention his wish to Commander Wagenaer.

Mauritius, the paradise, grew green in Peter's thoughts for a long time. As a chief surgeon he would earn a decent salary there, plus fringe benefits, and perhaps even a seat on the island's Council. Wouldn't that be by far the best for Eva and the children? But when he mentioned it to Eva, she scornfully dismissed it. He would never persuade her to leave the Cape, she'd already told him, she said. If he was ashamed of her, he could go there on his own.

A few weeks after the wedding Wagenaer asked Peter to arrange a small bartering trip to the Koina in the vicinity. Winter was setting in, and he'd heard that some Koina kraals had returned to the peninsula as had been the custom of old. Peter proposed that Eva accompany them. She made a bed of bushes for her and the children at the back of the tent-wagon, among their canvas bags with dry provisions, casked tobacco and a barrel of brandy. She would interpret and barter, and help to win the Koina over to tobacco and alcohol. There were some of Ngonnemoa's people still who knew nothing stronger than honey-beer. Some of those she brought to their wagon, and persuaded them to taste, until their throats were no longer burning so badly and the mouth no longer went numb. The throng around their wagon increased. She insisted on talking to each of them; from each she tried to trade a sheep or an ox or a cow, for brandy or tobacco.

During those few days Eva was content and cheerful. Here was her Peter, here were her children, there on the wagon was food and bedding, and around her were people grazing their fat cattle in lush green winter grass, and every day she could speak her own language and laugh with her own kind. In her morning prayer she thanked God for the joy. She had seventy-five cattle and two hundred and sixty sheep to take to the Fort.

For this service the commander gave them a good young cow in milk. Eva wanted them to sell it, but Peter built a stable next to the house, and laboriously learned to milk it. The fresh milk was for his children, the sour milk was for his wife. In the daytime their cow grazed with the Company's dairy herd, under the care of its herdsman.

At the end of the year a bright silvery comet appeared above Robben Island at dusk, and sank back into the sea each night. All through the midsummer it hung there, its luminous head over the island and its long tail reaching above the Fort, the houses, the mountain, the Liesbeeck farms and the black plains where the Koina had built their kraals. Night after night it was there, with the flaming, glittering head right above the island, and the tail like a white brush stroke across the dark sky. People were frightened of it. What was the meaning of the apparition? War. Earthquake. Perhaps the plague. One could examine one's life, pay one's debts, prepare for whatever one feared most. One could pray, but what more could one do?

Peter talked to Eva about the comet. He had to examine patients on board for bubonic plague, smallpox, leprosy. He feared that task, because a ship with one of those diseases had to leave for a quarantine station under the wind, taking with it the surgeon who had discovered the symptoms, and remain stationed there until the raging disease had spent itself. It could be six or seven months before it was declared clean. He asked her: if it were the plague or pox, and the ship had to lie at anchor behind the island, would it be hard on her if he had to remain on board for months? In that case she should ask the commander for help; perhaps he could lend her a slave, male or female. She had to protect her children against the pox and send them away, so that it wouldn't attack the girl's face and disfigure her.

The last night the comet hung over the island, the annual home-ward bound fleet arrived from the Orient. There were ten ships, two were still lagging behind, and one had exploded one night, more than a month earlier, on the back edge of the formation. There was only a huge, brilliant-white light, and no survivors.

Yes, they had been watching that comet at sea for weeks on end, and the sailors were uneasy. There was bad trouble afoot, Admiral de Bitter explained to Wagenaer. His fleet was transporting the greatest treasure that had ever been assembled anywhere on earth. The income from it had to pay for a final war against England. And now for the difficult part: the English were aware of this fleet, did Wagenaer know it? In one way or another the English had heard about the treasure, and their navy lay divided into three squadrons to patrol every access to the North Sea. Some of de Bitter's passengers and officers had asked him whether they could remain here on shore until the signs were more auspicious, among them his vice-admiral Borghorst, but he had refused. He suspected that this gentleman had jewels hidden in his baggage. That was how the stories went.

After the departure of de Bitter's fleet, a messenger yacht from the fatherland brought news of the expected disaster. They had met de Bitter's return fleet near St Helena, and had informed him as well.

Bubonic plague was spreading all across Europe and tens of thousands were dying in every country. London had burned to the ground, and England had declared war against the Netherlands. That was the message of the comet. And now God help the return fleet, and the poor fatherland.

On Robben Island the postkeeper had fired his signalling cannon several times during the night of 14 May 1665. It was the signal that there were ships abroad in the night that wanted to come in. But the sentries on the walls of the Fort could see no ship's lights on the outer roadstead. The shooting continued all night, and at daybreak they could see a dark column of smoke rising up from the fire hill. Moreover, the postkeeper was also desperately making flag signals. His national flag was upside down, his prince's flag was jerked up and down the pole, or the halyard was loosened to let the flag run out with the wind. Something was seriously wrong. An uprising among the convicts, thought the commander, and he sent over ten soldiers and a surgeon in the fast sloop.

It was the postkeeper's wife. Peter had met them before, the skinny sergeant Jan and his portly Maria from North Outer India. She had come to the Cape as a slave accompanying a sick-comforter's pregnant wife, where she'd been sold. Van Riebeeck had advised Jan and Maria to get married without delay, for soon afterwards they also had a child baptised. Now the overlong stay on Robben island was getting to Maria. She was thick as a barrel, suffering from water. Her body filled the whole *katil*, bulging over the sides. Her legs, like tree trunks, were too weak to carry her weight. Her eyes were shut, her large hands were tied together on her chest to prevent them falling to the ground. Under her dark skin she was bloodless, greenish in colour. Peter pressed a finger against her upper arm. A white dent appeared, remaining there after he'd removed his finger.

'She cannot breathe, master. She's getting weaker, and paler, and has kept her bed for fourteen days now. I no longer know what to do.'

'You're an East India farer?'

'*Oorlams.*'

'Then you know *beriberi.*'

'I was afraid of that. I hope you know what to do.' But they both knew there was nothing to be done. If only they could draw off some of her water, it would free her lungs.

'We must get her to hospital, Jan.'

'Can't you draw it here, master?'

'No. Is there somebody here to look after your child?'

'No, master. There's no women.'

He wanted to bring the patient round with brandy, but they could get nothing into her mouth as her throat was swollen tight; so he rubbed small quantities of it on her forehead and her wrists to evaporate.

'Cover her warmly. She'll have to go ashore. The child can stay with my wife.' The boatmen brought a few bags of shells from the beach on board, and then helped to lift Maria Zacharias on her *katil* and carry her from the house to the sloop that had to take her away. Peter, with the child against his shoulder and his medicine chest in his hand, was the last to step off the beach. The quartermaster called out a farewell to Zacharias. Then the sailors pushed the boat off, and shook out its two sails. The same afternoon Peter helped the Fort's chief surgeon to drain Maria. Three flagons of water, then she died under their hands.

Eva was annoyed because he'd brought the child with him. 'Give the child to the church,' she said. 'It's not my child. I have my own children.' He was disappointed that she wouldn't do the small favour for a friend, but without a word he took the child to the sick-comforter whose responsibility it was to find foster-parents, as the Cape had no orphan-house.

The commander called him, shortly after the woman's death.

'Two prisoners came here from Robben Island last night. Escaped, the godforsaken dogs, rowed all the way. And do you know what their story is? Came to complain against Postkeeper Zacharias. They allege that he maltreats them, and steals wine from the pantry, and sells the Company's sheep to ships' captains who send rowing boats to the island. They'd hoped that I would give them amnesty for the information, but they can bloody well go to hell. I had Zacharias brought here this morning and interrogated him in front of his accusers. At first he was stubborn, but later he confessed. In the end he asked me to release him from the island, but that is damned nonsense of course. The Council has decided to banish him, and now he's waiting in a cell until there is another ship to Mauritius. What grieves us most is that he allowed criminals to escape, and that he hadn't secured the Company's boat with a chain and locked up the oars. Master Pieter, it's not the first time in my life that I see a weak man losing a good wife and then falling to pieces all at once. And the same when a weak woman loses a good man. On the spot, everything goes to pieces, lock, stock and barrel. Now I'm looking for a postkeeper. There are a few men interested who deserve promotion, but I thought I'd ask you first. You have some experience, and you can look after the people's health. What do you think?'

'I know you can command me.'

'The goddamned devil knows that too. But what do you say?'

'I must think of my wife's health, and my children's. The rations are killing.'

'You can make a garden there. Vegetables and stuff. That's always been good for *beriberi*.'

'I have no desire to keep prisoners working. My heart is against it. I'm no slave driver.'

'You have your two corporals for that.'

'I don't feel like it.'

'So. Well, all right then. There is *beriberi* on our island. I want to know what causes it, and you're going to see to it that I find out. For this post the Company will promote you, and you'll be receiving a sergeant's pay. How does that sound now? If you succeed, you can count on it that I shall use you for other rewarding duties and services.'

It sounded good. Maybe, afterwards, at last, the Orient? Even if it had to be without Eva, but never without his children.

'All right, Your Honour,' he said, filled with hope.

Wagenaer shuffled round the table to shake his hand. 'So. Good. Pieter, you goddamned fellow, I know of no reason why you shouldn't one day become commander of a post like Mauritius. Keep your eye on that place, there are going to be lovely opportunities there, and then you mustn't hesitate to apply. You still need experience, particularly the kind you can acquire in a post in the East. Now go and talk to your wife. You have to leave for the island tomorrow.'

Eva's first question was: 'Pieter, will you be home every night then?' Then he told her about the cold, wind-blown island, the bitter water in the well, the broad stretch of dark seawater between their new home and this Fort, and of Postkeeper Zacharias's wife who died because no doctor could reach her in time. He had no more to tell her, and hoped she would refuse, so that he could report it to Wagenaer.

'Pieter,' she said gravely, 'Oedasoa has two hundred cattle and five hundred sheep for me. Remember that, if anything happens to me there.'

On the sloop which took them and their belongings across to the island, was their cow and a thousand bundles of thatching reeds to put a new roof on their house. The sloop returned with forty bags of shells, and a prisoner chained to the foremast shrouds. The corporals of the island, Peter soon discovered, were two giants who liked to kick and beat, and whose voices could send the gulls fluttering up screaming from the anchorage. They beat the Company's canes to shreds on the backs and buttocks of the chained prisoners. That was the way it had to be, they told the new postkeeper, that was how it was done.

Peter's day, every single one of them, commenced with the count-ing of the prisoners, the weighing out of food for the cook, the reading of the morning prayer on the icy, bleak parade ground next to the flag-pole, the inspection of the prisoners' stinking quarters after they'd been escorted to their working place, and visiting the sick. After that he went home, shaved, had breakfast, wrote his correspondence and copied it in the letter book, and kept accounts of the distribution of provi-sions. After that, if the weather was good, he went up the slope to the Fire Hill with the telescope, to talk to the sentry and make sure that there was fuel and oil. Then he climbed a little way up the brazier's scaffolding to examine the whole island with the telescope: the stone quarry on the Cape side where a team of masons was splitting the blue slate, the stone-pit in the middle of the island where blocks of lime-stone were cut, the chained labourers like ants in the north-western corner where for centuries the sea had thrown up a mound of broken shells on the beach. And if he swivelled the telescope further to the right, he could see his post house, the prison, the sheep pen and, last in the circle, a small colony of shiny seals on the black rocks.

This was his world, and it was meagre, impoverished and bitter. I won't ever be at home here, thought Peter, staring through the haze across the sea to the white smudge and the smoke over little houses near the Fort, at the foot of Table Mountain. 'I've made a mistake to come here. I'm trapped.'

He counted the Company's sheep on the plain, watched the labourer idling in the vegetable garden around the well, and adjusted his telescope to examine the ships at the Cape anchorage. Those from the East were deeply loaded, those from the fatherland rode high in the water. What flags, what distant ports, what places where the seawater was pale green and lukewarm and palm fronds rustled over white beaches, what strange green islands under a tropical sky, what foreign voices, what alien stars . . . Perhaps the Company would transfer him to the Orient one day. Through Eva he had grown fast to the Cape. Was he not already too old for the East, too deeply rooted in these parched dunes? Here, his wife fed chickens, his children drank bitter well-water, all of them breathed the sharp sea air laden with the stench of bird droppings and rotting kelp, and no one knew of anything better elsewhere in the world. They were all trapped. And poor Eva, without another woman's company.

Peter's daughter was four years old when she asked him to take her with him wherever he went, to the shells, the sheep, the Fire Hill. She no longer wanted to stay home. She never complained when he stayed in one spot for a long time, but patiently amused herself with small shells and little feathers. She was fleet of foot and agile. When she asked to be picked up, she clung tightly to his neck and examined the path before his feet with him. When he wrote at the kitchen table, she came to stand beside him and watched his hands. Like him, she rested her forehead in her hand, sighed.

'What are you doing?'

'Writing.'

She wanted a pen and paper. He had a neat thin slate split off for her in the quarry, smoothly sanded the four sides, rolled her a round slate-pencil under his boot, and took it home. She scrawled and drew on the slate, then she wanted to learn to write. But he didn't know how to teach her.

'This child of ours must go to school,' he said to Eva.

'She's lazy. She doesn't want to do anything, just wander around.'

'She will have her turn for hardship.' But he was worried. What would this isolated island do to his child? There was no other child around, except for her little brother who was crying almost ceaselessly, day and night. And no other grown-ups except for the miserable fifty-four who dragged chains along the ground and the more miserable pair who beat them.

The approach of a boat was first shouted from the Fire Hill: 'Boat coming!' Then Peter would finish his letters, seal them, wrap them in tarpaulin, tie them up. Empty water vats and oil barrels were rolled down to the beach, and the cook was ordered to empty his bread baskets. Then Peter would fire two powder charges outside the door to call in his sea workers to the posthouse. The children would go to the beach with the prisoners, but he, and Eva too, did not approach until the boat's quartermaster had come ashore. Then he went down to greet and welcome the man, and invite him to his house. The sea workers had to offload, carry home and stow what had been brought, and then load the mound of blue slate and bags of shells standing ready on the beach. Peter read the incoming mail first. This letter from the Fort was the main thing. What did the commander want of him? Usually it was simply: Send so many baskets of eggs, so many bags of feathers, here is another prisoner, last week's shells were not enough. He was desperately longing for something more. The letter he was waiting for would say: Your services are required at such and such a trading station on an island in the Orient. Start packing, I'm sending your replacement on the next boat. That was what Peter was hoping for.

Sometimes he sat thinking resting his elbows on the kitchen table. The letter would come unexpectedly. It would be a very ordinary day. Eva would be busy at the hearth stirring something in a pot or raking cinders from under the grid, one of the children would ladle a spoonful of drinking water from the vat, a prisoner would enter with an armful of chopped wood and his chain would tinkle on the slate floor. He himself would probably be with the sick in the kraal and someone would come to call him.

But the letter didn't come and, trapped on this barren island, he continued to wait. Sometimes he thought in dismay: There *is* a real world over there, isn't there, across the sea? Or has Copenhagen become a dead word, Batavia a series of letters in his imagination, like Monomotapa or Davagul? Every day boats arrived from the outside world to collect shells; and every time when the quartermaster handed over his letters, his excitement and expectation diminished.

Wagenaer, the man who had persuaded him and promised him promotion, had already left the Cape. The new commander was van Quaelberg, a military man who carried a sword at his side and wore a feather in his hat. Van Quaelberg didn't promise Peter anything. Peter was summoned to attend his presentation in the Fort, and that was the last he saw of him, except for his letters over the next two years. Seasons came and went, ships came and went, two years passed, sea-gulls flew and landed, and Peter remained trapped on his rock.

Two years dragged past on that bleak, bitter and barren island with its sharp ammoniac stench and cold storm winds. Only twice in all that time Eva saw other women on the island. The first was Theuntje of Bart, the Saldanha farer, Theuntje with whom Peter had played during his first winter at the Cape. She and Barbara Geens and Trijn Ras had been scarcely nubile widows, fifteen or sixteen years old, washed up here. They had barely known married life and would now never see the promised land, but the Company was to help them to return to their parents' homes. But for months there was no ship, and too many of those boring Sunday afternoons when the grown-ups slept and when the only soul alive would be the sentry on the wall outside. The few unmarried young people had sought one another's company to drive away their solitude and boredom. They were gay company, Barbara and Theuntje and Trijn. Usually they would play cards in his room on rainy days, or they would all lie on his bed, laughing, touching and squeez-ing one another the way penniless people would squeeze fruit at a market, and if they had nothing else to drink they would tipple from the Company's medicine chest. It was pleasant, warming the body when mixed with clear Cape rainwater, and most Sunday afternoons, thank heaven, it rained.

Now Theuntje arrived on the island as a convicted prisoner to serve her sentence. The letter carried a summary of the fiscal's case, and the Council's sentence against her. Peter entered it into the register next to her name. She'd been banished to the island for six weeks, her crime was slander. She'd told a group of farmers' wives that Hester, the wife of Burgher Councillor Mostert, had had two children out of wedlock in the fatherland, and that she'd murdered one. A complete fabrication, she admitted before the Council. The Council's sentence was: a spike through the tongue, forty lashes with the cane, rounded off with six weeks on Dassen Island. Peter was horrified by the thought. He remembered the sight of the prisoners' backs when he rolled them over on their bunks to listen to their hearts and lungs: rough ridges of old floggings, from the shoulder blades down until just above the strap of the breeches. But, the letter continued, on the unanimous plea of Cape women she had been reprieved. She was exonerated from the spike, the lashes were suspended for two years, and instead of Dassen Island where there was no living soul, she would be banished to the outpost of Robben Island.

He heard her at the shell boat, where one of the corporals welcomed her. 'You're not getting any privileges, missus, and mind you don't try to steal from us.' Peter looked through the window. That was Theuntje, slender, still young, but worn down. She carried her chain across the wet sand to the bank of dry driftwood above the high-water mark. In one hand, with the chain, she had a bag of clothing, in the other a bundle in a cloth.

'Stand still there!' shouted the corporal. She had to wait, until he'd explained his bags of shells and his piles of slate to the quartermaster. Then he approached.

'What's in that cloth?'

She held it out to him. 'For the people with whom I'm to be quartered.'

Then Peter had to step outside. Theuntje made it sound like curry-ing favour, her mouth was still her downfall.

'Fried chicken,' the corporal smirked. 'I'm truly fed up with penguin, missus.'

'No,' Peter intervened. 'It's her rations. Sorry, corporal, you and I are not having any of it.' And to Theuntje: 'Go up to the posthouse, at the flagpole there. You can knock, my wife is inside.'

He introduced her to Eva, and called to his children to greet her. 'You are welcome here in our house, Theuntje. The room over there is yours. Thank you for the present you brought. I appreciate it, but the Company does not permit us to accept gifts.' Then he went outside.

During the day his work kept him away from Theuntje, and she managed to keep out of his way. In the afternoon they shared a meal at table. She was more subdued than in her younger days; perhaps she wanted him to give a good report on her behaviour. From Eva he heard the tale she'd told: how she'd been tied to a post in the courtyard of the Fort, how the wives of the officials came to plead for her to be spared the disgrace.

Theuntje wanted to work. She milked their cow, something Eva had never managed very well and was happy to pass off to another. She dug a piece of ground in front of the house for plants she brought from the veld: marigolds, sour fig. She also promised Eva herbs and Dutch flowers from her own garden when she was home again, and mattress-bags full of fresh bush-bedding, which she'd give to the quartermaster for their beds. The children she took out to the dunes with a basket, to collect penguin eggs. She boiled soap from the mutton grease Eva had saved, perhaps with the thought of one day oiling herself with it, and baked rusks from lard and milk and coarse meal. Peter, and Eva too, occasionally offered her a drink, but she refused it. She wouldn't touch any drink. 'It's the demon drink that brought me here. I must stand firm against it. God have mercy on me.'

Peter was expecting that her husband would come to see her, as Theuntje had to provide for herself, and the fellow was nearly killed when he tried to come ashore one night after dark. What was his business? asked the guard. He had a canvas bag with him which he wanted to send ashore. The soldier unpacked it: clothes, a string of *bokking*, a loaf of bread, a bottle of wine, a bolt of unbleached linen with a rough file hidden inside. The soldier threw everything back into the bag. 'Take your arse back to sea, old one. No private boats allowed here.'

'Yes, that's my Bart,' said Theuntje when the guard came to report it. 'Never asks permission. That is his way.' A few days later he was back, this time with permission.

Bart Borms's two dark eyes stared deeply from a hairy face. Perhaps there was a Spaniard or a Frenchman among his ancestors, Peter thought. He was a short, wiry man, dark brown from the sea. A tarred plait hung between his shoulders. His blue canvas clothes were stained with brine, the tail of his breeches was thickly padded for the rowing thwart, his bare feet black from treading the tarred boards. He greeted Peter with a tug of the forelock, holding out a string of mullet to him. It was his thanks for the permission to visit his wife.

He was a naturally silent fellow. 'And he's got a lot to be silent about,' Theuntje explained. But he wasn't bad company. A glass or two warmed him up. He liked to have a drink, for the sea was a cold place, God knows, and a man got tired of its emptiness and silence. He'd been a sailor for the Company before their marriage, but then of course it became fashionable to turn free burgher. He couldn't plough or castrate a pig or stack a stone wall, so he became a free fisherman. Fishing was not work, it was a pleasure, by the dog's hairy skin. This Peter and Eva learned one evening at the dining table. Work came in at the brine vats, the cleaning and gutting and salting, with making *bokking*. The brine corroded your hands, wrist-deep.

During the time Theuntje was confined to the island, Bart turned up every Saturday afternoon, with the commander's permission, and he never came without a gift of fish or lobster, or a basin of roe, or a wind-dried snoek. On such evenings Theuntje insisted on cooking for them, and in a quiet, envious way Peter enjoyed the pleasure those two took from each other's company. Peter enjoyed Bart's tales, about his time as a sailor in the East and his experiences at sea, and he tended to Bart's thirst. Bart would sleep over, crossing back to the mainland late on the Sunday afternoon in his little sloop *Bruid*, which he'd taken over from the Company with sails, rigging, the lot.

Bart and Theuntje carried the children about, played with them, made them toys and told them stories. It seemed to Peter that they were sometimes more interested in the children than in him and Eva. One afternoon they were sitting beside the posthouse with the children.

'Master Pieter,' said Bart, 'Theuntje and I have been wondering if these two have godparents.'

'Are you volunteering, Bart?' He asked it as a joke.

'We'd be only too happy. We have no children. Nature has been against us so far. What do you think of it?'

'What do you offer for the two?' Another joke. Little Pieternella was sitting on Bart's knee, Kobus on Theuntje's lap.

'I have no money. I brought your predecessor Zacharias an English dog, and the prisoners ate it. No, I know you're only joking.'

'Then you'll just have to smuggle and trick and deceive until you're rich enough, Bart. Children are worth millions.'

'I know, master. I know.' The man was serious. 'But will you make us a promise? If the honourable commander agrees.'

'My children go to my people if something happens to me,' said Eva.

'No, they won't. They will go where they can go to school and get an education.'

In the brief, bitter argument between Peter and Eva the matter was forgotten, but Bart brought it up again the next time, and after Theuntje had been discharged from the island, Bart arrived one morning with two ostrich chicks in a bushel basket. 'A small instalment on this one,' he laughed, picking up little Pieternella. 'I'm taking her to the mainland with me.'

On another occasion he told Peter that he had a slave, an able man. And if Peter would give him a paper to appoint Theuntje and him as his children's godparents, he would let him have this first-class slave for a few rix-dollars. He would consider it, Peter said.

When Theuntje was fetched by the fiscal after the six weeks, Eva and the children were sorry about it. The silence at the dining table and the boredom of the barren yard became worse than before. Peter longed for the variety of food, for clothes washed clean, the tidiness of his house. The children kept on asking for Aunt Theuntje. And Eva was unhappier than she'd been before Theuntje's arrival. She nagged Peter to find work at the Fort, so that she could return to the mainland.

'I'm not going to ask. They sent me to find out about the dropsy, and I haven't found an answer yet.'

'How long is it going to take you?'

'I don't know. How can I tell?'

'Why don't you tell them you couldn't find it?'

'They won't accept it.'

'Why not?'

'That was the purpose they sent me for.'

'The one who sent you has left long ago. He's sitting in Holland, stinking rich and drinking wine.'

It was true.

'Pieter, I'm going off my head here. I must go to the mainland for a few days. I want to see my people.'

Once she'd left, he thought, she wouldn't come back.

Eva tried to dig in the flower garden Theuntje had begun, but in the wind and heat the young plants withered under her hands.

'Pieter, I have to talk to my sister about my cattle. There's a lot of money in them. And you can go and work on the mainland. You can do a doctor's work. We don't have to look after prisoners.'

He smiled at the thought. What would they live on? How could his patients pay him? Eva often was like a child in her arguments. She was unhappy on Robben Island, but where would they find something better that did not also mean greater poverty? It was a fantasy of hers, to think she could herd so many sheep and cattle from Oedasoa's kraal, something he had already refused him to his face. He'd heard that both Oedasoa and his wife had died, and he had to tell it to her so that she wouldn't cling to false hope, but the knowledge would make her even more depressed. He studied his wife closely as she stood at the big table, leaning on a broom. Her face had become rounder, her body heavier, her legs thicker. Was she pregnant again? She hadn't told him about it. *Beriberi*, it came to him; hence the listlessness, the inertia to move, as if everything was difficult.

'Eva,' he asked, 'are you pregnant?'

'No.'

'Are you feeling sick?'

'Yes.'

What could he do? He'd seen the *beriberi* come and go among the prisoners, and he'd never been able to do anything about it. Go? Only when they died. Even though it wasn't contagious, he hadn't been able to save a single patient. He remembered the water he'd drained from the mountainous body of Maria Zacharias, as she died under his hands. What could he do for Eva now? If she'd already contracted the condition, she would have one or two years left, no more, and there was no cure he could offer.

In the black night he went outside at his outpost, under the shimmering stars. The sea and the wind were booming cold from the south. Eva . . . How would she stand up to the *beriberi*? Here at the flagpole Jan Zacharias had made signals for a night and half a day to summon a doctor from the other side for his wife he was worried about. In vain. How much mercy would there be one day from the sentry, the guard officer, the commander at the Fort, when he made urgentsignals at midnight about Eva? Would they transfer him to the Fort if she died, or would he, too, be driven to stealing sheep before he saw the Orient? Beyond the black water were pinpricks of light which might be braziers on the bastions of the Fort. Apparently there was a big new castle to be built next to it soon. That was why there was now double the number of prisoners compared to the same time a year ago, that was why there were two shell boats per day, that was why the prisoners had to produce more bags per man, that was why the Koina would soon be told that it was time to pack up again and move deeper inland to make room for all the progress.

When he went inside, Eva had poured them each a *sopie*. 'You were right, I'm pregnant again.'

What pleased him was that the *beriberi* now took second place. With his arms around her he asked, 'Why didn't you tell me?'

'This was how it looked to me: If I'm sick, you will take me to the land. Can we go, Pieter? I beg you.'

'It is in the commander's hands. I cannot arrange it. But I'll write and ask.' With a sigh she left the room.

Their third child, Salomon, was baptised in the late winter of their second year. For those few days Eva and Peter and the children had gone to the mainland. Amazed, they stood on the quay with their baggage, looking at the new castle they were building. A long wooden building like Noah's ark sat among the white and yellow daisies in the dunes. He just *had* to have a look. He helped his wife and children to settle into the small room they had been allocated in the hospital. In the afternoon, while Eva was resting, he left Jakobus and the youngest in the care of a slave woman, and went to look at the ark with little Pieternella on the arm.

The place was teeming with labourers and noise. There were Europeans and Koina and Orientals and black slaves. An ox sledge loaded with heavy rocks was led past. To one side, under a lean-to, stonecutters were chiselling granite blocks into shape. The foundations of a five-pointed fortification were spread out in front of him, and now they were building one bastion at a time, one curtain wall at a time. Some walls were almost head-high. Wheelbarrows filled with wet clay were pushed up gangplanks. On top of the walls hoists were lifting up heavy rocks, swinging them into position, and lowering them into the wet clay. The law of Babel ruled: no talking on the scaffolding. Orders were given with hand signals. Only the foremen would occasionally utter a short, whispered word. On the beach Peter arrived at a gateway and gestured to the foreman: 'May I go in?' The man nodded, holding a hand over his head to signal: 'Watch out.' The wooden ark in the middle of the huge star, was a long, narrow building, wholly made of Cape yellow-wood. Its only door, below a clayed-up gable, faced the sea. Workers emerged from it, carrying scaffolding planks or beams on their shoulders or tools in their hands. For the time being it was a workshop and a warehouse, and on Sundays the hall in which church services were held. When the castle was finished one day the ark would be cleared away. Beside the ark was a well, covered with a wooden lid. This well was the central point of the castle.

Peter was impressed after he and little Pieternella had finished looking. This was to become a mighty castle, this first fortress before the threshold to India. In amazement he told Eva about what he'd seen. Just you wait, he said, a castle like this was going to be given a governor. That Sunday their son, Salomon, was baptised in the ark.

The other woman, after Theuntje, who shared their house on the island was Lydia Lacus. She and Fiscal Lacus were both quartered in the poshouse. Peter prepared his children's room for the two highly ranked exiles. He thought: If I do the Company this favour, it may be grateful to me. Eva refused to cook for them. The prisoners' cook had to prepare and cook the meals for Lacus and his wife, twice a day. It wasn't that Lydia did not want to cook, but she was a child of barely sixteen with a baby on the hip, and as housewife of the honourable fiscal it had never before been necessary for her to put her hands in cold water; for that they'd had two slaves, a man and a woman, from the Company.

For how long they'd be burdened with the Lacus family, Peter didn't know, because it depended on the fiscal's conscience. This man, appointed to balance the Company's books, had found ways to falsify them and to transfer the profit to his own pocket. Surely the young Lydia was innocent. Or was she? Peter, smiling in his bed at midnight, imagined a charming little ship on shining water, driven by light, fragrant little breezes, all frilly curtains and canopies and in full daylight, a multitude of little golden stars in the sky, surrounded by swallows circling around the masts. On the stern the loveliest little woman would be standing, delicately groomed and clothed, holding her dainty hands out to a poor sod, possibly her husband, stumbling after them through the water to catch up with her, his flat writing case under his arm. Sweat was shining on his brow, as the Bible would have it, but already he was too exhausted, his feet were sinking into the water and the wind was blowing more strongly, and he knew he would never catch up with the little ship. All the effort, the care, the haste, the early rising, all of it for the comfort and pleasure of the cherished little lady and her bored little children on the ornate little ship. For whose sake had Lacus stolen?

The quartermaster had whispered to Peter that a male and a female slave had testified how Lydia had pleaded with her husband to confess, swearing that if he didn't do it she would testify against him, but he wouldn't. Lacus had pleaded with her, she had persisted. The slaves had gone to investigate when they'd heard her screaming in the room. Lacus was beating her, on the arms, on the chest, in the face, and then he shoved her over a chair and a small table. Both of them smashed.

It left Peter cold with fear. How hopelessly scared would a man have to be to beat his wife? For without hope, what life was there? And what would happen to you afterwards, how would you redeem yourself, how could you repair the damage done to yourself? What would you say to your child one day, if he asked why his mother had left? You'll just have to bear it, Peter Havgard, he decided, bear it to the end.

At night he and Eva could hear the two of them quarrelling behind the wooden wall. One day Lydia brought him a note, asking the commander to save her from the cold, the bitter water, the undeserved punishment. The answer, two weeks later, was a burlap bag with blankets. But in due course she and her child were taken away after all.

Peter was bitterly unhappy. There were many convicts, much work. Except for the little girl, his own life was worthless, lifeless, hopeless. Eva was pining away, and regularly communicated it to him with a complaint, a groan, a look. She missed the bustling and colourful life at the Fort, as she had known it in her youth, the jovial laughter of cooks and their assistants in the warm, cosy kitchen, the crude remarks and glances of the soldiers, the proximity of the man who had the top authority, and her games with his children. Here on the island there was nobody who could ask her questions, or with whom she could talk about the Koina in her own language. Sometimes she cried on the bed in their room, while he yearned for long marches through an undiscovered landscape.

When springtime came and the long blue days drew the imagination to expeditions, Commander van Quaelberg summoned Peter. The commander was at the ark, the guard on the quay showed Peter the way. Behind the Fort a large limestone kiln was burning on the beach, and behind its billowing, stinking smoke, walls of another heavy stone structure could be seen. An ox wagon loaded with firewood was pulled in next to the kiln. Once again Peter was amazed by the massive, mighty new castle. That was where all the labour, the shells and slate from Robben Island went to. Workers with wheelbarrows, and masons on scaffolding moved over the stone walls; only the tarpaulin roof of the ark was now visible behind them. He stopped to watch the busy scene. Commander van Quaelberg, with plumed hat, knee-boots and sword, like a major on a battlefield, approached over the molehills from the building site.

'Ah, Meerhof, old chap. Come inside.'

They went through the main gate, across the courtyard and with the staircase up to the Kat. The old thatched roofs of the Fort had also been replaced with red tiles, and some of the most important window frames had been glazed.

'Well, Meerhof, old chap, I see you're having a look. Is it long since you've been here? Building everywhere now, the Company is building, the burghers are building. There's a good tavern at the back here, if you feel like washing down the lime dust. The hostess is Barbertje Geens. Dear woman, husband is a damned good-for-nothing. Ah, you know her?'

In the big hall where he and Eva had been married, the furniture was arranged exactly as it had been before, but the animal skins were gone. There were painted pictures in frames on the walls, and a woven carpet.

'Looking for something?'

'There used to be a big lion's skin, from my friend Piet Roman.'

'Ah, I had that sent abroad, old chap. They're very keen on such things.'

The commander invited Peter to sit opposite his desk. On his fingers he counted off the new buildings from one side of the town to the other, those of the Company, those of the burghers. Each building required so many loads of shell lime, so many loads of sand for clay, so many loads of fuel, so many loads of timber, so many loads of slate, so many loads of granite. And within ten years these numbers would double, as the Cape had to be safeguarded against the goddamned greedy Redcoats.

It's all about draught oxen, thought Peter. He wants to send me on a bartering expedition.

'It's about slaves, old chap. I want you to go to the East for us.'

'The East, Your Honour?' What would Eva say? What was he going to say to her?

'Ah, geographically, yes. But East Africa. It's an extensive journey, old chap. And we have a shortage of medical chaps. I must have a responsible man, and there are foreign diseases in those parts. So this is what I was thinking: I put a good military chap on the island, then you're free for the expedition. The clerk looked at the books, and he tells me you're the last of the old pioneers, so to speak. Others have died or are in poor health, or have left the country. Happens to the best of us, you hear, but you already know that, old chap. Now I want to offer you the position. And it will undoubtedly lead to further promotion.'

'May I think about it, sir? I must discuss it with my wife.'

'Ah, of course, the little wife.' The commander offered more details. They would be away for four, five months at the utmost. An interpreter would accompany them, a black from Madagascar who knew all the kings there and their languages. The ship would first go to Mauritius to deliver supplies for the new settlement, and on the way back stop over at Madagascar and East Africa, to purchase a full load of slaves for the Cape. The captain would receive an amount in gold coins, and had to bargain for the best prices.

Peter spent the night in his old room in the hospital. He wouldn't go to greet Barbara Geens. Or should he? She was married; he had to bed down with Eva in his thoughts. Once again the commander hadn't said a word about *beriberi*. How would he now explain to Eva that Mauritius was halfway to the East, and that this was perhaps his last chance of achieving something, anything?

It was difficult. The first two days back on the island he couldn't say anything because he was afraid of her reaction. Then he mentioned the possibility of promotion. Van Quaelberg wanted to use him for something different, he had to think about it, the extra money would come in useful, with three children in the house. Her resistance against his escape, like a small fire flickering between life and death, was slow to start.

'How long this time?'

'Less than three months.'

'Why must you go, Pieter?'

'Well, to find workers for the Castle.'

'No, why you and not somebody else? Why you?'

'I'm the last of the travellers.'

'What does a thing like that mean?'

'There's a mountain that bears my name.'

'Why you?' she insisted. 'I don't want to know about a mountain. Why you?'

He spoke to her about the children. Here at the Cape it was difficult to offer a child an education, and they really needed it. Van Riebeeck himself had had to send his two little boys to Holland, and probably would never see them again. Yes, the two boys she used to *abba* when she brought them up, he could see that she remembered them. In the East it was so much better. If they were transferred to one of the big stations in the East, it would solve all their problems. There the Company provided schools for its children. This was an opportunity for them all to get somewhere.

'A chance for you to waste your time again.'

'Eva.'

'You have another woman.'

'You know that is a barefaced lie.'

'For me to sit here while you go about with your friends? The sea is your whore.'

'Eva, I've been wanting to see something of the tropics all my life.'

'I tell you, Pieter, I'm not going to your East. I'm staying here.'

'We can come back again.'

'I'm not going. If you leave me here, I'll take my children to my people.'

'No.'

'I'm telling you. Why are you so besotted with your East?'

'Please, Eva.'

She stood facing the hearth and spoke with her back to him. 'I'm telling you. I'm not staying here, I'm going to my sister, and to Oedasoa. They always said I must come to them if you started messing around.'

'Messing. Do you even know what you're saying? And they're both dead anyway, both of them.'

'You're lying. You're lying, you hear.' She swung round and struck him a vicious blow across the cheek with a stick of firewood. 'Go away. Go to your whore.'

He thought: *Never again*. The words were as clear in his mind as if he'd spoken them aloud. And he struck her as hard as he could with his open hand on the side of her face, sending her staggering back several paces, stumbling over a bench and falling with the back of her head against a railing of the loft stairs, from where she slid down to the floor. He heard something break. It could have been his heart, it could have been her skull, it could have been the railing. He stood over her, panting. A pool of blood, glistening red, warm and liquid, was forming on the floor under her head, and seeping into the dry clay between the stones, until nothing but a dark stain remained. Then the heat faded out of him, and he was left dismayed with grief. What have you done to yourself, Peter Havgard? What have you done to me, Eva?

The children did not wake up. She'd lost consciousness by the time he picked her up. He shaved the back of her head, stitched up the cut down to the bone and bandaged it. After that he laid her on their bed, and cleaned the floor and the loft stairs. Her eyelids were shut, she was breathing jerkily and her body was limp. He called her name and lightly slapped her cheeks. He burned feathers under her nose, and dripped sal volatile into her mouth to bring her round, and afterwards undressed her and covered her, and kneeled beside the bed and prayed. The prayer became an accusation: See here what Eva has done to us.

Peter didn't sleep. He diagnosed a cracked skull and concussion and treated her for it, but then wanted a second opinion. In the morning the shell boat took his urgent letter to the mainland, and that evening the two surgeons and the fiscal were there to examine his wife. She was still unconscious. At the kitchen table around bottle and glasses they agreed that she'd stumbled over the bench and hurt her head against the railing of the staircase, resulting in a cracked skull and concussion. That was their report.

Only on the third day did she come to. She remembered everything, but it was as if she still didn't realise how much he needed to see Mauritius. He did not want to discuss the matter with her any further; he packed his sea chest and prepared the Company's medicine chest, and sent a letter to Bart Borms in which he entrusted to him and Theuntje the care of his children in case something happened to him and Eva, if the authorities approved. He had to go abroad without delay, and Bart had to bring the slave as soon as he could.

Bart brought the slave and a bagful of live lobsters, and promised to register the sale of the slave at the Fort. That set Peter's mind more at ease, Eva could not complain about fuel and water. The slave was an elderly man from West Africa, a friendly, grey-haired, smiling fellow. He was a fisherman, but also an able carpenter. His Dutch name was Jan Vos. His forearms, up to his elbows, were brine-bleached. He built himself a room at the back of the post house on the island.

A week later the quartermaster brought Peter an official letter, to prepare for departure. His replacement waited behind the quarter-master with a bag of clothes and a musket in his hand. It was Corporal Callenbach, formerly the postkeeper at Keert-de-Koe.

'When must I leave, corporal?'

'When the boat goes back.'

'Well. If it must be so, then.'

'That's good. I'll take a look around the island in the meantime. Can you show me a place to sleep?'

The soldier stood his bag just inside the kitchen door and introduced himself to Eva. She was sitting at their kitchen table, but did not look at the man.

'I have to go to shore now, Eva,' said Peter. 'They are ready to sail.'

She sank with her forearms on the table like a sailor at a bar counter, in her face a dazed expression as if she couldn't focus her two eyes.

'Hans Michiel is being billeted here, Eva. You don't have to do anything for him. Neither cooking nor washing. He has his own pan and bedding. He gets rations and will want a turn at the hearth.'

'Where does he sleep?'

He was sure she knew what she was saying. He felt humiliated.

'You decide.'

Coming and going, coming and going, and all because of the sea. He and the corporal went to supervise the emptying of the shell sloop, the prisoners carrying the blue slate and the canvas bags full of crushed shells on their shoulders down to the boat. His children were there. When he walked back to the posthouse he had a child on each arm.

'Eva, goodbye.'

He hadn't thought that she would cry. 'I'm sick, Pieter. I must go to the land. Take us with you.'

'Where can you live? You know we don't know anybody there.'

'Then take the children. Something will happen to them here.'

'Eva, they're waiting for me. Look, if you need anything, ask Hans.'

'I don't want him here,' she screamed, and grabbed his clothes in front of his chest in her hands as if she wanted to tear them from him. 'You're the Company's whore.' Screaming and cursing she hit at him. 'Get away from me. Get out of my life. Go to your whore!'

The ship *Westwoud* was a run-down flute from Enkhuijzen. It lay on the outer roadstead with its head to the open sea and its stern to the Fort. Its timber was parched and decayed by the sea air, its paint faded and peeling. Its sails were down, its tarred rigging broken and worn, and the flag on its mizzen-mast was flapped to narrow shreds. Under water its hull was packed with seaweed, a small shoal of fishes was feeding in it, as on a wreck. The quartermaster went alongside because Peter wanted to have a look on board. There were five officers, about forty sailors, and a guard of fifteen soldiers to be used in the slave trade on Madagascar. Below deck everything had been fitted for slaves. Shelves, as for merchandise, ran the full length of the ship. As wide as a man's shoulders and two feet apart, attached to both sides of the hull. That was where the slaves would lie on their backs, side by side, heads to the outside and feet inside. Apart from fuel and trade goods there was no other cargo in the hold.

Commander van Quaelberg signed their *Instructie*, and Peter and the ship's captain had to hear it word for word from his mouth, while the ship's council attended in a half-circle in front of his desk. Their route was fixed, from the Cape to Mauritius. At the south-east harbour on the island they had to fire a gun outside the reef to ask for a pilot. There they had to hand over provisions and letters, and take aboard all the unslaked lime and ebony that was waiting. Since the island had no medical orderly, Master Pieter had to ply his art there if required. Thereafter they had to cross over to the bay of Antongil on the north-east coast of Madagascar, and fire guns to inform the natives that they were there to trade. The interpreter knew the king of the region, as well as a number of his minor chiefs. Five different languages were used there. They had to offer the presents the Company had sent with them. Then Peter had to ask the king for slaves in exchange for linen, rope, nails, drink, tobacco, mirrors and gold coins.

The slaves would be prisoners, or prisoners of war, men, women and children. They had to be young, healthy and strong. Peter was to keep a record of every slave: name, sex, age, height, weight, state of health, price. He had to examine each of them in the presence of the ship's surgeon. No contagious diseases should be brought on board. The slaves had to be treated in a friendly manner, and they had to protect the women against men, white and black. That, too, was Peter's responsibility. There were rules about diet, exercise, illness, death, supervision, punishment. All those concerned were to bear in mind that the Company had acquired this property at great cost and much trouble, and that they had to be brought to market in the best condition.

For Peter the sea voyage was a pleasure, like his long overland journeys in the past. A light bout of seasickness during the first few days did not bother him, and once he was used to the motion of the ship, he went on deck and found that he was caught in the spell of the wide empty sea, just as by the land. Between sky and water was their ship,

and apart from the ship, nothing. He forgot about the Cape, and everything he'd left behind. They could not reach him, not even his little
daughter, and he could not reach her, even if he wanted to. His whole
life was here and now. Sometimes his daughter's face appeared in his
imagination, to change everything he'd persuaded himself to believe
into a lie.

Peter's first sight of the East were mountain peaks covered in clouds.
Mauritius Island gradually rose above the clouded horizon, like a grey-
green castle. How was it possible that there could be earth here in this
bottomless ocean? The island came as something quite unexpected,
after so many weeks at sea. The balmy nights, blue-green sea and strange
mountains enchanted him. Their stay was like a month in paradise.

And then, Madagascar. They sailed straight for Antongil Bay. Once
the first bartering with the chief had been done, without any mishap,
the ship's captain demanded that his sailors be allowed with the women.
He argued that it was an old concession that existed all over the world
and something that his men rightfully counted on.

'It says nothing about it here,' said Peter, taking out his *Instructie*.
'The commander said that the women had to be protected.'

'Of course. The commander is a decent man.'

'I refuse. I will not allow it.'

'Master, they're counting on it.'

'Captain, I forbid it.'

'They won't listen to you, master.'

The English disease, the disease of Venus, that was what was on his
mind when one afternoon he stood with four soldiers on the bone-
white shore of Antongil Bay, watching two boats with women and children moving off from the beach to where their ship lay at anchor in the
middle of the deep blue bay. Sky and water were the same colour, which
made it seem as if the ship was floating free in the air. He could hear
the screams and the boisterous laughter as the sailors grabbed at the
women and tore the clothes from them. He could see the ship rolling
from side to side from the wrestling. The soldiers on the beach with
him laughed and shouted encouraging remarks over the water. He had
to go back to the ship on his own, he thought, it was necessary to restore

order on board; he could not stay on land to barter if the captain shirked his duty with the supervision. He had spent a whole morning negoti- ating with the so-called king over here for some slave women, and had obtained these sixteen women at a very reasonable price. They were war booty, from the enemy just behind the ridge. The king had mentioned their original tribal name: the Red Coxcombs. They'd also shown him heads of the enemy, in the forks of trees surrounding his yard, with dark red feathers in the hair. The women had been hunted for his young men the previous year, but these sixteen had not yet borne children.

His two rowing boats penetrated deeper into the blue bay, and the noise in a foreign language wafted across the water. Some of the sailors appeared to be standing upright in the boat, looking at him, pointing. In all of nature, over the sea, in the air, came a motionless silence. All along the sides of the bay which tried to embrace the floating ship like two long arms reaching out, dark green palm trees stood bent over the narrow beach, as always in his dreams, but without this fear, this sudden cold that had come over him.

He was beaten down from behind and stabbed to death with twelve, twenty assegais. The triumphant spearmen pulled white feathers from their hair, dabbed them in warm blood and rearranged them in a line over their heads. Afterwards they dragged the bodies of the white people across the sand to the bushes.

It was late in the year 1667.

3

THE FISHERMAN

And the sea became blood; and the creatures which were in the sea
died, and the ships were destroyed
– The Revelation of St John VIII: 8–9.

BARTHOLOMEUS BORMS WAS floating in the limitless ocean north-east of
Mauritius. Alone. Today he was marrying the widow with the endless
womb, as Jack Tar says when a sailor drowns. On his forearm a blue
anchor was tattooed and under his feet was bottomless water. Limitless,
bottomless, it is the same. A skipper from his youth had once tied
together three deep-sea lines and all his finger-thick rope to plumb those
depths, but it was a place of which to this day the maps say: *No bottom.*

As usual after a storm, the sky was empty and blue, and the wide
sea lukewarm. His chest close, Bart gasped as he saw that day rise.
Daybreak, but not for him. He feared dying in this empty, almost
motionless ocean under the vacant sky. He had never been afraid of
seawater before. At seven, his father put the tiller in his hand. 'Stay in
the deep.' Just like that: 'Stay in the deep.' And he loved swimming,
which was something Dutch sailors tried to avoid, but the days of his
youth in the shallow bays of the East made him love the caress of water.
He feared drowning, that most painful death of all, and the terror of
sharks. This ocean, as always after a shipwreck, was teeming with sharks.
And he was tired of staying awake, afraid that the thong of the bamboo
tube that supported him might stretch and slip from him as he slept.
He was tired of holding on, of keeping watch. He knew that a man,
like rope, came to an end, and he was scared of dying. He was too
young to perish. What he felt was, his body was still too good and his
soul too bad. That was his second day of drifting.

There was no place to hide his face from the sun. Tired, suffering from salt water on sunburn, revolted by the bitter brine in his mouth, afraid of the last slow minutes of drowning, already his mind had left him from time to time. Once he imagined hearing voices in this soulless, empty ocean. In Batavia, on the square in front of the town hall where the gallows of justice stood planted, a pirate had been beheaded thirteen days before their fleet set sail. There had been a thousand witnesses. His Excellency the governor-general was there, with most of his councillors, the fiscal, the officer of the guard, a guard of sixty pikemen, a thousand citizens, Dutch, Javanese, Chinese, Indians, mestizos, freemen, slaves, from all faiths under the Eastern sun. Wasn't that enough? They could bear witness of how the bearded head had jumped from the block over the basket, rolled forward three or four yards, and stopped with the face turned towards the square. How much light, how much sight was there in the moment after you'd died? Bart wondered in the ocean as he drifted, that morning of his second day.

People had stood five-deep around the scaffold on that gallows square, pebbly and trodden to dust among the small *Kanari* trees on three sides and the stately city hall on the fourth. 'What am I seeing?' the head had asked, its voice a strange, high bleating. 'Ships. Ships.' There were no ships, for to the west were the blue-grey inland mountains. On the platform the body lay racked with spasms, spouting blood. 'It's ships sinking,' said the head on the ground. 'They're all perishing.'

In dismay the people groaned and keened, fleeing from the square. It was a terrifying thing that on the town square a man's head should lie and speak with the voice of a goat. They ran to the beach or to the city gate, their feet trampling up hot dust among the trees. Only the executioner's henchmen remained, the brutes used to meting out death in that place, and others who respected neither man nor devil. It was they who spread the tale, of how the head complained that it was cold, upon which one of the executioner's henchmen, the fool, went to pull a tarpaulin over the body on the scaffold. And how one of them tipped a basket over the head, and how it sounded as if the head was sobbing inside. When at last they dared to look, the hair and beard had turned grey as ashes.

All night long the town was filled with fear. From the Chinese *kampong* came the rattling of crackers, and in their quarters the Indians sounded a huge gong. The Town Guard was called out in strength, the High Council convened in secret, boatmen were rounded up, preachers were summoned for advice, the night watch was ordered to keep canals and streets empty until sunrise. Sailors who'd spent that night on deck examined the constellations of the stars and listened for distant earthquakes that might send tidal waves into the bay, but the stifling tail-end of the night was black and still, with nothing but flickering lights reflected in the dead water, the distant sounds of the town and the hiss of the sea, and the foaming multitude of stars overhead. In the early hours a fire was discovered in a thatched roof at the orphanage. That was the only alarm.

Ships, storm-tossed ships, started appearing in dreams that day. They were in the dreams of Bart Borms, and His Excellency Governor-General Johan Maetsuyker. On the seventh night before the fleet's departure Maetsuyker had a ghastly omen. He was alone in his room on the top floor, his windows were covered with gauze, there was a soldier on guard at his door, and in the room opposite the passage the Javanese servant of the top floor — that was how she was referred to in the house — slept. Her task was to respond whenever the master called her. He might want tea, a clerk, a chamber pot, whatever he felt like, but his bodyguard never left that door. That night it was just at the first crowing of the cocks that the soldier heard him talking behind his bedroom door. His Excellency is talking in his sleep, he thought. But then, a second voice. He started. Had he dozed off at his post, and had someone come past? But no, he had not fallen asleep. He counted the notches on the watch candle, and checked the figure in his book. He hadn't slept for a moment. He quickly crossed the passage and woke the woman on her *katil*.

'Who is in there with His Excellency?'

Together they huddled at the door to listen. There was a second voice. The lord was in conversation with somebody. The soldier knocked and immediately pushed the door open. A hiss of air from the warm room caused the candle flame to bend outward. The woman was the first to look. Maetsuyker was lying on his back on his four-poster; his hands were crossed on his chest, the sheet was drawn over his face.

The woman of the top floor uncovered his face to place her hand on his forehead. Then the governor-general opened his eyes.

'Yes?'

'My Lord was talking.'

'Yes.' He was calm. He looked the woman straight in the eyes. 'Aernout has just been here. They're perishing on the open sea. His ship has already gone down.'

'Is there anything we can do, My Lord?' asked the soldier, his candle raised high to keep the ugly shadows from the old man's face.

'No. They're past helping.' He straightened his gown and swung his legs from the bed. 'Call the clerk.'

'I dreamed I saw Admiral de Vlamingh standing on the water,' he recounted while the sleepy clerk sat scribbling at the side table. 'It was as clear as I see the three of you here now. He was beckoning with his hand. "Farewell, Johan," he called. "Wait, Aernout. What are you saying?" I asked. "We're sinking," he answered. "What are you talking about, what is going on?" I shouted, because it seemed as if he was sinking deeper into the water. "We're lost, Johan. A hurricane has sunk four of the seven ships." I couldn't understand it, because his fleet is only due to depart in seven days. I could see Aernout smiling as he waved for one last time. "There is no hope. Pray for our souls."'

After Maetsuyker had finished, the clerk read his words out to him. Maetsuyker took the pen from him and signed his name at the bottom, the clerk and the soldier signed as witnesses, and the woman of the top floor added her mark. The clerk folded the document and sealed it.

'In the strong room,' said His Excellency. 'And, on your lives, don't breathe a word to Aernout.' He reclined in the easy chair in front of the window which overlooked the anchorage, his forehead resting on his hand. The woman left to fetch him some tea. The soldier closed the door and resumed his guard. When his relief arrived he went to the officer on duty to report what had happened.

Bart Borms rested his weary head against the bamboo tube. God, how he wished he could sleep, but he was scared of strange dreams. Drink seawater and die, said Jack Tar. Yesterday the sea had tasted of coffee. Yesterday morning they'd lost their mainmast overboard after a night of wind such as he'd never in his life known to be possible. At sunset the previous evening – only there was no sun to be seen – the seven ships had still been together.

Since the afternoon a warm wind from the north-east had been blowing up a haze across the sea, and before sundown the admiral signalled the fleet to shorten sails, to show that they would be drifting down through the night, and to try to stay together. On all the ships sails were taken in and secured. Lanterns were strung up in the shrouds. Before it was quite dark the storm pounced like a tiger. All of a sudden the sky lost its stars. The ships had turned their heads to the north-east, in the direction from which they'd come, weighted down by the weather. The wind was coming from all over the compass; it felt as if it was pressing down on them from above. The officers brought their faces close together, shouting, 'Hurricane . . . bring in the sails, tie them up . . . send down the topmasts!'

Against the raging of the wind they drew in the sails and strapped them down, and before they'd finished the wind had begun to work loose the first ones. Then the ship's head dived down so deep that every time the bowsprit came smacking down on the water. White water came flying across the ship, and with every new shower they were up to the ankles and knees in seawater that went spewing out through the scuppers. One watch was below, there was nothing more they could do on deck. And as the wind grew heavier, moving more swiftly across the sea, it was as if the whole ocean was flattened by the force of the wind, so that there was much less of a swell, but the foam and water came flying like hail. Then all hands had to return to the deck to lower what had broken down, and secure what was left. For five, six hours they were driven back like that, head turned into the wind, with mostly all three watches on deck and four men at the helm; then the mainmast snapped at head-height above the deck, breaking its chains from the channels on the portside, toppling over with a heavy rumble and dragging with it shrouds and braces, and fell in a great splash on the starboard side into the sea. The ship reared up briefly, relieved of its mast, and continued to stagger back for another hour or two, still joined to its dragging deadweight, backing away before the wind. Outside, the mast, trailing its heavy load of yards and stays, continued to thunder against the hull as if a thousand soldiers were hammering a battering ram against the gates of a castle. The watch on deck went outboard in the rain to cut the wreckage loose. The rest of the crew was divided into groups to pump; there was already deep, deep water in the hold. They were only too relieved to have something to do, toiling away in the booming dark to help keep the black hurricane out of their souls. They hung on to their four pumps, taking turns, pumping and pumping, hour after hour to stay afloat, pumping and pumping, until black mud, thick with pepper, came spouting from the pumps. Soon, the pumps were clogged with pepper and coffee. And then they all had to hoist up the pumps to clear the blockage, and reassemble them, and then continue to labour at the pump handles, hour after hour.

About midnight there was an hour of less violent wind. It was the eye of the storm , they said; after this it would be coming from the opposite direction, worse than before. On deck it was quite clear how much the wind had abated, because the swell was again building up on all sides. Steep, shimmering black waves came hurtling towards them from the north-east, out of the dark, raising the bow, rolling it, suddenly dropping it. Then came the next mountain of pitch-black water, a full fathom of it washing over the prow. Now they again clambered over the gunwale and, secured with ropes around their bodies, began to hack and cut and saw at the tangle of rope and timber in the dark, while that mast kept on thundering against the hull like a huge hammer. Out there in the dark they were swept off their feet, off their precarious footholds. Some of them slid overboard, some of the others managed to crawl back over the dragging mast and matted cordage, to resume hacking in the dark at the thick ropes of their wreck.

When the watch below arrived in the hold to clear the pumps a second time, the water down there was hip-deep. Pepper and coffee were washing in a brown crust through the partitions on to the orlop

deck. Passengers, the families of lords returning home, were screaming in piercing voices, slipping in the thin gruel of seawater and coffee,
falling, grabbing at each other for help, then screaming at each other
again. Where the stump of the mainmast stood in the hold, a massive
knee had been torn from under the deck. Behind it the inner skin of
the ship bulged inwards under the heavy hammering of the mast against
the hull, and when the wind swung round to the south-west, pushing
the ship on to its other side, the hull was torn open, letting in the
sea. The sailors in the hold abandoned the pumps and leaped to the
ladders.

'Save yourselves!' shouted the boatswain. Bart stumbled through
knee-deep water on the orlop, over bales and boxes. With the rolling
of the sinking ship he was flung from side to side. Sometimes he staggered with difficulty up the steeply inclining deck, then he would be
scuttling and slipping downwards again. He groped to find a hold,
forging forward, past others who were fleeing backwards, screaming,
staring fixedly. In the forecastle messmates were milling like a flock of
wet and bewildered sheep in front of a gate. They were speechless,
unable to recognise one another, pulling open chests and throwing out
clothes, tying tarred bags around their bodies. Somebody pressed his
hands in a gesture of farewell. Two quartermasters attacked one another
with knives. All Bart could do was to hook his bamboo quiver half
filled with brandy over his shoulder, detach himself from the terrifying confusion, and make his way up to the deck, shivering into the
storm. He wasn't cold, it was shock and fear that shook him. Now it's
you and your Creator, *sapitahu*.

Beneath them the toppled ship was sinking rapidly starboard, the
white-painted tip of the foreyard almost touching the storming waves.
And every time the hull rose more slowly and more ponderously from
the water. Behind the rail around the waist at the foremast Bart held
on with a dozen others, up to their waists in milling coffee water, and
floating loose from the deck with the next wave. The entire well, from
foremast to mizzen, was full of floating human heads.

'She's going!' someone shouted. All of them together were lifted to
the peak of the next roller, from where Bart saw the glimmer of the

ship's lantern disappearing under water. Then they swiftly fell away into a hollow behind the brown shadow of the wreck. He did not see the ship again.

Alone, and floating in calm water, he saw, many hours later, the night turning into day, the light rising in a red glare from the ocean. The sunrise stippled with gold the calm, pale green sea. There were no ships, no survivors, no wreckage, no land to be seen. Daybreak, yes, but not for him. Through the dawn the sea gradually grew smooth, until there was no ripple left on the surface, and the sky was reflected just as blue in the water in front of his face. A wide brown lane like a muddy road stretched into the distance where it disappeared. Was there an island close by? The sea creates islands, and undoes them, but there was nothing and no one beside himself here.

For the first hour of daylight he floated gasping for breath, until he overcame his fear and relaxed his muscles. He wouldn't sink, though he might die of sunburn or thirst. People said that bamboo could drift right round the globe. He had to take care not to lose consciousness or go mad, there were still six other ships in the vicinity. There had been a woman washed into the sea at the last great flood, and fortunately she'd been found again, a single dark speck in a sea of yellow mud, kept afloat for twelve days by the bloated corpse of her child. There was a standing order to all skippers to turn back after a storm and conduct a search for a full day, before trying to regroup and resuming their journey. Later that morning Bart was wondering which other ships might have escaped. Even if there had been only one or two, they would be coming back the next morning to search in this place where the coffee was rising to the surface. Were there other people on their own in the water?

All day long Bart floated in the middle of the ocean. From time to time he would turn on his back, raise the quiver to his mouth and swallow some brandy. People used to say to him, 'Brandy will be the death of you.' By late afternoon the brandy was finished, and after that there were only the bitter taste of seawater, a burning thirst and his empty stomach. He kept his back to the sun, which by this time was reflected fiercely by the sea again, and he no longer thought about time. What would become of him? He was still drifting on the open sea. And so the sun went down over him.

In the night he heard sounds. The stars were bright and the swell low and even, but he could hear the howling of a storm, sails flapping, the tearing and crashing of breaking wood, the booming of a cannon rolling across the deck, screams of women, the spattering of flying spray against the hull. The air was filled with voices; he could hear snatches of sentences, exclamations. Those were sinking ships. I've gone mad, he thought, it was yesterday when this happened. Let me die, God. Do not let me wake up again. And in his head a clear voice said, 'Drink seawater and die.'

Before daybreak he was awakened by cramps. The cramps were pulling his calf muscles into hard, painful knots. He stretched his legs, swimming only with his arms. His limbs slackened for only a brief while, then he felt the cramp starting up in his calves again; it was becoming more and more difficult to relax the muscles. That was how the end began, with cramps like aching knots. Once his body was contorted into a bundle he would have to sink. And now he had to get out of this water or it would be all over. Frightened, he looked about him, turning round a second time. 'I'm still alive, God.' He was talking aloud to himself. 'Take a look below, I'm still here.'

He turned himself on to his back, and when he slowly stretched his legs the cramps in his calf eased slightly. That was a mercy. 'God,' he said, 'I don't want to stop drinking right now, but I'll immediately give up whoring and stealing and cursing and lying. From this moment I shall stop cursing. There's nothing else I can promise just now.' A little while later he changed his mind and said, without any idea of what he was saying, 'It will be good for me.' His body was too dead by now to regret these necessary promises, about taking his leave of soft brown Oriental girls. What did that matter in the middle of the sea?

He knew that miracles happened. He'd seen it with his own eyes. On the Company's galliot in Saldanha Bay, during the time van Riebeeck was in charge there, he'd seen a Bible containing the key of a sea chest, turn over in front of the eyes of twelve mates gathered there, when a certain name was spoken. How could he doubt, how could he, if that display had been meant for him? Behind him he could hear the sounds of swimming, and when he turned his face to look, there was a large gathering of people behind him in the water. Witnesses, yes. All the faces were turned towards him as they passed two oar-lengths away from him. There was resentment and hatred in their faces.

Look again, what do you see? Bart stared, incredulous. It was a large rowing boat, protruding barely two fingers above the water, which was why it looked as if the people were sitting waist-deep in water. And there were two or three people dragging behind. How could the boat stay afloat with so many people? He raised an arm, croaking with difficulty, 'Hoy, people of God!' They glided past in silence, removed from hope and charity. Right at the back, next to the helmsman, an old preacher was seated, wearing a white bib on his chest. Bart waved his arm, crowing hoarsely in despair as he saw them going past, trying with his cramping arms to swim towards them. 'I am Bart Borms. For God's sake, save me. Bart Borms from Woerden.'

The helmsman got up, stared at him, and shouted at his oarsmen, 'Hold water.' Then he leaned over the gunwale and stared into Bart's face. 'True as God,' he said. 'I've always been expecting to find you, you godforsaken scum. Now I've got you by the balls.' He called back over his shoulder, 'Back water, five strokes. We're picking up this piece of dung.' With the oars in the water the boat approached until it was right beside him. Relieved, Bart grabbed at a dragging rope. 'Thank you, mates.'

The helmsman leaned over him. 'You owe me a hogshead of brandy, you turd.'

'Aye, sir,' Bart gasped. 'Every drop.'

'Come, your hand. But this is the last.' As Bart heaved his chest over the gunwale, it immediately dipped under water, causing the sea to pour in smooth and shiny on either side of him. There were loud curses. 'We're sinking!' And a chorus of voices complained: 'Push him away. Row, row. Push his head under. Enough is enough, the wind may come up soon.' Without delay oars were splashing in the water. The man at the helm lifted the tiller from the rudderhead and swung blows left and right. 'Keep your order. I'm the captain here. This man was saved by Providence, how can we push his head under now?' He helped Bart on board by his collar. 'He owes me a barrel of brandy, and if he drowns it's all lost.'

But the people were angry. 'We took a vote: not another man on board, captain. We took a holy oath. We said it would be eighty-three, not a single one more. Why were the other twenty-three murdered? We took a decision, and we drew lots. The Almighty won't forgive us now.'

The helmsman threatened them again, and asked for silence, while Bart lay dazed and puking at his feet. 'Seamen. Brothers. Give me a chance. I don't want to taunt the Almighty. We said eighty-three, and my conscience forces me to abide with it. We did the right thing by putting others overboard, because it's better for a few to die in order to let many others live. Eighty-three. But Bart is a man of worth. There are others here who may go.'

The bent old minister next to him came to his feet. 'No. Thou shalt not kill. No more murders.'

'Sit down, fool. You're rocking us.' He shook the tiller in the pastor's face. 'Look out, *dominee*. Your two children here are not worth one man. They can make room for a good sailor. If you love them, then keep your mouth shut today.'

'Satan. Child of the Devil.' For that the pastor received a blow from a fist on his mouth, before someone plucked him down on his seat. The helmsman pointed forward with his tiller. 'Throw out the black.'

A powerful young Moor tried to get up in the bow, but his legs were grabbed on the spot, then his thrashing arms were tightly clasped. His eyes were rolling white, he threw his body this way and that as he shouted in a foreign language, but he was thrust from hand to hand to the gunwale and suddenly pushed into the void.

'Father, have mercy on his soul,' the helmsman said.

The Moor's head shot up beside the boat like a cork, his mouth wide open, gasping for breath. He grabbed the gunwale with two hands and threw a leg over it to clamber back. A blow from an axe split open his shin below the knee. One sailor fell on his knees to sink his teeth into the black man's fingers clutching the gunwale. His other hand was hammered and hammered with a belaying pin until his grasp let go by itself and he fell back in a cloud of blood as he sank beside the boat.

'Pull together, haul, haul,' shouted the helmsman. 'Pull together, haul, haul!'

In their shiny, smooth wake twenty paces behind the boat the Moor's head reappeared. Then he started swimming after them. They could see that he was an exceptionally strong swimmer.

'Pull together, haul, haul.' He seemed to be gaining on them. On the crammed thwarts the four rowers barely had space to move their oars, but more hands reached over to help them. Loudly and rhythmically the helmsman set the stroke, the rowers moved faster, and slowly the swimmer fell behind. Against the sinking sun they could still see the sparkling splashes of his swinging arms leaping up from the water.

The boat drifted for days. They were in a slow current which carried them to the south-west. It was *Aernhem*'s boat, its captain had personally taken the helm. They'd set out with a hundred and eight souls, but soon saw it was too many. No one could move, or the boat would fill with water and sink. The load had to be lessened to gain an inch or two of freeboard. It was thanks to the man at the helm, their captain, that they were still alive.

They drifted for days. Drink will be your downfall one day, Borms, they said. These proverbs were risible. Because he owed a man brandy, he survived. Because of that alone. But they could all die of thirst. Early in the morning, before the first heat, they licked the dew from the gunwales and the oars, and lay panting without shade in the daytime, while the sun, like a spider, sucked the moisture from them. Those who were fortunate to feel water in their bladders, painfully passed it into a cupped hand to moisten their tongues, which were hard as wood. Hoarse voices pleaded for a few drops in the mouth.

In the boat early mornings also brought the unexpected stiffened corpses that had turned their back on life, and had to be stripped and pushed overboard. Then, every time, there was a little bit more room, and a few pieces of clothing to hold over one's head for shade. The pastor wanted to say a prayer for each, but in more than one case they did not know the dead man's name. In the first glimmer of dawn Bart would see the faces of corpses as they floated past from bow to stern. Those lying in the glimmer of the sea, as well as those stretched out cold in the boat, were all pale blue. All the faces were dark, tense, darkly bearded. When he looked around in the boat again, he would think: But they are *us*, those are *our* faces in the water. Why are those who were still speaking yesterday dead now? We are dead. And this is the hereafter: to float for ever on an empty sea, hoping for an island.

There was less and less talking on the boat. At sunrise *Dominee* van Kerkhoven would come to his feet to say a prayer, and again at sunset. At the end of the first week his young sons had to help him to his feet. Every time his movements caused the sea to slide silently into their boat. His voice became weaker, dry and hoarse, and his words fewer. 'Sit, *dominee*. Don't cause trouble. You're scaring the people.' Once he tried to explain to the captain the justice of saving one soul from the sea and immediately drown another in the same ocean. But all the captain said was: 'Be quiet, *dominee*. For God's sake.'

For nine days Bart sat on the floorboards in the overloaded, stinking boat which lay low and motionless on the flickering sea, until his buttocks were chafed through and became inflamed in the brine. He remained near the captain's feet. Between them only did a contract exist; all the others, alive and already dead, were hostile to him. One blistering afternoon someone near the pastor screamed: 'We must eat the children.' A few voices rose in protest, then it grew silent again.

Those on rowing duty could barely lift their oars any more. Had there been wind, they might have contrived a sail, but the wind brought a swell, and then there was water spilling over the gunwale. At first they were grateful that there was no wind, but as more of them were put overboard they no longer cared. Slowly the boat drifted. Where was the wind? Every day there was more room on the bottom boards, so that another one could find some space around him, or a seat on the thwart. The ulcers on Bart's buttocks were yellow and scarlet with inflammation, but of them all he would have to wait until last for a place on the bench.

One day someone snatched a small fish from the sea with his hand,

and chewing it on the belly side, sucked the moisture through the holes in the skin. Bart could hear the greedy sounds, like someone eating watermelon. Past backs and shoulders he could see the man's eyes glittering in a hairy face, and he looked away at the cool melting of sea and sky on the horizon. Who was there in that boat who did not curse the poor man? Like the others, he lay with his head on the gunwale, dizzy with thirst, when he was brought to his senses by jostling, shouting and pushing. There was a wrestling in the stern at the helm. He could hear the minister's voice pleading, and the high scream of a child. He couldn't see who was fighting, the bodies came falling over him from all sides. He saw people trying to force one another over the gunwale, blades glinting, the rocking boat shipping water. What was it about? Then a body fell into the sea. He didn't look to see who it was; he did not care. The voices, hoarse and salty, were still shouting. Forwards and backwards the fight moved over him. It didn't concern him, he pulled his legs out of the way. Another body fell into the water. He closed his eyes and turned his head away.

Early on the eleventh day after the ships had perished, they caught sight of Mauritius. 'I thank you, captain,' croaked the pastor, struggling to his feet for a prayer of thanks. The island was a series of green mountain ranges. They drifted down along the east coast, seeing the sea breaking on a reef about half a mile from the beach. The captain called a sailor to the stern. The man scooped seawater with a cupped hand to wet his tongue and throat. Together they studied the mountains.

'Those are the islands of Kroonenburg. And there's the Black Rock. I can see it, skipper. And Third Corner, there to port, in front of us. I'll take a look from the bows.' The captain ordered four oars to be put out, and to row to the land. The healthiest ones, who were able to row, were seated on the benches. The faces of the rowers were contorted with pain as the pickled raw flesh of their buttocks chafed on the wet thwarts.

'Help the rowers. On your feet, four more men.' Bart was one of those who rowed standing up, facing the bows. Slowly they proceeded towards the reef.

'East Gap ahead, skipper. Keep to port first, a current sets in here.'

Bart could see the gap, where the sea did not break on the reef; behind it the water was a pale green, and behind the bay a dark green jungle, and behind the jungle mountain peaks, with clouds above them. 'Now in.'

Inside the reef the passage was shallow and perilous with gardens of red and white coral, reaching up almost to the sunlight. The water was so clear that they could see fishes and crabs down on the bottom. The man in the bows pushed them off the coral banks with the boat-hook. Then he gestured towards the islands to port again: 'Two Sisters.' Or to the lofty, pointed peaks to starboard: 'The Cat and Mouse.' For the first time there were smiles in *Aernhem*'s boat again. High against the sky, was a cat looking down at a tiny mouse before its feet. Happiness still existed.

The rowers were changed, not without the risk of causing the boat to water. 'Second Corner. First Corner.' The sailor pointed at another gap in the reef. 'South-east Gap, captain. Hard a-starboard now.' The boat was turned to follow the coastline. Once again the rowers were changed, and slowly they proceeded, struggling through the coral heads. 'The Sadelberg. The Fort.'

And so the boat ran on to the coarse white sand of the small bay at the foot of the Sadelberg. On a higher wall of a tumbled-down battlement, from the charred ruins of the Company's deserted post Fort Fredrik Hendrik, a black dog barked at them. The sailors held on to one another to climb out of the boat, stumbled through the shallow water (how curiously unsteady was the firm earth under the feet) and headed for the shade under the trees.

'Come and secure your boat properly, you'll be needing it again tomorrow,' the captain shouted after them. But they paid no attention, until he mentioned names. Here, on the beach, there would be conflict too.

In an overgrown ditch next to the ruined Fort ran a stream of fresh water from the Sadelberg. There they drank, and the captain made them listen to what he'd decided. He had removed the boat's tiller and was using it as a walking stick. He was there, with *Seur* van Hal, and *Dominee* van Kerkhoven, Ensign Evertsz and Seaman Stokram who had piloted them in. They would form the Ship's Council while they were on the island. It was also his duty to remind them of the Company's *Artikelbrief*, which before the voyage each of them had solemnly undertaken to obey. He expected them to do their duty towards one another as Christian people, as subjects of the prince and servants of the Company. There were sick men among them, and others who appeared to be in a reasonable state. For the moment they did not know what the island would bring them, but they needed food, and as far as he was concerned, he wanted to get back to the fatherland as soon as possible. Now he was going to divide them: some who had to catch fish and stand guard over the boat, and others who had to bring palm fronds to put up shelters in the old Fort, like the ones built by Javanese fishermen, as there seemed to be a storm coming up. Then others who had to look for fuel, and others who had to find food. Before sunset they would all gather here again with what they had collected. One final thing: he demanded of every man who owned a tinderbox to hand it over now.

Bart helped to cut palm fronds, and found himself a ripe coconut in the jungle and drank the water, but the fatty white flesh revolted his stomach, and he could keep in only a small morsel. Together with his palm fronds he brought back a few coconuts every time and put them on their pile of food. That evening they made a fire inside the walls of the old Fort, and the captain had the food roasted and shared out among them. There were pigeons, and a lean dodo, two large tortoises, an octopus and lots of coconuts. Somebody had discovered the old vegetable garden, and brought some overripe pumpkins. At the fire Andries Stokram told about small deer and pigs brought here by the Company, and about how they'd made palm wine when he worked at this outpost years before. From the wine one could distil a first-class arrack. The island of Kroonenburg was like heaven for the making of palm wine. That night there was heavy thunder and lightning with torrential rain, but they lay reasonably dry in their shelters.

To survive, one needs order and food, said the captain. You had to build up supplies, and for that you needed salt. If there were people among them who knew about extracting salt from seawater the way the Company did it in Amboina, they had to come forward. He was going to send them out again for fuel and food, and those who wanted to hack palm fronds for bedding, could do so. Tonight he would explain the plan the Ship's Council had decided on. He would like to hear what they thought of it. As far as he was concerned: as he'd already said, he wanted to get home as soon as possible.

In the long grass near the old vegetable garden they found the graveyard of the previous settlement. There were headstones with chiselled names. *Renier Por, Commander, died 7 January 1653*. The fellows who'd been out hunting had cut themselves spears and hardened the tips in the fire, and that evening they returned with a pig from the forest. They found the herd tamely rooting under the trees, surrounded them, and stabbed this one to death. Some wounded ones had got away. They dined well, as they also had dodos and fish. Already the conversation turned to something to drink. The captain demanded their attention.

'Here is the plan our Ship's Council regards as being in the best interest of the Honourable Company and every one of us. Our boat is in good condition. In a week's time I shall leave in it for Madagascar. Everybody here is welcome to sail with me, and those who choose to remain behind are welcome to stay. On the day I leave they will be released from their duty towards me. All I ask is that after that they will act like Christians towards one another. You need not decide now, there is a whole week left. Think it over well. Tomorrow we'll start preparing for the voyage. I want to try and make a sail from palm fronds, like the Chinese, and cordage from grass. And we must store enough water and food to last us for a voyage of seven days. Does anyone wish to say something?'

'Why are you now in such a hurry to leave, skipper?'

'This island makes a man lazy. I've heard that from many. In the end it is nothing but Kroonenburg and palm wine and young deer. Before it contaminates us, I want to get away.'

'Then why do you allow us to choose, captain? You can command us.'

'The fewer people we take in the boat, the better our chances of survival.'

'Captain, at the time the people were put overboard, we said we'd stand together.'

'Yes. That was my decision. Wherever I get to, Batavia or the Netherlands, I shall surrender myself for trial.'

'But then we no longer stand together. I can't face a court on my own.'

'If that is how you feel, you'd better come with me.'

'What do you think, skipper? What are our chances of being rescued from here?'

'I've heard of English and French ships coming here. Our own ships do not touch here, because it isn't on our route. Chances are that you may then end up from here in India. As far as I'm concerned, I have to report to Lords Seventeen about what happened to us. If I can reach Madagascar, I may be able to find a Cape slave ship. And from the Cape there are ships to the fatherland all the time.'

'And those who stay behind? What about our wages?'

'Wages are discontinued. You'll be leaving service voluntarily. For deer, palm wine and Kroonenburg.' From those words many jokes were later made.

'To whom does this island really belong, skipper?'

'To God,' said the pastor. But the captain said, 'The Company was here for twenty years. They didn't want to stay. I believe the English and the French will be interested. At the moment it's only us and the dodos here, and a pirate from time to time.'

Their fire was burning high. The dog, that was sometimes there and sometimes absent, came to chew bones in the night.

Every evening Captain Oosterwoud spoke to them. He helped them to decide. He encouraged Stokram to tell them everything he knew about the island. About water and fuel, good places to live, fruit to eat. There was food enough, Stokram said, depending on how hungry you were. In the early morning and at dusk large bats came out to eat fruit and berries; their meat tasted sweet. Then there were dodos and tortoises, and tame animals brought by the Company, like the pigs and deer. The sea had dugong, and all manner of fish. Then there was sugar cane, which could be used for a lot of things, and coconut palms. Tomorrow he would show them to make palm wine and cut heart of palm. The island was healthy too; they could see for themselves how the condition of the sick improved every day. One could live here, it could become home to you, once you'd come to know every spot and had given each thing its proper name, as had been done before. Cats' Island, Fisherman's Isle, Lady's Hat, Orange Tree River. It could become a very good home.

Those who were inclined to stay, said so openly. Bart was one of them. But the captain asked: 'Why do you want to stay here? When I arrive in the fatherland, the directors will take out their lists, and then they will. They take the list from the top, from the chief mate down to the little cabin servant. What has become of such-and-such? they ask. That's what the Company will want to know from me. But there will also be strangers knocking on my door: So-and-so was on *Aernhem* with you, he was my brother, or my uncle, or my son. Do you know what's become of him? So, what about your family in the fatherland? Some of you are married men, now you want to be abandoned here without wages.'

Bart thought: I must talk to the captain about the hogshead of arrack, and come to an agreement, or he will take me away with him.

The captain studied them all at length. There were no leaders among them. The oldest ones were incapable, the younger ones had no support. There was not one in this group who, in his youth, would have persuaded him to stay when the last boat cast off. Yet there were only eleven who'd come to ask to leave with him and *Seur* van Hal. He was content; the fewer there were in the boat, the safer the crossing. As long as he had three, his mind was easy. One for the sail and two to bail out. Still he went from one man to the next to hear what they thought. Bart rose to talk to him.

'Bart Borms from Woerden, skipper. I've come to thank you, for my life. I've emptied your hogshead of arrack into bottles, and sold it. All my belongings went down with *Hof van Holland*. I shall enter into your service, if you wish, but I'm asking you to let me stay here first.'

'Stay if you want. The blood I've shed cannot be washed off with arrack.'

Captain Oosterwoud warned them, those who didn't know, about what had happened in 1629 with the crew of *Batavia*. How on a barren island in the South they'd split into factions and clubbed one another to death in a bloody massacre. He spoke to the pastor. What advice did he have for those who stayed behind? Pray for one another? Was that all? Those who wished to remain, he called together for the last time, and asked them to refrain from choosing leaders, but to discuss their affairs, and then to act as each thought best. Then they would stand a better chance for peace. He distributed their tinderboxes. Then they could disperse. Each one would find a group that could make fire.

The evening before the boat left, *Dominee* van Kerkhoven prayed for those going to sea, a safe journey, an arrival on Madagascar which would bring blessings to the heathens. To those who remained, he said: 'My sons and I shall stay here in the old Fort. I pray in the morning, and again at sunset. Those who wish to, will know where to find me.'

Aernhem's boat left through the South-East Gap, fourteen days after their arrival. With the captain were *Seur* van Hal and eleven others. Far across the sea they could hear a dry rustling, like the wings of an insect. The palm-frond sail was tight and drew well in the south-easter. Some of them sent a message home, others didn't.

The total freedom was something out of the ordinary. They made tentative arrangements about the use of flints and steel, about co-operating in the hunt, and on the forwarding of messages, but the sheer volume of freedom was stunning. One could come and go, walk as far as one wished, stay in bed, build oneself a hut where one wanted, leave, return, stay away till noon. Everything was fine, no one would say a word. But there were some who felt offended by the way in which others infringed on their freedom. They all hunted with spears and clubs, and made shoes of skin to wade into the sea. In the shallow bay in front of the old Fort they pushed latticed fish-traps into the sand, and in the forest they set snares for deer and snags for the dodos. That was what caused the first problems, about someone stealing another's deer from his snare, or draining another's palm wine. Two fellows wounded each other quite badly with spears over palm wine.

At the first total ebb the inner sea practically drained away. In the evening they were sitting on the beach watching the almost full moon playing hide-and-seek among black thunderclouds. Here the sea never came rolling out on the beach in waves, but merely lapped at the sand like a dog drinking water. That evening the inner water was like black glass, smooth and still as far as the reef. Andries Stokram looked over his shoulder at the spot where the sun had set, aimed at the moon and said: 'I think it may be ebbing tomorrow night.' And the next morning the inner sea was almost dry.

'I'm going to try and walk to Fisherman's Isle,' said Andries. 'We managed to do it once in the old days. The dodos get very fat there.' Nine of them, all good swimmers, followed the beach all round the bay, knee-deep through river mouths, through muddy marshes with mangrove forests, swam through the broad Orange Tree River, arriving opposite Fisherman's Isle in the late afternoon. Fuel was plentiful, and they gathered a large pile of wood on the beach for a fire to keep the crabs away from them overnight. 'This place we call the Chalk,' Andries told them. 'In the old days we built a lime kiln here, and burned these mounds of shells and coral by the bushel, for a good building lime. We constructed the walls of the Fort from the burned stones and the lime. There's enough coral here to build a town.'

They spoke about the island; how there were places where you could see from the blackened, molten rocks that the place was once a volcano. Perhaps this island would erupt again one day. There were other islands close by where sailors had seen flames in the night. They spoke about where they might one day build their town, somewhere ships could come with trading goods. Here at the Fort, at the South-East Harbour. There were other good spots, like the North-West Harbour, but the English liked that place, and that would mean trouble with them every time war broke out. Black River Mouth in the west also had a good anchorage and a useful river. No, not Kroonenburg. Kroonenburg was only for palm wine and young deer.

When the sun went down behind them, the moon rose huge and yellow behind Tobacco Island. 'I think I'm right. We're going to have a low ebb tonight. Look, Fisherman's Isle is already clear above the water.' The island was shaped like a mushroom on its stem. Below, it usually teemed with fish, but now it stood with its bushy head in the sky and its foot in a small pool of water. They made the crossing, the hundred yards or so, almost dry-shod. Andries knew of a place where the rocks were shaped like steps, and there they pulled and helped one another up to get to the island. There was a forest of shrubs, palm trees, rocks with rainwater holes. Among them wandered goats, staring stupidly at them. Big, fat dodos stood scrabbling right in front of them, so that they had to be kicked out of the way.

'This is the place,' they said. 'It isn't Kroonenburg, but here we'll gorge ourselves.' The next flow cut them off from the land. Bart and his companions built a hut and remained there for two months, slaughtering and eating and allowing their palm wine to ferment properly in the coconut shells. It was a pity to kill so many trees, but the wine was good and strong and they all felt, once again, the joy of an evening in the tavern. In those two months they became good friends. They were all splendid fellows. They slaughtered the goats more for the skins than for the meat, as there was enough other food. From the skins they made shoes and breeches and waistcoats, all of them laced up with thongs. And they plaited large hats from palm fronds, like the Japanese. There was nothing a sailor could not make with his hands, they said. There was also an abundance of fish around their island, and the bones and meat and scrapings from hides which they threw into the water lured even more. The huge land tortoises were so fat that they could barely draw in their legs. They ate a lot, laughed a lot, swore a lot, but Bart was mindful of the oath he'd taken in the sea and counted his words. And to the captain who'd forgiven him for the brandy, he would remain true.

After the second full moon an English ship came in through the East Gap. It was wary of the narrow channel, brailed up everything and put out two rowing boats to pull it in right in front of the old Fort. Bart and his companions watched from the island. Five times the rowing sloops moved to the land and back. The same afternoon the ship went out again, this time under sail. No, they agreed, they didn't want to go with it, but there would be tobacco at the Fort now. Perhaps it was time to go ashore again.

They left all their things in the hut, and swam to the mainland. At the Fort they were surprised to see how few people were left. Some time earlier Ensign Evertsz and the pastor and a few others had made an agreement that they would take turns to live at North-West Harbour for a week, to keep a lookout for an English ship. On Fisherman's Isle they knew nothing about this. This ship was *Truro*, from India. It had already taken in refreshments in the North-West Harbour, fuel and water and numerous large tortoises, when the sentries met the English people in the forest. The English captain had been willing to go to South-East Harbour and pick up the castaways. He hadn't asked about who was going to pay. But no tobacco had been left behind. They had nothing to buy with, and the English sailors refused to part with anything; they still had to make do for six months at sea, with their own scant supplies. So the Reverend van Kerkhoven and Ensign Evertsz and eighteen others had left with the English. The *dominee* had said: 'I needed silence to thank my Lord, and now I long for books and a change of food.' His message to those who remained behind had been to make their escape if they had the chance, before the indolence of the island got the better of them, since idleness was the root of all evil. In the old vegetable garden was a large bed he and his sons had cleared and planted with pumpkin seeds. And without the others it was fine too. Fewer people would find it easier to live together.

Bart and his companions returned to Fisherman's Isle. The stinking carcasses of goats and tortoises lay strewn around their hut. It was strange how soon one stopped noticing something if you lived in the midst of it. They cleaned up a bit and threw the rubbish into the sea. After the English visit, their thoughts often turned to tobacco. They stuffed all kinds of dried grass and leaves into the thick thighbone of a goat and smoked it, without much satisfaction. They also built a raft of logs, fastened with thongs. The dodos were finished already, the tortoises were used up, the goat meat was tough and unpleasant to the taste, and curing hides was hard work. When the last palm wine was finished, the tops of all the trees on their island shorn off, each top hollowed out like a pot, and all the trees dead, they left Fisherman's Isle.

They had talked about where they might be going. Some spoke about

North-West Harbour, others about the old Fort at South-East Harbour, still others wanted to go to Kroonenburg. People had often said: Stay away from Kroonenburg, there you fall into bottomless water. Because it therefore had to be Kroonenburg, they dismantled the raft, and rolled up the thongs and stowed them with their leaf-mats to take along. Without sending their companions at the Fort word of it, they swam ashore at one high tide, crossed the Lemoenbosberg, and then had problems with several small streams and the great South-East River. On the other side of the river a level, stony plain stretched out before them to the north-east, and after three days of struggling across the plain along the river down to the sea, they arrived at a marshy beach overgrown with mangrove. Between the beach and the reef lay several yellow-white sandbanks, all of them thick with mature coconut palms. That was Kroonenburg.

It did not take long to gather enough wood for building another raft. With a large load of firewood from the land and their few possessions on it, they pushed the raft ahead of them while swimming alongside. The shallow water was lukewarm with sleep. The islands were as lovely as heaven. In between were deep blue pools in which shoals of small, brightly coloured fish swam. Young deer were grazing under the trees, approaching with big eyes to watch the people. What a pity to come and live here, thought Bart. It was such a beautiful place, almost like a picture of paradise in a children's book.

Each man marked five or six palm trees for himself, and then started chopping and hollowing them out, so that he'd be sure of a lot to drink. Afterwards they put up a hut, unrolled their mats on the sand and lay down on them to gaze at the breakers on the reef. They looked at one another, laughing. Kroonenburg was the best of places. Everybody had said so, and today they had finally reached it. What a life this would become, on Kroonenburg, without ever lifting a finger to work. You poured your wine, chopped down another tree, you slaughtered your meat, or took your fish from the water, and then you lay on the sand and ate and drank and stared at the reef. At night they made a fire to keep away the crabs, and ate and drank and slept.

Kroonenburg Island had a strange effect on Bart. He began to think of all the girls he'd looked at twice, painfully longing for their company. If he could have only one of them on this beautiful island, even if it were just for a while; it was all that was still missing from his paradise. With them in his thoughts he could not sleep; at night he lay awake with such a need that in the end he had to get up and assuage it in the dark some distance from the hut. In the daytime, in that endless languor, he lay on his mat under the rustling palm trees and thought of girls he'd known in Woerden, in Java, at the Cape and in Malacca. His memory became increasingly strong, their images more and more vivid. It is the real world beckoning me, he thought. Why must I go back? What does it want of me? Then he stripped off his clothes and went to float in the deep blue pool.

They spent much of their time swimming. There was a current that carried a swimmer among the islands for fifteen minutes, into a deep pool. There you got out, crossed the sandbank and went in again on the other side, where the current took hold of you again and carried you past all the islands back into the deep pool. Their days were spent drinking, sleeping, longing, swimming, eating and drinking. Why is that world beckoning me? thought Bart, for nowhere on earth have I seen a place like this. Yet at night he couldn't sleep because of the desire burning in him. He had never felt it before so persistently and piercingly, in the forecastle of a ship, or in the barracks and billets to which he'd been confined for months and years. That was what Kroonenburg did to him, and to all of his companions. He noticed, and all the others knew it too, that two of them would swim to the other island at night. He saw them walking naked on the beach; saw them holding hands. They did not discuss it among themselves. It was the unspeakable sin: nothing was said about it. Or if it wasn't the unspeakable sin, then what was it? One night he woke up because someone had spread a mat next to his and came to lie close to him. He got up and took away his mat. Who was it? It was this island, this Kroonenburg. That was what they had been warned against. To forget about these things, put them out of his mind, he started drinking more.

They'd been there for six weeks when a black frigate came gliding past beyond the reef, going south. Three masts, three black sails on each, three more black jibs on the sprit. It was a lean, swift ship, like a hunting dog, with ports for more than thirty cannon. Warship? Then they saw the black flag. Pirate. Bart ran from the hut to the edge of the water, waving his arms above his head. Dear Lord, thank You for this mercy, even if I have to escape with the help of the Devil himself. Andries Stokram was there too; he shouted, waved his arms and ran right into the water like a madman.

There were only the two of them out of the nine who wanted to go. The leave-taking was brief. Good luck. Safe journey. To you too, good luck. Andries knew the way all along the coast. It was a day and a half on foot. First swimming to the shore, walking some distance through the forest, then swimming across the broad South-East River below a thundering rocky waterfall, then above the high-water mark round Third Corner, passing below the Cat and Mouse, round Second Corner, then First. There the black frigate lay in the pool before the old Fort. Its sails had been taken in, its yards squared, the tops struck. Fore and aft, anchors had been laid out; it clearly intended to stay for some time. And the black flag was gone. Tired as they were, they jogged the last distance past the graveyard and the vegetable garden, laughing with relief when the black dog barked at them from the walls of the old Fort.

A few boats, their oars on the thwarts, had been dragged out on the beach. There were many strangers about, but Andries also noticed messmates from *Aernhem*, chopping firewood and filling water barrels. They conveyed the news that the pirate was willing to lift them all from the island. They didn't know where to, but they were going to work for their passage. His name was Hubert Hugo, he was a Dutchman from Delftshaven. At the moment he was in the forest looking for timber, and they would be wise to speak to his chief mate before the boatswains arrived with their rope ends. They were quick with their starters.

The chief mate was an Englishman with a grey beard. He wanted to know where they came from, why they weren't living in this bay with the others.

'Not enough food here for everybody,' Bart said. He could speak a few words of the language.

'You must wait for Captain Hugo. But go to that tree where you can see our barber, and wait in line. No tips to him, it spoils the sailors.'

By the time Hugo emerged from the forest, their hair and beards had been trimmed. A bulldog led the procession; he lifted his leg against a pile of pumpkins, and flopped down under a bush. Behind him were two large Moors with half-pikes on their shoulders, and behind these a man who must have been nearly seven foot tall, with blue ribbons in his beard and hair, followed by a girl and two boys of seven or eight years old. The chief mate waited until the pirate had been refreshed and the children had gone off to play; then he pushed Bart and Andries forward.

'Two new men, captain. Castaways from *Aernhem*.'

'Where have you been these two days?' It was Rotterdam Dutch.

'We were hunting and catching fish, captain. We beg you please to let us work for passage, wherever you're going.'

'And your names and occupations?'

'Bart Borms from Woerden, captain. Rigger's mate.'

'Andries Stokram from Haerlem, captain. Seaman.'

'*Oorlams?*' When they nodded he said: 'I worked for your Company for years. All right. Mister mate, take Stokram with you, and give Borms to the rigger. Now you want provisions for two more mouths. Get pumpkins and water.'

Bart told them about the goats on Fisherman's Isle, and if they had a fishing net they could draw a few barrels of salt fish. That won him and Andries favour with the chief mate. They said nothing about the seven companions at Kroonenburg. It was better to forget them there.

When the new spars arrived from the forest, Bart was surprised to see five black men with axes on their shoulders and chains on their legs. Black people from the dark heart of Africa were a rare sight. They were slaves, bought on the fever coast. Two guards with harquebuses followed the chain gang. The captain must have known how to select his slaves; these five were immune, salted as they say, against the bad air or east coast fever. That evening the pirates caroused around three big, leaping fires. The songs were German and Dutch, and there were two fellows with fiddles who played lively dances, but the Dutch men were reluctant to dance and preferred looking at the Germans and Italians prancing and turning. Pistol shots were fired into the night sky, and from time to time brawlers thrashed about in the grass, but in Hugo's tent outside the fire's circle, candles and a lantern were burning.

The next morning everybody was ordered to attend while the body-guards were spreadeagled between two trees and given eighty lashes each with a wet rope, because in the night the five Africans had absconded into the jungle with their chains and axes, and were not seen again. But after a few days men from Kroonenburg turned up unexpectedly, and wanted passage. Runaways had murdered their friend Piet Salomons, and the only way in which they had been able to save themselves was by swimming out to the reef. That day the tranquil island became beset by disquiet and fear.

The black ship's name was *Aigle Noir*, that is, *Black Eagle*. About mid-May in 1662 it left through the Eastern Gap, in a westerly direction. That was its direction, but only the captain knew its destination. *Aigle Noir* was an excellent ship, not particularly clean, but well appointed, well run and well sailed, and in every way equipped and organised like a warship. Sometimes it hoisted the black flag, and sometimes the white French flag with lilies, but there were other flags as well in the chest by the helm. The crew, murderers to a man, was divided into marines, sailors and gunners, as in the French navy. Just like the black slaves, the ship was Hugo's private property, and not that of any Company of distant lands. He'd had the frigate built in Rotterdam according to a new French design, and then sought official support for the plan he'd had in mind. The Duke of Vendôme, one of the French king's brood of illegitimate sons, had provided the papers he wanted: a privateer's pass in which Turks and Moors were declared enemies. That would save Hugo's sea dogs from the gallows, at least in France and the countries at peace with the French king. But it was for a portion of their booty, of course, and as a result Hugo had to commit twice as many murders and take twice as much loot every time, as only half of it ended up in his own coffer. With the other half, the Duke of Vendôme bought sweetmeats for his lady friends.

These things Bart learned one winter's day on the sunny side of a tavern on St Helena Island from Hugo's chief mate. The Englishman had met his younger brother there on a ship at the anchorage of St Helena, and asked Hugo for his discharge to go home. On this island, Hugo also left Bart and three of *Aernhem*'s men on shore. Each received a few gold Indian coins from Hugo's hand. Bart wanted to go to the Cape, Andries wasn't sure yet where to head for. The other thirty castaways from *Aernhem* entered into his service and left with him for the West Indies to see if Spanish silver ships still frequented those parts, as Spanish ships occasionally carried Moors on board.

The English village of St Helena lay at the bottom of a steep valley. There was a triangular fort and half a dozen houses. It looked as if one good downpour of rain up in the valley could wash the whole lot into the sea. In the back garden of the inn was an ancient tortoise. Fred comes from Mauritius, the innkeeper said, scratching the old creature's carapace. Bart stared into his beer mug. At the Cape tortoises were like fleas on a dog.

'Ten years ago Hugo was your Company's commander in Suratte, up in the north-western corner of India. There he married a pretty English widow. She left him later because of his temper, but he took the children and threatened death to anyone coming between them and him. The little girl in particular. He doted on her, as you saw. I pity the men who try to court her one day. Well, he returned home as vice-admiral of your Company's return fleet of '54, and was supposed to retire there. But it was just a design to get back to the Netherlands, to build that black ship. Because in Suratte he'd discovered something that meant much more to him than to your Company.'

'What?'

'Religion, my friend. There is money in other people's sentimentality. You just have to give shape to it. Look at the Pope, for example. I beg your pardon, are you Catholic? Our Pope is stinking rich, but the Irish stay hungry. Hugo's father was a French Huguenot, a dyed-in-the-wool Protestant. But it doesn't matter any more, as we no longer live in the time of the Crusades. In those days religion was a solid pretext for massacres. Christian against Mohammedan, and blood up to your shoe buckles, at least. Well, perhaps that business of religion for money, or Christian against Mohammedan, is still in Hugo's blood. In the ten years or so while he managed your office in Suratte, he had to keep an eye on the trade with Persia and Arabia. He would buy Arabian coffee and Persian carpets there for your Company, which were then transported to Europe on your return ships, to be sold at a profit of six to eight hundred per cent. For ten years he organised the profitable trade, for a meagre little salary of, say, a hundred guilders per month. Do you follow?'

'Yes,' said Bart and Andries.

'Innkeeper, three more large ones. Hugo told me that he used to look through his office window on the harbour, just like us here, watching the coming and going of Arabian and Indian ships. Not quite like here. Perhaps you know Suratte, it's built some distance up a river. But it's a huge port. And there he saw that for every ship with merchandise to or from the Red Sea, there would be two ships full of passengers. Pilgrims. Like sheaves of golden wheat they stood on those ships, ready to be harvested. Some of them he knew personally. This or that rich merchant, his sons, their wives. And their baggage. Sometimes merchandise and pilgrims on the same ship. Prosperous people, most of them. We, the poor, only go on pilgrimages when – ah, anyway. Sometimes he went on board to greet them, to wish them a good journey to Mecca. He saw what they were wearing in the line of jewels. Rubies, diamonds set in gold and silver. Emeralds and sapphires in gold. One day on *Aigle Noir* I was present when Captain Hugo had his chest unlocked. Three locks. One key is with him, one his little girl carries around her neck, one is hidden in the cabin. Only he knows where. My eyes almost popped out of my head; the King of England has nothing like that. Worth many, many millions. And those came from the fingers, from the necks, the ears, the arms, the clothes of those pilgrims camping on the decks of ships, on their way to the holy city.

'More beer, chief mate? Andries?'

'Yes, please. Three more, innkeeper.'

'And where do the pilgrims go to, chief mate?' asked Bart. The coins ready in his hand, were Indian money, with Indian writing.

'Thanks. They disembark in the harbour of Jedda in Arabia. Then they continue overland on asses and camels. There are two holy cities, Mecca and Medina. I don't know how they worship, but their prophet is Mohammed, and God they call *Allah*. And it's not just Suratte they come from, but from every harbour and village between India and Africa, and from the whole of East India. There are thousands of pilgrims on the water every day. They must all go up into the Red Sea, and its only entrance is past the rock Bab el Mandib, the Gates of Hell. That was where Hugo's *Black Eagle* nested. What he'd learned on the quay of Suratte in those days, was that a floating gold mine existed in the Red Sea, and no one had thought of it before. Hugo just wanted to get home, build his special ship, and then return to work that secret gold mine.'

The innkeeper called them to their meal. They took their beer mugs inside and sat down with others at a long table in the kitchen. It was good food: a large steaming flavoursome pie of beef, vegetables and boiled eggs, deliciously prepared by a woman. I am almost done with the sea, thought Bart. It's time for me to find a home.

'India is extraordinarily rich,' the Englishman said. 'You might think, the aristocrats of our kingdom, all ten thousand of them, with their fancy titles, and their sparkling little coronets and tiaras and sceptres, that all those jewels come from Europe? Not at all. There are no diamond mines in Europe.'

The rest of the story was too familiar. The merciless violence of pirates against innocents was recalled in forecastles and inns where sailors gathered. All of it, born from excessive greed. Their own hands, sailors' hands, were hardened by work, but remained empty.

Bart arrived at the Cape towards the end of the year 1663. He didn't show his gold. He knew he would have to buy food, and on the outward-bound ship that brought him to the Cape he'd exchanged Indian coins for Dutch currency. He got more than the face value of his money, because those raw crewmen were so keen, it was the first time they'd touched anything from the golden Orient.

Behind the Fort at the Cape stood a new inn, called the Elephant. He smelled the warm bread in their oven as he approached. The hostess turned out to be an old friend, Barbara Geens. But she was friends with everybody, one who had a kind word and a helping hand for all. When she saw him, she came to exchange a greeting, pressed her golden-red head against his shoulder for a moment, and said that they'd both grown older, and laughed about the injuries of time. She was glad that he was back, she said. She was married now: her husband was sitting over there in the corner, coughing. Yes, business was good. It was the quiet season now, but come *oorlammer* time, she regularly had to hire extra help. She sent Bart a second tankard to his table, with her compliments.

The day after his arrival Bart asked to speak to the commander. There was a new man in van Riebeeck's chair. It was the German they'd called Thunder Man in Batavia. Well educated, but very short-tempered.

'From *Aernhem*'s crew?' Wagenaer asked, surprised, when he told his story. 'You're not the only survivor who reached the Cape, you know. Captain Oosterwoud was here, earlier this year.'

'Has he left again, Your Honour? I owe my life to him.'

'He jumped overboard to drown himself, poor godforsaken soul, just at Hell's Door, three days from Amsterdam. What possesses a man?'

Bart thought: He was truly my captain. He was God in that boat. He decided who lived, who died. So, finally, he faced the question: Who then dares to be my judge? This will never do! And he took the decision upon himself.

'I was in *Aernhem*'s boat, sir. But I was rigger on *Hof van Holland*.'

'The Lords reported no survivors at all from that one, I am sorry to say. So. And where did you tarry?'

Bart told him. Yes, said the commander. Some months ago an Englishman brought the same information from St Helena. So Bart had been with Hugo the pirate? And what could he do for him now?

He wanted to stay here, said Bart. Previously, he'd been a farmhand on an allotment; first sailor and seal killer in the time of Commander van Riebeeck, then farmhand. Then the Orient beckoned him again. But this time he was finally done with the sea. Now he asked permission to remain here and become a free burgher.

'Back to farming?' Wagenaer waited for Bart to answer, for he didn't want to lose the man. Woerden was between Utrecht and Leiden, midway between Church law and free enquiry, even though the applicant was only a sailor. When he received a stupid grin in reply, he became serious. 'I must tell you, Borms, we expect wheat from our farmers. We can barter meat and other things from the natives, but we cannot import wheat and we cannot exchange it. We have to cultivate the wheat. Every clerk, every child needs fresh bread on the table daily. Every sailor must have his ship's biscuit. They work hard enough for it, the devil knows. And where must it come from? From the Cape's ovens. It means that our farmers must bend their backs over sickle and plough. A colony that cannot provide its own bread, is no colony.'

'I'd like to try, Your Honour.'

'Do you have capital, for seed money, livestock, implements?'

'No, sir.'

'So. That's how the Company treats its orphans. Bloody ship lost, everything lost. Damn it to hell. Well, I suggest you start here as a farmhand with one of the fellows who's already settled in. You sign a contract for one year, and that gives you an opportunity to see if you like the work, and if the work likes you. The other advantage is that you have very few expenses. You eat the man's food, sleep in his house, perhaps marry his widow, of which I can mention several examples. And one fine morning Bart Borms becomes the owner of a farm in Africa. Although it can be a goddamned curse, believe me. You may wish to pray against it.'

His final advice, as he took leave of Bart at his door, was to remind him that the Company's gold mine was situated in the East, but that this Cape was the hinge of the whole enterprise. Damned Cape lost, Batavia lost, the Company lost, the fatherland lost. It was as simple as that. If Bart asked for land to farm on, he was asking to become part of the pivot on which the Honourable Company and the fatherland rested. Did he understand that? 'So. Good luck then,' he said.

Barbertje gave him bread, cheese, beer and a clean bed, refusing money for it, but Bart pressed a gold coin in her hand. She put her arms around him like years before, and only said, 'Thank you, Bart.' She told him that she'd heard one of Tielman Hendriksz's farmhands was in hospital with a cancer. Tielman farmed on Den Uitwijk, right next to Coornhoop. His housewife was Maijke.

'What is wrong with your husband, Barbertje?' he wanted to know, deeply moved by the colour of her hair.

'I think it's consumption,' she answered. 'He has no strength, my poor man.'

Tielman was about thirty, his wife ten years older. They'd been married for four years. Their eldest was Catharina, a daughter of Maijke's with her previous husband. Their youngest was a year old, also a girl. Tielman had bought Den Uitwijk from van Riebeeck a year before. The land lay on the river in the most fertile part of the Liesbeeck valley. The honourable commander always had to have the best of every-thing in the colony, and he did not skimp on labour, with the result that the farm was a prime place when Tielman got it. For safety the lord also had the fort Coornhoop built on his farm. But, Tielman took pains to explain to Bart, there was a very big difference between commander and free burgher. The one could afford to hire labourers, the other quite simply not. If Bart was willing, they could appear before the Thunder Man the very next day and have a contract drawn up.

Bart did not want to be a shepherd and he had it stipulated in the contract. He could dig, and plant, and build dykes. Milk too; that was really a woman's work, but he didn't mind. Harness oxen and drive a wagon, he'd like to learn. But if he had to tend sheep, he might as well become a schoolteacher. All that he explained to the clerk who sat opposite him and Tielman, writing the contract. The clerk liked the neat little anchor Bart drew instead of signing his name.

The trouble, Bart discovered after a few months, was that Tielman wanted to play the lord as if he were van Riebeeck now. He owned land, had a horse and a slave and two farmhands, and now he felt justi-fied to ride out hunting while his labourers did the farming. Tielman was not the only one, it was the tendency all along the river, with only a very few exceptions. The people possibly recalled winter's tales their grandfathers had told of the old days: of a landlord who only meted out work and punishment, and spent his time hunting and riding about raping women with impunity. Now the small farmers along the

Liesbeeck wanted to play that game. Bart had no wish to be a farmhand for such a master, because there was absolutely nothing such a
man could do for him. From this farm, he saw, no good would come
for anyone. He had to work for himself, then he would respect his
master.

Maijke was pleasant and hard-working, but uncommonly thrifty. She
was still too bound by poverty. Every crust of bread was for the ducks,
every piece of pumpkin peel for the pigs. When they emptied a flagon
of wine, she turned it upside down and knocked out the last of the
lees on her palm. It had nothing to do with a love of alcohol, it was
only thrift. In the evening when they rose from the table, she blew out
the candles and put them away. The farmhands were given the stubs
that remained in the candlesticks, to take to their room. But she baked
an honest coarse loaf of bread, and she felt a need to trade: a bundle
of wood for a dozen eggs, the eggs for a cheese, the cheese for a small
bag of rice, the rice for a bolt of linen, the linen for an iron pot, the
pot for a lamb. Sometimes natives arrived in the yard, with bundles of
firewood, honey and the like. The farm dogs already knew some of the
people. Sometimes a native would come back with Tielman's shepherd
from the veld.

Bart and the other farmhand and the slave cleared the land, and
ploughed and sowed in the most fertile soil in the whole valley. They
fenced camps and planted vegetables, and seldom saw their master.
Tielman had little to say to his farmhands. Every few days he returned
from the veld with a buck over his horse in front of him. In the fatherland that kind of thing was the privilege of a duke. Then the farmhands
went to report to him:

'The Company's gardener sent a box of cabbage plants, master.'

'Yes, transplant them.'

'The roof of the sheep pen needs thatching, master.'

'What are you waiting for? Take thongs and sickles, and go and cut
reeds.'

'There were footprints in front of the sheep pen again, master.'

'Your own footprints.'

The farmhands were talking among themselves. Why had Tielman given his shepherd a linen bag with a full ell of tobacco in it? And why was there a Hottentot with Tielman when he came from the veld? The master is a smuggler, they said.

After Bart had been with Tielman for a few months, Commander Wagenaer called him in. Lords Seventeen had sent a letter to ask that the Cape send a ship to see if more survivors of that vast and costly disaster had arrived on Mauritius or the surrounding islands. To him personally it seemed like a goddamned waste of valuable time, but that was what the Lords had ordered and so it had to be done. Would Bart go with them and give the search parties a hand? He would have the work and wages of a rigger.

'No, thank you, I cannot, Your Honour. My master needs me. And another thing: I've drunk enough seawater for a long while.'

'The Company also needs you.'

'Then it is up to Your Honour to command me. My own feeling is against it.'

'On another day you may need the Company again, Borms, then you'll be coming to ask me for a favour. But all right, go back to your irrigation ditches and your bloody clods.'

Bart tugged at his forelock and put on his cap and took his leave. The Company disposed over hundreds of sailors to send. But he was now at the age where he had to put himself first. The man was right, of course, they should help one another. In fact, he had in mind a favour to ask of the Company.

Towards noon one day the short shadow of a young Koina woman arrived at the farm with a child on the back. The two were grey with fatigue. She found Bart in the beans. She undid the cloth holding her child and let her slide to the ground. She spoke Dutch: 'Is the master at home?'

'No, my master is out in the veld.'

'And your mistress?'

'She went up that way, to the Lyreman's place.'

'I'm so tired. We come a long way.'

'I'm sorry, there's no one here.'

'Are you Tielman's farmhand?'

Bart wondered where the woman had gone to school to know these parts so well.

'I'm Eva. This is my child. We've walked a long way.'

He could see that she needed water, and rest, and to feed the child. And the child was no Koina. It showed in the hair and nose. Could it be Tielman's child?

'Come, we've got sour milk in the outbuilding. Then you can wait for my mistress if you wish.'

In the dairy room were basins with cream and curdled milk covered with cloths. He skimmed off the cream and ladled out a bowl of curdled milk for her. Maijke could say what she wanted. The woman accepted the bowl in both hands and held it to her face. He watched while she drank, deeply. She was attractive. There were tanned sheepskins hanging from a beam, and he took some of them down and spread them on the ground for her to sit on. Among them he found a skin with the long hair of a Hottentot sheep. This was forbidden. And he saw how she looked at it, but said nothing.

'Come. You can rest here.'

She handed back the bowl and put the child to her breast.

'How far have you been walking?'

'From the Fort.'

'Who is the child's father there?'

'She has no father.'

'What is her name then?'

'Little Pieternel.'

As he thought: A white man's child. He went out to his work. When Maijke returned, she took the woman with the child inside.

In the flowering time Tielman told his farmhands to wash his wagon, and cut a load of grass and flowers too. His wagon was rented and that Sunday he had to ride a bridal wagon. The grass was lush, the marshes shimmered, and the world smelled of honey. Cows with large udders grazed hock-deep in clover and flowers. Bart was happy, but he was not satisfied. There was too little wind in this valley, his bed was too soft, the woman's food was too rich, they were too fond of making sweetmeats. He was wary of getting too comfortable. Ships and sailors rot on land. He was to attend the wedding the following day. According to the invitation brought by the messenger, Trijn Ustinghs and Hans Ras were to be married that Sunday after church, and the guests were invited to the festivities on Hans's farm. Hans was a hunting companion of Tielman's, a simpleton from the depths of Germany with the heart of a child and fresh grass seed in his hair. Weddings were good; one got the chance to dance with your neighbour's daughter.

On the Saturday they pulled the wagon down to the river, and washed the cow dung from it with pails of water and hard brooms, and left it there to dry. Then they cut a load of grass with scythe and sickle and made a deep bed on the wagon. There was an abundance of flowers. They pulled out armfuls. That was when Trijn and her friend arrived to decorate the wagon. Bart had seen Trijn with Maijke before. She was a plump little German farmgirl, barely twenty, who had been at the Cape for two years. The friend was Theuntje van der Linde. Bart, who hardly ever spoke to women, was shy at first. She was half a head taller than he, slender and although not pretty, attractive enough. She and Trijn chattered and plaited garlands of flowers to drape along the sides, and wove wreaths of flowers through the spokes. Bart laughed, and brought more flowers. It became a pleasant afternoon.

That Sunday Bart washed and combed himself, and put on clean clothes. He took one of his gold coins from its hiding place and cut it in half, it was to be his wedding gift. He and his workmate took the wagon to the church, where they outspanned with other wagons and hooded carts, and waited outside the Fort for the people to appear. There were few ships in the roadstead, only a couple that were outward bound, and then the Company's two lighters at the quay. The Sabbath was their only resting day too, when they did not sail to and fro across the bay with cargoes of slate and shells. Barbara Geens's tavern was closed, her white shutters were in the frames. It was a long church service. Bored, Bart and his companion stood beside the decorated wagon, kicking at dogs that came to cock their legs against the wheels. Next to the Fort a large new water reservoir of stone and brick was being built. They led the yoked oxen to drink from the stream above the tank, when a soldier shouted from the wall that they should get out of the water, it was for drinking.

What am I doing here? thought Bart. There's nothing for me in this game. I'm wasting my life in this awful place.

The Koina woman Eva came through the gate with her child on her hip. Both were beautiful in Dutch clothes, and she showed the signs of another advanced pregnancy. She came to stand expectantly beside the wagon, her face turned to the gate. 'They're coming out now.'

Bart took the child from her and climbed on the front box with her. 'Let's watch from up here, little Pieternella. You're not scared of going a little way up the mast, are you?' He held her tightly against him. A wonderful warmth came from her whole body. 'What do you say?'

A group of wedding guests were on their way to the gate, across the courtyard. But there the guards crossed their pikes to bring the procession to a standstill. That was the custom. 'The password first.' All cheered and laughed outrageously until the bride gave each soldier a kiss. Then they streamed outside. At the head of the group, Barbertje shouted: 'You look good with a child on your arm, Bart. You should have been a father long ago.' Behind her was her friend Theuntje.

People crowded around the wagon. Bart passed the child to her mother, and helped Trijn to climb up. For some reason she put her arms around his neck and kissed him passionately. Then he helped Hans up. The fellow's skin was smooth and shiny from shaving, wearing a suit too small for him, and he had grass seeds in his hair. Bart congratulated him with a handshake and helped them to settle side by side in the bed of deep grass. Branches frothing with white blossoms were thrown into the wagon, as well as gifts of pumpkins, a basket of eggs, a trussed suckling pig, more leafy branches. A soldier with a wooden flute and another with a fiddle mounted the wagon. Bart was still feeling the glow of Trijn's kiss in his body when Tielman shouted at him: 'What are you standing there for? Hook up the team. Take the lead rope.'

But he knew well that his companion had already hooked up the chain. There was nothing for him to do. The master was drunk, he'd been sitting drunk in church.

'All done, boss.'

Tielman's voice became louder: 'Then help Maijke up.'

Bart saw Maijke at another wagon, where they had put down a wooden box for people to step on, and she was helped up there. She had no wish to ride with her husband.

In a rage Tielman clambered up. 'Give me the whip. Mind your heads. Borms, take the lead rope.'

Their wagon was second or third behind the others. There were still people looking for seats on the wagons, and Bart waited for an opening so that he could lead his team through and go to the front of the row. Tielman flicked the whiplash dangerously close to his head. Bart got angry.

'Look what you're doing, master.'

From the Fort an earth road stretched across a green hill towards the Liesbeeck. There were six ox wagons in a row in the narrow road, with outriders in front and behind. Bart was in the lead, he couldn't see anything behind him, but he could hear the flute and the fiddle playing, and the cheering of the guests. Dancing began on the wagons, presumably flasks were passed round. Tielman cursed and shouted at the oxen, beating them with his long whip. Bart was wondering about Trijn's warm mouth. He should find out whether she felt like dancing tonight. Why was she so glad to marry old Hans? He led the procession down the other side of the hill to the river. Hans's yard was there at the little bridge; he could see the smoke from the chimney, where women were baking and men brewing.

Tielman bellowed and cursed, and Bart could feel the oxen straining forward under his lash. He had to step nimbly to stay out of reach of their horns. There were screams. He looked round. The wagon behind was forcing its way past on their port side to reach Hans's yard first, and Tielman wouldn't allow it. He was standing up, cursing and whipping, wanting Bart to run with the oxen to bring the bridal wagon into the yard first. The other wagon was beside them, its two starboard wheels on the bank beside the road, and the horns of the oxen striking together, people shouting and Tielman's whip whistling in the air. Holding his lead pair short by the head-thong, Bart jumped out of the way to take his team out of the road on the trot, allowing the other wagon to pass. When the oxen calmed down, the whole procession came to a standstill behind them. Bart relaxed.

Then Tielman struck him with the whip across the shoulders. Bart felt behind his shoulder blades, thrust his hand into his pocket and brought out his knife. 'By the hairy hound, master. Don't you do that again.' The bride was in tears. People came running towards them, thronging together. With the flat of his hand against the man's chest, the bridegroom pushed Tielman off the wagon.

'Drunken fool, do you want to kill all of us here?'

'Then get off, all of you!' shouted Tielman. 'Get off my bloody wagon, the whole whoreshop of you! If I and my wagon are not good enough, then you can walk where you want to go.' He snatched branches and gifts and flowers from the wagon and hurled them away. 'Move, get away from my wagon! You, Hans Ras, take your slut off my wagon before I kick her off. Take your goddamned cow off my wagon.'

In a flash the knives were out. In a flash they were stabbing, parrying, stabbing, parrying, stabbing. With a surprised grin Hans remained standing in the sandy road beside the bridal wagon, bleeding, a broken knife blade hanging from his ribs. His white shirt was slowly stained red, then his knees buckled. There were screams. Bart stood watching how Tielman was taken and led away, how the shrieking bride was lifted from the wagon, so that they could lay down her groom's limp body on the bed. His own shoulders were burning like fire. He held the oxen and spoke to them to calm them down. Filthy land swine. Never again.

The *secundus* and some officials and the pastor, who had gone ahead in carts as was fit and proper, had already been seated at the festive table when Hans was carried in. Master Pieter, the surgeon, went to Hans with his medicine chest. The *secundus* awaited the bride at the door and made her drink neat brandy. All who entered felt a need for brandy. When Master Pieter came to whisper to the *secundus* that he thought the patient was out of danger, but that he was taking him to hospital nevertheless, the *secundus* said to the bride: 'It would be a pity to send the guests home like that, Trijn. Come, let the flute and the violin strike up. Let the glasses be filled.' In the absence of her father, he spoke for the bride.

Bart unyoked the oxen, packed his yokes and chain in the back, took the oxen to drink at the river and put them in Hans's kraal. Inside Hans's hut he could hear the music. He wanted to collect his things from the farm and go back to the Fort on foot, to explain to Wagenaer why he could no longer work for Tielman. Then Barbertje and Theuntje arrived in the yard, each carrying a large pastry in a cloth on the head, and a covered basket in each hand. It might yet become a good evening, thought Bart. He would go to the Fort in the morning.

The next dawn he woke up between Barbertje and Theuntje in the deep grass on the back of the wagon. They'd slept well, very warm and very soft. He crawled out and walked through the bushes down to the river. Hans's dog went with him, and together they relieved themselves in the haze among the trees on the bank. The river water was icy cold. He rinsed his mouth, washed his face, drank a few cupped handfuls, looked round. Beside him the dog stood lapping water. He went some distance upstream, where the shrubs grew more densely. It was going to become a beautiful day. What a feast it had been. They'd eaten, drunk and danced until well past midnight, and the hut so full that half the people were dancing outside, until the farmhands and servant girls had to start thinking about getting back to their duties.

'You go,' Bart said to his companion. 'The master is in prison, and I'm coming to fetch my things after daylight. Tell the mistress I'm bringing the wagon, and I'll take my things.'

On the way back he went to check on the oxen. Hans's farmhand was there, to help with the harnessing. His master was in hospital, so he would first help all the visitors off the yard.

'Your boss wounded badly?'

'That's what they say.'

There were other people in the yard. The house was awake. Trijn Ras was getting a fire going in her new cooking place. She had helped everybody without asking anybody to give her a hand. Her voice was strong but amicable. She kicked Hans's suckling pig out of the kitchen door, threw a large meaty bone out for the dog, helped two old people on sticks to the bridge, flapped tablecloths outside and folded them over her arm, and stood in front of the door with Barbertje and Theuntje, laughing and laughing until it sounded as if they were crying. What was the joke? wondered Bart. Harmen the neighbour arrived and brought the empty beer barrel outside, pushing it along the path back home with his foot.

After Bart had harnessed the wagon, he went in to say goodbye. He would take the bridal wagon home, he told Trijn. And here was a present for her. He hoped it would increase. She gave him another of her hot, wet kisses.

'Thank you, Bart. I'll tell Hans.'

'Don't. You can see for yourself how it is with Hans.'

When she didn't answer, he asked: 'Those two, Barber and Theuntje. How will they get home?'

Some time later he led the oxen with the empty wagon along the river to Tielman's farm. Theuntje walked with him; the other one still wanted to help cleaning up. The early bees were busy among the flowers.

'It's funny to see a sailor leading oxen today.'

'My last time.'

'My late husband was a farmer. Hard-working. But it's always a struggle.'

'That's how it is with poor people like us.'

'What I mean is, look, my father was a fisherman. It's hard work, and dangerous, but farm animals are almost like people, they need you all the time.'

'Your late husband, recently?'

'Yes. He was to come and farm here. The Company told them to join up as soldiers, and when they got here they'd be free. The commander would assist them with land. He died at sea. Even before we crossed the line.'

'And the land?'

'It's only for men.'

'Are you going back, overseas?'

'It depends on my fortune. If I'm not staying, I'll go back.'

'Yes. Me too.'

'I don't have anybody here. Not even a child,' she said. 'I've got nothing left.'

At Tielman's yard he asked Theuntje to wait, he would be going straight to the Fort from here, if she wished to walk with him. His companion had cleaned out the calf stable, and Bart asked him to give a hand with the animals. Once the oxen were in the kraal and the yokes had been hung up, he collected his bundle in the farmhands' room, said goodbye to his workmate and walked off to where Theuntje was waiting among the white flowers.

Maijke came out into the yard. She said nothing, but gazed after them as they went. 'Come on, Theun,' Bart said. 'We are going to see the commander.'

Commander Wagenaer was on the far end of the quay. He had a staff topped with a crosspiece, like the saints in the pictures, aiming across it in the direction of his new stone tank. Bart waited until he and his clerk had finished writing. Then he tugged at his forelock and asked permission to speak.

'Ah, the man who would not do the Company a favour. And the lady?'

'Theuntje van der Linde, Your Honour.' Theun curtsied, and the old man touched his hat.

'Have you come to have your banns read? Excellent. The colony needs children. I wish you a dozen. Go with the clerk, he will write down your case.' He waved them ahead with his hat as if he were herding lambs. Bart stopped, pointing at a spacious, undecked sloop beside the quay.

'How much would the Company want for that sloop, sir?'

'*Bruid*? Not for sale.'

'Sir, I have a legal contract with Tielman Hendriksz. Then yesterday at the wedding he struck me with a whip and stabbed Hans with the knife. He is dangerous when he's drunk.'

The commander turned to them, his face grave. 'He is sitting with his backside in the Black Hole now. If Hans dies, I'll hang him. An example to other lazy bastards who want to hunt and drink and have their farmhands do the work. Is this what we took the Liesbeeck from the natives for? What the devil has that got to do with the price of the boat?'

Bart had a fright. What did the commander know? 'I'm not going to work for him again, Your Honour. I'm under contract, but I'm not going back. I want to be a freeman, working for myself, then I can respect the master.'

'So? And what about your legal contract?'

'I wanted to ask, as a favour.'

'A favour? What else will there be?'

'Sell me the sloop.'

'By my soul, man. Is there anything else I can do for you?'

'Easy terms for paying off, please.'

'You come here this morning to get out of your contract and wheedle our boat out of me and arrange for payments *and* marry this woman. All in one morning.'

'I'd like to discuss it with Your Honour.'

'Well, come to the office, the two of you. Strike the bloody iron while it's on heat, I always say.'

He made them sit on the upright pew in front of his desk. Bart knew the place. Theuntje was trembling, and grasped for his hand. He held it tightly. The commander wanted to know: 'Last time I asked you a favour, Borms, you turned me down.'

'I didn't want to go because Your Honour said it was a waste of time. Our last seven men became fat and lazy, and Captain Hugo left five blacks behind. What I hear is that the blacks have no respect for our people. I reckoned by myself that our companions won't be alive any more.'

'Why didn't you advise me?'

'The Lords had already decided to send a ship.'

The commander also wished to know: 'You come to the jetty and want to buy the first sloop next to it. Will a farmer buy a horse before looking in its mouth and lifting its four feet? Will he buy a cow without asking about her calf? He must first see it.'

'I know *Bruid.* I see it running every day, and it makes good speed out of every wind. That means its bottom is tight and clean, and its tackle in good order. When we were standing there on the jetty I had a look at the tackle. And the equipment, and the state it was in. I guess it's about five years old. Almost no water sloshing about the bilges. Its quartermaster cares well for it. Needs a touch of paint and linseed oil here and there. But I'd like to see it on the blocks before I sign.'

'You want to become a free fisherman. A Saldanha farer.'

'That's so, Your Honour. Fresh, wind-dried and pickled. In the early days, as far as I know, the Saldanha farers brought in mussels and oil and birds' down and everything.'

'Yes. The more slaves we have, the more fish we need. Cheaper than meat, which would of course gladden the Company's heart. But they prefer fish to meat. So do I, the devil knows, it's got more taste. You can bring fresh fish and oysters here every day, Borms, you hear?'

Bart smiled happily, pressing Theuntje's hand. He'd felt, that morning when he and the dog had emptied their bladders into the Liesbeeck, that this was going to be a good day.

'Our Fort is in a reasonable state right now, so we need less lime from Robben Island and I think we can now spare *Bruid*. We can look at the terms later, and first discuss your other bride. So. I assumed you wanted to have your banns read.'

After Bart and Theuntje had had their banns read in church on three successive Sundays, they were married in the hall with the lion skin on the wall. A messenger invited their friends, and the ward of the Elephant prepared a meal for them. Bart rented a fishing hut beside the Salt River and prepared it for Theuntje and him, and the evening after their wedding he opened the door of the hut for her. 'Come on board, Theuntje.'

In front of their door stretched a wide, silvery estuary. That was where Bart set his nets in the months that followed, and on the bank was the scaffolding on which he hung up his dried fish. On Saturdays and Sundays he sat with his back against the wall of his house mending his nets, and casting his eyes across the water. With his bent brown fingers and his broad cracked toes in the squares of the net, he was content. His wife was neat and industrious. She carried her keys on her apron with pride, and when she wrote her name it was Theuntje

Borms, Theuntje Bartels and Theuntje van der Linde. She was gay and confident in her new status. She put a broody hen on eggs, and planted a garden. She invited her friends, and took a basket when she went to visit them. She and Bart were surprised to find that they liked each other.

Bart felt a pinch of longing when he heard on the quay one day that there was a ship at the anchorage, sent to transport a new settlement to Mauritius. The ship *Waterhoen* lay at the inner buoy. There were a few of his old companions on board who were to form the core of the new settlement, since the Lords had advertised in the Netherlands that they would offer double wages to any of *Aernhem*'s men willing to join the expedition. They had to advise the designated commander on where to find the safest harbours, how to build huts, where the best ebony was to be found, where to burn lime, things like that. They would be the new commander's right hand. Bart did not want to go to Mauritius himself, but together with all the bad memories there were also good times to remember. It was years since he'd been rescued there, and he wanted to greet the old friends on board. He would ask to speak to the new commander.

He sailed out as if going to sea, and hove to alongside the hull of *Waterhoen,* and shouted up to ask if he could come on board. The officer of the watch told him no, it was against orders. Then could he speak to the leader of the people going to Mauritius, or to their officer in charge?

A middle-aged man with a bald head came to lean over the gunwale above Bart. The commander designate.

'Good day, friend. Jacob van Nieuland. What can I do for you?'

'Greetings, commander. I am Bart Borms. May I come on board?'

'The captain refused. How can I help?'

'Commander, I was in *Aernhem*'s boat that time.'

'Ah. Now you want to go with us?'

'Commander, I heard you have some of our old messmates in your group. Are there any of them I still know? I just want to greet them.'

'I'll call them.'

The commander returned with three sailors. Bart stared up, carefully studying the faces. 'They're lying to you, commander.'

They cursed him from above. One spat on Bart's head. 'To hell, you lying bastard. Who are you? We don't know you.'

'I'm going to fetch others,' van Nieuland promised. He brought three more. They leaned over the gunwale above him. Once again he carefully examined the faces. Time does terrible things to people's faces. Yes, two of them looked vaguely familiar, perhaps from those who stayed close to the vegetable garden and had been lifted off first.

'Good day, friends.'

'Who are you, mate?'

'Bart. I was with Andries Stokram.'

They spoke among themselves.

'Andries Stokram who wrote the book about his adventures?'

'The same,' said Bart. He hadn't known that Andries could write. And he regretted that he couldn't read, as he'd have liked to see what Andries had written about them.

'Never heard of you,' they called.

'I know.' With the oar he pushed his boat away from *Waterhoen*'s hull, until he drifted free. Then he jerked loose his headsail to catch wind and place water between him and *Waterhoen*. 'Commander, look out, for God's sake.'

'Thank you, friend.'

He did not tell Theuntje what he'd learned there, because occasionally he still had bad dreams at night about the island Mauritius, and then she asked him about it as if his distress was real.

When they'd been married for almost a year and Theuntje still was not pregnant, they began to worry. They heard about remedies and tried them, but nothing helped. What was wrong? What else could they try? Bart didn't want to discuss his bedroom matters with others, but from her he heard things she'd brought home from her friends, which made him suspect that she was telling them more than was prudent. But he understood her worry. What if they never had children? He tried to encourage her and joked about it, so that she wouldn't become depressed. They were still young enough, he said. He'd known a man who was a grandfather before his first child was born.

'As long as you don't mind trying, Bart.' And he certainly didn't mind trying, because he was fond of Theuntje.

He could see that she was impatient. She mustn't become impatient, he asked.

He listened incredulously the day the fiscal's messenger brought a letter to their door in which they read that Theuntje was being summonsed to appear before the Council on a count of slander.

'What? Theun, what is the man saying?'

She was as white as a gull. At first she tried to dismiss it, pretending she didn't know what the man was talking about, and later said that she would put her side of the matter in court. Bart needn't think that she would drag their name through the mud. But the messenger stood waiting with the summons and his writing box with pen and ink, for Bart to acknowledge receipt. As he drew his small black anchor at the bottom of the document she began to cry.

She lay beside him on the bed. 'It's because Hester has the four most beautiful children. I did an ugly thing. They're talking about their children every day, about their sons and daughters, and their babies. It's all they ever talk about. They look at me when they tell about their lovely daughters, and the dresses they've made for the children, and they laugh. They look me right in the face to mock me. It was to spite her that I told the lie. I am jealous.'

'Don't cry any more, Theuntje. It's me they're mocking, not only you. It is me too they're talking about.' He said it over and over. He might have said: 'You know, Hester Weyers was just a servant girl when she came here, and now she's bragging about being the housewife of wealthy Burgher Councillor Mostert.' But how would that help his wife to lift up her head in this town again? They would have to see this trial through, the whole scandal of public punishment, and then the humiliation of going about with downcast eyes for the rest of her life. It really was for life. 'It's both of us, Theuntje. I feel just like you.'

The Council summoned her best woman friends to testify against her. When one takes the oath in court, one takes one's conscience, one's living soul, in one's hand, standing there for all to scrutinise, one's judges and opponents, the executioner and the entire population. They asked

Trijn and Barbertje: Is it true that the accused stated in your presence that Hester Weyers had two children out of wedlock in the fatherland and murdered one of them? Yes, they said, it was so. What else could they say? What had been a silly joke one morning, among them and some others in the kitchen of the Elephant, had suddenly become something of horror and pain and blood, and lifelong rejection. What else could they say, because it was true.

The punishment was read out by the secretary from the stoep of the Kat. Bart was there in front among the assembled people. Theuntje stood facing him with a chain around her ankle. Trijn Ras and Barbertje were not there. The clerk knew how to make it sound solemn, as he had to stir up terror in them. Certain words, like numbers, implements and body parts he had to emphasise without fail. He read out her punishment: iron spike through the tongue, forty strokes with the heavy cane on the bare back, six weeks' solitary banishment to a desolate and unprotected island. But it struck no terror into these people; they wanted to see more, as if she were a kind of monster that had to be displayed and spreadeagled in public for their entertainment. After a suitable pause the secretary read the mitigation, following an earnest plea of certain ladies of the Cape. She was to be spared the torture, but not the banishment. Therefore the clerk summoned the jailer to take the prisoner back to the dungeon. The dungeon was right there in front of them, under the stoep of the Kat; they could see its little window. The soldiers called it the Hole. Bart could barely find words when he said goodbye to Theuntje. The spectators felt that they hadn't been given value for their trouble.

When Bart was given permission to visit his wife on Robben Island, he found that the Koina woman with little Pieternel was now wife of the new postkeeper. What a blessing, that Theuntje would at least have a woman with children to talk to.

Their lives changed after her discharge from banishment. He sailed from the bay in the morning, his thoughts at home with his wife. If only there could be somebody with her, it would have eased his mind. It wasn't about her safety at home, since everyone knew that no Hottentot or Hollander would harm a woman; it was because of her state of mind. You could not put a hand through a looking glass to touch what was behind it. It was the part you could not see when you peered into her eyes, like where the mercury had perished behind a mirror; there was something like a hideous cancer behind her face, behind her greeting, behind her smile. *There* Theuntje was alone with her thoughts. She could try to explain it to him, but he could never experience it, and what she did not tell him, did not exist. She stood on one side of an ocean and he on the other. Islands, both. For all eternity he could only imagine what his wife felt.

Visitors no longer came to their house. When he sailed out, to Saldanha Bay or Hoedjes Bay, both knew that she would be alone for fourteen days. Her friends were shy; they might come again later, but now was too soon, because Theun was a criminal who'd been exposed at the stake, Theun had been before the court, Theun had been in the dungeon. She was that against which people were sermonised, admonished, warned. Theun had to be avoided, otherwise one turned one's Bible and one's minister into liars. She had broken the penultimate commandment: *Thou shalt not bear false witness against thy neighbour.* And so, when Theuntje went with a basket of fish from door to door, they did not open, or they spoke through the shutter, and sent her away: they didn't need anything, they didn't want to buy fish. If Bart went with the basket himself, they needed fish. She was now keeping a little bird in the house, and two hares in the backyard, all of them in cages. She would clean the house and feed the chickens, perhaps go for a walk along the vlei, always alone.

Bart sailed out in his boat with his barrels and brought them back full of fresh fish he'd caught, filleted, salted, cured. There were more fish in these waters than he could ever catch. In Salamander Bay he clambered on the rocks and cut as much red-bait as he would need for one day. Then he would sail north up the narrows of Saldanha Bay in the direction of Table Mountain, and where he spotted fish shoaling in the shallow water he cast his net and hauled in hundreds of large mullet. It was a lovely place, with almost no sign of a human being. Sometimes he saw Koina on a distant shore, and they would shout a few words at him and wave a greeting. At night he anchored offshore in a quiet cove, ate his bread and fish, wrapped himself in a blanket, and shifted in under the forward half-deck with a bottle of brandy to sleep. He could hear the night sounds of lions, jackals and wolves, but he was safe and snug. But it wasn't good for Theuntje, alone. Perhaps they should think of giving up here, and go to the Netherlands where they were no longer known.

With his barrels filled, he would collect a few dozen black mussels and a couple of lobsters, and pack them into his seawater barrel to convey them to the Fort alive. Then he was ready for the return. It took him a day from Saldanha Bay when the wind was north, but a day and half a night with a headwind. Then he did not head straight for the Fort but first touched at Robben Island to see Master Pieter, with a gift of lobsters and fish. It gave him pleasure to see the man's children, and convey Theuntje's regards. For little Pieternella he sometimes took a bunch of blood-red flamingo feathers from the salt pan of Geelbeksfontein, or a large colourful shell, or the white glass earbone of a whale.

Behind Dassen Island Bart occasionally encountered a ship that had been blown past Table Bay, or because there had been no one left alive or capable of standing watch at the helm, and now lay anchored on its lee side. Most of the crew were black with scurvy. To the captains he offered what food he could, including fish, penguin eggs, sorrel or fresh scurvy grass from the island. If they offered cash, he allowed himself to be persuaded to take the foreign gentleman ashore and barter a sheep or two from the Koina. But that was only for *oorlam* ships on the way to the north, and out of these waters. To outward-bound ships he gave food and showed them where Table Mountain was, so that his name would never be mentioned to the commander concerning affairs beyond his contract. Sometimes the shallow anchorage at Dassen Island stood fouled by swaying corpses, sewn in canvas. He got them up on his anchor flukes or in his fishing nets. Once he brought up large lobsters feeding on the face of a corpse, and offered them to Tielman Hendriksz at the Cape.

As his service improved, his income grew, and Bart started thinking about acquiring a slave. He was no longer quite so indigent. Several of the freemen had acquired a slave or two to fish for them. The Company bought fish, the Elephant inn was a good customer, and there was daily commerce at the houses in town. Wagenaer treated him very well indeed, for mussels and lobsters and delicacies that ladies and gentlemen consumed with salt and pepper and white wine. With a helper he would fill his barrels inside of a week, then he'd get home sooner. And the slave could sell from door to door, instead of Theuntje who had become too timid to knock on doors.

'You can look up again, Theuntje. Lift your head.'

'I cannot put on another face, like the comedy players.'

'If it goes well, and we can salt away something, we can go back to the fatherland. Another while of this life, then we float again.'

Captain Bakker of the homeward-bound ship *Nagtegaal* hailed Bart in Hoedjes Bay to come closer, to ask if he knew of someone at the Cape who might wish to buy a slave. He was on his way to the Netherlands now with this man, and it was to his disadvantage, as he'd been blown past the Cape and they didn't allow slaves in the Low Countries. It was a good man, his name was Jan Vos, two years out of West Africa. He'd bought him on the way out as an assistant carpenter. The slave had the same build as Bart, average, black as soot, with a smile and a firm handshake. Bart paid for him with fish and penguin eggs, took him home to show his wife, and then to the Fort, to have him entered in the slave book. They knocked together a lean-to room for him on to the house, out of planks from the Company's galliot which had been wrecked on Dassen Island because of its quarter-master's incompetence. Out of fine duck Theuntje made clothes for the slave.

As Bart had expected, Jan Vos made his work easier by half. He lived simply, asked no favours, spoke little and worked hard. He was *orang lama*, a wise man who had seen the Orient, and his voice was soft. They would gather bait in the early morning, drift for a whole day with lines and nets, gut, fillet and tub fish, and barely speak two sentences to one another. Out of gratitude Bart treated him with care. It was Jan who proposed that they build a kraal of bushes near the beach and spend the nights on land. Jan built the shelter, Bart got on with his work on the water. With a fire at the entrance to ward off animals, they grilled fish in the evenings and enjoyed their bread and fish and wine, working on their nets and lines by firelight. Such was their life in that deserted bay, where there was more fish than the two of them could handle. It was the year the big comet appeared in the sky.

Once again all trouble came from the sea. First there was the fleet like never before, the so-called Bitter Fleet. It had the biggest and among them the most beautiful ships Bart had ever seen together. There were twelve of them laden with the treasures of the Orient. All deeply pregnant, as Jack Tar has it. Bart and Jan were drifting in the mouth of Table Bay when the flag went up on the Lion's Head, and shot after shot of brown smoke was fired from up there. Twelve shots, then Bart brailed up their sail.

'Wait, Jan. Haul in first. I want to see this.'

They approached, broad-chested across the water, from a slight haze. They were magnificent ships, ships like cathedrals, gigantic, dark brown, the masts slender and tall as towers, the broad brown hulls green with seaweed, the gunwales and galleries decorated with worn gold paint and carving, with a thin breeze from the south-west, with their topsails brailed, and their yards full of seamen waiting for the word to fling them out again. The tops were a feast of colour with flags of the father-land, the prince, the Company, the six different chambers, their commissioning pennants and the long white pennant of the admiral. On each ship an anchor team clambered outboard on to gunwales and catheads to cut anchors loose; on the quarterdecks stood, very satis-fied, some officers. They coolly gazed into Bart's eyes while their ships trailed in single file between his sloop and the Green Point, towards the anchorage. Bart saw signs that they had suffered sea damage: there was patching on hulls, missing lanterns, mended spars. He sat motion-less in his sloop as it rolled in their wake, thinking of the stately ships of de Vlamingh's homeward-bound fleet that never reached the Cape. Twelve ships – Jan Vos smiled at him – what a splendid sight. As the flagship passed the dunes, the Fort commenced firing its welcoming salute.

Should he sail out to Saldanha now, Bart wondered after the last ship had passed, or should he stay at the Cape today? Tonight the streets would be brimming with sailors. But Jan Vos pointed downwind.

'All right, here we go.' With that he shook loose the sail. Ahead of them was a long stretch of sea to Saldanha Bay. 'Get our foresail up too, I think.'

And when he came back, there was a notification that his sloop had been commandeered by the government. He had to help them replenish and refresh this fleet. Farmers' wagons and animals had been commandeered to carry firewood, and he had to assist by transporting wood, people, ship's biscuit, vegetables and still more people between the quay and these ships. The Company would pay, he was promised, for the use of his boat and his slave, but Bart knew it would not be a quarter of what he could have earned by sailing to Saldanha Bay. For three weeks he and Jan Vos ran a lighter service for the Company, taking their breakfast and lunch on board.

From the *oorlamme* Bart heard many anecdotes about these ships. What the admiral told his captain or his clerk today, his steward would tell his butler, and the butler the third mate, and he in turn the boatswain. Then the boatswain would fire up the ordinary seamen with the words: 'I hear we have three thousand diamonds on board, my hearties. But they don't belong to you. So up from your blankets. You've got to work for your biscuit and beans.' Bart also heard what the cargo was, and that the Cape commander had told someone that this was the greatest treasure that had ever existed in one place on earth, and that he had news from the Netherlands that the English already knew about every damned guilder and were ready to declare red war to get their bloody paws on it. One very wealthy passenger had gold nailed under the bilge water of his ship, and Mister Borghorst was carrying his whole fortune in diamonds in a small bag suspended in a place where no one but himself was likely to look.

The news of another war with England arrived soon afterwards from the fatherland. Bart heard it at the inn. What was to become now of this fleet, which had to avoid their hereditary enemy in order to reach Dutch ports? What was to become now of the five thousand sailors, the gold, the pearls and spices, the silk and the precious stones? What was to become of the poor fatherland? If England won, they would all become slaves, all the houses would be laid low.

While the Bitter fleet lay at the Cape, the market for fresh fish and pickled herring flourished, yet Bart wasn't in a position to do anything about it. For three weeks he and Jan Vos helped to equip the fleet to speed it on its way. And he wasn't paid in cash. The commander had written off a part of his debt on the books.

The ship that brought the news of war, also brought Inspector Goske. Wherever the Company wanted to establish a fort, it first sent out Goske. One morning the inhabitants of the Cape saw many small white flags planted among the dunes. Then they heard that here a huge castle was going to be built. They learned that the Company was going to send many additional artisans and would be renting wagons, oxen and labourers from the farmers. For Bart this was excellent news. If the garrison increased, the demand for fresh and salted fish would grow. Long live war, may it flourish, smiled the merchants. War was good for business, provided it happened far away from you.

A long boxlike structure was built in the dunes between Bart's cottage and the Fort. It looked as if Noah's ark had stranded there, right above the high-water mark. That building became the mother of the Castle: whatever was prepared inside went into the ground outside to become the Castle.

On the second day of 1666 the Company put its hand in its pocket to make a happy day for its workers. It was a day that would be remembered for years. There was no labour on that day. The deep and wide trenches for the Castle's foundations had been cut. Inside them, tables were placed on trestles, and for all who had lent a hand or were still to lend a hand with the work, there were meat and bread, pies and tarts, vegetable salad, wine and beer. Those who hadn't been involved in the building were ordered away. There were fireworks and music, more beer, and some short speeches, where the main business happened in the trenches directly in front of the gentlemen's table. There the cornerstones of Castle Good Hope were laid. Bart had already seen the stones on Robben Island, where they had been cut, engraved and crated for the crossing. All the honourable gentlemen stepped forward. The stones were big and imposing, silver-grey in colour, engraved in ornamental writing. One bore the name of Wagenaer, another that of Lacus. After the feast the tables were taken away and the stones covered up for ever, and it was a pity that other people from the Cape were not given a glimpse of them, and also that Theuntje had not felt like going with him to enjoy the happy day. The leftover food was given to the poor living in the dunes, where more and more homeless Koina had come to pitch shelters, to beg odd jobs at the new Castle.

After that, the new Castle became like a beehive: slow and dark it grew above the dunes, while hundreds worked on it in silence. In good weather and bad, service boats ran between island and quay, bringing more slate and shells. People were sentenced for small misdemeanours, to incur banishment to Robben Island, where they carried shells for the new Castle. There were times when Bart counted up to four hundred bags of shells, waiting to be conveyed from the island in one load. And on the same day they would be burned into lime, by which time the shell boat was on its way back to the island. He expected them to commandeer his own sloop for this task, or for transporting fuel for the lime oven or timber from Hout Bay too, if he wasn't careful.

Lords Seventeen calculated that if they dispatched a thousand soldiers to the Cape to build their Castle, gun in one hand and trowel in the other, they should also send out a soldier with a sword on the hip, a sash over the shoulder and a feather in the hat to oversee the whole enterprise. Bart, with difficulty, persuaded Theuntje to go with him to say goodbye to Commander Wagenaer one evening after sunset, when it was raining so hard that there was no one else in the streets.

'You should make friends with this van Quaelberg, Bartholomeus,' suggested Wagenaer. 'The man is a Hollander, and that means money in your purse. Go and talk to his secretary, ask for an interview. Don't get the cook's permission to go in through the kitchen door as you did with me. A soldier is a stickler for his honour. It's all they have, you see. So, take my advice, do it properly and ask to talk to him about the Saldanha fishing business. And you, Theuntje, you have suffered enough. Forget about the thing now. Have a couple of children, learn to laugh again. Children are a great joy, I can tell you. There's a German blessing: Beans in the pot, a rooster on the beam, children around your table. So. That is my wish for you.'

About that time Postkeeper van Meerhof's wife had another baby. A messenger came to their house about the christening, but they didn't go. It was Theuntje; she was sick with concern about something Bart no longer understood.

Commander van Quaelberg had been behind his plume for only three months when a French fleet sailed into Table Bay. They saluted the Fort with numerous volleys and acknowledged the humble reply from the Fort, and dropped their anchors on the outer anchorage. They were from the French East India Company, and their destination was Madagascar. The harbourmaster and surgeon of the Fort returned from their visit with reports of damage, disease, dirt and disorder, much worse than on any Dutch outgoing ship. Van Quaelberg visited the admiral on the flagship. As cadet he had learned not to trust a Frenchman, especially not when he was playing dead; before you knew it, *you* would be the corpse. Look at their flag, for instance, that white one: you thought the fleet had surrendered, then you discovered it was their flag of war. That was why he had to go on board himself. He was well received and entertained, and felt relieved. The French were to start a refreshment post on Madagascar and, like the Dutch, they wanted to trade in Oriental goods on the Indian continent. Madagascar would be their refreshment station, as the English were using St Helena Island and the Dutch the Cape.

Van Quaelberg welcomed the French as a possible ally against the English here in the South Atlantic. Whatever they asked for, he supplied to his guests: accommodation for the officers in the Company's pleasure house, ship's timber, fuel, food and wine from the Company's ware-house. Also carpenters, and treatment for their patients in the hospital. For all these favours the admiral paid him in gold coins.

Bart, at the quay, saw the Fort's lighters transporting the material to the outer anchorage. Carrying shells for the Castle was their real work. He knew the Company as a stingy employer, one that didn't suffer interlopers in its trade route. But under this new commander now, the French dined at the Fort one night, and the next night they all dined on board with the admiral. Then van Quaelberg, the commander, came with his sash and plumed hat, and other gentlemen, and at nightfall they were all rowed to the French flagship. At midnight farewell shots would be fired from the French flagship, and an hour later the guests arrived back at their own quay, noisy and staggering. The French were clearly hospitable, and the Dutch wanted to surpass them at it. Bart heard the whole story from the quartermasters, who had to wait with a cold and wet crew in the boat tied alongside, while the officers enjoyed their banquet on board. They were unhappy about this; they weren't the gentlemen's lackeys, they were tired and had no wish to row a ferry for midnight revellers. When the Company's cellars and warehouses were almost empty, the French departed.

Bart and Jan were cutting out red-bait from the rocks in Salamander Bay when the French entered the mouth with their white flags flying. What were they doing there? Madagascar, he knew, lay in the opposite direction. Perhaps the sea had brought him something today, but he had to be very careful. Jan pulled up the anchor into their boat, and Bart allowed wind and water to carry them to the open sea south of Jutten Island, right into the path of the fleet, where they cast out their lines. The fish fought for their hooks. There were yellowtail and large cob, as many as they could draw in; the hook barely hit the water before the next fish was fast. All the while they kept an eye on the French ships. The fleet followed the huge flagship in, tack upon tack. Then foresails and mainsails were taken in and secured, while anchor parties set to work preparing the anchors. They meant to anchor here, to talk to him. As the flagship loomed like a brown mountain over Bart's little boat, they all turned against the wind, and started dropping back. Then they let their anchors fall. Getting away was now out of the question. Seven massive ships lay anchored downwind from him. A fellow with a loudhailer and broad hand gestures hung over the quarterdeck rail to invite him and Jan Vos on board. Jan took a turn with their anchor rope round the flagship's cable, to prevent them from drifting off.

'Do you have someone there who speaks Dutch?' Bart called.

'Most of us speak Dutch if we want to.'

'Does your cook want to buy fish?'

There followed a conversation behind the gunwale. Faces looked into his boat. Then the hailer hung back over the side. 'He wants everything you have. We're letting down a barrel. The captain wants to talk to you.'

'No fish without cash.'

'All right. You can make a deal up here.'

A thick rope fell over the side. Bart made it clear to Jan: no fish without cash. Then he clambered up the rope with hands and feet, and climbed over the side. What he had heard about the dirt was true. He, who had first served before the mast at the age of ten, had never seen the like. People with food in their hands stood before him, eating. That was something seamen never did; they ate at mealtime, when they would go down to the forecastle to sit down around the mess pan, take off their caps, ask the blessing, and eat. Then it would be over until the whistle blew again. These people were raw landsmen. But then a real sailor with two feet thick with tar came to stand beside him and relieved himself against the foot of the foremast.

'Here, be off, you swine,' Bart told him. Had he been the boatswain here he'd have buried half his shoe in the man's backside. One shouldn't mess on board like that. In the bright sunlight on deck he could see bandages someone had plucked from a wound, covered in blood and pus. And there were chips of wood, shavings, fistfuls of oakum in the scuppers where a carpenter had abandoned his work. Here I'm not setting foot below deck, he thought, I won't step into human excrement with my bare feet.

What the admiral wished to know from Bart, he asked through an interpreter.

'Does Monsieur Borms realise that the Company's settlement in Table Bay is illegal?'

'No, how come?'

'Your Company's charter is from Cape of Good Hope eastward to Cape Horn.'

'Right.'

'Table Bay is west of Cape of Good Hope.'

'By the hound's hairy balls.'

'Pardon?'

'No, I'm not arguing.'

'Yes. Well, Commander van Quaelberg admitted that your Directors cannot have any objection if our Company founds an outpost in this bay.'

'Yes.'

'Fishing seems to be very good here in the bay. Has Monsieur Borms been paid yet?'

'I said no fish without cash.'

'Let us go on deck. We'd better take a look. Some of our seamen don't think anything of another's property. Does Monsieur Borms often visit this bay?'

Jan Vos had already paid out the head rope, so that he was lying some distance downwind. 'You watch out, Bart, these people mean to rob us.'

'Stay there, Jan. Keep ready to shake out sail the moment I jump. Get up the foresail.'

The interpreter tried to calm him. There was no danger. They wanted to negotiate in peace. If Bart called his fisherman closer, the cook would send baskets overboard and Bart would receive the cash here at the gunwale.

While they waited for the baskets, the admiral pursued his questioning.

'Van Quaelberg received us with the utmost hospitality and offered us all the help we asked for.'

'That is possible. He is a rich man.'

'We understand, we understand. Monsieur Borms will be paid for his services. But it is the principle we wish to bring to his attention. Commander van Quaelberg has no objection against our presence or our activity or our plan. He opened his warehouse to us, and bade farewell to us with a generous salute. So much is proven. And it is a worthy example to follow.'

'I shall bring Your Honour a few lobsters.'

'No need. But there's something else you can do for us. Stay on board for a few days while we explore the bay, and I will give you six of these louis d'or for every day's work.'

'Ten. If I break the law I'll be kicked out of this country without a stitch.'

'Then your commander will also be kicked out.'

'He's a rich man.'

So it was agreed. He guided the French East India Company's fleet into Hoedjes Bay where they anchored out of sight so that no one would discover them, unless by coincidence. There he showed them how to collect dunewood, not the branches of wind-blown shrubs, but the gnarled burls of their roots, thick as a man's thigh and so hard that the embers smouldered for a day and a night. That was what warmed a cook's heart. He took two officers overland to the Witklip, the White Rock, where there was a fresh-water spring, and suggested that they dig a trench to the bay to carry the water, if they were serious about their outpost. He took them to hunt, and to tracts of black earth where they could sow grain. He climbed rocky hills with them to show them the best views over the various bays, so that they could draw maps. He made contact with Koina, and made sure he was well out of the way while they bartered sheep and cattle.

Two of their sailing boats went out every day to sound different inlets, and two others, with provisions of food and water for the day, followed Bart's sloop, and he would point out the protected anchorages: Rietbaai, the reed bay which was laid dry twice a day by the tide, where it was easy to careen a ship; then the sweet-water spring on the Oostewal; and the brackish spring behind Bruidegompunt. He led them to the five islands where plump brown seals lay like sausages in a pan waiting to be transformed into oil. He showed them the eggs, the feathers, the wealth in building lime and granite of the region. For each day's work they gave him the ten pieces of gold. The day they examined the southernmost end of the bay near Geelbeksfontein, they came upon some of the Company's soldiers, pretending to be building a posthouse. Bart recognised young *Secundus* de Cretser, standing there with a bushpick in his hand, and he hung well back while the interpreter spoke to them.

The Company's tent was pitched there, with their pot and a pan, and beside it was a short piece of old ship's timber driven into the ground, with a board nailed to the top displaying the Company's monogram. The foundations of the building they were pretending to build were in the shape of a two-roomed house, partly staked out with large stones. It would take two men more than three months to build a post-house like that. But where was their boat? One couldn't survive so far from the Cape without a boat. Where would one go with sick people, what was there to eat once one's rations ran out, where would you escape to if you were attacked by lions or by Bushmen? Every time you would be driven back into the sea. And Bart could swear that these men had not been there two days ago. One only needed to look at how few bones lay on their rubbish heap.

But the interpreter and the two officials were arguing about 'primary claim' and 'closest existing headquarters' and 'first physical occupation' and suchlike things, on which their respective governments had prompted them. They parted with courteous assurances that they were one another's obedient servants, that their governments in Europe would examine the matter. On the way back to the boat Bart could hear that the French were annoyed. They believed that van Quaelberg was now trying to thwart their project. Clearly the commander had unexpectedly changed his attitude. Would he now be in trouble for that?

From there Bart and Jan in their sloop led the procession to the sweet-water fountain at Geelbeksfontein. They moved in among vast flocks of trampling flamingos, at which the French shot for their pleasure. Bart explained that the bird could be prepared like a duck, except that it always floated in an ugly layer of red grease. When he noticed that they were listening very attentively, he asked the interpreter to tell them, that if the French no longer needed him he would prefer to resume his work. Afterwards, he conducted them to the natural slipway at Stompe Hoek, where a steep beach rose from deep waters as if nature had specially prepared it for the needs of a loaded return ship. The French admiral angrily discussed with his officers plans to plant markers at several spots in the bay, bearing the device of their king. This excellent slope was one of them. After that the three boats left the bay on a long straight run before a south-wester, to where the French fleet rested under their white flags behind Hoedjespunt.

The next day, on the sea between Dassen Island and the Cape, Bart brought out his French money, counted out some pieces in his hand and offered them to Jan Vos, but Jan shook his head and dropped them back into the little skin-bag.

'I don't know what to do with it, Bart. If I know one day, I shall take it.'

Bart expected trouble back at the Cape. He and Jan carried their fish and nets ashore and tended the boat. Then Jan wanted to walk to the Fort to buy tobacco. Bart called Theuntje into their bedroom with its strange sense of emptiness, and emptied the small bag of gold coins on the bed. She had recently taken to wearing black; she was exhausted with loneliness, silent, depressed, wary of her own face in the mirror.

'There is enough here for both of us to go away.'

She wanted to know how he'd earned it, and what it was worth in Dutch money. She wasn't glad. She wasn't grateful. She wasn't excited. She barely smiled when she dropped the coins back into the doeskin bag. 'Thank you, Bart. It is yours. I shall go when you want us to go. I am afraid that may land us in more trouble.'

He buried the bag in the corner of their bedroom. The money would last them a while. So, even though he wasn't rich, he felt a bit more at ease about their old age. But he had to put that thought away, and not start playing rich. He had to stay poor, and live simply in the comfortable knowledge of having hidden something away in the corner. He and Theuntje talked about giving up the Saldanha Bay run. She wanted him to sleep at home more often, having her husband home once in a fortnight was not enough. He thought that if he sold the boat *Bruid* and bought something smaller, or built it himself, they could pay their last instalments to the government and still show a profit. Here in the river mouth at his door, with the blessing of the Lord, he could catch as much fish as he could possibly sell, fresh, dried and salted. And he needed to spend more time with his wife, at home.

It was hard to discuss this personal matter with Jan. Bart had come to like the man; they worked well together. He explained that he was going to cut down on his business; he wanted to live at home and carry his own fish to market. He wasn't the kind who could stay home and send out a slave to earn his bread for him. But there was one thing he wanted to ask of Jan, that was to help him build a yawl which he could use here in the vlei as well as out in the bay. Not as a slave, but as a hired labourer. After that he would set him free, if that was what he desired and if the Company would allow it. Jan said, good.

Commander van Quaelberg had grown grey since Bart had last seen him. Grey in the face, and somewhere he had lost his sword and plume. But he was happy to buy back the sloop *Bruid*. The Castle now required such an abundance of shells and slate, that there barely remained transport for servicing the ships. He had tried to buy boats from homeward-bound ships, but of course the captains wouldn't part with any, as that would be their salvation in case of emergency. So if Bart would bring the boat to the quay, he would send a quartermaster to assess it.

Then Bart enquired about the possibility of setting his slave free.

'No, that isn't permitted. The Company will buy the slave from you. We need many hands at the Castle, but no free slaves, we already have too many here. Tomorrow or the next day your freed slave lands in the lap of the Church Council as an indigent, or he commits crimes, and then has to work on the island in chains at our loss and risk. That's how it goes with free slaves. But your sloop we'll buy, as she stands.'

On the green grass in front of the cottage, Bart and Jan started building the yawl, with timber he had bought from his profit on *Bruid*. Right next to their nets and drying frames they laid down the keel and put the frame on the stocks. He explained to Jan what the commander had said about freed slaves. 'That's what they say, Jan. I don't want you to go into the Company's service. But the postkeeper on Robben Island is a friend of mine, and he's looking for somebody, because he's going abroad for a few months. Most of his work there is done by convicts. You know Master Pieter, and you know what his house looks like.' He gave Jan time to think.

Jan was working with the adze and the saw, very precisely. 'Do as you think fit, Bart. I'll be glad to get away from the sea for a while.'

'You can make a living as a carpenter.'

'I have no land. I need a house and tools.' And added to this was the certainty that it would take a long time for clients to give up their accustomed carpenter and bring their work to a free black. Only if the man worked for practically nothing would they do such a thing.

'I shall speak to the postkeeper.'

When the yawl was finished and its mast stepped and rigged, he and Jan crossed and recrossed the shiny smooth river mouth, for the boat to work itself loose. It was an ordinary yawl, with a fairly flat bottom and without much of a keel. The single mast carried a foresail and a small mainsail. It was meant only for shallow water, a one-man boat. They lowered sails, pulled to the shore, tightened the stays and hammered in the caulking more tightly until it no longer let in water. Then the bottom was smoothed with pitch.

One day the island's postkeeper sent a message that he should be leaving for Madagascar any day now. It would be good if Bart could bring the slave, so that he could pay him. For Bart the pleasure of visiting the island was that he could see the children, take them something Theuntje had baked, and come home in the evening and tell her how much they had grown since his previous visit. And the way in which Master Pieter and Jan Vos shook hands in front of him, there on the island, came as a relief. It was going to work out.

He asked the postkeeper to ask on the voyage, in case free burghers were now allowed on Mauritius, what conditions were like under their new commander, what kind of life a free man might expect, and to inform him of everything on his return. Goodbye, then. He would look after the wife and children.

The following spring was full of good weather and bad news. At first there were rumours of peace, later the truth became clear: the enemy had sued for peace; the terrible plague, a great fire in its capital and the Dutch fleet had temporarily brought England to its knees. There was much cursing about this in the town and new Castle. People who in one way or another make their profit from war loathe peace. One of the worst cases Bart came across was a man whose only daughter had married an officer here, and was now with the coming of peace expecting a transfer. All Bart personally expected concerning the Castle was that the garrison would be diminished, but that all work on it would be summarily stopped, leaving it lying half built in the grass around the ark, came as a surprise to all, and a most unwelcome one to most. Farmers, wood carriers, washerwomen, bakers, innkeepers, all were suddenly deprived of an income. All cursed the peace. Bart remembered his personal good luck, to be rid of his sloop before the market collapsed.

Next came the news of Master Pieter's death.

'What will become of the children?' Theuntje asked.

'No, their mother is still alive, remember.'

'You should go and ask, Bart.'

'I don't know, the woman has a sharp tongue. I feel it isn't right, the children still have their mother. If she should get angry now, she may turn against us. But I'll see if I can get a message to her.'

His trouble came three months later, when a replacement for Commander van Quaelberg arrived from the Netherlands, with powerful letters. There was good news and bad news. The good news was that ten ships of the Bitter fleet, the richest fleet ever, had safely delivered their cargo to the fatherland, after terrifying deprivation visited upon them by nature and man. There was a marvellous triumph in that. Then, the bad news. Lords Seventeen were disappointed that van Quaelberg had entertained the French, their adversary in the Eastern trade, had provided them with all forms of comfort and provisions, and allowed them to fathom and chart Saldanha Bay and explore all its natural resources. They compared van Quaelberg to King Hezekiah of the Old Testament, quoting the passage from 2 Kings: '*And Hezekiah said, All the things that are in my house have they seen: there is nothing among all my treasures that I have not shewed them. And the prophet Isaiah said unto Hezekiah, Hear the words of the Lord. Behold, the days come, that all that is in thine house shall be carried into Babylon: nothing shall be left.*' With that, van Quaelberg was summoned to Batavia. His replacement was Commander Jacob Borghorst. Concerning the Saldanha farer Borms, Commander Borghorst had to make it clear to him that he had committed treason and was no longer welcome or trusted at the Cape.

Bart remembered Borghorst. He had been vice-admiral of the Bitter fleet, the gentleman who had enriched himself through private trade and sailed home with his life's fortune in the form of diamonds carried on his body. Now the English had taken his ship and discovered his hiding place, and so here, old, embittered and impoverished, he had to start again as commander of a difficult little outstation. Instead of wealth he was given the Cape of Good Hope.

'Traitors get a bullet between the eyes, Borms,' Borghorst said to his face.

'I only did it as a favour, sir. I noticed how well disposed Commander van Quaelberg was towards these people, so I thought he would appreciate my help.'

'Such limp excuses did not help van Quaelberg, Borms. How much did they pay you?'

'They cheated me, sir.'

'I don't believe it. If you received anything, if the Company ever finds French money on you, your boat and your slave and other possessions will be confiscated, and you will be charged with treason. You will be flogged, and condemned to carry shells on Robben Island for twelve or twenty years.'

Could it be that the new commander envied him his good fortune? He had to devise a plan for the day this gentleman would drag him to court because of his French money. Only Jan Vos and *Secundus* de Cretser could testify against him. And, he and Theuntje decided, it would be best to leave the Cape. They could go to the fatherland, although tales from that part of the world had it that the climate was changing and the country was dying of cold. The North Pole was reaching ever further south, with more and more Europeans fleeing ahead of it. Canals were no longer navigable, the Haarlemmer Lake remained frozen all year round, the pastures were snowed under, drinking water turned to ice. All one's savings went into firewood and peat.

Then there was Theuntje, still going about with downcast eyes. He wanted to take her to a warm place where she would not recognise a single person. 'Mauritius,' Bart said to her. 'You will enjoy it, Theuntje. I was happy there, once.'

The new commander encouraged their departure. He'd heard that Bart's wife had been convicted of slander. It was the Directors' policy, he said, to dispatch drunken and useless farmers and other rabble to that outstation. He was prepared to employ Bart as a sailor, and place him and his wife on the next ship to the island. That would be *Lepelaar*. There Bart would serve in the garrison. The journey would be free.

Bart smiled under his beard. With this prospect he auctioned their plot with the cottage and the fishing huts Jan Vos had built, the yawl with its equipment and nets, and the salt fish he had in stock. The offer was not good, so soon after the war, but Bart had expected that, and regretted for a moment that he'd sold his valuable slave so cheaply. They were not nearly as affluent as he'd hoped on the day they left the Cape, but there was a little something hidden in a hollow bamboo, and he looked forward to the new home.

The hooker *Lepelaar* had been serviced and equipped to leave for Mauritius within days, when one blustery black night it was captured from the anchorage by five escaped convicts and sailed out of the bay. He and Theun were forced to wait for the time being, to stay at the Cape longer, to spend more money. In the end, no other transport was available except for the yacht *Voerman*. It had been equipped for collecting shells, and between decks it had to be demolished and rebuilt completely to provide living quarters. After that they had to ship drinking water, fuel, beer and other provisions for a second time.

'Our ship is small and the swell huge down there where we're going, Theuntje. We're not going to have an easy journey,' Bart warned her.

With them, a new commanding officer departed for Mauritius. His name was Georg Wreede. He was short, German and dark, and it was his second term on the island. In the forecastle Bart learned that he was the man who had initiated the sawing of ebony on Mauritius, and the one about whom his subjects had complained, on account of his love for the dark, bitter beer. But Bart remembered something else about him. When Wagenaer had been commander at the Cape, this Wreede had questioned Eva and Herrie and other natives and made a thick book of Koina words with their Dutch meanings next to them. The Directors were to have it printed, so that overland travellers could carry the dictionary with them in their bags to speak to the natives from it. Why had it not happened? And here Wreede was now, a second-chance man. What could one learn from it? Firstly, to devote your effort and trouble to yourself. Secondly, that there was no need to speak to a Hottentot in his language. They should speak Dutch. That was what the Lords wished everyone to understand.

Far to the south, *Voerman* battled against the sea, as it was winter down there and the ship hadn't been built for weather like that. Bart was rigger's mate. His bed in the forecastle had a hand-width of oak between him and the mindless blows of the sea. In the daytime he was at work, to tighten, to fasten, to repair or replace whatever wind and water had worn or loosened or carried away. The first watch at the helm was his every morning, and again first after sunset. For the first three weeks, day after day, they battled head-on against heavy rain under a low, leaden sky. Under small sail the ship staggered against waves, falling forward at the other side with the bowsprit turned downward, then battling up once more against the next slanting slope of glass-green seawater, the white foam streaming like rivers from it. Six days out of the Cape, the worst began. Two of them had to tend the helm as the sea was too strong for one. The weather was nothing to Bart, he'd known worse. When he ducked into the forecastle after his second turn at the tiller, in the musty half-dark hole where a smoking lamp and wet clothes on hooks swung in wide black circles, he was half dead. But there was no worry. Skipper and boatswain knew where they were on the ocean, there were two good helmsmen steering, the cook knew they had to be fed.

Bart was at home. He understood his work and did it well. Every day at sea was one closer to their port of destination. Theuntje, he discovered, was lodged behind a screen in the cabin, sick as a dog. There were other women too. He let her sleep, but knocked on her door from time to time to ask how she felt.

More than eight weeks out of Table Bay, they arrived in front of the South-East Gap of Mauritius. The captain wanted the galliot to be tidy on entering, the deck scrubbed, new sails tied on, everything stowed and secured, a lick of paint here and there to make up for what the sea had taken. The ship was small, it wasn't difficult. And when they went ashore one day, Bart was satisfied. Here Chief Wreede was master: he saw what Bart Borms could do, that he absolutely knew his work. And here was his captain, and captain and boatswain would give a good report of him.

It was seven years since he had last seen Mauritius. With the clarity of youthful impressions he could recall the names of peaks and islets. Kompasberg: as you entered the gap, Kompasberg would rise up like a finger behind the bay; it reached up straight behind the mountains in front, like a middle finger raised at you. That was how one entered the South-East Gap at Mauritius: you saw the middle finger and followed it until you dropped anchor in the basin in front of the Lodge.

In the rowing boat Theuntje looked around, with a smile of expectation. 'There are miracles here,' Bart had told her, as eagerly as a traveller before a journey. 'There you see Fisherman's Isle. The water is so clear you can see your supper swimming down below with its friends. You put in your hand, you pull it out. There is Cat's Island, there is Lady's Hat.'

Beside a rickety bit of scaffolding, partly of wood, partly stone, where two gentlemen stood looking down into their boat, hands behind their backs, the rowers held fast, so that their passengers could clamber out. Bart motioned at Theuntje to wait, the gentlemen had to do the welcoming first. On the rise above the beach a red-white-blue flag hung limply from a post. Next to it was a bell, dull with verdigris, suspended from a frame. Behind it stood a long wooden building, like the ark at the Cape. One would imagine that the two had been constructed from a single plan. The walls of the old Fort had been removed for the most part, and a number of shelters made of palm fronds on bamboo frames formed a semicircle on the lee side. There were people at work. On the land side was a jungle of young palm trees.

Ensign Smient and a clerk shook hands with Chief Wreede, the captain and boatswain, beckoned to two slaves on the shore to fetch Wreede's baggage, and escorted him on either side to the posthouse, as if they were leading a new prisoner to his cell. The captain and boatswain followed, assisted by their sailors. Then Bart helped Theuntje out. Their sea chests were still on board.

Inside they were welcomed by the head of the garrison. He introduced himself as Sergeant Philipe Col. He was a young man of perhaps twenty. He hadn't known about Bart's arrival, but a new face was always welcome. The married quarters were here down the passage. It was a single room, not the most wonderful accommodation of course, but when their chests arrived at the quay he would send someone to help. Chief Wreede would decide what Bart's duties were to be. And that was about it. The bell would ring for morning and evening prayers and mealtimes. The dining tables were in the big hall. There they would meet the rest of the staff.

'Theuntje,' said Bart, 'now we are free. Now you must look again like you looked when I first found you sitting in the flowers.'

'When, Bart?'

'It was on Tielman's farm.'

'There is now a lifetime in between.'

'We are starting again. If you think of turning back, it must be before the galliot leaves.'

First *Voerman* had to be readied for the return journey. There was a deep hole next to a stretch of sand half an hour north of the post, known as the French Church. It was hidden from the post behind a rough point. They brought the ship into that pool at high tide, where it would lie dry at the ebb. Then it was careened on its port side, scraped, burned and smoothed with pitch. At high tide the ship rose up and was immediately careened to starboard, for them to do the other side. At the next high tide *Voerman* was returned to the anchorage. And there Bart and two helpers served the rigging from forward to aft. All the standing gear was tightened and tarred, all the sheaves were greased, scuffed places were parcelled, deck joints were caulked and tarred, all the pumps were hauled up, dismantled, cleaned and put back. Then the superstructure, railings, masts, sprits, panelling and gunwales were saturated with linseed oil. Afterwards a cargo of ebony and lime and the ship's provisions for the Cape were loaded.

It was the last rigger's work Bart did on *Voerman*. Once the captain was satisfied and Chief Wreede had signed for it all, a leave-taking was prepared for *Voerman*'s officers. It was quite an occasion, the boatswain and one of the clerks wandered off the end of the quay arm in arm into the sea. In the early morning the pilot boat escorted *Voerman* through the gap out to sea. It required skill, as there was almost no wind.

The post's pilot was a Swede, slim as a dagger, slightly built, burned red by the sun, yet always without a shirt, as if through him all his cold ancestors still worshipped the sun. His bleached hair hung in slight wisps from his head. Sven was a seaman in his heart, but a woodcutter by trade. He could not be two things, the Company did not permit it. If there was no quartermaster available to pilot, Sven was called to the posthouse. If there was one, he had to put his axe on his shoulder and return to the forest. That was why he'd glared askance at Bart from the beginning; he could see from the black feet and the anchor on his arm that Bart was a sailor.

Theuntje wanted to work. She could, if she would, plait palm mats for her own use, but she needed cash for her work. She was allowed to help in the kitchen for her lodging. The cook and Chief Wreede both welcomed her help. And Bart said nothing, because sometimes he could hear her laugh with the cook and the two slave women. Then he felt that they had done the right thing, here they could forget about the world and the world about them, as the proverb has it. But proverbs so often lie.

Chief Wreede explained to Bart where he belonged. In the island's office were the chief and two clerks, and twelve soldiers, among them Philipe Col. Sergeant Col had had a good education, might even have be of good blood. He worked in the office and the warehouse. The soldiers were employed according to their trade or task, like black-smith, wagoner, hunter, tanner. The rest worked in the forest under Master Sven, chopping and sawing. Then there was the crew of the lighter. Its quartermaster was the cooper Daniel. After that, a cook in the kitchen, a surgeon, and fourteen male and female slaves.

On the plain of Lemoenboomsvlakte seven free families were strug-gling to make a few holes in the ground. It was hard work, for the island had a thick shell; you first had to break through that black skin of volcanic rock before you reached the soil, but by then you already had a pile of stones with which to build your house and the walls around your yard. The walls were necessary to keep deer from your vegetables.

The backbone of the island's economy was timber. Everybody knew it, from the commander at the Cape to His Excellency in Batavia. The old song says: *Holland stands on poles.* And Mauritius Island stands on ebony. There were several kinds of timber, but those from which the Company made its best profit were red and black ebony. The trees were felled here under the supervision of Master Sven, then they were dragged out on an ox sledge to a suitable harbour. The Kroonenburg Gap was the most convenient for that. The lighter brought the wood here to the post, where it was processed by hand into planks and beams. The export wood was piled up under a shelter to dry, until the Cape sent another ship to collect it. That was the story of the woodcutting. It was how Lords Seventeen imagined it to happen.

Chief Wreede told Bart outright: 'Sven's woodcutters waste wood. They waste half of it, and leave it lying at the roadside just like that. They take two or three planks from a trunk; anything more is too much trouble. The fuel stuff isn't brought in. The Cape gives orders because the Lords and Batavia give orders from the other ends of the earth, but here their words are wasted like water spilling into sand. I'm going to act against them now. Well, Bart, you were sent out as a sailor. Your place is in the lighter's crew. Report to Daniel.'

4

THE POSTKEEPER

*But the dwarf replied: Something human is worth more
than all the gold in the world.*
– Rumpelstiltskin

MOST GERMANS NEVER learned the cause of the destruction and despair
in their country. The main reason for that was that there were more
people under the ground than above, but the second and most important reason was that the living had never been told, because they'd
never asked about it. They believed that whatever happened originated
from a higher will. Moreover, their Lord was right; it had always been
so, and that was enough for them. Ah, that poor nation is so easily led
by the nose.

So, by the time Gustav had finished with Tilley, and Wallenstein later
with Gustav, there was left little of Germany, and when afterwards
Richelieu pushed in two more armies against the Austrian, the war
dragged on for another thirteen years, until its thirty years were full.
Full. Overfull. *Zum Kotzen.* But who were these lordy warmongers,
and what had it all been about? About the ambitions of parasites, the
scum that so enjoy calling themselves statesmen. One sees their names
in school books. Mark them there, don't ever trust them with your
life. And finally, the dear Church. In its darkest heart the Thirty Years
War was a struggle between the declining Catholic and rising Protestant
sects. With Germans, or with Germany, it really had little to do. When
will those proud people realise that they are easily misled?

Therefore, the fatherland was a rubble heap of burnt ruins, dese-
crated churches, felled trees, breached dykes, contaminated wells,
bomb craters half filled with dark slime, decomposing carcasses,

broken hedges, raped women, fatherless children, roads pockmarked with holes, unploughed fields overgrown with weeds, dug-up graves in which wild boars gorged themselves by day and shadowy wolves at night. (It is also known, you hear, that not only animals scavenged in the graveyards, but in those days it was easier for animals than for people to find food.) And lawlessness. The trees that had been spared became gallows for thirty, forty corpses. From a distance it looked like black sausages hung out by a butcher, but as you approached over the sticky clods of unploughed fields, you saw flocks of crows sitting on the branches, pecking. In those days a healthy body for a man or beauty for a woman was a curse. It was better for a woman to carry a face ravaged by smallpox, and better for a man to have no arms.

That was Germany, when Hans Michiel Callenbach was born near Lüneberg. The peace of Westphalia in 1648 left him an orphan of two years old. When the last skinny soldiers went home the next year, there was little left even of crows. You had to eat, and you were eaten; soldiers and crows knew that. The village pastor gave Hans to the widow of the prince's stable hand. Her husband was killed in His Lordship's service, her four children had died of poisoned well water during the siege of eight weeks by the French. She had one afterchild, a parting gift from six Spanish soldiers, but it had died even before the peace. The pastor had buried it inside the walls of the deserted nunnery.

'The child's father was a Catholic,' he told the prince who owned the village, 'and there is little space left for graves. There's a large number of orphans around, My Lord. If you agree, I shall place them out in foster care.'

'Billet them in,' said the prince. 'Today's infant is tomorrow's infantry. Every adult in this village can share his food with a child. And send me four or five good young lads to the castle.'

About Hans Michiel's origins there was no doubt. His father had been an ensign of pikemen in the Duke of Mecklenburg's regiment. His mother, the daughter of a Magdeburg baker, died of hunger in a poorhouse in Hamburg. The widow had fed Hans Michiel until he was six, and then took him by the hand to the village pastor.

'I cannot go on, Reverend. Hans Michiel must get food, but I cannot any more. If I had, I'd have given him.'

'It's enough,' said the pastor. For four years he taught Hans Michiel with his own children to write and do sums, and when occasionally his family went through bad times, he temporarily put the boy in the church poorhouse.

'We have more than enough savages, Hans Michiel. Anyone can shoot a musket. You're going to be a teacher.'

The prince, who also provided for the poorhouse, sent a message to the pastor every two years: 'Send up six or seven of the biggest lads.' That was how he came by recruits. When Hans was ten the prince said, 'The children of '44 ought to be big enough by now. Send me the healthiest ones.'

Hans was a tall boy and looked older than his ten years. He had run away from the poorhouse to the pastor.

'I also want to be a soldier, sir pastor.'

'Not a teacher?'

'My father was a soldier.'

Yes, the pastor thought, and where did it get him? 'I want to teach you to read and write, Hans Michiel,' he said in a bitter voice, but then changed his mind and placed his hand on the child's shoulder, smiling. 'All right then, Hans Michiel. Pack your bundle. There will always be soldiers as long as the Devil is let loose on earth.'

Before the castle's cornet arrived to collect the boys, the pastor spoke to Hans once again.

'What do you want to start now, Hans Michiel? Aren't there enough good people under the ground?'

Hans did not answer.

'You won't become an officer if you don't study.'

'I don't want to become an officer, pastor, but a soldier.'

'Have you no ambition then? Surely you want to go higher.'

Because he didn't know what ambition meant, Hans said nothing. Fifty years later he told a clerk: 'I still don't know. Never became an officer, never felt the need.' But the clerk noticed a self-conscious smile flitting from old Hans's face, and thought that the pastor had been right when he'd warned the boy all those years ago: 'You will regret it many times.'

Hans himself never regretted becoming a soldier. He retained a simple faith in the dignity of his calling. What could he do? The times thundered with drums and cannons, the daily smell was of wet leather and horse manure, the colour was brown beer and black and red banners, the taste was oatmeal porridge boiled with some salt to disguise the smell of marsh water. It was good, the world believed, to soldier.

'At least I could bear arms,' he gravely explained to the clerk. 'Your food and place to sleep came free, like any dog gets from his master. And when you grow old one day, you look back and see how you've tried to live like a dog. Always ready to bite, eat what you are given, bear the kicks.'

Hans Michiel became a stable boy in the castle. That was where he learned about horses: the coupling, pregnancy and birth, the feeding and grooming, castration, the hooves, teeth and bones, the courage, the fears, the equipment for saddle or harness, the training, usage and handling, and how to dress a horse with caparison and plumes for a procession. It was his first trade.

There he was selected as groom for an artillery officer. The wages were pitiful and the work hard. He had to wash and cook for the man, clean weapons, tend the horses, buy food for man and beast, find and prepare a place to sleep. At night the horses were secured with the halters to the ground line, the bit was removed from the mouth but the saddle remained on the horse. He slept for brief intervals between the head line and the haversack. After a skirmish he had to remain on the field, or return, if enemy fire permitted, to shoot the horses that could not be led away. If enemy sharpshooters allowed it, the victors came to cut out the best parts to cook before flies started swarming on the fresh blood. If you came tomorrow, you found worms.

That was the only schooling for a groom; you learned your trade as you rode through the mud and rain. But the fellow was too kind for words, so that one had to flee from it, and at fifteen Hans Michiel went over to the infantry. At eighteen he was a corporal with a cane under his arm and a red rosette on his hat. By then he was almost fully grown, strong and, as might be expected of a corporal, not afraid of using his cane. Only, food was still scarce and thin in their cold and famished land.

Hans Michiel was a serious young man. At the campfires he said little, but liked to listen. There sometimes was talk about deserting to the Netherlands. In his company were fellows with cousins in service of the Dutch. Life was better there. Food was plentiful and rich in butter, all trades were in demand, and your wages were given cash in your palm every week. That was how it was in Amsterdam. Cousins came home with stories about how they'd been to Japan and America. Although those exotic names meant nothing, their tanned faces and the beer money in their purses showed their prosperity. America and Japan? Strange things were told in the barracks. For example, about countries without borders or fences where wild herdsmen pastured huge cattle herds, countries where the women went about naked, countries where the savages pricked flower patterns on their skins with black ink, even countries without gods, and oceans where fishes glided from wave to wave. You didn't know what to believe. In Germany women would still remain scared for several generations of everybody who wore breeches, but Amsterdam was the place where all lusts could be satisfied. Hans's companions nodded their heads in encouragement: Amsterdam was the best of places, even though they had never been there themselves.

Sometimes when his company was drilling among leaves rotting in muddy water in the rain-soaked courtyard, the young Corporal Callenbach thought longingly of Dutch ships sailing south in the sunshine. If he could escape from this frozen castle with snow on its battlements, and its narrow, black arrow slits, and follow those brown ships to the south, he too might experience miracles. He did not want jewels, or a governorship in the East. His needs were simple: command over a smallish watch post in a warm climate, a corporalship of ten or twelve men, a good Swedish musket and a Protestant officer. That was enough for him.

Early in 1664 the prince sent him to the sea, in charge of a chain gang. The old man called him to his private cabinet in the cold heart of his draughty fortress.

'I wish you good luck, Hans Michiel. You have grown up here under my eyes. My cornet told me at the time: Here is a boy for the stables, he is used to straw. I am glad you chose right when our pastor wanted to make a teacher out of you. He is a teacher down to that clod of clay which he calls a soul, but not you. You are a born soldier, and you have eaten my bread. I tell you, there are few people I can trust nowadays. The best are dead, and I am left with a weaker lot than my father had in his service. Now some fool or other has told them that in India the streets are paved with gold, and today they just want to go to the East, the East, to the sea. Well, you know about the ones I sentenced last council day. Counterfeiters, thieves, murderers of old mothers. Scum from the ditch round the pigsty. I have a buyer in Holland waiting for them, and their passports have been written. If one of them sets foot in my domain again, he'll get the rope round his neck. You just watch out for them, Hans Michiel. They are chained, but true as God they're not crippled, and will cut your throat if you dare to sleep near them. Don't let them get loose.'

'I promise, My Lord.' That was the real Hans, a promising man to the bitter end.

'Hans Michiel, my secretary will give you two letters. With the one you can buy food and lodging on the way. With the other you will rid yourself of the bastards. The man in Delft will give you a banker's letter which is worth a lot of money to me. Don't lose it. The leg chains are included in the sale price; you can leave them there, I don't want them again. Make very sure you don't break any of the Dutchman's laws, Hans. You must watch out for that. The Dutch love hanging; it provides entertainment and education for their masses, and they take my money to pay the executioner. So use good judgement in everything you do.'

Hans listened in silence, and asked nothing that might spoil his chances to see the Netherlands, and that famous city Amsterdam. It was a pleasant prospect. Escorting the twelve convicts did not worry him. Why should it? They were ordinary folk, and he an ordinary corporal. He was relaxed and content.

'Good luck, Hans Michiel,' his companions said. 'When you come back, you'll become a sergeant.' In peacetime it wasn't easy to become a sergeant. It's all this damned peace, they said. They gave him advice. He would understand the language of Holland; it was like German spoken by an idiot. But food was plentiful there, and cheap, and the women too. And in some towns the sausage and the beer were passable. The water he had to avoid; it was black and bitter and smelled of corpses. The convicts didn't know it, but they were going to become galley slaves in France. That the Dutch were not allowed to know either.

When the flower shoots of April pushed through the snow and flocks of birds from the south-west began to arrive in the bare trees, he and his convicts left through the castle gate. With their bundles like humps on their backs, they dragged their ankle chains through the cobbled gate and through the muddy snow to the outer guard, where Hans Michiel gave the password and a final salute.

From Lüneburg they marched straight west across the black, wintry heath. From the outset everything was against them: the sky, the earth, the inhabitants. It snowed every day, with sleet. The roads were deep slush so that they had to struggle along slopes and break off pine branches at night to lay on the snow. The inhabitants knew more than enough about soldiers. They brought their animals inside and shut the doors when they saw the company approaching, and threatened with weapons from inside when he knocked.

His chain gang started talking early on. They promised Hans Michiel the world if he would give them a chance, if he would only turn his back for fifteen minutes and look the other way. He did not reply, except with cane strokes. Then they prayed aloud, as if this young corporal was the agent of the Almighty. The hypocrites wanted to soften him, he thought.

He said to them: 'Why are you praying aloud? The Almighty isn't deaf.'

'Let us get away together, Hans Michiel. Turn your back when you lie down.'

Somebody whispered, or perhaps it was in his thoughts between his restless sleep and the two or three times a night he walked around his convicts: '. . . *inasmuch as you have shown mercy unto one of the least of these my brethren, is more* . . .' More what? He wondered, but could not remember.

'Turn my back on you?'

'We are condemned to the galleys, to the treadmill under the Spaniard's whip, to the black islands at Peru to gather bird dung. Are you a Christian? Turn the other cheek.'

'Or just a person, Hans? A human being? Sell us in this town, and go and celebrate with the money. You'll be a man with a full purse, a hero among the whores of Hamburg.'

To five of the condemned he promised a piece of silver each if they arrived at their destination without any trouble. To seven others he promised a bullet. He suspected that they were hiding a stolen file. Closer to the Dutch border the attitude of the inhabitants was changing; they needed farmhands. All the farmers, the taverners, the women wanted his fellows. The pleading in the chain bored him, he drove them on with lashes.

'Be careful with your cane, Master Hans. If our blood falls on you, you are contaminated for life. Chained with iron.'

In Bremen, on the frozen Weser, he handed over his letter at the city gates and paid for quarters in the stable of an inn where there was a Last Supper painted on the wall. Before the Reformation it had been a chapel. 'A stable for Catholic horses,' said Hans Michiel. 'Behave yourselves, and pray softly.'

From Bremen to Papenburg was a five-day march, with two nights in the snow. It was the last German town on their way. On the flag in front of the castle, to the right of the main road, was an eagle with two heads. Hans bought bread, sausage and beer at the market and distributed it early.

'We'll be crossing the border soon. We're eating our last meal in the fatherland.'

'Who's your "we"?' one of them asked. 'Are you going with us, perhaps?'

'Don't be so forward, man. What is my coming and going to you?' Hans Michiel struck the man hard with his cane. He was confident, self-assured. His duty was almost over. Outside the town a woman with the bald forehead of a milker showed him the road with a hen she was holding by the legs. Two hours later they crossed the Eems, in full flood below a high stone bridge. After another hour, sliding and slipping down a long green slope, they reached a military post at the edge of a poplar wood. It was the Dutch border. Two elderly men sat playing cards on an open Bible.

'How many of you are there?' the older one whispered in his beard, his eyes on his companion's hand.

'A hell of a bloody lot,' mocked the youthful Hans.

'Do you have papers?'

'Two letters. With the one I buy food, with the other I sell this filth from the pigsty's ditch.'

The old man pointed a warning finger at his companion, raising his head a mere fraction to look at the convicts.

'An ugly bunch of godforsaken bastards. Where are you going?'

'To the sea.'

'For God's sake, everything is going to the sea. The river behind you can't wait to get there. Does the sea want *you*? That question is never asked.'

'Rotterdam.'

'That's best. Out of the country.' With his red, watery eyes still fixed on his companion's face, he motioned with his head: pass.

The weather grew worse; the convicts cursed and threatened. They wanted shelter, but he drove them on with his cane from dawn to dusk. In a cold, grey fog they marched for two days across the desolate Ellerts plain, and crossed the Vecht by a trim wooden bridge. With the town walls and church steeples of Zwolle ahead of them in the fog, a convict slipped from the chain like a fish from a net and ran across a ploughed field to the town gate. Hans Michiel aimed his musket at the man. He was a clear and easy target, running straight down a ploughed furrow. He would hit him high between the shoulder blades before he reached the end. But he lowered his musket and didn't shoot, because they were in Holland. *Other princes, other laws*, said the proverb. The chained convicts cheered the man on until he was caught by the guards in front of the gate and escorted inside. Hans went to inspect the chain. It had been filed through. The groove was rusty; the filing must have been done over several days. One of the others now had the file, and another groove had already been started.

With the permission of the mayor of Zwolle, Hans took his gang into the town and asked for the escaped convict to be surrendered to him. It was refused. The man had contravened no Dutch law, said the town clerk. Corporal Callenbach had been outwitted by a simple convict. There Hans Michiel felt for the first time that he had failed his prince, that he was not the capable and alert soldier people took him for. That night he locked up his gang in the cell of an inn, and with his own money bought a second chain from a blacksmith and paid him to attach it to his prisoners. He demanded the file and forced them to undress, but it was missing.

From Zwolle to Utrecht was three days. The detour across the bushy dunes of the Veluwe was fairly dry and they could make faster progress. Hans Michiel could hear their hate, sharp and piercing as glass; they made no attempt to hide it. With their whispers and sly looks they filed away at his self-confidence. He kept several paces out of their reach so that they couldn't overpower and strangle him, and take his keys. The morning after they had left Utrecht, three convicts filed off their part of the chain, broke loose and rushed at him together. He leaped out of their way. His face was flushed and his heart was beating fiercely; he felt eager to fight. He gave one of them a clean blow against the forehead with the butt of his musket. Then they turned away, and fled back to the town, helping the wounded man along. They knew that his lord had asked him to use his good judgement not to break the Dutch laws. His own neck was at risk here.

There was little left he could still do for his prince. Only eight men were left to be sold. Between Utrecht and Leiden they fell in with a section of an artillery battery which was marching to 's-Gravenhage. Hans Michiel offered his services, his convicts would help to draw the cannon in exchange for protection. The grateful cannoneers stepped out of the harness and with blows and kicks forced

the Germans into the first four places. Their route ran seaward, somewhat north of west, all along the bank of the Rhine. The ground was
low, moist and uneven. All day long a fine mist hung over the flat
landscape. On their right Hans Michiel could see the shiny shores of
great hazy lakes, and the dim western sun was a, pale yellow smudge
in the fog. First they went through Soeterwoude, then through
Katwijk. The villages were small and close to each other. In each was
a fortress, more like a fortified mansion with a moat and a tower, on
which a flag was lowered and hoisted again to acknowledge the passing
of the battery.

At night Hans Michiel chained his gang to the cannon wheels. He
took his turn at watch, and slept well for the first time in fourteen
days. There were soldiers on the roads, from single companies to
divisions of seven or eight hundred men, or a smart cavalry detachment in dark green uniforms.

'Is there war?' Hans Michiel asked the artillery adjutant.

'Yes, the whole world is against us, didn't you know?' said the man
and gestured with his pace stick to the four quarters. 'The English, the
Portuguese, the French, the damned little Japanese with all their cronies.'

'Who are they, the little Japanese?'

'Short little heathens. Small eyes. Tea drinkers.'

'And what are you fighting about?'

'Because they're so ungodly.'

'And no chance of peace?'

'Absolutely none. Heaven preserve us against such mercy.'

'Amen,' Hans confirmed.

Alongside them the two cannon were slowly rolling along an old
sunken road. It was even and well paved, so that the convicts found it
easy to march. Their leg chains clinked faintly on the mossy green
stones, beside the heavy rumble of the wheels.

'Without trying to poke my nose in it,' the adjutant asked, 'what
are these being deported for?'

'Everything. Every commandment in the Good Book, including your
lesser prophets.'

'Like what?'

'Theft, murder, perjury, armed robbery, whoring, high treason, arson. Counterfeiting. Heresy. Also the unspeakable sin.'

'You're joking?'

'As true as God. With a goat.'

'Which one of them?' whispered the adjutant.

'I don't know. It's a capital offence and he was to be drowned, but this year all our rivers are frozen solid to the bottom. Can you believe it?'

'I won't sleep again at night,' the adjutant said, grimacing.

Not far from the sea – Hans couldn't see far ahead, but he could smell the sea in the haze – the battery marched through Leyderdorp. The Rhine flowed right through the fortified town. Once they arrived at the other side, the city of Leiden was before them. A high wall with battlements and two towers stretched from north to south. The Rhine flowed around the town, then divided again and streamed through the city gates. On the waterways surrounding the city was a great deal of shipping; he could see the motions of masts among six or seven church steeples. A blue smoky hung over Leiden.

'What a city,' Hans Michiel said in awe. 'When was it built?'

'Not bad,' the adjutant admitted. 'But wait until you're inside. Amsterdam is something, but Leiden is beyond compare.'

Hans Michiel and his gang entered the city with the cannoneers through Hoogoordspoort on the eastern side. Here he had to show his letters. Then they rumbled along the Bree Straat, past an imposing city hall to the military quarters in the western part.

On that first visit Hans Michiel acquired a respect for the city. He who had grown up in a castle on a hill with scant knowledge of churches and burgomasters, could see that this was an example of how it should be done. The buildings were elegant, the streets tidy. Throughout the day scores of bells rang from the church towers. One knew where one stood. In a curious way the black-robed students in the streets drew his attention. They were fellows of his own age, but something about them made him feel that they were better than he. Why had fate caused him not to be one of them?

The adjutant pointed at the large painted targets of wood and straw in an open field. 'There are the Doelen. We'll be camping there. As soon as we have unharnessed I shall give you an escort to the Court of Justice.'

Hans helped to unharness his tired gang and again locked them on to the double chain. Later in the day two gunners accompanied him to show him the way. They passed the university where beardless young students with swords under black gowns slouched in and out below the gatehouse, then crossed the Rapenburg canal, and along an alley to the public square in front of the Pieterskerk. The church rose higher than his lord's castle in Lüneburg. Directly in front of it was the Court of Justice, where Hans Michiel presented his papers to the bailiff. Outside, the town guard watched over his convicts.

'You must go down to Delft. There is an office of the Honourable Company. The lawyer you're looking for works there. As regards your other request: you cannot take these people through the country under German law. Your lord should be aware of it. You say he sent convicts this way before? If he pays the prescribed fee to the government, he may be given permits, but not without that. The best I can offer you, is to lock them up for the night as dangerous elements. At nine o'clock tonight the curfew will sound, then you must come inside. At daylight I have to let you go.'

Hans Michiel watched gratefully as the convicts entered a row of dark cells of stone with iron bars, and went into town to buy food for them. In the Rapenburg was a baking house and a tavern under one roof. A painted signboard leaned against the wall. Next to it was chalked: *Gentlemen are requested not to piss over this.* The language was plain and easily understood. As he paid for his bread with German silver, a mob of students came stumbling into the tavern, dropped down on the benches and shouted for service. The baker gestured with his head.

'Scum.'

'Are they students?'

'Youth. They're all the same, rich and poor alike.'

'What do they study?'

'How to mock the Almighty, how to disrupt one's rest at night with their carousing, how to ravish young girls, how to tell lies to save each other's skins, and other marvels of the pagan world.'

'They seem to be such serious youths.'

'No, sir. You're a young man too, but I can see you work for your bread. These are the prodigal sons from a hundred homes. You know, the younger son who extorted an undeserved inheritance from his old father and took off to a far country?' He motioned with his head again. 'Here they sit.'

Hans missed their laughter when he distributed his gang's bread and had himself locked into a cell. Throughout that night, until shortly before the cocks' crow, he could hear their drunken singing reverberating among the buildings, their laughter and wild shouting. Hans drew his cloak and his blanket over his head, but later went to curse at the students through the bars of his window. He could see them thronging around a street fire. They urinated on a sleeping beggar, and screamed with laughter, staggering along the edge of the canal without falling in. Young gentlemen, the baker had said, drunken louts. With bitterness in his mind Hans lay down on his bunk again, while his stone cell became colder and darker around him.

The gaoler rapped on the door early. Hans Michiel showed his convicts the way without breakfast. He walked ahead of them to the Zijlpoort at the northern corner of the city, the remnant of his chain gang grumbling behind his back. Now that the journey had almost come to an end and escape was no longer possible, they were after his blood. Every now and then one needed to slip into a dark corner to lower his breeches, then they all had to stand and wait for him to finish. With their arms crossed over their chests, cold hands thrust under their armpits, they waited on the street corners, keeping Hans at bay with curses and open threats. They were filing away again in the dark, but he couldn't make out who had the tool.

Before daybreak he got passage on a peat boat, down the Vliet to Delft. The convicts lay on top of the cargo of steaming peat. His journey was almost over; he would deliver them in Delft as he had promised his lord. There were only two men on the barge, a father at the helm and his son with a pole in the bows. Their boat, loaded deeply, kept below the city wall and through the Koepoort, then out across the open plains to the south. There the sun rose for them. The broad canal meandered through the misty pasture, from one slowly turning windmill at a peasant's hamlet, with a wide curve of the stream to the next windmill on the opposite bank. At a bend in the stream, when the barge was alone in the silvery landscape and almost touching the bank, the front convict in the chain got up, stepped on the gunwale and leaped ashore. He was free.

Hans Michiel followed him with his musket. He landed with one leg in deep mud, but scrambled out on the bank and ran after the fugitive. He only glanced back once and saw his mistake. The barge was already against the opposite bank, and his last convicts were streaming overboard and running over the open plain. Hans Michiel realised that he had lost everything. It was more than the lost papers in his bundle on the barge, more than his lord's trust, that was slipping away from him here. He would not be a soldier any more. There was nothing left of his life, except for the musket in his hand and the man who had landed him in this misery. He pursued the fellow along the dyke, in the direction of a village in the haze. It was Voorschoten. There was a mansion with a moat and a drawbridge, and a guard on the wooden tower beside the house. The convict ran towards the bridge. Hans was panting with the effort to get there before they drew up the bridge. The convict reached the mansion, fell against the fortified door and slammed against it with the flat of his hand. As Hans Michiel reached the drawbridge, the gatekeeper had already raised it head-high. What could he do? He took aim at the convict in front of the foreign lord's door and shot him down so that he fell sideways with arms outstretched in a bed of red and white flowers.

He turned round abruptly, hurled his musket into the canal and fled to the north, away from the mansion at Voorschoten, away from his convicts, away from the barge with his papers, away from Delft, away from his lord, away from Germany, and if possible away from Hans Callenbach. He was lost. And in a strange way he felt free, free from his chains, and for the first time free, completely free, to choose his own course in life.

But it was not to bring him freedom. For where could he go? For weeks he moved along back paths from village to farm, and from farm to town. On street corners he begged from beggars, and followed from village to village behind companies of soldiers, to search in the grass of yesterday's camps for cabbage leaves or bread crusts. Sick from sleeping on wet earth, filthy and hungry and cold, he arrived in Amsterdam. There a soul-seller pulled him from the ditch beside the street.

'That's how we fall into the Company's service,' Hans in his old age told the clerk. 'Here we are today, both of us. I barely knew of any Cape, or about Hottentots. You get up one morning, you're still thinking of Delft, then suddenly you're on your way to the Cape. But I had to get to the sea, all the time, to wash up here. It is only much later that you understand it.'

'We couldn't help it, Hans Michiel. Our whole country was streaming down to the sea. The whole of Europe,' the clerk agreed. 'It was written for us: *Come away from the North, I am sending you out to the four quarters.* It says so in the Bible, I can show you.'

Hans Michiel considered, and nodded across the sea towards his own bitter island. 'It is so. Dragged to the sea, from all the corners of the earth. We, the convicts there.'

The soul-sellers of Amsterdam knew where to look for the material for the Company's navy and army. They foraged in the musty straw of inn stables, in the damp guardhouse of the city prison, in the gutters of the street behind taverns, and in the dark alleyways where tipplers urinated. But how had he, Hans Michiel Callenbach of Lüneburg, landed in the wet grass beside the gutter running from a tavern?

'Destiny,' he said to the clerk. 'From Boshuisen to Valkenburg, to Noordwijk, and so on upward. Then Haarlem. Sometimes on a milk barge, otherwise on foot. But always, Destiny. It *had* to happen that way: I had to go to the sea, the sea had to have me. Where it would carry me, I could not know. And until today I do not know. It is still washing around me.'

The soul-seller took bread and wine from a bag and waited next to Hans Michiel while he ate.

'This region gets cold, my friend. Everybody moves south, why not you too?'

After he had eaten, he offered him a place to sleep, then clothes, a few guilders in his hand. And Hans, ill, famished, and cold to the marrow, went to town with him, for a mug of pea soup he'd been promised, and to live on lice-infested straw in a basement with eighteen or twenty other indigents, and to wait. In the afternoons and evenings there was a slice of bread with a bowl of warm pea soup, for which Hans Michiel took off his hat and closed his eyes to thank God. It was little, but it was warm. The soul-seller brought him a sea chest of the exact dimensions, canvas breeches and a shirt with two old bullet holes on the left breast, against an advance on his first wages, for which he had to sign. In the daytime they sat there catching lice and shivering with cold, while they waited to be called. He had been in the dusky basement for four days when the soul-seller told them: Tomorrow they're mustering at the Company's office in Kloveniersburgwal.

They set out early, an unkempt, brotherly group. From a distance they could hear the snaredrum calling. Men and women were waiting, talking, on the pavement in front of the head office on Kloveniersburgwal. Applicants for the vacancies of packer were called in first, then applicants for the post of sailor, then those who wanted to become soldiers.

Inside, behind a table covered with green baize, were two clerks and an officer. An ordinary musket lay on the floor in front of the table. Hans approached. There was a new flint in the lock and rusting finger-marks on the barrel. The grooves of the lock plate were black with grime. Why was the flintlock on the floor?

'Take it,' said one of the gentlemen. Hans looked up and waited, but the voice remained silent. He took the musket by the neck just behind the lock, and swung it under his arm.

'*Ten . . . shun!*' shouted the officer. Hans was a soldier. There was no way he could hide it. He came to attention and placed the gun against his shoulder. Now all the gentlemen behind the table also knew it: he was a soldier. If the bailiff of Voorschoten was looking for the young German soldier who had killed the convict at his gate, he would know where to find him. The command had betrayed him; that was how easy it was to catch Hans Callenbach. The gentlemen behind the table grinned. So much this fellow was worth, so much his life was worth. Name? Place of origin? Approximate age? That was all.

Hans, shadowed by his soul-seller, waited in front of the table while the gentlemen drew up his papers and put their questions. So much, the soul-seller told them, Hans owed for his lodging, so much for food, so much for clothes, so much for a sea chest. And in front of witnesses the soul-seller swore: From today, until Hans went on board, he would provide him with lodging and kit, including tobacco and pipes, everything he needed. On Hans's first pay day part of his debt would be paid out here in Amsterdam to the soul-seller, and so on for the next sixty months. Hans signed the letter of debt. Caught again.

On his first pay day he was far, far away at sea. He'd been allocated to the ship *Roode Hert*. They were carried in open lighters from Amsterdam across a stretch of green water, northward to the deep behind Texel, where their ship was waiting. There the crew was mustered for the last time. To the last moment Hans kept on looking around to see if the bailiff from Voorschoten might yet come aboard to arrest him. Four ships were prepared. There Hans learned about working at sea, and a week later they departed together through Hell's Door. South of them were the green dunes of Den Helder, with the notorious three tall gallows on which swayed several corpses in a cloud of white seagulls. This was the gateway to the East, Jack Tar assured Hans. This was where hell began.

It was much worse than he'd expected. *Roode Hert* was a flute of three hundred tons, built ten years earlier in Amsterdam and with four passages to the East and back under her keel. The soldiers were placed under ship's routine. Hans hadn't expected it; back on shore they were to become soldiers again, but first they had to help to get this ship over there. The soldiers didn't work in the rigging, but at night kept watch like the sailors: four hours on duty, four hours off. Everybody had to help, on this fifth outward journey, everybody had to give a hand, and it was hard work. They were at sea for four months, and his back was purple from the beatings of the boatswain of his watch. Hans could understand that. When he was a corporal, he had also carried a cane. The pain was not so bad, but to restrain himself from hitting back was hard. The days were short, dark and cold, the nights black and icy. They kept watch, and when the sails were changed or the yards turned, sails secured or shaken out, the boatswain of their watch was there with his length of rope. 'To the mainsail haul, everybody at the falls to haul up the mainsail!' came the order. The boatswain pretended to blame the soldiers for not knowing what to do, and beat them indiscriminately. As a soldier Hans could understand the length of rope; it took him longer to learn the boatswain's jargon.

From Texel they sailed north-west, passing behind Scotland and Ireland. The sky was overcast daily; the sea was tired, slow, heavy, tinted like dull silver under a leaden sky. In rain and storm they were called out day and night, and the deck so deep under water that one could barely stay on one's feet. This *is* hell, thought Hans Michiel, looking up at the sailors clambering in the dark on yards higher than church steeples swaying over the heaving sea, and keeping his mouth shut. All around the sea and the wind thundered and shrieked.

The ship's diseases brought him down. He was sick in the stinking hold, and between decks it teemed with lice. This is hell, this is my punishment, he thought. Rat fever. He survived it. Food poisoning. He was one of six who survived a panful of rotten bacon. After a week of thinking he'd never see the sun again, he gratefully climbed up to the deck one sunny day. The weather was still cold, around them the sea heaved and sank, heavy and dark green, its surface glittering in the afternoon sun, and he had to hold on to stay on his feet. This was not home. Everything here was foreign to him, but he would adapt, willingly, to help them get to the end of their journey.

The longer they were at sea, the more putrid the food, the more nauseating became the smell in the gloomy darkness between decks. In the heat of the tropics, after two months at sea, the air that came up from the forecastle and the hatches of the orlop was thick enough to make one vomit. In four months at sea 104 of *Roode Hert*'s dead were sent overboard. Every day Hans Michiel was given more work, taking the place of the sick. All three of their boatswains died. The new boatswain's mates, ordinary sailors until recently, struck more often and more viciously than those before them. When the watermaker died, Hans Michiel was ordered to do his work. He had to scoop up ninety buckets of seawater per day and pour it into a gutter which led to a copper still in the kitchen. Three times a day he had to fill and boil dry the still, while the cook's fire was burning. The steam rose through a spiral pipe under cold water, where it cooled and appeared as a thin shiny stream of fresh water into a clean barrel. Ninety buckets of sea-water yield seven buckets of fresh water. That was Hans's job: scoop ninety buckets of water from the sea, fill the still, scrub the barrels. It was cold and wet work; the clothes on his body were rarely dry. Afterwards he had to do his turn at watchkeeping. Between watches he slept on deck in his wet clothes, pressed against the copper kettle with which he lived during the day, because of a memory of heat still lingering in it. At the same time it put him out of reach of the duty watch's feet, because in the fatigue and cold that pressed on them all like bitterness, they were always looking for something to kick.

In the documents of the Cape Council of Policy the arrival of *Roode Hert* is recorded wrongly. The ship arrived in September 1664, not in 1663. Nor is it the only error in the Cape records of those years; they are in fact bristling with inaccuracies. The quality of the Council secre-taries and – it may as well be brought to light – of commanders and governors is evident from them. Were they deliberate errors, to mislead the Directors? It will be to the Company's advantage if Lords Seventeen were to be more careful in future with their appointments made at all levels in the Cape office.

Afterwards *Roode Hert* went on to Japan, where it was burned the following year by the little heathens in the bay of Nagasaki. Hans Michiel was admitted to the Cape garrison at ten guilders a month. It was one guilder more than his previous pay. The work in the Cape Fort was much to his liking. It involved guard duty and foot patrols in a sunny climate. Because he could read and write he was made scribe of his section, with the rank of lance corporal. He kept a meticulous record of his detachment's strength, equipment, arms and ammunition. His sergeant mentioned Hans's name to the officer in command.

After two years in the garrison Hans Michiel was transferred to an outstation half a mile from the Fort. He was happy to get out of the garrison, because at that stage they were sawing wood and breaking stone for a new castle, which would replace the small Fort. This kind of work was boring and it would mean days, months of dust and sweat. At his outpost, it is true, Hans Michiel occasionally missed the colour and order of a parade ground, the smell and weight of a musket on his shoulder, the quiet of a turn at guard on the wall of the Fort. When the wind was right he could hear the distant trumpets at the Fort; he would listen how three or four of them took up the chord in the court-yard, and how others would fall in from far and wide, then their sound would reach him after some small delay, like echoes. The sounds were comforting, and made him feel content. I deserve this outpost, he thought. Outposts are for those who can be trusted, a rare gate to a new space, to new freedom. Sometimes he thought of the Netherlands, where the wide rivers placidly flowed through the even, green land-scape and the sun sank early in a haze of changing colour, and some-times he remembered his pillaged, famished fatherland. This Cape was good enough for him.

His self-confidence returned from hiding places. Only, the thing that had happened in Voorschoten he could still not understand. He had been corporal of a gang, who in the course of one brief march had lost everything, and so had to flee for his life. How was it possible that he had not turned out to be the first-class, born soldier people had spoken about since his childhood? In what way had he failed? That he had to flee, and where to, had not been his choice. But now he wanted to get away from his weaknesses, his disaster, and from all who know about that.

The wide circle of the horizon was one great loop, in which to catch a man. 'The enemy has two cannons, Hans Michiel,' the clerk told him in his old age. 'Their names are *Fate* and *Coincidence*. If one of them doesn't get you, the other will.'

What Hans learned was that yes, the enemy *does* have two cannons. There had been one occasion when he'd helped to bring in a casualty from the front line, a comrade from the infantry who had stopped a notched bullet with his face. He was a tall, laughing, young soldier, still under age. He was fully conscious; in the mud under a tented wagon a surgeon and a doctor worked on him. He could breathe, and swallow cupfuls of his fresh blood, but he could no longer speak. There were no tongue, mouth, lips or cheeks. The bullet had torn away everything as far as his spinal cord. The cheekbone below the eye cavities, the entire upper jaw, including the nose, were gone. At the front end of the lower jaw, like a bollard at the end of a quay, stood a single blunt tooth. What was left of a face, reminded Hans Michiel of the crescent moon on a standing clock. They'd stopped the blood; after such a wound the big arteries shrink shut by themselves. With two fingers the doctor was keeping open the air passage. He might live.

'A fraction of an inch,' the doctor said to the surgeon. 'To one side or the other.' Just so; if one of them doesn't get you, the other will.

The outpost Keert-de-Koe stood on a sizeable dune on the Cape side of the Liesbeeck, where the road to the interior crossed the river. It was a small fort with a flat roof, stone below and wood above. The lower room was a stable for twelve horses; from there a staircase went up to a room with two windows, seven bunks, seven chests, seven pegs on the wall for saddle and bridle, seven slots in the gunrack. In front of the fort the Company's flag flew from its post. On the right was a lean-to with an open hearth. The surrounding bushes had been cleared away, exposing a cairn of white limestones about ten paces from the river. On one side of the fort a palisade of tall yellow-wood beams stretched west towards the sea; on the other side was a toll gate in the palisade which followed the green bank of the Liesbeeck to the farmsteads higher up.

The post was manned by Corporal Callenbach and six horsemen. Their work was not demanding, but important enough. Every day they rode out on patrol: two men northward up along the fence, two down the fence to the south. Three had to stay home to open the gate, because it was the only gateway between the colony and Africa. On the near side was the colony, on the far was pure and endless savagery. Travellers and barterers of livestock camped the night at the post, and departed before daybreak. Men on overland expeditions went through with their pack oxen to distant regions, beyond the mysterious Tygerberg, which in the searing summer was dun-coloured with yellow spots and in the grey winter dark green with light spots. When it rained, the travellers slept in their posthouse. Bands of timid Koina entered with sheep in the morning, and went out boisterously with their worthless trade goods late in the day.

The Koina did not like the gate, especially because of a cairn for one of their heroes or angels in its proximity. They were afraid of his ghost. After sunset the *hei-nun*, or grey-feet, floated there above the ground. After sundown they would attack the guard and try to break down the gate, but they wouldn't tarry. A curious thing was that some whites had taken up the same story. 'Open up, we must get home before dark; the oxen are spooked.'

Hans Michiel spent some three years as corporal in charge at Keert-de-Koe. By that time he'd been there longer than any of his men, and he got along well with his officers in the Fort. The fourteen guilders were welcome, and the rare promotion thrice as much. He felt satisfied with the officers' choice. And he became friends with travellers who regularly passed through. They were the kind of person who felt secure on either side of the frontier.

Then he was transferred, with the likelihood of promotion. His new post was Robben Island, out in the wind-blown bay. He arrived there with his musket and pack, and the commander's letter in his pocket, for the island's postkeeper was being dispatched to buy slaves on Madagascar. His Hottentot wife looked tired unto death of that barren rock in the sea. Like others of her people she was probably a wanderer at heart, who became ill when you confined them. She was young, pregnant and depressed, and could not make conversation. Her husband's departure would sour her voluntary exile to solitary confinement.

Hans Michiel soon learned the tasks connected with the island's signalling and observation duties. The surveillance of the convicts was different from what he'd expected, different from his previous experience of the chain gang. The spirit of these men had already been broken through their public disgrace, and it was hardly necessary to keep them in check. When blows and kicks were required, there were two corporals to get the Company's message across. But they, the people of Robben Island, made Hans feel dejected. Nothing that any of them did there was for their own sake.

Corporal Callenbach did his writing at the table in the posthouse in the evenings. The postkeeper's children were restless, fidgety, unsure of themselves in the absence of their father, but they were not a nuisance, even though their mother endlessly scolded them. 'Your father is going to beat you, I will tell him,' were words he often heard there. Hans gave the children some of his rations, his prunes, biscuits and cheese, and took them along when he went outside to give the woman some rest, to the Fire Hill, or to the stone quarry, or the spot where shells were gathered. The little girl was a cheerful and bright child; she would jump from rock to rock, or scurry ahead with her tongue hanging out like that of a young hunting dog. He was less fond of the older boy, who was more withdrawn, unreliable, a troublemaker with sores on his legs, who would never be a soldier. The youngest was a boy of two, who stayed close to his mother.

There was also a slave, the property of the postkeeper. The man seemed to be wary of the posthouse. He slept in a shack built on to the house, but was outside before dawn to kindle a fire and cook his breakfast. After that he immediately left for the garden to turn over more soil, plant windbreaks in the ground, transplant seedlings, dig in manure, make furrows, stack higher and higher stone walls against the rabbits, and haul innumerable pails of water from the well to water his garden. The pails he carried two at a time on a yoke across his shoulders, almost half a mile from the posthouse. He provided the post-keeper's family with greenery, which was a blessing, as it kept them in good health. In the evenings after sunset, when because of the cold he could no longer remain outside, he came home with a bundle of fire-wood on his shoulders and immediately disappeared into his little room.

Hans hadn't been in his post for long before he could hear that there was some trouble between the woman and the slave. Among other things she wanted him to do their washing, which he refused to do. He washed his own few pieces of clothing and spread them over the bushes to dry, but he clearly resented the humiliating servility or the intimacy of other people's clothing. Hans could hear the woman ranting; she said that her husband was the postkeeper and would beat him. But that was none of his business; in another month or two Master Pieter would be back on the island, and he once more outside at Keert-de-Koe.

The woman seldom spoke to him. It wasn't that she avoided him, but she was lost in her own thoughts, unless she was entirely without thoughts. She cooked for them, and they had their meals at the same table. He said grace, and both of them spoke to the children, but not to one another. He would be there when her next child was born. One day, when he thought her time was coming near, he said to her: 'You must warn me in time, so that I can get somebody from the shore. There is a midwife at the Castle.'

'Yes,' she said, and that was all. Weeks passed, but she did not refer to it again. He asked the sloop's quartermaster to find out at the Fort what he should do in case she went into labour unexpectedly, but never received an answer. One evening when he arrived at the post after locking up the convicts, the woman had already gone to bed. The children were wandering through the dark house. They were hungry, cold, dirty from playing outside.

'Is your mother sick?' he asked the girl.

'Ma is lying in our bed.'

'Go and ask her if she's sick.'

She wasn't there. Hans Michiel went to look. The bed was crumpled as if the children had played in it. The youngest slept among the piled bedding.

'You stay here,' he said to the girl, placing a long candle in his lantern. 'I'm going to look outside, then I'll make us something to eat.'

But they left the house behind him. Their slave found Eva and the children in the woodshed on a pile of kindling. She didn't make a sound. Hans fetched his musket and keys in the posthouse and called the slave with him to unlock the convicts' lodge. There was loud screaming inside.

'Stay with me and keep the musket ready, Jan. I must have the old one with the wheelbarrow. Force the others back.'

The night wind at the door caused the light of their oil wick to shudder and shrink to a tiny, orange flame like a little *vygie* flower. Some of the convicts were bundled together at the back among the *katils*, engrossed in that game of taking turns to pull down their breeches, bending over, and forcing out a big wind. Behind them was one with a candle, and usually there was a blue flame of an ell or more long. The longest flame won bread, dried fish, a broken hacksaw-blade, or whatever they might have, to gamble on. Others were on their bunks. Everybody was cheering.

'Uncle Abraham, get up. Bring your wheelbarrow.' The man was one of two not locked to the chain, but to his tools. He was lying halfway along the room, an old man with long white hair. Hans Michiel waited until the old fellow pushed his wheelbarrow out through the door.

'To the posthouse,' he called, snapped the padlock shut and pushed him forward with the gun in his back, into the dark. Sighing and bent over in the cold night wind the convict walked behind his heavy wheelbarrow. With dull thuds the wooden wheel bumped over limestones. At the woodshed Hans Michiel leaned over to light inside with his lantern. The woman was crouching in a corner of the shed, her face contorted, her clothes hitched up above her hips. The two older children were sitting there with their mother against the wall. The little girl was comforting the sniffling boy. Hans Michiel put his lantern down outside, out of reach of the wind.

'Jan Vos, make fire and give the children some milk-and-bread. Come, Petronella, we'll help your mother. Can you come out, Mrs van Meerhof?'

No answer from that dark hole. The sea air was salty, cold over the rocky ridges. Hans Michiel stared far over the sea to the denser darkness where Table Mountain obscured the lower stars in the south. The lights of the Fort were invisible behind the swell, and only the guard ship on the outer roadstead to the east showed its small light. On all sides the night boomed.

'Can you come out there, Mrs van Meerhof?'

He did not expect an answer. This was life. Here was the postkeeper's wife, the children's mother, with him in the absence of help and advice. Hans was ignorant, and concerned about his responsibility. What he knew about birth, he'd learned in a stable. That had been bad enough. It started with a night watch that might last for hours: one man at the mare's head to whistle and whisper to her, and call the master if the contractions began. He'd held the lantern for the sweating and cursing stable master who, stripped to the waist, was working with a lathered arm up to his shoulder inside a mare to turn a foal that was lying badly, and sometimes there had been two or three men pulling the foal out with a rope, with two more at the legs of the kicking horse. Once they'd had to cut off the forelegs of a foal, on another occasion there had been a young mare that couldn't get her foal with two heads out. Hans had become used to it, but wondered about the cruel and curious ways of birth. Why with pain and blood, as if it had been planned by soldiers or the officers of justice? Someone spoke from the dark. Startled plovers flew up from the black shrubs around the woodshed. He leaned closer. What had she said? But there was nothing.

'We have to move her out and take her home,' Hans Michiel told the convict with the wheelbarrow.

'Let her be. That's all she needs.'

'Must I leave her there like a bitch giving birth on a sack?'

'She'll take care of herself. Just cover her to keep the child warm.'

'Advice of Jack Tar, old man. I need something better.'

'I had a wife, children.' The man with the wheelbarrow chained to his leg looked in through the opening of the woodshed. 'She wants to rest. All the Company's postkeepers and all the Company's convicts can't help her.'

Hans Michiel took the convict with the wheelbarrow back to the lodge and locked him up, then fetched the woman's blanket from the posthouse. Jan Vos had already fed the children and washed their feet and faces. They were tired and he carried them to bed. Hans Michiel poured Jan Vos and himself each a *muts* of brandy, gulped his down, and then went outside with the flask and the woman's blanket to cover her, should she need it. Blood and water came seeping from under the door of the shed and spread over the pale lime earth outside, fan-shaped like where the dark contents of a river mouth opens into the sea. The woman had lowered herself down the wall to the floor, her child had been born and she was holding him to her breast. In the lantern light he could see a bluish cable wound around the child. With his knife and lantern Hans Michiel crouched into the woodshed, cut the umbilical cord, stripped the contents between his fingers, rolled the end round his forefinger and knotted it, and washed the wound with brandy, as on the battlefield. The postkeeper's wife was lying there in her water, her soaked clothing bundled under her shoulder blades. From the contractions of her body he could see that her labour was not yet over. All he could do was to place the child against her again.

Outside he wiped his hands and the knife on the grass, blew out the candle in the lantern and, wrapped in his coat, with his back against the wall, sank down against the shed to keep watch until daybreak. Before him were the black sea and the dark and empty night. Behind them, Africa, even emptier, darker. What stars, what fate, for this child? He gazed at the stars and the black sky, sometimes swallowed from his flask and hummed softly: '*The old man's joints are full of pain, the brandy puts him right again.*' When the woman woke up, he would offer her some reinforcement. He knew of nothing else. Previously salt had been the answer, salt of the earth, for all wounds. The salt bag in his satchel was the soldier's salvation, for health, for food and medicine. Horses were given salt in the manger. But since brandy had come into the world, the soldier never gave a thought to salt any more. Brandy, for all problems. The child – it was a boy – might want to become a soldier, like him. Perhaps, one day, a famous name. Or more likely, a young corpse, hanging face down over a palisade, bayonetted. Or it may die here in the first winter, and in fifty years a gardener will dig up its tiny skull and y=throw it with the stones to build a wall against rabbits. Hans Michiel could remember his own childhood. It was fresh in his memory: a group of boys squatting around something bloody on the dirty snow, the nights on the road, paralysing hunger, the cold consuming all hope. Before sunrise, when the night was at its coldest, he woke up and heard the woman moving about.

'Can you come out, Mrs van Meerhof?'

'Take the child.'

The child, wrapped in a piece of her drenched clothing, had to be washed. He could smell it. Bent over, she came through the low door, took the child again and went to the posthouse without a word.

Jan Vos was at the hearth. There was fire under a pot.

'What are you doing?' she asked him, walking past.

'I'm making porridge for the children.'

'I look after my own children.'

Jan looked at Hans Michiel. 'Shall I go to the garden?'

'It seems to me the children need porridge. Boil water, perhaps she wants to wash.'

Hans Michiel unlocked a young Javanese convict, a ship captain's cook, from the work team and took him to the posthouse. The man had to cook. He left the ankle chains on, as well as the neck ring with the short chain that hung between the shoulder blades. He knew what the man's crime had been, but wouldn't tell it to Eva. He was satisfied that she and the children would be safe. Until the time this woman came to her senses again, the young Javanese convict would have to milk the cow of the postkeeper's family, wash clothes, chop wood, whatever was necessary. For Hans, conservative and cautious to the marrow, it was no easy decision. The commander might ask where he got the right to remove a shell-gatherer from the gang.

Eva soon called the cook a devilish Malay, and complained that they were all magicians and witches. Where could she have picked up such nonsense? Hans Michiel tried to stop her: she had to be careful. He had heard the Orientals had a terrible passion for vengeance and avenged insults with blood. She paid no attention, but beat the convict with sticks of firewood. She also shouted at Jan Vos, until he no longer wanted to enter the posthouse. At the dining table she was silent, morose. The duty of talking to the children while they had their meals fell on Hans Michiel.

Fourteen days after the birth, Bart Borms, the Saldanha sailor, sat in his boat under a shortened mainsail on the anchorage, shouting through cupped hands that he wanted to come ashore. Hans Michiel nodded permission. The guard beckoned to Borms, and he backed his boat stern first into the cove, flung his anchor stone into the surf, and held out a wooden pail covered with a cloth to Hans. His clothes were bleached and white with salt stains. His eyes were small, screwed up in his weather-beaten face behind his six weeks' beard. His bare feet were streaked with dirt and scabs of pitch.

'Come ashore,' Hans invited him.

'I don't have time.' But he swung his legs, with the breeches rolled up high on his strong brown calves, over the gunwale and dropped thigh-deep into the water.

'Good day, postkeeper.'

'Acting. Good day.'

'I brought Eva something.' Together they walked up the dune to the posthouse. 'My wife sends her this.' He gestured towards the pail. 'It's all she has at the moment.'

Eva was in her shift before the embers in the hearth. She'd risen late again. Salomon, the second youngest, played under the kitchen table with bits of wood. Hans Michiel waited while Borms spoke to the postkeeper's wife.

'The buttermilk is for you, Eva. Theun says it's all she has right now for a transition feast. She wants to come and see you one afternoon if she can get permission.'

'Yes, that's fine.'

'And she says if the children are difficult, they can come and stay with us.'

'Is fine,' Eva nodded. 'I'll ask Pieter.' She was reserved, as if she were hiding something from the fisherman.

'Some Cochoqua came up to my fish-house in Saldanha Bay. They also sent you something, but it is still there until the next time.'

'What is it?'

'Ostrich egg, some *haro*, some *chabi* for the transition ceremony.'

'Say thank you.'

'They would have liked to send a sheep, but old Oedasoa is still alive, they say.'

'He? Still alive? They lie.'

Hans Michiel saw the fisherman looking around curiously in the posthouse.

'News from Master Pieter?'

'No.'

'How is the little one, still healthy?'

'Yes.'

Why was she like that? Hans wondered. She let Bart ask questions, but said nothing herself, as if she wanted him to finish talking and leave.

'I'd have liked to see little Nella. My wife asks about her all the time.'

'They're outside.'

Hans Michiel took him by the arm. 'I know where they play. They were there a short while ago.'

Outside the dusty shell gatherers in their grey canvas clothes shuffled past, dragging a clanging chain through billowing lime dust round their feet, each with his canvas bag of seashells like the shell of a snail on his back. Bart waited for them to pass.

'Postkeeper, this Eva. She lies badly moored, in shallow water under a difficult shore. And she is sinking.'

'I cannot help.'

'Of course not. You are not her skipper. A man who takes a wife is like one who buys a sloop. A new captain comes on board, and you expect him to hold his hand over her and provide her with what she needs. But here, by the soul of the dog, her skipper has shrugged her off. Thrown her away here, is what my Theuntje says.'

'She isn't easy.'

'She goes off-course. But why? I say to Theun, perhaps she has a crooked keel, or perhaps her helmsman is hopeless.'

They found the children among the rocks on the beach. They were glad to see Bart. He first picked up the boy and kissed him, then the girl, and carried her on his arm.

'Your aunt wants to know if you are well?'

'When is Aunt Theuntje coming again? Did you bring the dog you promised?'

Hans Michiel intervened. 'No. The commander doesn't want dogs here. They chase the rabbits and the seals.'

'You two must come and visit me,' Bart pleaded. 'Then you can play with the pup. Ask your mother, and I'll come and fetch you for a few days.'

'We'll ask,' Pieternella promised.

'I brought you and Jan something. Come with me to the boat, then I'll give it to you.'

As they went down the sandhill to the bay, Hans Michiel pointed at Bart's small boat, fallen sideways in the shallow glittering wash of the tide.

'What has become of your sloop?'

'Sold. I'm tired of the sea, postkeeper. It is dead. By the yellow bile of the hairy dog, my good days are past, you hear. It never considers me any more. All my misfortune comes from that grey-green bastard.'

'But you still sail?'

'I used to be home for one out of fourteen days, and the other thirteen wet in the boat. There was no other way out.'

Bart lifted the two children into his yawl, and took out a string of large mullet, each the length of his forearm. 'This is for Jan Vos, postkeeper. Ask him to roast them on the coals, so you can taste. Jan has a way: he squats next to the cinders. A Hollander cannot do it.'

Then he took out a canvas bag from under the stern bench. 'This is what Aunt Theuntje sends you. Cookies! Look, these are with coconut, these with ginger, these with cinnamon. With her love. Give some to Jan too, give to your mother.'

Bart leaned over the gunwale of his boat, bailed two buckets of bilge water downwind and heaved his anchor stone into the bows. 'Come on, you,' he said to the boat, lifted the children out, pulled the foresail round, shook the mainsail out, pushed off into deeper water and climbed in. 'Aunt Theuntje is looking forward to your visit very much. Remember to ask.'

Hans Michiel thought that during Borms's hurried departure with hanging head, without saying goodbye, he'd seen something glisten in the man's eye. Impossible, it must be the sea air. But some time later Bart said to him: 'It's a sin and a pity about the children, Hans Michiel.' And when he asked what he meant, what was a sin and a pity, Bart said: 'Poor Theuntje. She's crying about the children. It's little Nella, little Nella all the time. Is it my fault that she cannot have children? And the girl is just as fond of her.'

After the child's birth Hans rarely spoke to the postkeeper's wife. They were the same age, equally lonely on the joyless island, equally unsmiling towards one another. A married woman might have a reticence of her own, he suspected. To the last day he called her Mrs van Meerhof, very formally, and for Eva he was a stranger without a name. They never became friends. He had his few soldiers, his thirty convicts, his visitors from the mainland, and the coming and going of ships for which he had fires lit or flags hoisted. And then, there was the little girl. But Mrs van Meerhof was utterly alone.

Early in 1668 Hans Michiel was summoned to the Fort. The sloop that came to pick him up loaded half the four hundred bags of shells standing ready above the cove, and it was loaded so deep that the sea almost slipped over the gunwale. Their luff against the south wind took from daylight to full noon.

He entered the gate of Fort Good Hope uncertainly, as if he were a stranger arriving for the first time. There was not a familiar face to be seen. To the east, the new castle had reached head-height around the wooden workshop, all slate and brown granite behind a lattice of scaffolding. A line of slaves, like black ants, carried the bags of shells from the sloop to where a stinking lime kiln stood smoking above the beach. Hans Michiel found the way to the commander's house; he felt at ease again. But on the stoep a sentry lowered his pike diagonally across the door. He had to be announced and wait there until he was summoned. This was new to him, the sentry, but the commander at the Cape was apparently becoming high and mighty and probably entitled to such a display. Then the answer was brought: Hans had to go to the secretary, there was a message waiting.

The secretary was a new man too, one prematurely bald, with a surprised expression on his smooth face. 'Postkeeper? Ah. Look, we had bad news with *Westwoud* which returned from Madagascar the day before yesterday. Very bad. Nine of our men were butchered there by blacks, and the captain came back almost without any slaves. Wasted expense, wasted labour.'

'Yes.'

'We heard it the day before yesterday. You probably saw the ship come in. The commander wants you to inform the widow.'

'Is it Master Pieter? The surgeon van Meerhof?'

'Yes.'

'What must I tell her? Was his body found? Was he buried there? Did they bring anything of his back? His sea chest?'

'I don't know. I shall go and find out.'

'And what is to become of the woman? She has four children.'

'I don't know. Her rations will of course continue until the end of this month, but after that I don't know. She cannot be lodged indefinitely at the Company's expense.'

'And her husband's accumulated wages?'

'Postkeeper, we're aware of that. The Company usually pays out after a month or two.'

'What can she do on the island to get her food?'

'Then she must move to the Cape, or return to her own people. I've been told that she is a Hottentot.'

'But she has four children with a European. Van Meerhof's children cannot disappear into the wilderness now.'

'Well, it's not for you or me to say where the children must disappear. The Council will decide.'

'It is for their mother to say. Her own people were Goringhaicona, but they no longer exist.'

'Where did you hear that?'

'I heard at the gate, Keert-de-Koe, we talk with the natives there. Her mother was Cochoqua, but that chief chases her away.'

'Well. There are some questions to which we'll have to find answers. Look, that was one matter. The other is that the commander wants you to remain on the island.'

'If there is a replacement available, I'd be glad to return to the garrison. Tell the commander.'

There was an hour or two to kill as he waited for answers, and while the sloop was emptied and reloaded. He chose his words drinking a pot of beer in the tavern. '*Mrs van Meerhof,*' he would say, '*I have bad news. The commander wants me to tell you that Master Pieter died abroad.*' But the commander had not said that, he hadn't shown his face. He left it to clerks to do the showing of faces. '*Mrs van Meerhof,*' he would say, '*come and sit here at the table. I am sorry about what I have to tell you. Master Pieter has died. His ship returned the day before yesterday with the news.*' And also: '*No, the Company has not said yet.*' '*No, your father is not coming back.*' And: '*Perhaps you should ask to speak to Commander Borghorst personally.*'

Perhaps he should get away from that island, so that others could concern themselves with the woman and the children. It was a pity about the little girl, a lifetime without a father. The others didn't matter, one way or another.

Hans Michiel walked along the sunny quay while the sloop was loaded with the monthly rations for his outpost. He waited for answers from that clerk with the startled expression, and thought perhaps he should speak directly to the commander about the woman's future, and mention that Bart Borms wanted the children. He looked at the village, at all the new houses, at the work on the castle. If he'd had money in his pocket, he could have gone to the Elephant for a cup. The hostess of the Elephant had bright green eyes, eyes like the sea on a summer's day; he'd never seen anything like that. She might be ten years older than he. If he'd worked on shore, he would have gone there more often, to see more of her. The Elephant was a merry place, because of her laugh.

Uneasily, he surveyed the village: all the strange houses, the bustling about the Castle. A clerk came out with letters, addressed to him. Borghorst had signed them. Hans stood there on the quay reading them. He was to keep the post on Robben Island until a substitute was sent. Further, it said that when he was relieved, he would be sent to Keert-de-Koe as sergeant in command. So, it was not to be the garrison, and that was a pity. Although Keert-de-Koe meant retracing a path he already knew, at least it was close to town. Also, it said that he should tell the widow van Meerhof that her late husband's grave was not known, that her late husband's accumulated wages on the Company's books would draw interest, and that she and her children should stay on the island until the Council had considered the matter more closely and come to a decision on her future.

He arrived on the island at sunset that evening and inspected the convicts before going to the posthouse. The kitchen was dark and the hearth cold. There was light in Jan Vos's little room, he could hear the children talking there. He lit the oil lamp on the kitchen table and took out his writing material to write to the commander about the island, but he couldn't think; the officials did not understand the situation. He abandoned the letter, and after a second or third glass of brandy called to the woman through the inside door, until she entered from the dark, softly, as if she had no feet.

'Good evening, Mrs van Meerhof.'

She held on to the door frame, looked over the short candle at the dark kitchen, past him, saying nothing. She smelled strongly of alcohol.

'I've heard bad news. Pieter died on Madagascar.'

Without a word she turned and went back to her room, into the dark. Later he could hear her crying; her voice rose and fell, and the sound was uninterrupted like wind keening through a crevice between roof tiles or the holes of a ruined house. Immediately the voices in the slave's room fell silent.

For the first time Hans Michiel went to knock on Jan Vos's door. The children were in his bed, covered with a kaross of buckskins. They stared at him with huge eyes.

'Your mother is feeling sad. She will feel better again.' To Jan he simply said: 'The postkeeper met with an accident.'

Beside the bed was a chest, made of a sturdy crate. On it were Jan's tobacco pouch, his candle and tinderbox, with a short pipe on the bowl of the candlestick. 'May I sit here? Have you people eaten?'

'Jan made us food.'

'Are you sleeping here tonight?'

Pieternella did the talking. 'Then there won't be room for him.'

'Perhaps they'd better go to their beds. Their mother will want them.'

He carried the three children round the posthouse and put them to bed and covered them up. They fell asleep very soon. Tomorrow he'd have to tell them, Hans thought, before their mother planted strange thoughts in their minds. He went back to the slave's room with a flask of arrack and his tobacco pouch and pipe.

They sat on the *katil* with their backs against the wall. It was only a sealskin stretched over a wooden frame, with a mattress of bedding-bush, and the skin kaross. They spoke about their concern for Eva and her latest child, and Pieternella and Kobus and Solomon who would be fatherless from now on. The Company had the power to strip people bare and throw them out. As long as Eva remained on the island something good might yet be done, but once she was on shore, there was no way of reaching her, except perhaps through the law. Because with her over there, you would have nothing more to do with her. And she could bring up her children as she wished and where she wished. Things would undoubtedly change, because Jan was Eva's property and what happened to her would happen to him. Jan's path and his were also parting now. And yet one never knew. This was very good arrack.

'Yet one never knows what the future holds,' Hans Michiel remarked, his thoughts with the bailiff of Voorschoten, and with sudden goose-flesh on his body as if someone was stepping on his grave. 'How did your road lead to this place, here, tonight, Jan?'

The slave gave a low laugh, and scratched his grey head as if he could not remember. 'I don't know the names of all the places I come from. But it's a long, long way.'

The biggest town there is Timbuctoo. The houses are of wood and raw clay, and they are not whitewashed like here. No limestone there, for whitewash. The world is green and full of water. They farmed with cattle. Very, very long horns. All around them is a desert, but that didn't bother them, for they had enough water, grass, trees, fish, meat, milk, everything. Twice a year the Arabs came from the desert on their camels to trade. Spices, coloured cotton and salt, in exchange for dried fish, hides, dates. From Timbuctoo the camel road led further to the coast, to Cape Verde. When the Arabs met the Portuguese at the seaboard, and heard that the Portuguese wanted slaves for their colonies in Brazil, they saw that there was a good thing coming. Then they no longer came with spices, but with muskets, and in every village they captured boys and girls, and bound them together with long ropes. They called it a *kafila*, a procession of captives.

I did the same, thought Hans.

'We had to walk to the sea, and they rode alongside with sjamboks. *Sjambok* is a word from the mouths of the Arabs. It went on for miles, miles. They rode on camels, muskets across their knees, sjamboks in their hands, while we stumbled along on foot in the white-hot sun, tied to the rope. The world there was naked sand, you wouldn't find a blade of grass to push through the stem of your pipe. We fell down from thirst, from fatigue, from sunstroke. Four, five every day. Then you heard the bang of a musket, and the dead were cut loose. So our *kafila* went through the desert, to the far seashore. At night the jackals laughed at our dead. The sea called me from far ahead; it wanted me. I had to go. I asked: How did you get hold of me, where have you heard my name?'

Behind the wall, in the postkeeper's room, they could hear the woman keening. It was strange to think that she'd been a widow for two months already, yet she only began her crying tonight. It was strange to consider that the children's lives would have been different if only their father were still alive. One death could change five lives. It was strange.

Hans Michiel did not speak to the children about their father's death. Before one week had passed, Corporal Jansz arrived to replace him. While the convicts walked up to their necks into the sea to empty the bags of shells in the boat, Hans Michiel escorted Jansz through all the buildings, showed him all the implements. On the kitchen table they signed the transfer. Of the Company, so many Christians, so many heathens, so many pots, so many pans, so many canvas bags, so many head of livestock, so many slaves. Then, there was the widow van Meerhof, with her children and her slave.

Hans Michiel had some raisins and dried figs left from his rations. The sun beat down from straight above when he found the children in the tall shrubs near the Fire Hill, where they were walking along the white dusty footpath, singing.

'I'm going away now, Petronella. Uncle Jansz is coming to live here in my place. I've told him about you. See what little jobs the two of you can do for your mother? And keep away from the convicts, as I told you.'

'I will, Hans Michiel,' she replied solemnly. Her brother nodded without a word. They cupped hands for the sweets, and stared after him as he went down to the beach. All that remained was to take his leave of his soldiers. He was glad to get away from there.

At Keert-de-Koe the pleasant, peaceful life helped him to forget about the poor people on the island. From time to time bits of news were brought to him. Eva's child had died. Why? Which one? Then could not say. A convict had committed suicide, and a ship's captain threatened to shoot one of the island's wardens. But his outpost Keert-de-Koe still remained the only gateway to Africa. The remaining Koina, fellows with tattered wide breeches and short pipes in their mouths, who passed that way to the Fort, could all understand Dutch. In the following months Hans and his horsemen patrolled the frontier, he noticed that the palisade had been broken down in places and was lying on the ground, and although he reported it, it was not put up again. The free farmers all wanted to graze on the far side of the river, right through the fence and over the young wild almond trees that had been planted there to mark the frontier. These were clear signs to Hans that the Company prospered. They were no longer afraid of the Koina, no longer needed the Koina for transport, or to provide for their ships. The Eastern frontier was open, the land was open to the European, and they multiplied and were ready to populate it.

From two of his soldiers who had spent a night in town, he heard that Eva was now earning her bread in a back room of a tavern, ashore.

'Did you see her there?' he asked.

'It's the truth, corporal. Everybody says so.'

'Everybody can lie too. You didn't see her.'

'The taverner tells that in just a few months she spent all her husband's wages there on lodging, and then she didn't know how to go on paying for her room.'

He was careful not to question them any further. What had she done with the children? He would enquire from the free burghers who passed through the gate in the daytime.

Then the commanding officer of the garrison came on inspection. He inspected the stable, their weapons, the horses and the barracks, almost finished their stock of brandy, and slapped a letter from

Commander Borghorst on the table. 'Promotion, I think, Hans Michiel. When you come back you'll be sergeant. You will go far.'

It was a transfer to the outpost at Saldanha Bay, two or three days' march to the north of Table Bay. Far enough, certainly.

Hans and two new men for the post were guided by two Koina with rucksacks and muskets, who would then lead the relieved men with a small flock of bartered sheep, back to the Cape. Hans Michiel enjoyed the walk, always in sight of the sea, under the cool, sweet wind that brushed the bushes and dunes in these parts. They were on the road for three days and two nights, and slept at places that had already been named, Gansekraal, Jakkalsfontein, in kraals of branches left by previous travellers, the ashes of their campfires caught in circles of blackened stones on the ground.

Saldanha Bay reminded Hans Michiel of parts of the northern German and Danish coast, with its long beaches and shallow waters. The outpost, his third command, lay at the foot of a steep rocky hill on the edge of a lagoon. The posthouse of stone and clay under a thatched roof, with a kraal added on, had been built right on the sea. It had a name, *'t Huis de Rust*. The tide had receded a long way, and an old rowing boat lay on its side in the mud on a long anchor rope, like a dead fish on a forgotten line. The guide took them to a well among the bushes to drink. The water was brackish, but not bitter like that of Robben Island. Over the warm earth among the bushes was the musk smell of striped skunk or genet. The posthouse was empty, and Hans had to wait until the livestock was brought home in the late afternoon, before he could meet his men.

When the two Koina and the relieved men from the post left for the Cape with their bundles and arms, driving before them twenty cattle and fifty-five sheep for which he had to sign, Hans was satisfied. Everything was in order; the commander was a long distance away from him. He wanted nothing more than that. About the silence he never complained; he did enjoy the silence of that remote post. He tended the livestock, looked out with a telescope from the rocky hill behind the posthouse, took turns at cooking. The herders brought home fuel. Fish was abundant, and occasionally some of the men asked permission to catch mullet in the inner water; their frames full of dried fish were next to the posthouse. At the end of every month a galliot or a sloop arrived with their rations, some gunpowder, some medicine and a letter from the commander. Hans diligently responded to it. He knew that his reports were being kept by the secretary, and whoever read them had to feel respect for the one who'd written it, even if it were years later.

At the Lookout Hill he sat with a telescope and surveyed the bushes and beaches on the far side of the lagoon. There was an empty stretch of white sand many miles long, shaped like a large scythe, and several stony outcrops on either side of the bay. In the bay were five brown islands, each with its white cloud of birds between sunrise and sunset. On the west, a bright blue sea thundered against shiny black rocks. But nowhere along those miles of beach, hills and rocks was there any sign of human life. To the south, Table Mountain lay in the far distance, the size of the first joint of his thumb. That was where his bosses ruled; there were a lieutenant, an ensign and five sergeants. He now stood a good chance of becoming a sergeant himself, but he could not relax about this. Fate, which had prevented him from carrying out his first independent command, which had caused him to kill a compatriot, and had unexpectedly driven him from his fatherland, was also in his mind. It would be by far the best if nothing at all happened, but something might intervene again.

Weeks of quiet isolation passed. There was the occasional visitor. Sometimes the Saldanha farers came to play cards and drink at their hearth, or a few Koina would arrive to exchange an ostrich egg or honey for a length of tobacco, or the government's galliot would bring their provisions and trade goods like beads, clay pipes, tobacco, sour wine, cheap stuff like that, which promoted dependency. From time to time a ship of the Company would anchor behind the islands, an outgoing ship unable to reach the Cape, or an *oorlammer* that had been blown past. Then Hans would provide them with what he had, like vegetables, fish and drinking water, send out a messenger to the Fort for them, and a week later the Cape galliot would arrive with a surgeon, a carpenter, a handful of sailors and provisions, to fetch the ship home to Table Bay.

In August 1670 the world discovered his hiding place, and came up to beat on his door. He thought: Now at last I can do something to compensate for my weakness. First, they saw a single ship behind Gull Island. It was a French frigate of some fifty cannon, showing that white flag which looked as if they were surrendering at a long distance. Hans sent out a messenger with a letter for Commander Hackius at the Cape. The Frenchman's boat was already in the water. They wanted fuel, to wash their clothes and fill their water barrels. Then they enquired whether Monsieur Bartholomeus was in the vicinity. Who? Oh, Bart Borms? But that one had left the country long ago. Then the Frenchman put in the high note. Their admiral had orders to take possession of this bay. The Dutch had no claim to it here. Their king had had the documents examined, and if someone did have a claim, it was the Hottentot king of this region, with whom they would negotiate or fight as he chose, but this bay they were going to occupy. And as far as he was concerned, it meant that Corporal Callenbach stood more or less alone against their whole fleet.

'Have you been to the Cape?' Hans Michiel enquired.

'No.'

'Perhaps you should report there first.'

'Unnecessary. We are on a free coast here.'

'Come into the posthouse,' Hans Michiel invited the officer. 'Let us drink to a happy encounter.'

The Frenchman entered, put his hat on the table, counted the beds and then the number of empty slots in the gunrack. 'What do you do here?'

'We assist ships that fall in here. And you?'

'We're sending troops ashore in the morning, and a flag party to take possession of this place.'

'And your authority?'

'From the French king. Admiral de la Haye has the certificate.'

'This bay has already been colonised. You will have to ask the Dutch king first.'

'Unnecessary. Your flag means nothing here. Your Company's charter stretches eastward around the globe from Cape Good Hope to Cape

Horn. And this bay falls outside it. It's as simple as that. You have no right here. Our East India Company needs a refreshment post for our ships, like the English on St Helena, and you Dutch in Table Bay. We are going to hoist our national flag here.'

'And build a fort, and lay out gardens?' Hans needed the information. If he was asked for a report, it could not contain any I-don't-knows.

'Naturally.'

'Livestock?'

'That we will get from the Hottentots, like you. Through barter or constraint.'

A rival French replenishment station for their ships trading with India, was cause for war between the two nations. 'The Company will not even allow another Dutch concern here,' Hans Michiel said with conviction. 'Not even other Dutchmen.'

The French lieutenant smiled politely, refused more brandy, took his hat, made a bow. He had to oversee his men, who were working with the water barrels. Towards noon Hans dispatched a second messenger with a letter to the Fort in Cape Town, and ordered the remainder of his soldiers to take up position with the Company's livestock on Gull and Sheep Island.

The following day three more French warships under their pale flag entered the bay from the north, and anchored on the deep side of the islands. Hans Michiel counted the gunports through his telescope; altogether there were now more than two hundred heavy cannon on this anchorage. No Company ship would be able to get in unopposed. Coloured flags played up and down the halyards, as they sent messages from one to another. Might they be saying something about him, and about the Company's herds on the islands, and here at the post?

That night, when he'd already put up the outside shutters of the posthouse, two natives arrived at the door. They were messengers from Couqusoa, the Bushman who hunted and fought for Oedasoa and Ngonnemoa. Couqusoa sent to inform him that he had thirty armed men to drive back the French, if they came ashore again the next day. Hans Michiel thanked him. He emphasised that they were not to attack the French, as they would then become enemies, but that the Company would reward him well if Couqusoa would keep in safety all the livestock on the islands and here in the kraal, until the French had left. When they departed, he gave in their care all fifteen of the cattle from the kraal to take away.

The sheep on the islands were removed at dawn the next day. Twenty Sonqua caught them, tied their legs and loaded them into the boat. Four soldiers rowed to and fro, while other Sonqua unloaded the sheep on the mainland, untied them and drove them to the posthouse. They had brought away a hundred and thirty-seven sheep when the French realised what was happening and sent four large boats with more than two hundred bluecoats, to stop them. Hans Michiel was satisfied. He had done his duty. Couqusoa's Sonqua had got away most of the Company's livestock.

From then, while he waited for help from the Cape, he had to look on while the French set up a camp of brown tents at Salamander Point, paraded daily on the sandy beach, mustered cannon and prepared for a march, while others dug in vain for water in the rocky soil. But nature was on the side of the French, because it rained well and they could spread sails between poles and fill barrels of fresh water almost every day.

Six days after Hans's first message, Sergeant Croese arrived at the posthouse on horseback. He had come to take over command. Hans Michiel had to take the horse back to the Cape; Commandant Hackius wanted to see him.

Was it mistrust? Hans Michiel was unhappy, as he'd wanted to see the matter through to the end. Whatever the French were planning, he wanted to be present there, to represent the Company in the matter. Occasionally came an opportunity for a good piece of work, waiting for a good man to do it, and the soldier on the scene should accept the opportunity. Now, it was to be Croese. What could Croese do here, better than he?

Commander Hackius kept Hans Michiel at the Fort for a few days. He wrote a report, leaving out nothing. His experiences at the outpost had given him some standing in the barracks. More news arrived overland from Saldanha Bay. The French had surrounded the posthouse, hoisted their king's flag and planted a post with his device painted on it. Croese had fled for his life, and his men were prisoners on the enemy's ships.

The commander asked Hans Michiel what he thought the French would attempt next. Was an attack on the Cape feasible? Yes, said Hans, especially because now in the wintertime there were no ships here in Table Bay. But there were other considerations: he felt that the French meant to establish a refreshment post, but not necessarily at the expense of a war against the Netherlands. Secondly, if they planned to attack this Fort, they would first occupy Robben Island. The island was the key to the Fort. There was a good anchorage, water, food, accommodation, and some thirty convicts who would support the French for the sake of their freedom.

'Good. Go out with the first shell boat in the morning, then prepare the island, in case the French try to land there. I'm promoting you to sergeant for the task.'

Sergeant. It was a pleasant feeling. He was completely satisfied with the commander's judgement. Now he could parade in front of a detachment and salute with the sword when they pass the honourable commander on the small stoep. Sergeant Callenbach gratefully bought his fellow sergeants a few pots of beer in the tavern. The hostess with the green eyes drew his first, took a sip, met his eyes over the rim, nodded and smiled her congratulations.

'You will go far, Hans Michiel,' said his companions, clapping one another on the shoulder, and banging their tin mugs together.

On the sloop with which he sailed to the island, were Eva and her children. She'd been banished to the island by the Council, on account of her repulsive behaviour in the Fort. She looked ill and covered herself with a tarpaulin in the very bows of the boat. Her face was wrinkled as if she'd aged twenty years in the six months since he'd last seen her. She smoked a short pipe, and had nothing to say. Her children appeared neglected, impoverished, with shaven heads, sore eyes and sticky noses. Their thin legs were covered with ugly sores. The baby was not with them.

The quartermaster told him the story, while the service boat was tacked out of the bay. Out of appreciation towards Master Pieter, the Company had given her a place to live in the disused pottery, six months ago. There, her infant died of the whooping-cough. A few times the commander had invited her to dinner, but what the woman needed was cash, as she was addicted to alcohol. For bread money she invited sailors home. One day, in full daylight, she hurled abuse at the commander in the courtyard of the Fort; in front of the whole colony, one might say. Hackius then warned her: he was going to send her to the island. She must have had a bad fright, because that very day she went off to the veld. The children were found famished and half frozen in the pottery, as their mother had left with all their clothes and blankets. In the dunes she exchanged them with some Hottentots for tobacco. The fiscal had her brought back from there. Her children were then taken into care by the Church Council, and they were not at all inclined to let Eva have them back, but the Council of Policy refused. Eva was the legal mother, and she had to take up her responsibility. Maybe the Council relied on the so-called natural love of a mother, but as far as the quartermaster of the boat was concerned: heaven help the poor children. If her conduct warranted it, she might occasionally go to the mainland on a day visit, but she was not permitted to spend a night on shore. Those were matters for the postkeeper, whose burden she was to become.

Hans Michiel was glad that the little girl remembered him. She spoke timidly, answered his questions and named all the diseases she'd had at the Cape: measles, chickenpox, whooping cough, and she'd shed a few milk teeth, gained others.

'And where is Jan Vos?'

'Jan works for the church.' The quartermaster shook his head, looking away, not knowing what she meant.

Well, thought Hans Michiel, Eva would not bother him. She and the children would have to live in Jan's outroom, as the honourable commander had indicated in his letter. She was not to be given alcohol. There was still a cow in milk on the island, belonging to her husband, and the shell boat would bring her provisions once a month. The postkeeper had to try to put her to work, it said. Hans Michiel thought:

Leave it to my successor to worry about care for her and the poor children; this time I shall be here for only a short while, a fortnight at most.

At the end of the flowering season he was still there. He himself provided the van Meerhof family with milk, for the children's sake, as Eva would have nothing to do with the cow. She wanted neither to milk it nor fetch it from the veld to be milked. Pieternella enjoyed feeding the cow and taking it to pasture, but Hans Michiel didn't like the child to walk about the island on her own, far away where the convicts broke slate or collected shells.

Eva was usually listless around the posthouse, but could scream vociferously at her children. When she came for her rations at the door, she was taciturn, often moody. Sometimes Hans Michiel could hear her shout threats and imprecations in a raging fit of temper outside. She would take her rice and beans without a word of thanks, walk off without saying goodbye, spit on the stone doorstep, hollowed out by many comings and goings, dragging her bare feet across the yard, sending the white lime dust billowing up. He could force her to rake the Company's shells into a heap and scoop them into bags, by refusing her her rations. Then she would mostly lean on the spade and gaze across the water to the north-east, where every day the smoke drifted up from different places, as the Cochoqua moved their settlement, and sometimes she would stare at Table Mountain and the smoke of the town. Her children were more disobedient than before; they would risk it on their own on to the dangerous Papenklip or into the veld, or on to the hidden, vertical sides of the stone quarry. One summer evening when the early stars were shining in the cool dusk, someone sent Eva a rabbit to the posthouse. Hans Michiel had it delivered to the outroom by a corporal.

With an acid laugh, the man came back: 'She says she takes cash only.'

'Throw it to the convicts.'

He thought of Bart Borms of old, when he saw the hungry and ragged children playing outside. 'It's because of my wife,' Bart had explained to him. 'We don't have children of our own. Perhaps a merciful fate willed it so, because a child will take after its parent. But this business is wearing Theuntje down. All she can talk about is other people's children, and it goes on day and night. Do you know what it is like, postkeeper? Have you seen a drinker wailing for his bottle? That's how she is. It is a terrible disease, the woman who wants a child.'

Yes, like an author with an unpublished manuscript, thought the clerk, when Hans repeated Bart's words to him.

One day the quartermaster of the shell boat mentioned that the French warships had left Saldanha Bay long ago.

'The French gone? Then the commander will summon me tomorrow.'

'No, postkeeper. He's forgotten about you. He has closed the outpost at Saldanha Bay. I think he is scared the French may come back and give him hell for that bay, seeing as it supposedly lies outside our borders. You will never get off this island again.'

He could not understand why they should have closed the post at Saldanha Bay. That was his post, now written off like that. Why was he here on Robben Island? His transfer would come through, he tried to persuade himself. He just had to be patient. For months he waited, but no instruction about Saldanha Bay or about his future was sent from the shore.

Hans Michiel went out to look for Eva when she wasn't home by dark. She had a dancing place in a hollow among the dunes. With dragging feet she would shuffle there in a circle, kicking up sand before her. She didn't sing, she just shuffled in the circle with drooping shoulders, stamping her feet in the dust. Her length of light chain came bouncing after her in the dust. Her hands were clenched in fists, she stared straight ahead of her, her lips were parted and her breathing came in shallow, groaning gasps. There were flecks of foam on her mouth. She wore only a skirt of skins around her hips.

'Missus van Meerhof.'

Her attitude remained unchanged. She wanted nothing to do with him. She was drunk from the dance, and he did not want to touch her. He left her there, and went to make supper for the children.

When Hans went out on inspection he took the children with him. If he could keep them with him like that every day for an hour or so, perhaps he could save them from the misfortune that fate had laid upon them. And there was something more, besides. Of all the people on the island, it was only the little girl's company and affection he enjoyed. That was something he did not get from anywhere or anyone else in the world. He took them with him to the far corners of the island, taking them on long walks around it. The sun reflected dazzlingly from the calcareous soil, burning their faces red under their hats. He spoke to them about whatever there was to be seen. Why were the mounds of seashells found only in this part of the island? What was the meaning of Papenklip? Why was the slate blue? How did the salt get to Salt Rock? Why did it look as if there had once been a beach in the middle of the island? What came first, the penguin or the egg? How did one count from one to ten in Dutch, in Koina, in German? How many pebbles did they have here, how many penguins over there? Where was Holland? Who were the Lords Seventeen? What had become of Jan Vos?

At the posthouse Hans Michiel recited rhymes to them in the evenings, the Ten Commandments, sometimes the plagues of Egypt, or the names of Jacob's twelve sons. 'Father Jacob said to his son Reuben: Forget it. You will never be it, try as you will. Make an extra effort if you think it will help. Give everything you've got; struggle as you wish. You're wasting your time. Hahaha! Others need only half try, but *you* will never win.' Then, he went to stand outside the posthouse, to stare across the black sea at the Fort.

Petronella was a questioner. Once she could count, she wanted to write. She already knew about reading and writing. Somebody must have shown her something. Hans sat down in the quarry with them where the whole wall of the slate quarry was one enormous slate, and he rolled them slate-pencils under his boot. On the bottom of the quarry the stonebreakers with their wooden wedges and sledge-hammers lifted out the doorsteps and paving for the new castle, or the slabs of heavy tombstone on which some respected name would later be chiselled. The boy wanted to draw on the rockface. The girl wanted to write. Hans Michiel taught her the way he had been taught. Cat was c-a-t. Her name was P-e-t-r-o-n-e-l-l-a.

One day he went to knock on the outroom door. He wanted to take the children with him to the veld. Their room was empty, stripped of everything that could be carried. His first thought was the shell sloop, that Eva might have evaded or bribed the quartermaster and sailed off on it. When he went to look outside, he saw smoke rising some distance behind the posthouse among the dunes. They were there, all of them, squatting round a fire. The striped blanket he'd given them for the girl's bed, was draped as a windbreak against their branch shelter; a few bundles had been shoved under the bushes. The little one was there, wrapped in rags. There was a tortoise on its back on the coals. He could hear them talk, but their voices were low. As they squatted there, their knees pressed against their chests, he could well believe that they were Sonqua. Eva raised one reed-thin arm from under her kaross to drink from a calabash. With her head thrown back, she let the last few drops run into her mouth.

When Hans Michiel stepped up to the fire, the girl greeted him, clasping her kaross to her chest. Hans Michiel took the calabash from Eva's hand and smelled the neck. It was a smooth brandy, not common ration stuff.

'Where did you get this?'

The girl replied: 'Is from a sailor here.' The cross-eyed older boy frowned furiously in all directions, as if he didn't understand what was being said, his face shrouded with a darkness. Eva grinned with her emaciated face. What disease did she suffer from? Hans Michiel wondered. He could ask for a surgeon to come over and examine her, but it was as if old age itself had clasped Eva in its embrace too soon, and that no medicine would save her from that clutch. He gave the calabash back to her, but she hurled it away.

'When you've had your food, you must come home, Petronella. Your mother needs looking after.'

The child nodded, but Eva screamed and cursed in protest. 'Needs? The hell with needs. What do we need from you? Leave my children alone and go to hell. We stay here, we didn't ask you for anything.' She stood before Hans Michiel and lifted up her dress. 'There, take it, there's your mother.'

'Missus van Meerhof, spare your children.'

Petronella took Eva by the arm and tried to pull her back to the shelter, but she shouted defiantly and broke loose. 'Go and look after your convicts. I'm not dying. I, I ate tortoise and hare.'

'Do you want to go with me, Petronella? Jakobus? Or do you want to stay here?'

But the child only shook her head. Then he walked back to the posthouse.

That night the children came home without their mother, with the clothing and bedding they had carried off. Her mother didn't want to come, Petronella said; she just lay there in the shelter and refused to get up, so they covered her with a blanket. Hans Michiel took a few soldiers and the convict with the wheelbarrow to fetch her. She lay beside a circular crust of vomit, covered with blowflies, and they had to pick her up. After they'd laid her down on her own bed, he went to speak to Petronella.

'Your mother is still young, but she's as weak as an old woman, and she needs someone to look after her. You and Jacobus will have to fetch wood and carry water and make the food. You must keep your mother clean, Petronella, because you can see she doesn't care any more. And Salomon.'

'She wants to get away from here, Hans Michiel.'

'She's not allowed to.'

'We can all stay with Aunt Maijke.'

'The Council won't allow it. You must look after your rations. I shall help you. And keep your room clean.'

During the following weeks Hans Michiel's concern about the children increased. From time to time, God knows how, Eva found alcohol and drank herself into a stupor. He could not report it, as the governor held him responsible for her. Sometimes she lay in her little shelter in the dunes, and sometimes she came staggering drunkenly to the yard and fell down in the bushes behind the posthouse and remained lying here. Then the girl came to call him, to help her mother back to her bed. Sometimes Eva's face was badly hurt in a fall; sometimes in raging sorrow she lay screaming on the stones. Once or twice Hans went out into the night with his cane and beat her, but when he saw the girl's face looking at him in horror he stopped doing it. Out of pity for the neglected child and what she'd lived through in her few miserable years on earth, he helped Eva across their threshold, and pulled their door to. He didn't know what more he could do for the child.

Sometimes she came to ask if he could send a soldier to look for her mother, she'd disappeared again. He couldn't; he suspected that the members of his staff were abusing the inebriated woman. The older boy was troublesome too. He wandered away from the other two and neglected the few tasks he had at home. Hans Michiel saw the girl drawing water from the well, or breaking wood in places where he'd asked her not to go on her own; it was Jakobus's work. But the boy went off to where the convicts were filling shell bags in the north-western corner, or among the stone-breakers in the blue-slate quarry. There a guard who tried to scare him off, one day – by accident, he insisted – threw a stone at him and hit him on the head. It bled quite profusely, and the corporal revived him with brandy and bandaged him with his own neck-cloth. People noticed Jakobus skulking secretively among bushes and rocks, and afterwards penguin chicks would be found at their nests with their necks wrung. The girl told Hans that Jakobus brought tobacco home, which he'd exchanged with the cattle hands for his mother's rations. Hans Michiel felt as if he was surrounded by opponents on the island; as if everybody except little Petronella had to be closely watched. His own corporals and soldiers were most likely behind the trouble with Eva.

At the kitchen table in the posthouse he told the children stories he remembered from his childhood. Everybody knew them; no one had ever been the first to write them down, no one the first to invent them. They had been thought up by grandmothers and told to children without parents to put them to sleep, just as grandpa's nightcap put *him* at ease against the coming night. Like those old tales about Little Red Riding Hood, Reinaert the Fox, Hansel and Gretel. For Eva's children the stories were splendidly new. For the first time, they looked in through a door where innumerable children had gone before. Spellbound they gaped at foreign lands with palaces, princesses, kings and dwarfs. At Christmas time, Hans gathered them to tell them what he'd heard about the birth of Christ from the parish priest, and with his own childhood in mind he described silent, dark northern forests, with pine branches bending under heavy loads of snow, a soundless white against black velvet. That one night of the year he took them outside to search the southern sky for the Star of Bethlehem, to see if perhaps it was around again.

The sloop which brought Corporal Janse to the island, returned Sergeant Callenbach to the Cape, and once again he became corporal. For another year and six months he served in the garrison, reminding himself how his prince had warned him to be wary of the Dutch, and always to use good judgement. On a wonderfully brilliant Saturday afternoon in early summer, he was corporal of the guard in the Fort Good Hope, in charge of two sentries at the gate and one on each of the four bastions. On the level ground in front of the gate the weekly drill was taking place, with Sergeant Croese in command. Like a horse trainer Croese stood in the middle, making the small garrison wheel round and round him with their banners, then to and fro; then in columns of three, and then in front formation; now at double time and then at a normal marching pace. He drove them with his commands from one corner of the parade ground to the other, shouting the names of the unfortunate select whom he couldn't stand, cursing those who had been in his bad books once, and then made the whole garrison run yet another five lengths, flintlocks high across the chest, as punishment for the clumsiness or ignorance of one or two. In this way he hoped to incite their companions against them, so that they would hear it time and again back in the barracks, and repeatedly suffer for it in body and soul. Hans Michiel pitied the sweating garrison, under their grey cloud of dust and the lash of Croese's tongue. Where he stood outside the gate with his two guards, the garrison was repeatedly driven past, so close to him that he could hear their panting.

'Corporal Callenbach, send those layabouts with you to me!' Croese shouted from the middle of the parade ground.

He did not react. His guards were not part of the drill session, and

Croese's call was unexpected, aggressive, and insulting in tone. Croese was undoubtedly aware of it.

'Stand fast,' Hans Michiel said to his men. 'I am in command here.'

Croese shouted: 'Roelofs and Krap, fall in here!' pointing with his cane to where he wanted them.

'Stay.'

Croese brought his parade to a halt and approached, swaggering, brandishing his cane. 'Damned dogs! When last did you have a flogging?'

Hans Michiel stepped forward. 'Leave the guard alone. The gate cannot stand unmanned.'

Croese stopped, staring at him in feigned surprise. 'Bloody fool. What have you got to say here?' And gave Hans three, four blows with the cane across the arms and shoulders. Hans warded off the blows, first grabbed the man's arm and then his cane, bent it until it snapped between them. Then he jumped backwards, into the guardhouse, where his musket stood. Croese followed on his heels.

'Keep off, sergeant. I'll kill you, I swear.'

Outside on the parade disorder broke out. The front line thronged closer, eager for blood, grinning. They tried to force their way through the gate. Croese heard the noise behind him and looked round. 'Back. Go and fall in.' And to Hans Michiel he promised: 'I'll be back in a while. Rub yourself with fat, because I'm going to tan your hide.'

'Look,' Hans Michiel told the gate guard. 'Pay attention. If he is disorderly when he comes back, I forbid him to enter. Arrest him. We are three to one.'

For another fifteen minutes Croese vented his temper on the garrison, and dismissed them. Then he advanced on the gate, with the 150 soldiers in his dust like schoolchildren, eager to see what was going to happen.

'Callenbach, come out,' he shouted from a distance, then drew his sword as he reached the gate, and bellowed: 'Come out, Callenbach!'

'Stand fast,' Hans Michiel warned. 'Say nothing, do nothing. His problem is the fellows behind his back. He puts on a brave act for them, otherwise they lose respect.'

Croese pulled off a glove and flung it inside the gate. 'I dare you to come outside, you dog with a pig's face. Come face my sword.'

'I am on duty. If you come in here with sword drawn I'll arrest you for being drunk and disorderly.' He raised his voice to the wall of faces in the background. 'You troops, you want him dead. This matter will be before the Council tomorrow. Take the man away, and don't incite him.' He remained standing with the cocked musket across his chest until Croese had replaced his sword in its sheath and no longer tried to force his way through the gate. Hans knew that a merciful fate had for the second time saved him from the gallows. He was trembling, he was frightened. Why was it after him? What did it want of him?

The case was decided in a most curious way. In Hans Michiel's old age a clerk brought out the original court documents for him to see. The court martial referred to an ordinance published in 1657 by the States of Holland and West-Friesland, on which the Company's statutes were founded, forbidding duels and declaring them punishable, as a result of which Sergeant Croese should have been stripped of post, rank and salary, dismissed as unfit to serve the Company, with confiscation of wages to his credit. So the following morning Croese should have been ordered by the commander to appear before a full parade where his insignia were ripped off his uniform and he was chased from the parade with a kick in the backside, according to the old custom. But no. It is recorded that at the court martial Croese admitted that he had been drunk at the time of the incident. He said it had been the first time in his eight years of service, and that it would not happen again, et cetera, et cetera. The court martial commuted his sentence to loss of rank and wages for three months, and a fine of four months' salary, of which one-quarter was to go to the fund for the poor.

After that, Hans Michiel was even more worried about his fate and fortune. He felt that he'd lost the favour of the garrison. They blamed him because they'd wanted to see Croese's blood and he had disappointed them. He had to get away from the Cape and try to reach the East, before something terrible happened to him. Croese got off almost scot-free, but *he* wouldn't.

The one official in the Council whom he personally liked, on whom he relied to deal honestly with his promotion, was *Secundus* de Cretser. Most people at the Cape were hoping that de Cretser would succeed to the command, some because they liked him, some because there might be advantage for them in it too. Then quite unexpectedly de Cretser had an accident with his sword. One moment he was still the acting commander at the Cape, popular, capable, and the next he was a fugitive, alone and on foot in Africa, a murderer with a price on his head.

That was why Hans was afraid. Earlier he'd felt: if only he could remain in the garrison where strict discipline regulated the behaviour and activities of his fellow man, he would prosper, since the work fitted him like the solid butt of a musket against the shoulder. Now there was no shelter left here either.

But first the sea carried him to strange shores. A good friend of his, Corporal Daniel Balck, had been left for dead on the east coast of Africa by the hooker *Grundel*, with eighteen other men. They'd been sent to buy slaves, and had marched inland to look up the natives, and that was the last to be seen or heard of Balck's detachment. The hooker waited for two days, firing guns every hour, and then left the coast. The commander was dissatisfied with that, and sent the captain back to search. This time Corporal Callenbach was in charge of the eighteen soldiers, as '*an expert land traveller and person of perception and knowledge*'. That was how it was phrased in his written orders. Recognition, therefore, was possible if he were successful. But he was doubtful, ill at ease.

Hans was set ashore with his detachment and baggage where Balck had disappeared, to march parallel to the coast for a week and fire a musket shot at intervals. It was already two months after Balck had vanished. Along that coast they saw marshes, many wild animals and black Africans, but not the least sign of Balck or his men. Hans Michiel and his entire group contracted the East Coast disease, and about half of them died on the return journey to the Cape. He himself had an attack of the disease, but only once, and not recurrently like the other survivors. So for four months of his life he sailed, marched, hallucinated and perspired with fever, without having anything but East Coast fever to show for it. Still, he was a corporal, at least that was something.

Upon his return the commander dispatched him, with two hunters, a butcher and an ox wagon with barrels and salt, to hunt hippopotamuses in the Berg River, and salt the meat and lard in tubs. They were slaughtering and tubbing in their camp, when about twenty Koina turned up to protest. The chief Ngonnemoa was there, with one who could speak Dutch. He told Hans Michiel that the hippopotamuses in the river and the game in the veld were his people's food. The Dutch had to remain behind that river and that fence they had put up, and not come here to steal his people's food. He regarded them as thieves, like the worst of the Sonqua, who were to be clubbed to death wherever you caught them. Hans should tell his chief that they had to stop this stealing of food. Hans said that he understood, and would convey the message.

'Will he listen to you, Hollander, or must I send your head back with that stuff you have in the pickling tub?'

With Ngonnemoa's message and only two tubs of meat, he returned to the Fort.

After this failure he was promoted to sergeant. It was the culminating point of his career. He was sergeant of the blue banner, the neatest and best turned-out thirty men, he believed, who bore the Company's arms. There were five banners in the garrison, each under a colour sergeant. White under old Sergeant Cruijthoff, red under Croese, blue under Callenbach, orange under Lubreghts, ermine under Bauw. Blue banner had the honour of leading the other four round at the Saturday parade, which meant that he himself followed in the footsteps of the commanding officer, walked in his shadow, and saluted the commander with the sword as they passed the stoep of the Kat. Only for blue banner did the commander doff his hat. Once this detachment had passed, he replaced his hat. It was a great thing for Hans.

Hans Michiel was snug in his post. He was able and happy and popular with his fellows, except for Croese. The food in the sergeants' mess he thought exceptionally good. He took guard at every fifth turn, and had ample time to work on his clothes. It felt as if he, the German, was more of a soldier than his Dutch companions, who were very good at drinking and swearing, but clumsy on parade and lazy on the march. One day the commander said, in front of the assembled garrison: 'It is on soldiers like Sergeant Callenbach that the power and honour of our laudable Company is built. I am grateful for your spirited example, sergeant. Well done, blue banner.' Of course, all the hats went up.

One day Hans Michiel encountered Corporal Jansz in the non-commissioned officers' mess, as the garrison sat down to their meal.

'Good day. How are things on the island?'

'Bitter. The water fills my kidneys with cursed stones. I'm finished, man.'

'I see. Routine still unchanged?'

'Unchanged. It kills me.'

'Your neighbours?'

'Eva and the children? The other day I beat Jakobus so badly that Eva had to keep him indoors for a week.'

'Why?'

'Stealing. He comes into the posthouse in broad daylight. First my food, because his mother is too stupid to feed them, and now my knife. I told her that I'm not bringing up other people's children. And my own tobacco for his whore-mother, that's how far she has egged him on. I brought them all to shore this morning. Eva wants to go back to the dunes, to wear her stinking skirt of hides.'

'Is that so?' Hans Michiel asked in surprise. 'Where are they now?'

'I left them on the jetty. I pick them up there again, first thing Monday evening.'

It was because of Oedasoa's death that Eva had asked permission to come ashore. The commander allowed it; perhaps out of pity for her, perhaps as a gesture to the Koina. It certainly was no longer because of the late Master Pieter; he was forgotten. A clerk in the office told Hans Michiel that the poor woman was having a bad time with her children. She'd sent a message to Maijke Hendriksz that the children

were at the Fort, and then she'd left, with the two natives who were
waiting to accompany her.

'Where did she go then?'

'To Oedasoa's kraal. Heaven knows where they're grazing this time
of the year. They immediately leave a place where someone died.'

'And the children?'

'I don't know. There's been no sign of Maijke Hendriksz.'

After the meal Hans Michiel started his search. He walked to
Maijke's house. She knew nothing about the children. It was an hour's
walk there and an hour back. It was late by the time he came back at
the Fort. Once again he went to enquire at the office, then he went
to the duty guard, then the main guard who had been on duty that
morning, then to the handful of layabouts at the gate, the Koina from
the dunes who carried bags and begged for tobacco. Yes, they'd seen
Eva, but the children were not at the Fort. Hans Michiel went to the
upper village behind the Fort, asking every passer-by, looking behind
every bush. The hostess of the Elephant promised that she would ask
around in her tavern, and Hans should let her know if he found
anything. When the sun went down behind Vlaeberg, and the number
of beggars at the gate dwindled, he emptied his pockets among the
remainder. He would give all his tobacco, his knife, his tinderbox to
the one who found the children. Drink, too. He would buy drink for
whoever helped to search.

It was completely dark when Hans had to return to the Fort. He
explained to Ensign Croese that he had to go on duty at eight the next
morning, and he wanted permission to stay outside overnight, in case
he could not trace the children before the tattoo.

'Yes,' said the ensign. 'But be in before the tattoo. You know the
governor.'

At dark, he found the night watch, the *ratelwag*, in the streets and
asked them to help him look. At nine o'clock he heard the drum
beating the tattoo from the battlements. If the governor was contrary
in the morning, then he, Sergeant Callenbach, would be in trouble.
For Hans it was as if the long drum roll on the battlement was meant
only for him, as if from now on he was walking blindfold to face the

firing squad, because his situation was such that one's feet were going one way, but one's road led elsewhere. From now on, whatever happened to him was pure grace, if it went well. The drum roll was rounded off with a last flourish, the flag was lowered, the heavy gate shut, bolted, the beam was thrown into the brackets. Hans, bearing a smoking torch in his hand, walked in the dark, calling. The few beggars, afraid of the *ratelwag*, had already gone off the streets. Around the village of twenty houses and ruins, dark bushes reached up the slope of the dark mountain. The air was cold, the sky heavily overcast.

Hans Michiel went to the Company's garden, and loudly called the gardener, to question him. The man was sitting down at his evening meal. From there Hans went to the slave lodge, then to the illuminated homes, then to the windy jetty, then to the cluster of fishing boats turned upside down on the beach. At each boat he bent over to look underneath. From time to time his road crossed that of the *ratelwag*. They had nothing to say to each other. They were standing on a gravel bank next to the Heerengracht, in a light drizzle. The guard officer had a small swallow of brandy in a pocket flask. This he offered to Hans Michiel.

'What time is it now?' Hans wanted to know.

'Past four.'

'Well, thank you.'

'Go to bed.'

'I can't. I'm locked out.'

'Go to my house.'

'I must try to find the children.'

'We're looking for them. Why don't you go to bed?'

At a late daybreak, on a wet and windy winter's day, he stood before the gate waiting when the pickets came out to open it.

'The governor wants you. He said: immediately.'

'I'm going to dress first.'

Governor Goske entered the sergeants' mess with his cane in his hand and his bodyguard on his heels, while Hans Michiel stood without his shirt beside his bed. The governor beat him with the cane over his back and shoulders, standing ready with the stick raised should Hans dare to lift his hand.

'To the guardroom.'

Hans took his clothes, thrust his boots and sword and blue scarf under his arm and crossed the courtyard towards the gate. The builders on their scaffolding, the clerks at their windows, the guards on the walls, could all see the governor giving him three more stripes on his back, before striding angrily ahead of his bodyguard towards the governor's residence. Hans did not go on duty. In the guardroom he remained sitting on a bed, waiting. He found a crust of bread in a tin plate under a chair and ate it. He wasn't angry, and he no longer cared about the children. It was fate which determined that things happened the way they did, and how could one word or another from him make any difference to it? He wasn't angry at the governor, because an example had to be set to the garrison. Nor at the young corporal who came to take the blue scarf from his hands and draped it over his own shoulder, or at Ensign Croese who wouldn't say a word to help him. They could lead him out of here and shoot him for all he cared, he wouldn't say anything.

Years later, when they were both old men, a former Council secretary told him: 'You Germans are the easiest people to lead by the nose. You are like slaves. Wonderful people, but as placid as sheep.'

Hans Michiel laughed. 'There are two reasons why you may be thrashed, but I respect your glasses.' His pain was lodged more deeply than the feelings he could control; it was a powerless, helpless prisoner in the deepest dungeons of his mind, it would never rise up in rebellion or try and break out in resistance or in vengeance. From time to time Hans almost forgot about that prisoner, his pain, to visit it only in rare moments of cynicism. But it remained alive inside him for as long as he lived.

Ensign Croese had Hans Michiel's sea chest brought to the guardroom. 'Your chest is packed. Here are your papers. You are dismissed from the Company's service. From here, you will go on board of *Henegouw*, to work for your passage. Give this letter to the captain. His quartermaster will come to fetch you at the noonday gun. Your salary to date will be paid in the Netherlands.' Hans thrust the letter into his pocket, but he did not want to look into his chest. His back would bleed if he were to bend over to look. The lock was broken open. It did not matter.

After that the sea took him again. It was under him, around him, over him when stormy weather transformed the well between fore-castle and quarter-deck into a foaming dam. And it was the cold Atlantic Ocean, not the gentle, warm purple-blue swell of the Indian sea he'd sailed at Mozambique. They remained at sea for three months. His back healed, he turned brown. In the early mornings he scrubbed decks, during the days he stood his turn on the lookout, helped to hoist barrels from the hold, to carry sails up from the lockers, bind them on and hoist them to nearly below the clouds, where sailors on the narrow yards were waiting for them. On the orlop, where he bedded down, he had to endure the itching of lice all night, the squeaking and fight-ing of rats over scraps of food, the noisy coming and going of quarter-masters and guards, and the furtive scurrying of secret gamblers. He was grateful that his humiliation did not turn into bitterness.

After a month at sea the captain called him aside. 'You have seen us bury a number of fellows. The officers tell me that you're a good worker. In your letter it says that you were a watermaker on your first voyage. Report to the chief boatswain at morning watch tomorrow. A hundred buckets a day, except Sundays. One more thing, Callenbach. What Governor Goske did to you I cannot change. But work hard, and I'll append a few lines of my own to your letter.'

The work was like carrying shells. Hans Michiel returned to the hundred buckets a day except Sundays, the red copper condenser, the wet clothes, the sleeping spot next to the warm bricks of the kitchen. With a rope around his waist he hung overboard from the chains of the foreshroud, flung his bucket forward, hoisted it up, emptied it into the still, dropped it again. There was only the sea to look at, but in almost every glass-green swell there was something to see, a patch of foam, a piece of cork, a feather, a strip of kelp was lifted almost up to his feet for him to look at. He was privileged; he saw every wave that came, and each one that went. If he wished, he could count them, like milestones in his life, from nowhere to nowhere. In the tropics he hung there without a shirt, but after the equator he had to cover himself against the weather. He wound rags round his hands so that he could clutch the bucket, for his palms were chafed red by the stiff rope and stung with salt water. Further north, his overcoat froze solid after the first breaker had washed over him in the dawn.

Behind Ireland the boatswain told him to stop; they had enough water to last them the remainder of the way home. In the icy wind that drew a silvery fog over the entire sea, he worked on deck again to scrub barrels with wire brushes, but it was good, he'd rather be there than up in the rigging, where the bundled sailors shuffled along frozen foot ropes to beat plank-hard sails into their folds with their fists. He told the cooper's mate that in the brackish water well on Robben Island green slime never formed. Perhaps a handful of salt with the filling of every barrel might counteract the forming of slime. The cooper's mate asked the victualler for salt. This Hans, he thought, would make a good seaman.

Far in the North Sea the Company's pilot boat discovered them in a steep, greyish-green swell, exchanged a few flag signals in passing, shouted a few words through the hailer, and swung her head back into the wind, to the south. The visibility went down to less than a cable-length; the flaming tar barrel on the mizzen-mast of the pilot boat was a smoky smudge in the grey haze in front of their bow. Opposite Terschelling and Vlieland the sea was turbulent under a leaden sky. Both ships laboured heavily against the sea; every wave was a massive blow against the bow, a roaring flood over the forecastle, a cloud of spray up to the masts over the ship, and a waist-deep, churning white maelstrom. It was fully three days of head-sea before the pilot boat could enter through the Hell's Door at high tide, and those who knew the sea could feel how the current took them there and carried them up into the greyish-green Marsdiep. To the north of them was the dyke of Oudeschild, a dark layer behind a grey sea-fog. To the south were the dunes of Den Helder, with its row of gallows hidden behind the low and heavy weather.

In the night Hans Michiel lay curled in his canvas round the cook's copper still and thought of the Cape, where it would be summer now.

There was no watch on deck, except for the man at guard watch and two nightwatchmen from the shore, because of their Eastern cargo. The whole ship was quiet, the masts stripped, their tops struck. It could be days before the weather cleared, when lighters would come for the cargo and then the crew. Hans sent his thoughts to Table Bay, and the arid island there on which he'd lived. Perhaps it was the cold which steered his thoughts like that. There, too, had always been more people imprisoned than free, more dead than living, more below the ground than above. He longed for his outpost Keert-de-Koe and for Saldanha Bay, where he had lived, a man with friends. Here he was washed up, back once more where he had started. How was that possible? What was wrong with him?

The crew were paid off in East India House in Amsterdam. They were home. There was the New Church, there the Weeping Tower, called Schreierstoren, there to the left the Naval Magazine with four new ships on the stocks, and right here in front on the Damrak, a black forest of swaying masts. At the Weeping Tower they climbed up on to the quay, sea chest on the shoulder, bedding under the arm, stamping their feet on hard ground as if to make sure about that. Unbelievable. They were home from the opposite end of the earth. Survived. Safe.

'Up to the Peperhuis, there you will find your captain and the *seur*,' the boatswain's mates urged them on. On unsteady legs they went into old Amsterdam, among hawkers, couplers, porters, tavern boys, women with children on the hip. So they headed for the Kloveniersburgwal, where East India House sat in a side street. That was the place where money burst from the windows, the place where Lords Seventeen sat around the table to roll the dice about Jack Tar. There they stood outside, all the way into the street to be paid off. The file of seamen crept forward as if the captain inside was winding them in with a capstan. A name would be called, a sea cap placed upside down on the table in front of the gentlemen, an amount read out, coins dropped on the cap, and then Jack Tar bent down to make his sign on the paper. After that his captain signed his name, and you were free. Sometimes the captain would shake the hand of a favourite, sometimes curses would be thrown to and fro, about fines and unexpected deductions. When it was Hans Michiel's turn, the captain took a letter from his inside pocket and put it on top of the small pile of copper and silver in his cap.

'Take this upstairs, to *Meester* van Dam. He knows about you. Good luck, young man.'

Hans carried his things upstairs. He had to wait for a long time in a cold passage in front of a closed door that had number four on it, with his chest at his feet. Through the window he could see their fellows forming small groups outside in the street, discussing where they would go to drink, exchanging addresses. One or two of them already had a woman on the arm. On the opposite side he saw families waiting for news, but too timid to approach. A carriage with six or seven rowdy sailors on top of their baggage went rattling past, away from the sea. One man had a long telescope pressed to his eye, another swung the whip, yet another was fighting the coachman for control of the reins.

A messenger called out Hans Michiel Callenbach's name, and escorted him to *Meester* van Dam. The gentleman's office was as plain as that of the secretary at the Cape. The same went for his clothing: simple black, without the lace at wrists and collar which Hans Michiel had seen worn on the streets. He was the Honourable Company's advocate. He asked Hans to sit.

'The deportation which Governor Goske issued against you is illegal. The Company uses Maetsuyker's *Nieuwe Indische Statuten* in its overseas territories, and the governor did not act according to them. Anyone has a right to a trial, ever if he is a murderer. I tore up your service record, and had a new one drawn up without Goske's remarks. It is a good record. If you wish to return to the Company's service with your previous rank and salary, you are welcome. As long as you don't go to the Cape while he is there, that would be asking for trouble. Would you like to go to the East?'

'Yes, Your Honour.'

'Just, *meester*.'

'I would like to go home first, to Germany.'

'All right.' Van Dam took his purse from his belt, and counted out ten silver coins. 'Go now, Hans. Ride where you cannot walk, but don't stay in Amsterdam for long. The place has a powerful charm; it makes you feel so much at home that you don't want to leave again.'

'Thank you, *meester*. This silver?'

'That I deduct from Governor Goske's benefits. I shall write to him about your case.' Van Dam led him to the door by the arm. 'Set sail, Hans, and get going. You don't have to be in a hurry to come back. The Company will still be here in a hundred years.' Both of them laughed, because both knew only too well how quickly everything could change: how heroes died, how governors came and went, how companies suddenly declared bankruptcy when profits declined. But this Company? Never.

Behind the door somebody asked van Dam what the sailor had wanted. 'What do we all want?' he replied. 'He wants to go East.'

Hans Michiel wanted to see whether his foster-mother was still alive. After that he wanted to join the army. Any prince could have him. The road east to the German border was one long slog in mud, but from time to time there were rides for a few guilders on a wagon or a barge, and once he spent a day walking with two farm girls behind a small herd of dairy cows. He ate bread and cheese with them, and he could see that they regretted it when his road turned off to the north. Later he was regretful too; he could have accompanied them to their winter grazing and given them a hand settling in there. But that would have been for their company only, for he wasn't a farmer. Farmers battle through their winters.

Hans Michiel felt rich. The purse at his waist remained full. When he came to the region where people spoke German, he couldn't keep the smile from his face. This was the land of his birth, after all. From Papenburg his money bought dark bread, strong beer and black sausage. This time he could afford a bed in an inn and eat a hot meal of sauerkraut and pork at the dining table in front of the hearth fire. But the travellers inside were silent, as if misfortune had entered with him.

He debated with himself honestly. The reason why he found himself on this road, was to find out what he had done wrong. He wanted to discover how it had begun, to follow the road he had taken, and look back with his experience and then tell that raw young corporal with the red rosette and the cane: Here you were too hasty, or too presumptuous, or too negligent, or too ignorant, or far too confident. This is what went wrong with you. This is why you run into trouble with your authorities, why you are still without rank, and why you had to waste years on an island.

Just as it was eight years earlier, the Lüneburg heath was covered under snow when he trekked over it along the black wagon track, alone. On the way were churches small and big, and chapels at bridges, but Hans went past, praying as he walked. In the environs of Kühnecke he heard the dialect of his home, and started enquiring about the old lord of Lüneburg castle and the widow of a stable hand. It had been eight years before, he said. But no one remembered her. Signs of the long war could still be seen. Beside the road were charred trees, a gallows fallen at an angle in the cursed and salted little square below, a broad stretch of dark green grass on a rise where had been the horse lines of an army camp. Only, the winter was equally cold, the sky grey, the ground mostly under snow.

Lüneburg's castle bore white ridges of snow on the battlements and over the narrow window ledges. A corporal and two young soldiers sat on picket guard, under a lean-to beside the gate. Hans walked up to greet them. They stared at him from under their heavy headgear, thrust their hands deeper into their coat pockets and pushed their feet towards the fire. In their pot a fragrant dumpling soup steamed.

The old prince, they told him, had died some years before. The castle had gone to a cousin, the son of his father's youngest brother. This man was now living there. Fond of hunting and horses, which proved that his bloodline was true. Hans enquired about his foster-mother. No, there were no old women working at the castle any more. Young things mostly, who enjoy playing around with the bodyguard in the corridors. But not old women. The village pastor? Yes, that was his house over there, but he was a Catholic now. The new lord had brought it about.

Hans knocked at the cottage. He was surprised at how low the roof was, how low the door, how small the windows, how empty the herb garden. He could easily rest his hand on top of the sod roof's overhang.

'Good day, sir priest,' Hans Michiel greeted the man clothed in black. 'I am Hans Michiel Callenbach. Years ago I lived here. Now I'm trying to find out if any of my family are left in this parish.'

'Welcome, pilgrim.' The priest opened the door to let him in, and escorted Hans Michiel to the room in which he'd had his lessons. The house was dark and spare, without decoration. It was clear that the priest led a life of poverty, but because simplicity is a virtue, he did it with pleasure. His parish was small, he said; old ones died, the young moved to the cities. If Hans wanted to, he could stay for the night. There was enough room for a visitor to sleep. And where did the brother come from?

They ate at the turf fire, burning with a low blue flame. There was black bread, pale yellow wine, white cheese. How had the parish changed so much? asked Hans. He remembered that after the war there had been much resentment against the Catholic Church, because of the Church's role in that terrifying struggle. Look now, barely eight years later. He would like to know how the priest experienced the changes. Would his reverence like to smoke?

Well, it hadn't been so long ago, the priest said. His memory was still good, and where memory failed there were, thank God, books in which the events had been written down. He was no learned man, and only wanted to do the will of the Lord and glorify His name, nothing more. When the village pastor had died, the prince had used the opportunity to return to the true Church. 'I was sent here and did what I could to spread the gospel in this impoverished parish. I could serve the Holy Sacraments to them, and offer them the comfort of confession. All of us, even our rulers, experience those great times of transition. We are human beings, whether you're Catholic or Reformed, and today's national politics barely leaves a humble man space to breathe. I did it with reverence.'

Hans Michiel enquired about the new lord, the strength of the garrison, the success of agriculture, and about the few townspeople he could still remember. Tomorrow morning, God willing, we can walk to the church, the priest said. The first Mass is at six. There will be a few people, as we're still in the twelve days of Christmas. We can look in the parish books if they have the answers you are looking for, and then the cemetery most certainly, the only place that has the full answer. The oldest graves are in the churchyard of the former nuns' convent. That is the oldest, but during the war scores were buried without stone or prayer.

When they left the house in the morning, the priest brought along a hymn book for Hans. Under delicate silver leaf patterns the leather cover was marked with pale green mould.

'This hymn book was left here by your village pastor. A gift from his father, as you will see written on the flyleaf. In Gothic writing, not so? And all the music notes. I found it in the pulpit. Perhaps he wished me to give it to someone. Perhaps he simply forgot it there after his last sermon. But the prince laid down the new policy. Take it, Hans Michiel. You know we use Latin in our church.'

'Thank you, reverend priest. I am in need of something like this.'

The little church was the one of his youth: cold, small, dark, with a few signs of the new lord's religion. There were an altar table, a heavy, black crucifix with a tortured Christ, and a blue and white Madonna and Child high on the wall. For the rest little had changed. In the bare, damp room behind the altar was a mouldy black chest filled with books. Of those, the priest took out three, which he brought to a table below the window.

'These were kept in the castle, during the war. Look to your heart's content, Hans Michiel, while I light the candles and prepare the Mass.'

There was a book of baptisms, a book of marriages and a book of deaths. All three began about ten years before his birth in the time of his old teacher. The Gothic writing he'd learned at school was faded but still legible. From the little church room next door came the sounds of prayer. Two or three people would sing, followed by the reading of the priest, which fell silent from time to time as he waited for responses. Hans Michiel drew his finger down along the date column in search of his parents' names. The entries started too late to show their baptisms or marriage, and he already knew that they had both died outside this parish. His own name was not in the baptism book. He checked the list of boys of his own age. He recognised the names of former playmates, but his own was not among them. That meant that he'd not been baptised in the parish. Perhaps he hadn't been baptised at all. In the book of deaths he discovered that of the old pastor, and about a year after his own departure from the parish that of his foster-mother. Then came the time of the Great Plague. It lasted for about five months, and every day three, four, five had been buried before the plague moved from the village. Three years later the language changed from German to Latin. It was curious to see how many people still died in peacetime; mostly the aged, but also young people, among whom were familiar names, up to two and three in one month.

Nothing. He was alone.

After the Mass the priest entered, stowed away his bread and wine, blew out the candles.

'Have you found anything, Hans Michiel?'

'I know that I have no home anywhere. Why are so many people dying here, sir priest?'

'It is since the cold came over this world. The people are freezing, and wood is almost unobtainable. Everybody coughs. Most of them die of the lung disease. But have you noticed, Hans Michiel, that children born here do not get married here later? The young move away; the sea calls them, and they go west to reach it.'

'Like the swallows, because of the cold.'

'Yes, and for other reasons too. Prophecies are fulfilled in various ways.'

Most of the walls of the former nuns' convent had caved in, and grass and young saplings were growing in the rubble. The chapel still stood, and was being cared for by a gardener, dressed in the prince's livery, who pushed open a door in the heavy gate for them. In the grass the priest pointed out one or two headstones of people who had been notables in the village. There were no others. Somewhere here a distant little stepbrother lay.

'What became of our nuns at the time, Hans Michiel?'

'Fled, those who could.'

Behind the altar in the nuns' chapel was a grey sarcophagus of roughly dressed stone, almost totally covered by an old-fashioned oblong shield, with a lance and sword crossed below, all of it cut from a single rock. A Latin epitaph was inlaid over the top section, but most of the letters had been dug out to be melted into bullets. The light on the floor was blue, green and yellow. In the windows above were still the coloured images of angels.

'Is this the old prince, here?'

'Yes.'

'It was he who sent me abroad.'

'People remember him as one who sentenced hundreds to death in this place.'

'And who didn't die with absolution as a Catholic.'

'Indeed.'

'Sir priest, from here I have to go back to the sea. Thank you for your hospitality and your help. Please take this, for the poor.'

The priest thanked him and wished him well, and as Hans left through the convent gate, he called hoarsely after him: 'Pray for me, pilgrim.'

Once again he took the snow-covered road to the Netherlands. He walked rapt in thought, sometimes singing a psalm from the book he had been given, sometimes studying the beautiful silver pattern on the cover. He would clean the cover, oil the leather. It had once been an exquisite little book; even if he became poor one day, he wouldn't sell the silver decoration. Some vague thoughts about the future came into his mind. Nothing was certain, except that he was alone in the world. And that he had failed once again. He had come to face the fate that had sent him to sea, and there was nothing. Now he had to find work for the winter.

That winter it went well with him. He never reached the Netherlands. He found the turn-off where the two farm girls had gone to their winter grazing with their cattle. There was an old, black, leafless poplar lane, a half-mile or more in length, at the end of which stood a small farmstead, barely more than a hut of sods, under a hill. It was a rather low home with a steaming turf roof, and a stable for twenty cows built on to the back. It was late afternoon when he arrived. As no one was present, he walked to the pine forest half an hour away to gather a bundle of firewood, and carried it back, casting one eye over his shoulder for the landlord's bailiff.

Their cheeks still showed the same glow, and from the way they greeted him he knew that he was welcome. They invited him in to the warmth under the roof, and showed him where he could put his bundle and his sleeping gear. The loft was spacious, with thick straw on wood. There he put down his burden. In the big room below, a row of boards had been set up, where basins caught the drops dripping from young white cheeses, suspended in nets under the beams. They told him that for the worst part of the winter they took their fifteen cows to a piece of rented pasture; that the cattle mostly stayed indoors. They mowed fodder where it stood, milked twice a day, made butter from the cream and cheese from the curdled milk. After three months their mother came to fetch the butter and cheese for the market in an ox cart. When there was new grazing in the spring, they took the cows back to the village.

He enjoyed the company of the young farm girls. They immediately had to work sparingly with their food, to divide their supplies for two among three, but when the weather permitted, Hans walked to town to buy provisions and some delicacies. And he told them about the Cape and the farms along the Liesbeeck (all of it free land, as much as one could manage) under year-long sunshine, where the cows grazed in the daisies and the milk tasted of honey. And he told them, when the winter cut them off from the outside world, of hippos in the Berg River and lions and rhinoceros behind the Tygerberg.

Evenings in front of the fire were the best. When they wanted to know about the places where the sea had taken him, they made a joke of it, asking: 'Where did you get so brown?' He told them about the shipmates, known as 'lords of fourteen days', because within two weeks they used to spend on drink and otherwise wasted what a sailor would earn over years in the hardest and most dangerous manner. In the heart of winter, when there were only four hours of light per day, all three of them would lie together in the deep rye straw in front of the glowing peat fire, and they would tell him new stories, of brave princes and beautiful princesses, magical castles, dwarfs and witches. 'Where did you hear this?' he would ask seriously, thinking of the princes and castles he had known in his life, and of old tales he had tried to tell to children. Were they the same stories all over again? Often he woke up in the morning with one of them in his arm.

When the weather improved, they sometimes took the cows outside, and Hans went to town for provisions, while the two girls with the shiny golden plaits wound around their heads, folded cheeses into white cloths like babies. The Dutch army, he learned in the village, was now fighting on all sides. The English, the French and the German bishops from this area had invaded the Netherlands at the first melting of the ice. The largest towns were already occupied; in the Utrecht cathedral the Catholic Mass had again been celebrated. The Dutch found themselves with their backs to the sea. They broke their dykes and flooded their country with seawater, and the prince stood with his army camp on the small high ground between Bodegraaf and Zwammerdam.

Why the sudden invasion? Hans asked in his fatherland. Well, because of the land; the damned Dutch were stinking rich. And for the restoration of the true Christian Church. Then that is what I shall do, Hans decided: soldier in the Dutch army, until Goske left the Cape.

When the snow melted, he walked with the two German girls behind the cows in young green grass and broad pools of snow water, from the farm to their village. It had been a great pleasure, he said, when saying goodbye to them; and on the way he thought how the medicine of the present healed the wounds of the past. Fortunately one remembered the good for much longer. Hans Michiel enquired about the road to Bodegraaf, where the Prince of Orange was camped. It was midway between Utrecht and Leiden, but he could not go there directly. The road to Utrecht crossed occupied territory, and without a pass no one could get through the French control posts.

He moved south behind the frontier on German territory, through Bentheim, Münster and Kleef, until he had passed the French lines and found himself behind their back and on the road to the flooded area. It was a long detour, a trek of more than a week along footpaths to avoid people and particularly the marching regiments. The farmhouses were already plundered, animals driven away, but he was well rested after his winter and survived on the black German rye bread and smoked sausage in his satchel. Something to drink was harder to find. The rivers were flowing strongly from melted snow and winter rains, but in the low territories where armies camped and marched, you couldn't put your mouth to river water. He hurried on, and only started looking for shelter in the late afternoon. Usually it was in a deserted farmhouse from where the farmer and his family had fled ahead of the troops. Land of Altena, Alblasserwaard and Land of Meuse and Waal were knee-deep under seawater; all traffic had to pass along the dyke. There were no horses or vehicles to be seen; the animals had probably been commandeered. And without a pass from the authorities travelling was a big risk. When he did encounter somebody, cripples or others unfit for military service, he wanted to enquire about the state of the war, which places had been occupied, which way to go to Bodegraaf, but everywhere people were too scared to talk about the war. The martial law of both the French invader and the Prince of Orange were in force here, in this place and over these people.

Hans caught up with the prince at Zwammerdam. He saw the tent with orange banners standing in the centre of the camp. That was the Kat, where the commander was housed. He immediately felt at home, like a boy relaxing in the care of a rich and important father and the company of twenty thousand brothers. 'I want to join,' he told a guard. 'Do you accept recruits?'

The guard looked askance at him, as if he himself did the preliminary selection. 'The drum beats at ten.'

While he waited, he examined the camp. The army was busy with field exercises some distance away. He watched them moving and concluded that there were not more than twelve thousand men about. Around the Kat were ten small tents for army chiefs, no more. In the artillery park were sixty cannon, large and small, each with the barrel turned down against the rain, like rhinoceros sheltering under a low tree, and that was all. There were two hundred wagons and carts, a camp with a hundred draught oxen, a small camp with livestock for slaughter, at the horse lines about two thousand horses, no more, were feeding from canvas mangers. They appeared to be in reasonable condition, and Hans

Michiel wondered who the horsemaster was, who wouldn't let the muzzles of his animals touch the ground of an army camp. Behind the horse lines was the customary village of tents for the cook, the wagoner, the blacksmith, the surgeons, saddle-makers and other tradesmen. Beyond the tents, downwind in a hollow, were the rubbish dump and latrine pits.

At ten o'clock twelve or fifteen recruits crowded together at the flag. Among them were a few darker-skinned fellows, French or Spanish, but they were warned rowdily: 'No Catholics here. Here we give Catholics hell.' When the drum began to beat the adjutant's tent flap was thrown open. In one cluster they thronged inside. Behind the table were a corporal and a sergeant. There a first selection took place. The suspect dark men from the south were escorted away, presumably for questioning. The second selection happened at the adjutant's table. All who had been soldiers before, had to step to the right; the rest were escorted away. Hans Michiel told them that he'd worked with horses since his childhood, and was sworn in as foot soldier in the army of His Highness the Prince of Orange. He was put into the horse section and equipped with a new musket and an unusually long bayonet. His new groundsheet was still sticky with linseed oil, and large enough to be buried in. He was satisfied. What pleased him was that he received a new full uniform. In the Company's service uniforms were not yet worn. At last he looked like a soldier again. It was better here.

Outside the tent drums were beaten again. With a smile of pleasure Hans listened. There were eight snare drums, two at each corner of a square. He couldn't see them, but knew what they were doing, and relished the fresh, rhythmic rattling. They were practising patterns and echoes, first clockwise, then diagonally, then anti-clockwise, always wonderful to the ear. Here were the drums, now loud, then soft, now near, then far, over there were the horses, over there the cannon. He was back in an army camp, and he was totally satisfied. It wasn't a castle, and this parade ground among the tents would be cold, as it was open on all sides, but drilling always sounded better on gravel than on stone. Hans Michiel could already smell the midday meal from the cook's tent; it would probably be a mug of hot vegetable soup and a large chunk of bread.

On Saturdays the prince inspected his army and then spoke to them from the box of a horse cart, as he wasn't a particularly tall fellow and barely twenty-two years old. They had to bear up, he said, and not lose heart. They were assembled here on high ground because there was almost nowhere else he could move to; neither he nor the enemy could attack through the water. They were going to move the camp between Zwammerdam and Bodegraaf to remain ready and active, while they were waiting for the outcome of peace negotiations, because much to his regret he had to say that a large part of the government and the general public was prepared to make concessions to the enemies, in order to avoid more destruction to the land. They were even willing to relinquish the eastern provinces and other parts already occupied, for the sake of peace. Why, for the sake of peace? He himself would never give up an inch of the fatherland, and would fight until the Netherlands was free, as before the invasion. He and his advisers believed that the fatherland's navy could beat the Englishmen at sea, and then he would invite the beaten English to join him in fighting against the French. The fleet was still intact, and de Ruyter was in command there. He therefore had good reason to wait high and dry between Bodegraaf and Zwammerdam, and in the meantime they collected supplies and exercised the troops. The weather was now getting warmer, the ground was drying out, and the navy could sail out. They just had to see it through and remain in complete readiness. In God's eyes being outnumbered meant nothing.

Hans's work with the horses kept him far away from officers. They were thirty men, under the sergeant horsemaster. They had to ride out with wagons to scour the environs and commandeer hay and grain-food from burghers with threats or violence. In the evenings before sunset they covered the horses with blankets, and removed and hung them out in the morning. They had to curry the horses, treat hooves and mouths, give them food and medicine, heal saddle sores and wounds, and on the march they had to drive wagons and carts, harness and unharness the horses, and repair and oil the gear. All this, in addition to guard duty, parades, patrols and field exercises. And shooting when the enemy showed himself.

Near Bodegraaf a man came to the camp to speak to the prince. In the hour following the morning parade the public was admitted into the camp to present petitions to His Highness. The memorandists entered the blue-and-white-striped tent one by one. Inside the flap was a table where they expected to find the prince, but they had to be satisfied with his orderly. The latter looked at pieces of paper, wrote down names and addresses, and dispatched them to a second table, where three gentlemen unfolded the letters, read them, and called out the names.

'Willem Willemsz.'

'Your Honour.'

'The prince will consider your request. Come again tomorrow.' There were various answers, like 'approved', 'turned down' or 'apply again later'. The soldiers reckoned that a prince ought to listen to the cases of his people, even if there was war, so that he could know if they were being treated fairly. It didn't matter that the prince did not see their letters personally, but only one of his councillors. In spite of the general suffering in the country, aggravated by martial law, there were people who thought they were treated unjustly standing in front of the tent every morning, hat in hand, with complaints against unmerciful landowners, cruel officers, crooked judges, unjust burgomasters and deceitful tenants. But it was only for one hour, then the tent flap was lowered and laced shut, because these petitions were a bloody disease in the land, like a swarm of flies following the camp wherever they marched. At every site the orderly would burn a drawer full of papers in the evening, and the brazier in the princely sleeping tent was lit in the morning with the petitions of the previous day.

Then, between Bodegraaf and Zwammerdam, the man once again turned up with his petition. He was still brown from the veld and caught the eye where he stood with rolled-up sleeves in the early spring sunshine when Hans Michiel passed following a manure cart with a spade on his shoulder. The man shouted at him: 'Postkeeper!'

The name, the rank he'd had at Keert-de-Koe, Saldanha Bay and

Robben Island, made Hans Michiel look round. It was Willem Willemsz, known as the Lyreman. He'd been a free burgher at the Liesbeeck. He was besotted with hunting, one of those who were tracking quarry more often than following a plough. His cattle were herded by a hired Hottentot.

'Come here!' shouted Willemsz. He did not want to lose his place in the queue. Hans motioned to his driver to ride on, and hurried closer.

'Are you joining, Lyreman? Are you coming to help?'

'I can't stay. The hired hand is fucking my wife.'

'What are you doing here then?'

'I've come to see our prince. The Council of Justice banished me. And you?'

'I'm in the army. Why were you banished?'

'Don't you know?' He leaned closer, whispered: 'Shot a bloody Hottentot.'

'Hey! Why?'

'Dirty bastard. It's the first time a white man's been brought to court for that kind of thing. Our government wants to pander to the blacks, now I'm being punished outrageously. But the prince promised me a pardon.'

'And you want to go back?'

'I must. I told you I've got problems at home.'

'I'm waiting for Goske to leave.' A sergeant was standing at his manure cart, talking to the driver. Sergeants enjoyed shouting a man's name in front of the whole camp for the officers to hear. Hans Michiel wanted to ask whether Goske was still in charge, who the postkeepers were at Keert-de-Koe, Robben Island and Saldanha Bay, but there was no time. He could land in trouble.

'Do you know what happened to Master Pieter's children, and to Eva?'

'I've heard that she went back to the Hottentots, taking them with her. Or otherwise she died. Or she threw them away. She was selling herself all over the town, from what I last heard.'

'Goodbye, Lyreman. I must go.' Then he ran. And when he was

walking behind the manure cart again on his way to the horse lines, Willemsz's words came back to him: '*Shot a bloody Hottentot.*' What had happened there? Which Koina, from which kraal? If the Cape court had banished Willemsz, why was he waiting here outside the prince's tent?

When the prince learned about the sea battle opposite Kijkduin, where for four days on end de Ruyter's fleet battered the English, he began his advance. Having reconnoitred the road, they started moving south one moonlit night, in the direction of Limburg and the German frontier. In the beginning there were delays, broken vehicles, complaints by the officers about the carelessness of petty officers, and failures of body and mind among the foot soldiers. The canes of the corporals and the cat o' nine tails of the provost repaired what they could, until everything was running smoothly and the men, animals and implements became one body. Hans Michiel marched with ease. From time to time he saw the prince, with a coarse canvas cloak over his shoulders against the rain, next to his driver on a horse cart, but always out in front, behind the small screen of scouts.

The French knew about their departure almost immediately, and sent reinforcements ahead to support the garrisons of towns on their way. The prince avoided small skirmishes. You don't go to the doctor for every cold, he said. He wanted the ordinary folk to see this army in motion, to inspire them with new faith. If the orange banner was shown to them, they would find new faith. These parts were used to the French and were no longer frightened, but filled with resentment against them. Along the way new recruits also joined, not young fellows – those had already been lost with the invasion – but boys and old men, tradesmen and farmhands, often in search of a warm meal, and sometimes with their own horse and side arm. They entered the region of Nijmegen, and moved south through warm fields of heath covered in flowers, where in peacetime one could see incredibly beautiful girls with dark eyes working in the vineyards and the fields beside the road, the prince told them.

Deep in Limburg the prince ordered them to make camp, with proper ramparts and outer defences, and on a sunny day he had two batteries of his cannon drawn up in a row, firing a hundred shots at the French garrison with a heavy stinking brown cloud and hellish noise. It was to taunt the French king and the bishop of Münster. The battle he tried to provoke nearly cost them all their lives. The enemy completely surrounded them and bombarded the camp, but the gunners of Orange responded while breaking up their camp and preparing their attack. When at dusk that afternoon the enemy stopped firing, the army, with the cavalry and the prince at the head, broke out and threw all their weight against one sector of the circle, and there made a breach among the enemy cannon with sabre and pike, through which the infantry and the baggage train poured, fighting as they went. Once through, they all turned round and chased the French from their positions with sword and bayonet; after that they forced their way into the French camp and baggage train, looting and burning and destroying, hooking up five of their cannon and hauling them away. After sundown they pitched camp on high ground, set out artillery and posted the outer circle of pickets halfway down the hill.

The next morning they started moving west in the direction of the French border. Now they could no longer avoid skirmishes. But this was what they had come here for, to taunt and beat the enemy in his backyard, so that he was forced to withdraw some of his troops from the Netherlands to reinforce his home front. Through Leeuven and Waterloo the French were on their heels with a growing force, and at Seneffe on the Pièton River, three day journeys across the French border, they were finally stopped. They were surrounded, attacked and driven back with heavy losses. Only with much effort could the prince reach high ground. When they could no longer get out, they prepared themselves to die and promised the prince that they would stand and fight.

The whole day of 11 August they kept the French out of their camp with sword and bayonet, while the enemy with his reinforcements surrounded them on the hill where they stood, but he had to keep his own cannon quiet, to avoid shooting his own people. The next morning the enemy withdrew his infantry, but from early his batteries hammered home a bombardment. The prince ordered them to dig: each man a hole for himself, to save him in while that bombardment continued. In spite of that they suffered losses, particularly among the animals and the baggage train, but also among the troops. The battering went on until noon, and then stopped. They expected a bayonet attack to follow, but the interruption was merely for the cannon to cool down, then the balls and bombs started again, and once more they had to dive into their muddy holes. Hans Michiel had long ago learned to keep on laughing and make silly jokes, and he also appreciated this reaction among his companions. If you didn't do it, you suffered damage to yourself. And after they had been under this bombardment for twelve hours, among torn bodies, thickly smeared with flying mud and horse manure so that it looked as if dirt was part of their skins, wet, cold and without food, he looked at his friends' faces and saw all roundness gone from them; all the faces were angular, with eyes sunken as in old skulls. They had all become old men, without any feeling, and might remain like that for the rest of their lives. And they laughed and didn't care much.

In the dark of the night, the prince said to the staring faces that there was nothing to eat, and there wouldn't be breakfast either. Early the next morning they should expect the last bayonet attack. He intended to break out from there at midnight, with everything they could carry with them; he couldn't say when they would rest again, but if they were scattered, they should reassemble at Halle, west of Waterloo, one daybreak later. This was their last chance. They knew where the cannons and the tents of the enemy stood. To this hour God had brought them. What had to happen now, was in their own hands. They should fight in faith.

They fed their campfires with whatever they couldn't carry, and while it burned they trekked down the northern slope of the hill, over stones and ditches, with the cannon and the wagons, and the horses, and a vanguard and a rearguard of infantry armed with pike and sword, straight towards the enemy's watch fires. Everything at speed in one great charge. *That way and through*, the prince had said. Remember: *that way and through*. Build up momentum until we are there, and keep it up until we reach the other side. Until their old age they kept on marvelling about that night charge. How had they managed to break through the enemy with some baggage and so many wounded? It had been their speed, their weight, their sustained momentum, they thought. *That way and through.* There's a weakness in the French, the prince had told them. They can attack, but do not like to defend. Remember that, turn them round and drive them out ahead of you. Keep on running with them.

After that they returned home. The French pursuit was half-hearted, clearly without any plan, as if something was lacking in the leadership. Could they have lost so many officers? Back behind the banner, behind the drums, behind the small screen of scouts, behind the prince, behind the cavalry, behind the artillery, behind the provision wagons, through Brussels, Mechelen and Antwerp, from town to town to capture and commandeer horses and transport as far as they went, until they were back home in the fatherland. Afterwards there was cheering along the road, new recruits, a schoolteacher with open-mouthed children presenting a recitation or a written address, or accepting a purse with a few silver coins for an orphanage from the prince, more aggrieved people with petitions, and the drawers filled with memorials emptied over a fire after sundown. Then Kuilenburg. Then Gouda, then Delft. There the prince attended church, to honour the father of the father-land, his ancestor who lay buried in the crypt. To bleach his soul, to pray that his fornication might be forgiven, his troops said. What? wondered Hans Michiel. This boy?

They were drawn up on parade on the market square, between the old-fashioned church, with its open tower in which twenty-eight bells struck music, and the still older city hall, built wholly from wood, within and without. Hans Michiel was on the right flank in the front row of his detachment. A beautiful town was Delft, even now in wartime. Behind the trees and houses their tents were set up in lines and squares. In the middle of their tent village was the Kat, the prince's multicoloured tent with its blue banners and orange flags. Masts and sails of canal barges moved past behind the tents, behind the houses. He could recognise the Company's large warehouse beside the canal, by the ship instead of a weathercock on the roof. A few fellows might desert here to look for work there; the corporals were warned to be on the lookout for that. Would the Company still be using the trick with the flintlock musket on the floor to catch their soldiers? They might just as well ask: 'Mr Callenbach, do you have any previous military experience?' But no, such openness was probably beneath them.

The lords of the Company's Delft chamber in their fur and plush accompanied the burgomaster into the church, at the head of the procession, behind the prince. To pray for commerce? Later he heard that the Company had granted the prince a loan of two million guilders on that day. Hans Michiel was completely relaxed as he stood on parade. In his mind, also smiling, content, at peace, were two German farm girls with golden plaits. Nothing bothered him. He could remain a soldier for ever. If he was promoted, good. Or he could go to the East, or he could return to the dairy farm. There he would be welcome.

For four months he marched with the prince, always on high ground between towns and cities. The prince occupied the best battlefields where he had the advantage, and the French did not show up. In the cities people massed along the streets to see them. Children trotted beside the procession. Down in Breda somebody threw a stone at the prince's carriage. The bodyguard caught a woman, and the prince handed her over to the burgomaster to be punished.

'Or must I give you to my bodyguard?'

'To the bodyguard,' she said.

'What, you must be the burgomaster's wife,' the prince mocked, and ordered her to sit in the stocks until sundown.

The prince was content when after the campaign of four months his army returned to The Hague, to prepare for the coming winter. The prince himself was more than a hero by now; he had become their beacon of hope for the future. They had fulfilled the purpose with which they had set out, he said to his army at the last parade. Now he expected, the prince said, that the English would ask for peace and afterwards come to an agreement with the Netherlands against the French. Most of the fear in the Dutch people had dissipated, and they were once again prepared for a prolonged struggle.

Once again Hans Michiel left The Hague with the wagons to gather hay for the winter. The garrison butcher went along, to buy pigs or sheep on the farms, to slaughter and salt them down. Trees were felled, branches sawed and thousands of blocks split, transported to the camp, and stacked to dry out. Every day he and other soldiers set out on trips with horse carts to find provisions. When their captain came to the horse lines for volunteers to fetch clothing material in Delft, he turned to Hans Michiel.

'Will you go, Callenbach?'

Hans was ready immediately. It was obvious, he thought, that the captain knew how to choose his men, and also exactly how to sift new petty officers from the troops. One asked for volunteers, then gave somebody an opportunity to recommend himself. That was welcome; he could now expect to be made a corporal.

Not Delft, but Leiden was the town for textiles. One might say that Delft was Leiden's port. If Leiden had had its own port, Leiden and not Delft would have been the Company's sixth chamber, but nature had willed it differently. There was no other place like Leiden for textiles; their weavers' guild was just as powerful as the town council. All linen was transported from Leiden to Delft along the Vliet, and there Hans Michiel had to load textiles for new uniforms, since the prince had advertised for two hundred recruits.

There were heavy rains in Delft, and the Company's warehouse master did not want to load baled textile. 'The guild totally prohibits it. The weather spoils the linen. And there goes Leiden's reputation.' He snapped his fingers. 'Just like that.' Hans and his companions had to wait under canvas on the wagon until the sky cleared. Behind the warehouse walls he could hear wheelbarrows rumbling on the wooden floors, but they had to wait, smoking their pipes.

In a fine drizzle he went to walk along the quay. Down there in the canal milk barges came past, and steaming peat boats, towards the town centre. The Company's boats against the quay were recognisable from its initials on the flags. There were two boats, of equal size. One had arrived from Leiden that morning, the other was loading Leiden wares to transport down the Vliet to the sea. Boxes were carried from a horse carriage by two sailors who balanced themselves barefoot on the gangplank. Last in the line alongside the quay was the barge that had arrived from Delft in the morning.

A student, judging from his black gown with the hood hanging between his prominent shoulder blades, poked his head through the hatch and when he saw that the rain had stopped, he climbed out on the deck. The fellow must have been eighteen or twenty, a scrawny chap with spindly legs in navy blue stockings, thick glasses speckled with raindrops and an eagle nose. He came up the ladder next to Hans Michiel and walked ahead of him through the warehouse door where he slapped his hand on the counter. There were black ink stains deep in the skin between his fingers.

'Service.'

The warehouse clerk stood directly in front of him and stared him in the eyes, then looking at Hans Michiel over his shoulder.

'The prince's order first.'

'Why do you ignore me, sir?' asked the student.

'Because your country is being occupied by an enemy and you are not in uniform. Because you fellows want to dress like monks, and that reminds me of eighty years of war against the Catholics and everything they stand for. And you students are not much different. And if you don't like it, then go and do what you students usually do when no one is looking.'

'That is a very unfriendly way of putting it, sir,' Hans protested. 'You insult the student because of the clothes he wears. He is not a lackey. Let him wear what he wants.'

'That does not concern you, soldier.'

'If I walk out of here, my captain will want to know why I was not served. Come, Mister Student, tell the man what you need.'

'I have come to collect parcels for the university.'

'Who sent you?'

'Professor van Rooij. Here is his letter.'

The warehouse clerk left the room.

'The Company's staff are getting impudent all over the world,' Hans told the student. 'I know them. They learn to be haughty with simple natives overseas, and then they want to come and lord it here.'

Some time afterwards a wheelbarrow with barrels and a box was pushed in.

'There's the university's stuff, and here's your consignment letter. Mark it off and sign for it. Don't take it and come back later to complain,' said the clerk. Then he turned to Hans. 'And now for the prince's order.'

While he waited for the material to be brought, Hans examined the crates on the wheelbarrow. There were four barrels containing live plants. The student peered through his thick glasses, then at the plants, then at the list in his hand.

'All of it Cape reeds, Mister Student. Thatching reed, Sonqua reed, broom reed, elephant reed,' Hans Michiel offered.

'Which one is elephant reed?'

'This thick one with the brown tuft, like an elephant's tail.'

'I see.' But the way in which he peered through screwed eyes made Hans feel dubious. 'You may open the box if you wish,' he offered.

'Yes, we'd better. Once a box arrived here filled with sand. Our plants had been stolen. Good prices are paid by collectors.'

Inside the box was dried grass, and in between were paper bags, tightly packed. In each were a few pressed flowers and some bulbs, and on each packet a name had been written. Hans opened one and read it out to the student: '*Blaauwe lelij, 1X bris, buiten post Het Rust Saldagna Bhaij.*'

'There's your blue lily. Where are these plants going, Mister Student?'

'The herbarium at the university. The Company sends it to our professor. From the Orient, and from Africa. There is much interest.'

'These plants grow in hot sun.'

'We have a glass house. Actually it's just thousands of glass windows, to let in sunlight, with an oven and hot-water pipes to keep it warm. The plants stand in barrels and boxes on wheels, so that we can push them in and out as the weather changes.'

The clerk behind the counter leaned into the conversation. 'Your professor hasn't heard that a consignment is rounded off with a bottle of wine.'

'No.'

'Then he doesn't know much, for all his so-called learning. It's a matter of good manners. I told your little friend that the last time round.'

'Why should it be necessary?'

'The Company transported it free on board and handled it halfway round the world.'

When they were both old men, Hans Michiel and the secretary talked about that day. 'And every time the professor sent a bottle, a green one, and the same evening the students emptied it. We took turns to fetch the plants, to get hold of the bottle.'

Hans Michiel, still a serious man and made humble by much adversity, did not see it as a joke.

'You robbed the man who taught you?'

'Yes. Students can be rather irresponsible.'

When the rolls of dyed linen and woollen material were pushed in, Hans Michiel went to call his companions from the cart, and examined the rolls as well as he could. Then he said goodbye to the student, and put their load on the cart and covered it with double canvases and tied it up, and rode away in the drizzle, to The Hague. Students. Prodigal sons travelling in the far country, and still without remorse.

On the way back under tarpaulins in the rain Hans Michiel's thoughts roamed over his life. His own youth was past now. What would he do with his remaining years? Perhaps hope, but probably boredom and the cold grey drizzle, made him believe that it would be better at the Cape. He could return as soon as Goske had left. There the sun shone every day, the days there were more interesting, only promotion remained most uncertain. There were three lost children, perhaps dead by now. If Eva was passing her life on the streets, she might not be alive any longer either. Her passport had been written: some sailor with the English disease would mean the end of Master Pieter's Eva. Where had Petronella been, the night he went to look for them? What became of an orphan with such a mother?

On the fourth day Hans Michiel arrived in the camp in The Hague with his wagonload of textiles. He had been relying on it that one day his captain would call him and tell him that there was place for a corporal in his squadron. And that was what happened upon his arrival. He could start immediately and the new salary would come into effect with it. Hans thanked him for it; he'd been looking forward to it for a long time. He knew he was a good soldier. That was something he'd been told so many times.

When the fifth year of his service contract was over in 1678, he was a sergeant. The English had been knocked out of the war, de Ruyter had seen to that, but French Louis offered them millions, bribing them not to enter into an alliance with the Dutch against France. So the Netherlands still stood alone against the French, but the people's morale was high. The French began to think that they might have made a mistake by starting this war, and clung to the towns they had occupied in the early days. For Dutch soldiers promotion came swiftly now; the older ranks gave way to the youth. Hans could speak and write Dutch well, and his German was an advantage, as almost half of his company were Germans. His captain said that if he hadn't been a foreigner, he would have been in the prince's bodyguard long ago. It's a pity, old man, but that is what the national government demands.

In the winter of that year Hans Michiel went to Amsterdam. North of Leiden the Haarlemmer lake was frozen solid. He made slow progress on foot in the narrow path. On the ice were skaters dragging loaded sledges, but he had only a bundle with a few pieces of clothing and the prince's letter in a cardboard tube in his satchel, and he was in no hurry. Old Amsterdam would always be there. And there was time to think how he would tell Master van Dam that he wished to join up again and sail to the East. Ten years earlier he'd tried to go there, but then he was stopped. He still longed to see the East. That was why he was here, he would say.

He discovered, when he stood in front of the VOC's advocate again, that he didn't need many words. The Company's book, the whole book of its origins, its framework, its commerce, its policy, its people, was in van Dam's memory.

'I remember you,' he said. 'You must have heard that Governor Goske has been replaced. I appointed his successor. And what do you want to do in the East?'

'Back in the army, Your Honour. That is what I can do best.'

'The four Fs, Hans? Fight, fornicate and follow a flag?'

'More or less, Your Honour.'

But when the advocate had to write that Hans should sail to the East, he put his pen down and said: 'Now that Goske has gone, perhaps you might wish to consider the Cape again. The Cape has also become a popular destination. They serve for a year or three, then they become free burghers. Free land is the attraction, if you ask me. There were dirt-poor fellows from the Veluwe, without a shirt to their name, who became landlords over there with properties as a big as a duke's portion here with us. It makes no sense, I say. But the Lords allow it.'

'It sounds good enough to me, Your Honour. But first the East. I am still *baar*.'

His letter was prepared while he waited, and he could report at the mustering point on the ground floor. He'd been a soldier for years, he told them there, and he understood the work of a watermaker, yet once again they tried to trick him with the picking up of a musket. So he was accepted for the second time for the Company's army.

On a bright day in March he arrived at the Cape, on the ship *Brederode*. The flag on the Lion's Head had appeared above the horizon the previous day. Outside Table Bay he remained on deck. The sky was slate blue. Before him was Robben Island, low, bare and dull-green under a haze of sea spray, through which white specks of gulls were turning. There was a flag on the Fire Hill to announce them. The opposite shore was a pale yellow ribbon around the whole bay, from Blueberg to the dunes.

There were no familiar faces on the quay. The Fort still stood, but somewhat dilapidated as if the Company did not have money for maintenance. Hans Michiel was directed to the new Castle. With his sea chest on his shoulder he crossed the beach to the Castle. The ark was by now gone, the Castle was standing on its own, detached from its mother. There was a simple gate on the beach, a few paces behind the lines of seaweed and bamboo left by the previous high tide, with a low ravelin, no more than a palisade, to cover the entrance. He stopped and looked around. It would seem simple to attack that little ravelin with infantry from the flank, but cover from above, from the walls, could ward it off. A bayonet charge, then. If the ships anchored closer to the beach and directed all their fire at the walls so that a musketeer couldn't show his head, four large boats full of soldiers could attack and raze the ravelin from two sides, exposing the entrance. If there were real in the garrison here, they would already have pointed it out to the commanding officer. And received a flogging for their trouble? Watch out, he warned himself. Not again. Look the other way, keep your mouth shut.

The new governor welcomed him, mentioning his name the way one soldier would to another – name is Bax van Herenthals – and put out a gloved hand to greet him. It looked as if he was hiding a skin rash, for his face was red, with swollen spots. He read the Directors' letter about Hans Michiel, in which they made clear that he should be appointed in his previous post and rank, should he decide to remain at the Cape. Fine, then in the meantime Hans should move into the sergeants' quarters until arrangements had been made to determine a function for him. There was a new outpost at Hottentots-Holland, and Saldanha Bay had also been resettled. This was better news than Hans Michiel had hoped for. There, on the frontiers of the colony he might hear where the children of Pieter and Eva van Meerhof were wandering among the Hottentots. When there was another ship ready to sail, he would go to the East.

Where would he begin with his enquiries? With the governor? The fiscal? He put his sea chest in the barracks and let his choice fall in between, on the *secundus*. He found the gentleman under a lean-to, where two woodcutters with a branding iron were burning the mono-gram of the VOC into the heads of heavy tree trunks. The wood was tumbled with thundering noise from a pile, then branded, booked and piled up in sorting lots: narrow-leaf yellow-wood, assegai wood, iron-wood, stinkwood. The Company's mark, smoking in the greenwood, was that one, already known worldwide, which stood in coarse white ridges between the wrinkled shoulder blades of old convicts, two fingers wide and one-half high, or painted delicately in blue on porce-lain, or in livid purple among the hairs on the rumps of horses and cattle, or finely engraved in brilliant silver buckles, richly embossed in gold on leather, or incised, heavy, black and deep, just above the touch-hole of a cannon. The sign of the laudable Company, the stamp of his famous employer.

The *secundus* took Hans Michiel aside and, to his surprise, shook his hand and enquired, his eyes on the woodcutters, how he could help? Hesitatingly, Hans began to tell about the woman Eva and her wretched poverty, her Christian children dragged about in dark Africa by nomadic herders, without benefit of church or school. Her own mother belonged to Oedasoa's people, the Cochoqua. They used to graze clockwise from Saldanha Bay through the Groenkloof to the Koeberg, and then up along the beach again to Saldanha. He had learned something about the life of the Koina long ago, he said, when he'd been postkeeper on the colony's frontiers. They were good-hearted people, the Koina, but their life was meagre and unblessed.

'The mother died here. She was a street woman and addicted to alcohol, and was banished to the island for her immorality. If the children were to live with her, what advantage could there have been in it?'

'Then she is better off now, Your Honour. She no longer gets anything to drink.'

The *secundus* was wondering what the soldier wanted, as the governor already had Robben Island in mind for him.

'She had other children too. From the men there on the island. She was the only woman they saw.'

'It is a bitter island for a man, your honour. Just like on the ships. But I never saw her looking at a soldier first. It all came from them.'

'Do you know that the children are now outside this colony? I myself have been here for only a few months, and I don't know all the details, but the government sent them away. I think the orphan master should be able to tell you about it. There was no prospect for them here at all.'

The orphan master's clerk was alone in his office. He had come to enquire about the widow van Meerhof's children, Hans Michiel explained.

'Yes, what about them?'

'I hear that they've been sent out of the colony.'

'When?'

'I don't know.'

'And where to?'

'No, I don't know. I arrived only yesterday.'

'Are you related to them?'

'No. A friend of their father.'

The clerk gestured towards a rack filled with piles of books. 'The committee for widows and orphans meets once in fourteen days. Whatever they determine is written up there. If you can tell me in what year it happened, I can try to look it up. And that means that from a given year I must read every single document from beginning to end. Sometimes you want only one paragraph in a resolution of fifty folios.'

'Is there no one working here who could remember their case? It could not have been more than six years ago.'

'It's possible. Where do you find the person? I'll start asking. Do you know whether it was a judicial matter, or were the people referred by the church?'

'How do you mean, referred by the church?'

'If they break a law, the government can banish them from the colony. If they're paupers, the church asks the government to do something.'

'And then?'

'The consequences are more or less the same. They are sent to friends or family.'

'But overseas? Their mother came from here. She was a native.'

'Well, I shall make enquiries. Come round from time to time to find out if there is news. We don't often send children away; it must be a really hopeless situation before the Council goes so far.'

Croese was a lieutenant now, the commanding officer of the garrison, and even a member of the Council of Policy. Hans Michiel saw him on parade once or twice, but avoided conversation. He was not assigned to a banner again. Two days after his arrival he was appointed postkeeper on Robben Island, with the provisional rank of corporal. If his service was satisfactory, he would be promoted to sergeant within a month. For the time being, Hans was satisfied. He was once again in charge of an outpost, the rest would follow. He was satisfied when the sailing sloop dropped him off in the small sandy cove, and when he unpacked his belongings from his sea chest in the new enlarged posthouse. Only years later did he realise how he had betrayed himself once again, given himself over in their hands once again, had once again been caught in the very same trap.

The number of convicts at the post, he learned at the transfer ceremony, had risen to almost a hundred. His detachment consisted of twenty-one soldiers under two corporals. New faces among the convicts interested him. Most of them were there for life. Each one's crime was entered in the books, but he could not link a man to a crime by looking at a face. Not one of them looked like a villain, but like men hewn from wood or stone, just as when as a young man he'd seen the prisoners for the first time. Murderers, runaways, reprieved homosexuals, arsonists, dark princes from spice islands fallen into disgrace, counterfeiters, smugglers, procurers, thieves. All of them were neglected, famished, suspicious, rude in speech and conduct.

Their work still consisted of breaking stones, gathering shells, looking out for ships, sending signals. His still meant driving them to work. What they ate out of burning hunger, revolted him. A dead sheep which he had thrown away, was dug up and cooked. One day there was a corpse sewn up in canvas on the rocks, and that night a human skull in their cooking pot. His first letter to Governor van Herenthals was to ask for more rice and bread. A surgeon arrived to examine their health, but the rations were not improved. Hans questioned the surgeon about Eva: she had been the postkeeper's wife here on the island, her husband had also been a surgeon, but he'd died on Madagascar and left her a widow.

'Yes, the bloody whore,' said the young man. 'She spread the English disease through the whole garrison. There was not enough mercury to treat them all. Good riddance that she died.'

'And her children?'

'No, were there children?'

He was never really in command on his island. Hans accepted that others would decide who or what was to be fetched, who or what dispatched. With every shell boat somebody was brought or somebody summoned to the Castle, but never he.

At sunset he read the evening prayer to the convicts from the little book of the parish pastor. He knew the words by heart. His book was open in his hands, but his eyes were on the four rows of faces before him. Contorted young men, gnarled old men with hair cut short and beards trimmed roughly and unevenly, with rotten sun-bleached clothes, unwashed, surrounded by the stench of human excrement, despising themselves with expressions of disappointment, or contempt, or mockery on their faces; some of them anchored to an iron ball, a wheelbarrow, a bed. They were his brothers, all of them unknown and lost, helplessly stranded between an illusion and oblivion, captives of the monster who inhabited the Cape rock for the moment.

Evening prayers were an opportunity for talking to the people, because during the day his soldiers guarded them at their distant working places and he didn't see them. Hans Michiel recited the prayer from his little book with great emphasis; he committed their souls to the protection of the Almighty for the night, in German. That he did while he stood before his soldiers and the convicts, all of them hungry, cold, grey with lime dust. They were his congregation: robber, smuggler, slanderer, thief, adulterer, arsonist, murderer, thief, counterfeiter, rapist, deserter, thief, perjurer, blackmailer, blasphemer, robber, thief.

The thief and the rapist had blue pictures on their faces. A passport to hell, this tattooing, and the ring in the ear. If a man felt the need to adorn himself, he usually had a nasty problem. A young man – his back covered in red stripes from a recent flogging when he first saw him, and so bad that he couldn't yet wear a shirt – said the whole prayer with him every time. His mouth formed the words, his eyes were shut, his hands folded together like a pastor's. This was how Hans Michiel remembered him: saying the evening prayer together for years. His crime was persistent resistance to his lawful authority. His name he couldn't remember.

5

RED DAWN

Red in the morning, a sailor's warning.

THE PROVERB HAS it, 'Cometh the hour cometh the man', and also, 'In the land of the blind the one-eyed is king.' This, people will say, was how it was when Advocate Deneyn became fiscal and hung his black gown in the Fort, but proverbs generalise and acknowledge neither the most senseless coincidence nor the cold handshake of fate. Coincidence is the unpredictable fall of a playing card or dice. Two sixes and a three, two threes and a six. No proverb can explain that.

Come and watch a group of card players in the barracks of the Fort of Good Hope, in the year of grace 1672. Three soldiers and a sailor are playing cards on a sea chest. From a beam above them hangs a smelly lamp, burning seal oil. They have pulled up three more chests for seats, and they laugh, slap down cards, pick up others. Notice how they laugh. Right now they're laughing, relaxed and content. The soldiers returned from the town just before tattoo, after leaning against a tavern's counter for an hour, drinking no more than two or three, or perhaps four beers. In the barracks one took a deck of cards from his chest, as it was too early to go to bed. They needed another hand. 'A fourth, anyone?' they called through the barracks. No one responded to that fatal invitation.

So they went to a sailor who had been lying with folded hands on his bed since sunset waiting for the bell to call him to night duty on the lighter. Now every action became a momentous deed. The waking of the sleeping man, the dragging of the chests, the opening of the deck, the cutting and shuffling, shuffling and cutting, all of it had a fatal edge. They cast coins on the chest to liven up the game, even though gambling was forbidden. Everything was done laughing, without a second thought, but all of it was fatal. They might be laughing now, but in half an hour they would be cheating, lying, cursing, killing, fleeing from the law, and you would be hard put to find a proverb to apply to any of them. You would see the chest and the cards smeared with fresh blood; there would be a body among the boots and cards and coins on the floor, and the smoking oil lamp would be swaying in circles like a priest swinging his censer over an altar.

We have a hard time digesting our proverbs. With a good deal of salt, *cum copia salis*, as the proverb has it. A stone's throw outside the barracks wall, a tarred rope stirs in the evening breeze on a gallows which will demand its share of the game in thirty days' time. What do proverbs mean? *He curses like a sailor? He's been brought up for the gallows? As drunk as a sailor?* The sailor was the quiet man and regular church-goer, the one who didn't drink a drop, never uttered a curse, yet there he lies bleeding on the prison floor, felled with a blow to the back of his head. It was, you understand, the fiscal's duty. The enemy has only two cannons, says the proverb; one is called *Fate*, the other *Accident*.

The Castle was a real man-eater, and not only because so many youths following the shining star of the Orient were ambushed here and compelled first to labour and build this curious monster. Accidents in the stone quarry and on the scaffolds were of little importance. There were wars about resources, Koina risking everything and losing all, prisoners on islands who should never have been prisoners, slaves from black Africa sold for rubbish by their kings, crimes committed on sea and land, people losing their jobs, children losing parents, people losing their lives. And this is where Advocate Deneyn appears on the stage, with his rattan under his arm.

Why the sea washed Advocate Deneyn ashore in this place is no secret. It was because of the fatal accident that befell the man who had been fiscal before him. That was Cornelis de Cretser from Culemborg, the outstanding official, none better. Like most he had begun as a soldier, and in the time of exploration he'd been a regular traveller by land and a regular comrade. The day when Piet Roman had been trampled by the elephant, he drew up Roman's testament in the veld. As witnesses to a single nod in the fragrant scrubland behind Meerhof's Castle, all twelve comrades witnessed it with their names right there in the veld, and de Cretser carried the document to the Fort, where it remained filed away, as Roman had had no relatives. Likewise, when the French first tried to settle at Saldanha Bay, it was de Cretser who was chosen, because he spoke good French, to hurry there and pretend he was in the process of building a posthouse on that desolate spot. If you inspect the notes passed between the two parties at the time, you will see that the French address all their threats and complaints to Monsieur de Cretser, completely ignoring Commander Hackius as if he didn't exist. That was the kind of man de Cretser was.

That kind of man was de Cretser, but there was something wrong with his luck, and that is all that matters. The commanders under whom he'd served, since van Riebeeck, had nothing but good to say about de Cretser. He was popular, energetic, successful, exceptionally blessed. He was promoted regularly: regimental writer, clerk, warehouseman, junior merchant, fiscal, merchant, *Secundus*, even acting head during Hackius's protracted illnesses. Such prosperous promotion does not happen often, not even to the most industrious and dedicated of us, but so it was destined in poor de Cretser's short life. Nobody begrudged him that, nobody was jealous; all were delighted with his progress and sincerely hoped that he would soon succeed old Hackius. There were those who would willingly lie on de Cretser's behalf, who were prepared to perjure themselves because of their fondness for him, for some of those living along the Liesbeeck hid him in their homes after his accident, fed him, helped him along, helped him to escape from the Cape. That shows how sincere their devotion was to good *Secundus* de Cretser.

To explain Deneyn's presence on the Cape stage, one may then begin with Commander Hackius, and say that if it hadn't been for the fact that old Hackius was ill so much of the time it wouldn't have been necessary for de Cretser to receive and entertain ship's officers on his behalf. But, the prime cause was the sea, that player on the Cape stage which is so readily overlooked by most. Look again. It was in 1671, and the return fleet was in the roadstead. *Secundus* de Cretser hosted passengers and captains, among them Adriaan Drom of *Wimmenum*. Drom and his passenger Isak Fonteyn brought a long-standing quarrel about the favours of a little Oriental slave girl to the fatal dining table. De Cretser's convivial reception had a pleasant calming effect on the two middle-aged roosters, and their host had time to plan his brief speech before sending them home. But before the closing prayer, and just after brandy and tobacco had been served (there was no hint of unsteadiness yet), the two roosters suddenly sprang to their feet, and a rapier and a long dagger flashed in the candlelight. What could the host do? He had to do what had been destined, what else? He parted them, and escorted Captain Drom, who was the drunker of the two, to the door. Outside the door Drom attacked him with a knife. So de Cretser drew somebody's sword which was hanging with a cloak behind the door, and stuck it in below Drom's breastbone until it protruded two hand-widths behind his shoulder blades. That was how it happened. For weeks afterwards he hid in the veld, and with the farmers. Those who helped him knew what the law demanded, but they helped him nevertheless. They couldn't believe that their *Secundus* de Cretser would have to swing from a gallows. The law was one thing, justice something else, and in between them a human touch was lacking.

This business with de Cretser was only the prelude, and not even all of it, to Advocate Deneyn's arrival on the scene. It had started earlier. Deneyn had already been posted to the Cape at the time de Cretser was promoted to *Secundus*. When Deneyn arrived, de Cretser had escaped from the gallows, and Secretary Crudop, acting as chairman of the Council after Hackius's death, was acting in the post of fiscal. Crudop had to draw up the summons, the warrants and the proclamation with the reward for the life of his fugitive friend Cornelis de Cretser. But de Cretser had fled the country. It is now known that he made it back to the fatherland, on *Stermeer*. Fiscal Deneyn's first case was against Willem Willemsz van Deventer, a free burgher who had killed a Hottentot and he, too, had fled the country. But Deneyn's appearance on the Cape stage that day, his arrival in the Fort of Good

Hope, his real debut, was something exceptional. It is rare for a player to make such an entrance.

Deneyn was irritable about something. It is possible that he expected some kind of welcome on the quayside, but honestly, nobody had been expecting his arrival. The Council did not know that Lords Seventeen would be dispatching a new fiscal. The Cape had never before had a fully qualified advocate as a fiscal, and the Council wasn't sure that such a learned official could be destined for the Cape; after all, this wasn't Amsterdam or Sodom yet. A sailor from the lighter carried his chest from the jetty and put it down before the main gate. That had been his instruction: goods and people should not be left standing on the landing stage.

Deneyn was a slightly built youth of twenty-two, with the golden-blond looks one associates with Scandinavians. His sea legs had trouble with the loose sea-sand, and he approached leisurely with his walking stick under the arm, stopping to study the castle which was being built. The vast ark stranded among the dunes, surrounded by low stone walls destined to become a castle, had him guessing at words. How would he describe this arrival, his first impressions, in his journal, or in the travel book he was working on? 'Behind everything, like the backcloth on a stage, stands Table Mountain . . .' Theatrical? Undoubtedly. Then he came to the Fort where his chest was waiting, and there were two soldiers on guard in the shade just inside the gateway.

'Where will I find the commander?'

'The commander is dead.'

'Who is in charge?'

'The Council, collectively.'

'Who is the executive officer?'

'We don't have one.'

'Are you trying to mock me? Bring my chest, fellow, then I'll show you who's giving the orders.'

'Sorry. Can't leave my post.'

The other soldier spoke: 'Come on board, My Lord. A guard of honour and a band are ready to welcome you.'

Deneyn smacked the soldier's legs with his stick, and the soldier pushed him with the flat of his hand on the chest causing him to land on his backside in the sand. A corporal came from the guardroom, asked what was going on, and helped Deneyn to his feet.

'Come along, go inside. That man will bring your chest.' He beckoned at a Hottentot who was waiting for small tasks, but Deneyn, red in the face, pointed at the soldier. 'I want his name. And you,' he pointed at the other soldier, 'you will be prime witness.'

'Lick my arse first,' the soldier replied, but the corporal intervened. 'Please calm down, Your Worship. He was attacked while on duty. Come, follow the man with the chest. You can convey the matter to the Council.'

This was how Deneyn made his appearance, and, honestly, the circumstances in which his name was first recorded in the Cape documents. But that was not yet the whole of his entry, it was barely the beginning. That evening, at dinner with the other councillors and their wives, he mentioned that he would take his place at the next Council meeting. The councillors looked at each other and quietly went on eating, as they had no knowledge of the man, except what he'd told them himself. Chairman Crudop responded quietly, 'It may well happen.'

Crudop had no wish to vacate his rewarding post to a new fiscal. The next day he felt more courageous, and intimated that they would certainly obey the command of the Directors, but that there were a case of assault and other accusations made against the fiscal which had to be cleared up first. In the meantime, they would do everything they could to ensure that his stay would be comfortable.

The return fleet was late that year, and only reached Table Bay in April. And its arrival was a relief to the Council, which had had no idea of what to do with Deneyn. Now they could pass this problem on to the admiral of the fleet. The admiral was Aernout van Overbeke. He and Pieter Deneyn were as like as two coconuts, with a few insignificant differences, for example that Aernout was an *oorlammer*, a Dutchman who had been East, and Deneyn still a greenhorn from Holland; and that Aernout was ten years older and had served in the Council of Justice in Batavia. What the two had in common was that both had studied law at the University of Leiden, both had been admitted to the Bar in Holland, and both had written down their experiences with a view to publication, for Europe was reading avidly whatever was written about the newly discovered world.

There was something else both had learned in Leiden, and not in lecture halls, but in the four taverns surrounding the Justice Square in front of the Pieterskerk. That was to drink deep into the night, smoking, talking, and to spot pretty girls at a distance and quickly arrange for a meeting, the way a pirate would plot the boarding of a prize ship the moment it appeared in his telescope. Not all the Cape councillors were amused to learn that Admiral van Overbeke had been known as Drunken Nout as a student, and when they listened to him telling Deneyn of what had happened one night a decade earlier in the tavern De Gapende Regter (The Drowsy Judge) and heard the two learned gentlemen's belly laughter, the Council felt that their problem was turning serious.

The four Cape councillors got together to formulate their case against Deneyn. To begin with, he had assaulted the guard at the gate; secondly, he had about twenty barrels of wine smuggled on board of the ship Gouda before his journey; and thirdly, he had neglected to post the Company's prescribed proclamations on board or to have them read to the crew. But the wronged guard wanted to withdraw his accusation, and as for the twenty hogsheads of wine, half the Gouda's crew declared that they had taken in twenty barrels of wine from a galliot on the high sea on Deneyn's orders, but all the officers testified that they knew nothing about it. The same happened in connection with the printed Articles supposed to be posted on board, but which still lay unused in the ship's desk. The sailors testified that they had neither seen nor heard such a proclamation. The officers stated that Deneyn had personally read it out to the crew every day. The case ended as a pile of affidavits and counter-affidavits, and eventually died of old age. Van Overbeke, as chairman, and the assembled captains of the return fleet, oorlammers to a man, requested the Council to acknowledge Deneyn as fiscal and councillor, and given the majority of votes, this resolution was passed.

On the same agenda was a constitutional case. How strong was the

Company's legal claim to the Cape? It was useful to have jurists at the table, and Admiral van Overbeke had much experience in constitutional affairs. Should the fatherland be drawn into war in the near future, the chairman argued, it might well be against the combined forces of France and England, since they wanted their share in the Oriental trade and had to break Holland's stranglehold on it. Neither kingdom was strong enough to undertake this on its own, consequently it would have to be as allies in a joint operation. After the fatherland itself, the Cape was the second target. Therefore work on the Castle had to be speeded up. All the captains present had to send work teams ashore daily. But how certain, how legitimate, how internationally acceptable was the Company's claim to the Cape and the Cape coast? A few years earlier the French had demonstrated that the Company had no legal claim to the Cape coast; it was even admitted in the Company's own charter. Then the Dutch West India Company sued, demanding a hundred million in damages because the VOC had been operating in its territory. Legally they were right, and it was costing the Directors a court case dragging on for years and much money to keep these matters under control. An invader might yet acknowledge the claims of the natives, but not those of the Dutch. If the Hottentots had the first legal claim, the Company had to settle this matter with them well in time.

'We need to own this land legally,' said Deneyn. 'I can defend a land claim provided I have seen the owner's title deed.'

'Do we posses anything of that kind?' Chairman van Overbeke asked Crudop.

'There are two peace treaties from van Riebeeck's time.'

'Possibly extorted. It won't stand up in court. We must try to buy the land from the natives. We must get the deed of sale in our own name, for this is the dawn of the white man in Africa.'

'The Cape,' suggested Deneyn. 'We do not want Africa. The Portuguese have been in Africa for years. We're interested only in the Cape.'

'Just as far as a twenty-four-pounder can reach from an anchored ship,' a captain suggested.

'Further. That is not far enough.'

'The further you move inland from the coast the weaker your grip becomes.'

'Then the answer is infantry with field guns.'

Deneyn's proposal was accepted. The Council would decide what territory the Company required, and what price they were prepared to offer. With the aid of the chairman and those councillors with some knowledge of the Cape natives and their history, Deneyn would draw up a proper, formal deed of sale, with a map. Then the Lords could justify their claim in European courts of law.

Pieter Cornelis Deneyn drew up a single deed for the transfer of the Cape Peninsula and Saldanha Bay, between the United East India Company on the one hand, and Captain Schacher, son of the late Gogosoa on the other. The price was low, a mere eight hundred guilders, and was paid in goods like tobacco and coloured beads. A second deed was between the Company and Captain Kuiper, for the transfer of the entire Hottentots-Holland. The two documents were properly signed, in the presence of witnesses. Whether Schacher and Kuiper had any understanding of what they were involved in, was from a legal point of view their own concern. It was all the work of Fiscal Deneyn. His signature appears on both. He rose in the esteem of the councillors, and the Lords Directors acknowledged his purchases as useful and well done.

After the departure of the return fleet, it took the new fiscal a while to settle into the quiet routine of the Cape. Initially he felt out of his depth. Perhaps it was because he could not relax in a tavern in this place, for the Cape was too small. The companion on the bench beside one tonight might well be your accused criminal tomorrow. He may simply have longed for Leiden; that is a familiar malady. Seeing Deneyn with his wig and gown in the courtroom, one might never expect such a jolly fellow in the tavern. He couldn't help that; perhaps he was like that bewitched prince in the fairy tale, a monster by day and a prince after dark. The second reason for his dislike of the Cape was the total lack, an almost unnatural absence, of young girls around him. He was obliged to go to church on Sundays to see what there was to be seen, and that wasn't much. The prettiest was certainly Gisela Mostert, daughter of the burgher councillor, but he was the fiscal and she still wet behind the ears. It remains a fact that she was very attractive, and often he would see her young face in his mind's eye. He wrote a poem for her, on her birthday, one of his better compositions. It can be read in his book to this day.

New brooms sweep clean, says the proverb, but Deneyn's beginnings at the Cape were difficult. He was interested in his work: law was in his blood. His grandfather had been a student of Huig de Groot, the Moses of Holland, as far as legal matters were concerned. His father, Advocate Cornelis Deneyn, was still practising in Haarlem. Fiscal Pieter opened his first case ('*Pr de Neijn, fiscal of this Residence, ex officio, pltff vs Carbet, 13 April 1672*') and abandoned it because he could find no grounds for the accusation against the fellow, while two councillors strongly insisted that Carbet should be packed off to the island. The Cape Koina were a very serious problem for Deneyn, as the defender of law and justice in wildest Africa. Judicially they were regarded as subjects of the Company, and the law was one level on which their existence overlapped with that of their white neighbours. Do the Spaniards in America regard their Mexicans, the English their Redskins, the Portuguese their Negroes, the Dutch their East Indians, as being under their law and jurisdiction? If so, by what right? The *Statutes of India* vaguely offered some help, but one thing only was certain, and that was that everybody first checked how strong the natives were before deciding whether they were one's subjects or not.

Then there were interesting exceptions, like the woman on Robben Island who had asked the postkeeper there to write a letter, protesting against her confinement. She'd been born a Hottentot, was baptised and married a Christian, and was banished to the island without any formal judicial process. She was simply exiled for life without any ruling by a court, or the benefit of a lawyer to act on her behalf. The law was on her side, thought Deneyn, and should she appeal to Batavia she would win her case, but this Cape Council would never forward her papers. What about her children, since there were three children, who were Dutch citizens after all, and probably born in wedlock. Why should her children share in her banishment? He would see to it that they were removed from there.

The situation at the Cape was complicated, fascinating. There were officials of the colonial staff, or servants as they were called, and free burghers, slaves and natives. How could one law be applied to such a diversity? One law for both the lion and the ox amounts to oppression, and the cross-application, like that of a Batavian statute on a Hottentot, might be a grotesquely misguided act. The *Corpus Iuris Civilis*, Damhouder's *Praxis Rerum*, Maetsuyker's *Nieuwe Indische Statute* and the thirty-nine other titles in his book chest might not be enough for this place. It was an interesting time, the dawn of the white man in Africa, as Drunken Nout had called it, but he was not at ease here.

The return fleet had departed and Deneyn was unhappy and, to his mind, unwelcome in the community, when Chairman Crudop asked him to draw up a summons against the free burgher Willem Willemsz van Deventer, for the shooting of a native. Murder or manslaughter? Deneyn wondered, and within fifteen minutes he had the accusation ready for Crudop's signature. He summoned a surgeon and arranged for two horses, for an autopsy on the open veld.

The small farm where Willemsz lived was on the eastern bank of the Liesbeeck, near the Ruiterstal. There was a simple house, a kraal of poles and branches, a rectangle of untilled land, a woman and two young children. She was probably no older than seventeen. The corpse, she said, was at the Ruiterstal, where the soldiers had covered it with bushes.

'Where is your husband, Mrs Willemsz?'

'He's not here.' As if that was something she often said.

'And your farmhand?'

Her eyes quickly scanned the yard. 'Ockert has gone to the veld with the cattle.'

'Where did the accident take place?'

'Here.' She stood in the door, raising one bare arm to point up along the river. Then she raised her other arm as if she was pressing a gun to her shoulder. Deneyn watched the movements of her body. She saw what he was looking at. 'Willem was standing right here. And the Hottentot was over there, where the *dienders* planted the stick.'

'What *dienders?*'

'From the mounted guard. They picked him up there and planted the stick.'

'Well, I'm first going over there to have a look. If your husband comes home, don't give him any help or comfort. Tell him to report to me without delay. All his possessions may be forfeited, so no sheep or cow or article may be sold or bartered. I want to speak to your farmhand too. Tell him what I said.'

She looked past him and the surgeon towards the river, and across it, at the green veld.

Only the corporal of the mounted guard was home; his troopers were out on patrol. He was Lorenz Fischer, locally known as Lourens Visser, but certainly no relation of the Vissers around here. Deneyn asked to see the corpse. It was covered with branches, downwind from the posthouse. The body lay face down, clothed in a short skirt and a kaross, and there was a blue wound high up between the shoulder blades, presumably a bullet wound. The surgeon muttered his observations as he probed the wound with lancet and forceps: the cadaver was that of an adult male Hottentot, about thirty years old, without visible defects or signs of illness. Rigor mortis had already set in, which meant that death had occurred at least three hours earlier. The cause of death was, with reasonable certainty, a bullet from a flintlock musket which had entered between the lowest vertebra of the neck and the top vertebra of the spine and shattered the spinal cord. 'And here's the little devil.' Using the forceps he extracted the flattened bullet, a lopsided star with four points, turned to Deneyn, and placed it on his palm.

'I've finished, *meester*. You may bury the cadaver. I will write my report.'

'Wait, fiscal,' said the corporal of the guard. 'Your Excellency must decide: the Koina asked for the body. They want to bury it in their own way. They will come and fetch him here.'

'All right. The Council won't have any objection. Can you tell me something about this Willemsz fellow, and about the accident?'

'Fiscal, let us make quite sure about the Council. The Cape is a strange place. And I'm saying that with due respect to my superiors. We have a proverb in that part of Germany where I was born, *Beware of the land where they strike the bell by hand*. I always think of that first before I undertake to do anything.'

'I know. It's true. But I am taking it on myself. Bury him; if the Council complains we can dig him up again.'

'Good heavens, fiscal. Is it war and murders you're looking for now? No, rather leave the carcass here.' Lourens went to collect bushes and branches and dragged them to cover the corpse. Deneyn and the surgeon helped him. Then the surgeon returned to the Fort, with his small chest slung around his shoulder on a canvas strap.

'Now, postkeeper. Can you tell me anything about the accident?'

'We heard the shot. It was about eleven this morning. I sent a man, because people aren't allowed to hunt here. He came to tell me that Lyreman had shot his herdsman and run off into the bushes. He still has the gun with him.'

'The Lyreman is Willemsz?'

'Yes, I don't know how he got that name, he doesn't make music, he's a hunter. He remains in the veld for weeks at a time to shoot. If you want to know about his hunting you must ask his old father-in-law, the two of them are in it together. The old man lives on the Wynberg. Now you must come with me, fiscal, I'll show you where I stuck the marker in the ground this morning. Sixty-three paces from his doorpost. What does that tell you?'

'That he's a good shot, and meant to kill. It may well be a count of murder, not manslaughter.'

'That's what I reckoned too.'

'You're about his closest neighbour. What do you know about the family?'

'They've been living here next to us for about four years. Lyreman married that girl when she was fourteen. Her father, old Jan Visser, was his neighbour on the farm up there towards the bend in the river. The old man was the Company's huntsman, and he and Lyreman became close friends because of the hunting, but of course there was old Jan's daughter too, an ignorant child still. Right from that time Lyreman is rarely home. He makes a better living from hunting than from farming. Gives him more pleasure too, than home.'

'Who is the farmhand?'

'That's Ockert Olivier. He's about twenty years old. Fiscal, I don't want to gossip, but he sleeps more with her than her own husband does.'

'Can you prove that?'

'Yes. He himself goes about saying the children on that farm are his. Lyreman is away from home for weeks on end.'

'Well, postkeeper, you've said here to me what you may have to repeat in court. Are you prepared to do that under oath?'

'I am.'

They went to the stake in the ground, where the man had been shot down, and Deneyn looked up towards the cottage beside the river, where the woman with the bare arms stood watching them. It was remarkable. Could anyone hit a target at such a distance? It could only have been an accident, thus manslaughter, not murder. Deneyn took his leave from the postkeeper, promised to let him know the Council's decision about burial, and asked the way to Lyreman's father-in-law.

Jan Visser was a blacksmith by trade, but a hunter at heart. Fifty years old, and as weather-beaten as a barge that had been left lying on land for too long. His hair was long, grey and dirty. There wasn't a single tooth in his upper jaw. His anvil was set up under a tree. There were two or three wagon wheels propped up against the trunk, with the steel rims detached and waiting to be tightened, and he had his leather apron tied round his waist, but his bellows was still, and his hammer lay on a cold fire. They spoke beside the anvil.

'Mr Visser, I'm looking for Willem Willemsz. Is he here on your farm?'

'No. We haven't seen him. That's my wife over there; you can ask her.'

'Do you know where he is?'

'No. He's off into the country. He's got to keep away from the Cape now.'

'But how will he survive in the veld? Who will give him food?'

'No one, but the fellow can shoot, Master Fiscal. He'll look after himself. If Willem were lying over there now, behind that flat black rock over there, he'd put three out of five shots right between your eyes. Just as he wants to. Side wind, twilight, uphill, damp air, it makes no difference to Willem. His hand is as steady as this anvil. We've been hunting together for ten years now. When we're out looking for hippos, he takes one bullet; for a rhino he takes two; for lions perhaps three, because they go about in packs. We used to earn premiums on wild asses, on rhinos, on lions and tigers, and on wolves. All of it clear profit, for there was almost no expense except for powder and lead. I'm not a bad shot when it comes to buck and things that stand looking at you, but Willem likes to hunt something that runs. That Hottentot now, you must agree it was a beautiful shot. First shot, on the run, at more than sixty paces.'

'How do you know these details?'

'The mounted guard was here to look for him.'

'You must warn him, Mr Visser. He must give himself up. We're going to outlaw him.'

'You expect Willem to give himself up, to be hanged?'

'One other thing. Do you know why Willem killed his herdsman?'

'The bloody fellow broke his blue beer mug.'

'I have to ask you one more thing: is it true that there's twenty years' difference between the Lyreman and his wife? And furthermore, that Maria has a relationship with the farmhand?'

'Yes, everybody knows about it. I know what you're thinking, Mister Fiscal. You think perhaps Ockert gave the gun to Willem and said, "Here, boss, you give him a scare, there's only powder in this thing." So that Willem would get into trouble about the Hottentot and get hanged for it. But no, anyone can see that was my Willem's own shot.'

So it was murder. On the way back to the Fort, Deneyn thought he should look in on Maria Willemsz again. What pretext could he use? Should he say, I have to see the shards of that amazing mug which was worth a human life? Because what he wanted to see was a woman who at the age of seventeen was prepared to take turns with two men in her bed.

Three Koina chiefs came to the Fort with a gift of five sheep for the Company. The Council met to listen to them. Van Breughel, Crudop, von Breitenbach, Deneyn and Surveyor Wittebol were present. The Koina were represented by Kuiper, Schacher and another. Deneyn was surprised by their good Dutch. Their case was clear: they were asking the Council to ensure that the murderer was punished. They had sent out search parties and found his tracks, but now he appeared to be on horseback. Who had given him a horse? There were people who said that farmers along the river were giving him food and shelter. They said: If he didn't turn up, revenge should be taken against the wife and the father-in-law and others who helped the murderer. Their cattle should be given to the dead man's relatives.

The councillors agreed: the man had to be found and brought to face his accusers. Deneyn shook his head: 'There can never be a question of revenge.' Suspicious, in silence, they listened to him. 'Willemsz must be brought to trial. The court will decide,' he said. Then the Koina reminded the Council that only a month or two before, five young boys had been caught, branded and flogged by the Company, each receiving fifty lashes on the bare back, after which all five were clamped to a single chain and banished to the island, there to carry shells for the building of this Castle. Three of them for fifteen years, and two for seven, and what they had done was to steal a few sheep from a farmer. Now, such a heavy punishment meted out to five children for an act of little import, meant that a murderer should be punished much more harshly. How could there be some kinds of punishment for the Koina and others for Hollanders? That was what the people wanted to know.

Deneyn did not have an answer for them, but at the time he had clearly put his personal view on paper, to prepare his plea for the five boys' punishment. *The African natives, known as Hottentots,* he had written, *have been found by all European nations, wherever they might travel on earth, so far the most brutish of all, who according to the authority and conviction of historians exceed all others in ignorance and reprehensible morals. As regards their education, nature and way of life, they appear to be more like animals than humans. They have the appearance of rational beings and consequently possess a rational soul, but I am uncertain whether the principles of inter-national law are applicable to them.* There it stands, in his handwriting.

Chairman Crudop assured the Koina on behalf of the Council that he would continue to search until they had found the man, and if the court were to find him guilty of murder, he would be severely punished. By death, yes, if there were no mitigating circumstances. This they had to accept, and also convey to their people. Crudop ordered arrack, and pipes and tobacco, and while they smoked and drank he again assured the Koina that the Company would severely the punish the man if a court found him guilty. It was the Company's wish to live as good neighbours in peace and justice with the Koina.

As prosecution slowly turned into persecution, Deneyn continued to build his case against Willem Willemsz. He called witnesses, placed them under oath and took down their affidavits. His summons was read from the top of the stairs for a second time, and posted on it, and thereafter also for a third time. The appointed time elapsed, but Willem the Lyreman did not surrender himself. Then the Council of Justice met to hear and consider the fiscal's plea. In his absence Willem Willemsz was sentenced to lifelong banishment, with the confiscation of his property, of which two-thirds would go to his wife and one-third to the government.

Another problem, ominous, unseen as a sunken wreck adrift on the open sea, was the illegal detention of three Christian children in a working colony for criminals. The law could not tolerate it. It was not acceptable, and had to be corrected. In England the children of convicted bankrupts and indigents had to go to prison with the parents, but thank God England did not yet rule over Dutch territory. In Holland the children of incompetent parents were adopted by the congregation of their church and placed in an orphanage or the care of selected guardians. Against remuneration.

Now, who had placed the van Meerhof children on the island, and when? Fiscal Deneyn only had to walk from his office next to the Council chamber to the room on the western side, the so-called secre-tariat, to put a question to the clerks and clutch a few bundles of docu-ments under his arm. He could make sure about his case, because the

Company's system operated in the secretariat. One might say of the Company what one wished, but one need never look very far for its documents. Deneyn's answers were right there; he found them without the least trouble. The woman and her three children had been placed on Robben Island by Commander Borghorst as a result of her misbehaviour and public indecency, to labour on the public works for an indeterminate period. Borghorst? That was the fellow who'd strung his life's fortune in small bags of diamonds around his what's-its-name, which then turned out to be the first place the English looked for it. So the children and their mother had now been on the island for more than three years. Who were they, those van Meerhofs?

The mother was Eva, who had been brought up as a daughter in the household of Commander van Riebeeck. Her own name was Krotoa. She should be about thirty years old by now. She'd been baptised in the Christian faith and catechised, and had married the surgeon van Meerhof in 1664. He'd died in the Company's service in 1667. There had been no cash payout to the widow in compensation for the loss of the breadwinner, but after almost a year she'd been granted a free house on shore. Then she'd begun to abuse alcohol and neglect her children and turn to prostitution.

There were three children. There used to be more. The oldest was Pieternella, born out of wedlock, probably in 1662. Then Jakobus, born out of wedlock, probably in 1664. He was an epileptic. Then Salomon, born in wedlock in 1666. Then one who died in infancy, while the father was overseas. More than a year after her husband's death Eva gave birth to a son, Hieronimus. The father was unknown. The child died after a year and was buried on the island.

The father, Pieter van Meerhof, had left two wills. In one of them his possessions were bequeathed to his old father in Denmark. The old father apparently died, because in the second will Pieter left everything to the poor at the Cape. Both wills had been drawn up before his marriage, and because they'd been married in community of property, both were now invalid. The widow had no will in her favour, and owned nothing of any value except for a slave.

The slave was Jan Vos from West Africa. He was a carpenter; that certainly was worth something to the estate. Everything they used, bed, table, clothes, slates, pots and pan, belonged to the Company and had to be returned one day. The father's accumulated wages still stood on the books. The surviving children should therefore benefit from it.

When an occasion arose to sail to Robben Island, Deneyn arranged with the quartermaster of the boat to allow him time on the island to talk to the widow Eva. First he had to discuss matters with the post-keeper, concerning certain prisoners the postkeeper wanted to free from their chains so that they could work better, and about a case where a convict who had died had been buried in his chains. After that he would see the woman. The quartermaster had to be patient; he promised to keep an eye on the wind and the tide.

'It's true, fiscal,' the postkeeper explained, rummaging in a small flat box among old letters from the shore, and copies of replies written by his predecessors. 'I had him buried in his chains. That's true. But look, here's the letter I've been looking for. Here it says, *The prisoner shall never under any circumstances be freed from his chains*. Is that not what it says?'

'Yes, that is so.'

'I was sitting beside the body with my hacksaw in my hand to take off the chains. And do you know what I thought? Better not, I told myself. Just do what the lord ordered. People have lost their jobs for less than this. If the Council is not satisfied now, I can show them the letter.'

'I understand. I'll explain to the Council, but there's no need to dig up the body now to salvage the manacles.'

Afterwards they looked for Eva and the children. The children liked to go down to the slate quarry, the postkeeper told him. There they play around and chat to the stonebreakers. It is better for them there on the south side than on the north, where the prisoners go about with the bags of shells. Deneyn and the postkeeper walked from the posthouse up the Vuurberg, the Fire Hill, and down the other side to the quarry. It was useful to see the island from this height. Opposite them were Table Mountain and the Lion's Head, and in between the green stretch of seaway, the road to the Table Bay anchorage. The Castle was invisible behind the white line of the dunes. Those dunes were a good place, a natural site for planting an outside gallows, so that seafarers arriving in and departing could see the gulls swirling around the bodies, and know that the system they'd left behind at Den Helder was in full force here.

At the foot of the Fire Hill was a large rectangular pit, excavated into the blue slate. It was long, wide, and deep enough for a big ship, like a blue dry dock in the earth. A hammering of wood on wood came up from the hole. Down on the floor a team of stonebreakers was toiling. Their water barrel and bags of rations stood behind them against the wall in the shade, where the day's stones had been piled.

'That's the children, down there.'

'How do we get down?'

'They'll put up a ladder for us.'

The foreman climbed from the hole to greet them, and together they descended the steep ladder. Deneyn wanted to see what the stone workers were doing. They flaked off the stones, two or four or six fingers thick for floors, a hand's width deep for window sills and thresholds, three feet wide for a tombstone or a beacon. The blue stone could be split neatly along a seam, as much as eight feet long. The seam was sawn along a scored line, into which wooden wedges were driven from below, after which it would be lifted from its bed with wedges and hammer. It was a beautiful dark blue stone lined with silver, this Robben Island slate which was found nowhere else.

'You can order your tombstone if you wish, Master Fiscal. We measure your length and your shoulders, mark it with your name, and keep it ready for you. You can write your own text right here; just keep the last date open.'

'Thank you. But I have work waiting.'

The three children were playing against the wall, far away from the workers.

'Why are the children playing here?'

'It's good for them, I think. We keep an eye on them. The foreman here is like their father.'

'I want to talk to them alone.'

'All right, let me go there with you. Just approach them slowly. It's like with animals. Once the boy hurt himself very badly on the cliff.'

As they approached, Deneyn asked, 'Are there more children like these at the Cape, with a native mother and a white father?'

'That I can't tell you, *meester*. But there are no other couples like them around who are married. If there are children they may be in the veld with the mother. I must say I doubt it, because the Koina don't allow sleeping-around.'

'But those two, the oldest ones, were born out of wedlock, weren't they?'

'Is that so? No, then I don't know, *meester*. But their mother grew up in the Fort. She has our ways.'

'Then they must be the first of their kind.'

It was like with animals. They could see the children looking left and right in alarm, making nervous movements to escape, but the biggest one said something and they huddled together, their backs pressed against the dark stone wall, their eyes on the fiscal, and when he reached them, they kept their eyes on the short walking stick under his arm. A beating. They were scared of him.

'This one is Pieternella. This is Jakobus, and this one is Salomon. And this is *Meester* Deneyn. Say good day to *Meester* Deneyn.'

So, these were the children of the red dawn. They tensed their faces, mumbled, whispered hoarsely, and glanced at the stick again. They were dressed like the slave children of the Company, in something like a knee-length sack of coarse linen, with holes for the head and arms. All three were thin, flat as oars. The little one was wearing an oily hat that nearly covered his whole head. From under the hat came a coughing and a sniffing, and he was breathing through his mouth. The boy, the older one, was a mixture of people. He was shorter than his sister, his hair was curled yellow and tightly against his skull, small ears, broad nose bridge, his skin dark, his eyes a smoky blue like the sky. The girl was the tallest, and nothing like the ordinary Dutch girl with red cheeks. Her face was pointed, with high cheekbones, dark Oriental eyes, wide mouth, pointed chin, small nose. Six or seven years from now she might be something exceptional, but at the moment she was bony, covered in dust, with scabs on the elbows and knees. She lifted her face sideways when he spoke.

'Good day, P'nella. Good day, boys.'

'They don't talk easily, *meester*.'

'Thank you, postkeeper. I want to try.'

Pieternella's first words were, 'Where's Uncle Otto going?'

'He has to speak to the other people. And what are you doing here?'

'Playing,' said the boy in a deep, hoarse voice.

'That's good. I'd like to see what you're doing.'

Without a word, Pieternella motioned to the blue wall of the quarry. There, right at the bottom, were drawings and words scribbled as with a slate pencil on a slate. He could make out fishes, and ships, objects like animals with two legs.

'Chickens?'

'Gulls.'

'And who draws so nicely?'

'This is mine, that is Kobus, here's Salomon.'

Deneyn pointed at a ship, fully rigged. On the afterdeck was a stick man, taller than the masts. 'Did you draw the ship, P'nel?'

'Yes. It's our Pa.'

'Who did this writing?'

'All of us,' said the boy. But when Deneyn asked him to read, he couldn't say a word, and the girl had to step in to defend him: 'I'm still teaching him.'

'I understand. And what did you write here?'

Her finger gestured vaguely at a few scratches on the rock face.

'Hans Michiel.'

'I see.' She stared into his face for a long time as if she was trying to make out what he saw. 'And can you write your name too?' But if she could, she wouldn't.

'P'nella, how's your mother?'

'She's sick.'

'I'd like to talk to her.'

'About what?'

'About you three.'

'What do you want to say to her?'

'I want to talk about your slave too. Do you still have him?'

'Uncle Otto works him in the garden.'

'You get some of the vegetables. What does your mother say?'

'She wants to sell Jan.'

'That won't be a good idea,' said Deneyn, looking into Pieternella's eyes. 'No.'

'No,' she said, looking him in the eyes too as she spoke.

'Then I must talk to the postkeeper and your mother, when she feels better. They mustn't spoil things.'

He put out his hand, and greeted all three children. The questions he'd meant to ask her, whether she and her brothers would like to live with people in town, play with other children and go to school, had to wait. She would not leave her mother behind. And would it really be such an unfortunate thing for her to grow up on the island? He wasn't sure about that.

Eva lay on her bed, covered by a sheepskin spread. She was awake. From the door Postkeeper Raling called, 'Eva, the fiscal wants to speak to you.' She half raised her head and turned her face to the door.

'Can I go ashore now?'

Deneyn's eyes examined the dusk. So, this was Eva. She looked older than he had expected.

'I don't know, Mrs van Meerhof.'

'Did you bring my Pieter's money?'

'No.'

'Did you bring something to drink?'

'Totally forbidden,' said the postkeeper.

'I must have it. I'm dying.'

And the fiscal remained quiet, because he knew what she meant. He could understand the urge, but there was the government's law. And the law was he.

'Then why did you come to wake me?'

'I want to talk about your children. I want to remove them from the island. They are not prisoners. They shouldn't grow up among convicts.'

'What are you trying to pretend? I never had any say over my children. So what do you come to discuss today? Take them away if you want to. They're the Company's children already. Everything belongs to the Company. Take them, go away.'

'Eva,' exclaimed the postkeeper, 'the fiscal wants to help your children.'

'But not me. I can die here for all he cares.'

'Let her be,' Deneyn said. 'She only thinks of herself. Come, we can talk outside.'

Back in the open, the keeper said, 'There are bad things coming, fiscal. Very bad things. I know she has the English disease. The Council sent me word about it, because our fellows admitted it to the surgeon who examined them. But now, God help her poor child, it seems to me she's pregnant again.'

'Do you lock her up at night?'

'What would be the use? She does it in the daytime. And it's no use rowing against the current without many oars in the water, *meester*.'

'I see she has a shackle on her leg.'

'That was ordered by *Heer* Borghorst. I do what they say. That's the best.'

Well, what could one do in this case? 'I want to see the slave that belongs to this woman.'

The slave was carrying pails of water on a yoke over his shoulders, walking between the well and the vegetable garden when they met him. He was an elderly man, under a straw hat.

'This is Jan Vos, *meester*. Jan, the fiscal.'

And now, thought Deneyn, they were moving to another code of law. First they were with the rights of orphans and widows, and now it was the rights of slaves. It must have been under the Romans that the Dutch had last owned slaves. And he, Pieter Deneyn, hadn't shaken hands with a slave before, either. Watch out, Advocate Deneyn, the water was getting shallow under your keel and before long you might be stuck. The Cape was a trap for an inexperienced man.

'How are you, Jan Vos?'

'Well.'

'I've come to find out if there's anything you want to tell the Council. I heard the woman was wanting to sell you.'

The slave lowered his pails to the ground. 'Yes. That will be a mercy.'

'How does she treat you?'

'She never says a word. But I'm not a convict and I've been on this island for a long time. If it wasn't for the children I'd have run away long ago.'

'You think you can get away?'

'Yes.'

But the postkeeper laughed. 'No, *meester*, they cannot.'

'The law must punish you if you run away.'

'I'm already punished here.'

'Why do you want to get to the land?'

'I was a freeman's slave, and now I have to work in the garden for the Company without any wage. They're turning me into a convict. On land a slave gets a wage when his master hires him out.'

'It is unjust. Did you learn a trade?'

'I don't have papers, but for years I was a carpenter. I can earn my own bread.'

'I shall take up your case, Jan. As long as you don't try to abscond.'

'When you're finished here today, *meester*, will you stay, or do you want to go ashore?'

'Look, you've asked me to be removed from here. I shall see what I can do. For a start, don't mention it to anyone, especially not to the woman and the children. And another thing: it's possible that Mrs van Meerhof may be pregnant again. Have you any idea who the father could be?'

'I don't associate with rubbish.'

On the dusty road to the posthouse the keeper said, 'Jan has become bitter. He used to be an affable man.'

'If he escapes, he will have to be punished. But don't put him in chains or lock him up.'

'All right, *meester*, but they cannot get away from here, even if that is what he thinks. So shall I rather use one of the convicts in the garden? We need the vegetables.'

'Wait until you hear from the Council. When the Council writes to you about Jan Vos, they'll let you know about a convict for the garden.'

And yet it was possible to escape from the island. A few weeks later five young Koina, all locked to one chain, disappeared from there.

The sea captains, who in 1672 brought news of a new war against England and France combined, could give no reason why England should have declared war. The case of France was clear: France had an agreement with England to declare whenever England declared. The Conspiracy of Dover, it was called. But why should the English hoist the red flag? The reasons they advanced were so ludicrous that the declaration could hardly be taken seriously. Allegedly the king of England felt insulted by a painting now in the city hall of Dordrecht, depicting Admiral de Ruyter setting fire to the Medway River, and he was further insulted because his ship *Royal Charles,* captured there and towed off, was now in Amsterdam where the ordinary citizens could pay to visit it. But such pointless pretexts suggest that one should look elsewhere for the reason, and the most likely was that they colluded to break the Dutch hold on the Eastern maritime trade. But the Dutch were not frightened. They had the water line, they had de Ruyter at sea, and young Prince Willem on land, appointed as army chief for one campaign. Since the Cape was the gateway to the East, the Cape Council was instructed to declare martial law.

Deneyn discussed the matter of the children and the slave with councillors, as he wished to hear their opinions before he tabled it at the Council meeting for a decision. He persuaded them that Jan Vos was being used illegally for his labour. But the Council refused to consider offering him payment, as it hadn't hired him. In that case, Postkeeper Raling should pay. Jan Vos could come ashore on the next boat, provided somebody could be found to hire him, but his income had to be used for the maintenance of the woman and children.

Deneyn was not satisfied with that. 'We are now in the domain of poor-relief and as you know, in the fatherland that is a matter for the Church. Let me ask the Church Council for advice.'

His proposal to the Council would be that the slave be used to earn an income for the whole family, under the supervision and control of the Church Council. He submitted his proposal in writing and was invited to attend when it was to be discussed. Would the Church Council be prepared to act as guardian for the under-age children of the late surgeon Pieter van Meerhof and their mother, Eva, who was incapable of looking after them, and would the Church Council itself become administrator of their estate? It wouldn't cost the Church Council anything, as the family had its own source of income. This offer the Church Council could not refuse. They unanimously accepted it, and forwarded it to the Honourable Council. The Council appended only one condition: the woman had to remain on the island. The decision was taken on the advice of the surgeons.

Deneyn was satisfied. He hadn't told them that the woman might be pregnant again, but began to enquire about good foster-parents.

When work on the Castle had begun six years earlier, there was silence on the scaffolding. It had been the rule, ever since the time of Babel. Now it was no longer observed: people called, shouted, cursed, objected, bickered. From a distance one might distinguish as many as five languages at any one time. The old foremen were baffled; they did not understand what had happened, or what to do about it. Perhaps it was hunger that made the men light-headed, and fatigue, because if you had to break rocks from sunrise to sunset, and carry them, and hoist them up, and stand guard at night on a half-empty stomach, then fatigue and dizziness prompted you to talk back. That was what the Cape was like. Perhaps it was the corporals with their canes themselves who started all the shouting, but the officers were dissatisfied. Noise wasn't acceptable. Order on the scaffolding, they instructed the foremen. This was military construction and talking and complaining should not be tolerated. Particularly now under martial law, it wasn't just improper, but dangerous for discipline.

Over at the Castle, as usual on the first day of the month, the soldiers did not return to work in the afternoon after the bell, but gathered in front of the office window in the ark to collect their food money and rice rations. There one of them said, as was subsequently confirmed under oath before Deneyn: 'I have not eaten for two days and I'm so weak now I can barely stand. The Devil take me if I have to work any more today.' Just then, Sergeant Croese arrived to tell them they had to return to work, the pay-out was postponed until four o'clock.

The disappointment was expressed in one long sigh. The silence began to seethe, there was whispering and mumbling all around. Someone called: 'First rations, then work!' The sergeant laughed and tried to calm them. They thronged around him and shouted in unison: 'First rations, then work!' He struck a few blows with his cane around him, and blew his whistle. Lieutenant von Breitenbach had arrived late at the office, which was why the money was not ready, but he was already inside by the time the uproar started. He was resolved to teach these troops a lesson they would not soon forget. He took up position in the door of the ark and told the three sergeants closest to him with their backs to the wall, facing the troops: '*You* name two, and *you* name two, and *you* name two.' He raised his two hands as if to bless them, and as they fell silent, he said: 'Each of your sergeants is now going to call out two names. Those people are to come up to me here.' And when the six stood still in front of him as if expecting a promise: 'I'm arresting these six for sedition. Take them to the cells. Corporals, drive the rest back to work. Use your canes.'

Deneyn worked on that case for weeks. He had scant experience of military law, and in a country under martial law, military rule replaced the civilian. He did not have the right books either. The acting commander here had sole discretion over life and death. Deneyn had the accused brought up from their cells, placed them on oath, and interrogated them. The charge was mutiny against the legitimate authority. They denied it. Deneyn agreed. Disorder, disobedience, uproar perhaps, but not mutiny. And their motive? Fatigue, hunger, despair. Neither were they the only ones, or even the first, to start the shouting before the ark; everybody had shouted together. Deneyn told the Council that he could see no grounds for a charge of mutiny. Mutiny was a capital offence. The Council insisted, they demanded a capital trial, as an example to the others. And should sacred justice now act as schoolmaster? Deneyn wondered. But he had to do as he was ordered, since they were all under martial law. My hands are now stained red with blood, he thought. And I am changed into an executioner. But he would do his duty to his country. After the accused, he called witnesses. But they refused to remember anything. Everybody had been shouting, there wasn't one who'd shouted more loudly than the rest, but it had all been out of fatigue, hunger, despair.

The Council found all six guilty, as charged. In wartime mutiny is never tolerated. Now for the example. The six were called in, and told that they were guilty of mutiny in wartime. They fell on their knees, pleading for mercy, their hands clasped in supplication in front of their faces. And the court was merciful: four of the six would draw lots for life or death. The two who drew death were hanged three days later. Both had been in the country for only a few months. The two who drew life, were flogged and sentenced to hard labour in chains for twenty-five years. Of the last two, one was flogged and had to work in chains for three years, and Magnus Pietersz had to straddle the wooden horse for three days: the first day with weights of twenty pounds on his legs, the second day with ten pounds, and the third without weights. On the fourth day he was unable to walk. That day the bodies of Jeremias Brommels and Martin Glockner were removed from the gallows and buried behind the cattle kraal.

Such was martial law. The reason for it was the war the fatherland was waging against the English and the French. News from the Netherlands was bad. The country was on its knees. The French king personally was at the head of a hundred thousand men from the south, and his general, Turenne, from the east with forty thousand men. Nijmegen, Zutphen, Culemborg, Arnhem, Bommel, Doesburg, Naarden and Utrecht were already in French hands. Young Prince Willem took on the French with barely ten thousand men. His last hope of retaining the western high ground of his country, was the water line. If his government gave the word, the sea dykes in the north and south-west would be cut to flood the country.

In Lords Seventeen's letters, the Cape Council was warned to keep close watch on the coast for English and French ships, to place the burgher militia on a war footing, and to avoid hostilities with the natives for the duration of the war. Should the enemy enter Table Bay, the Council had to evacuate Robben Island and destroy everything on it.

This possibility gave Deneyn the opportunity to remove the van Meerhof children from the island.

There was a carpenter of the Honourable Company who worked on the Castle, a Rotterdammer called Long Gert. His wife had come out to join her husband, and their house stood next to the large garden behind the Company's stable. Deneyn selected Gerrit van der Byl, and asked the Cape *dominee* to find out from the man and his wife whether they were prepared to accommodate the three children. There would be an income for his family, and he would have first option on hiring the slave who did carpentry. The *dominee* went to talk to them.

'When our heavenly father looked for a home for His only son, He also chose the house of a carpenter. He could have chosen the palace of a great warlord like Julius Caesar or Alexander Magnus, or a humble shepherd's shelter, or of course the luxurious mansion of a merchant. I do not know why, brother and sister, but in the gospel I read that He chose to place His son in the house of a carpenter. The Church Council does not come to you today because you are a carpenter, Brother Gerrit, but because of the life you and Sister Sofia are leading. The Church Council prayed for guidance in the matter of a home for these three children, where they can grow up in the Dutch and Christian reformed way of life, and it was as if a star positioned itself above your house behind the stable, to show that this is the chosen place where Pieternella and the poor children will be brought up.'

Long Gert was one of the old-fashioned kind of carpenters who refrained from speaking on the scaffolding. In his throat a large Adam's apple moved when he listened, but he rarely said anything. His wife Sofia was barely thirty, almost as tall as he, and just as quiet. Their only child, after twelve years of marriage, was a tall, quiet boy called Pieter.

'We feel honoured that the church has thought of us, *dominee*,' Gert answered. 'Sofia and I will discuss it, and pray, and then let the church know.'

Deneyn was in his office planning by candlelight how to shed more blood in ways the congregation would remember for ever, when Sofia and Gert went on their knees in their house to pray about the van

Meerhof children. The next morning Long Gert looked in at Deneyn's office, and told him they would lodge the children.

For Sofia the next four years, when she had a daughter in the house, were the most pleasant of her life. Never before had she smiled so much. She dressed the child as prettily as their allowance made possible. As for the two little boys, she simply saw to it that they washed, put on clean clothes and went to church with her and her husband. From her husband they learned to say please and thank you, to eat with others at table, with a knife and fork, and to pray and say grace, all according to Dutch custom. With time and patience it all worked out. But they were easy children, who ate anything, wore anything, did anything one asked. Of course she and Gert had to keep an eye on them, and repeat everything two or three times, but that was nothing to her.

She could see that in a quiet way they were close, the three children. You could find them standing in front of Pieternella, but without exchanging a sound, and when you approached they would quietly disperse. A few times soon after their arrival the eldest boy had attacks of epilepsy, but Pieternella let him thrash about on the floor until it was over and then covered him to rest. What was it, Sofia wondered, was it a devil or an angel that went at him like that? What did they want of him? And it was impossible to make him put shoes on his two feet, in sickness or in health.

Her son Pieter had always made friends quite readily, but now that there were children like brothers in the house, she saw that he found it hard to share his room. For the others it must have been just as hard, but they didn't show anything. She thought: They'll get used to each other.

Her husband was very happy with the slave. The fellow could plane, saw, hammer, make trusses, boil glue, fashion nails, sharpen and care for his tools, always with a smile. Long Gert found that he could now take on profitable outside work to augment his pay. The Company and the free burghers wanted to build and extend, and there weren't enough carpenters at the Cape. Gert could leave everything to Jan Vos. The slave was a real asset to him, and for the first time he and

Sofia could put something by for the day they would become free burghers. He hoped that day need not be too distant, and he knew to whom he owed it.

Their son had a private teacher, a soldier from the garrison, but the other three went to the Company's school. It was a small room in the Fort. Jakobus struggled, as he had a short memory. Pieternella and Salomon found it easy to learn. They were just as clever or better than those of their age, and when the *secundus* or the *dominee* came on inspection once a week, they were the ones who were asked to stand and read from the *Huispostillen* or to recite a piece of catechism. Pieternella wanted to know what Pieter was taught by his private teacher. It included long prayers and also the orations of dead emperors; if she wanted to, she could also have learned to recite it. But she and Pieter sat at the table at night writing on their slates for each other, sums and riddles, or just the names of countries. This was how one wrote *Batavia*, this was how one wrote *Charlemagne*.

On Sundays they all walked to the ark together to attend church, except for Jan Vos, who lay on his *katil* smoking.

'Don't you want to come with us, Jan?' Long Gert asked.

'My soul cannot bleach, master. I prefer to rest.'

Pieternella noticed that Jan was given clothes, and tobacco and wine, as they had been promised. He lived on his own in the backyard, made his own food, washed his clothes and hung them out to dry. Jan earned the food for the four of them, like a father who rises before daybreak, winter and summer, to work for his family.

'Wouldn't you like to have a wife, Jan?'

'Not any more, my child. When I was young, I liked thinking about a wife. But it is no longer necessary. I'm doing everything myself.'

Sometimes he spoke to her about her brothers. 'You must listen, Kobus swears at the little one.'

'I think he learned it from my mother.'

'Then you must tell Long Gert, so he can speak to the child.'

'I'll speak to Kobus.'

'Don't you ever think of your mother?' he asked Pieternella.

'Yes. I think it's better for her without us.'

'That's good. It's her life. Your life still lies ahead. You're getting on now, and in ten years' time you won't remember Jan Vos either. I'm thankful that the fiscal took us.'

Jan Vos's wages of 200 guilders per year were more than twice the income of a soldier. He had few expenses, as he led a simple life, but he insisted on having shoes. The Church Council refused to comply. Slaves went barefoot; that was how one recognised a slave.

'Bart Borms also went barefoot. In those days he and I worked on the sea. Now I work on houses.'

Fiscal Deneyn saw Pieternella in church. It was as he'd suspected: once one had washed away the dust and combed her hair she would be a pretty child. He looked up her date of birth as close as possible, and saw that she was about twelve. He would like to speak to her. He went to the house late one Saturday afternoon when he knew both Long Gert and Pieternella would be there. He had tea with them, and talked to Gert and Sofia, and enquired after the children and the slave. He would like to exchange a few words with the girl. She was called.

'P'nella, I must tell someone in your family about your mother's situation, and I think it should be you. The Church Council and the government are looking after your mother, but I want you to understand how it works.'

She nodded. But he wanted to hear her speak. 'How did it come about that you were called Pieternella? That is unusual. Petronella is more common.'

'It was my father's name.'

'Was he Pieter?' But he already knew that. 'Then there are quite a few of us who have the same name. Your father, and you, and I. Our name means rock.'

'And Pieter van der Byl.'

'Yes, indeed. I want to tell you about your and your mother's and your brothers' affairs, as if you are the mother, and you will remember it until they can take care of their own affairs later. All I want to ask you is not to discuss it with anyone. All right?'

'Yes.'

'When your father died, he left a small sum of money. It belongs to your mother and you three children, together. The Company, that is the government, had to give the money to your mother, to look after you. But the government thought she might spend the money, waste it, and neglect you.'

Her face was sombre.

'Do you remember the time when your mother went away and left you behind in the old pottery? According to the books you were naked when you appeared before the Council. Without any clothes.'

'I can't remember.'

'Who told you to go to the Council? Was it you?'

'I don't know.'

'Well, anyway. That was what the Council was afraid of. They are still keeping your father's money, and you should know that it isn't much. The years you lived on Robben Island, some of it was used to pay for your food and clothing. But what remained has now been invested so that it can grow. It slowly becomes more, almost like a child growing. I saw to it. Something else that is added to it, is Jan Vos. He is now working for you, and everything he earns, goes into your fund.'

'Is Jan working for us?'

'Let me explain it: he works for Mr van der Byl, and the money he earns, goes into your fund. But it is fair to say that Jan is working for you. Isn't that so?'

'Yes.'

'It's like the fresh-water barrel in Sofia's kitchen. Jan is the only one who works to fill the barrel, but there are five people who drink from it: the three of you, your mother, and Jan. All of you must have food and clothes. Jan gets almost nothing, because he's a slave.'

She looked him in the face and asked him: 'What do people call you?'

'Fiscal, or *Meester* Pieter. Friends just call me Pieter.'

'Can Jan have shoes?'

'Anyone can.'

'Will you tell them to let Jan have shoes?'

'I shall remember. But if you're not watching carefully, the barrel will get empty.'

'Yes.' Her mouth was as unmoving as her face. Lovely eyes the child had. I'll still make you smile, he thought.

'I'm now going to have a few words with Jan. Give your brothers my regards, and our namesake, Pieter van der Byl.'

He shook hands with her, and let her go through the door ahead of him.

That afternoon she heard from young Pieter: the fiscal was the one who had people branded, and shot, and hanged, and locked up, and beaten. Who drove nails through their tongues, and cut off people's ears, and pinned them to a post with a knife through the hand. Who sent people to work in chains on Robben Island for life. It's him, Pieter Deneyn.

Some people never learn. There was a woman called Maijke Hendriksz who had been in court several times, and had to be punished yet again. Deneyn examined her record. She was Maria van den Berg, housewife of Tielman Hendriksz, and in her case there was no question of crime because of poverty. They owned a farm along the fertile Liesbeeck. It was Den Uitwijk, established by Jan van Riebeeck himself, so it had to be the very best. Maijke was fifty-one, Tielman ten years younger. They had children, of which one girl was still at home. It looked like a good-for-nothing family. Not one of them belonged to the church. Tielman did not want to farm, but tried to earn his bread in easy ways, like hunting and smuggling, while the farm went to ruin in the care of a hired hand. Both had criminal records. In nine years Tielman had been to court six times, for assault, smuggling and the illegal sale of livestock. A violent fellow to boot. Once at a wedding he very nearly killed the bridegroom. He was the one who started the fun, as the saying goes at peasant weddings. His fines were considerable, and Tielman was close to bankruptcy.

Maijke's first contravention was insulting a neighbour and then assaulting her with her fists. The court tried to settle it, and withheld a verdict and punishment. After that Maijke appeared three times in two years, respectively for assisting a culprit, theft and illicit stock bartering. On this occasion she and her farmhands stole sheep from the natives and sold them.

This time, Deneyn asked, in his argument, that the court should consider the previous contraventions and sentence her to be severely flogged, tied under the gallows with a rope around her neck, followed by twelve years' labour in chains on the island, with confiscation of all her money and possessions. And for each of her three helpers, a flogging, and three years in chains on the island. The Councillors looked from the fiscal to the old woman, and back to the fiscal, and adjourned the court. They decided: concerning the second, third and fourth accused, his plea was granted. As for the first accused, she would stand with a cane in her arms and witness the punishment of the others. She herself would be confined for three years, and had to pay a fine of four hundred rixdollars. Deneyn was most satisfied. The sentences were executed on a school day in the front courtyard of the Fort. The children could hear the sounds through their window. Pieternella knew Aunt Maijke well. She was the only friend her mother had left.

The German proverb, *Beware of a land where the bell is struck by hand*, had been made for the Cape. The garrison and its free population were both so small, the government so strict and the examples of heavy punishment so regular, that one would expect little serious crime in the tiny colony. Deneyn remembered what Commissioner van Overbeke had said about the country's red dawn. Red it certainly was; a lot of blood was flowing. Andries Vries was flogged because of a stabbing, branded with a glowing knife and sent to the island for two years. Some runaway slaves were hanged, their bodies dragged afterwards through the streets by the hangman's rope to the new outside gallows in the dunes, and there hoisted up, eventually to fall prey to the birds of the air. Two soldiers who had drawn their knives against the constable of the Fort, were each given a hundred stripes and five years' hard labour in chains. Jan Tenger had to stand in the gallows' rope on the scaffold for a full day for stealing sheep, followed by ten years' labour in chains on the island.

When there was an execution, Long Gert mentioned it to the children, as it was on their way to school in the morning. He explained the cause to them, and if he could find something applicable from the

Bible, he would read the passage to them. 'The punishment is for us,' he said. 'It is an example to you and me.'

And he himself believed in a good example. That drunkenness ran in families, he also believed, and as long as the van Meerhof children were under his roof, they never knew that he also kept wine and brandy in the house. He tried to set a good example to them.

His wife Sofia also believed in a good example. A good example and good health were all she'd inherited from her mother. She mended her and her husband's and their child's clothes herself, and taught Pieternella how to hem a piece, how to make buttonholes, darn socks, patch the knee or the seat of a pair of breeches, how to stitch hooks and eyes to the back of a dress. The children's clothes were made by a tailor and paid from their fund. Sofia would take the one who needed clothes and tell the tailor what she wanted: a red cap for Jakobus, green cotton hose, a canvas cloak against the rain, or for Pieternella a blue dress, a red bodice, a coatee, two aprons, a wide collar and three shifts. Sofia chose the material herself, measuring the lengths and widths across the child's body. Then the tailor would climb off his table, take out slate and slate-pencil to figure out the price of material, buttons, thread, hooks and eyes, and the labour, and show Sofia the sum. 'And one ell of red ribbon for the child's hair,' she ordered, pulling an ell and a half from the roll. She wasn't stingy with the children's clothes, but when it came to looking after them, keeping them clean and tidy, she was stricter than a chief boatswain.

From Robben Island the postkeeper complained that Eva was not looking after herself, and needed help. The Council proposed that a Koina be hired to chop wood and carry water for her; the wages could come from the children's fund. Deneyn prevented it. He wanted to protect the children's money; it shouldn't be spent on Eva. He discovered that there was a decrepit old slave woman in the lodge who couldn't be used for anything else. If the Company placed her on the island, ostensibly to carry shells, they could provide her with bread at convicts' rations, and Eva with a servant. He wanted to make an investment. It was time to plan ahead.

First he asked Long Gert what he thought of arranging for Jakobus to begin learning a trade, as the children would need a larger income one day. Jakobus was now twelve; a trade would take four or six years of his life. Long Gert thought it was a good idea. He himself had been that age when he started learning as a helper to his father.

'There's a difference. A helper receives wages. I want him to become an apprentice. That costs money.'

'Then I don't know, *meester*. It may be throwing good money after bad.'

'Do you think he can't learn?'

'He can if he wants to, but perhaps he doesn't want to.'

It was not unusual for an apprentice to be unwilling, but the master had the duty to punish him. And money was paid in advance so that a master lost nothing if his pupil turned out to be unwilling and did not finish his contract. Then Deneyn took his idea to the Church Council. This body wanted to know whether he could suggest a trade which would be within the boy's capabilities. There were tailor, surgeon, shoemaker, carpenter, locksmith, blacksmith, coppersmith, tinsmith, bricklayer, wagoner.

'Shoemaker.'

'And is there a shoemaker who would be willing to take an apprentice? What about sailor, perhaps?'

'For heaven's sake, no.'

'Why so, *meester*?'

'It will be his death.'

'We'll find out if there is a shoemaker who needs an apprentice. You know what that means, *meester*. If it's a bad shoemaker, he will be wanting for a pupil only for the income. But we'll try to persuade Jacolini.'

Only then did Deneyn speak to Pieternella. He could take the decision on his own, but he went to her to see her lovely eyes again, and that quiet, serious mouth of hers. He didn't tell her that her mother was pregnant again, that another consumer would be added to her list, and that once again there was no father. He only said that they were going to need more money. Everything was getting more expensive, and Jan could not go on for much longer, earning money for all of them. Boys had to work. What did she think, he asked: could one expect Jakobus to lend a hand?

'I shall find out from Jakobus what he thinks.'

'We can call him here.'

'I'll talk to him myself.'

Deneyn was satisfied. He felt sure that she trusted him.

Then Maijke appeared before Fiscal Deneyn again. She came to claim a reward. A notice had been posted offering a reward of thirty rix-dollars on the heads of two young runaways from the garrison. They wanted to flee the country, but for quite some time now there hadn't been any ships. They'd been on the run for almost a month and had been forced to break in to steal food. Some gave them something, out of pity. One day they emerged from the bushes behind Table Mountain, in the kloof known as the Hell, to ask Maijke's farmhand for food. The hand had already had his noonday meal, but would come back the next day to chop wood in the same place, and promised to bring them food. Watch this tree; when its shadow touches that rock, you must come to the wagon.

That evening the farmhand made a bad mistake with Maijke. He told her about the two deserters who'd been to the wagon, and asked her whether she could spare a crust of bread and some of the hippo meat for them. She put extra food in the cloth with the farmhand's, as he had asked. Tielman was still out hunting, and Maijke still in confine-ment, but that evening she walked to the Fort and told Fiscal Deneyn where and at what time he could nail the two runaways. And that was exactly how it turned out. From an early hour, well before the farm-hand came to the wood, Sergeant Croese with twelve men formed a large circle around the place and waited while the sun moved over the trees, and caught the two runaways where they sat eating at Maijke's wagon. One of the two was hanged, the other sentenced to flogging and twenty-five years' labour in chains on the island. That was why Deneyn told Maijke in his office that day: 'Here are your pieces of silver.'

Lords Seventeen had sent advance notice that they were dispatching a new commander to Mauritius, but the man they sent was least expected. Pieternella and her brothers were on the beach in front of the Fort, the school had just come out, when the young lady approached from the quay. Fiscal Deneyn came from the gate, his walking stick under his arm, and stopped beside Pieternella to await the visitors.

'What do you see, P'nel? Or what do you think you see? Have a close look, tomorrow I shall ask you.'

How prettily she was dressed, Pieternella thought. She was half hidden among sailors with chests on their shoulders, two half-grown boys, and a black-bearded giant with a slight limp, but the young lady turned her eyes to Pieternella and then spoke to the big man. She was attractive, not like the angels in the Bible, but like the French girls who some-times came here. Although the weather was warm and there was no slave with an umbrella on the quay to meet them, she had done well to put on her green velvet. And emeralds, it had to be emeralds in the heavy silver ornament on her breast. Their ages must have been four or five years apart, hers and the young lady's. Was she of noble blood? Her father was a real gentleman; one could see it on the wide strips of lace, the silver buckles, the curved, decorated scabbard of the sabre, the coloured ostrich feather in the hat. But if you looked at the boys, you might wonder if they really were her brothers. The older one was more attractive than the young lady, the younger one more like an Oriental around the eyes, with the blue-black hair, the pale brown skin. That was what Pieternella saw. Who were these people? Fiscal Deneyn shook hands with the gentleman, bowed, smirked; shook hands with the young lady, bowed, smiled; shook hands with the boys, bowed, smirked.

'That was Commander Hubert Hugo and his children,' he told Pieternella the following day. She was on her way home from school; he on his way to the slave lodge. 'He was a pirate to begin with, but now the Lords have put him in charge of Mauritius.'

'What is the young lady's name?'

'She is Mary. Her mother was an English lady.'

'And what are they doing here?'

'Repairs, refreshment, before they leave. Would you like to have a look at his ship? If you wish, I can arrange for you and your brothers to go on board.'

'No. Hans Michiel told me how they murder people.'

'Look, he isn't a pirate any longer. That was years ago.'

'Are they forgiven? Will *Secundus* de Cretser and the Lyreman be forgiven if they come back?'

I shall teach you to smile, Deneyn thought. 'No, they won't be forgiven. But it's different with this man. He didn't rob our people, for one thing. Another thing is all that is now past; and the third thing: the Company needs him for a difficult task.'

She looked in his eyes while he spoke, but said nothing. If she'd had the words, Deneyn thought, she might say without a smile: 'You have one law for poor people, *Meester* Fiscal, and another for the rich and those with powerful friends.' But she didn't say it; she was too young, she didn't know about such injustice. Yet she suspected it. She had the feeling that Deneyn was not frightened of her, but he was of the man with the black beard. And she was right.

'Our Company needs him, P'nel. They're sending Hugo to perform a particular task. Not everyone can do it, which is why they gave him the rank of commander, and independence from our governor. That shows how important his work is.' Deneyn pointed with his stick. 'It has everything, everything to do with our Castle. We must have slaves to build it, for the soldiers are getting angry if they have to do it. Their work is to stand guard, and to fight. And we need much more building lime. There are mountains of lime on Mauritius. Over the centuries the sea has washed up banks of coral and shells there; now it's lying there waiting. And also, we need a tough leader on Mauritius, so the English or the French won't take the island.' All the while he is walking beside the child, explaining with much seriousness. He wants her to think well of him. Why? He cannot tell. Perhaps he will know later.

'Are you going to turn Mauritius into another Robben Island? Catching people to carry shells, for this Castle?'

'Yes, something like that.'

'Will the young lady stay behind here at the Cape?'

'No, she's going to Mauritius with them. Unhappily, I think.'

'Because there are no other young ladies there?'

'There may be one or two, but none of her class. She will be lonely.'

'Will she see Bart and Theuntje?'

'Who?'

'Bart and Theuntje Borms. He is a fisherman. Will you tell her?'

'I promise.'

They arrived at the Company's slave lodge. Deneyn bowed to her and shook her hand. She walked on, past the Company's garden, past the Company's stable, to the carpenter's house.

She saw Mary Hugo a few times. Sometimes on the beach, sometimes in the big garden, walking with her father at sunset, sometimes on the square in front of the Fort, sometimes with her very handsome brother, and a few times with Fiscal Deneyn. Mary was always richly dressed, always in good spirits. When she walked with her father, they were arm in arm. Pieternella could see how her father enjoyed her company. She envied Mary: the beautiful clothes, a father to take her arm. One day while she was in school, they left for Mauritius.

Deneyn came to tell Long Gert that the shoemaker Jacques Jacolini was prepared to accept Kobus as his pupil. Kobus asked no questions when they explained the contract to him; he was glad to get out of school.

'Now you must remember, P'nel,' Deneyn said, 'we will be drawing money from your fund to pay for Kobus's apprenticeship. He will have to work hard. You must encourage him. If he fails or runs away, your money will have been wasted. The work is not difficult, as far as I can make out. But he must be patient and serve out his time. There are also fines and corporal punishment for a pupil who runs away.'

'Jakobus doesn't like shoes.'

'I can see that, P'nel. But he must try. And Jakobus, you've finished school now, but you still have a lot to learn. Master Jacques will show you how to earn your own bread, and for your sister and your brother who are too young to earn for themselves. Just see it through; one day you will be a *baas* yourself, with a pupil.' What he meant was: Keep the fund solvent, until P'nel is big enough. One day I shall take care of her. At the moment I'm not yet allowed to.

Free burghers on a hippo hunt in the Berg River tried their best to persuade the government, and their wives, that theirs was an urgent and important enterprise, and extremely dangerous too. They had large families to provide for, and slaves to feed, and they couldn't afford to slaughter their sheep or cattle for food. The farmers' families were dying of hunger left and right all the time, which was why they had to hunt hippos to keep body and soul together. Then they would come to the Castle for a permit to pass through the gate at Keert-de-Koe, and provided with that little scrap of paper four or six men would set out, with a barrel of wine, a half-muid of coarse salt and some empty vats on an ox wagon for the Berg River. Two slaves had to go with them, one leading the team, the other driving it with the whip. Apart from that the slaves had to yoke and unyoke, build branch shelters, graze the oxen, carry wood and water, cook, tend the wagon and gear, pitch the tents, and perform other tasks, like running messages back to town.

There is a lovely long valley that starts below the Paarl Rock and runs northward towards Riebeeck Kasteel, with an abundance of small game and occasionally even lions and elephants. In winter the river in the middle of the valley was full of water, and there were deep pools frequented by hippos. Winter was the time for hunting. The hippos used to graze in the long grass beside the river, and they were tame and fat. There the farmers would camp, and start to save their families from famine. Every day they would shoot one or two hippos, cut up the carcasses and salt away the blubber and meat. They roasted and ate the succulent meat and marrow, and drank wine, studying through their pipe smoke the high mountains on the opposite side of the valley, looking for breaches where a man might get through with a wagon and slaves to the next hunting ground, once the game was depleted here. That was the way to hunt hippos. Once the licence period was over, you prepared to go back. When the hippo pools were empty, or the ground became so soaked with blood that it began to attract lions, and if you still had time left on your ticket, you got the slaves to shift the wagon further north, to the next pool.

The Koina living in those parts were subjects of Ngonnemoa. They subsisted on milk, and sometimes at a transition feast they would eat meat. Only very rarely did they kill a hippo. One reason was that their assegais did not penetrate more than a hand's breadth into the skin;

they didn't kill. There were also Sonqua, the Bushmen, who didn't herd cattle or sheep but lived on venison. They would shoot a hippo with poisoned arrows and then camp beside the meat until it was finished. They were the ones who complained to Ngonnemoa that the Dutch were now killing the last hippo. One wagon after the after was coming this way; they shot until the moon changed, and when they left the pools were empty. What were the Bushmen supposed to live on? And Ngonnemoa agreed, because he'd been present when van Riebeeck had said the Dutch needed the Liesbeeck valley to survive, and had made them drink brandy and arrack from a pot until they threw up. Now they wanted to drive their pegs in here too, and kill all the game with their shooting. What about tomorrow?

Gerrit Cloete, Hendrik and Ockert Olivier went to the Fort with their empty hands to complain about how Ngonnemoa had treated them. Deneyn had to take down their statements. The first day, they'd just barely shot when the bloody Hottentots came across the river with forty or fifty spearmen and took away their muskets, powder, lead, tobacco, oxen and harnesses, even their pot of rice from the fire. They had a dog, which they'd borrowed from Gys Verwey, and Ngonnemoa had said to them: 'Look here,' and stabbed the dog to death. Then he said in Dutch: 'Dutchman, one word, *kalem. Kelem.*' Those were his exact words, which meant: Shut up, or we'll cut your throats. And they took the axle-pin thongs from the wheels and cut them to pieces and said: 'Now walk back to your homes.' That was what Ngonnemoa had done to them.

Governor Goske had been appointed over the Cape for the duration of the war, the first to carry the grand title of Governor. Goske wanted to send some of his garrison or his burgher militia against Ngonnemoa. The burgher militia now comprised three companies of almost a hundred men, and they were skilled and well trained with their muskets, a pleasure to behold on parade. Goske often stood at the edge of the parade ground to watch the burghers while they trained, and then smiled, thinking: I am a privileged man. Here I am looking at troops that will become famous in the world. Even the Prussians won't stand up to the children of these men. He wanted to send the burgher militia against the Cochoqua, but Lords Seventeen told him to avoid actions against the Cape aborigines and concentrate on building the Castle and protecting the Cape against the European foe. But Goske couldn't ignore this insult of the Company's subjects by the natives. There were even firearms in the hands of the natives now, and bartered cattle could no longer be expected from Koina in the Peninsula, or from Ngonnemoa. For draught oxen he would have to turn to friendly Captain Klaas, far across the mountain in the east. He told the Council: If a criminal sees that he can get away with something, he will do it a second time. Ngonnemoa had to be repaid with war for his arrogance when the time was right. There would be a second occasion, and if there wasn't, it could be arranged.

Goske started by imposing his authority on the neighbouring Koina. According to their custom, Captain Schacher and his leading men came to meet the new *souri* and share a glass with him, but Goske sent his servant to inform them that they were shameless beggars and shouldn't waste his time. Next he sent his fiscal and two burgher councillors to Captains Kuiper and Schacher in the nearby Tygerberg, to order them out of those valleys and to stay away from them in future, as the fiscal had assured the governor: 'We possess the legal title deeds to those parts.' When Schacher's people brought twenty sheep to barter a few days after his first visit to Goske, the governor kept them waiting while he attended church twice that Sunday and afterwards inspected the parade. Late in the afternoon he sent a message postponing the transaction to the next day, and then he sent them home on the pretext that their sheep were too thin. From that they could see whom they had to deal with, and to what nation the Cape now belonged.

The letters from Lords Seventeen were heavy with bad news. The enemy were advancing in the fatherland, from town to town. Several cities were occupied by French forces; their troops were billeted with townspeople. Surrounding farms were stripped bare. Only the intense cold, the rain and the muddy roads prevented the enemy from moving faster. At sea the English had the upper hand with their endless numbers of ships and sailors, while the fatherland was already calling on its last reserves. Extensions to the fleet had been neglected by the national authorities, and as a result the French were ensconced in the country while the English dominated the sea. Such were the fruits of negligence. Out of panic and distress the Dutch tore the councillor de Wit and his brother limb from limb with their bare hands, a hundred and seventy-one pieces all told, and their remains were strung up in a tree by their heels. That was fear, in its most hideous form. It was becoming clear that mastery at sea was the major prize of the war. Control of the North Alantic Ocean would ensure power in the East. Were the Dutch to lose the East, they would be losing the bread on their tables.

Governor Goske's reaction to the bad news was to order his officers and artisans to accelerate even more their building on the Castle. It was as if he wanted to pull that new fortress upward from the ground with his bare hands, the way a sail is hauled on to a yard. And could the Cape support itself with bread and other food during a war? For this purpose twenty soldiers were dispatched to occupy the green hills and cool valleys of Hottentots-Holland, construct a posthouse there and plough fields for wheat along the river.

'We possess the legal title deeds to it all,' Deneyn repeated with conviction.

A survey was made of how much wheat, rye, oats and barley every free farmer had sown and how much he expected to harvest. A census was held under martial law. The fisherman who had the monopoly to catch fish in the mouth of the Salt River had the audacity to play the clown.

'How can I tell you what I'm going to catch next year?' he told the clerk. 'Step into the sea, and ask the fishes which of them are planning to take the bait next year.' Then Deneyn personally explained the matter to him, telling him that his privilege was being suspended, and that the Company was taking his hired servant back. This was how the Castle was now controlling the people.

Think of the Castle first, was Goske's message to employees, freemen, wood gatherers, all. Always the Castle first. He placed the oldest slaves of the lodge and Indian exiles who were good for nothing else in a team of workers under a corporal to gather shells in the bays behind Lion's Head, for lime. From the beach at the dunes round

boulders were transported to the Castle. The Company hired thirty
Koina, from those lying about idle at the Castle gate, to carry building lime and stones and hoist them up the scaffolding. They were paid
with two meals of rice per day, and tobacco and arrack in the afternoon to lure them back the following day.

During that time Deneyn reported another curious thing. He
attended an autopsy on a sail-maker who had fallen to his death off the
jetty while half drunk. It was ordinary low tide, witnesses reported.
The man had walked off the edge and fell on hard sand at the bottom.
How were shell boats and loaded stone boats to get alongside at low
tide? People who had been at the Cape for ten or fifteen years showed
him the dunes in the south and east, stripped bare for the Company's
lime kilns, and the clouds of white sand that blew from there into the
bay. Each dune had a flowing white mane in the strong summer wind.
It was not that the quay had become too short; the beach had become
wider, the bay was shallower than ever. The Castle stood further away
from the sea.

So the Castle with its unappeasable hunger for fuel and timber was
beginning to gnaw at the land. One day it would start gnawing at the
Company itself; Saturn devouring its own children, the present gnawing
at the future, the beginning gnawing at the end. But think about the
Castle first of all. Now the quay had to be lengthened. The beams had
to be brought from Hout Bay by sea. Teams of axemen were sent into
the old yellow-wood forest at Hout Bay to cut firewood for the lime
kilns and long beams for the jetty. Every two or three days, without
interruption, a hooker or a flute brought the logs and fuel from Hout
Bay, and laid it at the Castle's feet, as if on an altar.

Ships, outward or homeward bound, arriving at the anchorage, had
to provide boats and men to collect shells and slate from the island,
for this Castle. They were also obliged to send soldiers and sailors
for labour on shore. If a ship's captain refused, Goske pressed the
Artikebrief in his hand, and threatened to remove his ship from under
his backside. A team of thirty sailors from *Hasenberg* with good seaman-
ship and common sense hauled a flagpole and a cannon up Lion's
Head, and planted them up there. From then on, lookouts, so-called

sea-watchmen, had to climb the steep rock every day to stand watch on the top. In this way all the Cape was entrusted to these sea-watchers.

While subjects and slaves hauled the Castle up from the soil with their bare hands, troops with muskets and field cannon drilled on the even patch between the Fort and the Castle. Both tasks had to be done, both were important. Twenty-five sailors from *Saxenburg* were sent to construct a redoubt for four cannon at the small bay behind the Green Point. The Cape burgher council offered to build a similar one for four cannon on the foundations of the former Duynhoop redoubt. It became a race: the burghers against the sailors. Both were finished in fourteen days, but the green branches were first hoisted over the burgher redoubt, and there the victory was celebrated with farm wine. Goske made ample provision for festivities at the sailor redoubt. When later in the war the farmers were commandeered to stand guard at Burgher Redoubt at night, they changed its name to Farmers' Regret.

When Goske wanted the admiration of his troops, or wished to placate them when they became restless, he improved their liquor rations. He had some old stock slaughtered, ordered four leaguers of strong beer to be brewed, and threw a happy day for one-half of the garrison in the kraal behind the Fort, where they could feast and entertain themselves with all kinds of tomfoolery until dusk. In addition, each man received a *muts* of arrack as a nightcap before tattoo. Then Goske would be everybody's hero again. The singing at the bonfires soared up to heaven. The next day the other half of the garrison, the boat crews and the outposts, were granted their happy day.

'Just turn a blind eye today, *meester*,' Goske told Deneyn. They stood on the wall watching the soldiers in the kraal sing and carouse and beat one another's teeth out over the graves of companions who had recently been laid to rest there. Turn a blind eye, Lord, Deneyn thought, as if in prayer, it is all for this Castle of Good Hope. My hands are covered in blood. I work with blood; it is the red stream that makes my mill-wheel turn.

His contribution to the war against France and England was that he did his work diligently and precisely. He could help to win the war in a courtroom, he believed, and he made sure that heavy punishments were inflicted. The land was ruled by martial law, the Company needed labourers, and within the framework of the law he could provide them. He had no wish to be a schoolmaster with a lesson attached to every sentence, but he could make a worthwhile contribution to the war effort. On one day he imposed the following sentences: Jan van Nes, for stabbing with a knife: keelhauled thrice, loss of six months' wages, and one year of hard labour in chains on the island. Dirk Lubreght, for manslaughter: to stand blindfolded on the scaffold, having a shot fired over his head, loss of six months' wages, and five years' labour in chains on the island. Barent Jongman, for hitting back at his captain: a thrashing, keel-hauled thrice, loss of six months' wages, and three years' labour on the island. Paul Bernardi, for insulting a burgher councillor: blindfolded on the scaffold, a shot fired over his head, loss of six months' wages, and five years' labour in chains on the island. Cornelis Potman, for manslaughter in self-defence: death by firing squad, and in mitigation to be buried immediately. Steven Botma, in whose tavern the manslaughter occurred, loss of his liquor licence.

On 1 January 1673 Skipper Freyn and the officers of the flute *Helena* were given a send-off to fetch lime and ebony beams from Mauritius, which the Castle was waiting for. At dinner that evening Goske said he had no doubt that Commander Hugo had already made a big difference to that island, and everybody was looking forward to Freyn's return with a cargo of good news for the Honourable Company. For Deneyn, there was a fleeting memory of the commander's fair daughter. He had really enjoyed her company. As a pretext to join her on Mauritius, he might propose that it was time for the island's judicial procedure and documents to be inspected, for which he would be just the right person. But not yet, for as long as the Castle needed him here.

And for Goske it was good news when in that same month there came a message from friendly Captain Klaas across the mountains in the east that all the Hottentots in the world, that was to say those of Ngonnemoa and those from Saldanha and all in the peninsula, were waging war against his Chainouqua, because he was still trading with the Company. The Ngonnemoas were even carrying muskets, and they had stolen most of his people's women and all his livestock. He wanted the Company to confiscate their muskets. Now Goske saw his chance for retribution against Ngonnemoa, and he sent Sergeant Croese with six soldiers against him. Only six: not too few, not too many; the number had to stir up just the right thoughts in Ngonnemoa, and Croese was by far the coarsest of his sergeants.

Croese found the Ngonnemoas beyond the Berg River. He accused Ngonnemoa of being a troublemaker and a thief, and demanded all firearms. But Ngonnemoa brought only one musket; it was all he had, he said. He had received it from a burgher in exchange for an ox. It was such a fat, ugly ox, he said, while his people burst out laughing, and the burgher had slaughtered and pickled the unwieldy beast. So Croese came back with one musket and a mocking message, and information Goske was eager to have: there were some four thousand cattle grazing under Ngonnemoa, and a few thousand sheep.

After Croese's visit to the Cochoqua, livestock in the care of farm herders were stolen away and several farmhouses were burnt down in quick succession, as if the same hand was responsible for it. In one of the fires a farmer's wife died. Everybody knew it was Ngonnemoa's doing. Goske still waited.

He asked Deneyn: 'The last time our people caught the five Gonnemans red-handed, they were sent to the island. And they escaped. If it's a capital offence, we must punish them with death. An eye for an eye.'

'I cannot confirm it, Your Honour. Justice must be done.'

'Then I take it upon myself.'

At Postkeeper Raling's request, Deneyn had visited Robben Island in the flowering season, as Eva needed to speak to him. He asked Long Gert and Sofia whether they thought P'nel might want to see her mother. Both of them said that Pieternella was a very sensible child. If she wished to speak to her mother, she could certainly do so. Pieternella was eager to go. She would like to take her mother some clothes and soap and perhaps buttermilk. And her mother would wish to see Salomon.

'That is fine,' said the fiscal. 'Ask Aunt Sofia to help you.'

'We don't have money.'

'I shall pay for it.'

The three of them made the crossing in a shell sloop, together with a surgeon. Deneyn said to Pieternella: 'The surgeon and I will speak to your mother first, and afterwards the two of you.'

It was spring on the island. The plain behind the dunes was covered with white and yellow flowers. Postkeeper Raling was glad to see the children, and to have an opportunity for sharing a glass with visitors in the morning. He had become indolent and fat since Deneyn had last seen him, and his hair and beard were long and unkempt. He met them at the landing place and walked before them over the dunes and the dusty scrub to the posthouse. The house was dilapidated, the thatched roof tattered, and on the south side a sandbank had blown up as high as the window sill.

Raling took arrack and three chipped glasses from a cupboard.

'What can you offer the children, postkeeper?'

'I wasn't expecting them, *meester*. And their mother's cow has died. What about tea?'

'What about tea, P'nel, Salomon? With sugar cubes, postkeeper.' Deneyn enquired about the convict numbers, their clothing and rations, their conduct. For how long would the supply of shells still last? For how long would the slate quarry last? When the children went outside, he asked: 'What is wrong with Mrs van Meerhof? What does she want?'

'She is close to her time, and the English disease is ravaging her. Her room is reeking with it.'

'Has she shaken off the liquor?'

'Yes, as far as I know.'

'And more reasonable in her speech?'

'She is more reasonable.'

'And the old slave woman?'

'She doesn't want to work with the woman. Most of the time she is outdoors. She sleeps in the woodshed.'

'Is she doing her work?'

'Yes, that she is, but Eva has been bedridden for some time now. It's a mess. She's rotting like a Portuguese fo'c'sle.'

'Do you think the children can see her today?'

'I wouldn't if they were my children.'

To Pietcrnella, Deneyn said: 'I'm going to see how it is with your mother. Put your things here on the table, and stay with the post-keeper.'

In Eva's room Deneyn opened the door and window to let in some air and light. The place was putrid from her illness and her unwashed body, and untidy. Her face, arms, hands were covered in sores. The surgeon walked around Eva's bed, pressed his thumb against the soft flesh of her upper arm and pointed at the dent it made.

'Dropsy, fiscal. And eight or nine months pregnant too. And the English disease. Can you see the red flames here inside her elbows and in the corners of her mouth? Look at the eyelids, the nose, the lips.'

'How far is the disease?'

'If you care to turn your back, I shall have a look. Mrs van Meerhof, I have to examine you. Will you cooperate, please?'

Deneyn asked over his shoulder: 'How far is the dropsy?'

'Too far. If I have to drain off water, her constitution won't bear it. Think of her child. All right, Mrs van Meerhof. It's done.' He poured water in the ewer, washed his hands and patted his palms dry against the legs of his breeches.

Deneyn straightened the blankets around Eva. 'What is it you wish to tell me?'

She groaned, exhaling revolting fumes over him. 'You must give my child to Maijke to bring up if I die.'

'I shall find out from the Council.' But of course he would propose that they turn it down, with sound reasons. So he already knew what the Council would say.

'If I live, I want to go to shore to have the child baptised.'

'When are you expecting it?'

'In two weeks.'

'I shall discuss it with the governor and the *dominee*. Is there anything else?'

'What does the child of a mother with the English disease look like, *meester*? Is there any hope?'

'Is there hope for any of us?' he asked bitterly. Then he regretted what he'd said. 'Look, I brought Pieternella and Salomon with me. They would like to see you.'

Eva started up in fright. 'Let them stay at the door,' she groaned.

The surgeon had a few phials in his chest for her. 'Something for the stomach. Something for the kidneys. All pregnant women need it.' He showed her how to use them. 'I shall ask for a midwife to visit you, Mrs van Meerhof. She could stay here for a few days if the authorities are willing.'

'Good,' said the fiscal. 'The Company will pay. Have you finished here then, surgeon? Please ask the children to come.'

He went outside with the surgeon. 'What does the child of a mother with the English disease look like?'

'It depends on how badly the mother is affected. The child is born with it, and usually does not survive. You cannot treat a newly-born with mercury. Don't let the children touch her, *meester*. Kiss her face, that kind of thing.'

The children stood crying in the door, barely an arm's length from their mother. Eva sobbed, groaned. Deneyn put Pieternella's parcel in Eva's hand.

'How beautiful my children look,' she said. 'Where is Kobus?' While she unfolded the small bundle with fingers swollen like sausages, Deneyn explained about the boy's apprenticeship.

'Yes,' said Eva. 'You're planning things for him again.'

Pieternella told her about the schooling.

'Now where did you find this?' asked Eva, taking a dress from the bundle.

'I sewed on the buttons myself, and we adjusted it, Aunt Sofia and I.'

'Who's paying?'

'It comes from Jan Vos's slave money.' That was how the fiscal had prompted her.

'Come closer, let me touch you.' But Deneyn held the children back.

'I'm going to have another baby, Pieternel.'

The children stared dumbstruck at their mother's sores.

'You must come when I have it christened.'

They didn't know what she meant. Deneyn smiled at Pieternella. 'They are in church every Sunday, Mrs van Meerhof.'

The child, if it survived, was to be a burden on their fund. Deneyn had decided not to remind the woman to have a will drawn up. He would have her certified as incapable. That would be better. He would take care of P'nel's affairs himself.

On a Thursday at the end of September the child was baptised in Deneyn's office. They were brought on the first shell boat that morning, and returned to the island on the last boat in the afternoon. Eva gave up the name as Anthonie, and because the father was unknown, it was registered as Anthonie Evasz. In the books of the Church Council it later became Evertsz, and sometimes even Everaerts. The van Meerhof children were not told that their mother was in town.

In the autumn, some six months later, there was a small uprising among the convicts on the island. Deneyn went to inspect matters, to ensure that the supply of shells and slate would not be interrupted. It was a wet, windy day, and although he was thickly wrapped against the weather, he felt ill and cold. The island was totally repulsive to him. He first went to see Eva. She was in bed, and the old slave woman was holding the child on her lap, on a chair in the corner.

'How are you?' he asked. Eva said nothing. He asked the slave woman.

'This woman is very sick. This child is very sick.'

'Does the doctor come here with medicine?'

'He comes.'

'How are you?'

'I am sick. You must take me away.'

'What do you need, tobacco or sweet arrack?'

'I must get to a fire, but they don't have a fire for me. You must take me away.'

'You must help the woman.'

'I don't want this woman. I don't want this child. It is the child.'

'What about it?'

'The child cannot see.'

'Is that so?' He went to look. The child was sleeping. He asked Eva: 'Why didn't you tell me the child was blind?'

'The child was born like that. What can you do about it?'

'Do you nurse the child?'

'Yes.'

'Then it must stay.'

He spoke to the postkeeper about the quarrel among the convicts, and accompanied him to the shell banks, where 139 men had to shovel crushed shells into empty canvas bags and carry them on their shoulders across the island to the boats. Those who were aggrieved were leaning idly on their shovels. He could have them beaten on the spot, or he could take them to Goske to remove the grudge from them in more sophisticated ways.

'What is the matter?' he asked Raling in front of the convicts. 'Why are they not working?'

It was all about food. There were two camps among the convicts, those of Dutch blood and those of foreign blood. Now it appeared to those of foreign blood that the Dutch were receiving more rice than they. They had friends in the other group who confirmed it.

'Sergeant Raling, I want you to put a stop to this bloody nonsense,' Deneyn said aloud in front of the convicts. 'Make sure it stops, and don't interrupt the Company's work with such confounded nonsense again.'

That evening he sat in front of the fire in his room, disgruntled and alone, warmly wrapped against the early winter weather. He smoked and drank brandy, and wrote a poem about the island to while away the time. Drinking was becoming a habit without any pleasure here at the Cape. There were days when the island appeared quite attractive, but mostly it repelled him. Could that have harmed P'nel's spirit in some way? He had to tell her about her mother and her half-brother, he had to break the bad news to her in such a way that she wouldn't fret about it. If only he could get away to the East, or otherwise Europe.

When he went to Long Gert's house late that Saturday afternoon, he took her the poem. He sat with her and Pieter and his parents at the big table, and read it to them. He didn't ask them whether they understood what he read, but appreciated the smiles it elicited from Sofia and Long Gert.

'You don't seem to like my little poem, young lady. You ought to understand it; you lived there for such a long time. I went there yesterday to speak to the postkeeper and the convicts. Keep it, and read it again, if you feel like it. Perhaps our namesake Pieter can explain it to you. But there's something else I must tell you, P'nel. I visited your mother, there. She is still ill, and the baby is not well either. I just want to assure you that our surgeons will be doing their best. Please don't worry.'

'I shall explain the poem to you, Pieternel,' the boy said. 'It's easy to understand.' Deneyn was grateful for it.

The winter of 1673 was a difficult one for the fiscal. News and rumours of wars, and reports from distant battlefields arrived at the Castle, but the very sounds of war were heard in town. Every evening when the labourers handed in their tools, a soldier waved a red flag at the edge of the village. Then there would be loud explosions in the quarry in the hillside above the dunes to break loose rocks for the next day, and those who cared to could go and watch the cloud of dust and the flying stones. The noise shuddered through the town, and if the wind was slightly north – always a sign of rain – it sounded like the distant rattle of drums drifting over the houses with the smell of black powder like rotting cabbage. It was the smell and the sounds of Zwammerdam and Bodegraaf and other places where the prince was fighting for the freedom of their fatherland.

Another unusual phenomenon for the Cape was the blacks brought from the sea. Two hundred and forty Africans, meant for West India, were brought ashore from an English ship taken near St Helena Island, to help drag the Castle up from the ground. It was strange to see so many blacks, where they had been wholly unknown before; foreign here, like camels, like palm trees.

On the third of July the sea brought Willem Willemsz back and allowed him to come ashore, to present himself at Deneyn's office in the Fort. In his hand was a roll of parchment sealed with orange ribbon and black wax. Deneyn had him arrested before unrolling the document.

'That is not for you, fiscal,' said the Lyreman. 'It is for the governor.'

The seal in the wax was the lion of Orange. Amazed, Deneyn read the signature: *Guglielmus*. There was the signature, there the seal. The Prince of Orange had given the Lyreman royal pardon for the murder of the Hottentot. With the rolled parchment in his hand, and followed by the Lyreman between two soldiers, the fiscal crossed the courtyard and knocked on the governor's door.

Goske stared suspiciously at the seal and the signature. 'Forged, I'm sure. Lock him up, *Meester* Deneyn. And start writing in your Latin to inform His Highness what has been perpetrated in his name.'

It took him nearly a month: the interrogation of Willem Willemsz, new research into a matter long cold, the exposition of the Council's diplomatic quandary caused by the unusual circumstances and, finally, the courteous protocol rounded off with an elegant handwriting. Goske decided that Willemsz was to remain on Robben Island until there was a reply from the Netherlands, to prevent the Cape natives from think-ing that he had been set free, since the Koina never forgot anything. Hypocrite, thought Deneyn, he goes about free without asking what the natives had to say about it.

When Goske issued a hunting licence to Tielman Hendriksz and his companions, he advised them to form a strong group, so that Ngonnemoa would leave them in peace. Remember what happened to Cloete and Olivier; form a strong group. And that they were: Gys Verwey, Tielman Hendriksz, Hans Ras, Barend Gildenhuijs, Frans Schanfelaar, Wynand Bezuidenhout, Pieter de Noorman, another. Impossible to form a stronger fighting unit. The eight of them left for the Berg River in two wagons, up along the long valley between the mountains, past the Vogelvlei to the nearest pool where hippos had last been seen. First came rumours that they'd been surrounded by Gonjemans for a whole week, and then that all of them had been murdered there at the pool. Gonjemans, is what it says in the journal. First it was Ngonnemoa's people, then Gonnemans, now it was Gonjemans. And on the eleventh of that month a horseman arrived at the Fort to report that their jackal-torn bodies and the burnt-out wagons were strewn about on the spot.

In the evening Sergeant Croese left the Fort in overcast weather with seventy-two troops on horseback – half of them soldiers, the other half burghers – and a horse wagon with powder and provisions. The outriders carried torches in the hand, and they were going at a hard pace. Towards nine o'clock they arrived at Hoogekraal in the Tygerberg, and reached Captain Kuiper's kraal in the Koeberg when it was raining so hard that they couldn't move any further. In Kuiper's kraal Croese caught a Gonjeman whom he threatened with castration if he didn't lead them to Ngonnemoa. There the rain came down so hard that Croese distributed the powder, lead and flints, so that each man could keep his own things dry. Because of the torrential rain they were forced to spend two days between the Tygerberg and the Mosselbanks River, and on the fourteenth they camped at the Paardeberg. At that place Croese stood before his army under the flap of his tent to read from Goske's *Instructie*, which ordered them to ensure that the Gonjemans would be given a lesson their descendants would remember. Then Croese added: Here were two commanders, the burgher captain and himself, but there could be only one leader. If the joint forces agreed to name him as their chief, he would continue with his task. Once they had done that for him, he merely said: 'Keep your powder dry. I shall punish the man who cannot give fire.'

From there they trekked in the rain to Riebeeck Kasteel, and still in the rain to the Berg River. The river was in flood and almost a hundred muddy, rushing paces wide. They pitched camp, and built a raft, and crossed the river with all their possessions on the morning of the sixteenth. Then Burgher Lieutenant Diemer arrived on the far bank with eighteen more men. Croese called a halt, while the raft was rowed back to collect Diemer and his men. He had bad news. Two days earlier the Saldanha boat *Bruid* had brought in the only surviving soldier from the outpost of Saldanha Bay. They had been attacked by Koina at the posthouse. Four men were stabbed to death, and he was the only one who could swim out to the fishermen's boat to save his life. The posthouse had been plundered and burned to the ground.

The guide, at the end of a thong tied to Croese's horse, led the augmented army to Sonquas Drift, where the horses splashed girth-deep through water, and then on to the Vierentwintigriviere, or Twenty-Four Rivers. It took them a full day to cross all the streams. There the rain stopped. Croese forbade them to make fire, which meant one more plain meal of brandy, dried meat and rusks. And in the twilight they could see smoke rising at the Moeras River, directly under the mountain.

Their attack began in overcast conditions soon after first light. The Gonjemans were camped about a mile ahead of them, in a patch of dry thorns. The morning fires were burning there, and the livestock would soon be driven out. They led their horses closer, behind a low ridge from which the guide could see the campfires. There they mounted to the saddles, and charged at Croese's command. As the horsemen topped the ridge, the Gonjemans flung open gates and took flight with people and stock. At the sound of the first shots they abandoned a small flock of sheep to slow down the army, followed by a few head of cattle some distance further on. By that time the Hottentots in the van had reached the foothills. Croese brought his army to a halt and called them together to collect the cattle and sheep. They took the stock back to Sonquas Drift and crossed there, and on the way they were to shoot the wounded Hottentots scattered in the veld.

They made slow progress with the stock across that heavy veld. The Gonjemans came back out of the mountain, waylaid the livestock, shooting arrows and hurling assegais from the front and the flanks, which caused the cattle to turn, mill about in panic, break away and scatter in all directions through vleis and streams. The horsemen broke rank to head off the cattle in one place and help companions in another, which gave the Koina an opportunity of moving in among them. They had to load and fire, load and fire, leaving the cattle for the time being to run away into the rain.

It was eight o'clock and pitch dark by the time they reached the deserted Gonjemanskraal with the remaining animals. Then, for the first time in days, they made fire from the wood the Koina had kept dry in a hut, and cooked their food. But there was little sleep that night; the guards stood two by two in a circle around the camp, being relieved every half-hour. And it was barely light when they had to saddle up again, swallow their breakfast, and after their brief parade and morning prayer, start driving cattle, after setting fire to the kraal behind them.

Soon the Gonjemans were back in force around them. But, obviously, they were fatigued. Their numbers had been weakened, and they had few spears left. Even so they managed from time to time to cut out an ox. While crossing the Vierentwintigriviere, Croese suffered particularly heavy losses of sheep and lambs, as the streams were deep and the horsemen had to dismount to follow the sheep on foot through the marshes, and as soon as the flock stampeded, the Koina caught up to scatter the horses and cattle. At dusk they were at Sonquas Drift, and pitched their camp on the river bank. There was no dry wood to be found, and throughout the night they stood a double row of guards: the inner row around the cattle and horses, and the outer around the camp.

When at daybreak the first horsemen rode down the steep river bank to lead the procession, some Koina leaped from under the bank to stab at the horses above them. It turned into a wild, splashing, foaming crossing. Croese drove them on from behind at speed, so that they could get out from among the bushes and bulrushes and from the water. There was shouting and firing, and the livestock caused an unearthly din. On the plains at the other side of the river, the enemy closed in on the rearguard, causing the army to turn and form front, and fire three volleys at them. There seemed to be no end to the pursuit of the Gonjemans. Soon afterwards it started raining again; softly at first, but after a few loud thunderclaps it fell down icily and heavily like a breaking wave, so that it was impossible for anyone to use a musket. And the cattle stumbled and fell in the mud from exhaustion. Those that fell had to be left behind while the remainder were driven on, against wind and hail, as fighting man to man against the Koina was no longer possible.

For two days and two nights the rain continued unabated, and then one morning they found themselves in bright sunshine at Hoogekraal, where a wagon with two bags of biscuit and a barrel of arrack had been waiting for them in a barn for a week. When the sun went down behind the island that evening, the army was back at the Fort with eight hundred cattle and nine hundred sheep.

Goske announced that any Hottentot seen with a spear would be regarded as an enemy and shot on sight without exception.

'They also carry spears in self-defence, Your Honour,' Deneyn ventured. 'Against lions and leopards. Apart from that, there is war among the tribes. I doubt whether your proclamation is legal, and would like to request advice on it from the Netherlands.'

Was it war? Deneyn wondered, but without feeling any guilt about his complicity in the crime. How could one justify Croese's expedition? Wars were declared through the exchange of official notes between governments, and in this case the Netherlands had descended to the level of the savages, responding to robbery with massacre. Who had decided on stock theft?

There was nothing in the Council's minutes about that. The crime committed could become genocide within weeks, because the Koina depended for their lives on the products of their livestock, and now Ngonnemoa's people and their children would be left without food in the heart of the winter. Or, was genocide Goske's real intention? He would deny it, that was to be expected. Why had he issued the hunting licences after being warned to maintain the existing contract with the natives? He would say: The Company has carried out punitive expeditions in East India before this; Governor-General Coen's rape of Banda Island is my example. Or he would say: We have martial law in the land. But martial law applied to the states of England and France, and Lords Seventeen had requested him to avoid clashes with the indigenous peoples. Deneyn was convinced that there were serious grounds for a judicial inquiry against the governor.

'*Meester* Deneyn, I take it upon myself.' That was Goske: strike first and then take cover behind his rank.

With so many new widows suddenly at the Cape, Deneyn helped to found the Cape Orphan Chamber, and had a large chest with iron fittings made to be placed in the front porch of the ark, in which people could put their spare coins. He also had the fund and account of Pieternella and her brothers transferred from the Church Council to the new Orphan Chamber.

The Captains Schacher and Kuiper and friendly Klaas from behind the mountains to the east now all turned against Ngonnemoa, as they were afraid that Ngonnemoa's war against the Dutch might affect them and destine them for annihilation. For that was what Goske intended, they believed. Rather hide, like chickens under the wings of the hen, when the falcons were about. About a month after Croese's orgy of robbery and murder Kuiper and Schacher and about a hundred of their followers arrived at the Fort with four Gonjemans, caught spying on their kraals. Now they brought the four men for the governor to determine their fate. Goske summoned the fiscal, but Deneyn recused himself. The case was beyond the scope of his knowledge and experience, and clearly mattered only among the natives.

'I take it upon myself,' said the governor.

In the presence of Schacher and Kuiper, Goske had the four interrogated by interpreters, and persuaded two of them to confess that at the Moordkuil and also at Saldanha they had acted illegally against the Company. Then Goske told Kuiper and Schacher: 'Well, you brought the men here. They admit their guilt. I don't want to interfere in your matters, so I am handing them back to you to be punished by their own people. Take them outside and do with them as you think fit.'

Goske had Deneyn called from his room. 'Before the guilty are executed, I want to know whether in your capacity as fiscal you wish to say anything against it.'

'I'm telling you that I doubt if it is legal. They do not belong among us. I regard these prisoners as soldiers like ours, who carry out the orders of their superiors, and not as criminals. Have you had witnesses and interpreters sworn in?'

'Then I take it upon myself. And if you wish to learn something about justice in Africa, then come to the wall with me and observe from up there.'

What Deneyn observed from the wall, was the slow, deliberate beating to death of four men by strangers who had nothing to lose or to gain from it, with sticks somewhat thicker and barely any longer than his own cane. This was illegal, was his first thought; the men had been sentenced to death, but not to torture. He believed that an executioner at an execution had no grudge against his victim but was merely trying to earn his bread. On the beach before the gate a hundred or more executioners were playing cat and mouse with the condemncd. They made mock charges against unarmed people; they whistled and waved their sticks in a circular dance, leaped into the circle one by one, dealing light blows to ankles and elbows, which hurt, but without drawing blood. Or they would aim at a knee and then strike a crushing blow against the head, or four or five of them would concentrate their blows only on the kidneys, or only on the nose. They danced and strutted, and skulked about; they stared the victim right in the eyes and struck at his genitals. Together they would cheer at a good blow, stop to rest, and when they got tired they would withdraw to drink water, and return to the ring with a swagger, drawing the process out for more than an hour, until Goske, white in the face, brought his cane rattling down on the rail of the battlement, shouting at them to get it over with in the name of the Devil.

'Now they're killing for their pleasure, *Meester* Deneyn. That is why I think nothing of these savages and their so-called indigenous justice. Do you still want to go on watching? I'm tired of it.' So they went down. In the courtyard Goske ordered the officer of the guard to have the corpses dragged by a rowing boat to the outer anchorage, and to make sure that each of the natives was given a good draught of arrack at the kitchen door. 'Do you want to summon such as these before a court of the fatherland, *Meester* Deneyn? Revolting people.'

In the absence of intelligent company that evening Deneyn described the killings in his diary. The men had been tortured for an hour before they were released by death. The Dutch style of execution was supposed to set an example to others, it had to contain an element of deterral, but what example was set when a condemned man was rewarded with death? It is much better, he wrote, to sacrifice healthy people to the Castle, so that they could help with building rather than fill a hole in the sand with their maimed bodies.

That was what Fiscal Deneyn did. He studied every case. He consulted the notebooks from his undergraduate years for guidance. It was easy to say: My book knows nothing about slaves; my book makes no mention of Hottentots; my book doesn't know about Goske; my book has no knowledge of a commercial company that holds the world by the throat; my book says nothing about a castle which has to be dragged upward from the arid dunes with force and bare hands. It was easy to find excuses for himself. Reading his old books, looking at his student's notes with a sketch of a gallows to warn himself of a pending examination, and the names of girls scribbled next to examples of important trials he was supposed to look up, he would tell himself: The book speaks only of my youth in Western Europe. I cannot see anything which could help me here. This is the Cape; I am trapped and banished on a barren island; here I stand alone, I have no guide or guidance.

Then the thought occurred to him: he would like to return to the university now to tell the students: 'Wait. Watch out. What your professors are telling you, what you read here in books, looks different outside the city walls of Leiden, different in a storm at sea, different in Africa, different in a barracks in the East.' And were they to answer: 'What must we do? Can you offer us any advice?' then he would have to say that he didn't know, he was merely trying his best in the place where he found himself.

Deneyn was a prisoner of that Castle. It was a wet, wet, wet winter, that first one of his imprisonment. The great kilns were rained out, the builders on the scaffolding pushed wheelbarrows filled with mud, it was getting dangerous on the wet planks. The grumbling became worse, louder, open. The people were cold and ill, and looking for shelter against the heavy rain. And the corporals with the canes were scared to touch them. Four slaves deserted. Two of them were the Company's property. Late one day they sheltered against the rain in an extinguished lime kiln, failing to come out again when the others returned to their work. When night had fallen properly, they slipped out and fled up the coast. The other two slaves belonged to Broertjie Louw. It was impossible to understand why they should have deserted, as they never worked harder or for longer hours than Louw himself, they slept more than nature required, and ate at his table with him and his children. Deneyn was unable to find any extenuating circumstances for those four, and he asked for them to be hanged. Their bodies were dragged through the town by donkeys as a warning to slaves, and then hoisted up again at the dunes as an example to the Company's seafaring men.

A few weeks later five white soldiers appeared before the court of justice. They were deserters. According to martial law they were to be hanged, and Deneyn knew that the governor wanted an example to restore discipline, but this time he pleaded for only the leader to be hanged. The Council accepted. Perhaps they were becoming worried about those men they had forced to draw lots, on Goske's instigation, for life or death. Therefore Jan Niels was to be hanged alone for desertion. His four companions would witness his execution from under the gallows, with the ropes around their necks; after that they were flogged and sent to Robben Island to labour in chains for six years. The same day Deneyn sent a sailor who had stolen a half-*aum* of arrack to the island, also to labour for six years in chains. The crime was not so serious — sailors inherited the need for alcohol from their ancestor Noah — but someone had to pay for Jan Niels's solitude before he'd been pushed from the ladder. The winter of 1673 continued until the whole place was practically under water. The veld was shimmering with vleis and pans, the frogs were croaking by day, and the Liesbeeck came down so strongly that one could haul fresh water from the outer anchorage. The clumps of rushes it dragged down to the sea took root on the far side of the island.

Late in November Captain Klaas and twenty of his Chainouqua turned up at the Fort with a gift of fat cows, to enquire whether he should remain at hand for the joint attack on Ngonnemoa which Goske had talked about earlier, or whether he could move back to his Overberg territory. What mischief was to come out of this? Deneyn wondered, because the Gonjemans had not done anything wrong lately, and in fact had not been heard of in months. But Goske told Klaas: All right, you may start reconnoitring. Following that signal other tribes also began to move closer, like chickens around a hen. Kuiper and Houtebeen settled down so close to the Ruiterwacht that Corporal Visser had to order them further away.

And in the name of what justice did a governor plan a raid on the cattle of a broken people, or punish a widow for stealing two ewes? Deneyn felt sorry for the old woman who was brought before him. She stared at him like a dazed sheep. There was nothing he could do for her. Everywhere there were people who refused to learn, and she was one of them. He requested the Council this time to take into consideration all Maijke Hendriksz's previous contraventions and sentences in order to determine her punishment, and not to accept any plea in mitigation. The Council agreed. They remembered the previous occasion, not so long before, when they had tried to give her a serious warning against theft. At the time her husband had still been alive, but she shouldn't think that her widow's cap and black dress now raised her above the law. She and her farmhand Philip Builings, and through them the whole of the Cape community to whom they were to set an example, had to feel once again the heartless, icy weight of the law.

Builings was the first man ever to be banished to the island for life. Few people were aware of that, few knew Builings, few felt sorry for him, and he was forthwith forgotten. On the island he became but a single shell gatherer, of which the Company needed hundreds. Maijke and her farmhand were both sentenced first to stand on the ladder under the gallows for an hour, with a chain on the leg, the gallows rope around the neck and a sheepskin nailed above the head. After that they were both flogged at the stake, branded behind the shoulder, and sentenced to labour for life on the island. The property of both was confiscated by the state. When ordered to sign her sentence, Maijke wrote with trembling hand her baby name Maja, as if she were once again six years old. After his punishment had been administered, Builings was taken to the island, but the widow was allowed some months to arrange her affairs.

What else? Hendrik Evertsen accused Catharina Kients, Pieter Visagie's wife, of slandering him by spreading a story that *he* had been the one who'd reported Maijke's theft. He demanded a public apology from Visagie. Deneyn had to enforce it. Visagie's argument was: What man can control his wife's tongue?

In January 1674 the flute *Helena* arrived in the roadstead, after a year's absence. Where in the blue world had this ship been, and what had its people lived through? What had the sea done to them, and what did their arrival mean to those living under Table Mountain? One could see smiles on the faces of the first seamen arriving at the quay. Their ship's hull was overgrown with the luxuriant seaweed of tropical waters, and their faces brown from the tropical sun, but why were they laughing? Was it caused by thoughts of the East behind them, or the Cape before them?

For Deneyn there was a letter from Mauritius, from Mary Hugo. His heart felt warm when he saw his own name in her handwriting on it. He had never expected to hear from her. Her image and her voice were still clear in his mind. What could her letter mean? Was it merely loneliness? He sat at the table in the cabin of the flute *Helena* at the inner anchorage, together with Captain Frooij and the Fort's surgeon. From ship's mugs they gulped rations-brandy mixed with Cape rainwater. Their enquiries into the health of the crew had been made, the flute's waybill compared with the contents of the hold, the inspection of the ship's journal completed. On deck, above their heads, the tops and yards were lowered to the deck to be repaired and cleaned after a journey of seventy days with dull sounds of thuds and cracks.

'One thing,' said Frooij. 'Commander Hugo's letter reports that I have Philipe Col on board. Col is not on board. Let the governor tell you what that letter says, *Meester* Deneyn.'

'That's all right.'

'I have a packet of letters for you from Mary Hugo. She made me swear with tears on her cheeks, Fiscal Deneyn, with tears on her cheeks, to give it into your hands. There you have it. Here is my witness.'

'Captain Frooij, what are you worried about? Is something wrong?'

'Not a word, *meester*. It's your business.'

'But with tears, can it be so bad? Surely she has her father, if she is in trouble?'

'No, *meester*. No, *meester*. Come, drink up. I have to go on deck.'

He carried her letters in his coat pocket. Of course he was anxious to read them, but he kept them for later when he would be alone, and the anticipation sweetened the pleasure. He would love to hear how she was faring on the Cape's other island. He had hoped for a few words of friendship, perhaps a sign of something personal between them, but he had a vague hunch that she might have something like jewels to sell, and wanted him to be so kind as to allow Captain Frooij to trade on her behalf. Obviously Goske was not to hear about that. That was what Deneyn supposed, but his heart was young enough to hope to the very end that she would remember him for something pleasant, and perhaps be prompted by loneliness to exchange a few words with him as a friend. But he could not calm his fear, because there had been a hint of disaster in Frooij's voice.

There was not only one letter, but five or six. The top one, thirty pages long, was to him. For the moment he put the attachments aside. Her handwriting was large and unformed, her spelling simplified: *Your honnour de Neijn, you will find it strange that I rite to you* . . . He turned over a few pages. Somewhere in the middle his eyes caught the words '*where are the promises he made me if I went with him to mouerisius?*' and followed them to the end of the line. That was how she wrote the name of the island, '*mouerisius*': *Oh mouerisius, mouerisius, I pitty myself that I ever set foote on you.* Later he was struck by the words *recquest from someone who onse was your frende.* Again he paged on and on until he reached the end: *Have pitty on a pore womman who is saddened unto dethe.*

Then Deneyn swung his legs from the bed and started reading, holding her letter close to the candle.

Your honnour de Neijn, you will find it strange that I rite to you, but I am driven by distres. I beg you on my nees and with tears in my eyes please to helpe me. Show pitty to a womman who is sad unto dethe. I want to declare befor the worlde and will dye my dethe upon it that it is true. I am not writing to accuse my father, but to liten my consins of the iniustis he did to Pier Fieleep Col on my behalffe. All I aske is that you kepe my leter and not showe it to my father.

Her fear was evident, but why was she concerned about Col, and what kind of relationship could have existed between them for an injustice to be done to him on her behalf? Deneyn took up the attachments and examined them separately. There were four letters she had written to Col, but none from him to her. The fifth letter was from Col to him, Deneyn. Perhaps Col was still alive, but the date at the bottom was more than four months earlier. The case of a living man was more urgent than that of a dead and so deserved more attention, as the suffering of a living persisted while that of a dead was over, according to Damhouder's codex. But who was Pierre Philipe Col?

He took up Col's letter. It was written in reddish-brown ink, the writing so small and crabbed that he could barely decipher any words in it. It reminded him of a confession he had once used as evidence at a trial, written in the dark with a blade of straw dipped in blood, by two hands clamped close together. That poor fellow had hanged himself from the legs of his breeches on the back of his cell door that same night. But Col's letter was several pages long, and would take time to complete. Then he noticed from the dates in the margin that it had been written over several months. What was going on here? What was the relationship between the prisoner and Mary Hugo?

Her letters to Col had been folded several times to fit into the palm of a hand, the folds worn and smudged. He unfolded one:

Beluved Col, I never dard to anser your letters becose I fered that you turned agenst me mecause father treted you so badly on my behalfe. The captin assured me that you do not rite to blame me but from luve. Therefor I beg you with much fere that when you have finished redding it you will returne it to me. The captin promised to putt it in my hands. You must knowe . . .

The rest was her business. It was her heart, those were secret words she had whispered in Pierre Philipe Col's ear under rustling palms on the golden beaches of Mauritius. Whoever Col was, whatever had happened to him, he had conquered Mary Hugo's heart. And I'm not jealous, thought Deneyn. Now he knew why none of Col's letters to Mary had been preserved. They had arranged for every letter to be returned to the writer, and his had been confiscated in his possession, possibly in his cell. But by that time the contents had been safely sowed in her heart. *Plase your trust in God. He will help you. If God does not deliver you, do not give up hoope. One never knoes if perhaps God decided that Sven and Zacharias must get there reward from it.*

Deneyn already knew, before he had been properly informed about it, that there was nothing he could do for her, as she lived beyond his jurisdiction. As long as Hugo was in command there, Mauritius did not fall under the Cape. That was what Hugo had demanded from the Directors as he refused to be under Goske. It was purely a matter of pride. So he went free, and that was how easy it was for Fiscal Deneyn to be himself absolved. Then what was it that Hugo's daughter could possibly expect of him?

He brought tobacco, a pipe, a carafe of brandy and a good thin glass to the table, lit another candle, put on his floral Japanese gown, and arranged pen and paper within reach. Perhaps he could make a few notes. He started reading her letter from the beginning: *Your honnour de Neijn, you will find it strange that I rite to you, but I am driven by distres . . .*

She told about their arrival on the island more than a year before. Col had welcomed them on the quay. By that time he had been acting commander for seven months. Originally he had been the soldiers' corporal, and had taken over the administration after the accident in which Chief Wreede had been drowned. Her father had been instructed to inquire into Col's administration upon his arrival and examine possible complaints against him before taking over the island. After his inquiry, he was so satisfied that he asked Col to stay on as *secundus*, with the rank and salary of a sergeant, and he undertook to write to Batavia for approval and confirmation.

Her father had originally promised her that she could proceed to Batavia on the first ship that stopped at Mauritius, to enjoy something of the Oriental way of life before he retired and they all returned to the fatherland together. After they had been on the island for a month or two, and she'd reminded him of his promise from time to time, he started finding excuses, and she thought he was afraid of being lonely in their house after she had left. When the first ship came, she asked whether she could send her possessions on board, but all he said was: No, not this time, but with the next ship. And during the first year there were only two. When she asked whether she might send her possessions on board this time, he started ranting at her. And she saw that he would never let her go.

Thereupon she made an arrangement with a sea captain, and asked *Secundus* Philipe Col if he could spare a soldier to transport something for her. She gave the soldier her sea chest, with everything she wished to take with her, and paid him to carry it to the house of a free fisherman, who promised to take her on board during the night before the ship was to sail. That evening at the farewell dinner the captain told her that he no longer saw his way open to take her, whereupon she had to have her chest collected from the fisherman again.

After the ship had left, she told Col what she had done. He had a fright, and told her that he would have to disclose it to the commander, but she pleaded with him, for her own sake and that of her poor friends on the island, not ever to tell it to her father. He agreed, on condition that she would not go away.

She had no rest after that. She had no one to talk to, and found no pleasure in anything she did. She cried a lot, and sometimes Col saw her when she was so dejected, and tried to comfort her. Col was a good worker and the commander often summoned him to talk to him, so that they often saw one another, until an affection developed between them. After some time they began to talk about love, and exchanged rings upon a promise of marriage, but they still had not informed her father. Then one day her father asked her what ring she was wearing, and started shouting at her when he heard that it was from Col. But she promised to sever relations with Col if he did not approve.

The next morning her father summoned the Council, ordered Col to vacate his seat at the table, suspended his rank and salary, and dispatched him to the Vlakte Post where he was to remain. He was forbidden to speak to her. Thereupon her father called Jan Zacharias who was on guard outside the door, and appointed him acting sergeant on full pay. This man was a former postkeeper on Robben Island but was scourged and sacked for stealing sheep. If he worked without his shirt, one could see the signs of his disgrace.

She gave more details in her letter about the councillors, to arouse

Deneyn's suspicion about their judgement and fairness. Jan Zacharias went about all day with a tankard of arrack in his hand; he was hardly ever seen without it. One night he removed the victualler's keys from the head of his bed and stole wine from the pantry, as well as some of the venison her father had had smoked to send to the Cape, and with that he and Master Sven and Master Pieter Walrand and Daniel the cooper caroused all night in the house of the freeman Bart, while it was against the law to leave the Lodge at night. From all the liquor Master Sven and Daniel drew knives and challenged one another to come outside, but Bart separated them. The next day Master Sven was unable to work. Jan Zacharias stayed in bed for two days from the carousing, and so did Master Pieter.

The second councillor was Sven Telleson. *Baas* Sven (Mary wrote *basvent*) was the island's head woodcutter. He had already been caught three times for stealing from the Company's magazine and warehouses. Once he had roamed in the bush like an animal for four months before they could catch him. When Chief Wreede drowned, Master Sven was there first to break open his chest and steal money from it. He was illiterate and simply signed with an S and a T.

The third councillor had previously worked a ferry boat in Amsterdam. His name was Jan Claasen, and he was their *secundus*. When he was in command of soldiers and they refused to obey, he would draw his knife and want to fight them.

This, your honnour de Neijn, is the Counsil that sat here on the iland over Monseer Col. She was afraid of what they might do to Col, and sent him a message with a freeman that she wanted to speak to him, and would wait behind the garden one evening after sundown. That evening they dined outside under a canopy as usual, and while the others were still sitting around drinking and smoking, she asked her brother Gerrit to take a walk with her. Near the garden, she told him that she was hoping to meet Philipe Col. There and then he turned back to tell her father what she had said. Before she and Col had exchanged four words, the *secundus* and Sven the woodcutter arrived to take her to the Lodge. Col was simply told to get back to his designated post.

At the Lodge she was treated wretchedly. She had to stay in her room and nobody was allowed to go near her. Her window shutters were nailed shut to prevent her having a view. The next morning Col was called in. In the meantime her father had broken open his sea chest and removed his papers, as well as seven or eight ells of serge and twelve ells of ribbon she had given him as a present. When they saw this, the councillors told her father how Mary had previously dispatched a heavy chest from the Lodge, and he demanded the full story from her.

When Col arrived in the afternoon, the Council was summoned, and they decided to keep him in custody until a case against him had been prepared. Her father wanted to have Col tortured. He then wrote three letters, purportedly from Mary, and handed them to her with threats about what he would do to Col, forcing her to copy them word for word in her handwriting. These he then sent to Col as if they had been sent by her, one after another, and each time Col recognised her handwriting, and replied to the letter, telling her everything her father wanted to hear from him. Col's answers never reached her. She only saw what her father had brought her to copy, but she believed that Col would notice the difference between her spelling and her father's, and realise that the letters had been written under duress. One thing the letters said, was that Col should deny everything of which they accused him, and she would do the same.

When Col appeared before the court, they asked him if he had received the serge and ribbon from Mary, which he denied. They asked him if he had written letters to her, and he denied it too. Then her father said: 'You cheat, here you stand and lie to us. I've had enough of you, I'm going to punish you properly. I shall make the charge as heavy as I can. Here you wrote everything down for me. Can't you see the letters did not come from her? The vixen cannot write in such a style. I dictated them to her. Look, here are the originals; the ones you received were only copies. Go back to your cell. I am going to make an example of you.'

A day or so later Col was placed on an island on bread and water, and kept there for sixteen days. When the ship *Helena* arrived, he was taken off and locked up in chains on the flute until the day of his trial.

Some of the officers took pity on him, and asked how they could help him. Twice Captain Frooij brought her letters from Monsieur Col, but because she was too depressed and frightened, she did not respond. When he brought her yet another letter, she started answering, and told him what she'd seen in the books about the accusations against him, and sent him what she could to help him in his defence.

And I pleded with Father, like a person who pledes to God for his sins, so I pleded for Col, but I coud not do anything. It was as if Fathers hart was made of stone. And Col, becose of the hevy leg irons in wich he was keped day and nite, his legs began to fester and swoled up so terribly that the mark of the iron was pressed into his legs. Master Walrand, our surgen, asked a few times for the irons to be taken of, but it was not allowed. From the festering he got a hevvy fever, and so he sat in the irons for almost four months. If he dide there it wuld have been to Fathers liking.

She sent Col twenty hen's eggs, because she was afraid that he would not survive on the thin rice gruel. And because she knew of his love, and that he was suffering because of her, she wrote that she would never abandon him, signing her name underneath in blood. And Col wrote her to pledge her his faith, signed in his blood.

The yacht *Wittenburg* was at the anchorage. In the evenings the ship's officers dined on shore with her father. The young men were eager for her company, but she did not come to the table. When they were outside for supper, she slipped into her father's office and searched among the papers for the charge sheet against Col. She let him know what he was being accused of: he had stolen textiles, he had abandoned his post, he had prepared to hand over the island to the French fleet, he had insulted the honour of the commander and his family by paying court to his daughter, he had attempted to seduce the girl and gave her a potion to make her fall in love with him, and he had lied under oath.

She took the captain and the *seur* of the yacht *Wittenburg* into her confidence, and told them why Col was being imprisoned and what he was going to be accused of. They said that they refused to have anything to do with it, and turned down the commander's request to take their seats in the court.

On a Sunday the Council was summoned and Col was brought in. He could barely stand before them. When they asked him something, he asked to be allowed to call witnesses, and for the papers that had been removed from his chest to be returned to him. Some of the charges were not mentioned there in court, but they were written on the act of accusation that was forwarded to the fatherland, and there they would remain, as if they had in fact been heard. She sent him papers into the Council room, which she had prepared for his defence, but her father seized them. Six or seven times Col requested that Miss Mary be heard, but they refused. And when at last she herself asked one of the guards to let her in so that she could address the court, she found that they had already adjourned and were standing about in small groups discussing a hunt planned for the next day. In one half-hour Col had been tried and sentenced and the sentence signed.

Col was returned to the flute *Helena* in leg irons. Once again she slipped into the office to read what his sentence was to be. He would be forced to stand at the stake for an hour with a notice above his head, he was stripped of rank and wages, and banished to serve in chains on Robben Island for three years. Justice was to be meted out to him on the Saturday, but by the Monday her father already regretted not having demanded a heavier sentence. He wanted to have the man scourged, so that he would never forget his disgrace. Her father came to cajole her to find out whether they were still corresponding, and then threatened her, but all in vain. Once again he had Col's cell on the ship searched for letters or other tokens. This time they found a few pieces of eggshell, with figures and dates written on them. This was what he wanted, for the dates had been written on Hugo's instructions by his servant. The key to his pantry was in his own room, and only Mary could have taken it.

She refused to admit anything. In that case, her father said, Col would have to confess. I shall torture him, even if it is unto death. Ten or more times he came to her to say: Mary, I'm going to torture him, even if it is unto death. I'm going to string him up by the arms with weights on his legs. She trembled in her heart, but refused to say anything, because if she admitted that they were corresponding, he would want the names of the persons who carried the letters. At last Hugo summoned *Seur* Hasselberg, the *seur* on *Helena*, and asked him if he would have any objection if he tortured Col to extract a confession about who had sent him the eggs on board. He said: No. The sailors were already in the boat to row the whole Council to the flute, when her father came to tell her that he was now on his way to force Col to confess, even if he had to tear him into four pieces. Then she admitted that they were still exchanging letters, and that she had sent him the eggs.

The Council sat on board the flute *Helena*, and Col's sentence was increased to forfeit his post and pay, to be flogged and branded, and thereafter to carry shells on Robben Island for five years. The eggs and the letters were the cause of the aggravation of his sentence.

When his justis was meeted out to him, Father had me rowed to the yot Wittenburg *so that I coud not free him. If they left me on land, I woud have shouted and shouted to all the poeple that it was not true what they accusd him of. Col sufered his justis, sufered it pasiently, and he was flogged and branded, on mouerisius, for my sake and not becos of crimes. After he sufered his justis, a chain was put on his leg to sale to the Cape on the flute* Helena. *Father was sory that he coud not hang him. If he had a chance he woud have hanged Col. So he sat in the preson for seven months altogether for my sake.*

Now she threw herself on the mercy of Commander Goske, so that he could summon Col to appear at the Cape, because even though Col had been sentenced to Robben Island, her father had decided at the last moment to keep him on Mauritius. If Col wasn't rescued, her father would kill him, even if it were to cost her life. She begged Deneyn and Goske not to inform her father that she had written to them; that would spell Col's death.

She asked Deneyn to interrogate Captain Cornelis Frooij. Captain Cornelis had assured her of his help. He was the only one in the entire Council who had voted against her father. He had proposed that the young man's backside be properly thrashed and that he be keelhauled from the foremast, but nothing more, and for that the boorish councillors had jeered at him. He was the only one, and there were five others and her father had two votes, so it was seven to one. *Seur*

Hasselberg of *Helena* would have liked to stay on the island, but when he saw what her father was doing to Col, nothing could keep him there.

She wanted to get off the island. All the officials stared at her when she came outside. She wanted to get out from under their eyes. She couldn't go to the outhouse without their following her. Furthermore, she begged that the few friends she and Col had, would be protected. There was a freeman who had taken a drill and a file to the flute to free Col, but Col had refused. Then there was Paul the tanner, the helmsman and the captain of *Helena*, and Master Walrand, and Trijntje. Those six.

Oh God, your honnour de Neijn, do not let Father know anything I rote to you. I shall be greatful and obliged to you all my live. Tomorrow I leave on the yot Wittenburg *to Batavia. Please send me a leter. The adres is To the mis pelgerom, widdow of mister Arent pelgerom, to be handed to me living on the Tijgersgracht in Batavia. 27 November 1673.*

That was how it went, how the sea worked. And it had been barely a year before she had walked across the paving outside his door. He could still hear her laugh when he'd said to the beautiful child, to win her favour: 'The more I see of men, the more I pity women.'

Deneyn folded up her letter and put it aside. Her case was well and clearly set out. Her letter was three months old. To write to the father-land now would mean four or five months. To write to Batavia, three months. Add to that at least six months for help to arrive from anywhere. His only witnesses were Frooij and Hasselberg. There was no hurry. He had time. He looked for Col's document and opened it.

The writing was so small and the words so cramped together that the letter was difficult to read. Would Col have been afraid that the paper, or his ink, would run out before he had told his story? He said that his name was Pierre Philipe Col, he was twenty-four years old, and came from the town of Lokeren in East Flanders. Undoubtedly French-speaking, thought Deneyn, possibly a Catholic and perhaps a spy; that might explain her father's animosity. This was important, as the Honourable Company was no less unsympathetic. Col had joined the chamber of Middelburg, had been in the Company's service for five years, and was until recently *secundus* of the post Mauritius, with the rank of sergeant. At present he found himself in the hell of the flute *Helena*, and humbly requested to be summoned to the Cape or Batavia to justify himself before a court.

So far so good, thought Deneyn, feeling more and more at home in the situation. Col requested permission to appeal against a sentence. That was something the Cape fiscal could respond to. How had the prospective appellant signed his request? He turned to the last page. *Your slave, P. Philipe Col.* Oh merciful God, why must a man be so humiliated?

Mary's letter was about personal matters from beginning to end. Now, what did Col want to convey to the Cape fiscal? Col realised that his letter was evidence that had to go to Batavia, and took trouble to reveal his contribution to the development of the island, paying special attention to charges of maladministration which might be brought against him. They might argue that he had allowed the island to deteriorate, and that he let the hooker *Goudvink* return to the Cape empty. In his seven months as officer in charge he had burned more than 200 bags of charcoal, tanned 450 cattle hides, undertaken a variety of building projects, among them a stable for horses, a chicken run, a stall for thirty cattle, a house for the gardener of sixteen feet by twelve feet at the garden. There he had also made improvements to all the labourers' cottages. Furthermore, he had two heavy wagons made, with four more wheels and their axles in stock, a boat of eighteen feet long, twelve new wheelbarrows, twenty-five axes, numerous spades and shovels. He had ebony wood cut and dried, and had 557 planks sawn from it, and dispatched to the Cape on the *Goudvink*. He mentioned the small number of labourers available; of these he had to apply a certain number every day to find food.

It was curious, thought Deneyn, to see what somebody had to say about himself and compare it with what others said about him. About his unfortunate relationship with Mary, apparently the only cause of his downfall, Col wrote very little, as if it was of no importance to him. Perhaps he was pushing it to the background to spare the lady. Or did he want to forget about all the unpleasantness, and her part in it, her sweet provocation which had caused him to fall into disgrace?

Would he be aware of the fact that she had already left the island and was at rest in the golden East tonight? Perhaps Col was lying in his cell at this moment thinking of her, wondering whether his Mary had done enough to save him from the executioner. How strongly had she really appealed to the councillors? How scared were the councillors of Commander Hugo? Deneyn had seen before how much servility could harm the Company's concerns.

From such a distance there was little he could do for these people. Here he was on the safe side of the danger line, and they on the wrong side. He felt as if he were on a raft on the open sea, watching people slipping from a sinking ship and drifting away, seeing them scream. They put out a hand to him, pleading for help. Maijke Hendriksz had been here in front of his desk, but already she'd been too far away for him to touch. He might yet be able to help Sargeant Col. He would try, purely for the sake of Mary Hugo, the damsel in distress, as in the tales of chivalry. First he would write to her at that familiar address in Batavia. He had never seen the Tijgersgracht himself, but he'd heard about it in a lecture on private trade. The late merchant Arent Pelgrom had been one of the greatest scoundrels ever in the Company's service. He had robbed the Company of hundreds of thousands. Everybody knew about it, but the innocent Mary apparently did not.

For days Deneyn went about with the thought that he should show their letters to the governor. He didn't do it. His attention was distracted almost immediately by mundane matters, all of them shortly after the arrival of the flute *Helena*, among them the fact that natives from Schacher's kraal had burned a thousand bunches of thatch, which had been cut, bound and stacked to dry with much effort at the Rietvlei.

'They're looking for war, Your Honour,' Ensign Croese said in Council. 'The garrison is ready. I can ride out this afternoon with thirty men.'

'They're telling us that we should leave their thatch alone, as they have to build their houses from it,' was the opinion of *Secundus* van Breughel. 'I wish we could do what they want, but we need the thatch ourselves.'

Deneyn first wanted to have more information about the matter of the thatch. It was possible, improbable but possible, that the reed cutters might have been ordered to set it on fire and place the blame on Schacher, because then the Company could forcibly expel Schacher once and for all from the peninsula. He did not say it in Council, but instead spoke of insufficient evidence, and voted against action.

And there was Francijntje van Lint, a stowaway on the homeward-bound fleet from Batavia. After six weeks at sea and at about the height of Madagascar the sergeant on *Gekroonde Vrede* brought a young soldier to the captain. 'This Franciskus, captain. I think he is a woman in man's clothing.'

The captain said: 'Franciskus, you can take off your shirt here in front of us, or you can do it in the cabin in front of one of the gentlemen's ladies. You can choose.'

Some of the ladies on board took Francijntje in their employ, and gave her clean clothes. At the Cape the captain handed her over to the fiscal. Deneyn interrogated her on board. She was strongly built, not very attractive and burnt dark by the sun. And she looked the fiscal in the eye across the cabin table; she was not frightened of him. After all she had been through, she was no longer afraid, but she needed help. Here was a Cape free farmer to whom she was engaged, she explained, but they had no money for her passage.

'I must know how you managed to get on board, how you passed the muster in Batavia, how you could masquerade as a man every day. Did you get help from other people, on board or on shore?'

She answered all his questions in full. In Batavia she had asked an ex-soldier for advice. He had told her what to expect, warning her to do her work in such a way that she would never be singled out. He had applied under her name to register for the voyage to the father-land, but on the day of the selection it was she who went on board and responded to her name. At sea she had kept away from the others as much as possible, never talking, and praying a lot.

'I still have to know, miss, how you managed to relieve yourself. The sailors empty their bladders in the copper pig's ear against the gunwale. You couldn't act any differently. I'm asking so that I can warn the captains about how you manage it.'

She agreed to show him, if he would allow her to fetch something from the cabin.

'I must say the ladies speak well of her,' the captain confided when she was out. Francijntje returned with a small silver bowl, a boat with a spout two fingers long, and held it before her, with the spout in her hand.

Deneyn smiled, the captain laughed out loud. 'What have we here? Look, *meester*, this is how she brings her dowry, in silver.'

'I hope it brings you luck, Francijntje. I shall make my plea to the governor, but you must stay on board in the care and the service of the ladies until I have spoken to your free farmer. After that it is for the governor to say. I shall not prosecute you. Is the captain happy with that?'

The captain still laughed: Don't let our boatswain find out.

There was a slave who had attacked a free burgher with a sickle. Why, is of no concern. He was flogged, branded, and placed on the island in chains to carry shells for two years. And there was Jan Hamboes; his crime was stabbing with a knife. Who was he? It is of no concern. His punishment was flogging and three years on the island in chains, carrying shells.

In this way a few busy days went by, in which he could do nothing for Mary Hugo and her Philipe. He was reluctant to mention their case to Goske, because it was a matter in which he could easily burn his fingers. Goske might dismiss it. The acquisition of a new pair of free burghers for the Cape was one thing, but to interfere in the family affairs of the pirate Hugo, an independent commander at an outpost, was something else. But he, Deneyn, wanted the home-bound fleet which lay at the anchorage to take his plea together with Col's appeal to the fatherland, and he did not want to send a half-baked case abroad. Frooij and Hasselberg were the only ones he could use to testify for Col and Mary, and their evidence would determine his plea. If both were to testify for Mary, he would demand an inquiry and support Col's appeal. But if both were to support Hugo's charge, he would abandon Mary and her Philipe. She wrote the name *Fieleep*. So much for the education of girls.

Captain Frooij took *Helena* to Hout Bay to fetch wood for the lime kilns, as the dunes at Table Bay were already stripped bare. The remains of the tall yellow-woods felled at Hout Bay for the Castle, had to be collected, and shrubs with fairly sturdy trunks chopped out; most importantly, the hard root had to be dug up. It was unbelievable that a puny, wind-blown little shrub could have such an extensive, solid, heavy root system underground, but that was the real hard root, thick as a man's thigh, iron-hard with age, and the best kind for coals to burn seashells down to the ash-grey lime for the building of the Castle, the wonderful new Castle, that had to defend the Cape for the fatherland against English, French and whoever else might come. When Frooij had a boatload of firewood, he had to send it in his sailing sloop to the ship. Once its hold was full, he had to bring the wood to Table Bay. Once a week it was expected of him. In this way the dunes of Hout Bay were despoiled of vegetation, the root systems eradicated, but the Castle had to grow and live.

Deneyn went to search for Captain Frooij and *Seur* Hasselberg in Hout Bay, taking the coastal road, a shorter but more difficult route than the one through The Hell. In the valley behind Table Mountain he could see from afar the smoke of a wood fire above the tree tops, and hear axes ringing in the still air. A slave armed with an assegai was guarding the oxen against lions. Two wagons stood next to a camp of tents and sawing trestles where a team of twenty woodcutters and slaves were transforming huge yellow-wood trees into beams and planks for the Castle. The foreman pointed out a rivulet. Follow the stream to the sea and he would find Captain Frooij's sailing sloop. Why were the boards being transported overland, but the firewood by sea? Deneyn asked him. The trees sank, it was impossible to get them aboard, the foreman explained. An ox wagon was the only way of getting them to the ark, even if it meant working the oxen to death over cliffs, sand dunes and the vast stretches of rock. All they could do, was to make the trunks a trifle lighter. But the oxen were worn out quickly, and were caught or broke their legs; every fortnight he needed twenty new oxen. Then the foreman said a strange thing. He said: 'That Castle devours oxen. I'll put my head on a block that a month from now we'll have another war against the Hottentots.'

Deneyn left his horse there, and went to look for Frooij, carrying his slender rattan and his writing equipment under his arm. Near the sea he could see how the dunes had been dug up for hard root. At the river mouth stood a tent. There were men working. The sailing sloop lay in shallow water, and beyond the sheltered bay the flute under bare spars had turned its bows against the south-wester. Frooij was in the tent, but he came out when he heard that there was a visitor.

'Are you coming to see if we're wearing out our backsides, fiscal?' asked Frooij. 'I can assure you we really don't need that.'

'I wasn't sent for that, captain. It is something else. I have begun an inquiry for an appeal case. I'm summoning you and your *seur* as witnesses. You can have it in writing, if you wish.'

Frooij slumped down against a round white dune, as if his legs were exhausted. 'What do you want? Which case?'

'Philipe Col of Lokeren against the Council of Policy of Mauritius, in respect of sentence passed against him in August '72.'

'Ah, the youngster. No, I don't know anything, fiscal.'

'Captain, are we going to do the interrogation here on the beach or shall we sail out to your ship? I find it too windy and uncomfortable here.'

'I cannot leave before we have a boatload of wood.'

'In your tent.'

'No.'

'All right, then let me unpack my writing material and prepare a plume, and I'll ask you a few questions.' Deneyn shook his inkhorn and stood it in the sand, shaped a point to his quill, and rested his box on his knees. The folios fluttered in the wind.

'Have you noticed, captain, that everybody here talks about the south-east wind, but that it blows without fail from the south-west?'

'Everybody usually lies.'

'How so?'

'If I want to know which way the wind blows, I look out of the hatch.'

'But what do you mean with: everybody usually lies?'

'I think the way I think, not like everybody. Something is as it is if I think so. Then I don't care what everybody says.'

'Does your opinion often differ from the popular one?'

'Often. What about it?'

'I noticed that you were alone in your vote against the Council on Mauritius.'

'And what about it?'

'It seems to me there are two sides to that case. Now, for how long were you at that anchorage, captain? How often did you see Mary? How often Col?'

'I was at the anchorage for four months. You saw my ship's journal, the day I arrived back here. It is written there. Or were you just paging?'

'Did you go ashore every day?'

'Yes.'

'Saw Mary Hugo every day?'

'No.'

'Col every day?'

'No.'

'And the commander?'

'Yes, every day. My business was with him, not with his children.'

'You were at the anchorage for four months, but Col's first contravention had occurred two months earlier. That was the occasion when he went off to meet Mary. Now what did you see or hear that made you decide to vote against the commander?'

'I have two eyes in my head, and two ears on my head. The way I reason is this: If I place a lookout in a mast and then find him in the forecastle, I give him a hiding there and then as an example. And if you put out a pikeman with a musket, and you find him in the tavern, then you can hang that man for all I care. That was how it was.'

'But is the Vlakte Post so important?'

'No.'

'And that was what you told Hugo, that he'd sent Col away just to get him out of reach of his daughter.'

'That was what I thought. I didn't say it.'

'Then why did you vote against the accusation?'

'At the Vlakte there is nothing but palm trees and vegetables, but Hugo wanted Col there. Col broke the rules when he left. That is right. What is wrong, was that the girl's father wanted to play the judge over two lovers. That is wrong. He interferes where nature has brought two people together. That is unnatural. That was what I voted against.'

'And did you discuss your feeling with the other councillors?'

'Discuss? Telleson and Zacharias are crept so far up Hugo's backside that you won't find them to discuss anything. Telleson staggers about in a haze of liquor, and Zacharias receives a sergeant's pay for as long as Col stays in prison.'

'What about the opinion of *Secundus* Claasen?'

'An irresponsible fool.'

'Then what about your *seur*? Didn't you talk to him?'

'I give orders to my *seur*, and I expect him to report to me. For the rest we seldom talk.'

'Ah,' said Deneyn. 'Ah, no love lost in the cabin?'

'What? What are you saying? Wait a minute. Come, we can sail on board this moment if you have to see Hasselberg.' Frooij got up suddenly, dusting his breeches behind. Without looking back, he strode to the beach, shouted at the sailors, helped them to shove his half-loaded boat into the sea, hung the rudder himself and shook out the sail. Deneyn was still asking questions, but the captain was busy with the sail and the helm, and his answers were curt and evasive. To Deneyn he seemed upset.

Bookkeeper Hasselberg was not of much use. He spoke to Deneyn in the cabin, while Captain Frooij and his boatswain were hoisting the bundles of firewood from the sloop and lowering them into the hold of the flute.

'How regularly did you go ashore on Mauritius?'

'We dined ashore every evening. They invited us. Much better than ship's food. For the rest I often came to the Lodge for my work. Refreshment, fuel, repairs, cargo, that sort of thing.'

'And who were at dinner?'

'Hugo, Claasen, Zacharias, Telleson. Who else? Master Walrand, but he was a married man. And Captain Frooij.'

'Was Walrand the only married man?'

'Well, the others had certainly not been married in church.'

'You mean they kept concubines? Who?'

'I'm excluding the commander from it.'

'Are you talking about slave women and convicts? That is illegal at a Company post.'

'I was not involved.'

'The others break the law.'

'Fiscal, you know what the law says, but do you know what nature says? How does the law expect young men to remain without female company for months and years?'

'Would you therefore say that the commander is a man of high moral principles?'

'I don't know about his principles; I just think he is too old for it. Perhaps there's a crack in his bowsprit.'

'I assume the children were at the meals?'

'The boys. The miss stayed inside while we ate, and we didn't see her.'

'Never saw her?'

'Well, sometimes she came past. She had friends among the free burghers.'

'How was her relationship with her father?'

'They never spoke.'

'And did you meet Col?'

'No. He was in chains, the four months we were there.'

'So why did you think Col was guilty, if you knew neither him nor the lady?'

'The commander told us what was going on.'

'You believed everything he said?'

'I was only a visitor there. What else could I say?'

'Col is asking for leave to appeal. He will probably be tried in Batavia. Then everybody who found him guilty before, will be called to justify themselves. How will you defend yourself?'

'I must stick to my story. I believe Commander Hugo will stick to his.'

'I want to defend Col. It is my duty. Will you testify in his favour?'

'No. No, fiscal. That I cannot do. I believe what the commander told us. He was present at the whole business.'

'You will not get another chance to rectify your error.'

'Do you think Batavia will blame Hugo? A man like him? He gets away with murder.'

'Really?'

'No, it is just a saying.'

Deneyn put his papers together and stowed them away. It meant that he now had only Frooij as a witness.

He looked down the forward hatch, where Captain Frooij was at work.

'Have you finished with Hasselberg? I thought I should speak to you. Let me finish here, then you can come to the cabin.' Frooij told the boatswain to continue with the work of hoisting, swinging in, lowering and stowing away until it was done. As soon as the sloop was empty, he would send *Seur* Hasselberg to the shore with them to fetch the next load. He would hoist his blue flag when they were to come on board, then they had to take the fiscal ashore.

Deneyn thanked Hasselberg and took his leave. As the *seur* with his hat and oilskin was lowered over the gunwale into the boat, Frooij called his servant. 'It is noon. Time to eat and drink something in the cabin. Will you join me for the meal, *meester*?'

'Indeed. Thank you for the invitation.'

The cabin boy flapped a checkered cloth open over the table, set out plates and knives, and put a blue dish under a damp cloth and a large fresh loaf before the captain. He cut the brown crust off for Deneyn.

'This is what our seamen call "south-east", fiscal. Hard, windy and full of sand, but healthy. Have a taste. It is the genuine Cape bread.'

The cloth over the dish had the same pattern as the curtains in front of the cabin window. It was rare for a service boat to have curtains in the cabin. The servant brought glasses and a bottle, drew the cork and poured wine, heavy and purple like the sluggish fluid in the lungs of a drowned man. Captain Frooij leaned over to him. 'To your health, *Meester* Deneyn.'

Deneyn raised his glass. 'A long life, captain.'

'You saw yourself that the wind is always south-west, but they talk about a south-easter. The bread must then be wrongly named as well. It just shows, you can be sure of nothing.'

They pulled out chairs on either side of the table. The cabin boy offered a bowl of butter, but Deneyn shook his head.

'Who bakes this delicious bread, skipper?'

'A woman called Barbertje Geens.'

'Oh yes. With the green eyes. It's something to behold.'

'Exactly. I go there personally to buy my bread. Unusual, very. That may be why there is no man she can live with, because she is not your ordinary woman. She deserves a baron with a castle or a nobleman with a double surname. What do you think? Heaven knows, she deserves a bit of comfort.'

'I don't know,' said Deneyn. 'She likes working. She asked for the contract to supply bread. She rents a house because of the big baking oven in the yard, but other necessities like a baker's trough and tables she bought for cash. I think she gets on well without a husband.'

'Do you know what they say? They say she gets up at cock's crow to make fire in the oven. And she mixes dough for a hundred loaves. Then she strips herself naked and gets into the trough, and for an hour she treads the dough. That is how this bread gets to the table.'

'That is what her competitors say. Plain envy.'

'Delicious to me. I believe every word. That is why she has such a lovely figure. Now look, I want to tell you what I know about Col's case. Boy, put the bottle down here, we can pour for ourselves. Ah, this lobster our cook took among the seaweed yesterday. I prefer it cold. Bring a damp cloth, boy. And then leave us alone.'

Deneyn had to pardon him, Frooij said as he broke the lobster open with his hands, but this was how he ate. It was the easiest way, and there was a damp cloth for his fingers.

They broke the bread, ate the lobster with their fingers, poured more wine. In the Company's service the sailors ate like dogs and the officers like kings, Frooij said. This lobster, with fresh bread and wine, was the tastiest he knew. One could easily eat too much.

On Mauritius old Hugo was just as keen about his favourite dish. There was a Javanese cook, a convict; at dusk every day he fetched Hugo an octopus from the reef, and curried and peppered it, serving it with rice. *Orit* it was called, delicious, fresh from the sea. Hugo had sent him, with the chain on his leg, in pursuit of octopus. One day he clambered into a hole on the reef after an octopus, and there his chain got caught on the coral. Tide came in over him, and only at the following low tide did they see him again. Mauritius was like paradise, but there, precisely there, one should expect to find devils lurking. Was Deneyn familiar with the proverb that power corrupts? Yes, on Mauritius it happened that much sooner. It was as if something good in that place could never mature, but rotted instead. Deneyn had to forgive him; he had become embittered by the injustice he had to witness under the pretext of the Company's justice. He wanted to recount what he knew of the honourable Hugo's crime against his daughter and the boy.

Deneyn: 'Mary writes to me that you promised to help her.'

Frooij: 'She told me her father had screamed, those were her words, that the dog should die, he wouldn't get off that island alive.'

Deneyn: 'What does her father have in mind for her? Must it be money, or rank, or status?'

Frooij: 'All three. But there's no one like that on Mauritius. Col shaves every day, he washes himself more often than the ordinary soldier, irons his clothes with a hot iron. And he is a handsome boy.'

Deneyn: 'Have you read her letters, the ones you brought me?'

Frooij: 'It was I who suggested to her to put her case to you. I promised to bring the letters. She wrote day and night, in the cabin on *Wittenburg*, just a pistol shot from her father's lodge. Crumpled it, started again. I asked her captain to wait. Hugo sent word from the shore to find out what the matter was. She had Col's papers there too. I was surprised to see them, because at that moment Col was in the hell on *Helena*. One of my own people must have taken them there, behind my back. I still don't know who. The day after she'd finished, *Wittenburg* went out to Batavia. Not one of them, her family or councillors, went to see her off. Freemen sent fruit, buttermilk, sweet biscuits. I myself took *Helena* to sea a fortnight later.'

Deneyn: 'And could you help her in any way, except with the letters?'

Frooij: 'I couldn't give her passage without her father's consent. It would be abduction, as she is under age. But it makes no difference. I don't want her for myself. Col too: I had him on my passenger list to bring him to the Cape, to carry shells on the island for five years. That was his sentence, but the day before we put to sea, Hugo sent his boat to fetch Col. After that there was nothing I could do for him. Been in chains for a year now, if he is still alive.'

Deneyn: 'Who do you know among the settlers whom I could perhaps call as witnesses? Are there soldiers in the garrison favourably disposed to Col?'

Frooij: 'No. Too scared to open their mouths, the last one of them. There are a few free burghers, and one or two servants. But you shouldn't, because if Hugo hears their names he will destroy them. I take it upon myself, he always says. I take it upon myself. Then he does as he wishes, and woe betide the one who opens his mouth.'

Deneyn: 'What about her brothers?'

Frooij: 'No chance. They are just boys of this world. The little one is innocent. The pretty one bursts into tears if his father farts.'

Deneyn: 'Seventeen years old?'

Frooij: 'Yes. The child also writes a wonderfully fine hand, like the letters of a booksetter, you must have seen those, but they're all scared of their father. What would become of them if they testified against the old man? Would they be struck dead? The whole settlement is scared of their father. He carries black blood on his two hands. Was a pirate in the Red Sea for years. I think it was because of him that the poor girl sought out a man's company. Do you understand?'

Deneyn: 'Do you think Hugo will ever forgive them, and allow them to come together?'

Frooij: 'Hugo told her that Col would not get off the island alive. But what sin have they committed? All young people feel like that. He should be honest: if his daughter led Col on, he should drag her to court too, and try them together.'

Deneyn: 'We can try to persuade your *seur*. He supports Hugo.'

Frooij: 'Leave Hasselberg out of it. If he finds out that I'll testify for them, he will turn against them, and the other way round.'

Deneyn remembered Frooij's reaction when he'd asked if there was bad blood between them. Therefore he did not question him any further. Sometimes captains and bookkeepers did not see eye to eye.

In the late afternoon, with the sun behind Karbonkelberg, Frooij had his blue flag hoisted. They had eaten and drunk well, and were good friends. Frooij proposed that they lie down in the cabin for a while until the sloop arrived. Deneyn still had to put into writing what he'd heard, but drank another glass or two of dark wine with the captain. When he left, Frooij hung over the gunwale to shake his hand, while Deneyn descended into the sloop on unsteady legs and unsure of his grip, his writing box under the arm.

'Don't fall overboard, skipper. I need you.'

'And I you.'

In the following weeks slaves, Koina and soldiers carried the Fort to the Castle. Whatever was loose was taken from the Fort and transported on wheelbarrows, stretchers, or by hand or head the distance of five hundred paces east, to where the Castle rose broad and brown like a young rising loaf among the dunes. Everything that was carried across, was swallowed by the half-finished Castle. The black cannons, too, were transported by hand, as there were no oxen. The flute *Helena* once again returned to Hout Bay, for more firewood.

The good Captain Klaas of the Chainouqua sent people with the message that the Gonjemans were camped at the Little Berg River, three or four days from the Castle. The Council had arranged with him for an attack before the start of the rainy season. The Company would contribute fifty soldiers, the burgher militia had to provide fifty, Klaas would give 150 and Schacher 250. The rains usually started at the first full moon in April, and already it was late March. That was his message. Use commiseration in respect of women and children, Goske wrote in Ensign Croese's *Instructie*. The gathering spot was once again Hoogekraal in the Tygerberg.

They marched north for four days, finding Ngonnemoa's kraal in the same difficult terrain as the previous time, where the half-dry ditches and empty waterholes of the Vierentwintigriviere criss-crossed a barren plain. There Captain Klaas's scouts found the Gonjemans, and led Croese's army behind a series of ridges to a point close to water, where they had to spend the long night.

But the Gonjemans had seen them, and made their bundles and prepared everything during the night, and early the next morning they were in full flight with their stock and mats and everything they could carry. Croese's charging vanguard arrived in an empty camp. There they shot a sick dog and looked for tracks to follow. The tracks led towards the mountains. That pleased Klaas and Kuiper, because when people fled into the mountains they left their cattle behind. The horsemen rode out ahead to lead the pursuit. Quite soon they could see dust rising from where the Koina were driving on their cattle. As they gained on the fugitives, small flocks of sheep were abandoned again from time to time. When they were within shooting distance, firing a number of shots ahead, small herds of cattle were also thrown away. All morning it continued like that. They did not manage to shoot a single Gonjeman, and at the foot of the mountain it was already too late in the day to venture into the kloofs and bushes. Schacher and Kuiper didn't want to continue the pursuit either; they were content with a share of the four thousand sheep. At the Cape, the eight hundred cattle were divided between the Company and the burghers. Croese brought back a young Hottentot under arrest, one of Kuiper's troop who had stabbed his cousin to death with an assegai. Deneyn declined to get involved.

One day in church he heard that Francijntje van Lint, spinster from the congregation of Batavia, had died. She was the one who had come to her fiancé as a stowaway. But she was so fit and healthy, why should she have died so suddenly? Throughout the sermon Deneyn thought of her. From the moment she had first appeared before him, he had believed that she was someone who deserved help, and he had done his best for her. Why should she die? She had shown courage, determination, thought Deneyn, and had been destined to become a mother of heroes. She hadn't. How could the death of the poor, plain woman make an iota of difference in God's great plan? He was alive, and others were alive and grew old, but Francijntje had to die young. So little he understood about the right and wrong of things. On the Tuesday she was buried under the floor of the ark. Deneyn was in attendance; there was one grieving farmhand, and almost nobody else, but for him it was as if a sister was being buried, though he had hardly known the woman.

On the Thursday another stowaway appeared before him, a youngster who clearly hadn't started shaving yet. Deneyn immediately had him sentenced to three years in chains on Robben Island. Was justice really blindfolded, Fiscal Deneyn? He wondered. You seem to have one law for women, another for other weaklings. After the youth, a black slave appeared who had wounded a Dutchman with a knife. This man he had flogged, branded on the left shoulder and sentenced to carry shells on the island for five years. In due course a letter from the Lords Directors arrived on the outbound ship *Zieriksee*, that the escaped Cornelis de Cretser had been employed again, as a merchant at eighty guilders, to become *secundus* at the Cape. At the same time van Breughel was transferred to East India. Now what was going on here? wondered Deneyn. De Cretser had stabbed a sea captain to death, but was being pardoned, returning with a clean shirt and a broad smile. A month earlier he had destroyed a slave for a flesh wound. How did one balance the scales of justice? Look out, look out, Fiscal Deneyn. Was justice blind, or only you? And he came to the conclusion that he should be as consistent as possible. In Africa he could still not find any light.

On 13 July 1674 the ship *Couwerve* arrived on the roadstead. Its hull and spars showed a long and difficult voyage from the fatherland. There were masts without sail, masts without yards, and long seaweed dragged alongside like green beard. But volleys of salutes from the temporary bastions of the Castle were fired that day, and a clerk with a hailer was sent through town behind a guard of honour carrying banners, drums and trumpets, to announce peace. The clerk with the hailer shouted: 'News from the fatherland: Peace with England. Peace with England.'

Governor Goske summoned Deneyn. The population had to realise that the war with France was still continuing. Equally important: the letters made it clear that the peace with England might not last long; the English only wanted to catch their breath. So the work on the Castle and other fortifications had to continue with all speed.

In these circumstances a capital trial turned up, which brooked no deferral, as Bookkeeper Hasselberg of the flute *Helena* had reported his captain. It complicated matters. Seaworn *Couwerve* had to be attended to, and half of its crew were in hospital. *Marken* had to carry news of the peace to Java. *Helena* had to be prepared as from the next day, for a voyage over Mauritius to Java. It was midwinter, the worst time of the year for long voyages, but it could not be helped, they had to go to sea. But *Helena,* with her skipper in jail, could not remain without a captain. Consequently Deneyn could not tarry with this case; he had to try Captain Frooij and the two sailors, so that the Company's work could resume. He realised that it was Frooij's right to have others of his occupation and station on the bench. Here Captains Claas Voogt of *Couwerve* and de Keizer of *Marken* were available, to augment the Council.

What did all this mean? Captain Frooij, his only witness in the case for Mary Hugo, the only man not afraid of her violent father, stood accused in a capital trial, and Philipe Col was still in chains. Capital cases usually ended under the gallows, and he could not lose Frooij. He told Goske about Col and Mary Hugo.

'If *Helena* leaves for Mauritius immediately, it may be an opportunity to inform Commander Hugo that Col has appealed to be heard in Batavia, and that his papers are being forwarded from here. Then it will be wise for him to release Col, to proceed to Batavia on the *Helena*.'

'What papers do you have ready to forward?'

'Personal statements from Col and the girl.'

'Is that all? It won't stand up.'

'Captain Frooij promised to testify. He was an eyewitness.'

'My dear fellow, the man is in danger of his life. What hope do you have?'

The next day, the Sunday, a thanksgiving for the peace was held in the ark. The three prisoners were in cells in the old Fort, beyond the stretch of destroyed veld which had become a parade ground. That was where Deneyn went to conduct his preliminary investigation. In the name of the honourable East India Company, Pieter Deneyn, fiscal at the Cape of Good Hope *versus* Cornelis Frooij of Vlissingen, forty years of age, Klaas Steenhouwer of Hoorn, eighteen, and Joost Jansz of Schoonhoven, fifteen, all from the flute *Helena*, presently in Hout Bay, accused of sodomy and attempted sodomy.

On guard in front of their heavy cell door was a child of perhaps sixteen, dressed, armed and standing to attention as a fearsome soldier. Deneyn interrogated Jansz and Steenhouwer together. The two sailors wanted to push the blame on Frooij. Deneyn began with the usual questions and taking the oath. Were their names such and such?

'Yes.'

'Have you been on the flute *Helena* in Hout Bay over the past months?'

'Yes.'

'And why were you sent there?'

'To fetch wood for the building of the Castle.'

'How long were you there?'

'Since January, when we arrived from Mauritius.'

'What were your duties on board?'

'Steenhouwer was butler, Jansz cabin boy.'

'How often did the sailors go ashore to fetch wood?'

'Every day.'

'So you two were the only ones on board all day?'

'Yes.'

'Did the sailors return in the evening to sleep on board?'

'Yes.'

'Where did each of you sleep?'

'In the forecastle.'

'Why and how often did you go ashore?'

'Once a week, when the captain told us to. Then somebody else watched the anchors.'

'And what did you do on shore?'

'We went with the captain into the dunes to find the best firewood. Afterwards we served the captain in his tent.'

They were accused of having committed sodomy with one another and with the captain. Did they know what that involved, and what punishment could be expected for it under Dutch law?

Jansz did not know.

Before the Council of Justice Deneyn introduced his argument. 'Since the creation and the origins of humanity we have the example and the testimony of tens of thousands of generations of our forebears, that God in fact created woman as a helpmate for man. She is attractive and alluring in shape, for a man to find his fulfilment in her, and through the centuries of our existence on earth this has been the natural principle and motivation of our human existence. Therefore those who despise or reject femininity and use a man for this purpose, strike a blow in the face of the Creator, insulting and rejecting every woman made by the Creator. Sodomy is unnatural, even among animals. It is only reptiles, the adder and its spawn, that copulate in the digestive tract of their kind. Where it appears among human beings, it is an evil with dire consequences. And the Creator endowed Moses the lawgiver with the insight and wisdom to forbid and combat it. In the Book of Leviticus it is stated clearly, in the eighteenth chapter, verse 22, and just as clearly in the first epistle of St Paul to the Romans, first chapter, verses 26 to 27. Other biblical references can also be cited. The second epistle of St Peter, chapter 2, verses 6 to 8. The first chapter, verse 7, of St Jude. There can be no doubt.'

Deneyn was solemnly convinced of his case. His deep yearning for female friends, known and still unknown, was the conviction in argument and the urgency in his voice. He could hear some of their voices, feel the warmth of their bodies. There was one who had put her arms around him, not around his waist, but from below upwards, so that her palms were on his shoulder blades, and then she would pull him tightly against her, breast to breast, hips to hips. Some wanted to drink, some wanted to go to church, some wanted to sing, some were sleepy, some wanted to walk hand in hand down the Breestraat in Leiden of a winter afternoon when there were lights in the shops. He remembered some better than others; he could see their faces, how their eyes became large and incredibly soft on his pillow. He was grateful for the pleasure they had brought to his life, and believed that he understood what he was talking about.

Before the court he interrogated the boys separately. Joost Jansz testified trembling that one evening the captain had called him to blow out the lamp in his cabin. The *seur* was already asleep, but his cabin door across the passage was open. Then the captain called him to his bed, and touched him. He pulled away and the captain said: Well, if you don't want to, then get out of here.

Klaas Steenhouwer leaned against the rail with an open mouth.

'Did Captain Frooij ever attempt any bodily advances with you?'

'What?'

'Did the skipper try to make love to you?'

Yes, but that had been only once. About ten or eleven weeks earlier the captain had ordered him to go ashore with him. There they walked along that long beach, past the scrub and the dunes, beyond the river mouth where the sailors worked. Then the captain took him by the arm. 'Klaas, you've been here for a long time. Have you learned something of the Hottentot language by now?'

'Yes, in a way.'

'Can't you find me a *meid*?'

'Where will I find a *meid* here, skipper?'

'You will also do.'

'Skipper, listen! There's a God above us.'

'Forget about it.'

But as they walked on, the captain first put his hand over his shoulders, later around his waist, so that he had to tell him to stop. And nothing like that ever happened again.

Christiaan Hasselberg of Westkiel, bookkeeper on the flute *Helena*, testified that he was lying on his bed one evening with his door on the hook as usual, when the skipper on the other side of the passage called the boy to blow out the hanging lamp in his cabin. Once the boy was inside, the skipper said aloud: '*Seur*, are you asleep?' But he remained silent, listening.

'Here, boy, come closer so that I can feel you.' After a long silence he heard the captain again: 'Come, get into the bed.' He didn't know what Joost had said, but the skipper's voice was quite clear: 'Well, if you don't want to, then get out of here.'

Then Frooij was called.

'Cornelius Frooij, you are captain of the flute *Helena* which has been at anchor in Hout Bay for the last six months to fetch firewood.'

'Yes.'

'You are accused of having committed the unspeakable sin with Joost Jansz and Klaas Steenhouwer. How say you to this?'

'Not guilty.'

'You know Jansz and Steenhouwer. What was their work on board?'

'They watch the ship. Prepare food for the crew. Adjust the anchors as required. Watch for signals from the shore.'

'Where did they sleep at night?'

'Sailors sleep where they find space.'

'In the cabin?'

'Of course not.'

'Is it so that you mostly remained on board yourself, and sent your bookkeeper ashore with the wood gatherers?'

'Why not?'

'Is the answer yes?'

'Yes.'

'Five days out of six?'

'Yes.'

'The Company sent you personally to fetch fuel for the Castle. You could have supervised your men better on shore than the bookkeeper could. What were you doing on board during the day?'

'Watched ship. I examined every piece of wood and cordage on the ship. There are fifteen miles of cordage.'

'Found anything amiss?'

'A crack in the bowsprit.'

He would not progress with Frooij. Because there had not been witnesses on deck, Frooij could find any pretexts. He'd worked on the maps, he would say, he'd measured the angles of the sun, he'd examined every piece of sail, wood and cordage on board. Deneyn had to try a different approach.

Witness Elias Tack of Vlissingen, 18, sailor: He had gone to the cabin three weeks ago to report that there was a tear in the bowsprit, when the captain touched his manhood. He jumped away, and directly went to the forecastle to tell it to the fellows. That had been the break-through.

There are three degrees of interrogation. The first occurs in an open court session, but for the second and third you need permission from the bench. You submit your list of questions, and if the majority agrees, the presiding official writes at the bottom: *ad torturam*, signing it with his name. The second degree of interrogation takes place behind closed doors. Because the new Castle as yet lacked a cell with the required equipment, the workshop in the ark was used for this purpose. The members of the court of justice, its secretary, the fiscal as prosecutor and an executioner attended. The questions are read out point by point, and the prisoner's responses written down. If he refuses or gives unsatisfactory answers, the prosecutor asks for sharper methods to be applied. On the instruction of the chairman the interrogated person's wrists are bound by the executioner, and he is hoisted up with a rope over a pulley hanging from a beam. If he still persists in his refusal, weights are attached to his ankles in multiples of twenty pounds. The form may be varied by suspending weights from individual toes, or by hoisting up the person with his arms tied behind his back, or by using special instruments like thumb or ankle screws. It is desirable, preferable, not to draw blood or maim limbs.

Under the second degree of interrogation Joost admitted that one evening at dusk, when the bookkeeper had been ashore, his captain had invited him in the cabin to commit the unspeakable sin and that he had acquiesced. It had been only that one occasion. Klaas confessed that while they had been walking hand in hand, beyond the river among the dunes where they were alone, the skipper had produced his manhood and asked him to play with it. He had first done it with his hand, and had later taken it in his mouth, until the captain was finished. But that had been the only occasion.

Cornelis Frooij did not wish to add anything to what he had already said. The boys' confessions had been procured under duress, that was obvious; they merely wanted to escape the pains of torture. He maintained his plea of not guilty.

The third degree of interrogation is applied to capital cases where the state or authorised authority, in this case the Company, is already convinced of the accused's guilt. The purpose of interrogation now becomes a confession of guilt. His life is regarded as already forfeited to the state, and the procedure as if he is being executed. Should he, for example, die under interrogation, this is precisely what is entered on the act of accusation: *Died under interrogation*. The members of the bench and the secretary, prosecutor and executioner are present. The questions are read out, and on the request of the prosecutor the chairman authorises the use of harsher methods, like glowing irons, pins, the extraction of teeth, toenails, fingernails, or the rack.

Frooij confessed that he had committed the unspeakable sin three times with Klaas and once with Joost. After these confessions the court found all three of the accused guilty and sentenced them to be dropped into the bosom of the sea and be suffocated by seawater until death ensued. Deneyn took the certificate to the governor, for his confirmation and *fiat*.

'Six days, and all done,' smiled Goske. 'And on the seventh, he rested. Were you not in too much of a hurry?'

'The confessions came quickly.'

'What about mitigation? Or deferral with a view to appeal? You wanted to use Frooij in a case against Hugo. And Frooij is not exactly what you would call a scoundrel. My wife liked him, he often dined here.'

'He put his private parts into places where I would not put my walking stick.'

'You must realise how it will weaken your case against Hugo. You said there was an innocent man in irons on Mauritius. What about offering deferral, for appeal to Batavia? Then I can immediately appoint someone over *Helena*, and send the ship on its way.'

'No. No. In one word: sodomy stinks.'

'And Hugo? Without Frooij's evidence Col may rot in his irons.'

'It could take months, years. We can all die.'

'You are a hard man, Fiscal Deneyn.'

'That is what I heard them say about Your Honour. You are my constant example.'

The three convicted men were taken to the Council chamber in the morning, and the sentence was read out to them. Was there anything they wished to say to it? All three asked the court for mercy. Then they had to sign their sentences. Joost Jansz made a small cross, the others grimly wrote. Deneyn had them taken back to their cells immediately, and made his preparations for the execution: the captain of *Marken* had to take the necessary manacles, chains and weights on board the same morning. The condemned would arrive after dark; they had to be locked up separately in the hell, with a guard at every door. They would eat at the usual time, and were to receive no extra liquor, tobacco or other privileges. They were not allowed visitors. They could be given candles and writing materials, but the guards had to look out for arson.

At about ten o'clock that night he had them all rowed to *Marken*. It was pitch dark, overcast, with a cold northerly wind. He sat on the stern thwart, the lantern between his feet. Beside him the quarter-master, ancient, puny and shapelessly bundled up, was at the helm. His voice carried no further than the first oars. 'Pull, and . . . pull, and . . . pull.' Opposite them were Frooij and the boys, wrapped in blankets.

'Execution is tomorrow evening before sunset,' Deneyn said close to Frooij's ear.

'St Paul to the Ephesians: ". . . *let not the sun go down upon your wrath.*" Day after tomorrow I'll quote you chapter and verse.'

'I packed writing materials for you. The *dominee* will come in the morning. Is there anything you need?'

'Air.'

'I have a request, skipper. You know that Mary Hugo is waiting for the affidavit you promised.'

'Pity now, isn't it?'

'*Marken* is leaving for Mauritius in a few days. If you wish, you can write the affidavit, for their sake.'

'Is the word of a monster of nature accepted in court?'

'There is no other hope.'

'I see.'

'Pull, and . . . pull, and . . . pull,' sighed the quartermaster, and stroke by stroke, like the ticking of clockwork, the splash of the oars in the uneasy sea brought them closer to *Marken*.

Deneyn did not go on board. He held the lantern's light to his face, and waved. Captain de Keizer was there, and some of the duty watch to help the prisoners over the gunwale. 'Heavy weather coming, fiscal!' called de Keizer, as Deneyn's crew held their sloop against his flute.

That night he worked on Col's case, against Commander Hugo. It was nearly daybreak by the time he went to bed, and when he got up in the late morning, it was still dark, with a northerly wind carrying a strong smell of living seawater over the whole land and into his room in the Castle. Since daylight the soldiers had been razing the old Fort from van Riebeeck's time, and when he woke up, only the stone Kat was still standing. Deneyn took his tarred hat and black oilskin, and at one o'clock met the *dominee* and the two delegates from the Council. With the *dominee* was Ensign Croese, who had just been appointed head of the garrison. The executioner, a silent, shiny black bundle, waited with three sailors in a sailing sloop against the jetty.

The crossing, against the cold wind and a steep sea all the way to where *Marken* was pitching in the heavy swell, took an unpleasant hour. He clung tightly to the gunwale. Deneyn always felt suspicious of the sea, like a man in a bitter marriage; he mistrusted the woman, but couldn't do without her. On the boundless ocean was ample opportunity for an awful mishap. Ensign Croese was seasick and pale; they had trouble getting him up the ladder and on deck.

'You fellows can wait in the forecastle,' Skipper de Keizer told the boatmen. He himself led the *dominee* forward, and returned to ask Deneyn whether they should wait until sunset.

'We should wait at least until the *dominee* has finished.'

De Keizer took them to the cabin, lit the hanging lamp from a candle, called for brandy and placed a deck of cards on the table. But the wintry weather could not be kept out; the groaning of the anchor cables and the anguished creaking of shrouds and masts shuddered through the ship. Deneyn shuffled the cards and dealt them round the table.

De Keizer fanned his cards open in his hand, rearranged them, and pushed a rix-dollar forward. 'A few guilders on the game?'

They concentrated on the game, took cards from the hand and discarded them and looked for better ones and stuck them in their hand. The golden liquor tilted from side to side in their glasses.

'The widow's lap will be bitter tonight.'

They flung down cards, picked up others. 'And cold.'

'Always. How can you expect anything else? Ah, I've heard stories, of those who almost got away. Perhaps it's true, about the English captain who went down east of Mauritius. Pass me the bottle. As he jumped, his foot caught in the bight of a rope and there he dangled overboard by one leg, and a fat old woman in the sea grabbed him by the other foot, and there he hung, spreadeagled over the sea, and the rolling of the ship ducked him and ducked him, until he drowned.'

They played a round or two in silence, pushing small piles of coins across the table, handing round the bottle. Croese pushed his cards away and lowered his head in his arms.

'Those English. Once they sailed from Ceylon with an elephant on board, I heard, and right there at Mauritius they also went down. Some sailors fashioned a raft from spars, and threw it overboard, and jumped on it. Then the elephant jumped on top of them. Blood and splinters. Nothing left. Pass the bottle.'

'Up? A dollar a round? Or three?'

Croese pushed his chair back, and stumbled through the door with a hand over his mouth to retch over the gunwale.

'Downwind,' de Keizer shouted after him. 'Another round? Three dollars from now, right?' He dealt another hand.

'I remember one skipper, when he saw it was time to go, the widow was waiting, he transferred all the silver from his sea chest to the belt around his stomach. Then he threw the chest overboard and leaped after it. The chest floated, but he sank like a stone.'

They played for an hour, increasing the stakes once more, and twice called for another bottle. Then they became silent. Deneyn felt the slow onset of nausea, he gripped the edge of the table with both hands. His eyes were streaming like the windows of the gallery. The sea pushed green-white over the small windows, the ship sank down, the windows grew dark, it staggered up, went down again, struggled upward. He felt the liquid pushing up in his throat. He swallowed and swallowed to hold it down. His mouth filled with water. Fathoms down Leviathan stirred in thin, green slime.

'Where's the *dominee* staying?' asked the captain. 'We'll be working in the dark.' He tugged at the door; the light spilled outside, the storm tore coat and door from his hands, splashing water inside.

The *dominee* came in, put his sea-drenched Bible down among their money and wet glasses, looked into Deneyn's eyes and said softly: 'Here are a few letters for family. Will you forward them, or shall I?'

When they came on deck, it was raining hard. Deneyn accompanied de Keizer to the forecastle. A mournful song came from the low hatch, high, urgent, shrill against the thundering wind. Perhaps it was a hymn, but Deneyn did not recognise it. During a lull the captain bent over and shouted: 'What are you singing down there? What blaspheming is that?'

'A hymn of thanks, skipper.'

'What for?'

'For the blessings bestowed so generously on seafolk every day.'

'Quartermaster, pipe both watches to lee side to witness the punishment. Boatswain, hoist the red flag to the mizzen-top. Provost, bring along six men and follow me down to the hell.'

The prisoners were hauled from their narrow holes, pushed up the stairs, manacled and weighted on deck. Sailors padded past, to crouch with their backs to the rain against the gunwale, trying to stare through the grey rain to an invisible, grey shore. The lesson was for them. From his pocket Frooij pulled a sheet of paper, barely one-quarter of it covered in writing and without date or signature, and passed it to the fiscal.

'I was too sleepy. I have not slept for two nights, you know.'

The executioner descended the rope ladder into the boat, followed by three sailors. The shuddering prisoners were given ropes around the chest to help them down with their heavy irons. When the last of the three ropes were flung off and became slack, Deneyn motioned to the quartermaster to push away. The executioner looked up at him, and he nodded. In the sloop the two sails were shaken out and caught the wind, flapping and jerking wildly. The boat immediately buried its head into a wave. On deck they couldn't hear when the condemned were pushed overboard, but waited in the driving rain for the boat, now nearly empty, to return.

It rained for three days and three nights. A winter storm from the north brought work on the Castle to a standstill. On the quay nothing moved, except the waves, green as bottle glass, that broke and ran foaming over it. The streets were streaming channels of mud. In the Company gardens trees were torn from the ground and a pomegranate hedge of a hundred and eighty paces long was blown down. Outside on the anchorage the Company's ships bucked and staggered on double head-ropes.

On the morning of the fourth day, it was 29 July, there was not a cloud in the sky, not a breeze in the air, the sea was still and smooth as glass. The face of Table Mountain streamed with white waterfalls. How miraculous the contrasts of nature, the secretary expressed his feelings about the beautiful morning in the journal, that three days of raging storms could be succeeded so suddenly by such an exquisite stillness? The whole world washed so clean? Shortly after daybreak there were shots from Robben Island, calling for help. Deneyn had to go out there to see, Governor Goske instructed him, and he had to take a surgeon with him.

It was Eva van Meerhof again. There was a new postkeeper, an old sergeant with a grey beard and wide clothes he had made from canvas. 'I shall tell you every word of it, *Meester* fiscal, the way it happened. You know that woman, and you know it is hard to contain her. I heard that she used to be the postkeeper's wife here on the island. Her husband was also a surgeon, but he was murdered on Madagascar.'

'I know.'

'When I took over here, the postkeeper told me that the bloody whore was spreading the English disease among the convicts. I asked for her to be sent ashore, but the governor was afraid she might infect the garrison, they had no more quicksilver to treat that bunch of adulterers. Then she had the child here at the post, and he is a year old now, but he causes a lot of work. They sent us an old slave woman, but the old crone has given up. She tries, but she cannot. It is as if it's against her faith. I must confess to you now: I gave Missus van Meerhof arrack.'

'What!'

'Yes. Only little sips to begin with, with water. And do you know what I succeeded in doing? I made her get up from that bed where she'd lain for almost a year. She gets up now and comes to the posthouse for her morning tot and her midday tot and her evening tot. That was what I succeeded in.'

'You have no right.'

'No, I know. Last week the shell boat came here, and the quartermaster saw her here in the house, and he greeted her. She answered with a curse. You must beat her, postkeeper, he told me. Otherwise she won't listen. It is the only language she understands. But then she began to whine about her children. I told her I didn't know where they were. She looked through the door here over the sea to the shore, and swore at me through the gap in her bottom teeth, a word that sounded like a hiccup. The quartermaster took my cane from the table and gave her four or five blows on the back and arms.

'Well, the surgeon here can say if I am right, because he told me so himself: the disease gives them ugly sores on the body which bleed easily, but there isn't much feeling in the skin. So you can beat them to death, and they don't even know, but they're bleeding all the time. So the quartermaster said to me: You must beat her, postkeeper. She is totally possessed by the Devil. Look, she's still swearing. Because Eva had lowered her head, but we could see her mouth moving. Let her be, coxs'n, I said. She has made up her mind. You can thrash her to shreds, but she has already made up her mind.'

Because he'd felt sorry for her, he had then given her an extra cupful that morning, and by noon when it was feeding time again, she was like a woman possessed. 'She screamed, she swore, she howled like a dog; she lay here on the flagstones whimpering and foaming at the mouth until I had to go outside to get away from her. I walked down to the beach.'

'What was she crying for?'

'Liquor. And Master Fiscal, that was the last I saw of her, alive or dead. Until the following evening.'

'You searched for her.'

'The old slave woman was the first to come and tell me. You know how it became cloudy that morning, and by late afternoon it started raining. She told me the child was hungry, and she didn't know where the woman was.'

He'd left with the duty guard. Spread across the width of the island, they walked up against the gale, head on the chest and oilskins clutched at the chest. The scrub and dunes were soaked; on the clay soil surrounding the stone quarry a large marsh had formed. Before them the sea smashed against the rocks, sending curtains of spray and shreds of thick, beaten foam flying far inland. The dark came down early and quickly. They grouped in front of the hearth in the posthouse to talk. The rain beat against the wall and clattered against the single window shutter, and sometimes a gust of wind swept down the chimney, causing the embers on the hearth to glow for a while, and sometimes with a handful of heavy drops flopping down in the ashes.

It was still raining at daybreak. He allowed the convicts to sleep until it was nearly daylight, and when he went to read their prayer, he explained what he wanted. They had their porridge with prunes, and all together went out into the miserable weather, accompanied by their guard of twenty soldiers. The rain was cold in their faces and the wind shook them as they struggled against it across the island, towards the northern beach. There every thundering wave came storming green and white over the black rocks, splashing in their faces, churning around their legs. They searched up and down, probing the holes with sticks, then divided into two groups, one to walk eastward round the island, the other west. The meeting point would be the Fire Hill. He himself led the group with the longest and hardest route, on the side of the island that faced the open sea. There they found Eva at the Salt Rock in a pool of seawater, behind the piles of foam left by the night's high tide. Perhaps she'd fallen in there in the dark. They carried the body to the Fire Hill. He knew that one shouldn't touch a body if you had wounds on your own hands, because then her sickness would pass into your blood, so he and others who had healthy hands carried her home on their oiled overcoats. And they were drenched to the skin by the time they arrived at the posthouse.

They could all see that the weather was going to continue for days. No boat could be expected before it changed. So they contrived a coffin and covered the body with half a bag of raw sea salt, keeping the coffin in the woodshed for the fiscal.

Deneyn went out to identify the corpse. The surgeon scraped the salt from her face with a small plank. 'I cannot say here, fiscal. She must be put on the table. It might be drowning, as the postkeeper said, and we must open her lungs. As you can see, the English disease has broken out all over her.'

He asked the postkeeper to nail an old boat's sail over the box. Then the convicts carried it on their shoulders to the shell boat. The old slave woman, carrying the child bundled in blankets, was delighted to climb into the boat. It was her day of salvation.

On shore the fiscal summoned a slave with a wheelbarrow filled with lime bags from the kiln, to push the coffin to the hospital. Just before the end of the quay its wheel sank into the sand. A sailor tied a rope around the axle, and with the rope over his shoulder pulled in front while the slave pushed the wheelbarrow behind. Deneyn followed, with the ancient woman and the bundled child.

The secretary concluded his journal entry for the day with a few remarks on Eva's life. Some of the children from her marriage had already died, but three were still alive. Since her husband's death she had given birth to just as many illegitimate children. She had been placed on Robben Island several times to take her out of reach of liquor, but there abandoned herself to immorality. Her innate evil could readily be seen from her behaviour.

Deneyn went from the hospital to the Castle, to speak to Long Gert about the children. He found him among the roof trusses of a building against the western wall of the Castle.

'Welcome to the future governor's house.'

'Such a huge place for one man?'

'No, he will have only the three rooms here at the back. The front portion is the Council chamber, and on Sundays it will double as church.'

'What will become of our ark then?'

'For the moment it will remain. This hall won't be ready for months.'

'I have a funeral for the ark tomorrow.'

'Whose?'

'It is Pieternella's mother. She died the day before yesterday.'

'Oh no. What do I tell the children?'

'It worries me too. But you will know better than I. The first thing is to reassure the children that their life will not change. Naturally they will feel bad for some time. The other matter is about money. Their father's small credit now goes to them. If you will take care of the first matter, I shall handle the second. And rather you than your wife. Or what do you think?'

'No, my wife has already suffered losses. She is better with such things. I'd rather have her speak to Pieternella.'

'Good. Now look, the funeral. I won't be sending messengers round, I don't want people there. I prefer to keep it simple and poor, as the children must pay for everything. No deep mourning, please tell Sofia that. So we'll have one body, a *dominee*, a fiscal. Two foster-parents, your Pieter and three orphans. Did Eva have friends among the people at the Cape?'

'There was Maijke Hendriksz.'

'Leave her. And no meal for the guests.'

'Sofia and I would like to offer something, at our expense.'

'Good, and thank you. Until tomorrow at four then, at your house.'

Eva was buried under the floorboards of the ark. Deneyn paid for the gravediggers, the shroud and the coffin from his own purse, and spoke to the *dominee* in advance about a simple service for a wife and mother who had been baptised, confirmed and married in the Reformed faith. The three children sat in the first row of chairs of the church, neatly dressed and combed, Pieternella forlorn in pleated black, and the boys with black cravats on the chest. The only other difference he could see between them and Long Gert's young Pieter, was that the three of them were weeping into big black handkerchiefs. Jan Vos had entered with them, but shuffled past to sit in the back row on his own. The coffin was made of pale pine and without handles, standing on a low pedestal like a flour chest. The *dominee* announced the hymn, but set it in too high, and only he and Sofia reached the end. His service was brief, the bare formulary in crape without a lesson. Upon the *dominee*'s sign the two gravediggers lashed their ropes round the ends of the coffin and lowered it into the grave, hand over hand. Deneyn caught a mother-of-pearl shine of fish scales glimmering on the sea-worn rope. As the *dominee* approached the end of his prayer, Deneyn nodded at them. 'Shovel in.'

The *dominee* walked back to the house with him; he and Deneyn were the only guests. He opened with a prayer of thanks, and drank two bowls of tea while comparing the miracle of life with the miracle of death, and the children at a corner of the table sadly shook their heads when Sofia or Pieter offered them sweetmeats. Later Sofia asked Pieternella: 'Won't you take Jan something?' All four children used the opportunity to get to their own worlds. Then the *dominee* could enquire about the children's progress at school, and Deneyn about Jakobus's progress in his trade.

The sun was almost down when he and Long Gert sat round the table with Pieternella to discuss her estate. Jakobus, her eldest brother, was to become the estate keeper, but until he came of age would have no say in the estate. The Orphan master would administer it on his behalf.

'What does it mean: when Kobus comes of age?'

'If he has enough years under his hat. Everybody receives it at twenty-five, but for a hardworking boy who supports his brother and sister, the Company will issue the certificate at eighteen.'

'But if he cannot?'

'If he dies young, or if he is too careless with money, or becomes a drunk, or lands in prison, then the duty falls to the next son.'

Her face was serious, as if she had already assumed the responsibility, when she asked: 'How much do we have now?'

'That is why we are talking to you rather than to Jakobus, for you can explain it better to him.'

He calculated it for her with a pencil on paper. Her late father had left 917 guilders to his wife and children. The church had divided it: a half to their mother and a half to the three children. Their mother's portion had been invested with the money lenders, and earned a monthly interest, but because she had spent more on food, clothing and medicine than her interest brought in, her portion had become less and less. At her death she had only these few guilders left. Deneyn wrote down the amount in large figures on the right side of the sheet. 'This was her credit. It is now yours.'

The other half, which she and her brothers had inherited from their father, was 458 guilders. A soldier of the Company earned such an amount in six years. It had been invested, and earned interest. It was their credit, so he wrote that down on the right hand too. Thirdly, they were fortunate in inheriting a good and healthy slave from their father. Every month the man earned twice as much as a soldier in the garrison. This was their credit, so it was also entered on the right. Now if they added it all up, this was how much she and her brothers had to their credit.

'Does it look like much to you, Pieternella? But first let us look at what has to be deducted from it. There are three of you, and Jan Vos, but your mother had other children as well, like Hieronimus and Anthonie. You all need food, clothes and a roof over your heads. You are growing up, and now wear more expensive clothes. When I saw you on the island for the first time, you were barefoot. Today you are dressed like the best in Amsterdam. You and Salomon have to pay school fees, and Kobus his apprentice fee. Last month we bought Kobus an ivory comb. He is growing up and wants to look good. If we add up all your monthly expenses, we must write it on the left here. We call that the debit. You see, you are already using more every month than comes in. Every month we have to use a little bit of your inheritance too, otherwise there is not enough for your needs. How long is your inheritance going to last?'

'Spoken like a schoolmaster,' grinned Long Gert.

Pieternella stared at the figures for a long time. Among the Koina there was no money or credit or debit. But she understood how it worked. There were five of them who had to live, but only Jan Vos who earned anything. One day their father's money would be finished and one day Jan Vos would also die. And then? Lost in thought she put out her hand for the pencil.

'We shall have to live very frugally.'

'Indeed, Pieternel,' said Long Gert. 'But in four years or thereabouts you will get married, then your husband will take care of you.' She silently stared at him, until he laughed. 'Now don't be scared, my child. Nature will prepare you.'

It remained a mystery to her. Would she have to get married in four years' time? And what about Kobus and Salomon? She still had to learn to live with the knowledge of not having a mother or father any more.

Deneyn saw the doubt on her face and wished that he could help her gain assurance. He had done it for others before. Pieternella was only eight or ten years younger than himself.

Long Gert spoke while he had the child's attention. 'Pieternel, believe what I tell you. Work and save, those are the words. Hard work and a tight grip on the neck of the purse will bring you to the top. My mother was like that, and so was her mother.'

'Yes,' said Deneyn. 'It can help, for things are against us everywhere. But let us proceed. There is still the matter of Anthonie. The Church Council hired Jan Heere's wife to look after him. You know where Jan Heere lives, in the Sea Street. Perhaps you may feel like looking at how it goes with Anthonie, but my advice is: don't. I must tell you, it is not a pretty sight. He was born with a very contagious disease. If you were to get infected by him now, you will be very unhappy for ever. You must never touch Anthonie, and never put anything in your mouth that he has touched, and never kiss him. Tell it to your brothers. Make sure they understand, these are matters of life and death.'

'What disease?'

'They call it the English disease. I think it would be better for you not to visit him.'

'Must Anthonie die?'

'Yes. You and I must also die, but he will go earlier because of the disease.'

She began to cry again.

In the following weeks Deneyn had sentenced a sailor to be keel-hauled and carry shells on the island for four years for drawing his knife from the scabbard. Two soldiers convicted of theft he had flogged and put on the island for three and five years respectively, and four runaway slaves he sentenced to scourging with the loss of their ears, followed by lifelong labour on the island. And a Javanese who had resentfully resisted a guard, he sentenced to the latter with the loss of his two thumbs and his tongue.

And Maijke Hendriksz had now had time enough to organise her estate. Of what use could her provisions and transactions be any more? The time had come for her to go the island like the others. She still had to evacuate the farm. Den Uitwijk had once been the best farm along the river. Van Riebeeck had personally chosen and developed it and ensured that there would be proper surveillance of what his slaves did there. The soil curled rich and black behind the ploughshare, the river was full of water all year round, the vleis covered with young grass, and no wind blew over the wheat in that valley at all. Tielman Hendriksz had been van Riebeeck's farmhand at the time he bought it from his master, but once he had it, he only used it to sleep there at night, hunting by day and leaving his farm-hand and two slaves to look after the farming. After the Gonjemans had cut his throat at the Moordkuil, Maijke tried to continue on her own, but what could she do? She couldn't hunt, she could not trade, and her farm would not prosper. Had she been younger or more attractive, her remaining farmhand might have taken more trouble for her. The lands and the vegetable garden were a messy wilder-ness of weeds and unkempt shrubs, her plough stood abandoned in the middle of the field, and the house needed thatching and plas-tering. One might say that those were her own concerns, not for anybody else to bother about, but how did she manage to let a good farm go to ruin like that? Van Riebeeck's hair would stand on end if he were to see Den Uitwijk.

Deneyn rode to the valley with a clerk and two assistants to enquire how far she had progressed with her arrangements. The plough still stood in the middle of the overgrown fallow land. The house was in disrepair: sheaves of decaying thatch hung from the roof, and patches of plaster had fallen from the walls. An unpainted window shutter drooped from a single rawhide hinge. A man looked out from the outbuilding when the dog began to bark, and crossed the yard ahead of them, pushing open the door of the house.

'Missus, show yourself. The fiscal is here.'

Deneyn handed the horses to the farmhand. 'Walk them, give them water, put them in the stable. Do not off-saddle. Be at hand if there is anything I want to know.'

Slow and broad like a herring boat in a narrow stream, Maijke came into the front room.

'Good day, Maijke.'

'Good day, Justice.'

'How is the farming going?'

'It is easier to trade than to farm.'

He had to put an end to such talk immediately. 'Then you must get out of the Company's dominions, because our prince gave all trade from Cape of Good Hope eastward to Cape Horn to the Company. And it has the monopoly. Go to America if you want to set up shop.'

'Yes, I know, Justice.'

'What does your farmhand do?'

'He is repairing the plough.'

'Why aren't you farming?'

'I know I have to leave this place.'

'You will be leaving in a fortnight. I have come to make an inventory of your possessions. You need to have an auction.'

'I need more time.'

'You've had more than enough time. You must come with us. Now.'

'Go on your own, why must I follow you?'

'To make sure you don't hide anything behind my back, and so that you can't say I stole anything. Come, you know how these things work.'

In the farmhouse were a few rough tables and chairs, a pot rack, a long kitchen bench, a wide bedstead and a *katil*, pewter plates, some pieces of crockery, a spit and grill on the hearth, barrels, pots. The walls were bare. Outside in the yard were a small number of ducks and chickens, a washing barrel, and under an old tree an anvil and a sturdy wagon.

'How many sheep and cattle?'

She mentioned some figures.

'Slave?'

'Yes, a very good one.' That was worth something. His eyes wandered over the well-situated farm. The harvest was worthless, the haystack was small and trampled down, but he could get something for it. He went to inspect the outbuilding, wrote down the farmhand's bed, table, chair and musket, then went into the workshop where the farmhand was cutting at the plough handle with an adze. There were gardening implements, a hayfork, some carpentry tools, a few barrels.

'Does the musket belong to you?'

'No, Your Honour.'

'Leave the plough, and start thatching the roof today. And once that is done, immediately start plastering and whitewashing. I must sell this place.'

'I don't have any thatch.'

Deneyn gave the farmhand four blows with his cane across the arms and shoulders. 'Then go and cut some. And get clay and lime. You've had years to get thatch and lime ready for today. I'm coming back for the auction in a fortnight, and I'll strip the hide off your back if I don't get two thousand guilders for the place. And mind you go and find other work. Your contract expires next Friday. Otherwise you're back in the barracks.'

'Yes, Your Honour.'

'How many sheep and cattle do you have here?'

After the farmhand had told him, he had to change Maijke's figures. 'Why are you lying to me, Maijke?'

'I didn't know any better myself.'

He took her outside under the tree, and enquired about heirs for her estate.

There were a son Hendrik with her late husband in Holland, and two daughters. The elder, whom she'd had with her first husband, was Cornelia, married to Pieter Jansz van Nimwegen, living on Mauritius. They had a child, Hester Pietersz of Mauritius. The younger daughter had been born here and was married to Gerrit Visser, known as Gerrit Grof, that is, Gerrit the Blacksmith. With Tielman she'd had only that one child. Young, but already mother of two.

'The son and your two married daughters are out of the estate. The Company claims everything you own.'

On the day of the auction Maijke's slave, a man from India to judge from his appearance, fell on his knees before Deneyn and grasped his legs with both hands.

'Justice, in the name of Jesus. Give me justice.'

Deneyn called for help, for someone to pull the fellow off him. His servant was there first and gave the slave a blow on the head with his stick, which sent him bleeding, half unconscious, and still whimpering, to the ground. 'Give me justice.' The blood flowed down his neck, dripping over his greasy jerkin and Deneyn's shoes.

'Help him up.' The man got up on his own, pushed away the servant, and asked Deneyn: 'In the name of God, give me justice.'

'What do you want? Who are you?'

'Jakob from Colombo.'

'So. Mrs Maijke's slave.'

'No. I am a free man. There are witnesses.'

'Where were you when I came to make the inventory?'

'I was in the veld with the stock.'

'And why should you be free?'

'I swear, when Master Tielman was sick, I prayed him back to health. There he promised that I would never be sold. I had to serve the woman, but when it came to selling, I was to be free.'

'You prayed him back to health?'

'He was dying. The surgeon sat with the little mirror in front of his mouth. His shroud lay ready there on the bed. That was where I prayed for him.'

Deneyn nodded to his clerk and took the slave aside, to the water barrel under the tree, so that he could wash his face. Fresh blood mingled with the water in the barrel. Deneyn shook out his kerchief and handed it to him. 'Wet this. Stanch the blood.'

It was a strange tale they heard there, once the man had finished drinking and washing. He was a Catholic, and had made himself a rosary of seeds on a thong so that he could pray in the veld. One evening Tielman came to his room and saw him praying with the beads, and told him that nobody would ever hear this from his mouth, but he'd been a Catholic himself in his youth. But here it was forbidden, and if they were to find out, he could expect them to make life hard for him. When Tielman fell ill and they came to tell him that his master was dying, he went in and prayed beside the bed; it was St Thomas he invoked to intervene for the sick man. He prayed there in silence, without beads. The woman, the surgeon and the farmhand were all present around the bed, keeping their vigil with a bottle of brandy and tobacco pipes. At daylight the fever broke. That same morning Tielman promised him that he would never be sold again.

Deneyn told the clerk: 'If the man is a Catholic, he is free anyway. The Company's policy is: no Christians in chains. We shall not put him up for auction, I am going to discuss the matter with the governor. Take statements from the woman and the farmhand and find out which surgeon treated her husband, so that we can enquire about his story.'

Maijke contradicted the slave, saying that he was a sworn liar, but such a hypocrite one could whitewash the house with him. But when the clerk mentioned the other witnesses and demanded an oath from her, she only said: 'A hundred guilders to the Devil, how is one to make a living?' and then corroborated what he had said. 'Now you have stripped an old woman bare, fiscal. Are you pleased with your work?'

Jan Mostert, the father of young Gisela who was growing prettier by the day, secured an advantageous contract with the government to rent Den Uitwijk, with an option to buy after a year. Fourteen days later Deneyn had Maijke conveyed to Robben Island on the shell boat, for life. The postkeeper had to give her work suitable for a woman. He arranged for her married daughter to take charge of her weekly rations, as the Company was not going to give her anything.

It occurred to Deneyn to place the child Anthonie in Maijke's care, as it was already being passed on from one caretaker to another. The foster-parents tended to last for only a few months, before they asked the church to find another home. First it was Jan Heere the sick-comforter, then Frans de Bruin and his wife, and then Cornelis Adriaansz, whose wife likewise informed them that they wanted more money, otherwise they couldn't manage, as they had exceptional trouble and expenses with the child. All of that within a year. Deneyn had kept it from Pieternella. So, perhaps the child should go to Maijke, since she and Eva had been friends before.

About this time the governor told Deneyn to investigate, at the request of the Church Council, what was going on in the household of Willem Willemsz van Deventer. He had been on the island for eighteen months now, and had asked on several occasions to be returned ashore, as there had been problems in his house, and so far the governor had only written to the postkeeper to tell Willemsz he shouldn't bother him with his letters, and bear in mind that he himself was the cause and source of his misfortune. Later the man had written to be brought ashore so that he could be seen by a doctor for his dropsy, and the governor had refused. Then the postkeeper wrote if he could remove the chains from the man's legs as the legs had swollen so much. Some time back the church had requested that the law be summoned to act on what was going on in Willemsz's household, and possibly set an example to the congregation. Now there had even been a letter from Lords Seventeen regarding Willemsz. Would Deneyn please go and see and report on it?

Deneyn cast his thoughts back over the matter, and requested the relevant volumes from the Secretariat. Willemsz was married to Maria Visser. Oh, that one, adulterous since girlhood. At the time there had been a farmhand who had slept with her. Now the church wanted to make an example of them. It would not be of any use to speak to

Willemsz about it, as he was no longer present on the scene. The lock and key of the story was Maria Visser.

She was now nineteen, thickset and unwashed, already overblown, bare to the waist in the spring weather and with a short pipe in the mouth when she opened the door for him.

'Go and put on your clothes. Or is this a brothel?' She muttered something about Ockert, and pushed the door to. He paced up and down outside the door, later knocked again and shouted against the door: 'Justice! Fiscal Deneyn!' and went inside. She was not in the front room.

'Maria Visser. Appear before the Law.'

She entered with a dirty child on the arm, a greasy sheepskin around her shoulders.

'Are you Maria Visser, housewife of Willem Willemsz?'

'Yes. You know me.'

'Don't tell me what I know or think, or whom I know. You cannot see inside my head. Maria Visser, your husband has been on the island for eighteen months now. Is this your child, how old is he, and who is the father?'

'Ockert Olivier.'

'Have you had more children born out of wedlock?'

'One other.'

'Have the children been baptised?'

'The *dominee* turned Ockert away.'

'Your husband is the Lords' prisoner on Robben Island, and has asked the governor to enquire into the misconduct in his house.'

'I don't want Willem any more.'

'Then you have to sue for a divorce and see that your children are cared for, but not persist in adultery in his house while he is in chains. I am telling you, if Willem doesn't bring a case against you, I shall, but you will end in the spinning house on Batavia, among others of your kind.'

'Then I'll go to your spinning house.'

'All right, if that is your choice. I shall initiate the arrangements. In the meantime, let your fellow adulterer know what I told you.'

After that he went to the island one day to take a statement from the Lyreman and to see how old Maijke fared. They spoke among the flowers on the bank behind the mounds of broken seashells. Willemsz's legs were thickly swollen with water, but he could still stand and handle the shovel.

'Is it painful?'

'Yes, my whole body is aching.'

'What medicine do they give you?'

'Nothing.'

'I shall see what I can do.' He told him that his wife now wanted to divorce him. He marvelled at the man's patience.

'The people here on the island have told me about the children, but I have forgiven her. I'll raise the children as my own.'

'She wants a divorce.'

'That I cannot. Even if we have to live in disharmony for ever, I won't let her go. That is why I went to seek out the prince, and came back. It is to be with her; she was so young and beautiful to me.'

'She is going from here to the spinning house in Batavia. If you won't lodge a complaint against her, I will.'

'Lodge, if you must. I can't. What will you charge her with?'

'Adultery. Public immorality. Indecency.'

'And my two children?'

'The church will propose something.'

The postkeeper took him to Maijke, where she was pretending to work in the vegetable garden. She had other work too, she went to show him. There were a few rabbits in a cage, and in the evenings she helped the cook. To his surprise she seemed satisfied and almost cheerful.

'I feel young again,' she said. 'I work hard, and I feel healthy. I have lots of time to think about my faults. Yes, I've also started praying again.'

'You must let me know if you get dropsy. Or if you have any other request.'

'Yes. I have a request right now. The men have their habits, I was married twice myself, but I am no longer in the mood for their stuff.

Everybody who comes past here has something to say. It is: "How about it, sweetie?" And: "Two *stuyvers*, my buttercup." I am a Dutch woman, not one of their tarts.'

'I understand. I shall tell the postkeeper to forbid them.'

'The next I'll give a smack in the face.'

'Don't. They are violent men. Just keep quiet and tell the post-keeper.'

'In that way a man is worse than an animal, because an animal doesn't bother you all year.'

Her hypocrisy irritated him. Was she hoping for a remission of sentence, for her good behaviour? Really, she couldn't think much of his intelligence. With his information he returned to the governor. He suggested that they oppose a divorce as there was more advantage to the Company in keeping married couples and their children together in the hope of reconciliation, and aim at eliminating the interloper Ockert Olivier. It could possibly be achieved through negotiation and discussion with all parties. But the governor wondered who would listen to a human being when nature spoke? Deneyn was young and had much confidence in himself. Yet he promised to take Willemsz's case to the Council.

As Jakobus began to grow up, misfortune struck. At that time Deneyn was getting the feeling of simple, comfortable times slipping away; of something coming to an end, the way fine weather disappeared behind a horizon when heavy clouds moved in and cast their cold shadow over the sea. The shoemaker Jacomo Jacolini came to him, carrying his pride like a shield before him.

'Have you been informed about the business? It is bad for my shop.'

'What are you talking about?'

'Jakobus. Have you heard about the thing? It is not in the contract, *meester*. If I'd known, I would not have taken him. Can you imagine what will happen if there are ladies and Jakobus falls down?'

Deneyn made him sit down, and asked him to tell it from the beginning. A sad picture unfolded. Jacolini had been at his workbench; he was stirring a pot of glue over a flame and drawing twine through the green berry wax to thread a fine needle for a girl's small shoe. Kobus was astride his bench, clamping a boot between his knees, leaning slightly forward. With his weight on the awl he pressed holes through sole, inner leather and uppers, when suddenly, bellowing in a deep voice like a giant, he slid off the bench. His head hit the floor. It was the roar of a madman that made Jacolini look round. There the boy was on the ground, his legs kicking, his arms flailing, his face white and contorted with tension. His mouth was wide open, his tongue a hard purple lump deep in his throat, and his eyes rolling white in his head, and he jerked and screamed, while all the time stabbing about him with the awl. Jacolini splashed water, trying to hold the boy and grab his arm, but it was only when he lay still of his own accord that they could do something for him. Once he'd calmed down, his colour returned, and then it took an effort to prise that awl from the fist. His hired help and the neighbours' slave carried the boy to hospital on a door.

'Epilepsy?'

'Exactly. That is what everybody assures me.'

'Was he hurt?'

'I don't know. He hasn't come back. For all I know, he is still there. But what I wanted to say, is that there is nothing about that in our articles. I was deceived. I demand justice.'

'I don't think something like that is bad for business, Jacolini. If the boy works well, he is a boon to you.'

'There's my shop. Have you seen the chairs I had made, and the mirror? I want the ladies to enjoy having their feet measured and their shoes fitted. I pour them tea. I come from a country of shoemakers. They will get a fright and faint, perhaps get hysterical. This sickness will give my shop a bad name.'

'Perhaps it won't happen again.'

'It will happen again and again. Somebody can get hurt with that awl. What about the glue pot? It is boiling. Think of the ladies.'

'I shall find out from the doctor.'

He went to the hospital. Doctor ten Damme had dripped brandy into the child's mouth to relax the muscles, but there was little else he could do. Epilepsy was a rare condition and little was known about it, but he was convinced it had something to do with the nerves. He would like to experiment with different medicines to see what he could do to prevent such attacks. Deneyn asked him what it would cost. The boy was not an official and had to pay for his services, but he was an orphan and poor. Hopefully the doctor could adjust his tariff?

Something else he arranged, before going to Long Gert's house to talk to them and Pieternella, was finding another master for Kobus. There was an old shoemaker called Kees Backer, who could use a cheap helper.

Sofia and Gert understood that it was neither the Good Lord nor the Devil who visited the child, nor was it a contagious condition, but something like constipation which could lie heavily on you today and be gone tomorrow, and that all Kobus needed was a bed to lie on and a friendly word when he came round again. He had heard that Emperor Julius had also suffered from epilepsy, and look how far he went. Perhaps he would outgrow it, the doctors said. At his age most children had nerves in one form or another. Doctor ten Damme's treatment would draw another two hundred guilders every month from Pieternella's fund, but there was nothing they could do about it.

What Deneyn regarded as the end of easier times, became worse with the illness of the slave Jan Vos. He had been complaining of fatigue for a long time, and became slower and slower in his movements. Long Gert noticed how he would clutch a ladder and take three or four long breaths before placing his foot on the bottom rung. When he walked on the eaves of the roof, he would shuffle a foot at a time from one spot to the next. At the saw, he could only give nine or ten pushes before he had to rest. Later he could no longer work. Long Gert took him to a surgeon. The man listened with his ear to Jan Vos's chest. He palpated the whole arm from hand to shoulder to feel a heartbeat, as well as under the left ear and other places where a pulse was supposed to throb, but there was no sign of a pulse.

'It's the heart. It is run down. Otherwise there is nothing wrong with Jan.'

Gert took Jan home. It was the end of his income. 'Jan Vos, I have to hire other people in your place. See what tasks you can do here around the house.' He bought a young house slave, and took in a German apprentice to learn Jan's work. The apprentice's first task was to measure Jan for a coffin, without waking him up, as he lay on his bed for a large part of the day with his shoes on and a red cap on his head and his eyes closed. Pieternella and her brothers sometimes went to speak to Jan and took him his soup when he was awake. His hair had long turned grey, but she could see his skin becoming pale. She told him that she knew how he had worn himself out working for them. He had helped to bring them up, and she would never forget it. Jan gently pressed her hand.

'The doctor says I must take the strong red medicine.'

'I shall bring you some.'

She told Sofia that Jan asked for a draught of wine, and Sofia sent Pieter with an earthenware pot to the tavern. Jan had a wooden mug like the one used by sailors, a small length cut from a spar, hollowed out with a pocket knife and decorated on the outside. Pieternella filled it three-quarters full. He sat back up against his pillow, took a deep draught from the mug, inhaled with satisfaction. Then pain struck him in the face. She could see it tearing through his body as if a meat hook had been driven into his chest and he had been hoisted up by it. His right hand held the half-empty mug out to her, before he turned his face to the wall and vomited the dark wine over his blanket, and died.

Pieternella mourned for a long time, and wore her black to school. Her brothers wore their crape only on the first day, after which they became unwilling. She asked Long Gert for Jan to be buried beside her mother, but that couldn't be done, as the ark was for the baptised only. Moreover, the ark was to be removed soon, then everybody would have to be laid away somewhere else.

'Will Jan Vos go to heaven?'

'I believe so. But perhaps he didn't want to. He told me their souls belong with the spirits of their ancestors. It is somewhere in the north.'

'Mister Heere says a black man doesn't have a soul. *Meester* Deneyn says it's an open question.'

'What would he mean by that?'

'He cannot find an image of one anywhere.'

'Confounded Catholic.'

The fiscal came to their house on Sunday, and spoke to Sofia. If they had no objection, he would like to take P'nella for a walk. 'I must tell her what her family's future looks like. And I want to make a few suggestions to her.'

The girl, as she grew older and developed, became increasingly attractive to him. The day would come when he should speak openly to her about his feelings, but she was still very young, barely fourteen, and ought not to be burdened with husband and children and a household while still in her childhood, like the young farm girls in the village. He would allow her the opportunity to live and to learn, and he would help her grow up, but he was determined to keep her for himself.

The veld behind the Company gardens was gold and white with spring flowers. They picked some and walked through the flowers to the outer canal at the western edge of the town, following from there the stream to the sea, as far as the slaves' graveyard, where they placed flowers on Jan Vos's grave. Some graves had a stone at the head, but not one had any inscription. Together they brought a big stone from the veld, which they placed at the head of his grave.

'I shall ask my brothers to come and cover the whole grave with stones,' she said, while he resolved to send convicts that coming Monday to do it. They walked still further outside the town, past the shelters of homeless Hottentots at the dunes. Pieternella carried Deneyn's short rattan under her arm. On the beach to the right of them stood the gallows and wheel of the outer justice, where the executed were displayed. There were no corpses, but three large crows examined them from the cross-beam as if taking their measurements. In front of the gallows lay a vast vlei, thickly sprinkled with the white dots of water hyacinths. Beyond the wide stretch of green seawater was Robben Island, a place on its own, but attached to the Cape in a woeful way.

She pointed to the flowers. 'This used to be one of my loveliest spots, here.'

'I'm sorry about the gallows. It became necessary.'

'But why so many? It wasn't here before. People say you have blood on your hands.'

He was surprised to hear it from her, and disappointed. He wanted her to think better of him. 'Do you believe that because there is no smoke going up here, P'nel, there is no war? Let me try to explain, if it is true that I'm being accused of blood. Wait, stand first. Listen to me.' He became agitated. 'I am a soldier of my prince. I do my duty. Our country was attacked, we were caught in the most uneven war in the entire history of Europe. The kings of France and England colluded to divide our country between them. Six years ago they made a conspiracy to acquire our harbours and our commerce, because I swear we have nothing else, no mines, no agriculture, no forests, no large population. Do you know the proverb: *The Creator made the earth, except for Holland*? Because what we have, we scraped together from the sea with our own hands. A French army invaded our country, and in one month they conquered ninety-two towns and cities, up to Utrecht, the city where our ancestors built our first church a thousand years ago. What was here in your country a thousand years ago, Pieternel? The French king rode at the head. His holy brothers in arms invaded from France and Germany, and overran that whole region along our eastern frontier. Three provinces, the largest part of our country, are now in their hands. We cut the dykes, and submerged what was left of our land under water. Rather no Netherlands at all, than a Netherlands under a foreign flag, we say. The prince has already lost most of his soldiers; now he is fighting with farmhands and tradesmen against overwhelming odds. Do you understand what I mean if I say that this Castle of Good Hope is the first fortress of India, and I am one of its officers? Please try to, P'nel. No Dutchman can be accused in these circumstances of having blood on his hands. There! A long plea, but it is important to me that you understand. And I don't care what the Cape says of me, as long as you understand how I feel about my work.'

'I believe what you say. But it was so beautiful here long ago. My mother used to say it was one of the best pastures of their people.'

'It is only part of a battlefield. The whole Cape is a battlefield. And all the sea around it.'

She kept gazing at the shining marsh, as if she was trying to imagine shouting hordes marching through smoke with banners and cannons. She could not succeed.

'Don't think, because you do not see smoke, that there is no war here, P'nel. It blazes all around us.'

From then, he looked up Pieternel's company and took to walk with her whenever the occasion presented itself. Sofia did not insist on a chaperone. Pieternel believed it was because she trusted them. Deneyn imagined that Sofia would be happy for P'nel to get betrothed to a prominent young man.

She invited Salomon to walk with them. He was unwilling; he was afraid of the fiscal. She had to plead with him, and bribe him. One day, while they were passing far behind the gallows, Salomon asked Deneyn: 'Why do the soldiers call that thing the widow with the wooden legs?'

'They're just mocking. They figure that a man who has been hanged, has married the gallows.'

'But married, so quickly?'

'It's like chickens.'

'Is that what you think of marriage?' asked Pieternella. 'Like chickens, and like a gallows?'

He heard how serious she was. He had to watch his words. She was intelligent and sensitive.

He would walk her in the direction of the Kloofnek, or to the Salt River mouth and other places where they would not see the gallows. In all directions the landscape was pleasant, and quiet, and safe. He would tell her about the Netherlands and the East, about Rome, Paris, England. It was very easy to talk to her. She listened to what he said about books, writers, about what poets wrote of gods, kings, war and marriage. There was Donne, the English minister, people were discussing his work right now. Donne was unusual, surprising in his thought. As regards fidelity in love, Donne said that no beautiful woman could be faithful.

'A strange thought,' she said.

'Well, here is something you cannot quarrel with. He writes in his devotions: *No man is an island, entire of itself. We are all involved in Mankind. And therefore never send to know for whom the bell tolls; it tolls for thee.*'

'Do you believe it?'

'Oh yes. A poet must speak the truth.'

'But it isn't true.'

'No?'

'I know people who have no one at all. Islands, all.'

'Name one,' he challenged her.

'Hans Michiel. A soldier.'

One day he read to Pieternella from the little book in which he copied his own poems, and asked her if she liked it. She answered cautiously: 'You will have to explain.'

'This first line, *The day was red since break of dawn*, describes the situation in this country, you see? In all parts of the world a new dispensation begins with blood, almost. It is like birth. *The day was red since break of dawn. A fiery hue the moon did spawn.* How does that sound?'

'The first line is nice. The second you just made up to rhyme with it. What could it mean?'

'It is the future.'

'We don't know the future. You cannot write about it. All of it is a mystery.'

'That is so, but I put the history of the whole world and of humanity on earth, from beginning to end, in those few words. Creation started with fire, did it not? God said, "Let there be light," and suddenly there was an enormous ball of fire. And, in the end, the moon will also be red as blood, says the Bible. And still, between beginning and end, it is red. That is what I meant. We are still experiencing creation, it is not complete, it still is going on all the time, everywhere around us.'

'Is that what students learn at university? I can understand if you explain, but I'm not clever enough to see it by myself.'

'Oh, you're intelligent enough, P'nel. Believe me, if you were not, I would not have been able to talk to you. But the words I wrote just came from talking to students. Friends, in boarding-house rooms, taverns, or walking along the canal from one lecture room to the next. We read, in many languages, all the time. Do you read?'

'Pieter and I read to each other from the Bible.'

'Yes,' he said, 'there is beautiful poetry in it, much of which I can recite from memory.'

When she told that to Long Gert, he said: 'Oh dear me, when they start on poetry they're in love. I wonder how it will go? Refined young men are not easy to live with.'

She looked at the carpenter in surprise, as she was interested in what Deneyn had talked about. Did that mean she was in love too? It was possible.

One Sunday after church he walked her through the Company gardens. It was forbidden to the public, but Deneyn wanted to show her that councillors had privileges in which their lady friends could share. Pieternella was impressed by it, because the slaves watering the plants took their caps off to them.

'P'nel, this young fellow, Pieter van der Byl. He is a pleasant lad. Quite handsome too.'

'Yes.'

'I hear he kissed you the other day.'

'Did Gisela tell you?'

'No, it was Sofia. But watch out for boys of seventeen. They fall in love beyond all measure.'

'That is what she told me.'

'Now that Jan has died, your family's only income is the bit of interest. It will be years before your brothers start earning. I have often thought about what we can do. Your expenses are high. Have you thought of marrying?'

'Yes.'

'Do you have anyone in mind?'

'No.'

'If you married me, we could go to Batavia. The chances for promotion are far better there. Or we could buy Den Uitwijk, and start farming. Or we could live here in the Castle, Master and Mrs Deneyn. We shall be quite well-to-do. I work hard. I may become governor one day.'

'Are you asking me?'

'I am serious.'

'Even though I'm born out of wedlock, and half-Hottentot, and even though my mother died of the English disease, and I am an orphan without a dowry, and without education?'

'Yes.'

'Then tell me why, because those are the reasons why Aunt Sofia wants to keep me away from Pieter, now that I'm growing up.'

'I enjoy your company. You are quiet, but your thoughts have been to places where the thoughts of others will never reach. Your face is fascinating. I can look at it for hours.'

'Is it love you feel?'

'I don't know what love means. I know there are signs and proofs of it. Do you know?'

'No.'

'Do you know anyone who does?'

'Pieter.'

'He is lucky.'

'I think Uncle Gert and Aunt Sofia also know.'

'You may be right. But I am not asking you for an answer. I am eight or ten years older than you. I shall not ask you for a lovers' meeting before you're older, and in the meantime you can think about what I said.'

'I will.'

'Sofia says she is worried that they cannot give you the best, because they have little themselves. Jan Vos's death was a loss to everybody. And she said she was afraid that you and Pieter might be getting too close. That is why she hopes you will marry soon. She hoped the two of you could remain like brother and sister.'

'Then I must leave her house.'

'Not for any of the reasons you mentioned.'

'She is afraid that I will destroy her only child's future. Like my father destroyed my mother, and my mother afterwards herself. She is afraid for my sake.'

'There are other people who care about you.'

'While others are scared of me. I'll have to go away from here.'

'Look, P'nel. I give you this rattan as my gage. Do with it what you will. But if you ever feel lonely, by this token you will know where to find a friend.'

'Thank you.' She examined the small silver knob with Deneyn's initials in a circle under a woven coronet. 'If they transfer you away from the Cape, you will forget about me.'

'Only if I ask for it. Because the man in whose post I was appointed is not coming back. Do you remember *Secundus* de Cretser? He was pardoned by the Lords and sent back here to become *secundus* again. But his ship was captured by Barbary pirates, and he died in a prison in Algeria, after waiting for years for a ransom which the Lords refused to pay.'

'I remember him well. That is another friend less.'

He allowed her to fall silent. They walked along a straight avenue of young camphor trees. Then she raised her face to him.

'And will children with brown eyes be welcome in your family?"

'I doubt it. If they reject me, I shall also be poor in family.'

He put his hands, at arm's length, on her shoulders as he spoke. This is how he shows that he is serious, she thought, looking him straight in the eyes as she listened to him. But it was so that she could get used to the touch of his hands, and already he was considering putting his arms around her. After which his fingertips on her back would start on their own accord to look for an opening in her clothes.

Maijke had been on Robben Island for three years when a new governor arrived, and as was the Company's custom, he announced a happy day for labourers and studied the list of prisoners for one or two to set free, for the sake of creating an impression of mercy and amnesty. He wanted to know from Deneyn what Maijke Hendriksz's crime had been.

'Smuggling and stealing. She never stops.'

'How does she get by on that island?'

'She is elderly, not dangerous. She performs light tasks.'

'Would she be able to sustain herself here in town?'

'She could get a brewer's licence, if she wishes, or keep a boarding house.'

Governor Bax had her brought to shore. He wanted to see her and talk to her. Maijke walked with a cane, on two swollen feet that would not fit into shoes. Her body was painful and heavy, with a swollen face and bags the size of eggs under her eyes. The hand with which she greeted the governor was thick and round all the way to the elbow; she could barely bend the fingers. With her swollen hand on the Bible she promised never to steal or smuggle again. First, she would like to go to her daughter, and spend a month or two with her. If she could be cured from her dropsy, she would open an inn and sell sugar beer.

After she had left, Governor Bax asked Deneyn about the convicts' rations. The old lady was suffering badly from dropsy, and should have been brought ashore earlier. Fresh vegetables were what was needed for dropsy, he said, fresh from the garden every day. It was something the Council should attend to; he was surprised that Governor Goske had allowed the situation to deteriorate so far. If the island was too arid to produce vegetables, then they should send the vegetables there.

But it was too late. They had waited too long. That year and well into the next, the dropsy brought work on the island to a standstill. The shell boats no longer ran, and those that went out with vegetables came back loaded with sick people. Twenty convicts were carried to hospital on stretchers. Among them was Willem Willemsz. Some of them had their water drained off to remove the pressure from the lungs, but a body cannot lose so much water at once, and their kidneys collapsed.

Deneyn visited Willem Willemsz in hospital. Here lies the hero who shot down a Hottentot at sixty paces, and was honoured with a pardon from his prince written in copperplate Latin, now prostrate on a bundle of straw in the Cape hospital with his legs swollen to the circumference of tree trunks. On that beautiful parchment the prince's secretary had wasted a lot of ink. No, there was no chance of Willemsz going to the farm, but his family could visit him in hospital. He warned the Lyreman time and again: If the Koina drag you from your bed on the farm, we will have serious problems at the Cape. Don't then come and complain to me.

Once again Deneyn and his sergeant rode out to the Lyreman's farm. There were a slave woman and two children in the yard. Their mother wasn't home, but after some effort Deneyn discovered where to find the farmhand Ockert Olivier. Ockert and Maria were together in a warm stretch of rushes not far from the river. He had Ockert manacled to go to the Castle, and took the woman home and explained to her where, in a manner of speaking, her hearth fire and her front door were.

When he returned to the Castle towards sunset, he had Ockert Olivier brought up from his cell, charged him with adultery, and wrote to the church secretary to have the bastard's children placed in foster care. The best would be to sentence Olivier to the island, and send both Willemsz and his wife out of the Cape, where one would be beyond the reach of a lusty farmhand on one hand and of Koina bent on revenge on the other. He would try to find out what Willemsz's prospects of recovery were, and whether he would survive a long sea voyage.

Bax found four petitions from Willem Willemsz in the file, begging to be brought ashore, and two more in which the postkeeper requested a permanent surgeon for the early detection of the disease. When Maijke appeared before Deneyn again, she was partially recovered from the dropsy. During that interval relations between Deneyn and Governor Bax had deteriorated. Perhaps Bax van Herenthals had a young nephew in Holland studying to be an advocate whom he wished to bring out to the Cape, because he indicated that he did not agree with Deneyn's methods of applying the law.

Perhaps Fiscal Deneyn had been at the Cape for too long, Bax suggested, and his career might benefit from working closer to the Council of Justice at Batavia, as the Cape was an isolated island, alone and remote between Europe and the East.

It might be true. Of course it was possible, Deneyn thought with a feeling of vague unease, as when a ship lying anchored in calm water is unexpectedly hauled back by a current, causing the entire vessel to strain and groan. Anything was possible.

A clerk presented Maijke, and her file with the latest charge sheet on top.

'Not you again? Sit down. Let me see what you've gone and done this time.' When he'd finished reading the charge sheet, he asked: 'What drives you to such things?'

She slightly raised one shoulder. 'Poverty. You don't know what we suffer.'

'If you wanted money for food or clothing, why didn't you tell me?'

'I've had enough of you.'

'So? Then I am not sorry to hear that I have inconvenienced you. I wanted to make an example of you for others to learn from, but you do not even learn from your own disgrace.'

'Do you talk about shame? You're a learned man all the way. Why don't you mix with your own class? If there's a rich man's daughter, your kind spend months licking the father to a shine, and she is carried to your banquets with a coach, but if the girl is a poor man's daughter, you're after her like dogs after a bitch to seduce her for your pleasure.'

'Who are you talking about?'

'You know exactly. The whole town is talking about how you're after a mere child to lie with her.'

Her voice was shrill: he hadn't realised how serious she was. He hoped to laugh it off, to spare them both every embarrassment. 'Everybody loves girls, madam. Unfortunately boys are popular only until they're ten, after that they become ugly. It has to do, you understand, with the worship of beauty.'

'What are you trying to make me believe? You think the governor doesn't know of it?'

He was speechless. What did she mean? Would P'nel know what was said about her, and would the townswomen and farmers' wives be gossiping among themselves only, or insult her to her face? He had not expected this kind of thing at the Cape. But were such places any better than a backward European hamlet, because the sky is always clear here and the veld covered with flowers? Don't you know any stories, old hag? he thought. Stories are about beautiful princesses. That is what all stories are about. But he did not say it. And the fine rattan with its silver button was no longer on his desk.

'I am releasing you on your own responsibility, madam, and I shall summon you to appear before the court,' Deneyn said. Then he rang for the clerk.

The charge he brought against Maijke on behalf of the Honourable Company, concerned the buying and selling of stolen goods. It had started with the discovery of ten bags of rice in the shallow water of the stone quarry beyond the slave graveyard. Ten were too many; had it been one or even three, it would hardly attract any notice. People would think that slaves had stolen the rice, but ten bags of rice had to have a story. The governor had a notice written, and announced a reward for information about the rice. Rewards usually worked.

Lammert was quartermaster of the lighter which had brought *Croonenburg*'s cargo of rice ashore. The work had been in progress for two days when he'd encountered Maijke Hendriksz on the road to her house one afternoon. He'd crossed himself and passed above the wind, but she had called him to ask if he could find her a few handfuls of nails; old rusty nails would be fine. Or perhaps some rice, from his work in the landing boat? She would reciprocate with eggs, milk, cash. Lammert had mentioned it to his crew, and they'd said: yes, they could help her with rice, but not with nails.

That Sunday, during the church service, they carried a few bags of spillage rice from their quarters behind the jetty, and put them over the hedge into her yard. She paid them two rix-dollars in cash. The last Sunday they carried rice during the sermon, they knocked on her door for their money and drank some sugar beer in her house on the success of their enterprise. On the landing boat they divided the seven rix-dollars. It never occurred to them that it could be a crime, or that Maijke would sell the rice. Their attitude was: spilled rice belonged to them. Everybody knew how the soldiers on guard at the Castle entrance took handfuls of rice from the slave women carrying the baskets between the quay and the Castle. They kept it in the guardroom until they went off duty, and carried it home in their breeches pockets. Nobody ever said it was wrong. But trading in rice was the Company's prerogative.

On different occasions they had deposited thirteen bags altogether over her hedge; each weighed twenty pounds. One evening the lighter-man Cornelis came to warn her: her house was going to be searched, she'd better get rid of the rice. It took her a whole night to do that. She and her helper Jacob walked to and fro seven times to throw the rice in the stone quarry. Three bags they opened to let the rice run out over the edge, the last ten they just dropped in.

Fiscal Deneyn wanted to make an example of her and of them. He asked the Council to have Maijke Hendriksz throttled to death at the stake. They approved it unanimously. As for the other accused, he asked that the quartermaster be flogged, followed by six years of carrying shells on the island in chains, while the sailors had to be flogged and carry shells for three years in chains. The Council accepted his demand and pronounced it as their sentence. The governor had to sign it.

Deneyn had not expected that everything would continue without change, and was not surprised when the new governor called him in to discuss the sentences. Governor Bax had different views from Goske, and felt the need to interfere where Deneyn had previously acted independently. First Bax wanted to know whether Deneyn knew what had become of Philipe Col? No, he didn't, there was no communication with the island any more. Then the governor wanted Maijke's punishment to be mitigated. Deneyn thought: The man is looking for an opportunity to demonstrate his mercy in public, so that people will think he is something wonderful. I'll be glad if Maijke dies, so that she can never open her mouth about P'nel again.

'I suggest that we moderate her punishment, *Meester* Deneyn. As follows: she must witness the punishment of the others with the hangman's rope around her neck, then be flogged and branded with a gallows on the shoulder, thereafter to be banished from the Cape for life.'

'That was what she was given a year ago.'

'But your demands are harsh. They appear inhuman to me, *meester*, if you ask me. Apart from this case against Maijke Hendriksz and others for which you want my signature, I must tell you: I have drawn the court records of capital trials in which you officiated under the government of Governor Goske. In every case you were the prosecutor. It appears to me that you do not see much difference between violence and justice.'

'On the contrary, I see very clearly the difference between justice and the law. The law has a strong arm and must use it. Sometimes the dividing line is very thin, but it exists.'

'The number of people you have sentenced to labour on the island could be smaller.'

'It was necessary. The Council passed the sentences, and Governor Goske never disapproved of it.'

'Change your view. I take no pleasure in blood and in rows of corpses on a gallows.'

'I do as I think fit. It does not concern me what anyone else thinks of my work.'

'In that case, *meester*,' Bax said, out of breath, as he pushed the files away from him, back towards Deneyn, 'if you do not care for my wishes, you would do better to keep your chest packed for the first outward-bound ship that comes past. You will go to Batavia, whether you want to or not.'

6

SAPITAHU

When they asked: Who is the father? she said: Sapitahu,
who knows him? It also means sailor.

DANIEL AND BART travelled from Batavia with the return fleet of '76 to
complain to the Cape governor about the way in which Commander
Hugo was running Mauritius. They would have preferred the governor-
general to have acted himself, but His Excellency sent the secretary to
show them the sea road to the Cape.

'You must lay the right courses,' he said. 'Jan Bax is in command
over Hugo. And if you cannot obtain satisfaction from him, and you
do not wish to return to Mauritius Island, you will be better placed
there to set your sails on a different course. You can either remain living
there under Bax, or you can take a ship to the fatherland.'

They knew that he was right, but would have preferred His
Excellency to act personally against Commander Hugo; after all, he
was closer to Mauritius and much higher in rank than the Cape. They
had no desire to go to the fatherland. If free men had to travel for nine
months to the fatherland to complain about the commander of a tiny
island at the back side of the world, then they were wasting more time
than they could afford to. As a last anchor, they could indeed remain
at the Cape – Bart and his wife had experience of the place – but they
would have to think well before they did so. The reason was simple:
they wanted Mauritius, but it had to be Mauritius without Commander
Hugo.

Daniel questioned Bart and his wife about the Cape, and then it was
as if Bart himself didn't quite recognise the place. Since when were

there corpses swinging on a gallows behind the dunes, as he'd seen at Hell's Door and in Batavia? What big castle was that behind the dunes? What had they done with the Fort? What did all these white houses mean? Why was the sea so far away from the dunes now? Why did everything seem so dry and dusty? Whose fishing boats were all these dragged out on the beach? Bart shut his mouth. He had no answers for Daniel, and from Theuntje's startled face he could see that the Cape looked strange to her too, and he knew that she felt ill at ease and frightened.

Daniel enquired from the quartermaster of the lighter about where to look for lodging. There was an abundance of it, he was told. It was strange to hear, because usually the boat crews would only advertise the landlord who gave them the best fee, but they also learned the reason for it. It had happened before that a fiscal had ordered a quartermaster to be keelhauled because a landlord had paid him a fee. Since then they had to give all the names if they were asked.

'Name some?'

Only one was known to Bart, and his wife looked up when she heard the name, but said nothing. She was still a silent person, Theuntje. So it happened that when the Hottentot at the quayside offered to carry their sea chests, Bart asked him: 'Where does Barbertje Geens live?'

Barbertje was glad to see them. How long had it been? They looked so brown. And what kind of place was this Mauritius? Was it, as people said, a paradise? She had the inn now, for taverns give too much trouble. She had people from all countries coming under her roof; she heard news from half the world every week. And from time to time she brought up an orphan for the church. It was a service of love.

Daniel didn't know the woman. He usually remained quiet among strangers until they had a chance of getting to know him, before he joined in the conversation, but he watched her as she threw over a tablecloth and put out knives and spoons and mugs for them. She wasn't young any more, she had been friends with Bart and Theuntje in their youth, but she had a face no one would tire of. She had a haystack of red hair, without a bonnet. What was unusual, was her bright green eyes. He had never seen such a green in the world. Like wheat, like the mature leaves of trees in summer.

Bart told him that men were constantly following Barbertje, giving her no rest, yet then they would seem to be scared to touch her. Perhaps it was her eyes. Cape women liked to gossip about her. They couldn't understand how she worked, all alone, while their men all stared after her. There was the story about her bread, her way of baking. And once a fellow who was eager to woo her, told in the tavern how they were happily holding hands, but when he wanted to light another candle, Barbertje went to the kitchen, saying she thought the bread was rising. Yes, there had been a court case concerning her. At the time she still had the tavern, the Elephant, right up against the moat at the Fort. The lookout on the wall testified that a soldier stood a ladder against her window one night and climbed up, and opened her shutters. Her screams woke up the whole world: murder, robbery, help. And the soldier shouted back just as loudly: 'Then open up, in God's name, everybody knows you're a whore. I'll pay you three *stuyvers*.' And then the tongues were wagging again, relentlessly. Once a woman's name was broadcast in taverns and barracks, how could it be bleached?

Perhaps her eyes were her undoing. She'd come here, little more than a girl and married to Rosendaal, the Company's gardener. They had a daughter, who was herself a mother now, but he died before the child was a year old. Later she took another husband, one years younger than herself; Henk Reijnste was his name. Bart and Theuntje, and others too, found it a pity that she should have taken such a one, so colour-less, worn out and thin, with a little cough, not eager to lift a finger, and almost like a dog in her company. And barely ten months, then Henk died. People started saying she was a witch, it was those eyes again. And just as well Reijnste had no money to his name, otherwise she would have been badly slandered. So Barbertje had to go through life without friends. Perhaps it was different now, as youth could no longer be held against her.

'I'm sorry I arrived too late,' Daniel said. 'I like a witch. Beautiful eyes she's got, I'll never tire of them.'

When Barbertje came to clear the table, Bart asked her: 'My friend here will be looking for a wife while we're at the Cape. What is the harvest like in the field?'

She laughed with Daniel: 'Where have you been all these years?' For the rest she merely said that she couldn't believe he needed help, and went into the kitchen.

They had to wait until the third day, while the governor's secretary compared their simple petition with the governor-general's voluminous missive from the East, and prepared a minute for the Council, which met on Thursdays.

'Bart and I are free burghers from Mauritius,' Daniel told Governor Bax van Herenthals. 'We are farmers. I'm trying with tobacco and sugar. But Your Honour, the commander makes it almost impossible for us.'

'And his hand is too heavy, too heavy,' Bart nodded, as if he was afraid that Daniel might forget to mention it.

'I may have good news for you, but on whose behalf are you speaking? Who are the plaintiffs?'

'We are about twelve farmers. Your Honour will find their names on the letter. And seventeen Company servants, but they won't put pen to paper.'

Bax searched among the letters on his large table, and later called over his shoulder for a clerk, who took it from the top of the pile and handed it to him.

'Ha, this one. Difficult handwriting. Yes, you complain that he moves you from tilled land and established farms, forcing you to start from the beginning.'

'Yes, Your Honour. House and everything lost. The main thing is our land. There isn't arable land on that island. You have to break out stones for months before you get to the soil. Then you have a spot the size of this room,' Daniel explained. 'You must first break through the shell before you get to the soft stuff.'

'Why does he do it?'

'He made a law: nobody may farm or sail out of sight of the Lodge. He is afraid that we'll trade with the ships. Your Honour will understand, it takes time to break through that crust.'

'What else? Is there more?'

'Your Honour will see what we complain about in that letter. He had a slave of Bart's caught, and hanged him. It was Bart's only slave. Now he is on his own.'

'Why was the man hanged?'

'The unspeakable sin, with a goat.'

'There are prescribed punishments, you know that.'

'But Your Honour, there is another man on the island who was sent from Batavia for the same thing – the only difference is that he did it with a dog. And he lives.'

'That I cannot explain to you. I can understand that you are unhappy.'

'And his hand is too heavy, Your Honour, too heavy,' Bart said with downcast eyes.

'I understand.'

'He had an innocent sailor shot.'

'How did that happen?'

'The Council sentenced a man to a shot over the head. Your Honour knows, as a warning to us all; the way a sheep thief stands with the skin above his head, but without being hanged. And on the day of the sentence they shot the man between the two eyes. Right between the eyes, and all our commander said: Sorry, it was an accident. That was when we felt, on Mauritius you're not sure of your life with a commander like that.'

Bax called the clerk, and told him to take statements from the two about the case of the sailor.

'I assume you are willing to do it?'

'I shall do it under oath, Your Honour.'

'Well, is there anything else?'

'It's Commander Hugo, he trades for his own account. He buys slaves and sells them to sea captains, to look for a profit overseas. That is illegal, isn't it? And the thing is: the slaves were meant for us free burghers on Mauritius. We had to get those labourers, that was the intention of the Lords Masters. We were promised that.'

'Can you prove what you say, the illegal trading?'

'I shall make another statement, under oath. But there are other things too.'

'These matters will be resolved between the Company and

Commander Hugo. It may lead to civil claims, but at the moment I can tell you what I know, and that is that Lords Seventeen have appointed his successor. It said in their last letter that they are sending his replacement on the Easter ships. And some four or six weeks later I shall send the new man off, to Mauritius. If you want to go back with him, I suggest that you remain patient. I believe you can look forward to a better life over there.'

With a satisfied smile Bart turned to Daniel. 'Get sail up, friend. The sun is shining again.'

They rose together, nodded, tugged their forelocks. 'Thank you very much, Your Honour.'

'Good day. What are your trades?'

'I'm a cooper,' said Daniel. 'My friend is a fisherman.'

'You have my permission to work.'

'Thank you very much, Your Honour. Thank you ever so much.'

In Barbertje's inn, at the long kitchen table in front of her hearth, they ate with Arie Koningshoven, a regular client. He comes here because of Barbertje, said Theuntje. How do you know? Bart asked. Can't you see? she said. Arie is a widower. He became head carpenter a little while ago in somebody else's place, because people don't last long on the Castle. It destroys them, worse than the sea. Arie wants to become a free burgher and try to farm. On the one hand it will be a pity, now that he receives good wages for the first time, but the Cape farmers seem to be doing well. There's lots of land which the Hottentots vacated, Arie said. There's already an outpost of the Company at Hottentots-Holland, where they farm with wheat. That means twelve guns against the wilderness. For the time being he himself was still cautious to cast loose his mooring rope, because beyond the frontier you try to live among lions.

Arie and Bart were the same age. Arie had three children at home; the oldest was nearly six. He enquired about the East. He said: as far as the East was concerned, he felt like an uncircumcised Jew. The Cape was his new fatherland, so it seemed as if he'd have to be content with being halfway East.

Daniel thought: Why should a *baar* man with three little ones pay court to such a woman? He was looking for someone to bring them up for him, and he would see to it that there would regularly be a new little boat under construction above the slipway. She had wondrous eyes. Sometimes she looked directly at him with a smile. She wanted to know whether he'd been a soldier before he became free. He said no, no. He'd been a sailor, since childhood. Had he been to the East? Yes, he'd completed four returns: fatherland, East, and back again. She kept looking at him with that smile.

'And what does one learn in the East?'

'Wonderful things. I am thankful to the Company, because otherwise I would never have seen it.'

'Tell something?'

'Bart here has experienced many strange things. He can tell you stories that will make your hair stand on end.'

'But where did you learn your trade as a cooper?' Arie asked. 'It takes five years. Yet you're still a young man.'

'On board. From apprentice to cooper I was with one master.'

'And today my friend is strong on sea and land,' Bart said proudly. 'I was too dumb to be anything but a sailor.'

Arie offered to help them find work. The Company did not accept people without a three-year contract, as they knew well, but if they had the governor's permission, there were freemen like the Saldanha farers who took on hands. Tomorrow after work he would introduce them to some of his friends.

After the meal they sat in front of the innkeeper's hearth. She teased him and Bart. 'A Dutch sailor is a truly wonderful piece of work. He takes his merchandise, his language and religion and his diseases right round the globe. He carries death in his musket. He empties a region and fills it with half-bloods. And he gets nothing out of it all, except for seven guilders a month on the book.'

Theuntje heard something which made her ask: 'Are Eva and her children still around, the Koina woman from the island?'

'No, she died some years ago. Her children are here. The church is looking after them.'

When the widower left to put his children to bed, and Bart helped

Theuntje to wash the dishes, Daniel stacked the wood box at the hearth and filled the water barrel in the kitchen from a well in the yard. He heard Barbertje asking Theuntje to help her at the inn, for a wage.

'For the company, Theuntje. I want to hear about your East, and about your island. I would so much love to see that part of the world.' Later she brought out a bottle of brandy and glasses and said: 'Come, let's talk at the hearth. There is still some warmth.' But Theuntje and Bart wanted to go to bed.

They carried the long kitchen bench to the hearth and she let Daniel talk through half the night about his childhood in Vlissingen and about his parents and his brother; how he'd been barely ten years old when he went to sea; about his first years on the local trade; how he'd learned from sailor friends to read and write; of the first time and the times afterwards when he'd heard the call of the East. Ever since then his floor had been a deck, his walls bulkheads, his window a hatch, his brothers messmates, his father the captain, and his church the wide ocean with the three crosses of foremast, mainmast and mizzen always against the skyline. When he'd arrived at Mauritius and seen the black earth and curiously shaped mountains, the land had called him back, and there he'd cast his anchor ashore.

Late in the evening he stacked fuel on the coals again. 'We must go to sleep,' she said, but poured more brandy into his glass.

'Say when you want to go.'

'I want to stay here. Tell me about Coromandel and Malabar, about their camphor and rubies, and their coloured cotton. What does *salem-puri* and *bafta* look like, and the *fota* and the *niniqua*, and the flowered *chintsa*? And how is our cinnamon brought from the forest?'

He laughed, in the bright green of her eyes ablaze with fire. She was like a child asking for stories because she couldn't face a lonely night. He moved closer to her, and later took her hand. She wanted to hear about the mysterious East, and from her mouth he wanted to hear about human life, brief and dark and meaningless as it was, if one thought about it properly. He could tell her some things, but there was much he wanted to know, and she was the one from whom he wanted to hear it. She would know how to say it.

She certainly knew how to say it. The night grew old around them. The fire changed to ashes. They saw it happen, but refrained from adding more wood. Towards midnight she said: 'Now we must really go to sleep, Daniel. Tomorrow night more of the same, please.'

'I will. You would have liked to become a sailor if you could, it seems to me.'

'I'd love to go to the East.'

'Come with me to Mauritius. You won't regret it.'

She put her hand to his face, and turned it towards her to look into his eyes. 'You cannot enter my life now. You arrived twenty years too late, and you need someone younger. But I want to do something for you so that you won't forget me.'

'Why?'

'Because I'm sorry that you are too late.'

'I accept your offer.'

'I want to present you to Pieternel van Meerhof.'

The next day Daniel walked through the town to look for coopering work, and found his companion at the fishing boats. Bart had been told about a widow who had a good boat with trappings, sail and gear, but no one to take it to sea because she asked too much for her share. He and Bart went there and examined her boat inside and out, discussed it and then went to knock on her door. Daniel said that they understood it was her only income, but they did not want to buy a share in the boat. They were prepared to rent it for a few months, and would deliver one-tenth of the daily catch to her fish-house in addition. She wanted a guarantee. He said they could not give any, but would pay her rent in advance and deposit a sum in her name on the Company's books, which she was to repay when they returned her boat. If she was willing, they could go to the office together and have the agreement drawn up.

In a tavern they drained a few mugs of beer, smoked a pipe and read their copy of the contract to make sure that everything was in order. They would not be allowed to go to Saldanha Bay, the clerk had said, since that contract belonged to others, and from Robben Island everybody had to stay away. But otherwise the sea was open to them.

Bart was eager to get to work. 'You will see, this sea is not as pleasant as the one at Mauritius, my friend. The water is cold, and in the afternoon the wind comes up, but we can earn our bread with a dragnet and a few handlines before the sun comes over the mast. On rainy days we'll work on the nets, and make bloodlines for the snoek run.'

Daniel was cautious. There were seven other fishing boats at anchor before the small beach. Those people were competitors. The market wasn't big; had there been more Catholics around, more slaves or other fish eaters, it would be a different matter. But Bart reassured him: they would start catching from before sunrise, and by noon when the wind came up, they would return, count out the widow's portion, then put aside their own fish for eating and sell the rest on the beach. If there was any left, they would go from door to door with baskets. And lobster, he knew the lobster holes, but it was really only the poor who ate lobster, and they always wanted to buy on credit. They had to watch out for that.

Daniel was still unsure. He would prefer to make barrels, but there wasn't much work at the Cape; the only free cooper already provided for all. Then rather back to the sea, grateful that they still had bread and an income.

Every evening he and Barbertje spent before the hearth. She wanted to hear him tell about the sea, about captains and ships, spices and storms, snakes and fruit and flowers, and she stared him in the face and watched his mouth, and listened how the sea made Daniel known to her. Sometimes Bart was there too with his strange tales, like about the time on the Saldanha Bay anchorage when a Bible turned over in front of his eyes. There were six or seven messmates with him, but they took an oath among themselves to deny everything. Witchcraft was a capital matter, inviting death. And the commander had ordered them to keep quiet about it, upon the threat of severe punishment. So they appeared before the fiscal to take the oath with the hand in the air, and everything they swore there was perjury and lies.

Daniel let Bart speak. He was content to let his eyes rest on Barbertje's golden head while she questioned Bart in detail about that strange thing he had experienced. Whose Bible had it been? Had they risked it a second time? He kept his eyes on her, on her glowing hair, on her ear, on the line of her face as she turned it towards Bart. Did she believe him? He would always believe *her*, even if she told him that an angel appeared at daybreak to knead her dough.

'And how far did you go in the world, Daniel?'

He let Bart speak, so that he could enjoy her fiery red head at leisure. She listened intently, her chin turned slightly sideways. Once Bart had floated for a day and a night in the open sea, but thoughts of life and death had helped the time to pass. But he had certainly ventured far into the world, yes, so far that there were no people living there. There was an island, well beyond Banda-Neira. It was fairly big, mostly mountains and high rocky peaks, covered with dense jungle. Here and there one could see flashes of yellow beach between the jungle and the sea. Their ship was behind the island waiting for a typhoon to pass; sky-high cloud castles sailed past behind the horizon. They were anchored there for a day and a half. He stole a coat and slipped away from a party of wood gatherers. With a canvas bag on his shoulder he went to look for a man of whom he had been told. The jungle behind him was cackling with monkeys; nowhere a sign or a sound of human life, no footprint in the sand, no mark of an axe on a tree trunk, no carving or implement of stone or steel. All the time he felt as if he was the only living soul in the world. Yes, he had the impression that the Creator was still at work next to him in the bush. Hour after hour he walked between that clamouring jungle and the empty blue mirror of the sea, until he arrived at a hut of decayed wood, hopelessly caved in like a wreck falling to pieces on a reef. Beside it were old frames of *trepang* makers, and the skeleton of a shallow sampan dragged out under the trees, everything deserted, desolate.

There was a man, crooked and yellow, who tattooed him for a *stuyver* and the brown overcoat. He had heard about the old man; he had a name for blue ink, not the soot-black everybody else used. It came from a rare seashell which lived in the coral before his hut. Look here on his arm, still bright after thirty years. Perhaps Bart had been his only visitor in months, yet they did not speak to one another. And after an hour he went back without a word, along that stretch between jungle and sea, across the whole island where no one lived, to the bay where his ship lay anchored to its own reflection. Surely that had been the last and the most remote place on earth. Yes, he was punished for his desertion.

'And you, where did you feel the loneliest?' Daniel asked Barbertje, his face almost touching her golden-red hair that smelled of fresh nuts. She pointed to her bedroom door. 'In there, between midnight and daylight.'

Because they had to go to sea in the dark of night before dawn, they went to bed early, but there at the fireside, when they were alone, Daniel held Barbertje against him to feel the softness and the warmth of her. That was what he wanted, before returning to Mauritius. He was old enough and had waited long enough. She remained pressed to him for as long as he wanted, and in the days on the fishing boat on the open sea he kept thinking about her. She was something beautiful. Did it matter at all how old they were?

One afternoon they walked home with a half-bottle of wine and a small string of fish they'd had to buy because there hadn't been a catch all day – something to do with the wind, most likely. From the shouting and laughing in Barbertje's front room they thought something was being celebrated in there.

'Do you think it's the peace, my friend?' asked Bart. 'I reckon the French surrendered.'

Daniel went to the yard at the back to hang the fish in the shade, before he went inside through the kitchen. He remained standing in the door with his cap in his hand. In the middle of the room Theuntje was laughing and crying with her arms around a young girl, and there was a half-grown boy too, clearly a brother. Theuntje turned the child round to show her to Bart. 'Look who's here, Bart. It's little Nella. Look how she's grown.'

Bart studied the girl at arm's length and kissed her on the cheek. 'My child, my child.' Once again he held her at arm's length. 'How glad I am to see you. You're the image of your father.' Then he took the boy by the hand, shaking it as if he was pumping bilge water. 'Old Salomon, goodness me, how big you are. How are you, people, and where is Kobus?'

From the far side of the room Barbertje arrested him with her eyes, fetched him and took his hand to lead him closer. 'Daniel, meet my friend Pieternella van Meerhof. Pieternel, this is Daniel Zaaijman, from Mauritius. And this is Salomon.'

He nodded. 'Pleased to meet you.' But his attention remained with Barbertje and he moved past the talking people towards her. He heard Theuntje say: 'And do you have a beau?'

Pieternella laughed, shaking her head shyly, but her brother said loudly, as if trying to embarrass her: 'Yes, you have, it's uncle Long Gert's Pieter.'

When Barbertje prepared to serve tea and went to the kitchen for boiling water, Daniel followed her, but she told him straight: 'It's no use following me around, Daniel. I invited Pieternel so you could meet her. She will make the best wife for you.'

'It's the first time I've seen her. I don't know her or her parents.'

'Her parents are dead. She is a foster-child of a friend of Arie's, but heaven knows, if ever I had a second daughter I would have wished it to be her.'

'She looks like a mere schoolgirl.'

'She is. I've told her what a woman ought to know, but life itself has made her wise. After school she comes here to me; I bake sweet-meats for her, and we talk. I don't have many friends, for which I thank God. She can cook and make clothes, and she can talk about anything.' Then she took her teapot and a sugar bowl. 'Come inside. We can talk later.'

At the dining table that evening, in Arie's presence, she told Daniel about Long Gert van der Byl and his wife Sofia. Long Gert worked hard, but it was difficult to raise four children on his income. And she had a feeling that the two of them were against Pieternella coming here to her house. At the table she asked Theuntje directly why they didn't take Salomon and Pieternella to Mauritius with them. They could at least mention it to the Church Council.

Theuntje and Bart looked at one another. Theuntje said it was her dearest wish. 'I'd really love to, Bart. If Nella wants to go.'

'Perhaps van der Byl will not let the children go.'

'I believe he will,' said Barbertje. 'He has reasons.'

Arie said: 'It is for the governor and the Council to say yes.'

'He'll want to know if we can afford it. I'm only a fisherman.'

'Other fishermen have children, Bart.'

'And then about their education. Mauritius is a place without church or school.'

'All countries started like that.'

'And the men, white or black, are not used to young girls,' Arie added.

'Bart and I will look after her,' Theuntje answered quietly.

Daniel listened to them making plans to get the children away. The first thing was to speak to the foster-parents, and once that was arranged, one should go to the Castle. He wondered whether they should not first ask the children what they felt, but it wasn't his business, he should remain quiet. Later he learned that Barbertje and Theuntje had already discussed it with Pieternella. Was that how the mysterious voice of the East worked? Perhaps the East had as many voices as there were people, all of them mysterious, and all with hidden meaning.

One evening at twilight Bart and Theuntje put on the best clothes from their sea chest and went to Long Gert's house. Barbertje sent a bag of rusks as a gift; Bart thought a nice string of fish would be acceptable. Daniel told Barbertje that the two would make good parents, but he had his doubts about the children. Children growing up in a town had friends, and wanted pretty clothes and to sit in the front row in church to boast. On Mauritius there were few, big or small, who didn't go barefoot, and it was so hot that people wore loose clothing, as in the East. These children would miss the Cape.

'Pieternella is not a child, Daniel.'

'Is it so that she takes after her father?'

'Bart says so, but they were friends. I can see both her parents in her.'

After that Daniel once had to go to sea alone, so that Bart could accompany Theuntje to the Church Council. Barbertje had prepared the words for them. They should ask for the girl and the younger boy;

the children had known them since birth, they'd grown up in front of their eyes. The elder boy had to be seen by the doctors for his epilepsy, and there would be no help for him abroad. They were prepared to sign any papers. That was what they proposed to the Church Council.

The Church Council looked at the children's accounts. Their small capital had been used up; there was only enough to help the oldest to a trade and, God willing, provide food and lodging for the youngest, their half-brother. The Church Council wanted to know from their schoolmaster: How were the children doing in their lessons? They were among his best, he said. The boy, especially, was bright. He would be sorry to lose them; they were easy children and paid regularly. The Church also wanted to consult Long Gert and his wife, and sent a Council member to discuss it with them. Long Gert said he would be sorry to say goodbye to the children, but he granted them a better life and wished them all the best. He would provide a home to Kobus here, for as long as the Council and the boy wanted it. Sofia said quite frankly that the girl was growing too fast; much as she loved her, it was time to give her over to another. She was sorry, but the child had become too pretty. Her son was infatuated with Pieternella, and now it was reciprocated. There lay incest ahead, and she could see no other way out.

'Is she a girl of loose morals, madam?' the Council member wished to know.

Long Gert rose to his feet. 'What the devil do you mean, sir? To speak about the child like that?'

'No, I beg your pardon if I offend you. But why else would Mrs van der Byl want her out of the house?'

'You know how it is with young people, Mr Councillor,' she apologised. 'They get attached to one another. Puppy love turns the head, and before you know it, the children are in trouble. The church is acquainted with such cases.'

Long Gert looked his wife in the eyes across the table as he said to the councillor: 'The only reason, sir, is that she is a half-blood. Whether my son gets her into trouble or whether they enter into a respectable marriage, makes no difference. My wife and I are worried of what may befall our family. Sooner or later there is a little one who reverts to its ancestors. I'm talking about Eva.'

The councillor understood. Once you had brown eyes in your family, how did you get it out again? He felt sorry for the girl and the boy who were forced apart, and who would never forget one another for as long as they lived. He had recently lost a child, and knew about death and longing. He returned to his office, and told Bart that the Church Council would have no objection if they submitted an application to adopt the children. After that Bart had to approach the governor, and supply him with the necessary assurances about the education and protection of the two minor children.

Daniel and Bart were in their boat behind Dassen Island halfway through the morning one day, taking in yellowtail and cob so big that both of them had to lift the fish on board. They kept an eye on Table Mountain in the distance. The wind was from the south; once the cloud came over the top, they had to up anchor and get home before the wind became too contrary. The usual haze covered the whole north behind them. They spoke little, but ate, smoked, drank water or wine according to their need, and tested their four handlines in turn to feel the tug of fish.

On one occasion, Daniel got up to stretch himself and pull his breeches down over the stern of the boat, when he stopped speechless, staring at three Dutch ships luffing up from behind at a cannonshot distance. He couldn't hear the sails yet, but in his mind was the sound of the groaning masts and yards, the whisper and whistle of the wind in cordage, the hiss and sigh of it in sails, the bubbling of strong seawater along the hull, the familiar smell of wood and rope and warm pitch, the stench of the forecastle, the long, straining creaking of the stays and the dry groan of spars. He could not take his eyes from the three ships.

'Bart.'

'What?'

'Look at this.'

Bart turned on his thwart, and stared in silence. He held his breath, his mouth half open in awe.

'Daniel, shall we finish for the day? Ask them to take our head rope.'

'We cannot do that, Bart.'

'The fish will bite again tomorrow.'

'It would be a sin.'

Bart moved his feet a bit, took off his hat and raised both his arms in greeting.

'First pull in our lines, Bart.'

They waited for the ships, and Daniel started shouting when the nearest one was a rope-heave away to starboard. 'Hoy, *orang baharu*, how fare you?'

Hands were raised behind the gunwale in greeting, and an officer with a hailer shouted from the afterdeck: 'Hoy. Are we set right to enter the bay?'

Daniel pointed at the mountain. 'Two, three glasses, the way you're set. Keep to lee of the big island and anchor at eight fathoms, right in front of the gallows.'

'Enough refreshments there?'

Bart got up with a fat cob. 'Are you asking me, *orang baharu*? Am I the governor? Tell your cook we'll be alongside in the afternoon with fish. More than enough for everybody.'

The officer with the hailer talked over his shoulder, and an attractive woman with curly brown hair and a young man with a wig came forward to lean over the gunwale.

'*Seur* Lamotius wants to know if Governor Bax is in good health?'

'The best. What news about the war?'

'The French still occupy the country. De Ruyter is dead.'

Surprised, Bart stared first at the officer and then at Daniel, and sank down on the thwart with his fish. Their boat started rolling and pitching in the wake of the ships.

'That's a lie!' shouted Bart, but Daniel realised that it must be true. He had felt the weight of bad news on his heart. Something must surely have come to an end. Was it the end of Holland?

'Is Vlissingen still holding out?'

'Yes.'

'How is the courage of the people?'

'Good. They live from the sea.'

The ships sailed past, keeling over to starboard on the other tack with a booming of sails. The voices became small.

'And Woerden?' Bart cried through cupped hands.

'Occupied by the enemy.'

When they were lying alone in the sea again, Bart asked Daniel: 'What now?'

'There is the Easter fleet, which will take us home, my friend. Mauritius is the only home we have now.'

Bart took two, three gulps of brandy, and remained sitting with the bottle close to his mouth. 'De Ruyter dead, the man said. Friend, is that possible?' He drank from his bottle again. 'It must be the end of Holland. Perhaps I shouldn't let Theuntje hear this. She still has people in Woerden.' He unrolled his two lines, peered at the bait, and hurled the lines out wide on either side of the bow. 'De Ruyter is dead, they say. I was a child, when he was already admiral. What is going to become of us?'

'Come, we'll sink this boat under the fish.'

'We now belong to Mauritius. Theuntje and I, if we can get those two children, will have nothing left to hope for. It is our only home.'

And mine, thought Daniel. And mine.

Daniel asked Barbertje: If the girl is in love with the carpenter's son, how can one expect her to move to Mauritius? Perhaps Bart should invite the carpenter's son with them too, otherwise she'll pine for him too much and make everybody unhappy.

'He wouldn't want to go, Daniel. He knows his life still lies ahead. Think about it: Would you have wanted a wife when you were sixteen? He will fight against it a little, but it will just be for show, because he knows he has to let her go. He is far too young to get her. He may even feel relieved to be free.'

'I don't understand it. Love is love.'

'Daniel, what are you talking about? Do you know what love is?'

'I think so.'

'I don't. It is not a word I use. You think you know, because you've heard stories here and there.'

'I have seen something of the world.'

'Seen love? What are you saying? You told me about the sea, and about the East, your wonderful, mysterious East, and about the stern sea with which one dare not play games. You think you understand it. Bart said: in the heart of a storm he found God. The good man. And I asked you – do you remember? We were sitting here at the hearth, you and I and Bart, and I asked: What does the sea and the sky look like in Mauritius at sunset? You said it was a heavenly sight. How lucky you are, Daniel, who often see what was not permitted to Moses. Now you want to talk to me about love. I experience my ocean and my whole East in this house. Men have come here to talk about love. I must live off what wanderers bring here. Am I to love in stories? That is why I have always asked: Please tell me what you have seen? I must know the truth. Go out, search around, and then come and tell me where you have seen love.'

'How can you not know what love is? Have you never felt something for a man?'

'Once or twice. Three or four times. Sometimes stronger than others, depending on the man. A lovely feeling, only too seldom. The last time it happened I was forty-two, and a married man of twenty-four woke it in me. We knew we couldn't stay together, and it was good, but it wasn't love. I think: if you can see an end, it isn't love you are looking at.'

'What advice do you have for me?'

'Go search. Don't wait for it to come to you.'

'How do I begin?'

'Where are your brains, man? Do you think I'm going to explain to a man your age how to get hold of a girl?'

'No. Because it's you I need.'

'You have no right to want that, Daniel. It will be a sin. When we sat here together, I've often longed to be young again, with you. I would have been very happy. But it isn't possible. I am for ever too old for you.'

'It doesn't matter to me.'

'It does to me. You are full of the force of nature. I felt it in your body, here at this fire. You must have children. But I am already past the age. Do you understand? I am not going to make you unhappy, because you have come too close to my heart. Go find yourself a wife your own age.'

The first Sunday, he went to knock on Long Gert's door, where he was expected. They spent the afternoon in the dusky living room. Everybody was in their Sunday clothes. There were Long Gert and Sofia, and Pieternella, but she did not join in the conversation, her eyes were cast down over sewing. Daniel was glad to see that they were not like some families, spending the Sabbath with folded hands. The lad Pieter was a tall, strongly built fellow of sixteen or seventeen. Her brothers Jakobus and Salomon were also there, but they soon went outside. Daniel's eyes wandered over the furniture. Oak in the front room, pine in the kitchen. One rarely saw oak; it must have been stripped ship's timber. And shaped expertly, simple in line, practical. Pieternella was privileged to grow up in such a home. His own hut on the island was made of palm mats. Long Gert's eyes followed him, challenging him with a look to talk about his trade. Perhaps Long Gert would want to know if he could make furniture, but he was a cooper who worked with an adze, not a carpenter with plane and chisel. He hoped the man would explain that to Pieternella.

Sofia enquired about Mauritius, and he told about the hard life under Hugo. The island looked like a paradise, but in every paradise the Devil came to stir up trouble.

'Are there free farmers living there? Families with children, like here?'

'Ten or twelve families. We try to farm with sugar and sweet potatoes, and tobacco.'

'And are there towns?'

'No.'

Then Long Gert started asking about timber. Daniel was cautious. What furniture wood grew there? Long Gert wanted to know. He had heard of red and black ebony. The new commander had arrived on the Easter ships, as Daniel would probably have been told, and he'd heard that the man had brought with him a marvellous invention, specifically for sawing ebony.

'No, what kind of thing could it be? It's the first I have heard of it.'

'Pieter here wants to become a free farmer once he has finished school,' said Sofia. 'Would the government help him get to his feet, on the island?'

'No. Rather don't. The island has too many worries.'

'*You* are doing it,' said the son with his father's straight challenging look. 'I can too.'

He would stay calm, Daniel thought. 'Come and try. There is a difference. I have a trade. In the daytime I farm, at night I earn my bread.'

'I can teach.'

'The children live a long way from the Lodge.'

'Then I can enter the Company's service, as a clerk.'

'Perhaps, but they may send you to Batavia.' He said it as a joke because the boy was so persistent, but he couldn't quite contain the resistance in his mind, as the boy was looking for a quarrel.

'Does the island belong to you? Or are you a kind of chief?'

'Pieter, you shame us in front of the stranger. Leave the room if you cannot talk properly.'

'No, my lad,' Daniel said. 'I just live there. You know, don't you, you can do as you like.'

Long Gert and Sofia were sitting there, studying him. Like other parents they were wondering if he would be a good husband for their daughter, and they also knew exactly what was wrong with their son. He might just as well have told the boy that the ocean was big, then all his questions would have been answered. He couldn't care if the boy felt unhappy. He took his cap and said that if Long Gert and Sofia were willing, he would like to invite Pieternella for a walk with him.

'All right,' Long Gert said. 'Pieternella?'

She looked at Sofia, waiting for her nod. Then she put her sewing in a basket with a lid. 'I shall ask Salomon to go with us.'

Sofia went out with her. Daniel and Long Gert waited in silence for them to return. It was customary for a member of the family to be sent along if one walked out with a girl, but as far as he was concerned, the fewer there were to consider, the better. Pieternella was the one he had to get to know. Pieter sat there, waiting to be invited too, but he refused to ask him.

On that first occasion they walked round the back of the Company gardens to the sea, beyond the mat houses at the dunes. The town was asleep. Daniel asked the children to show him the Cape. Whose nice house was that? Which wreck was that, washed out on the beach? Could one eat these berries? He had the feeling that he, an *oorlammer*, was taking a walk outside with two schoolchildren. That they were poor orphans, did not bother him. He had no status himself and had never looked for it – quarterdeck or forecastle was all the same to him – but he knew that there were others who, for the life of them, *had* to sit in the front pew in church. The children, he decided later in the day, were pleasant company; they could tell him about the houses, the wreck, the name of every flower and shrub. Salomon was a cheerful talker, walking like a gentleman with a fine rattan decorated with a silver button. At first he carried it neatly under the arm, but later he started hitting at grass and bushes. Then Pieternella took it from him and carried it in her hand.

There was a graveyard for slaves at the edge of the town. He wanted to walk past, but she and Salomon entered the enclosure and went to an old grave to pick up the headstone that had fallen over.

'Whose grave is this?'

'Jan Vos. He brought us up.'

He helped them to prop up the headstone with stones, straightened the edges and stacked rocks against the footstone to keep it in posi-tion. There was no name or sign on the headstone.

Behind the dunes was a *kampong* of twenty or more mat houses, and a few cooking shelters from which, here and there, smoke was going up. Outside, Koina were sitting in the wintry sun catching lice. Those were Koina who worked in town, said Pieternella. They had neither chief nor cattle, and they didn't put up their homes in a circle; each one was his own master. A skinny dog raised its voice against the passers-by, and an old woman shouted at it to shut up. Salomon called something to her in her language, and when she got up from her mat to look at them, Pieternella went to her to talk. Daniel and Salomon waited in the footpath.

'Does Pieternella know her?'

'Yes. I think she is related to us. An aunt or a cousin of our late mother.'

Daniel compared the two women from a distance. The young one was the kind one saw in Batavia every day: a half-blood girl, in Dutch clothes, baptised and educated, and more popular than full-blooded ones with men who believed they could tell the difference between the women who shared their beds. But the old woman was from the Cape. He had seen Moors from the north, and blacks from the fever coast of Africa, but the people of the Cape were unique in appearance and easily recognised. He couldn't see that these two were related.

'The older she gets,' said Salomon, 'the uglier she gets.'

'It is the same with my old aunts. Do you understand what they say?'

'No, they talk too fast.'

When Pieternella came back, Daniel tried to find out how she had learned the language, but all she said was: When I was small. And it was Salomon who told him that they sometimes lived with Koina and that during their mother's last years she had refused to speak anything but Koina to them.

A path turned off to the gallows. The gallows field was surrounded by a whited wall, with a small gate, closed, chained and padlocked. The square was overgrown with chalk-white daisies. It is the garden of death, Salomon said. Only the fiscal and his henchmen were allowed in there. And murderers.

They walked around the gallows, never far from the sea, with the dark island like a dun-coloured smudge on the horizon, until they reached a large shiny vlei where seagulls and wild ducks were paddling together. Herds of cattle lay in the long grass, and herdsmen were sitting together in twos and threes, smoking. Salomon thought he could recognise Uncle Long Gert's milking cow, but there was a strange herdsman with it. Pieternella had to forbid him to throw stones at the birds, and she immediately dropped down on the bank with him to take off their shoes and stockings. She pulled up her dress to her knees and waded into the water first. Salomon went off to one side, after the ducks. Daniel remained sitting on the bank, gazing at the shape of her leg and ankle. Pretty, as he'd expected.

She came to stand in front of him. 'Are there vleis like this on Mauritius?'

'Yes.'

'Do the people there throw stones at birds?'

'We catch with nets.'

'Do you wade in the water there?'

When he saw the smile on her face, he took off his shoes and stockings, rolled his breeches to above his knees and went to her. 'We live in the water. You'll see.'

They walked side by side until the water became too deep for her, and from there they waded further up to their calves, while he told her about the lukewarm, blue-green inner water at South-East Harbour, where one could reach the reef at low tide, an hour and a half away, sometimes waist-deep and sometimes up to one's neck among coral and brightly coloured fishes. Big fishes, so tame they barely looked at one.

When they returned to the village in the late afternoon and had to cross the canal of the Buitengracht, which lay dry in the early winter, he held out his hand to help her across, but she looked past his hand and clambered over on her own, following her brother.

Governor Bax sent a letter with a messenger to summon Daniel and Bart.

'Hound's bile, man,' Bart said deeply worried. 'What does he want with us now? Tomorrow we have to deliver a full day's catch to the widow.' But they went to find out what it was, resolved to keep their mouths shut and their ears open. It would have something to do with the island. If one helped the governor today, he might help you tomorrow.

It was high tide when they arrived, neat in their shoes and hose on

a weekday, and the spring tide was almost up to the Castle wall, dangerously close to the sea gate. 'We're here to receive the governor today,'
Bart announced haughtily at the gate. 'Let us wait inside, friend. Our
shoes are getting wet.' They entered the new fortress, and stood gazing
around while somebody went to get a reply from the governor. There
was a hive of people against the walls: stonecutters, carriers, helpers,
bricklayers and foremen on the scaffolding, porters across the courtyard, soldiers on the battlements, and in a barrel secured to a mast on
the sea bastion a fellow with a telescope studying the roadstead.

It was the gentleman with the pretty wife on the Easter ship, seated
next to Bax behind the table. The governor presented them to *Seur*
Lamotius, and offered them chairs. *Seur* Lamotius was to be the new
commander of their island and was spending a few weeks here to famil-
iarise himself with the affairs of the Cape and Mauritius. The governor
assumed they still wanted to return to the island?

With their caps on their laps they sat waiting. The gentleman was
young under his fine powdered wig, with a smile on a wide mouth,
and a sallow skin and dark eyes suggesting a French ancestor. He looked
like a pleasant fellow and offered a firm hand, Daniel thought, but
rather on the young side. In his mind he compared the *seur* with the
massive Hugo who, like a pirate sloop with a loaded cannon in the
bow, never went about without a curse and a threat ready on his tongue.
How could this pleasant young man save them?

Lamotius wanted to question them about the woodcutting. He had
heard that they were experienced inhabitants, and wished to know their
opinion. Listening to an opinion is different from asking for advice,
Daniel knew. Well, how could they help? He and Governor Bax were
eager to hear what the Company could expect from Mauritius in this
regard, said the *seur*. Wood was the Company's only hope for the island,
and if the island could not deliver that, the Company would close the
place down and vacate it.

'Close and vacate? And what about us, *seur*?'

'No, I don't know about you, friend. I presume you will then be
given a passage back to the fatherland.'

'The fatherland?' exclaimed Daniel and Bart in surprise, and Daniel went on: 'The fatherland is flooded, and the French command the high ground.'

'Well, there you have it then, friend,' the *seur* said with his smile. 'You and I *must* succeed on Mauritius. We have got to make it work.'

I don't want to make the island work, Daniel thought. I am a free man and my only interest is my plot. If the Company cannot make the island work, all it has to do is to go away and leave us alone. But he told the governor and the *seur* at length about Sven Telleson, about red and black ebony, and stinkwood which, when sawn, smelled of human excrement, of the rainforest, the Natte Bos, where only ferns grew, about distances and steep forest tracks where people had to walk in single file, about Black River's impossible ravines and cliffs, about difficult creeks and Commander Wreede's accident when the boat capsized in Vuile Boght, about Commander Hugo's severe punishments, about hurricanes. But manpower, messieurs, that was the word. It meant healthy young men, and enough of them, under a strong commander. That was how de Ruyter had achieved his fame.

The governor and the *seur* looked at him in silence.

Bart had another good idea. 'In Commander van Riebeeck's time we had free woodcutters here. And I don't know whether you still have them, but I reckon the Company can save a lot of money in pay and rations if it used freemen to cut and work the ebony.'

'Why not?' said the *seur*, looking at the governor, but the governor handed it back to him. 'You may recommend such a thing once you have investigated the matter over there. The privilege was discontinued here because the men work without supervision, wasting and spoiling more wood than they deliver.'

Daniel wanted to find out about the invention the *seur* had brought with him, but it was not mentioned, as it might be a secret matter. At any rate, they would find out in due course. Lamotius wished to know about their agriculture, rainfall, natural food resources, the free burghers. Two of them had now come here with complaints against their commander. Did they think the problem would disappear with the honourable Hugo's departure?

Daniel replied: 'We trust it will happen, *seur*.'

'So?'

'Who knows tomorrow? Who can say what is destined for him?'

Then Bax took the word again. 'Then there is still the matter of the two orphans to be adopted.'

'It's my wife and I, Your Honour,' Bart said.

'The Council received the recommendation of the church, and I see it has the approval of the foster-parents, and of our Council of Policy. My one concern is that there may be unhappiness among the Cape natives if we send the children out of the country. The children are minors and have no choice in the matter. The Hottentots may have a claim to them; there may be cousins and uncles and aunts who may have a claim according to our Dutch national law. But because the oldest boy will remain here, the Council decided not to make enquiries, nor will they inform the Hottentots. It is possible that there will be no objection. But it would be in your own interest not to let it become known too widely.'

'That is in order, Your Honour.'

'Now, next matter. For the sake of the children we have made enquiries about the prospective foster-parents. I asked the fiscal to look it up, and he tells me that you, Bart, and your wife both have criminal records.'

'Yes, Your Honour.'

'We are taking the children away from a church elder and placing them in your home. Is that prudent? I am saying it here in front of Mr Lamotius, so that he will be aware of who lives in his colony and what is going on there. If I have to ask for a testimonial on you, Bart, whom should I ask? The honourable Hugo?'

'Your Honour can ask my friend Daniel. Here he is.'

With a slight smile Bax asked: 'Zaaijman?'

'Two trustworthy pieces, Your Honour.'

'Well, then. The children's papers are being prepared, and you and your wife must come here to sign. Commander Lamotius will keep an eye on them and inform me how they are. That will be all, for the time being. Or is there something else the two of you wanted to say or know?'

Daniel spoke. 'Your Honour, we know how much trouble the Company takes for its people, and the burghers on the island have told me to ask whether it is possible occasionally to send a *dominee* on the fleet going to Batavia, to stop over with us. For communion and baptism.'

'I saw that in your letter. I understand your need, and our Council will consider it. We shall see,' Bax said, getting up to signal the end of the interview; and Lamotius confirmed it: 'Yes, indeed.'

'There are half-grown lads, still unbaptised,' Bart added, without getting up.

'All right. We are preparing the hooker *Boode*, and you will leave by the end of this month. I presume you want to work your way over?'

Bart and Daniel confirmed that they would like to work for their passage, took their leave with broad smiles, and went to sit in a tavern, laughing and drinking a mug, before going to break the news to Theuntje and Barbertje. The new commander looked like a good fellow, they agreed. Did you hear what he said about closing and vacating? Just like that: close down and vacate. He hadn't even been there yet and was already talking about closing down. 'One day,' Daniel told Bart, 'the shell of a turtle said to the turtle living inside it: I'm going to close down and vacate.' They laughed and knocked their mugs together. They were going home, the only home there was for them, and good times lay ahead. Make sail, full and by.

If the weather permitted, he and Bart put in a whole day's fishing for the cash, which they immediately had to exchange for groceries. Daniel bought a few tools and implements, some clothing, a roll of white duck. The Church Council informed Long Gert that Bart and Theuntje were taking over as guardians of the children. During those last weeks the children often visited them, and Bart had clothes and shoes made for them, and bought for himself and his wife what they needed, with the children in mind. Who could tell when they would get to Batavia or the Cape again? They needed medicines, coarse stuff for mattresses and pillows, finer stuff for clothing, extras for the voyage, like cheese, wine, some bags of rusks, as well as ink powder, plumes and paper, slates and slate pencils for the children's schooling, tobacco to smoke and chew, scented snuff, stockings, crockery and cutlery for the table, scissors, needle quivers and thimbles for sewing, the comforts of Bulaeus's *Huispostillen,* hundreds of fathoms of fishing line, flatlead, garden seeds, and a razor with its strop and brush, bearing in mind that Salomon would need it one day. Blankets, Theuntje had assured Sofia, would be required only for the sea voyage, not afterwards. Sheets one had to have – one needed something to cover yourself since the mosquitoes made their appearance over there, but coverlets were not necessary. Sofia found it hard to believe.

Daniel and Bart were fishing behind Dassen Island when the hooker *Boode* went past to Saldanha Bay, to be careened for scraping the bottom, burning and caulking. And a week later they were in the same place when it approached from behind towards the Cape, and Bart, pretending to get a fright, said: 'Dog's hairy collar, friend. I thought it was a state yacht, with the prince himself on board.' It was trimly renovated, its paint gleaming, its standing gear freshly tarred and swathed in wrappings like babies. To the eye it appeared ready for the long haul to Mauritius, and a white pennant at the foretop intimated that it was under commission, its papers written and in the captain's chest. But it wasn't, they knew that. Bart gave a shrill whistle after the hooker, high and low, like a sailor at a prostitute.

'Painted whore of Babylon.'

'Yes. Its crew are a hard-working lot, I see. We don't know about the officers.'

'But you and I, friend, we won't get in their way.'

They were to find out that the hooker's men, *baar* and *oorlams,* laboured under their boatswain's rope, and all of them got in the boatswain's way and in the way of his rope's end.

The two remaining Sunday afternoons Daniel continued to walk out with Pieternella after church. On both occasions Kobus and Salomon accompanied them. The first time Pieternella wanted to walk down the Table Bay beach, past the Castle to the river mouth. The sea was low and the sand hard. The children carried their shoes and stockings in their hands. Salomon was at the tide line to inspect what had washed up. He picked up shells and objects and brought them to show, or called for them to come and look, and wrote his name in large letters on the sand with Pieternel's silver-tipped cane. For long distances Pieternella walked ahead on her own in the shallow water, but Kobus kept mostly behind Daniel, quiet in his shadow, and when he said something, Daniel usually either didn't hear or didn't know what he was talking about. Opposite them, against the background of the Lion's Rump, the three outward-bound ships and a hooker lay under bare spars with the bows turned against a north wind. Daniel knew each one of them, he was beside them with fish every afternoon, but feigning ignorance he said he wondered what their names were. Pieternella pointed out the hooker *Boode*, and Salomon knew all the outward-bound ships: *Huis te Velsen*, *Sumatra*, *Westeramstel*.

As they walked, he asked about the fortifications among the dunes. Salomon was able to say: this is Houte Wambuis. Exactly like an under-shirt, a *wambuis*, ironed flat. How many cannon? That one was Santhoop. Over there Duinhoop, and then the Uitkijk. Every time he asked: How many cannon? And every time Salomon could give the answer.

At the river mouth Bart and Theuntje's old house stood long ago. A crooked plank from one of his frames still remained, half entangled in a bush, but the house had been dismantled and carried away. Here was the scraping block at the door of the fish-house. Look, here was a thick crust of fish scales, caked into the sand. Here their garden had been. Theuntje had grown Dutch flowers. Look, here in the tall grass there was one. Pieternella showed it to Daniel.

'They're Theuntje's flowers. They left here when I was small.'

'You can pick it and show it to her.'

'No. I don't pick flowers from a grave.'

'From now on you must say *Aunt* Theuntje,' Kobus reprimanded her. 'She's going to be your mother now.' But when they went away, Kobus followed with the flower in his hand. 'For Aunt Theuntje of course,' he said when she looked at him. But she said that the seed should have gone into the ground. Now it was dead for ever.

At the vlei she showed Daniel the houses of the free farmers in the Liesbeeck valley. In the distance they could see cattle grazing in the river.

'Are there still Hottentots hereabouts?'

'No, no longer. Only at the Tygerberg over there, and at the blue mountain in the distance. This river mouth is for the Company's cattle only, and the Liesbeeck for the free farmers.' Behind them the boys threw stones at the birds. Daniel looked at the distant mountain range to the east, calculating in his mind that the whole of Mauritius might fit in between here and those mountains. In that direction, and further to the east, land might still be available, if the island had to be closed down and vacated.

They wandered along cattle paths through the veld, until they reached the Company's wagon road which took them back to the Castle. Pieternella asked him about Mauritius, about lions and snakes. In this very road people and animals had been caught by lions. Everybody coming this way is armed with a musket. She isn't scared, she said, looking up with a lovely smile, but they had to take care. Salomon assured them: if a lion charged, you had to stop and stare into its eyes, you must never run away.

'I hope I'll remember.'

On the other occasion they walked along the beach, and when they arrived back at Long Gert's door, Daniel, remembering something, asked Salomon: 'Where's your cane today, old fellow?'

'It was Pieternella's. Kobus broke it.'

'I'll mend it,' he offered. But she refused, with a firmness which made it clear to him that she didn't want it. She would probably keep the silver. And he noticed that in her refusal she had called him by his name for the first time, and repeated it just afterwards.

'Thank you, Daniel. I enjoyed the walk.'

'The company made it. Another Sunday again?'

She nodded gravely and said goodbye, and called the boys after her.

Once the departure date had been set and became known on the streets, Daniel and Bart filled their boat with fish one last time and settled with the widow, and gave part of their share to friends, to Barbertje and Sofia and Long Gert, and the chairman of the Church Council. Afterwards they sold the rest and took three days to wash out the boat inside and to scrub and burn and lightly caulk it outside, darn the sail and mend holes in the net, and cut two worn sections from the anchor rope and splice it on again. Then they anchored the boat with the seven others in the shallow water of Rogge Bay, placed the four oars with eight thole-pins and leather bailer on the widow's stoep, and knocked on the door. She returned their guarantee money and tore up their contract, and they thanked her and took their leave.

That last evening Barbertje came to Daniel with a heavy, old Bible. Scuffed edges of loose pages protruded, the back had collapsed, the leaf-patterns of the silverwork on the corners and the hinges were worn thin and smooth.

'Do you have a Bible?'

'Only my Testament.'

'Take this with you. And write me a few lines from time to time.'

'What about you?'

'You know, don't you? Now that I see that you and Pieternella can get along, I'm letting you go with a happy heart.'

'Perhaps she will reject me in the end.'

'If that is what she decides, it will have been your own fault.'

'She's a child, unsure of herself, and ignorant.'

'Whatever is childlike in her, she will outgrow. You will have to be patient, and help her to mature. Give her a chance to enjoy her youth too.' She took Daniel's two hands and held them in hers. 'Lead her by example, otherwise leave it. That is my experience. Everything else comes by chance.'

'I don't understand.'

'Life passes quickly. Think of it. Help her to enjoy this little span.'

'But what can I do, except to earn our bread by the sweat of my brow?'

She put her arms around him. 'You will never lord it over her, Daniel. And you will help her to find what she asks of you. And you will laugh a lot with her. And you will not keep her away from other people for any reason at all. Promise me that. If I have your word for it, I'll be at peace.'

He wrapped the Bible in his clothes and put it in his sea chest, and once they were at sea he made a white canvas cover for it, so that one could open or close it without removing the cover. Whenever he opened it he remembered Barbara Geens and the favour she had done him, and sometimes in his mind he saw only her lovely golden head with her pale skin and bright green eyes, and remembered her voice.

From early in the morning the drum was beaten in the streets to call in the sailors. One could see for which ship it was; it was the one with the flag at the maintop, which had hung out its foretopsail. It was *Boode*, the hooker. Daniel and Bart waited till last, and hired Hottentots to carry their chests and those of Theuntje and the two children to the jetty, paying them at the rope barrier where the land people were stopped. There the clerk with the branding iron and red brazier burned the Company's mark on each chest as it was put down, and there they took leave of Long Gert and his wife and son and of Kobus, and Barbertje. Daniel climbed from the jetty into the boat to take their baggage. He had been looking forward to this voyage, but there were others who were afraid of it, or who took leave with sorrow, and he preferred to be out of the way. In the lighter he said to Pieternella: 'From now on it is sea all the way until we get home. You mustn't worry.'

Once on board, he and Bart helped Theuntje and the children into their accommodation, deposited their own chests in the forecastle, and then reported to the captain. They were freemen from Mauritius, they said, Daniel Zaaijman and Bart Borms. They had been signed on to work for their passage. The captain consulted his list: Zaaijman and Borms. They had to report to the boatswain.

The boatswain was a youth with sparse beard and long, dirty hair, and infatuated with his length of rope. It was two arm-lengths of tarred half-inch manilla; the bottom end had been spliced back a palm's width, and the top formed an eye that fitted tightly round his right wrist – a tidy, even piece of work. One got the impression that the fellow slept with it. His face was tattooed with black curls around the eyes and across the cheeks, in each ear was a ring attached to a larger ring. His name was Lubbert Franz, boatswain. To Daniel he said, without any greeting: 'I'll see you in the foretop.' And to Bart: 'Mizzen.'

'Bo's'n,' they replied.

'Up there.' He motioned with his head, slapping the doubled rope lightly against the leg of his breeches. They went up the shrouds to their places of work ('Perhaps the man wants to see if we can get up the mast'), moved out along the foot rope below the yard to the furthest point as he motioned out wide ('Now he wants to see if we're scared') and stood there with their bare feet on the rope while the boatswain was talking to somebody on deck, before he ducked under the poop, without coming out again. Daniel gestured at Bart: back to the mast. They lowered themselves to the deck, and mingled with the crew beside the gunwale.

'Who ordered you down?' the boatswain came to ask. 'If I put you somewhere, uncle, you stay there,' he said to Daniel. And then: 'Did you hear me, uncle?'

'Yes, bo's'n.'

'Well, goddamn you, uncle. Don't waste my time.' Then he turned to Bart. 'Grandpa. The same to you. You heard me?'

'Yes, bo's'n.'

Behind him were the faces of the seamen, waiting, row upon row, as in the stalls of a playhouse.

The last lighter of the evening had the fiscal and his henchman on the back seat, and a few women and children and a thickset man on top of their baggage in the hold. The ageing fiscal, writing-case under the arm, came over the side first and headed straight for the poop as if somebody had shown him the way. Then a young woman came up the ladder followed by two small girls, then the thickset man in leg-chains, and while there were loud calls from the boat for a chair, the boxes and bundles were handed up one by one. The chair was let down into the boat from the foreyard to hoist a corpulent woman on deck.

From the stern a quartermaster walked forward shouting, rattling a handspike against the woodwork: 'All hands, gather at the mainmast!' And at the forecastle door he turned round and came back: 'All hands, gather at the mainmast!' His last rapid blows were against the cabin door. Bent over, the fiscal and the captain emerged from the poop door, and moved in behind the rail from where they could look down over the crew and passengers in the well. After them Theuntje and the children came on board. Daniel beckoned them to him, where sailors and passengers all thronged behind the mainmast. In the oblique light of early sunset they looked up at the captain as if expecting him to read a sermon. When all the faces were turned up, the fiscal motioned with his hand to his servant, and with a club in his fist the fellow left on a meticulous tour of the forecastle, the forepeak and the hell, the afterdeck, the orlop and the hold, in search of stowaways and contraband.

Unfolding a large sheet of paper, the captain nodded a few times towards the forty, fifty faces before he began to speak: 'Johan Bax, surnamed van Herenthals, governor of the Cape of Good Hope and its dominions, including the island of Mauritius, hereby order and instruct the captain of the hooker *Boode,* in the service and on behalf of the United East India Company, to sail from here to there with crew, passengers, provisions and cargo as described in the undersigned and attached list of persons, baggage and cargo, under command of Captain August Wobma and lesser officers, who have been duly granted authority and permission according to the general Article Letter issued by the Lords States-General, signed and dated . . .'

He continued reading. He recited it partly from memory, as sea commissions differed from each other only with respect to some names, dates and numbers, and he could see their attention slipping away from him, to the sun on the late-afternoon sea, to the village and the rectangular greyish-brown mountain behind. They were all still linked to the land, Table Mountain still loomed in a brown haze above them, their clothes were fresh, some still remembered the smell of hay in the manger and the taste of butter in their mouths. Then he nodded at them a few times and said: '. . . and for this purpose the ultimate authority for the duration of the voyage is vested in the person of Isaac Johannes Lamotius, designated commander of the outpost, without diminution of the rank or station of the aforesaid captain.' Again he nodded in their direction. Had they heard it? He said: 'Commander Lamotius and his family are coming on board early tomorrow morning. That is when we will depart from here. Until then

I am first in command. Now pay attention while the fiscal calls the roll.'

The old fiscal started calling in a reedy voice, his finger at the top of the list.

'August Wobma, captain.'

'Present.'

'Lubbert Franz, bo'sun.'

'Present.'

He read the roll all the way down. Such-and-such, cook. Present! Such-and-such, cook's mate. Present! Everybody had to respond: the crew, the paying passengers, the two prisoners, who responded to the names Willem Willemsz van Deventer, exile, and Maria Tielemans Hendriksz, exile. 'But that's Aunt Maijke, isn't it?' Theuntje said to Bart. Their chains, the fiscal added, were not to be removed while the ship was in view of the land, and the leg-rings were permanent. After he had finished reading, the fiscal's man was there again, to whisper that he had not found stowaways or contraband. In conclusion the fiscal wanted to hear from the captain: Are you satisfied that you have been properly provided with crew, equipment, firewood, food and drink? And the captain had to sign for his word at the bottom of the page.

Lamotius arrived early in the morning, with his wife and child. The captain was at the ladder to welcome them, with two quartermasters to pipe them in, and while the pipes shrilled and the captain made his bows, the seamen stared, for the commander's lady was a most attractive young woman. A wide hat was tied over her head with a kerchief, but one could see curly brown hair, a delicate skin, large brown eyes, a wide mouth. She carried her child, a little girl, in her arms. The sailors watched her hips as she followed the captain across the deck, and made big eyes at each other. The anchor was about to come in; there was more than enough wind to get them out of the bay and into the main, and they were standing by for it. They remained on deck, staring at her.

Boatswain Lubbert approached cursing from forward. 'Don't you have manners?' he railed. 'Damned randy swine!' hitting out with his length of rope in all directions. They should have made sure that they'd had enough of it; now it was too late, goddammit, to stand slavering. They had to man the capstan to get the cable in.

'To the capstan!' he shouted, lashing the nearest crewmen with his starter. 'To the capstan!' They hauled the hooker's cable in until the ship stood on its anchor, then he beat the sailors up the shrouds to shake out the sails as the captain called the commands. After that he shouted and cursed them back to the deck to haul the anchor from the ground, bring it aboard and secure it, all the while striking out to his heart's content. Daniel scrubbed the mud from the anchor with a wet broom as he was ordered by a quartermaster, and received two strokes with the rope over his back. He lifted the broomstick and told the boatswain: 'Keep your hands off me, you louse!'

'Think what you're doing, uncle. You can be flogged for your attitude.'

'Keep your starter off me unless you want this broomstick up your backside.'

'Did you hear me, uncle?'

'Yes, bo's'n.'

The captain had the commissioning pennant hoisted with five cannon shots, and the new Castle gave them farewell with three. The boatswain shouted all the passengers out of the way. He tacked the hooker out of the bay against a northerly wind; the third tack brought them directly below Robben Island's lee. Daniel was in the foretop and saw Pieternella and her brother at the stern gunwale, pointing at the island and waving as if they could recognise people on shore. Boatswain Lubbert was right behind them and must have said something to her to make her turn round, because she took fright and pressed her hands to her mouth. Daniel and three others were hanging over the foreyard with their faces to the bow, pulling up the sail with their hands and folding it over the yard under their stomachs; they needed both hands for the work and couldn't look round at what was happening behind. He dropped his head and kept his eyes on his work, deciding to bring the matter of Boatswain Lubbert to a head once and for all as soon as he came on deck.

When his watch was over, they were on the open sea to the west of the Hout Bay's mountain. The deck had been cleared, and they were running with a good wind under full sail and a spritsail at the bow. In the forecastle he gave his knife to Bart and asked him to look after it for him, until the end of their voyage, and throughout the next watch he remained on deck until he saw Commander Lamotius walking behind the mast; then he went nearer to greet him.

'Ah, Zaaijman. At last we're on our way.'

'Yes, Your Honour. I wish you and your lady a safe passage.'

'Thank you. Are you married? Do you have a family on the island?'

'No, Your Honour.'

'We have quite a few newcomers travelling with us. I suppose you know them. Who speaks on behalf of you Mauritius farers?' If the commander had been more experienced in the customs, he would have said: Who is the oldest among you? So he and Daniel looked at one another until Daniel made up his mind and said: 'It is I. I came to complain about Commander Hugo's rule.'

'I remember. I hope it will go better now.'

'Your Honour, I came to ask that Bo's'n Lubbert's rope be taken away from him. Bart Borms and I have been freemen for years now. We cannot take his assaults.'

'That is understandable. Yes, you are my burghers. Are you off duty now? Come, let us talk to the captain. He is chatting to my wife, and she is not feeling well.'

Captain Wobma was not happy with Daniel's request. They were still in sight of land and already the sailors were trying to meddle with his affairs. He would prefer to turn the ship round right here and return to Table Bay. He reminded Daniel that he had registered to work for his passage.

'I shall do my work, skipper. You can watch, I always try to be first in the shrouds. Day or night, in any weather. But that man's starter is a wickedness of the Devil. It tempts me to strike him back.'

'That sounds reasonable to me, captain,' Lamotius said.

'I will not take away his starter. There is no ship on which this doesn't happen; the rope's end is to spur them on.'

'Captain,' said Lamotius, 'please instruct Lubbert to keep his rope for proven laggards. Please make sure you do it.'

'I shall take the helm at every watch,' said Daniel. 'I shall steer. I'm asking this for Bart too. I read the compass, I have years of experience. And I am a cooper.'

'For how long can you steer?' asked the captain. 'After one watch at the helm of this hooker, you have to rest for three.'

'Not I, captain. But I must get out from under your bo's'n, otherwise I won't take responsibility.'

Annoyed, Captain Wobma spoke to Daniel, but it was meant for Lamotius. 'You Mauritius farers are full of complaints, the lot of you. I've been there before. Always want this and that and live like kings. You are never satisfied. Be well warned, commander, by what you see here today. They will turn your hair grey over there.'

'Like kings?' Daniel asked the captain without hesitating. 'You are lucky to have a king at your helm, captain.'

After that Daniel spent his every watch, day or night, at the helm, as he'd undertaken. Sometimes Bart stood the watch with him, but usually it was with other quartermasters. Helmsmen were off duty for four hours out of eight, as it was hard work. The helm was an oak beam too hefty for one man to get his hands around. From the head of the tiller it stretched forward all the way across the poop almost to the mainmast. At one end the ocean strained and jerked at the tiller, as the other two sailors kept it in check. Every swell passing under the hooker tried to wrench the tiller from their hands. The two helmsmen – it was rare for the sea to be so calm that one man was enough – were straining there at the tiller under the open sky in rain or wind to keep the ship's head on the compass according to the captain's instructions. Sometimes, in heavy following swell, the sea broke green over the stern, burying the helmsmen chest-deep in water.

On the first afternoon out of the Cape seasickness struck the passengers, and it was three days before Daniel saw Pieternella again. In that time *Boode* went far south, down to almost forty degrees, where the strong westerly winds blow month after month and the great western current flows around the globe. This was where Wobma wanted his ship. It was mid-season, the winter trade wind blew constantly, the days were dark and cold and the rain came viciously and ceaselessly from the north-west. By day they sailed under the foretop, main course and reefed maintopsail with the mizzen way over to port, and at night only under reefed topsails and mizzen. The cold and rain, occasionally with hail, lasted for weeks. The sails were soaked and heavy and white water poured from the ship as it rose from one swell, to be buried again by the next. In those conditions helmsmen worked with lanyards around the body, as the watch huddled behind the weather gunwale.

The captain and the boatswain were together on the deck at daybreak, and again at noon to measure the height of the sun and calculate their progress. When there wasn't a sun, they observed the evening star, then once again the captain and his boatswain were together at the compass. When there was no sun or stars for days, he drove the ship forward to escape from under the weather, reckoning purely by the hourglass. Without time an officer could not make his calculations. A helmsman was also the ship's timekeeper, he had to turn the glass over in its container and strike the bell on the half-hour. Daniel was expecting Captain Wobma to find fault with his steering. The captain said nothing to him and rarely responded to a helmsmen's greeting as he emerged from the poop door. He would bend over the compass to see how the ship's head was pointing, and went off to his position at the lee side of the poop deck to examine the horizon through the telescope. Helm, rudder and helmsmen were mere implements to a ship's captain, apparatus to control the sea. It had to work, there was no need for a greeting.

When the boatswain's turn at watch came round, he would walk from starboard to larboard, hitting out at the men hauling at the ropes, cursing the watch sheltering behind the gunwale against the hail-rain. He never spoke to Daniel, merely speaking the course he wanted to be steered. With Bart he occasionally exchanged a few words as if they were friends.

'So, you're a helmsman now, grandpa. Did you get scared of the mizzen yard? It's swaying rather dangerously, isn't it?'

'No, bo's'n.' That was Bart's only answer. But one night in calm weather under the slowly tilting sky he and Daniel spoke at the helm, and Bart told him that on his first voyage to the East, a boatswain's mate who'd used to follow men up the mast with his starter, had been trampled in the teeth and kicked from the foretop shroud, and beaten until he'd fallen into the dark sea from that height. After that the other petty officers had been more careful. But Boatswain Lubbert came back time and time again to talk to Bart in order to make friends, so that Daniel would be isolated, in disfavour with himself and the captain.

'Why do you carry two knives, grandpa?'

'A messmate asked me to keep it for him. He has a terrible temper.'

'Who?'

'Bo's'n.'

A helmsman's work had some compensations. The two of them were the only ones to receive a tot of arrack at the beginning and the end of a watch, against the fatigue and the cold.

In the day, when the weather was calm, Pieternella, or Theuntje, or Lamotius and his wife, occasionally walked for a while behind the mainmast. Daniel appreciated their friendly greetings; they were people from the warmth of the cabin, but he could not talk to them. Either the captain or the boatswain would be there at the compass and he had no wish to earn a harsh word from them. When his watch was over, he would eat his food, usually cold in congealed white fat, and wrap himself in his damp blanket, and lie down on the deck to sleep, out of the way in the dripping forecastle.

He had news from the cabin through Bart, and sent his own messages through Bart. 'Ask Theuntje about their accommodation.' Half a day later he would hear: 'It's fine. Theuntje and Pieternella have the constable's room, and Tieleman's Maijke and the convict's wife and children sleep with them on the deck. The old woman shouts and curses something terrible, making life most unpleasant for the convict's wife, calling her a slut and so on all the time. Salomon sleeps with the captain's cabin boy. The new commander and his two have the captain's cabin, so captain and boatswain have to make do together. By the mangy dog, those two are birds of a feather.'

Then Daniel would ask: 'How is Pieternella?'

'You can see she's fine.'

'Tell her, Bart, she must never walk on her own. She must watch in the cabin at night, and fasten her door. And she must remember: no women in front of the foremast.'

'I'll tell her.'

'Sound Theuntje a bit, if she thinks Pieternella will marry me.'

'What is the matter with you? You have to teach the child what she needs to know.' But three days later he heard: Theuntje said she would think about it.

Then there was the convict Willem Willemsz, nicknamed Lyreman. He was swollen round with dropsy. The boatswain called him Pigface because his cheeks were so round and his eyes reduced to slits. The ring around his leg had become encased in his flesh. He was too heavy to go into the shrouds, and the captain excused him from it, but the boatswain paid him with his rope. The captain made him pick oakum; his two arms were covered with tar up to the elbows, and he crawled about on deck caulking seams as he went. And because he was swollen so badly he would pass wind all the time, and the sailors closest to him would make sure that he was kicked every time as was the custom. So it might be said that he was booted across the sea from one country to another.

When the height of the sun at noon one day showed that they had fallen far enough south, Captain Wobma plotted a course for the east, adding sail, and the hooker lurched ahead like a donkey kicked in the backside. They were right in the great western current, which carried the ship like a dry leaf in a mill-race; there was green sea ahead and a beautifully strong westerly wind from behind. The hooker ran, its keel water bubbling loudly as if it was boiling, and far behind, above the endless white track of their wake an albatross came to hover. It remained hanging in one spot, as if it had been pasted to the sky. It should have meant good luck, but it wasn't, as in that time the firewood got soaked through an open hatch and for two days they had to eat cold food, and the water barrels knocked about in the hold, causing staves to spring, so that they lost drinking water. It was the carelessness of some unhappy sailors; their hearts were not in the work.

Daniel kept his eye on their wide, white wake over his starboard shoulder. He wanted to draw a straight white line across the sea. There were some who noticed it, like the captain, and one day Salomon pointed it out to Pieternella and said, where *Seur* Lamotius was present to hear: 'It looks as if we're unrolling a ribbon across the sea.'

'The Company draws hundreds of these ribbons over the ocean every day,' the commander remarked. But his wife said to Pieternella: 'I don't think they're all as straight as this one.'

There were good days at the helm. In the southern hemisphere the weather clears from the south-west. For a long time the sky had been blue; they'd hung out every scrap of sail. The course was due east. In the morning the sun was obliquely above the larboard bow, during the day it remained overhead to larboard, and in the early afternoon it went down over the larboard quarter. At night, waning or waxing, there were shards of moon, with its cool golden light from the starboard side. The sky was cold and clear, the heavens pulsed with stars, and every time there was a shooting star, Daniel mumbled the helmsman's incantation to invoke the good. '*Here we sail, with God on high . . .*', the entire, long hymn.

And from before daybreak they ran with a morning star before the bowsprit, due east. There was no end to the seawater, and the captain's chart bore no sign of land ahead. Now there were fewer changes to be made to the sails; at sunset the watch shortened sail, and before sunrise the next morning it was shaken out, and running gear was tightened and again secured. Then the ship dipped its head and ploughed on more deeply, causing its bow wave to curve, bright, white, with dull, heavy thuds on either side over the two anchors.

'Thank you, merciful Father,' Bart said, 'now at least the one whose voice you can always hear above the wind has become quieter.'

The captain had the watches changed to eight-hour shifts, and one day said to Daniel: 'If you cannot keep it up, tell me, then I can put someone else in your place.' And Daniel thanked him and turned his head towards the white line of his wake, so that the captain could see what he was looking at.

Six weeks after they'd left the Cape, the captain said: 'Now we'll see how well you tended the glass.' He made them veer north-east, and after ten days on this course where the sun couldn't be seen for days on end, they had to deduce from the stars that they were back at the height of the Cape. After that, one day passed like the other; sometimes with a feeble wind from the south-east, and sometimes with a strong westerly. The night air became warmer, and there were fewer days when it looked as if one were observing the world through clear glass. On the fifteenth day the captain posted lookouts in the foretop and the maintop, but they had nothing to report. Sometimes there was a school of whales, and once or twice they saw the topgallant sails of ships from the north behind the horizon. The officers measured their heights, made their sums, and diminished the water rations for the crew. Those who knew something, realised that it meant they didn't know where they were.

'If we miss Mauritius now, we can go straight through to Batavia,' Daniel said aloud to his mate. He flung a bucket on a rope overboard, and tested the temperature of the seawater with his elbow. 'Your butter will be melting before the week is out, doctor,' he told the cook. 'You'd better start working in more salt, otherwise you'll lose the lot.'

Seven days after the lookouts had been posted in the masts, Daniel noticed a dull red glow in the distance over larboard, one dawn when the morning star was already beginning to fade. He pointed it out to his companion at the helm. 'I think I recognise that, friend. Tell your bo's'n: you think you can see the volcano on Île Bourbon.'

'I don't like talking to him, Daniel. He comes at one with his rope's end without any cause or warning.'

'Then we'll shout, friend.' He cupped his hands in front of his mouth: 'Bo's'n, there's a light, thirty degrees over larboard.'

'Where?' asked Lubbert, opening his telescope at the compass box. 'Show.'

'Thirty degrees over larboard is about there,' Daniel said, pointing.

'Bastard, you are looking for me,' grumbled Lubbert. Then he shouted up: 'Masthead! What do you see, thirty out to larboard?'

'That will be the daybreak, bo's'n.'

'Nonsense,' said Daniel. 'You know at what time the sun will rise. Notify the captain, otherwise we'll have to turn back in a week to come and look for this spot.'

'Who are you ordering about, uncle?'

'We're too far east and will be passing below Mauritius. Skipper will be grateful to you.'

'Grateful or not, I owe you a hiding from the start.'

'Below!' the lookout called down. 'Below!'

'Then you'd better start, bo's'n.'

'Below! I see a light there!'

'Below your grandmother. Keep your eye on it as if it's a whore mincing round a corner.' The boatswain called forward to a sailor: 'Go and wake the captain. Run, before this rope's end gets you.'

'I reckon,' Daniel said aloud to his mate, 'we can change course so long, and fill the sails to go and see what it is. The captain will be grateful to me.'

'For God's sake, Daniel, don't provoke him. Why are you needling the man?' whispered the helmsman.

'It's what the Devil in hell is planning for me, friend. That is what he wants of me. Perhaps it's my fate to be hanged because of this piece of excrement.'

At sunrise the captain took the height and sent Daniel up the mast with a telescope. He came back to report that he believed it was Bourbon, he could see the smoke from the mountain. Thereupon the captain scribbled calculations on his slate and changed their course. Two days later they saw Mauritius. It was high day, and the ladies and gentlemen were on deck.

'Deck! Over the bow, ten to starboard. Land clouds.'

'You go up, Zaaijman, and say what you see.'

In the cross of the mainmast he wrapped his arm in the shroud and steadied his glass against the mast. The clouds were hanging over Pieter Both's Head. Through the telescope the head stood halfway clear of the sea, blue under a sky of round white clouds. That was home. Mauritius, his only home.

'Masthead?'

'Mauritius, skipper. I can see the south-western corner, Pieter Both's Head.'

'Come down.'

'How do we go from here?' the captain asked him at the compass box. Daniel remembered that the captain had once told about having been in these waters before. Perhaps the man was making a last attempt to trap him in a net.

'With sail and wind the way we are now, the course should be due east. Sunset will bring us to the South-East Gap, half a mile outside the reef.'

Sundown found them becalmed in front of the gap. It was high tide and foam broke over the reef. The sky was a bright orange, and the kloofs in the mountain deep in shadow. The passengers had been against the gunwale for quite a while to gaze at the land. A land boat, its patched sail hanging limp against the mast, lay rocking right in the gap. A black man stood in the prow, and through a hailer his helmsman called at Captain Wobma to let down his boats and man them, so that they could haul his hooker in. Wobma objected; he preferred to wait out at sea and go through in the morning.

'Can't you see it's high tide? Commander Hugo says you must come in, he's not sending out a pilot again.'

Wobma passed his telescope to Daniel and said: 'Who is that fellow? Impudent dog.'

'It is Sven, the pilot.'

'Then we'd better put out. Bo's'n, call both watches. Bind up every-thing, we're putting our boats out. Then you take one, and appoint somebody for the other boat, and tow us in. Zaaijman, you have the helm.' Two drag-ropes were laid out over the prow of the hooker. One watch pulled up sails, folded them in, tied them down; the other watch swung and lowered the boats. Twelve oarsmen were counted out and sent to their places. Oars were passed down.

The pilot boat slid in under their lee, as if there was no wind in its sail, touching the hooker's hull so that its black man could leap aboard. Then the pilot raised his thin, red face and recognised Daniel at the helm.

'Whited wall.' And he let his boat glide away in the current. His black man moved forward silently, efficiently, out to the tip of the bowsprit.

So they went through the gap in the reef: the pilot boat in front, then the two longboats with their teams of rowers lifting the oars from the sea in unison, leaning forward and at the coxswain's call cutting the blades into the water, pull, lift, lean, pull, lift, lean, throwing their bodies back, all together to the coxswain's call. Like long-legged spiders the rowing boats crept across the smooth water behind the pilot boat, close, close to the island on starboard. On the hooker's bowsprit the black man lay stretched out, staring down to the bottom of the sea, raising an arm to starboard or larboard as he wanted Daniel to steer, among the coral beds and shallow.

Commander Lamotius and his wife were at the gunwale close to Daniel, their keen eyes on the dark green coast below the crimson sky, Theuntje and Salomon were beside them. The Lyreman's wife and Maijke Hendriksz stood, their backs to the land, talking about slaves. Pieternella saw Daniel alone at the tiller, and came to him with a smile. From far ahead the splashing of oars could be heard, and the coxswains' shouts giving rhythm to the rowers.

'Will we go ashore tonight?'

Daniel replied softly, not to attract the captain's attention. 'It will be dark by the time we have the anchor out. No, I don't think the skipper will open hatches tonight, and without our chests we cannot go ashore. Tomorrow morning, I think.'

'It is a warm evening.'

'If you stay on this island, you will never be cold again.'

'I am far from home, Daniel. I don't know other places. What is going to become of me, and of Salomon?'

He was quiet while he pushed the tiller to starboard as the *serang* indicated, waited for the ship to settle on course, and then straightened the rudder again. He had to concentrate on his work here. 'I shall show you everything. Look, there's the Lodge, below that round rock. You will see the flag in a moment. There you can see Compass Point coming out, right in front of the bow. It stands in the middle of the island, and you can see, old Sven is heading straight for it. The man on the bowsprit we call *serang*. I'll show you everything. There is the Lemoenbosvlakte, where our house is.'

'Our house? Do you have a family here?'

'I mean: if you will marry me.'

'Are you going to ask me?'

'I'm asking you now.'

She gave no answer. Beside the ship four dolphins leaped from the water, green and blue below the water and glistening silver above, one after the other, to enter the gap before the hooker. Daniel also was silent for a long time, his eyes on the *serang*.

'Very good luck for us, Pieternella. These dolphins.'

He steered the ship down the channel, following the serang's arm and hand signals. He knew the channel himself, with its cat's heads and branches of coloured coral on either side and a sandy bottom over which the tides moved in and out, twice a day. Coral always grows to its lee side, and is much steeper on that side. But one sees it best when the sun is at its highest, with some little breeze to ripple the water. A reef with half a fathom of water has a brown colour, at one fathom it is greyish-brown, deeper down the water becomes darker, pale blue, dark blue, purple, until a lookout in the mast is no longer aware of a reef below the keel. Here in the twilight, with the sea like a dark mirror, one needed a good man on his belly on the bowsprit, and a very steady hand at the tiller.

Pieternella placed her fingers on the pole as if to feel the weight of the ship. 'I don't know what it is, Daniel. I'm afraid of getting married. I'm still too young.'

'We can help one another. I shall look after you.'

'I'm very poor. I don't have any dowry or inheritance. And very few clothes.'

'Those are things we can get. We are both young. I won't let you down, Pieternel.'

'Well, when should I marry you?'

'Once we've unpacked the chests?'

'I'll find out from Aunt Theuntje.' Later she said: 'Sooner or later you will have to kiss me, Daniel, if I understand it correctly.'

He put his hand over hers on the tiller, so that they were steering together, and nodded. 'You understand correctly. Can you wait until we are anchored and the tops sent down and all secured?'

The ship was in the pool in front of the Lodge. At high tide there was water under it, but at low tide it was almost all mud. Daniel lay on his bedding without a shirt. From tomorrow night the crew will be sleeping out on deck, with the stars as their only cover. It was his first full night off watch for fifty-three days. He was tired, but the silence throughout the darkened ship, the close heat of the forecastle and the deathliness of the motionless ship made him restless, so that he remained between fully asleep and fully awake. In the heat and dusk he longed for Pieternella. He was still surprised by the strength of her narrow hand on the tiller, and when she said goodbye to go to Theuntje and Salomon. They were betrothed now. He had to give her a ring or some other token, for people to know. The boatswain would come to look for him; his kind did not rest after they'd been challenged before inferiors. They always had to be on top, to maintain their standing, what they liked to call their honour, among the workers. What would have become of poor Sergeant Col?

He thought of going for a swim, or maybe watching on deck all night. After they let go their anchors fore and aft in the pool before the short jetty, Sven brought the pilot boat under the bowsprit to take off his *serang*, and in passing turned to look at Pieternella. The commander's wife was next to her, older and prettier, but Sven looked at Pieternella with a frown, as if he thought he recognised a lost relative. Commander Hugo and his younger son came aboard before dark, and carried away Commander Lamotius and his lady, to the shore. Skipper Wobma did not go with them. Which was a mercy from heaven, otherwise the boatswain would have come looking for him.

When the boat returned from the shore deep in the night, Daniel was still awake, restless. He took the lantern from the hook to look for Bart among the messmates lying in a close bundle like caterpillars against a tree trunk, and asked to have his knife back.

The first night on shore, in his house at the Lemoenbos, he couldn't sleep either. The world seemed to be lying wrong for him: north was now rather more west than he could remember, and his mattress was too soft, and he felt that the earth was a deck which was supposed to move, yet there wasn't the slightest movement in the ground, and the twittering of geckoes on his walls was different from the sound of the ocean below his head. Barbara Geens's face haunted his dreams. The time was wrong too. When they'd left the Cape, the sun rose at almost eight o'clock; now it rose at six. He would have to change the clock to keep his head. Time, he knew, is something which exists only on clocks. If you don't have one, there is no time. A farmer abides by the sun: he looks when his chickens go to roost, when his cattle come from the pasture to be milked, when his rooster begins to crow. A day or two from now he would hopefully be all right.

There was no wind; the forest behind his house lay in a deep sleep. Pieternella would be just as confused, probably also awake, more worried than he, listening perhaps in the warm night. For what? For the heavy wings of bats in the trees, and for geckoes in the thatch. What would she be thinking of? There hadn't been young girls on this island for years. Commander Hugo's daughter nearly went out of her mind from loneliness, and grey-haired at seventeen, and look how Hugo had treated her and the poor lad. He himself had been lying alone at night now for long enough. He wanted a wife, and children, and nature was ready to give it to him. He wanted to hear people in his house. There were those like Sven who fled into the forest when they saw people, but Sven went to slave women, or convicts, when he felt the need. He couldn't go to slave women like Sven and *Seur* Jongmeyer and others. If a child were to be born, it would be his child born into slavery. Bart said, when he'd told him that Pieternella had said yes, 'I'm happy for your sake, friend. Now Theuntje loses the child again.' But Theuntje had Bart, so she should be content.

It was for his own need too that he'd gone to Batavia, where he'd been shown the sea route to the Cape by the late Secretary van Riebeeck. It was a merciful destiny, because that was how Pieternella had now come to this island. They had a habit, the gentlemen, of placing your feet on a certain course and then to die behind your back, so that you couldn't go to look for them afterwards to blame and accuse them.

When they'd gone to greet Commander Hugo the day before, after the public induction of Commander Lamotius, he'd presented Pieternella as 'my intended', and the gentleman had said, 'Ha, there's a wedding at hand. When do we sail, skipper? No later than three weeks.' Hugo could indeed look forward to his departure, he who'd refused to let his daughter go from under his eyes. Now he had to go to Batavia to search for her. And in Batavia the Cape letters would be waiting for him, accusing him, and among the letters were affidavits from Zaaijman and Borms and a petition from the island's citizens and almost the whole garrison, and from Sergeant Col, about the way in which he and they had been treated. But he would escape after all. The rich escaped everything.

He'd promised Bart that he would help him to build a room for Salomon. And afterwards Bart would come and help him here. He would make this house spacious and comfortable. All day tomorrow neighbours would turn up to greet them. They would drink Bart's arrack, and later Bart would have to start adding sugar water, for where were they going to find new supplies? He and Bart had expected Hugo to burn down their houses while they were away, but he hadn't. He had become cautious, the gentleman. What had frightened him? Was it what he'd done to his child and to others?

In the daylight Daniel inspected his withered sugar and tobacco. For six months it had never been irrigated, and in that time not much rain had fallen, so the soil was like black powder and most of the plants had withered away. He would have to start over again with the planting. And likewise his vegetables, with the new seeds he'd brought from the Cape. His house had been ravaged by the wind, more than Bart's, and somebody had stolen a long piece of his fence. Fortunately there had not been a hurricane this year, but it made it more likely that there would be one coming the first autumn. Then he put on his hat, and went into the forest with his chopper to cut palm fronds.

'I see you're not sleeping,' Bart said, when Daniel dropped the first load of branches in his yard. Bart's house had been made mainly of old ship's timber, which in some places still showed the curves of a boat. 'You're an early man. Good dry stuff. Come, let the womenfolk lie.'

He picked up a skin-bag and a machete at his door, and they walked back along the footpath to the forest. That day each of them brought home five more bundles of fronds, accompanied by Salomon on the last three trips. Bart called the boy 'little scholar,' because the child had so many questions.

'Did you sleep badly, Pieternella?' Daniel asked her when they rested for a while under the shady tree in front of Bart's house.

'No, we made clothes last night, Aunt Theuntje and I. And talked a lot. We burned up a candle. Then we slept late this morning.'

'What did you talk about so late?'

'Having banns read, things like that. Do you know about it?'

'Yes. It means you and I must walk to the Lodge to speak to the commander.'

'That's not all. We must appear before the congregation three times.'

'I'm not afraid of that. I must still give you that pledge that comes from my heart.'

'Where do you find the words?'

'Heard them somewhere. Long ago.' He did not say it to her, but for a moment Barbertje Geens's golden head had been vividly in his mind. 'Will you be pleased with a nice big fish?'

She laughed at him, and he was grateful for it, and grinned back. He would have liked to hold her against him, but he was sticky with sweat. Visiting time was after sundown, after he had washed.

'Aunt Theuntje says if we still want to appear on two Sundays, and get married on the third, then we have to give notice tomorrow, because the day after is Sunday. She says she and Bart will give a reception, here at their home. We must invite the people, and we must book the musicians when we're at the Lodge.'

From that moment, from those words, Daniel's own life was taken away from him. Previously there had been little apart from his sugar and his tobacco in his mind, and every day was long, simple and clear ahead of him, and his to use as he wished. He could set out and hunt with his dogs, and anywhere around the island he could lay down his musket and take off his clothes to swim in the inner water. In the evening he could go to neighbours to play jass and wager a guilder, drink a few rummers of arrack and bet a few guilders, and return home at any hour of the night. Only his dogs knew or wondered where he was, and if they cared about him, they didn't often show it. From that day on it was like when one became a ship's captain, and you no longer had duty watch every four hours, but all of the twenty-four. You are never at ease again. As long as there was land in sight, there was no sleep for the captain. He and Bart would have gone to cut wood to finish the framework for the room that day, that was what they had agreed, but now it was changed because of the banns. His whole life had to change, from here.

And over the next months the feeling steadily grew in him, that he was no longer a captain on his own, and independent. There was a second hand on the tiller. And as if it was a warning, he began to feel that he was caught in a terrifying current and dragged away to where he did not want to go.

And Pieternel? What was it like for her, to be living in Sofia's safe home one day, and then to cross the ocean to open her eyes on a strange island in Bart's fishing hut? He asked her this as they walked to the Lodge, the next morning.

'What does our world look like to you, Pieternel? What do you think of us?'

'I cannot understand so many new things at one time. It is beautiful. It is very beautiful.'

'And our people?'

'So far I know only Bart and Aunt Theuntje. And you. But I am happy to be here.'

'And I, Pieternella. I was looking for the East, but here I found paradise.'

'Have you seen snakes around here yet?'

'Those on two legs. As in all other countries.'

He took her to a part of the Lemoenbooms River, where it flowed shallow and wide over a bed of pebbles, and picked her up and carried her across. She held her breath until they reached the other side, and asked: 'Didn't we cross by a bridge yesterday?'

'Yes, but I like it more like this. The bridge is just around the corner there. I helped to build it, in the time of the late Commander Wreede.'

'Are there more rivers ahead?'

'Yes.'

'With a bridge?'

'You can say how you prefer it, with or without.'

When he put her down, she wanted to know: 'Am I too heavy for you?'

'Like a lump of lead. Can you swim?'

'Are you going to drop me?' she asked. 'Daniel, have you ever seen a woman swim?'

'In the East everybody swims. But here you may well be the first. It is easy. And on the whole island there is nothing better. I want you to see Kroonenburg.'

He explained the place names as they passed. Here was Lemoenbosberg, the Orange Grove Mountain. There were orange trees growing all along the river, planted almost a hundred years ago by Hollanders. They had spread up the slope of the mountain. This time of the year the oranges were ripe, but the free burghers were not supposed to pluck them. They belonged to the Company. There to the right, as they went, was Fisherman's Isle; and the Kalk, or the Chalk; and Modderbaai, Mud Bay. And there was Kattieseiland, Cats' Island; and the Juffershoedje, the Lady's Hat, near the pool where the hooker lay at an angle. After that they reached Roode Krans, Red Cliff; and Franse Kerk, French Church, where the island's boats were hauled up. Behind the Lodge was the Sadelberg, the Saddle Mountain. He showed her how melted rock had streamed black into the sea long ago, when the island had been born from a volcano. Beyond the Lodge was the vegetable garden, and then Brandende Hoek, Breakers Point, the only spot in this bay where waves broke.

When they came near the Lodge, he offered her his arm. 'We shall cross the square together, so that everybody can see us.'

The clerk was Commander Hugo's elder son. He was an exceptionally fair youth, his face should have been a woman's. Daniel was glad to see him; he always had a friendly word for people. He came round the table to greet them, and helped them to carry the long wooden bench closer to his desk. Yes, he had received all Pieternella's papers from the Cape. And how were things at the Cape? Did the wind still blow so hard? His father had cursed the place because his hat was blown away all the time.

'No,' Pieternella said seriously, 'there isn't much wind.'

The youth looked surprised. 'The so-called south-easter, even though my father says it's south-west? Well, I assure you, my father often curses for nothing.'

'People from the Cape do not think of it as wind. It's just the air.'

'I understand. Have you come from the Lemoenbos now? I want to get us something to drink. Fresh orange juice, our slaves pressed three thousand yesterday. Excuse me for a moment.'

While he was out, Daniel whispered to her: 'Some of the others treat us free burghers with disdain. But blood counts, this one is a true gentleman.'

Did they come to have their banns registered? he asked. Yes, he thought as much. Everybody could see it from afar. He knew their names, and wrote down the particulars of their banns for them with a fine hand. The announcement would be made on Sunday after the service. It cost four guilders, but if they didn't have it in cash they could bring it later. And what did the young lady think of this island?

When they were outside again, they heard a huge voice shouting in the office: 'This office is not a confounded taphouse.'

'His father,' Daniel said. 'The lad is a great disappointment for him. But just look at the handwriting, Pieternel. It looks as if it's been done by a book printer.'

At the exit from the square the two guards lowered their pikes and barred their way. '*Tabetje*,' they asked, grinning. They wanted either a few guilders or a kiss from the bride-to-be. Pieternel knew the custom from the Cape, and lifted her face to the nearest one, while Daniel looked for coins in his thin purse. The corporal, a sallow foreigner, hugged Pieternel and kissed her as if the pair were going to be married.

'Hey, Jacomo. Your hands off my betrothed. The child is only fourteen, and I myself have not yet kissed her like that. Stand back, Pieternel, this fellow is like an animal.'

'Fourteen years, my friend? Indeed, young Giulietta of my home town was also only fourteen when she became the world's princess of love. Shame on you, Danielo, you're neglecting your duty to this little dove.'

'What Giulietta?' asked Daniel, but the sallow corporal kept on staring into Pieternella's eyes, so that he could swear the man wanted to seduce her.

'Ah, little dove, one night by moonlight I must tell you the story of Romeo and Giulietta, two young people from Verona, very close to where I was born, and where young love now blossoms eternally.'

'As long as I am present,' said Daniel, but not without pride. Right there he arranged with Jacomo for music at the wedding. Jacomo had a friend who could play the flute quite reasonably, and there was a new woodcutter, a savage from Armenia, with a saw. You wouldn't believe it. He played his saw with a bow, a sound so mournful that the dogs howled all the way to Noordwyks Vlak and tomorrow he would saw the raw red ebony with the same instrument. Not dance music at all, but very popular; all the farmers and their wives would break into tears, and wail as one might expect of uncouth barbarians. Jacomo Baldini and his companion, fiddle and flute, would provide the real dance music. And the corporal gazed into Pieternella's eyes and assured her that Jacomo Baldini was her future husband's best friend. He, too, was to become a free burgher; the Dutchmen in this place knew him as Jaap Baldyn. A soldier chiselled from one block, was Jacomo. He had taken an Indian wife, and he would bring her to the wedding and present her to them.

The Sunday when their banns were read, the hall, entirely of timber, was full. People had come to see the new commander. In the front row to the right of the desk were the officers: Lamotius, Hugo, his younger son, Wobma and Franz from the hooker, and the councillors Telleson, Claasen and Zacharias. On the left, next to Lamotius's lady, were two married women. Behind them, men to the right, women to the left, were the lower officials, the soldiers and sailors, then the free burghers, then a few slaves and convicts, sunken down on their own small benches and seating blocks. Among the convicts were Maijke Hendriksz and Willem the Lyreman. Hugo's elder son played the clavichord, read the chapter, started the hymn with a rich tenor. The congregation did not let him down; they all rose to support the younker in his singing.

After the psalm Lamotius took the word. He read a long text from Bulaeus, and one could see that he had prepared, as he left out a considerable amount. Then he asked them to sing another hymn. Afterwards he presented his discourse. To those who had not yet seen him, he wanted to say that he was Isaac Johannes Lamotius, the new commander, and here on his left was his wife. They were planning to visit the whole community during the coming weeks. He had been inducted formally, and the Council would be meeting the following morning under his chairmanship. If the congregation had requests or petitions to submit to the Council, they could present it at the office for consideration, as had been the custom in the past. He hoped that the community was entering a blessed period. The hooker *Boode* would be leaving for Batavia on the thirtieth, weather permitting.

Then Lamotius opened another small book and called Daniel and Pieternel to the front. Daniel went cold.

'With doors opened as required by law, I hereby announce for the first time to the congregation that Daniel Zaaijman of Vlissingen, bachelor, and Pieternella van Meerhof, spinster from Cape of Good Hope are of the intention to enter into the state of matrimony. Let those who have any objection, speak now or for ever hold their peace. The announcement will be repeated on the following two Sundays.'

Daniel felt light-headed. He remained standing in front of the congregation, staring at their faces, until Pieternel took his hand and pulled him forward. As a new ship on the slipway, when the blocks were loosened and removed, slides down into the water, it now happened to him. He was still dazed as he shuffled down the narrow aisle. Where was his life taking him?

Under the palm trees the black-clad congregation milled around, kissing Pieternel and shaking Daniel's hand, and for the first time in months he greeted old friends and introduced them: these were Hein Karseboom and his wife, this was Fockje Jansz, this was Noordoos and his wife. What is your real name, Noordoos? He invited each person who came to shake his hand to come to the wedding. When it was all over, he bowed to Pieternel. 'And I am Daniel Zaaijman from Vlissingen.' For the first time he pulled her into his arms and kissed her, and he was amazed at how soft her mouth was, and how she held him there against her and wanted to remain pressed to him.

There was one other, with a crumpled suit of brown canvas hanging from his body in folds, who approached to touch Daniel's shoulder with the back of his hand and, without speaking, shoved a red paw in between them. His weathered face was the brown and red of dried wood; his hair and beard, which in younger years had been a golden red, was mostly bleached a yellowish white. His appearance reminded one of smoked fish.

'I have some dogs for you. At least three.'

'Pieternella, this is Sven.' They looked at one another, without greeting, without nodding, as if they had known each other all along, thought Daniel. 'I cannot train dogs now, *baas*. I have too much to do.'

'And how will you get food?'

'My business, *baas*.'

'The other matter for you is: Hugo is not going to leave *St Hubert* here. He is going to burn it.'

'I don't believe it.'

'I'm telling you his own words, Daniel. If you want it, we'll take it out one night and hide it in a river mouth, like at Klimopberg. We'll cover it with branches until the gentleman has gone. Or we sink it.'

'Hugo is not one to play with, Sven. He will hang you to be done with you.'

'Then go to the Devil.'

'Come to our wedding, *Baas* Sven,' Daniel called after him.

On the long road home between the sea and the mountain, together with Theuntje and Bart and Salomon, they talked about the wedding: how many guests, what to eat, and also, whether the notables chose to honour them or not, it was their duty to invite those people.

'What did Sven want from you?' asked Bart, and Daniel pointed at Salomon's back, placing his finger on his mouth. 'He wants to sell dogs. But first I'll build my house, then get the crop in the ground, then perhaps train dogs.' He was grateful that Pieternel had not said a word, and when they were alone, he told her so. Piracy was a hanging matter.

In the following week he and Bart and Salomon set up the frames for the outroom, clad its walls and roof with plaited palm fronds, laid a floor and made Salomon a *katil* of bamboo, with a canvas mattress stuffed tightly with coir.

'A Dutch sailor,' Bart boasted before Pieternel and Salomon, 'can sew, and do carpentry, and cook, and do anything you ask of him. We learn it at sea, and in the East, and wherever we go. You, little scholar, cannot do better than become a sailor.'

'Softly, Bart,' Theuntje said. 'You're talking about a child with a head on his shoulders. Don't listen to him, Salomon. When you're old enough, you can make your own choice.'

'And in the meantime his best learning years go by.'

'You can also learn a trade,' Daniel told the lad. 'That way you can rid yourself from anybody who tries to dictate to you.'

The following Sunday their banns were read for the second time. After the gathering Daniel and Pieternel spoke to the commander about their wedding the next week. It was to be his first wedding, said Lamotius, but they could rely on him. All they had to do was to arrange for two witnesses and ten guilders. Daniel thanked him, saying: If the commander and his lady were agreeable to attend their little celebration, they would be honoured. Outside, where new faces and old friends came to congratulate them, more invitations were extended, and Daniel spoke to people about a wagon and oxen to bring on the guests.

Bart warned him: Don't invite Hugo, don't invite an insult from the man. But Pieternella reminded them that Commander Wagenaer had attended her parents' wedding; they could not act anything but decently now.

Daniel went to knock on the gentleman's door. He opened himself, big as a giant, without overcoat, his shirtsleeves rolled up over his heavy, black forearms.

'Ah, Zaaijman. And the intended. Marya, Maria, what is your name? Come on board.' He went ahead of them down the passage to his quarters. Everything, walls and doors and floors and ceilings, were of wood, like the city hall in Delft. Twenty yards further he opened a door. It was a beautiful room, once again fully of wood, with broad Dutch furniture, Oriental carpets on the walls, and the world's arms exhibited against the side as in a knight's hall. 'Everything in here must be packed into boxes this week,' he said. 'Look, when I come out of church, I have a drink to restore my balance. Sit down, if you wish. I want to tell you, Zaaijman: I know you went to lay charges against me. I resent that. Now, something to drink.'

'Beer, please, Your Honour.'

'Marya?'

'Pieternella, Your Honour. Nothing for me, thank you.'

He thumped with a staff against the wall. 'French brandy, and Liège beer, Tony,' he told an Oriental servant at the door.

'Tobacco and pipes, *tuan*?'

'No. It's a strange bunch that arrived here on *Boode*, Zaaijman. Almost like Noah's ark, a real menagerie.'

'There are people who know of nothing strange, Your Honour,' said Pieternella, looking the commander in the face.

'So? You should see their papers.'

'Your Honour, Pieternel and I have come to invite you and your sons to our wedding.'

The servant brought liquor, offered the tray, bowed to Hugo, left backwards through the door. Hugo swilled a large gulp of brandy around in his mouth, then Daniel raised his mug to Hugo, nodded, and took a sip of his beer. Bitter, perfect. Outside the fatherland he hadn't tasted this in years.

'That man, Tony Robson, I gave the name of my English servant who'd died the day before. I found him as a baby alone on a raft in Sunda Strait; you will know, Zaaijman, where the blue sea ends and the green sea begins. South China Sea, the maps call it. Alone in a basket on the float he drifted, thirty miles from the nearest land. What was he: a fisherman's throwaway child, or a prince hidden in a basket among the rushes of a river mouth? Like that Jew. I shall never know. But no thank you, Zaaijman, I do not attend weddings. I made the mistake once. I wish you all the best, and little Marya here. If you'd been twenty years earlier, Zaaijman, I'd have made you rich.'

'Another thing, Your Honour. I want to make an offer to buy St Hubert.'

'No. It is not for sale. And it was because I'd forbidden you free burghers to sail around the corner that you and Borms went to lay charges against me. Now you're trying again. No, I'm not selling the boat, and I swear I'm not offering it to the Company, even if it wanted to pay. What must I do with money? My life is past. No, I'm going to set fire to St Hubert. It's a good sloop; you will know, you were my coxs'n before Telleson. Did you know my first name is Hubert? People, if you can call them people, gossip about that sloop bearing my name. Well, why shouldn't it? But it's just a barefaced lie to annoy me. Saint Hubert is patron saint of the hunt, in our church. The old soul was buried a thousand years ago in the cathedral of Liège. I took my son there to look at the tomb. Why, I don't know. Pride? Gratitude? Yes, heaven knows, I was a good hunter, here too. And I must thank you, Zaaijman. The game has not yet been scared off; a good shot can enjoy himself. It is the only pleasure I've had on this damned island. No, I'm going to set fire to my sloop. The hunt is over.'

When they took their leave, without shaking hands, he said to Daniel through the half-closed door: 'Tell Sven I wish him good luck with Lamotius.'

'What does he mean, Daniel,' asked Pieternella, 'if you'd been twenty years earlier, he would have made you rich?'

'He was a pirate at the time.'

'I think something human is worth more than all the riches of the earth, Daniel.'

Just as among reefs in the ocean there run strong currents one would not suspect in open water, taking hold of your boat, jerking it forward, turning it round and throwing it sideways so that you have your work cut out with sail and rudder, fending off from rocks with oars and boathook to avoid capsizing, the three weeks before his wedding turned Daniel's life upside down. He had a single aim in mind: to enlarge his house. He needed help from Bart and Salomon, and if they couldn't help, he wanted to proceed on his own, but without being hindered. His house had to be finished before he was married.

Theuntje was the one who helped him most. It was *her* child's wedding, *her* daughter's house which had to be finished. She made sure that Bart and Salomon were there to help Daniel, and to prevent their coming home in the evening, she arranged for them to spend the nights there. She would stay with Pieternel. She sent food for them with Pieternel. If neighbours came to speak to Bart, she said: You'll have to talk to me, Bart is busy. She hired women to bake and cook for the wedding, and men to brew and slaughter. She sent messages and money to secure wagons and oxen for the guests, and had a seamstress fetched to make a dress and nightclothes for Pieternel. It had to be of silk, and bolts of floral silk she had selected for herself in the East were taken from the camphor. She told Pieternel: Choose whatever you wish to have made; what is left over, we'll put away for your children.

She told Daniel and Pieternel that if they had no objection, she would like to invite people like Aunt Maijke and Willem the Lyreman. Daniel was worried: those were people who had stood on the pillory, and surely Commander Lamotius would not wish to sit down with them. But Theuntje said: We come from the Cape, all three of us have stood on its pillory, and one day we shall all be pilloried before our Creator. He could not follow her explanation, and said nothing more, not wishing to oppose her. And she refrained from telling him what Maijke had said to her: that this Pieternella had been so hot for the young Fiscal Deneyn that Barbertje chose to let her leave the country. To get betrothed here to an impoverished cooper. She could have had gentlemen officers for company, with cake and pastries on the table and a slave woman behind her shoulder. And what about Long Gert's poor boy who now had to wander across the globe, forever desolate? How could Barbertje be sure that she had done God's will? That was what Maijke had told her; whether there was any truth in it, she did not know, but she did not care about Maijke's sorrows.

In the cool of the afternoon Pieternel brought them their meal and drinks, and sometimes clean linen for Bart and Salomon. Daniel took her through the extended house to show her each day's progress, and when they were out of sight he would embrace and fondle her, and they laughed and looked forward to the time they would be living here together. On the east side he added a large room with outside shutters, and in front of it a veranda as he'd seen in India, which overlooked the whole bay and the foaming reef behind it, from Breakers Point all the way across to Fisherman's Isle.

'In the East people spend their evenings until late outside on the veranda.'

She tasted the word with her tongue. 'Veranda. And what do they do here in the dark?'

'I'll show you. I used to pick out every little light from here at night, the one at the Lodge, the hooker's. But you can also talk to friends or guests. I hang the lantern in that corner, so the moths go that way.'

'What turns the inner water such a strange green, Daniel, and so inky-blue just outside the reef?'

'That I shall explain to you when we sit here in the evening.'

'We'll finish all our work before sunset. Then the evening will be ours.'

'Where would the child get such wisdom? Now you must tell me if you have any good ideas for our house. Think about it. A small room there, a dividing wall there, perhaps a hatch in the roof.'

During the last days before the wedding he and Bart worked on a broad bedstead with poles like a tent, over which one could drape a net. Everything was of bamboo, as were the roof joists and trusses, the window frames and shutters throughout the house, all the joints sturdily and neatly fastened with cordage, as on a ship.

'What do you want to do inside here?' Bart asked. 'It looks like a place for one of those Indian kings, with fourteen wives.'

'Ask Theuntje to explain to you. Come, let us measure the canvas for the mattress.'

'The bed is as big as a room,' said Salomon, and when Pieternella visited again, she stared in amazement at the huge *katil*, and then at Daniel.

'In Vlissingen, where I come from, this is the way we do it.'

'Why do you think they wear such wide breeches?' Bart said to Pieternella. And years later, when Daniel and Pieternella lay on the bed with two little girls between them, and the older one said, 'The bed is as big as a room,' he would remember his childhood in Vlissingen, and she would think of her brother Salomon.

Commander Lamotius was considerate enough to hold his church service on the Saturday afternoon, immediately followed by the wedding. The Sunday was a day of rest for the colonists, but the second high tide was in the afternoon, which was when the hooker *Boode* departed for the East. So he had a ready-made excuse: his lady and himself wished them many blessings, but they could not attend the wedding feast on the Saturday, as the farewell party for the hooker had to be given that evening. This meant that neither they, nor Commander Hugo or his sons, nor Captain Wobma and his officers, could attend their wedding celebration. Daniel didn't mind, it came as a relief to him, but Bart was indignant, and Theuntje said that was a gentleman's idea of courtesy, and the answer to her prayers. And the bride was withdrawn and without appetite, as if she was not feeling well.

The church service was long, the hall was packed to the shutters, the commander read the full chapter from Bulaeus, and the congregation was grateful for younker Hugo's fine tenor when they rose to sing, for the afternoon was stifling and they had little air in there. When Lamotius called them to the desk, Daniel was concerned about Pieternel looking so wan. The commander read the formulary. He was a fluent reader, and when he asked if they swore before God and these witnesses, Daniel felt as if he could feel the deck fall away under his feet as of a ship sliding down a steep slope, and hear the waves thundering in his ears, and he could barely hear his own voice respond. And who speaks for this woman? I, Your Honour, Bart was prompt to say. Then the commander asked: And you, Pieternella, do you promise to honour and obey, and slowly Daniel's own thoughts took over again and the sea became quiet when he heard her answer. Then I pronounce you husband and wife, and may God bless you. That much he was permitted, not being a *dominee*.

Outside on the square the commander's wife came to them, and offered them a gift, wrapped in blue and white cotton. 'Pieternel, this is for you. Why are you so pale, child? Must I call the surgeon for you?'

'No, madam. I am all right.' And she thanked her with a smile and a curtsy.

They were carried home on decorated chairs under a tent of palm fronds on the bridal wagon. Behind them were two wagons with women and the musicians; the men went on foot, all with their muskets over the shoulder, followed by two or three riding on oxen. It was one of Hugo's laws, only knights and gentlemen travelled on horseback.

In Bart's yard the tables stood laid under his shady tree. Two slave women were busy over pots and grids at his smoking cooking place. Daniel and his bride had to pass a guard of honour with rattling muskets under a canopy of green palm branches, the muskets and branches intermingled. Theuntje seated the guests: here was the bridal table, here married couples, there unmarried people. Their decorated chairs and green palm-frond canopy were taken from the wagon and put in place. Pieternel, he could see, was relieved to come to rest. Theuntje handed round a pitcher and a glass.

'Pour for Pieternel.' Then Daniel saw Boatswain Lubbert. I cannot drink, he decided on the spot, not one drop, and may heaven beware that I get hold of a knife.

The guests stood in line to shuffle past the bridal table with their good wishes and present their gifts. Those were untied, and cloths were unfolded, first of all that of Mrs Lamotius. It was a thick bolt of blue and white cotton, with inside it a green silk gown, and inside the gown a Delft dish with its lid, brand new. The guests envied her with much acclaim. Daniel also saw a small box with scented Japanese soap, a tart dish, a hand grinder, two slightly used Delft plates, a bag of rusks, a bedpan, a skein – brand new, still with its seal of red lacquer – of forty fathoms cod line, a Weesper flagon of Dutch gin, a *riempie* chair, a churn, a woven Indian bedspread, and other marvellous things.

Everything was shown around, and admired, and packed aside by Theuntje, proud and possessive. A farmer told her he would bring round a broody hen on two dozen eggs on Monday. Daniel and Pieternella thanked and thanked them all, the women and most of the men kissed Pieternel, and she smiled and thanked them, but the smile was stiff, nervous.

There was a mingling of people in Bart's yard, white and Oriental, half-blood and Indian, looking for something to drink and a seat at the table. Daniel kept his eye on Boatswain Lubbert, loud among some others at the barrel under Bart's tree. He didn't know who had invited the man, but among the strangers there certainly were other uninvited ones, like sailors and garrison soldiers coming for a drink and some merry company. An open canteen at a Christian wedding was nothing unusual. Theuntje and her friends carried food around; the talking and laughter grew louder, shouts rose up. Under their own green canopy, Baldini's musicians tossed about their first unsteady notes as they tried to find one another, and the sun was preparing to set behind Lemoenbosberg.

Jacomo started by playing light, fast music on the violin to loosen up the guests: dance tunes, peasant songs, occasionally a march from the military camp, when all the soldiers would drum on the tables with their hands. The noise grew merrier. Dishes of food were carried about on a door, empty mugs and plates were sent back, and around the canteen where the drinkers stood with their heads bunched together, the laughter occasionally erupted in a screaming. At sunset Jacomo waved his arms for silence, so that the barbarian with his saw could show his art. They cheered the foreigner and drank to his health, shouting for more, and more, and *Baas* Sven took the saw away to examine it in the firelight.

But Jacomo wanted them to dance; that was why he had been hired. He climbed on a short tree stump where he pranced and cavorted to make the guests forget about the mournful saw. The farmers formed a circle, stamping their feet, turning and clapping their hands above their heads. Then he remembered a wild tune, something with a coarse sea rhythm, which caused Sven and Lubbert to wail like wolves and fall to the ground where they drummed their fists on the grass, before jumping up again with wide grins, squatting down opposite one another in the circle, each with a bared knife clenched between his teeth.

The farmers stood back for them. First Sven, still on his haunches, hopped forward. He swivelled his shoulders, aimed with his head, his clawed hands grabbing and tearing the air, grabbing and tearing, while with a distorted face a much afrighted Lubbert retreated to his side of the circle. Then they danced back: Sven retiring and Lubbert advancing, hopping, knife between the teeth, pretending to catch and kill him. And back again. And again. The two dancers couldn't stop. The guests cheered. This was truly wild, they were like animals. It would end with one of them stumbling and the other falling on him with the knife, they thought, that was how this would end.

'Haven't seen *Jut Swart* danced for a long time, Daniel,' said Bart. 'It always makes me think of penguins in rut. Aren't you eating anything?'

'No.'

'I'm going to turn down your coverlets,' Theuntje came to whisper between him and Pieternel. Daniel had seen that morning what she'd placed in the new room. It was her own best linen, scented with ambergris Bart had brought from the East. She had been too reluctant to use it as it was impossible to buy, but this morning she'd found the opportunity.

Amid the noise Daniel said to Pieternel that they might put on the ring if she was willing. Her shoulder trembled under his hand and her skin was pale and cold in the warm night. 'What's the matter, Pieternel? Are you sick?'

Bart stood up beside her to discharge a shot from his musket. The guests flocked together before the table. This was the great moment: the fitting of the ring. It was a big ring they had borrowed from Theuntje, and in the silence Daniel slid it over her finger. Shouting, whistling, clapping, cheering and randy howling broke out around them. They bellowed like cattle. Lubbert was in front; sweating and heated by the dance he pushed in between Daniel and Pieternel to kiss her. She called out, warding him off with her hands, and screamed before Daniel could pluck him away by the collar.

'Off my wife, you scarecrow.'

'I didn't get a kiss.'

'You can kiss my arse.' He was standing ready, his knife in his hand. He knew what he was doing. He had known it for a long time. Theuntje led Pieternel indoors. The violin started singing again.

Sven approached Lubbert to tell him: 'You're sailing tomorrow, friend. Rather go on board.'

'Who says so?'

'I am a councillor here. Go on board.' And Daniel picked up Bart's musket, motioning to the man: get out of the yard.

'Remember what I promised you, uncle,' said Lubbert, staggering drunkenly as he spat at Daniel's feet, helping himself to a bottle of wine from the table and going off into the bushes.

Daniel remained outside; he loaded Bart's musket and rested it against his decorated chair. The flute and violin sang, the saw whined along, the farmers laughed, and there was black murder in the balmy air. Daniel badly wanted to take a gulp from the arrack on the table because his heart was beating so violently, but pushed away the glass Bart held out to him.

Inside the house Theuntje whispered to him: 'Daniel, I don't want to ask my child this, but is she pregnant?'

'From what?' he asked, propping the gun against the wall, pushing past to where Pieternel was lying under the thin coverlet on the *katil*, and sat down beside her on the bed.

'Are you sure you're not sick, Pieternel?'

She took his hand and said: 'It's just the crowd. All the eyes staring at us, and the laughter behind hands when they talk about us, and the shouting about our ring. It has been going on for weeks now, at the Lodge and here. Bart with his jokes, and Aunt Theuntje worrying and bustling around me all the time. Why are they mocking us? Is something wrong? I don't know what it is about. I'm only fourteen.' She began to sob. 'And then that ugly dance, and the painted face. Why did he make himself so hideous? I never saw anything like it among the Koina.'

Daniel put his arms around her, and comforted her. 'Some people are like that. We'll talk about these matters tomorrow. Calm down now and rest, there are only friends around you.' He kissed her on her forehead. 'Tomorrow I'm taking you home.'

Lusty music met him in the yard. The circle laughed and danced, stopped to eat and drink when they felt like it; men went beyond the lantern light into the bushes to empty their bladders or to vomit behind trees. Daniel patrolled the perimeter of Bart's yard with Bart's musket. Death was out there in the dark, part of the dark, and he had to track it down and settle it before it trapped him here while he relaxed. Now, Bart and his oldest friends lounged in the decorated chairs behind the bridal table, eating and drinking and laughing noisily.

In the late evening another guest turned up out of the dark and approached Daniel where he stood under the trees among the outer lanterns. It was the young Hugo, in his dark blue linen suit, with a brilliantly golden starry sky behind him. The guests moved away from him as was their custom; he was so fair of face that women and men were embarrassed to speak to him.

'Thank you for your invitation, Daniel. I know you're closing down, but I came as quickly as I could, for a dance with the bride, and to offer my gift.'

'You are most welcome, Sir. Unfortunately the bride is not feeling well, but let us clink a glass. Come, have a seat.'

He asked for dry white wine, which they didn't have. Cape brandy, *jonker*? Yes, just a small one, with water. 'And what happened to the bride?'

'Too much tension. Her standing rigging was set too tight, but it will loosen up after a few days. And then she was badly upset by Bo'sun Lubbert of *Boode*. Was he not supposed to be at your officers' farewell?'

'He was told to keep away. Mrs Lamotius cannot bear his face.' He raised his tumbler. 'To you and Pieternel!' and drank half of his brandy and water. 'I have dined, thank you. Monsieur Lamotius gave us a fine banquet.' Once again he raised the tumbler: 'To the free burghers of Mauritius!' But he put his glass down without drinking.

'Is the young lady too sick to see me?'

'She is asleep, Sir. Come, I'll wake her.'

'No. She may never sleep again.' He pulled a small golden crucifix on a delicate chain from an inside pocket. 'This present is from my late mother and myself to her. She need not be a Catholic, Daniel. And this is for you, so that you can look far.' From the deep inside pocket of his overcoat he brought a brass telescope in a leather case. 'With this you can make out Jupiter's three moons.'

Daniel thanked him, wrung his hand warmly, and passed the gifts along the old men at the table. Then he refilled the young man's glass. But he pushed it back. 'Thank you. I had better say goodbye, friends. Tomorrow I must balance the Company's books before I leave, and pack my things.' And he laughed, the only one at the table to catch the joke.

Bart brought him a lantern with a long candle, and Daniel walked with him to the dark rim of the yard.

'I must say I am very glad to get away from here.'

'That was what Commander Hugo also said.'

The younker turned about before him. 'How did it come, Daniel, that Chief Wreede had his fatal accident in your care, to create a vacancy for my father here? You were the helmsman.'

Daniel thought: He wants me to take responsibility for the accident in Vuijle Boght, for the horror which later befell his sister. I'm happy to reach out a hand to someone sailing with me, but what can I assume of what had happened in Vuijle Boght? My hand was on the tiller, but the thrust and scend of the tide and the current belonged to the sea.

'I could not prevent it. Just a terrible current where there hadn't been anything when we came in at high tide. No signs, not a wrinkle on the water. It wrested the sloop from my hand and lifted it on the reef all in one swell. We were loaded deep with timber; the sloop simply capsized on the coral, and the next swell smashed right through us.'

'And so Hubert Hugo was given the position on Mauritius.'

'That's life, Sir.'

'Thank God it's over now.'

'And how will it go with you, Sir?'

'Good, I trust. At last I'm going to the East, you understand, *orang lama*? There I shall try to find my sister, to ask her forgiveness, and if that is not possible, back to the fatherland. *Mea maxima culpa*. My great transgression. It is my fault. It was all my fault.'

They shook hands. 'Thank you for your hospitality,' the young man said, going off silently into the dark with his small light.

At the Sunday's second high tide Daniel and Pieternel were sitting on the bench on their veranda watching *Boode*, with the black sloop *St Hubert* in tow, reach towards the open sea. There was much work in their house, and two wheelbarrows full of presents they had pushed from Bart's house, all of which still had to find its place, but Daniel did not feel like working. The previous night he had only found sleep at daylight on the coir mat before Picternel's *katil*. Bart had come to ask him whether it was an acceptable hour, as he couldn't really make out how it stood with the stars. According to his calculation it might be two o'clock. Bart fired two shots to indicate that it was time, and the two of them began to clear up. The last guests were ready to go, the canteen had been sucked dry. Two guests, making love in Bart's sugar, were stopped by the shooting. Two brothers who had been in an ugly fight at midnight, lay asleep together under the hired wagon. In Bart's tobacco stood the hamshackled ox of somebody who had gone home on foot. Sven lay in Bart's barn with his crumpled overcoat folded under his head, his clothes unbuttoned and his knife exposed in his hand. Daniel and Bart scraped out cooking pots, emptied and stacked dishes and carried them inside, poured out half-filled mugs in the grass, folded tablecloths, gathered shards of broken bottles, and doused the lanterns and the last of the cooking fires.

'We can calculate costs on Monday, mate' said Bart. 'But now a glass of French brandy before we turn in.'

'I haven't had a drop of liquor all night, Bart. I'm expecting that bastard here.'

'A single mouthful to you then, for luck. I shall help keep watch.'

In the two decorated chairs under brilliant pre-dawn stars they emptied a half-bottle and agreed that their eyes were falling shut from sleep. It was broad daylight when he and Pieternella arrived home with all their things and Salomon and Bart following with the wheelbarrows.

They went outside when they heard the shots from the Lodge, giving farewell to the hooker, and watched the two ships from their veranda, drank the tea which Pieternel had made, and ate from what Theuntje had sent.

'My hair will lie down again once I see the hooker go. I do not fear any man, but I feel the hangman's rope pressing around my throat as long as that rubbish is around.'

Beyond the reef the hooker slackened sail. What now? Daniel went inside for his new telescope, set it, and handed it to Pieternel. 'Lookout, report what you see.'

She put a foot on the bench and rested the telescope on her knee. 'Nothing, skipper.'

'Take your fingers from the opening. Now tell me what you see?'

'But that's Sven. And there is Commander Hugo. The sailors are hauling the sloop alongside the hooker. There Sven and Commander Hugo are clambering over. It looks as if the sailors have dropped an anchor. Yes, there they're climbing back. There is smoke, Daniel.'

'Let me see.' *Boode* fell away downwind from the sloop *St Hubert*. There was grey smoke at its forward hatch, then two explosions in the heart of the sloop, hurling the hatch into the air, immediately followed by yellow flames breaking from the hatch with dark smoke. Then the stern of the sloop sank slanting into the water, the flames turned and swept upward, burning a black banner on the mizzen-peak to ashes. Then more explosions. In a short time the black sloop was under flames from fore to aft, like a bushfire on an island. By then, the hooker *Boode* was already far downwind, on its way to the East.

He passed the telescope to her. 'Behold, lookout, what man is. Consider his folly, and learn to be wise.'

'I see the pilot boat, skipper.'

From Sven he heard the next day that the dogs he had promised him, the best on the island, he'd been ordered to shoot. He'd asked, but the commander said: 'The hunt is over, and St Hubert's Festival is past.'

Daniel went back slowly to his work. It was because of the joy he took in Pieternel, of whom he could not get enough. He gave much time to the work around the house, to be close to her. For more than a week he did nothing but saw and split firewood. He built a coop for poultry, and then a bleaching shelter. He was at home, and they were together all day. Then he remembered that he would have to repair the fence around his yard against deer again, and he took her to the forest with him to collect palm fronds and bamboo. For the first time in more than six months he opened his chest with cooper's tools, took out his chisels and adzes and inspected them, honing those that required it. Once he felt a desire to tackle something big, like a wagon, or a yawl, but the urge vanished when he closed the lid of the box. That evening, as they sat outside, he carved the year and Pieternel's initials next to his into the lid.

For milk and sweet potatoes or vegetables and meat they walked to their neighbours, and bought what was needed. Daniel introduced his wife to those who had not yet met her. 'But you're only a little girl,' old Noordoos's wife said. What a mere child Pieternel had been when they got married, he discovered when a year or two later she still grew in height and in womanly form.

Pieternella loved walking in people's gardens and among their vegetables, looking at their cattle and poultry. Daniel had assured her that they could have gardens just as good or better, and a milking cow, and a pig to fatten up. She went home with sweet-potato tubers, geranium cuttings or pumpkin seeds, or a duckling people had given her in her apron. When her garden was green around the house, Daniel reopened his furrow from the river causing the irrigation water to run past right next to the house, like in earlier times. The broad shining water beside his house was a sight to behold.

He and Bart went to the Lodge together to hire a plough and draught oxen from the Company. Between the two of them, as on a ship, working together always made labour easier. Afterwards he bought tobacco plants and sugar shoots from the Company's garden, cleared his fields, burned the old stuff and planted everything anew. Bart did not want to plant new sugar, he felt there was a big hurricane coming. For the time being a vegetable garden was enough.

Once their crop was in the ground, Daniel spent the days felling ebony and dragging it home to cut it with the saw and work it into staves with the adze. In the evenings he made barrels. The Company asked him to provide barrels for water, beer or vinegar, or old used vats for raw lamp oil. He showed Pieternel: here were buckets for water and milk for the burghers, and if he burned pitch inside, they were turned into sanitary buckets for the outhouse of the Lodge. These very shallow ones were intended for provisions, they were for the meals in the barracks and for sailors. He could deliver as many barrels as they required, but he did not want any slaves or servants around him. More work meant more helpers, who had to be watched and fed. If he took on more work, it would also mean seeing less of her. He only wanted her with him, no one else. Look, he could plait his own hoops from rattan, and if people wanted iron hoops he would have to buy a slave and teach him to work a smithy. He was content, he felt that they were living comfortably. Wasn't that so? His crop was in the ground, his wife in his arm, the bay lay blue in the distance, beyond the bay was the Lodge, much further away still was the Cape.

Daniel seldom received cash for his work. The farmers paid with cheese or eggs, and the Company with reductions on his account. Commander Lamotius wrote to order a deep vat to bath in. Daniel made it, filled it with water and climbed into it with Pieternella. They could sit up to their necks in the water. It would be an excellent thing for cool evenings. For them a shallow vat was enough, and cold water refreshing in the heat of the climate.

Later, when in his sixtieth year Daniel looked back, he said to his son: This is just like the sea: you sail for a few weeks in good weather with topsails to your masts, and no two days are the same, and then you have bad weather for a time. Then the good days come back, of which no two are the same, and then storms again for a time. You get through, but every time you are more worn, your ship more weathered, and you lose some of your people. Yes, you lose some. And it is strange that you forget the good times, of which there have been so much more, but you remember the storms. At the end you look back and all you see is a turbulent sea behind, and a turbulent sea ahead, and the night so dense that you have no idea of what you will do with helm and sail, and in its box your compass light burns down smaller and smaller.

Of Mauritius he could recall the difficult times best. Mercifully his family had come a long way before disaster struck their home. Those at the outpost Mauritius had been together for thirty-two years as if on one ship, under different captains of course. That was more than half of his life. There were Wreede, and Hugo, and the unfortunate Lamotius, and then Roelof, and last of all Momber. Some of them were good fellows, others less good, but all landsmen at heart, unfortunately, and more than once it was their own captain who ordered them into a storm. At such times a helmsman must pray and be vigilant. And heaven knows, in those times he himself just about scraped across the rocks before he reached open water again. A merciful destiny, he had.

The difficult times and the most difficult people stood out in his memory, like buoys in a well-known roadstead. He sometimes said to Pieternel: Do you remember the French lieutenant's wife, or the day the sawmill was blessed, or the hurricane at the mouth of Black River? And he understood: if you name the people and recall their deeds and misdeeds, you come to understand the fateful journey of the ship *Mauritius*. Its journal, as they say, the journal of the ship *Mauritius*, which sank and had to be abandoned by its crew, was also the journal of his own life.

What can be said about guilt? No one is to blame, it was nobody's fault. If it had been the commander's fault, one could go and reason with him, or take up arms, as some had done, and beat on his door. One could do that when there was a human being behind the mis-adventure, but if God Himself brought the disaster, there was nothing you could do and nowhere you could complain.

There were more than enough mischief-makers, and as it goes with woodworm in the skin of your ship, you had no inkling of the very worst among them. Their kind were abroad, behind desks, scribbling thoughts on paper for the attention of the Directors, without ever setting eye on the green and blue island. And it only came out when there was a heavy swell before your bow and you ran the risk of getting wrecked; that was when you heard what had been decided abroad about you and your family's future. Among those there was even a governor, whose father had been born on the island, both of whom should have understood the profound yearning in these free burghers. But Mauritius had produced enough of its own weaklings, and there were others, godforsaken scoundrels who reckoned that this island was too much of a paradise and should not be allowed to continue like that. What could you do? Your ship was small, and the ocean huge. You could but go overboard, and swim, and try to save others you cared about, if you could.

The prophet of doom was Sven. A few weeks after the wedding he started coming to Daniel's yard to say that he was on his way to the forest and just wanted to fill his water flask in the furrow, or carve a piece of tobacco for the day, or hone his axe on Daniel's stone. Then he would remain for an hour, drink what he was offered and tell what was happening at the Lodge, what this one or that one or the new commander had said. While talking to Daniel, he would turn his head to look after Pieternel. They knew that Sven came to look at Pieternella. He told her: the first time he'd seen her, he'd thought that she was somebody he knew, his late sister, no less; he almost got a big fright. Later he said that he'd heard from Maijke she was Pieter van Meerhof's daughter. He had known her father, they'd been together on one voyage. Havgard was the name. It meant: garden at the sea. Meerhof was the Dutch form; some people in Holland simplified it to Hougaard. There was another councillor here who had also known her late father. Jan Zacharias was his name.

It was Maijke's loose mouth which had caused them to be stuck with Sven, thought Daniel, and to Pieternel he said that he was going to chase Sven away, but she said the man wasn't bothering her, and she liked hearing about her father.

'Aren't you friends then?' she asked.

'We were, at first. He taught me to hunt here. You know how a sailor is better with a knife than with a gun. One day when I was taking time to load, he said: No wonder you Dutch waged war for eighty years. It was *Baas* Sven's drinking day and night which made me become a free burgher. One night he drew his knife against me. If Bart hadn't separated us, I would have gone to the gallows because of this Sven. I no longer trust him with my life. He's just a good-for-nothing.'

So Sven brought news from the Lodge just to look at Pieternel, and Daniel made sure that the man wouldn't keep him from his work. But when Councillor Sven put a paper bag of Arabian coffee on their kitchen table, he said thank you, but first show me your receipt for it, otherwise I won't accept it. This Sven might be in a useful position, but he was an apostle of evil.

Willem the Lyreman and Maijke Tielemans, on the other hand, were small, poor, unhappy people on Mauritius, and from the outset it had been their own fault. The Cape Council had said, upon the honest advice of Bart and Daniel at the time they had been questioned by Governor Bax, that the new commander could place Willem with his wife and children on Noordwyks Plain. Parts of the tough crust on that plain had already been broken by the Company, and there were several steady rivers. The Council showed even more mercy to Willem by allowing him to farm for a half-share with the Company. It provided plough, oxen and seed, and received half his harvest; the other half it bought from him. All it required of Willem was bread-wheat, since bread, like seagulls, one seldom saw on Mauritius. And following that instruction the Lyreman, with his leg-iron and a heavy heart and swollen with dropsy, was taken on the post boat to the shallow bay of Kroonenburg with his wife, daughters and their few chests, and from there with the post wagon through the forest to the plain, where the house of one of the colonists was cleared out for them. Commander Lamotius waited hopefully for the first wheat.

In terms of the same proposal by Bart and Daniel at the Cape, Maijke had to work in the Company's garden near the Lodge, and with the help of two or three slaves plant and maintain a new palm forest. At his wife's suggestion Commander Lamotte – that was another characteristic of Sven's, to make free with other people's names, as Commander Lamotius sometimes, but very rarely, signed Lamotte –

ordered Maijke's leg-iron to be removed. He walked with her through the sugar cane to the cleared land, to show her what the Lords wanted done. He pointed out to her three different kinds of palm that thrived on the island, but it was the coconut palm she was required to plant, the one with the thin trunk and the large yellow fruit below the crown. The coconut palm is one of nature's greatest gifts to man, he said. While Maijke was watching a few cattle being driven past behind them, Lamotius enumerated: It provides shredded coconut, coconut oil, coconut milk and coconut shells, as well as fronds for houses, mats, shelters, hats and brooms, and coir for mats and mattresses, and of course there are palm wine and palm arrack too, and fresh young palm heart to eat. But man is an ungrateful receiver, for every palm tree tapped for arrack must die. Which means that every tree should be allowed to bear its fruit a few times otherwise it dies without offspring. All Aunt Maijke had to do, was to ensure that her slaves brought her all the ripe fruit, wherever they found them, and plant and tend the shoots after they had germinated. Palm trees grew where they could see the sea. Did Aunt Maijke understand? Here in the Company's private garden every tree belonged to the Lords. No one was allowed to cut down fronds from these trees, or pick nuts (or pick them up from the ground!) or tap arrack or cut palm hearts. Understood?

'What about Sven?'

'Why?'

'He is *baas*.'

'Of what or whom? Not of the garden, nor of you, nor anything else, including his own soul. Tell whoever told you this that that is what I said. All right? Now, how is your leg today, Aunt Maijke, without the ring?'

It was a dry time when the new commander started looking for a place to build his sawmill. To establish a profitable sawing concern on the island was his ideal. And the Lords expected it of him. Just as Hugo had been given the post because he'd promised to supply them with hundreds of cheap slaves, the new commander was offered his after he had demonstrated a model of his secret invention to them, persuading them that it could make a profit from the sale of black and red ebony.

Lamotius and Councillor Telleson went to explore the kloofs near the Lodge in search of the right site for the mill. The streams were weak and nearly empty, but Sven knew of a deep gully with a sharp drop, in which there was still enough running water to keep a dam filled. It was only a half-hour from the Lodge, just beyond French Church. He would show him a small island in the stream where the sawmill could stand, and an ideal narrow stretch in the gully for the dam above.

And the sawmill was a first-class construction, big and strong, built to stand almost until doomsday. With contract work Daniel earned a few guilders from it. They sealed off the eastern stream and allowed it to run dry, then built a wall of indestructible oak beams across it. A few yards lower down they erected the millhouse of heavy oak on the small island, its wheel in the gully and a wooden gutter running from the dam over the wheel, and a bridge over the gully for wagons to reach the island. All of stout Dutch oak. And they dug open the dry stream for the dam to fill. When the work was done the commander announced that everybody who had worked on the mill would have a Happy Day on the Sunday after church.

Daniel and Pieternel went with the procession from the Lodge, carrying palm branches instead of a flag, behind the French Church to the Happy Day at the sawmill. Commander Lamotius was in front, with a guard of honour and two snare drums; his wife fell in among the common people next to Pieternel. She was a beautiful young woman. She wore the island's big hat of plaited palm fronds like the farmers' wives and the slave women following behind with food baskets, but her posture was different. She did honour to the hat with her straight back and narrow shoulders. And her clothes were simple as theirs, but again her manner of wearing them was different. Daniel often looked at her face, where she walked beside Pieternel, the two of them talking and laughing like close friends. She was more than beautiful; she was born of blue blood, the way one found it among the oldest families in the fatherland. Always calm, humble and a friend of the humble, never vain or excited. One barely heard her voice; she was gentle, the smile never far from her lips. One tended to feel that she wasn't human, perhaps an angel or a member of alien nobility, but not one of us. And yet she was a friend. Any official or soldier would lay down his life for her, because she would give hers for them. They knew that.

At the mill that day they learned what her first name was. When the meal was spread out under the trees, and the glasses filled with the Company's beer and other liquor, Commander Lamotius led his wife to the sluice and raised his hand for silence. She turned her smile to them, winking at somebody in the front row.

'I, Margarethe Andrea d'Egmont, hereby open this mill to the honour of God.'

'And in the service of our Honourable Company,' the commander reminded her, and her merry laugh mingled with the sound of falling water as she opened the sluice causing the shiny stream to strike the wheel for the first time. From that Happy Day the stream nearest the French Church became the Molensrivier, the Mill River.

In the late afternoon, as Daniel and Pieternel walked home, he said to her: in one respect he felt himself the equal of Lamotius, and that was that both of them enjoyed an equal measure of happiness and pleasure from their wives. He also told her that the Duke d'Egmont had been the first hero of the fatherland to die in the war against the Spanish, and how his property had been destroyed and his family persecuted and impoverished. That he had learned at school. The new rich in Batavia loved to boast with inherited slaves and sedan chairs, but they would never match the lady's quality, as that could only be inherited in the blood.

'She says she is expecting another baby. Nobody else knows it yet.'

'I didn't know you were such close friends.'

'She knows I will not tell anyone. She invited us to visit her.'

'Ah, I'm not one for commanders, Pieternel.'

'I'll go alone. She is one friend who doesn't look at clothes.'

Pieternel went to visit several times, when Daniel was off to the mill to give a hand with the carpentry and the moving parts. It was a difficult process, as they had to work from a drawing; there was a new invention with lots of ironwork and supports which Daniel had never seen before, and for which they first had to build a smithy downwind from the mill. He and Pieternel walked together as far as the mill, and from there she went on to the Lodge. He could see how much pleasure the new friendship afforded her, and she always came home with novelties, like how to make tea the Japanese way, how to cook rice with every grain separate rather than one grey mush, how to prepare a *karri* sauce. She told about the lady's little girl of two, and two young Indian slave girls of her own age, girls like princesses in their dress and comportment. The commander and his wife spoke French to one another, and Portuguese to the slave girls.

'Is something wrong with our mother tongue now?' he asked, and she couldn't understand that he felt annoyed.

'Would it be all right to invite them to our house, Daniel?'

'Invite, if you wish. Of course the neighbours will talk, because their women are jealous and their men worried. They don't like seeing officials around. They will ask: What is Zaaijman up to, inviting the commander to the Lemoenbos?'

When the lady did come on a visit, her two Indian slave girls were with her, walking and talking next to her as if they were sisters. And the neighbours did gossip. Sven came to tell them that the neighbours said Daniel was no longer the man they had known, and it spoiled slaves to drink Japanese tea with them in your home.

Daniel laughed. 'Tell them to count how many of our people are married to slave women. Do they think you may marry one, but not drink tea and talk with her?'

In the time they were working on the sawmill, the new commander began to show his fangs. Some months after Commander Hugo's departure the flute *Hasenberg* arrived from Batavia with provisions and convicts. Among them was a convict Goulan and a Chinese Tianko, and a family: Ansubu and his wife Inabe, and their daughters Bau and Iba, who had been banished from Timor for fomenting unrest against the Company. One night somebody heard that slaves in Ansubu's house were plotting to kill the officials, burn down the Lodge, and escape on the sloop. When Ansubu's house was searched, pistols, powder and lead that must have been stolen from the magazine, were found under the floor.

A soldier called Hans Beer was summoned, because he had an

interest in the older daughter. The commander had Goulan, Tianko, Ansubu and Hans locked up, and the Council started formal interrogation. Goulan and Tianko hanged themselves from the beams in their cell on the first day. That was what was said: died under interrogation.

Commander Lamotius's wife sent word to her husband in Council that they shouldn't interrogate Hans Beer together with the others. It was wrong, since there was a relationship between him and the daughter of a fellow accused. She even wrote a formal letter about the matter to the Council. She explained that the father might say, if Hans did not testify in his favour, he would avenge it on his daughter, and if he testified against him, he would do the same. But the Council met only on Mondays, and by the time her letter was read, Hans was already dead, deceased during interrogation, as the phrase goes.

'A strange world in which a commander's wife can prescribe to him,' Sven commented. That was how he came to gossip with them, straight from the Council.

'That is when words do not help,' Pieternella replied. 'Your Council has no right to use the third degree. Only a fiscal may request that from the authorities.'

'Where did you hear about third degree?' asked Daniel. 'Please don't come between a commander and his wife, Pieternel. Think before you speak.'

'Do you believe that Hans meant to murder us all? Do you believe the slaves wanted to see us dead?'

'How must I know? I would say that they might try, one day. The commander has to demonstrate that he will not tolerate treason, otherwise you and I can no longer sleep in peace.' But he thought: Here it begins again with another bloody commander, just as it was under Hugo. Why then did I go to the Cape at the time?

One day the lady came there with her slave girls, carrying working baskets and a roll of textile, and for three days the women chatted and drank tea in Daniel's house while they made a large gauze tent to drape over the bedstead. She had such a drape of fine gauze over her bed in the Lodge. That kind of net came from the East. It was a gift from her to Pieternel and Daniel.

Wednesdays Sven's woodcutters brought a load of ebony to the sawmill, unyoked their oxen to graze, and sawed the tree trunks on the sawing trestles above the pit into planks. Two men used a double-handed saw on a trunk, and with their best skill they could cut three or four planks from most trunks. Some days they made beams, straight, square and up to thirty feet long. These were meant for the Castle at the Cape. The planks were nailed up in pine boxes and taken to the Lodge on the wagon, and stored in the warehouse for the day the Cape would send its hooker again. The woodcutters used the opportunity to examine the inside of the new mill, they wanted to know where the saw was. Here were the usual paddle wheel, the axle, the cogwheel, but what about all the other wheels and where was the saw?

The builders on the mill knew where the saw was, since the commander had explained it to them from the outset. The saw blade was of steel, and round, three feet across, with teeth all along the edge. They built that strange shiny serrated disc so solidly into the gear that it wouldn't buckle, and Lamotius answered all their questions, about how fast the disc should turn, how the wood would be brought evenly to the turning blade, and how the teeth would have to be sharpened regularly, as young wood erodes steel.

For Lamotius that circular saw was a matter of pride. It was his own design. He acknowledged that there might be problems, for it was the first if its kind. The speed of the blade had to remain high, and the wood had to be fed evenly, so as not to disturb the balance of the blade. One needed constant strong water behind the wheel. If there was no water in the dam and the wheel stopped turning, they would have to revert to sawing by hand. But his career and his life were linked to that blade. If he did well here, he could expect promotion to Batavia, perhaps *secundus* at the Cape, and the distribution and sale of his invention in Europe.

With the first rains the dam overflowed. Now they would see if the paddle wheel produced enough power to lend speed to the blade. They fed dry wood through the saw and made experiments, but the commander was not satisfied. The blade was skew, one could hear it whistling. Why? The floor of the millhouse was uneven; they had to dismantle the whole machine to level the floor, and then reconstruct the machine from the beginning. But something that worked properly from the first, and with which Lamotius had had success over and over again, was that he could attach the shaft to a lathe, and easily turn out heavy table legs and posts for a bedstead. But it wasn't for a lathe that he had been sent to Mauritius, but for a sawblade.

Lamotius spent days, sometimes on his own, sometimes with one or two helpers, in the mill to make that saw work. He worked on it every day until sunset, because he'd made a promise to Lords Seventeen. Then something more terrible started bothering him, and that was his faith in his own ability. The small model he'd demonstrated to the Lords in Amsterdam had worked well. He had to go on searching until he'd found what was wrong with his invention. He could not send word to the Lords that his invention had failed, and could they please offer him another post. His mill *had* to work. If only he could work undisturbed and in silence, he thought he would find the answer. He wished he could move his other tasks, like the office work, aside for a while. What he did move aside was his administration, his staff of frustrated young men, his free burghers, his wife, his child.

Sven Telleson, councillor and master woodcutter, could not help him. Lamotius was glad when Telleson took his cynical face off to the forest, leaving him alone with the saw. Then Sven would go and tell Daniel that this much-vaunted invention they had been promised would never work. It had all been a lot of words. With all the cogs it looked like the inside of a watch, but it couldn't saw wood. He, Master Woodcutter Sven, would have to keep this island going with his handful of men, to prevent the Lords from closing it down.

Boode returned to the anchorage, bringing the annual provisions and loading timber and building lime for the Castle at the Cape. Lamotius was nearly caught with empty hands. He had to set his labourers to make lime; his woodcutters had to abandon the ebony for the time being, to chop firewood. With *Boode* came two letters, from Sofia van der Byl and from Barbara Geens, for Pieternel. It was good news. Everybody was well, and they were just anxious to hear how she and Daniel were. Pieternel read the letters to Daniel, and started writing a long answer to each, to go back on the hooker. Daniel hoped that it would depart soon, so that he could put Boatswain Lubbert out of his thoughts.

From Lemoenbos Daniel could see banks of grey smoke rising from the limepits near Vissers Island for weeks, and smell the stench of quicklime on the south-western wind, while *Boode* loaded the boxed ebony, and then remained at anchor quiet and empty with crossed spars on the polished surface of the inner water. The ship's cooper turned up at Daniel's house one day, the same affable and capable man from their crossing two years earlier. Lamotius sent word that all his men were burning lime, and could Daniel find the time to overhaul the Lodge's vats to exchange for those of *Boode*? Daniel needed the work, but if Lubbert saw him at the Lodge, he would look for an excuse to provoke trouble. In his reply he said: if they could deliver the barrels at his house and collect them again, he would do it. Lamotius agreed. It took two months before *Boode* had its full cargo. The limepits were extinguished, the workers returned to the Lodge. But *Boode* remained.

Sven came to sit on their veranda to tell them how the commander had given Captain Wobma his sea letters and a proper farewell, but to their surprise *Boode* remained at anchor in the pool. What was the man waiting for? Lamotius sent Sven to find out whether Wobma needed a pilot, and Wobma took offence at that. Was Lamotius suggesting that he couldn't pilot out his own ship? What did Lamotius know about navigation? There was no wind here, how was he expected to sail? Sven told the captain, as politely as possible, that he believed he could take the hooker through the gap; a month ago he'd taken a flute out in almost windless conditions.

Captain Wobma turned against him. 'Are you saying, *Baas* Sven, that you took *Hasenberg* out of here with less wind than we're having now?'

'Yes, that's what I did.'

'That's a lie, you bastard.' He pulled a belaying pin from the shelf at the mast. 'Get off my ship, you drunkard. Fool. I'll break your neck for you.'

'Who, you, skipper?' Sven put on a show of bravery.

When Wobma shouted: 'Take him, bo'sun. Take him, men!' Sven jumped into the pilot boat.

But why was Wobma keeping the ship here? What did the man have in mind? Lamotius could think of no reason. What did Daniel think?

'You have to figure that out, *baas*. I'm just a cooper.'

Daniel slept well under the new net over their bedstead. In the hottest nights they could now cast off the sheet without being plagued by insects. That night he was awakened by gunshots near his house. It wasn't Bart, it came from further along the mountain. Sitting up, he could hear, above the sound of a westerly wind in the palm crowns and the dull booming of the reef, a number of cannon shots as well.

Pieternel turned over in her sleep, took his hand and woke up.

'I think I'm expecting a baby.'

'What makes you say that?'

'I can't tell. What do you hear? Is it thunder?'

'No. I think it's the neighbours shooting.' Together they went outside on the veranda. The morning star sat bright above the sea, but to their left was a white glow in the sky as if the sun was about to rise behind the Lodge that day.

'Sadelberg is burning. The wind is still westerly. It will move away from us.'

'No, it's the Lodge. Look at the sea shimmering at the anchorage.'

He pulled on a shirt and breeches, and ran out with two leather buckets in his hands to see what he could do. Along the way he met neighbours, one with a coil of rope, the other with a spade. They told him about a huge explosion, fifteen minutes before. It could have been the magazine blowing up. When they emerged from the wood at the French Church, the Lodge was in flames in front of them. Left and right palm trees, stables, outbuildings, fences, lean-tos, everything was burning.

There was absolutely nothing they could do. The fire was unstoppable. Captain Wobma, his hailer in his hand, shouted orders, warning people to stay away. Around them the fire raged, one could see the hooker lying brightly illuminated in its pool. The sailors from the hooker remained standing with their buckets empty in their hands. The heat was too ferocious for them to approach and they could only wait for it to abate. The people of the Lodge, sick with shock and the hot smoke, were laid down in the grass beside the stream and revived. The surgeon from the hooker crawled among them with his medicine chest and linen. Daniel tried to find out from the bystanders how it had started. The people were horrified, depressed, silent. He learned that it had been burning for over an hour, and that the commander's lady with her child and two slave girls were still inside, amid the flames. Lamotius was terribly disfigured.

Daniel and three or four of the free burghers offered their services to Captain Wobma. He ordered them to help form a wide cordon around the place with his sailors, and nobody was allowed to go inside or out.

Tents were brought from the ship and pitched for the injured, the hooker's *seur* arrived with writing material, and the cook and his helper had pots and provisions brought ashore. At sunrise the Lodge was a low mound of black, smoking charcoal and wet ashes. Wobma called the sailors together: almost all of them suffered from burns or inhaling smoke. Lamotius, they heard, was being treated on the hooker. *Boode's seur* drew up lists of names. The only dead so far were the commander's family and his servants. Wobma commandeered the free burghers to fetch tools and call up their slaves and neighbours, with provisions for two days. At ten o'clock they were to present themselves here with his crew. Those who remained absent would be hanged here, on the square. He placed Zaaijman in command of one-half of them, and his boatswain in command of the other. One lot had to dig up the mound of rubble, while the other was to chop bamboo and branches to provide shelter for the people.

Daniel told his group: 'Go and get your own spades, crowbars, picks, wheelbarrows, water buckets.' Whatever was here, is now ashes. He had time to think, as he walked home, what to say to Pieternel. She would have a fright, she would cry, she would be sorrowing for a long time. In almost two years she had still not made any other friends here. The commander's women were like sisters in her home. Barely a week ago they had been working together on the big curtain of net for her bed; he could still hear them laughing and talking. Pieternel had told him that she thought she was expecting. She might suffer from this loss for the rest of her life. God should help them with their houses of leaves, if one day a fire were to sweep through the Lemoenbos. The poor Lamotius; if he survived, he would want to return to the fatherland.

When he arrived home, he told her that the Lodge and everything had been destroyed by the fire, and that they still didn't know the fate of the lady. He was afraid of saying more. He put sweet potatoes and meat and a bottle of brandy in a canvas bag, and asked her to pack herself a basket so that she could accompany him to Theuntje's place. From there he and Bart walked to the Lodge, pushing a wheelbarrow.

The free burghers were assembled at the flagpole. Daniel asked the skipper for a scribe and a guard, and the captain looked on while Daniel made a drawing on the ground of how the Lodge was constructed, indicating the different rooms in the smoking mound of ashes. The rear bedrooms were on the mountain side. They would first clear the eastern and western sides simultaneously, and then work their way through from north to south. Places dug open would start burning again, so water had to be ready to douse them. The young *seur* from the ship had taken his seat with his book in a tent, and whatever they took out, had to be brought to him to be sorted and written down. If there was something that couldn't be lifted, they had to stop digging and call him. Charcoal, broken porcelain and ashes were carted away to the ditch. What had to be saved was ironwork, nails, pieces of books, unbroken objects. The skipper would say when it was time to rest or eat.

In the middle of the day *Baas* Sven and the woodcutters arrived from Noordwyks Vlakte in the sloop *Vanger*. There they had caught a slave and drawn his story from him. Sven took his men to the forest to fell building timber. There was no place to sleep where the Lodge had once been.

The free burghers were dismissed the second day. Their work was done. Lamotius, wrapped in linen, was brought from a tent to identify the four bodies. The funeral took place at twilight on the third day. The next morning *Boode* left for the Cape with the news. In later years

Daniel and Pieternel would remember those few months of sorrow and change as the time of the first fire. Do you remember that first fire, Pieternel? Do you remember the ointment against burns *Boode's meester* prepared at the time of the first fire? Do you remember what bloody Lamotius said, at the time of the first fire? The first fire was more than a flaming beacon on their seaway, it changed the lives of most of the people on the island, and those of people still to come to the island.

Pieternel spoke to Daniel about Bart. From his fiftieth year his condition deteriorated. He wasn't ill, but his force dwindled, and he became thin: an old dark brown bag of bones with that small bright blue anchor on his forearm. Most afternoons he slept through, and in the evenings he and Theuntje retired early, as had been their custom. In the morning one could see him standing in front of his house in the Lemoenbos with a bowl of tea, looking down the hill over the small farms to the muddy marshes in the direction of the Chalk. In front of his feet lay his garden with vegetables and some tobacco, and in the Modderbaai, or Mud Bay, he kept a sampan with which to earn his bread. He caught his fish behind Fisherman's Isle, which he sold in the Lemoenbos from house to house. At the Lodge there were unhappy people, and likewise among the free burghers, but Bart and Theuntje had all they needed. One might say that their old age was assured. Why should he slave, if there was good French gold buried under his floor? In all the years he had spent little of it. But to the very end he had to pretend that he was a poor fisherman, never ever appearing well off at all.

Now Bart needed to simplify his household and retire peacefully, like a gentleman. His body and soul needed it. In his kraal were six plough oxen of the Company which he no longer wanted and about which he had to speak to the commander. There were other matters on his mind too. When he spoke to Pieternel about Salomon, she was immediately prepared to do as he asked; she and Daniel would be happy to take the boy in with them. She thought Daniel would welcome it. Theuntje understood Bart's need, and knew that the boy would be well placed under Daniel's roof. But Bart also had to discuss it with the commander.

The commander was furious. He told Bart: The boy is your legally adopted child, now you want to abandon the child who has grown up in your house and regards you two as his father and mother. What is Theuntje's role in this child neglect?

'No, commander. She is against it, but there is nothing more I can teach him. From Daniel he can learn the cooper's trade, and he has to be taught from the gospels. Moreover, he will be lodged under his own sister's roof.'

'I see only one thing, Bart. You are a sluggard who wants to empty your hands of the child. You say you want to return your oxen and plant just enough for your own table. If all the farmers want to do that, who will produce food for the garrison? You are healthy enough to produce food for the island, but now you want to spend your time sitting on your stoep and smoking. Look, personally I don't care how you free burghers wear out the seats of your breeches, but I'll be damned if I turn Mauritius into an old-age home. You've got to work, everybody must work, for the benefit of this community, otherwise I'll throw the lot of you on the first hooker to the Cape.'

That was how the commander spoke to him, the way he spoke to everybody these days. So he thought: he would undertake to build a good boat for the Company, against payment. That was something he enjoyed. He could work without any help provided it didn't get bigger than twenty feet. That changed the commander's mood. He needed a shallow boat to carry logs from the Lodge to his mill, and bring back the sawn planks to the Lodge. The Company would provide pitch and planks for the hull, and a mast and rudder and cordage, but Bart had to make the knees and ribs and the bowsprit and sternpost and the keel, and rig the boat. Agreed? Fine, Bart said, then he would keep the boy for the present and bring the oxen round in the morning.

Bart tended his plantation in a calm manner, which was more characteristic of the sailor than the farmer. What he believed was: if the wind blows strongly, you shorten sail, which was why he pruned his plants short. That didn't produce much fruit, but saved work, so that he could spend a full day working on the boat. He took Salomon with him to select the timber in the forest, showing the boy: from a crooked branch like that we take two ribs, in this trunk you can already see the bowsprit, over there is a first-class fork for the knee beneath the stern bench. He was in no hurry. It wasn't necessary; he had money under the corner of his house.

For altogether five months they toiled on the boat. When Lamotius came round to see how the boat was progressing, Salomon would run home when he saw the commander. From the outset Bart wondered whether the man's bandages would ever be removed from his body and the crutches from under his arms. For months afterwards he wondered when the ridges of scar tissue would disappear from the man's face, whether the holes in his lips would close up, or the hair grow to cover the stubs of his ears, or nails return to his fingers. Theuntje took the child's side; she said that Salomon was not the only one who could no longer look at their commander's face.

'How come you're working so slowly,' the commander asked, 'as if you have money buried under your floor?' And when Bart gave no answer, he said: 'Rich or not, we both have to labour as if we're poor. I need that boat, and damned soon too.'

That made Bart think: Perhaps I'm not playing poor enough. I must convince the commander that I have no money at all.

In those days *Boode* returned from the Cape, with a new *secundus* for the post, some bricklayers with material to rebuild the Lodge from stone, and chests with implements ranging from pots and pans to writing material, to replace what had been lost. The hooker would remain for the crew to lend a hand, until just before the next hurricane season. Bart made friends with the ship's carpenter; he invited him to his home and entertained him with what he had, like fish, some vegetables and arrack, and the carpenter never came ashore without a double handful of brass nails in his breeches pocket for Bart. Until one day, when Captain Wobma ordered the carpenter to empty his pockets. And that was how Bart was called before the Council.

That same day Willem Willemsz van Deventer also appeared. He was an impossible man, that Lyreman. The more he recovered from his dropsy, the more ill-natured he became. He was impertinent, defiant and enjoyed humiliating people with word or deed. Sven came to say:

According to Commander Lamotte the Cape was sending its rubbish to this place, but he wasn't going to take nonsense from this Lyreman. When the commander went to talk to the Lyreman on the plain, he was away hunting with the slave the Company had given him to help with the wheat. Lamotius asked his wife to prepare a room, because he was staying until her husband returned. Sven and the commander looked around the disorderly yard: there were the oxen he'd been given, there the plough lay abandoned in the yard, as the man had evidently not lifted a hand to clear the land or to plough and sow. When he returned, with the slave carrying the hump and fat of a bull in a bag, and the commander asked where the wheat was, he replied that if the Company wished to farm with stones, they were welcome to try for themselves. Thereupon the commander asked whose ox he had shot and what had become of the meat. And the fellow answered: You can go and look for yourself; these two legs can't carry me back all the way. The commander took umbrage at that. He said: I am confiscating your musket and on Monday I'll send a wagon to remove you and your household to the Lemoenbos Plain. Perhaps you'll do better, closer to the Lodge.

So the Lyreman was moved to Lemoenbos Plain, but there was still no wheat for the Company. Daniel himself knew what happened after that. He was present, and put his hand on paper with his neighbour Willem van den Hoeven and Willem's Grieta against the Lyreman when they were asked to do so: how they had spent a companionable evening on Daniel's veranda with some neighbours. Then the Lyreman stood up, glass in hand, lifting one leg to vent a resounding fart, and said as if it was a joke: This one goes right up Lamotte's nose, and wait a moment, here's another one for him. Then, there was the matter of the Lyreman's slave who had disappeared off the face of the earth. They'd gone out hunting as two men, but he came back alone. Run away, he said, he had no idea of the slave's whereabouts. Perhaps he'd killed the slave, but there were no witnesses, and he was brought to the Council for no more than the wheat and the bull and his disdainful impertinence.

When Bart appeared before the Council, and the commander asked why he had stolen the nails, Bart simply said: 'I needed nails, sir. For the boat.'

'I can understand that you are poor, and I am sorry about it, Bart. But I cannot forgive you. I have to punish you as an example to the free burghers.'

'Yes, sir.'

'But I shall commute your punishment.'

The new *secundus* was eager to demonstrate that he was also an officer at last. On the day of his arrival he already refused to assume charge of the warehouse, as there were no papers about the contents. So he intimated. And Commander Lamotius was careful and gave him rope, because such a small boat, which was so top-heavy, soon capsized and caused everyone sailing in it to drown. And he was right to be cautious: here, at his first Council session, *Secundus* Drijver said that he felt the Council had neither the right nor the power to flog free burghers and so he elected to recuse himself. But they were three to one, and decided on corporal punishment for the accused. If people wouldn't listen, they should feel. The ship's carpenter would be given fifty stripes, the Lyreman forty, and Bart Borms twenty, reduced to fifteen because of his age. All three, as an example, at *Boode*'s mainmast.

Pieternella felt that Daniel ought to try and do something for Bart. He should go to the Lodge and speak to the commander. Daniel said: How can I interfere with the case? I complained against Hugo because it concerned me personally, but this has nothing at all to do with me.

The neighbours came to complain too; there was a general feeling that there were heavy times looming again, and if anyone could speak to the commander it was Daniel. When Bart lay broken on his bed, staining it with his blood and water, Daniel asked the commander, on behalf of the free burghers, that punishment should be meted out with a lighter hand and with more caution, to prevent it degenerating into assault and manslaughter again, as it had been under Commander Hugo.

'What are you talking about, Daniel?'

'I'm referring to the way Bart was beaten, sir. He is lying there with a heavy fever, and he is bleeding from below.'

'I wasn't present, but the *meester* was. He didn't say anything to me.'

'Now it is too late. Bart needs a doctor. We are worried that he may die.'

Sven had been present, sent on board as representative councillor. He had seen it all. He sailed out as pilot, put on a different hat, and went aboard as councillor. It happened at the main shroud of *Boode*, starboard side, in front of the entire crew, for their carpenter had to be set up as an example to Jack Tar. The flogger was their boatswain, who applied his lashes with force. The carpenter squirmed with pain, groaning and biting on the rag between his teeth, and taking his fifty lashes, but his breeches and back were caked with blood. Then it was Willem Willemsz van Deventer's turn, and from the moment he'd been seized up the stay, he ranted against the Company and cursed the skipper and commander for the whole anchorage to hear. The captain called on the boatswain to stop so that he could reprimand van Deventer about his cursing. Then the flogging began. When the captain stopped counting at forty and reached the words: 'Let this be a lesson to all in God's name, and a final warning for ever . . .' van Deventer spat at Sven. Then it was Bart's turn to go up to the shroud.

Bart walked forward on his own, raising his hands to be bound. Boatswain Lubbert greeted him with a hoarse voice: 'Good day, grandpa.' Then he rolled up over his shoulder a sleeve that had come down, and poured the bucket of seawater in a thin stream over Bart's breeches and buttocks. Captain Wobma read out the details of the crime and the sentence, and intoned: 'In the name of the laudable Company, let justice be done. Bo'sun, lay on as I count. One. Two.' The boatswain seemed to linger longer between blows to make sure they cut in more deeply, which automatically made the skipper count more slowly. At the eleventh or twelfth the captain said loudly: 'Lower, man, not across the kidneys.' Only then did Sven look up. It had been a mistake, he admitted, as he'd been sent as the councillor to make sure that everything was done properly.

On his return from the Lodge Daniel looked in at Bart's house. Bart lay face down on a square of canvas on the floor surrounded by the bloody stain of his water, his head resting on that blue miniature of an anchor on his arm. He was feverish, dazed; sweat glistened and pooled between his wrinkled shoulder blades. Theuntje applied green herbal poultices to his buttocks and lower back, and wiped his upper body and his legs with a damp cloth.

'The commander says he's sending the surgeon with ointment and medicine. I told him the blows go as high as the first rib. If he wants to beat us, he should know what he's doing. I told him: "Lashing is one thing, flogging something else. If something happens to Bart, we shall make ourselves heard in Amsterdam."'

'I don't care, Daniel. If Bart has to die, there is nothing left for me.'

'The rest of us who want to stay here, we do mind. The commander says he's coming to speak to you. And the surgeon says that bruised kidneys can recover if the damage is not too deep.'

From that day the farmers on the island turned against Lamotius. They came to Daniel's house with their complaints because he was the one who had gone to the Lodge. Daniel didn't want to hear their stories, he didn't want his house to become their meeting place, and he wanted to keep peace with the commander. To him personally the man had only done well, and he'd ensured that Daniel always had enough work to make a proper living.

Most of the free burghers who called, bored him with their tales, but Sven, with his news and his friendship with Pieternella, was different. The spirit had not yet died in Sven, and he enjoyed praising the most beautiful spots on the island, calling them miracles of nature. He loved the beautiful spots, that is to say if he ever loved anything besides liquor, but he didn't call them works of the Creator. One never heard any of the names of the Creator from Sven's mouth, neither in respect nor as a curse. He told Pieternella about every one of the island's miracles of nature, among which had been Commander Lamotius's wife too until her death. He spoke about the waterfall in the Great River, and the sky-high twin falls in the Black River Mountain, and the unbelievable mountain peaks known as Three Teats, and the lovely Vermaaklikheidskiel, or Entertainment Keel, and the green Bokgat, or Deer Hole, and the delightfully warm swimming hole at Kroonenburg. He offered to take Pieternel and show her each of those places.

Daniel could see how Sven desired his wife's company, and also, because he was a man, more than her company, and it disturbed him. He told her that he knew she had been here for almost two years and had still not been beyond Lemoenbos and South-East Harbour. If she wanted to go with Sven, she should do so. One day when he could afford a slave, they could explore the island, but now he had to work for their living. She said, she'd like to see the beautiful spots, and if it wasn't possible for them to go together, she would consider going with Sven.

One Saturday the hooker's cooper told Daniel that this was the fiftieth piece of his work he was now taking back on board: four leaguers, eighteen *aum* barrels, ten half-*aums*, twelve water barrels, six pickle vats, and he'd delivered the account to the Lodge for payment. That in itself was reason to celebrate, but there was more. It was his fiftieth birthday and he wanted to invite Daniel and Pieternel to dine with him on board. He told Pieternel that it was full moon that night, she should see how beautiful the bay and the Lemoenbos Plain shimmered in the moonlight, and how the lights of the Lodge were reflected in the black inner water.

Daniel borrowed Bart's sampan, and just after sunset they rowed from Modderbaai directly in the line of moonlight to the illuminated ship, past the dark silhouettes of Kattieseiland and Juffershoedje with its single palm tree like a stylish black plume. Pieternella wore an Oriental gown, which Margarethe d'Egmont had given her. It was a warm evening, and she dragged one foot in the cool wake of the boat, excitedly pointing out the torches and braziers of the Lodge, the phosphorescence on the reef, and the few big stars hanging above their house against the dark mountain. She had never been on the inner water at night before. She held the gift for their friend, which Daniel had made: a small tobacco barrel of red ebony to take one pound's weight of contents, with a tightly fitting lid.

Except for an anchor guard of six, playing at dice on the forward hatch, the cooper was the only man on board. He had the captain's permission to entertain guests in the cabin, and the cook's favour to use his kitchen. The hatches of the cabin were wide open; they could hear the water playing against the hull and around the stern anchor cable. Like officers they ate and drank at the cabin table, talking about the cooper's two years at the Japanese post in Nagasaki. ('A terrible place. You live like a bird in a cage, but it's a lesson no Protestant will ever forget.') And the man could cook. ('How else can a bachelor survive, and what else can he do with his money but buy the best cheese and wine and share it with friends?') He prepared sour fish for them, in the Japanese manner, with a salad of bamboo shoots, raw green peas and cold palm hearts. There was also a hot, strongly spiced octopus with *karri* sauce and rice, and a few bottles of wine he'd obtained from the ship's bottler. ('Slightly past their best because of the heat.') But he knew how to cool a bottle under a moist canvas in the wind. Late that night he served them sago with brown sugar and a golden ginger syrup ('Another of the palm tree's manifold blessings, this sago'), followed by black, bitter coffee from Java and cigars from the West Indies.

From the position of the stars it was past midnight when they went on deck, standing behind the gunwale to gaze at the dark land, and to say goodbye. A slow rowing boat came splashing across the pool towards the gangplank. From its zigzag course over the strip of moonlight they suspected the rower had one long and one short oar, so they waited in silence for him to tie up and clamber up the rope ladder. It was Boatswain Lubbert, hopelessly drunk. He turned back on the plank, humming a tune, and took his time to unfasten his breeches and urinate into the sea. His shirt was unbuttoned over his painted chest, hanging in loose flaps over his breeches.

Daniel took Pieternella by the hand. 'Come, down the ladder. Goodbye, friend. And many thanks.'

'Ah, our helmsman,' Lubbert called with a thick tongue, stumbling across the deck in the dark as he struggled to do up his trousers. 'Right here on our bloody hooker. Welcome aboard. And this whoreson of a cooper. Come, come and drink a glass with me in the cabin. I've done some splendid eating and drinking on land, you swine. Now you can go to your bloody bed, cooper. One glass, helmsman. Come down. Or go to hell and leave your tart for my pleasure.'

He went stomping down the ladder. The cooper said goodbye to

Daniel and took Pieternel's face between his hands to kiss her on the forehead. ('If there had been ladies like you in my youth, Pieternel, my life wouldn't have been so lonely. Thank you for your company, friends.') From below the boatswain shouted: 'Where the devil are you? Hell-hound.' They could hear him climbing up again. Again he raised his painted head over the hatch-coaming. 'Why must I keep on talking?' He scrambled on deck and stood before Daniel, grabbed his hair in both hands and said: 'I'll throw you down on the orlop, you dog.'

His voice brought the sailors up from the forehatch. Daniel broke away. 'Watch what you're doing, bastard.'

Lubbert stood swaying on his legs before Pieternella, leering at her. 'I see your tart has a loaf in the oven, helmsman. That's how I fucked her for you, last passage.'

Daniel's blood shrank in his body. Tonight the gates of the hereafter were gaping wide for him or for this man or for both. There was no hanging back. The pig had defied him, for he was now glowing with the food and drink of his friend, and not prepared to die. He said, making sure the sailors could hear him: 'Spare my pregnant wife, bo'sun.' His friend was already helping Pieternel into the sampan, before he threw loose the head-rope and called at him to get in. ('Come down, in God's name!')

'Come ashore, you mongrel,' Daniel invited the boatswain in front of the assembled sailors, throwing his cap down on the deck. 'Bring it ashore if you have the gall.' Then he climbed down into the sampan.

The watch pushed forward in the dark, in a huddle behind their boatswain, as Lubbert hung screaming over the gunwale, holding his member in his hand and swinging it before Pieternella. 'With this. Fucked her!'

They rowed ashore, moored to the jetty, then hurried ahead to find safety in the Lodge. The Lodge lay asleep. The braziers were burning low. Lubbert, following them, was cursing and screaming at the top of his voice from the dark night-sea, that he was going to castrate Daniel and drape his guts over the bushes. Daniel had Pieternel by the hand, dragging her forward, while the ship's cooper shouted from the jetty that he should flee. Here and there in the Lodge shutters were flung open and lanterns hung out. The night watch at the gate struck the cracked bell, a dull and dead off-key tone.

On the small acre of grass at the land side of the quay Daniel stopped, pushed Pieternella away, wrapped his waistcoat around his forearm and took his knife from its sheath. Pieternel was crying, shouting his name, pleading that these were hanging matters, he should give her his knife. The heat was now so intense he could barely breathe. His mouth was dry, but his eyes were accustomed to the light, his muscles were relaxed and his grip on the knife solid. He was ready. When Lubbert stumbled up the grass embankment with half a dozen sailors in his wake, there were already two or three people from the Lodge as well, and the porter with his torch.

Daniel tried to ward Lubbert off, saying: 'Now, no knives. Let us fight it out with fists.' And Pieternel, wielding a length of bamboo, tried to keep Lubbert away from her husband, but he pushed her off, making a sudden stab at Daniel. The blow cut right through his rolled-up waistcoat into his arm. Like a sword fighter Lubbert tried to keep distance, stabbing with a straight arm; the next blow cut Daniel from the lower belly up to the shoulder. He felt no pain, but he was startled by his own blood in his palm when he reached for his heart. He was the one who should live, not this dog. He charged forward, felt Lubbert's stab low and deep in his thigh, and grabbed him by the shirt. Now they were wrestling chest to chest, each grabbing at the other's knife-arm, stabbing, parrying, cutting, panting in each other's faces, pushing the opponent away to gain distance, stabbing again. Lubbert's shirt was torn from him. The sailors egged him on, laughing in the background; they wished he would die tonight. Swaying and heaving, covered with blood, Daniel fought against Lubbert, staggering across the square, slashing, stabbing, warding off blows, chopping, cutting. When Lubbert raised an arm above his head to pull free, Daniel managed to grab it, burying his knife three times into the armpit. Lubbert retched out a stream of blood through mouth and nose, slumping into Daniel's arms, his face against his chest. Three, four, five times Daniel could plunge his knife into Lubbert's lower belly without any resistance.

'Pig,' he said, pushing Lubbert off, causing him to fall. Blood flowed from Lubbert down the grassy embankment, but nobody approached to help him. Daniel turned away. Here he still was, and although he was badly wounded, he felt he would survive. His heart would beat slowly again, his breath would later cool, his mouth grow moist, his wounds would heal. He would be back on his feet. He would report to the commander. It was sweet, this heady feeling of freedom, even if he were to hang for it. He said to Pieternel: Pieternel, Pieternel, overwhelmed by gratitude.

'You're in arrest,' said the guard, holding out a hand for Daniel's knife. 'Regard yourself as the Lords' prisoner.'

The surgeon from the Lodge returned from Lubbert's body with a lantern in his hand. 'He is dead. Come into the *corps de garde*, so that I can have a look. Immediately.'

After a week, Lamotius visited him in his house at Lemoenbosvlakte. It was the first time the commander had gone there. Daniel lay in his large bedstead, parts of his body in bandages. Lamotius came to tell him that the Council had met, and it would not be necessary for him to come to court. After testimony from various people, they had decided on self-defence, and no thought of manslaughter. Lubbert had been buried outside the graveyard fence. The skipper had wanted it to take place at sea outside the reef, but that was ruled out, as Sven told them that at this time of the month the tide brought everything back inside. Now he was writing his report to the Cape, and he just wanted to know, before concluding, if Pieternel hadn't had too bad a fright? A woman who received a fright during her pregnancy might suffer misfortune in labour. Was Daniel sure he wouldn't have lasting damage from his wounds? And were the inflammation and fever truly over? These points had to be cleared up before he could conclude the case. The Cape was dissatisfied with his handling of Hans Beer's case. In that affair he'd been convinced that he was doing the right thing in the Company's interest, but they wrote that it was illegal to push interrogation to the third degree, and a grievous error for Beer to be displayed with his head in the fork of a tree on the Breakers Point.

Also, *Baas* Sven had requested to be released to the Cape. It saddened him; as the man was supposed to be his right hand. There would now be a vacancy for a master woodcutter, and attached to it, a seat on the Council. Would Daniel consider taking the post and returning to the Company's service? There was ample time.

'Thank you, commander. I prefer to work at home. Being together is important for me and Pieternel.'

'I understand.' The commander commented on the drape of fine white gauze on their bedstead, and said he also wanted to look in at Bart's, to find out how the old man was.

He, Daniel, eat the Company's bread again? Never.

Their days passed without their being much aware of it. Seeing Bart on his crutches rowing along the forest road down to the beach road, did not remind them of the passing of their own lives. For them, life had barely begun. From dawn to dusk they were occupied with their work. And when later on there were occasions they remembered because they had brought sorrow to their home, in those distant times there were still more occasions for satisfaction and joy. And Daniel never gave a single thought to dinners with gentlemen and important passengers in the Lodge which he never attended, because he'd said no thank you to the Company, or to discussions at Council meetings, or letters to the Cape and Batavia about the future of the island and the well-being of free burghers. He chose to let such go by him.

Before the birth of their first child Salomon came to live with them. Daniel taught him the cooper's trade, and the boy was not unwilling, only clumsy, because he was left-handed and most of the tools were shaped for the right hand. He was eager to read, and took their house apart in search of books. He told Pieternel that the whole world could be found in books. Pieternel knew about lots of books in the Lodge of old, but in the first fire everything had been turned to ashes. Daniel offered the boy his Bible; it was all he had in the house. In the evenings after supper the dark sometimes weighed on them, and then Pieternel asked Salomon to read for them from their Bible. Daniel shaped staves with adze and spokeshave, Pieternel mended clothes by lamplight, and Salomon sat at the head of the big table reading.

He started on the first page: *In the beginning God created the heaven and the earth. And the earth was without form, and void; and darkness was upon the face of the deep.* He was a fluent reader, and from time to time he stopped to say something or ask a question.

'It says here about the Creation, that when the work of every day was finished, it was good. *And God saw that it was good*, it says here, five times, six times. Right so, but where does the serpent come from?'

They didn't know, but that was how it was. The serpent was there, among the good.

Daniel also said: 'Look, if Salomon read correctly, my understanding is that God said it was not good for Adam to be alone, and so He put Adam to sleep, and then Eve was made from a rib. That is what I heard, but I don't understand it. God Himself knows how lonely it used to be here in this house at night. Anyone who looks at how a man is shaped, will immediately see the need for a woman there. I say what I believe: all the time He was making Adam, the Creator already knew there would be an immediate need for a woman, and not some time afterwards, as Salomon tells us, when He saw how lonely Adam was at night. Are you sure you read it right, Salomon?'

'Word for word.'

'I believe it the way it's written,' Pieternel said. 'For me that is the truth.'

'I first need to find out more. Perhaps we'll understand later,' said Salomon. In the front of the Bible where there were two blank pages side by side, he entered on Daniel's request their names and Daniel's date of birth, and their marriage date. And, as their children were born in due course, first Salomon and later Pieternel wrote down their names and dates of birth. And night after night Salomon read to them, for as long as he lived with them. Theuntje came to listen how he read, and she kept on saying to Daniel: 'You really should send Salomon to study. Just listen to him. You must send him to the fatherland, Daniel, like Commander van Riebeeck's two little boys. I remember them well, they were like my own. Bart and I will help with Salomon's passage and his school fees.'

'He must say what he wants to do. I won't force him. Except if he wants to enter the Company's service, then I'll tell him his compass has gone wrong.'

After the birth of Pieternella's first child, Theuntje sent word that Bart's back had given up. He could no longer work in his garden, watering or hoeing. Daniel and Salomon went to visit him. Bart, on his *katil*, told them that he was lying at his last anchor. He was content, but complained about small injustices done to him. It had been a mistake to build the boat for Lamotte. By the dog's hairy grave, look what it had brought him. He'd had enough money all along, French gold coins, real *louis d'or*. Please learn, little scholar, from this lamentable example. Do not work unless it is necessary; it only leads to misfortune and sadness. The surgeon had come round from the Lodge the day before, to enquire whether he had any pain. Yes, he had, but there was no need to take any trouble now. His water came out as pure blood and there was no cure for it. Daniel need not be concerned about his plantation, as long as everything was cropped short, nothing could be blown over. Perhaps he himself might go out to sea in the morning to catch fish.

'Safe journey.' They said their goodbye.

'You too, *sapitahu*. A jib to the bow.'

Lamotius visited Daniel once more to ask whether he would help to put the sawmill into full production. He managed to get small numbers of planks sawn at a time, but his figures on paper suggested that it should be much more. He had so much work accumulated at the office that in Sven's absence he could not attend to the mill's speed.

Daniel was at the time making a coffin. 'I can leave my work here, commander. I can leave this every day to work at the mill. It will bring in wood for the Company, but it would be no use to the island. I'm saying this with respect: if the Company cannot solve its problem with that saw, we'll all of us be in great trouble. To think that I am asked to help the mighty Company off a lee shore is a poor joke.'

When Sven returned from the Cape with the hooker, he had a wife, but he didn't look happy. Griet Ringels was the oldest of a ditch-digger's daughters. In a dry land there wasn't much work for a ditch-digger, and she had a hungry face and a habit of taking what did not belong to her. While they lived at the Lodge, she took somebody's laundry from the line. The commander moved them to Lemoenbos, and there she found somebody's free-ranging hen and a clutch of chickens in the forest and drove them to her own home. She had been under the impression that they were wild, she explained.

Once again Sven came to sit on Daniel's veranda, like a dog that wasn't fed at his own house. 'She is not as pretty as Pieternel, and several years older than me, but we'll get used to one another. I want to become a free burgher, cooper, and perhaps have some little ones, that is the main reason why I married her.'

Every time Daniel saw him, Sven was skinnier, redder in the face, shorter of breath and temper. Daniel gave him his mug of arrack early, so that both of them could go to work, but from that time Sven would wait for a second mug, and returning from the sawmill in the evening, he would once again stop over at Daniel's place. Lamotius wouldn't hear of making him a free burgher, he said, he first had to serve out his contract and help to get the cursed sawmill right. Production had to be increased fourfold, otherwise the Lords were closing down the island. But Sven couldn't care a single damn for the island or the Lords, just as they had never cared for him.

'We're only sawing by hand these days, cooper. Always back to my handsaw. If there is enough water in the dam for once, to turn the wheel, then it's the cogs slipping or the blade vibrating. Then I have to hurry to pull the brake, and try to repair it, before one trunk has gone through the saw. Why should I mess with such equipment? I've given up on the mill, cooper. By hand I can do it, but Lamotte refuses to listen to me.'

Soon Sven was staggering by the time he came from his house, top-heavy like a sloop rigged and loaded too high and in danger of capsizing. Then Daniel would laugh. 'Take another look, Baas Sven, maybe it's not the sawblade that's wobbling, but you.' But he felt sorry for the man, because they'd once been messmates. And who could tell that liquor would not one day get the better of him too?

Most summers, when the rivers dried up and formed stagnant pools on the plains, dysentery broke out among the island's people. It became a common occurrence in dry years. The whole island knew about it and expected it in such seasons. Every housewife learned that from October you worked with boiled water and regularly washed your hands with soap. Drinking water and water for washing you hoisted from a well or scooped from a running river, but if it came from a stagnant pool, it had to be boiled before use. Clean well water would be safest, but there had never been a well at the Lodge, as Sadelberg was one solid granite rock all the way out to the sea.

The cause of that disease was that people with dysentery had to wash themselves and their clothes more often than healthy people, in order to rid themselves of the smell of excrement. That was the entire cause of the disease. Infected people who were fortunate to have a house, could wash in a tub at home, or when they were too ill they could be washed with warm water, but a hunter rinsing his breeches in the river, a slave bathing his body in the river, a single slave woman taking a family's laundry to the river could infect a colony. And there were exiles from India who solemnly stood waist-deep in water pools because of their religion. It was a regular occurrence in the dry seasons. A ship with convicts from India in the dry season was an early warning. In that way the disease reached the hands of the woman washing in the river, and the water in the kitchen where the slave woman was rinsing the dishes.

Sometimes the attacks were mild and the fever broken within a few days, but on other occasions they were heavy, with severe stomach cramps, high fever, bleeding stools, and then the whole colony would fall ill. *Secundus* Drijver with his holier-than-thou attitude, who had taken an oath not to sign books or letters, was one who died in this manner before the next arrival of the hooker. Put differently, after barely a year of collecting affidavits against his commander and other underhand business, the island was rid of him.

Dysentery was familiar in the East; it was as much part of the East as rice, hot dust, or the smell of *karri*. The honourable gentlemen and the whores of Batavia both knew it. It was also something that drove the Dutch in the tropics East to get rich fast, so that they could afford the slaves to carry water and hew the fuel with which to boil it.

But there was another disease on Mauritius which Batavia did not know of, for which they had no medicine, and which the Lords could not imagine when Lamotius tried to describe it to them in his letters. The time would come when they were to experience it themselves, and that time was drawing near.

Just after the hand of God had grasped Batavia and shaken it – *Enough, Sodom! Enough, Gomorrah!* – the other disease crawled from that city's canals, floating through the streets on windless nights like a cloud of bad air. Out of ignorance they then called it bad air, *mal aria* if you tried to be more clever than others. *Malaria* – bad air. The Dutch East India Company would never again forget that disease, nor was it to survive it. Perhaps Commander Lamotius misled apothecaries like Doctor Cleijer and the professors of Leiden about its symptoms, because apart from excruciating headache, dizziness, high fever and muscle pains he compared it to '*equilepsia* or *St John's evil*', adding that four comets had been seen over Mauritius, that first hot year of stagnant water pools. After that, no professor would risk a diagnosis, since the Church was powerful and the stake for heretics not forgotten by any means.

Lamotius himself suffered from malaria. He was suffering from it when he wrote to Governor van der Stel at the Cape. He was dizzy, his hand had difficulty transporting the pen from inkwell to paper, shaping with difficulty the inky words for the remote and strange van der Stel. Did the good governor by any chance recognise the symptoms, having spent his youth here on the island? Van der Stel pretended no knowledge of it. Perhaps Lamotius was exaggerating his strange diseases, as in the same letter he begged for a transfer. In his reply the governor did not even refer to the disease.

Coughing and wheezing from a lung disease he'd brought from the Cape, Sven came to tell Daniel what their commander had written to the Cape about the malaria. Sometimes word for word, as it had been written in the letter, because councillors read and signed documents; only in Sven's case it had to be read out to him, and then he would draw his two block letters below, each as long and as wide as the first joint of his thumb. And his eyes followed Pieternel as she moved across her yard while he spoke.

'I went on two voyages with Commander Hugo to collect slaves, and on the coast of Mozambique I saw blacks prostrate, with a disease resembling this, or the very same. The Arab who was our go-between said he never slept on shore, he slept on board, because at night the bad air comes up from the marshes, that was what he told me. And something else one sees there: the blacks don't live near swamps and marshes, they build their houses on high ground. I told Lamotius about the stagnant marshes here behind the Chalk, and the man said to me' – Sven's voice rose in disbelief – 'he said he couldn't help it. That was what he said. He was working on a model of the sawblade now, somewhat smaller in diameter but heavier, to go to the Cape, he couldn't be bothered with marshes now.'

In that first season of the new disease eighteen people died, black and white, adults and children, among whom Salomon was one of the last. Pieternel grieved for her brother, going about clothed in black as she tended her child, moving through the house with thoughts about her own mortality. She walked to Theuntje carrying the child in a cloth on her back to commiserate with the old woman.

'Now you and I will have to read our Bible by ourselves,' she said to Daniel. She was expecting their second child by then. As her time approached, her familiar smile returned. Daniel was happy to see it. He had liked Salomon; the boy had been a pleasure to have in the house and a favourite with the neighbours, but very surely the day was now approaching for his wife and himself that they too should die. One lost one's people along the way as the journey continued; he himself had lost parents and brothers when he was young. And what did one have left in one's hand at the end? All you really had was what you possessed at this moment and what you were doing now, where you found yourself at this instant.

'All we have is here and now, Pieternel. Today there are you and I and our child. Perhaps, by the next hot season, one or two of the three of us may be gone.'

Sven was practically useless after his return from the Cape. Lamotius came to ask Daniel if he knew how Sven had drawn his map. The man had walked away from his job; not even his woodcutters knew what had become of him. His wife said she didn't want to have anything to do with the drunken rubbish. To the holier-than-thou Drijver, a man of no descent but plenty of pretence, and much flashing of white linen at the breast and around the wrists, Sven had made false statements about Lamotius's conduct, so that these could be forwarded to the Cape. To every Tom Fool and free burgher Sven would relay what had been said about them in Council or written to the Cape. His lung disease had worsened, he was constantly exhausted. He stole liquor from the warehouse and even drank the rations of his workmen. Fourteen days before he had abandoned his men in the forest and deserted from the lumber yard to old Noordoos's distillery at Kroonenburg, where he lay in a drunken stupor for a week. And all that as a member of the Council. He had spoiled four axes on the grindstone, cutting grooves into them so that they were wasted. The woodcutters came to Lamotius to complain about the axes. The Council tried Sven for misconduct, and halved his wages. Instead, he had slunk off into the forest again, four days ago.

Daniel discovered that Sven was working for Willem Willemsz van Deventer, because he owed the man money. He told the commander about Sven's whereabouts.

Lamotius's messengers found Sven in the Lyreman's yard, splitting red ebony for firewood. *Firewood*, no less. Unperturbed, Sven went on standing small stumps on the chopping block and splitting them with his axe. Without looking at the clerk he said in his whistling voice that he didn't want to hear about the Company. The clerk asked whether he could take down a statement to that effect. Sven raised himself to his slight height with the axe on his shoulder, and answered gasping for breath: 'I wipe my arse on you, and on Lamotius. And if either of you cross my bows again with your orders, I'll chop him to pieces with this axe. I regret that I haven't done it long ago. Take that as my statement.'

For that, Sven was suspended from the service and his possessions were confiscated. He came to Daniel's workplace carrying under his arm only a hammock painted in many colours. Could he come and live in the outroom?

'Now I need freedom, cooper, otherwise I'll kill whoever gets in my way.'

'Where is your wife?'

'What do you want with her?'

'I want her to come and take you away, and keep you at her own house.'

'I'm staying. If Pieternel doesn't want me, I'll go to the Lyreman, even if his wife is a poisonous bitch. Otherwise I stay. Please, cooper.'

Daniel thought of how the old man never stopped ogling his wife, but he told Pieternel that he would like to employ Sven, if she wouldn't mind his sleeping in their outroom. Sven had to promise to remain outside in the yard; he didn't want his wife or child being infected by Sven's disease. But she never paid any attention to it, and went outside to speak to Sven whenever she wanted. She also gave him food from their table, but usually Sven did not want to eat. Tobacco was enough, something to drink, and if she didn't mind him lighting his eyes by looking at her.

'It doesn't appear as if you and I will visit those marvels of nature, with our bodies, the way we look now,' she said, eight months pregnant, to this acquaintance of her late father.

So Daniel and Sven spent their days in the yard, sawing staves from logs, plaiting hoops, making vats, burning tar. Sven could not work for longer than half a day, before he was exhausted and had to lie down. In the shade of the palm trees Sven and he discussed the possibility of getting a proper cooperage going, with an assistant. Undoubtedly, they should have done it long ago, they said, knowing well it was too late. He gave Sven arrack morning, noon and night, and a bottle for Sundays, because he knew how the man's enormous need had him trembling by eleven, sweating large drops and shaking like an epileptic by noon, until a second and third mug calmed him down. When Sven became too weak to climb into his hammock, they made him a bed on the outroom floor. There Pieternel tended his wasted body during his last months, while he coughed blood, drenched his bedding several times a day and gradually drank himself to extinction.

They scrubbed Sven's hammock and slung it between two corner posts of the veranda where he could lie in the breeze, looking out over the bay. The hammock was a beautiful piece of work. The canvas had been cut and hemmed by a sailmaker, which was evident from the small even stitches, seven of them to the length of his needle; it was painted blue and green, with white, sharply rounded lines representing waves. In the middle, in a double circle of rope, between which the name Sven Telleson and the date 1632 were painted in large, ornate letters, King Neptune ruled with his trident. Around him the sea teemed with ships, whales, coral gardens among which mermaids and octopuses swam, with white gulls over the water, and at the head a compass colourfully executed with a red arrow pointing north and a golden cross indicating east. There was no sign of land anywhere, no mountain peaks, trees, town or quay. The overall picture was such that when someone lay in the hammock, it was as if he'd sunk into the sea, with a border of birds and clouds right at the top, then the sea with its ships, and under it the bottom with fish and coral and shells. The sixteen nettles at the head and foot were artfully knotted from eighth-inch rope, plaited, spliced, made into all the pretty patterns known to a sailor. Who would have painted it all for Sven? His own name he surely couldn't write.

One sunset, when the foam on the reef showed that the tide was receding, Sven departed. The clerk who came to examine the body, asked whether there was a testament, or an inheritance. There was nothing, except for a knife, canvas breeches, a hat of plaited palm fronds, and that hammock. The *seur* moved his fingers across the bright pictures.

'What is this date? Is it his birth date?' But they did not know.

'The widow might want it.'

'She can come and fetch it,' said Daniel. But the widow wasn't interested.

Do you remember Sven, Pieternel? Where in the mind of his wife, among everything she had experienced, would there still be a place for Sven? Daniel had to think, and calculate how old Pieternella would have been at the time. When they moved to Black River, she was as old as Commander Lamotius's wife had been at the time of the first fire. Pieternella did the housekeeping, controlling her household and her children just as well as his late mother had done it. And she was no longer worried about giving birth, no longer apprehensive about sick people, no longer avoided old people, no longer afraid of corpses. She spoke to chained slaves and cloaked commanders, her eyes on their faces and her voice even and calm. He was proud of her way of coping; in her habits and manners she was like the commander's wife. When her hands were on him, he could feel a force flowing from her into him, he could feel it easing his nerves and relaxing his muscles. Her hands healed his wounds and injuries; she healed his losses and his disappointments. She had to be old, ancient to have so much power. When had Pieternel grown so old?

Lamotius came to Daniel, accompanied by Jaap Baldyn who had been discharged less than a month before. They sat on the veranda.

'Ah, isn't that old Sven's hammock? Impudent rascal. Drew wages, never did a thing. Good riddance. Who would have written his name for him?'

The commander had a proposal to make. He had a new sloop named *Europa* on the blocks at the French Church – Daniel knew about it – a beautiful, spacious sloop and a first-class sea boat, and it had to be put to work. He wanted to make a proposal and asked Daniel to consider it in the interest of the island.

Until now, the island's main products had been ebony and building lime. The Castle at the Cape was being completed, and no longer required so much lime. So he'd thought of other ways in which this island might be of use and profit to the Company; to prevent its being closed down. There was tobacco: most of the free burghers were now producing tobacco for the garrison's use, but it could be expanded, also for export. The Cape used thousands of pounds of tobacco every year to exchange for draught oxen from the natives, and as all tobacco went up in smoke, it meant that the demand was constantly renewed. Then there was arrack; they knew for themselves that there was arrack made of sugar syrup, and the *arak apè* manufactured from palm juice.

Nowhere in the entire world did sugar cane grow taller, thicker and sweeter than on this island. It grew luxuriantly on Lemoenbos Plain, and several free burghers by now had their own handmills: little more, in fact, than two rollers and a handle, to press the juice from the cane. And at Kroonenburg old Noordoos was distilling cane arrack, keeping a licensed tavern, much to his own detriment, one should add. Fockje Jansz had tried to do it surreptitiously here at Lemoenbos too, but it had been discovered and confiscated. He, the commander, had written to the Cape governor about arrack more than a year before, and now at last he'd received a favourable reply.

If Daniel and his family, and Jaap with his, were to move to Black River Mouth where the palm forest grew, to distil *arak apè* for the Company, the Company would buy their whole harvest. Jaap here had experience of making brandy in the land of his birth, and Daniel was a cooper. The Cape had sent the necessary implements, like a still with head and coil, and the Company would make it available to them free of charge. As well as provide a pair of slaves to chop firewood and gather juice. Also the knives, spoons, barrels, funnels and buckets, all the necessary tools, would be provided by the Company. The two of them would have to tap trees and make wine, and distil the wine into *arak apè*. They would constantly have to compare the taste and strength with the product from Batavia, which the Company called good arrack. They could plant sugar too, if they wished, and try to blend the cane arrack with *arak apè* to provide more volume. Or flavour the cane arrack with aniseed or cloves; the taste was popular with some. But their main product should come from the crown of the coconut palm. He offered them the monopoly. If the quality was good, he would collect their filled barrels with the new sloop. Please think about it? Here was also a private letter for them, which had arrived with the hooker.

Daniel was already smiling at the thought. This was the change, the improvement, he needed. But what about Pieternel? She was in an advanced stage of pregnancy, she could not have more than a month to go. What about her vegetable garden, and the house she had furnished here around them? He told Lamotius that he wished to call his wife to be present at their discussion.

With his eyes on Pieternel, Lamotius briefly repeated his offer about the distillery at Black River Mouth, the so-called Molucca Anchorage, while Jaap explained the working of a still and the tasting of heads, heart and tails. Might Daniel be interested in undertaking it, with Jaap Baldyn as his partner?

'Is that the full offer?' she asked.

Well, there was another choice. The Company wanted to rent out the major part of its outpost Noordwyks Vlak to a few interested farmers, to provide vegetables and bread for the garrison. That meant cabbage, carrots, turnips. And starchy food like sweet potatoes and manioc. He wanted to experiment with mealies and Natal wheat, and whatever else could be ground for bread flour. There were fifteen morgen of tilled land and some sturdy buildings, there. And it was fertile soil, for herbs as well. Rue, sage and rosemary thrived there. The Company would provide ploughs, draught oxen and implements. The posthouse would be reserved for its people, the official palm-tree growers like Robert Hendriksz and Aunt Maijke. Well, they could have a week or so to think about it. They were the first ones he'd approached. There were others who would be interested. The new sloop was almost ready for the sea, it could not lie idle at the French Church.

That afternoon, as the loose, round clouds that had been hanging motionless over the south of the island all day turned orange, Daniel and Pieternel talked about the proposal, as they carried on with their work. There were three choices: they could stay where they were, or go to farm at Noordwyks Vlak, or move to Black River.

Pieternella said that she would like to go to a new place, but preferably not close to Aunt Maijke. One of the last stories told by Sven, the island's oral newspaper, was how Aunt Maijke had appeared before the Council to ask permission to marry Robert. Lamotius asked why the bridegroom had not come with her. And Robert, when the commander discussed it with him one day, simply said that he didn't feel like getting married; he hoped the commander would not compel him. It made Aunt Maijke an even more difficult person, they all knew.

Daniel, reconsidering, preferred to stay. Here was the house he had built himself, it was comfortably appointed, and he was close to the Lodge where his work came from. His sugar was almost ready to harvest; why should he abandon it and place everything at risk for a new arrack distillery, a completely new life, in a remote spot beyond the mountains?

When it became dark and they heard the first mosquitoes, they went inside, placed the shutters in the frames, ate their supper and put the little one to bed. She was two years old, and happy with her doll in her child's bed of bamboo and palm fronds, covered with a hood of fine gauze. Right beside her the cradle stood waiting for their next child. After supper Pieternel read a chapter from their Bible, covered in canvas, with its picture of a ship her brother had drawn in brown ink. *Hoeker Boode* had been written below it in brown, and you didn't realise that it was a Bible before you opened it and read from it. She read about the strong man Samson who had caused trouble wherever he went, among friend and foe alike, and of his wretched end. Could it be possible for a man to kill a lion with his bare hands? asked Daniel. He had heard about a farmer at Katwijk who had crushed a crazed horse to death against the city wall, and then there was a German who was said to have throttled a black bear. Pieternel said she didn't think it had anything to do with force; a thin man could receive strength from heaven. She felt sorry that a man like Samson, with such a gift, could amuse himself with loose women. His poor parents. Fortunately there was no widow or child. And Daniel kept gazing at her in wonder.

Pieternel closed the Bible, in which a new name would have to be written in a month or two. The first name, under those of the parents, was that of a girl, Catharina Zaaijman, with the date of her birth, in the thick tome with a ship on its cover.

'Have you thought of a name, Daniel?'

'Your father's name if it is a boy? I know it's the custom for my father's name to come first, but it doesn't matter.' He pushed the lamp towards her, and gave her their letter to open. It was from Barbara Geens, her name was on the front on the cover, with the words: *With a friend guided by God*. It was a long letter, filled with news about the Cape and about Barbara herself. Daniel thought of her face with a smile: the wide mouth, the green eyes and the stack of red hair. I'm getting on, she wrote, here in the young colony of Stellenbosch, surrounded by young people. People are taking risks, everything is making progress. She was with her daughter Sara, married to Adriaan van Brakel, and they already had a good assortment of children, but she wished she could have gone on with her work at the Cape. Yet she wasn't feeling strong enough. The government was now distributing farms and town plots wherever you wanted. The farms here were fertile and the soil rich; everybody was getting married and having children and their livestock multiplied. Long Gert van der Byl and Sofia had also become free burghers. Young Pieter was still living with them; he had grown taller than his father and was a great help to him. The two were really making a success of farming together. Pieter would probably claim a farm of his own when he got married. Something noteworthy was that the Company was allowing the free burghers at Stellenbosch a measure of local government, with a council of *heemraden*, so that they could solve their own problems. The people appreciated that. The four *heemraden* were Long Gert, Henning Hüsing, Hans Grimpe and Henk Elberts. All very important, and amazingly enough the wives were not yet going about with upturned noses. It was beautiful there among the mountains, and it had been raining all winter. People are beginning to talk of our town, our church.

'Do you know where this Stellenbosch is?'

'Do you remember that day, Daniel? We walked to the mouth of the Salt River, and then you showed me the mountains in the east and wanted to know if there were people living there already? I said: There are Hottentots living there. I wonder whether they have driven out all those Koina?'

If people were making such progress, they didn't want to remain behind themselves. It was all God's mercy. A weak person, with strength from heaven, enjoyed mercy. There at the table they decided to move to Black River Mouth, and Pieternel would wait here until after the child had been born.

Fourteen days, the commander had said. They walked through their house and across the yard, discussing what should go and what should remain. They could break down practically the whole house and take it along, but at the other side he would build them a stone house. His sugar he would certainly harvest, but his young tobacco and some of the vegetables could remain for the new owner. There were no graves yet of which to take their leave; their dead were in the graveyard at the Lodge. Their nearest neighbour was Aunt Theuntje, who would be sad about their leaving, but she would be happy for Pieternel to come and stay with her until after the birth.

Daniel told Pieternel what he knew about the west side of the island, and Molucca Anchorage, where they would be going. One went round Both's Kop, then north for three or four miles, where one found the river mouth pushing black mud into the inner water. The climate there was somewhat drier, with a sea breeze cooling the land. There were almost no mosquitoes yet. The Black River forced its way strongly into the sea, through a deep, wide mouth in which boats could lie safely or be rowed upriver for half a mile. The gap in the reef was rather difficult for anything larger than a hooker, but not impossible if one took care. Years before the flute *Molucca* had gone in there; that was why it was called the Molucca Anchorage. Their house and garden would have to be built upriver, out of reach of the saltwater tide.

One morning Lamotius sent word that the hooker's captain wanted to go to sea, and if Daniel's mind was made up, he had to come over, while the sailors were there to help. Pieternel said she thought her time would be in a fortnight. She would pack and prepare everything, and if Daniel had to leave before she was ready, he had to go. They packed what they could, the fragile things wrapped in palm grass, and put ready for the sailors to collect.

On the Saturday he took Pieternel and the little one with their things to Theuntje, walked to the Lodge where there were a surgeon and midwife to help her with the birth, and told the commander that he would be ready by Monday. On the Sunday he told his soul: Today it's you or the sugar. And everything he had he cut down short above the ground, binding the thick, juicy canes in bundles to take with him to Black River. All their domestic possessions were transported by the new sloop in one week, but Pieternel had to wait with Theuntje for more than a fortnight for her delivery.

At Black River Mouth Daniel found four slaves working without supervision at a lime hole above the beach, with a few vats of coarse building lime intended for immuring the Company's arrack stills. Why would these men work without supervision in that heat? With what threats or promises had they been persuaded? The panels of his house were unloaded from the boat on the grass bank above the high water. He stood the sides of his house upright with tackle and pulleys and fastened them, hoisted the flat roof over them and tied everything down, and laid the floorboards in position and nailed them down. On the lee side of the house he put up a cooking shed. When his boxes with furniture arrived, he had them carried inside, and carrying a water kettle in his hand one day went in search of a spot where coconut palms grew close to drinking water, far enough above the spring tide's reach to ensure that seawater would never reach there. He found an even patch under a cliff, beside a deep pool through which the river ran. There he measured out a wide yard, stacking stones at the four corners where his big house was to be built. To one side was still ample protected land for Jaap Baldyn, and for the Company's still. Then he took off his clothes and spent a half-hour swimming in the deep pool. He would make a rule for that: Drinking water was to be taken from above the swimming hole, and no one would be allowed to put a foot in there, and no one would draw water from the swimming hole or below it.

The slaves working without foreman or supervisor reminded him of how he had built his house and afterwards had cleared his land at Lemoenbos ten years before, all by himself. Now everything had to begin again from scratch, but he was looking forward to it. The slaves he had been promised and their supervisor arrived while he was digging the foundations for his stone house. He did not welcome their company. He preferred working on his own. He sent them off to carry building stones, and after they'd spent a week on that, they were sent down to the beach to dig a limepit, and bring baskets full from the hip-high bank of bleached white coral on the high water mark, to the lime pit.

In the meantime Jaap Baldyn brought him the news that Pieternel had had a little girl. Another daughter, but thank God, they would follow him here. Jaap and his workers pitched their tents a hundred yards closer to the sea. In the daytime his yard was resounding with calling and shouting at the work, and in the evenings, after Daniel had had his swim and walked back to his house at the river mouth, Jaap played the violin, while the slaves beat drums in the firelight.

Pieternel and their two children were on board when the commander came to brick up the Company's still. The sloop *Europa* lay anchored head-and-tail against the tide in the river mouth, and Daniel rowed out to bring Pieternel ashore. She had a slave woman with her; on free loan from the Company, the commander assured him. Now he had to take charge of a slave as well; he'd never wanted to have that, he already had more than enough to think about.

Daniel was concerned about the increase of his household. There were four of his own people on the site now and five of the Company. How was he going to feed them all? He had to plan: using one slave for part of the day catching fish, and another digging in the garden and planting vegetables along the river, while he himself hunted deer, dodos and land turtles, and still worked as much as possible on the building. His days were too full. He was working much too hard, Bart would have said. He should rather start slowing down. The slaves cut fuel, carried rocks, made lime, mixed mortar, but he himself had to do the building, make doorframes, doors and shutters. And he collected all suitable pieces of wood to build himself a sampan.

Lamotius brought news that the Company's farm at Noordwyks Vlak had been rented by the burghers Michiel Romond and Gert van Ewijk. And the versatile commander also had capable hands. He placed their still dead level and walled it in, and built a water furrow from the river to cool the still, in such a way that the water appeared to flow uphill, but that was of course just an illusion.

When his house was finished and they had carried the old house from the river mouth and put it up behind the new one as an outbuilding, Daniel continued to miss the simple life and tranquillity of earlier times at Lemoenbos. He and Pieternel could no longer be alone together like before, as much and as intimately as they wanted. Now, for the first time, there was a partner at his workplace with whom he had to discuss business, a slave woman in his yard, the crying of two children inside. Less than a stone's throw away, between him and the sea, was Baldyn's house. Baldyn's wife liked visiting, bringing different kinds of cooked food as gifts, rice with a pot of *karri*, *rutti* and strongly spiced *ketjap*. But uninvited, and unwanted. Daniel felt that every time he had to catch a few extra fishes or find a bigger deer to shoot to repay her generosity. Was this the life he wanted? What was it that life wanted from him? Surely not this. Where was the precious simplicity of the life he'd known?

Pieternella enjoyed the voices and bustle in their yard. She joined her yard to her neighbours', with their children running and laughing together to and fro. When in the twilight she watered her herb garden by hand, their slaves talked together under the trees. Daniel thought: Pieternel needs family, she longs for cousins, aunts, sisters and sisters-in-law as other people have. He himself continued to go in search of silence, with an axe in his hand into the forest behind his house to look for ebony, or on the plains between sea and mountain to look in the palm forest for adult trees to be sacrificed to the Company's thirst for liquor. Adult trees with ten or fifteen large coconuts. 'No virgins, Daniel,' Jaap had said. 'You must look for married trees.'

Sometimes Daniel went to sit on the rocky ridge behind his house, watching their yards and distillery from up there: the two houses with their outbuildings, cooking shed and stables on the lee side, the people and animals moving about there, and the river mouth, the blue-green inner water beyond, the reef in the distance, the open sea purple as ink towards sunset. Something was wrong. Something had made an about-turn here. His face, used all his life to look east, now had to look west. Was it a watershed in his life, had he passed a turning point, and was he now at the beginning of his return journey? 'Barbara,' he said, to hear the sound in the silence against the slope of the mountain. What is going to happen to us?

Palm trees thrive on coastal plains. They like growing where they can see the sea. Sven believed that palm trees came from the sea, their ancestors arriving from who knows where, the descendants following a current, washed out like sailors, shooting root on strange shores, founding a colony. You, too, *sapitahu*, you like putting roots down in mother earth and staying close to the sea, without taking the trouble of dispersing over the mountains and exploring the hinterland. Look how long you have been living here, and your wife has still not been to Bokgat or Kroonenburg?

On the plains of Black River Mouth, as far south as Pieter Both's Head, grew thousands of palm trees. There Daniel selected the oldest trees. He and a slave stood a ladder and chopped off the head, causing it to crash to the ground with all its nuts. Three of the ripest nuts were buried under the tree so that they could sprout and grow; the greenest ones were carried home in a net. Then the man on the ladder hollowed out the decapitated trunk with his knife, as deep as he could reach with his forearm, that was the pot. For two days the stump stood bleeding – or crying, as Baldyn said – into that pot, and on the third day one brought a mug and a barrel to empty it. Then it had to bleed inwards again for another two days, before it was emptied once more. He and the slaves went out every day to empty pots; some for the first time, others for the second or third. Some trees could be bled up to five times, then its blood turned sour and dark brown. And from the fermented juice palm wine was made, to be distilled to *arak apè*.

Distilling was Jaap Baldyn's task. He did it with the ostentatious secrecy of a major cellar master. He spoke of old family recipes whispered from father to son, the necessity of copper stills, the taste that soldering gave to alcohol, of heads and tails, of too weak or too strong. He would catch a few drops on a fingertip at the end of the coil to taste, closing his eyes to consider it in silence, comment that he tasted lead, this run would have to be flavoured with aniseed. Or he would spit it out with a shout: Cobra venom! Daniel trusted him; their arrack tasted good and strong to him, and Commander Lamotius came to taste, and congratulated them on what they had achieved. He promised them that he would order another still if they could keep two going at the same time, and at his first visit he took away six leaguers with him to the Lodge. One of those was to go to the Cape as an experiment.

Watching Jaap, Daniel discovered how to work with slaves, or how to get them to work for you: a slave had to eat and he knew it. Consider his needs, give him a full stomach, a full night's sleep, a bedtime drink and an opportunity of meeting a wife. Make a study of his weaknesses. Greet him, thank him for a piece of work, look after him when he is ill. Put in more work than him, longer hours, so that you can honestly look him in the eyes. Keep a loaded gun behind your bed. But it was still far, far better the old way, without slaves.

The Company's hunter, with his official green hat, bugle and three hungry hounds, came for a shoot in the vicinity every few months, arriving on the boat *Vanger* which Bart had built. At the river mouth he flung down his anchor in the shallows and pitched camp on Baldyn's land, with his bags of salt and empty vats. There he also off-loaded provisions and barrels for them. Sometimes he brought a letter from Lamotius, or a kettle the Lodge had sent to be patched. Then he hunted in the hills and ravines for a week, his slave slaughtering and salting on the beach. In the evenings he brought a dodo or two home to roast, and came over to drink and tell them news of the Lodge. He was full of praise for their product; he liked strong liquor that caused flames to belch from your mouth and smoke from your ears. He wouldn't go near their flavoured drink, no offence intended, but aniseed arrack was a whore's portion.

Daniel and Jaap tried their arrack on the hunter, because their liquor was intended for the garrison, neither too fine, nor too crude, and one which would still have the ordinary man on his feet after four rummers, talkative but happy and without a headache the morning after. Sven had told them about a taverner in the East who sank two fish heads in every leaguer, leaving them there to disintegrate. Another swore by a full scoop of gunpowder. Baldyn refused to consider it. He would invite the hunter in, sat him down and poured slowly. He gave him a meal, fish and rice with onions fried in turtle oil, and left him to talk, and drink.

So, who had died at the Lodge? The old ones passed away, the young ones grew big. What could one do? Old Fockje Jansz and the Lyreman and Willem van der Hoeven, all three dead in one month. It was the dysentery again, many had been struck down by it. But there were ugly stories at the Lodge. The garrison was divided between those who were loyal to the commander, and those who were not. The division ran all the way from the head clerk to down among the soldiers. For a long time there had been bad blood between the commander and the new *baas* woodcutter Abraham Steen, as Steen couldn't get the sawmill to work. It wasn't his fault; most of the rivers on that side of the island were stagnant. Three of the young clerks, Molijn, Swaanswijk and Geel, had resisted the commander for a while, mocking him behind his back, spreading a story that Lamotius was jealous because Steen received more favours from van der Hoeven's wife than he. Also that the commander had tried to seduce Molijn to commit the unspeakable sin. They even went and gossiped about crimes he was supposed to have committed in the fatherland. They no longer respected the commander. As for the commander, he cared nought for their nonsense. He was quick with his cane. And he increased his bodyguard from one to four. That is a sure sign of trouble. And the whole settlement could sense it. The three had been arrested to be tried at the Cape, and the commander had them marooned on Tobacco Island by *Vanger*, to remain there until the hooker called again, but they'd escaped without delay and were now hiding in the bushes, begging food from homes. Nobody was allowed to help them. But the commander had ordered him, the hunter, personally: If they refuse to stand, shoot at their legs. But Adam Cornelisz said he would help those boys and he'd beat up the official who tried to prevent him. So, the split had now gone all the way from the Lodge to Lemoenbos and Noordwyks Vlak. Almost everybody was against the commander. As far as he himself was concerned, he knew that it was the Company's bread he ate, and he always had his musket.

Just after New Year's Day in 1685 the hunter reappeared at the Molucca anchorage, bringing a surprise. It was Pieternel's brother Kobus. The hooker had arrived two days before, and was anchored in South-East Harbour in front of the Lodge. He had a letter from Lamotius, but none for them from the Cape Church Council or the Orphan master about Kobus.

Pieternella was glad to see her brother. How was he? How was such-and-such? Why hadn't he answered their letters? Daniel welcomed him, but was disappointed, at the first greeting, with the fellow's handshake:

a weak, limp touch, not a grasp with which to lift a drowning man into a boat.

The hunter had to take Daniel aside to talk. The commander wanted him to know that the skipper had said he had twice been forced to have the youngster given twenty stripes. Once for malingering, because after he'd been seasick he wanted to stay in bed. Skipper had done everything he could for him because of his falling sickness, made him bottler's assistant, and on day duty only, but the bottler could get no work out of the lad and the surgeon could find nothing wrong with him. But the second time he stole tobacco and a knife from the rigger's chest and hid the knife in his bedding. That was the Commander Lamotius's message. And this, then, was Pieternel's brother. He did not know what they had done to the boy at the Cape, but he was not well. The dog that is kicked the most, often becomes the most treacherous.

The note from Commander Lamotius was to inform them that one of the three condemned clerks was still at large in the forest, and that if the accused was to show himself he should be arrested and delivered on board, with his fellows. Violence was unnecessary, the fugitive already showed remorse for his deeds, but was naturally too scared to hand himself over. From the Cape, Governor van der Stel sent word that Daniel's brother-in-law had been sent to Mauritius at his own request to live with his sister. He had been trained as a cobbler, but could not make a living. His behaviour was unsteady, and he had no testimonials. Commander Lamotius planned to send an *aum* of arrack, some of their best tobacco, butter, soap, hides, barrels and other examples of the island's produce to the Cape on this hooker. He hoped that with Governor van der Stel's support they might find a market at the Cape. After all, their governor had been born on Mauritius, he should understand their needs.

With this letter Daniel went to Jaap Baldyn. Why not try? The hooker would remain here for more than a month. They could supply a few of those products, and buy some others, to keep in boxes and vats so that it wouldn't be harmed at sea. His wife's brother was here now and could give them a hand. Daniel and neighbour Jaap gave one another the handshake of agreement. Their wives, too, were happy about the opportunity of earning cash.

But it was much more difficult to win over Kobus van Meerhof. He had to be encouraged, reprimanded, warned. It made him resentful and brought on his epilepsy a few times. The slaves avoided him, and the women pitied him, but all one got out of the fellow, was that he was a shoemaker and didn't really understand cooperage and arrack.

'I don't understand it either,' Daniel said. 'I just *do* it. Do you want to make shoes? Then why did you not bring your last and tools?' He soon reached the end of his temper. The youngster was a natural shirker. From the outset he said to Pieternel: 'He likes arrack and tobacco even if he doesn't understand them, but when you look for him, he's gone. And he sits in the sun too much, it's bad for our slaves.'

Pieternel thought that Kobus might look after their few dairy cows, but he wouldn't do that either. He would bring the cattle back from pasture too early, just after noon, with one or more missing, and driving them unnecessarily fast. It went on every day, even though Pieternel spoke to him about it. If one could see how a cow's stomach had been voided behind on its shins, you knew it had been unnecessarily hurried. But there was no need! Pieternel was displeased with it, because her cows were lamb-tame, hand-reared. His screaming at the cows was bad for them. She believed: one didn't shout at a cow, and one didn't beat a cow. And the boy could not learn to milk; he came back with half-buckets of milk from cows with large udders, so that she herself had to go and finish the milking. And the cows didn't like his hand. One could immediately see if a cow didn't like the milker's hand; they were restless at the manger and drew away. She would much rather do the milking herself and send her cattle out to pasture without Kobus.

One early morning when Daniel came outside, there lay an English ship before the gap, in eight fathoms of water. From the shape he could see that it was an English ship: in recent times they had a lighter appearance, less angular than those of the Dutch or the Danes, less broad on the water, and rigged much higher to carry more sail. He went in to tell Pieternel, dragged his sampan to the water and floated downriver to the sea, while he set up his little sail. It was a ship of the English Company; their red-striped flag was hoisted for him on the mizzen-peak as he approached. This was the arch-enemy, five months under way from the Thames without stopping over anywhere, and they required a pilot to bring them in, as they were in need of water, fuel and food. Could he help? Yes, he could guide them in, but they should be ready to move out again should the weather come up. He believed he could supply what they needed.

The English had departed by the time Commander Lamotius arrived on a visit a fortnight later. He and the young clerk Ovaer lodged with Daniel, the other clerk and the sailors were with Baldyn. Daniel told him what he had done. He had had his children baptised by the English pastor, caulked their vats, and sold cattle for slaughter, poultry and vegetables to them. Their sick had been in his care on land, in tents. The English had taken in water and fuel and felled two trees to brace a cracked foremast. They'd buried one sailor, flogged one, and one had deserted. The deserter had come out of the forest after his ship had left, and Daniel had given him food and showed him the way to the Lodge.

'How did they pay you, Daniel?'

'Jaap Baldyn and I each got four bags of rice, commander. Jaap's wife served food at a table here under the trees, at noon and in the evening; she likes cooking for people. They also gave Pieternel cheese in exchange for butter and buttermilk, and various medicines, and vinegar, and so on. For the rest they paid in silver.'

'Try to get a message to the Lodge if another ship comes this way, Daniel. The Company doesn't lose much if you carry on a bit of trade with strangers, and it would be better for them to get refreshments here rather than to be left to themselves. But I want to know what is going on. And we shouldn't sell arrack to strangers. I rely on you in that respect.'

'That will be fine, commander.'

They sat on the veranda in the warm evening, drinking young arrack. There was some lightning in the west, far over the sea. It was delightful here, completely free of mosquitoes. Daniel questioned them: What

did Adam Cornelisz and the others of Lemoenbos say about the opportunity of sending samples of tobacco to the Cape?

The farmers were happy and grateful, Lamotius told him. They soaked
the leaves in strong brandy sauce before drying and twisting them, and
then turned them into a tight coil, which they secured with small wooden
pegs. It was quite an art, some couldn't get it right. He suggested that
Adam coop his best leaves, all of them young leaves, open in vats like
the Virginia tobacco brought from America to England. It wasn't the
farmer's task to cure and roll it, but the merchant's. If the attempt was
successful they would plant three, four times as much for the next
season. Perhaps tobacco would save the island, in addition to ebony and
arrack. He also told him that it was severely dry on the eastern side.
The sawmill had been standing still for months, and the staff and slaves
were once again afflicted by dysentery and the strange disease caused
by poisonous vapours. It was a pity that this beautiful island should be
plagued by such a disease. He himself suffered from it intermittently;
the terrible headache and dizzy fever continued for several days every
time. He would like to found a permanent colony here on Mauritius,
as van Riebeeck had done at the Cape, but he couldn't invite people to
their death in this place. These days the Company only sent out exiles,
no-good scoundrels, outcasts; one could see it on the scourged backs
when they worked without shirts. Already the Cape is regarding this
island as its penal colony. A convict had also arrived on the ship, a French
lieutenant and his wife banished to Mauritius for twenty years. He
was not in chains, but was restricted to the Lodge. And such people
were here against their will, they would never become settlers. The
commander told Daniel: 'Perhaps it is you free burghers and your children who should inherit this island, instead of the Company.'

'That is my belief too, commander.'

Speaking of no-good scoundrels: the young lady at the Lodge, the
French lieutenant's wife, was lonely and might appreciate Pieternel's
company, should Pieternel wish to come on a visit. They were the
same age. Personally Daniel thought that she had been done a grave
injustice. Pieternel, sitting with them on the veranda, enquired in the
dark about the young lady at the Lodge, as Daniel watched the distant

lightning approaching. He was vaguely listening to the story of the French lieutenant's wife who had followed her husband into exile here, and quietly pitied Lamotius who had been without wife and child for so long now. Thank God, something like that had not happened to him. But he would remain on guard. The weather was threatening strongly. His own sampan had been dragged far out. After midnight he would walk down to the anchorage to see that the Company's sloop was secure.

For Jean-Baptiste Dubertin, Daniel had never felt sympathy. He had come to know him as a braggart, a vain man rigged like a small galliot but with the noise of a frigate of forty-eight fire-mouths. Who were those people? Dubertin was an elderly officer from the garrison at Ceylon, married to the younger daughter of a good Utrecht family, and they were on their way back, returning to Holland, but fate intervened, saying: Let us play the fool with these silly people, let us put them on one ship, and most of their luggage on another, and watch what happens. That was why Dubertin and his wife had to go ashore at the Cape and wait until the other ship arrived from Ceylon with their possessions, as they needed clothes and other things. While they waited, for nearly two months, Lieutenant Dubertin accepted a post in the Cape garrison to pay for their lodging, as he wasn't rich, but loved entertaining according to his rank and status, and cash was scarce. Dubertin was made a warehouse master, where he helped himself from the warehouse as he had learned to do in Ceylon.

Was fate laughing at these two people behind its hand? Never. It couldn't care less, it had already found others to play with. First Rijklof van Goens arrived from the East as commissioner appointed to inspect the Cape and became an enemy of van der Stel and a friend of Lieutenant Dubertin, whom he knew very well from his own Ceylon days. A fortnight later Baron van Reede arrived from the fatherland as high commissioner, also to inspect the Cape, and became an enemy of van Goens and a friend of van der Stel. The latter saw a chance of avenging himself on van Goens (doesn't one deal an enemy a double insult, by insulting his messenger or his favourite?) and forbade Lieutenant Dubertin to leave with the home-bound fleet, ordering his books to be inspected for embezzlement and theft of Company property. Thereupon Commissioner van Goens began to worry that the gemstones he had brought with him might also be confiscated, and arranged with the young lady Aletha Uijtenbogaert, that is Dubertin's wife, that she would travel to Holland with a small pouch of jewels, hidden in a spot where no man would search. Her explanation was, she wanted to go to Holland to arrange family matters before returning to the Cape permanently, and nobody suspected anything.

For that piece of chicanery van Goens rewarded her richly. But after her return to the Cape, her silly fool of a husband one day bragged: 'Borghorst is not the only one to have carried jewels on his person.' When those words reached van Reede, he desired revenge on van Goens, and he had Dubertin arrested and dragged before the Council. Since Dubertin had always been obstinate, moody, domineering and cruel to his subordinates, and fond of beating, there were many witnesses to confirm his transgressions. His punishment was exile to Mauritius for twenty years. And Aletha, ignorant child, instead of going home, or trying to bribe van Goens to help her, followed her braggart of a husband to an island on the backside of the globe.

That much Daniel deduced from Lamotius's narrative. That an injustice had been done against the woman was obvious, but it had been her own choice; moreover, who had wronged her, the Company or her own husband? And he wondered if her feeling for her husband might be love, real love? That evening, Lamotius said he wanted to place them on Noordwyks Vlak, so that the French lieutenant could farm if he so wished; and the master woodcutter would keep his eye on them there. Should Pieternel want to visit the woman at the Lodge, he would arrange transport for her.

That night of blustery wind and lightning without rain, the commander fell ill again. Daniel and Pieternel could hear him groaning in his bed. He was confused, hallucinating, sometimes almost driven to distraction with fever, and now hot, then cold, and he kept on kicking off his sheet, moaning of headache, drenched with perspiration. Daniel pulled off the man's soaked nightshirt and covered him with the sheet.

He called Pieternel to look at the burns the commander's body had suffered: the scars of his wounds lay over the front and back of his body like flames of red, white and purple, burned into it. They lay him down him on the floor and sponged him with river water over and over again, until his groundsheet and bedding were wet with sweat and water. Sometimes there was a respite for half an hour, then he came round again, and when they returned to him, he was shivering and his teeth chattering from cold as he pulled the sheet tightly over him again. They would make him tea to drink as he regained consciousness, but there was no medicine for his affliction.

The following afternoon the commander was carried to the sloop by sailors, still weak and quite yellow in the face; even his eyes and his nails were yellow. Daniel piloted them out on the tide, clearing the reef. He said to Pieternel: The poor man, how can he do his work with such an illness? She said: It is like our Kobus. But it wasn't. Lamotius had promised the Lords to save this island from closing down. Their own survival depended on his great enterprise, that sawmill with the circular blade. He told Pieternel: as far as he was concerned, the commander deserved their support. What did it matter if the man had promised his wife gowns of flowered silk and huge riches and an early retirement, and now his dream had gone to ashes? He was an honest entrepreneur who had brought a good plan to the wrong place at the worst time.

Daniel was ashamed to talk to Pieternel about her brother. There were things she already knew, which she had discovered herself, or about which he'd told her that evening when he had first talked openly to her about Kobus. He could see that something was bothering her, as she read to them from their old Bible with the ship on the cover. Her voice showed it first, and soon he noticed that she was on the verge of tears. She had chosen the piece about the prodigal son to read, about the wastrel who returned to his old father with a nice story, and how the old man forgave him.

He abruptly interrupted her: 'What is the matter, Pieternel?'

She closed the Bible, then opened it again, at the beginning, where their wedding date and the names and birth dates of their two children were written, and turned the book towards Daniel. A large number of names had been scribbled on the page, an untidy list of strangers, covering the whole of it. And there was the cause sitting at their table, staring at his handiwork with his mouth half open.

'It isn't me.' But it was, because the name of his half-brother Anthonie was there too, misspelled but recognisable.

Daniel told him: 'Keep your hands off our things, or get out of our house. I've spoken to you about your idleness, and about beating Baldyn's dog almost to death, but I am now getting tired of talking. I'm telling you for the last time . . .' He did not finish the sentence. The Bible said that the old man had forgiven, but that old man had to watch out, for the rest of his life he and his workmen would have to keep an eye on that boy.

What Pieternel told him, was that their slave woman had come to her to complain that Kobus wanted to lie with her. When she went into her room, he would be sitting there. What could she do? She would ask Kobus: 'What do you want?' And he would say: 'You know what I want.' She told him outright that if he needed a woman, he should do it like an honourable young man and keep to his own kind, but it was no good. The woman was no longer young, and she was unhappy and frightened. It was time for Daniel to speak to Kobus.

He began by attaching a strong barrel-bolt to the woman's door and showing her how to open and close it, but after he had spoken to Kobus, the lad ran away. Five days later two of Adam Cornelisz's slaves brought him back, with his hands manacled. He had tried to pounce on a slave woman in their yard.

Kobus's habit of stealing arrack landed him in trouble with the government. Jaap Baldyn was suspecting it and kept his eyes peeled, seeing him draw half-distilled arrack from the still and going off to the forest with it. Then he followed the tracks and discovered a hut where the clerk Molijn was holed up, and there it came to light how Kobus had been stealing food and drink for a long time to keep him alive. Daniel was relieved that he was not required to take Kobus and Molijn to the Lodge. Jaap was the first witness, and returning from the Lodge he reported that Molijn was in chains, and the commander was sending

Kobus home with forty strokes on his wet breeches. Daniel was embarrassed for his poor wife's sake.

The hunter's gun went missing, while he was lodging with them overnight. The man suspected that a slave had stolen it and hidden it in the wood, and to satisfy him they questioned all the slaves, but they already knew where every slave had been that day, and the hunter's musket was not seen again. Daniel confided to Pieternella that he was worried about Kobus and that gun, and he would be required to account for it personally, since it had disappeared from his house, and the Company's mark was on it. Then, a week after the musket, Jaap came to tell him that he'd found Kobus behind a closed door in an outbuilding with his little girl on his lap. He'd lost his temper and given the fellow a severe hiding with a thong. He now came to apologise to Pedronel and Danielo, but he and his wife never wanted the man at their place again. Perhaps the Company might employ him at the Cape? That same night Kobus's outroom went up in flames. Twelve people came running with buckets of water from the river, and they managed to save Kobus without injury, but he was hopelessly drunk and barely knew what was happening.

That was when he warned Kobus that it was his final word, that out of respect for his sister he would not lift his hand against him, but this was the last time he would let him bring danger, damage or shame over their house. Soon afterwards an English ship arrived at the anchorage, and he and Jaap and their wives did well out of supplying it with provisions. After he'd piloted the ship through the gap and they'd already been paid and thanked and offered a farewell with a cannon shot, the chief boatswain appeared at the gunwale holding Kobus by the scruff of his neck. 'Does this belong to you, Mr Zaaijman?' And he threw Kobus into the sea. Seldom in his life had Daniel felt so humiliated; what was to become of his name among seafaring men? For his wife's sake he helped Kobus from the water into the boat, and decided on her advice to take him to the Lodge and ask the commander to keep him locked up there until the hooker arrived, and send him back to the Cape.

Only then did they have peace in the house again. The time passed quickly; almost imperceptibly their children grew up, and new little ones were born. Jaap and his wife grew grey and plump, yet every other year a new little boat was launched: each tawny child as beautiful as the other with jet-black hair and dark eyes. Life was now pleasant. The distillery was doing so well that they could pay off all their debt at the Company's office, buy their own still and equipment, and start building up a credit. Cash they never received from the Company, but twice a year they could expect English ships that paid in silver or with Indian merchandise like coloured cotton, rice and spices.

There were setbacks, yes. These shook them awake, to prevent their becoming complacent. One had to be alert, and look ahead: What was the enemy planning against you? What had fate decreed for you? Beyond the mountains, beyond the sea, harm was plotted against one, or against one's leaking sampan, or maybe something against one's patch of beans, or one's child. And one never knew who the adversary was or when to expect him, but as the Book says, it might well be the Lord Himself. It could barely be otherwise. Be on guard, exercise your trade so that every tenon fitted its mortise precisely, and pray, and be watchful. Therein lies your salvation.

Two years after they had dispatched the first samples of their products to the Cape, Lamotius came to them on a visit. He came personally, because he knew how great their disappointment would be, which was why he brought them this letter from Governor van der Stel, to see with their own eyes. There it was: their samples of the island's products, like butter, arrack, hides, barrels, et cetera, described in Lamotius's letter and entered on the hooker's waybill, had not arrived. Their dried beans the crew had to eat at sea in their distress. The captain had died at sea, and his successor said he knew nothing. What was there that Lamotius could say to them now? Furthermore, he had to inform them that Kobus had also died at sea. The way in which Lamotius said it made Daniel suspect that something untoward had happened, but for his wife's sake he did not ask. And on his own he never spoke about Kobus again, but he kept in mind that Pieternel now had no relatives left. She was all on her own.

They could try again, Daniel said to the commander. Baldyn now made a particularly fine aniseed arrack which was popular with the English and would find a ready market at the Cape. And as everybody knew, the farmers of Lemoenbos made a passable tobacco. Look, here all three of them were smoking it, the English visitors smoked it, and the whole garrison chewed it. They simply had to try again, that was the only way out. What else was there to do?

A few slaves had been brought this time, Lamotius said. Daniel and Jaap could each have one on credit on the book; the rest he had to keep for sawing ebony. He didn't know what it was with the mill; after the last rains the river was running again and the dam was full, but he could not get sufficient speed in the cursed cogwheel. And the parts kept on breaking down: here a few teeth from a wheel, there a chip from a blade. Very often one lost heart, then you just had to pray and make yet another precise model for Batavia or the Cape or Holland. Somewere in the world they should be able to cast or repair that circular blade.

'We also have a serious problem at the Lodge with that French lieutenant. You probably know about it?'

'We heard, from free burghers coming this way.'

'I need your word that you won't help him to escape from the island.'

'Is he on the run then?'

'No, but he is most boastful. Will you promise?' And when they nodded, he said: 'I must inform you about the situation. If you listen just to Dubertin or the free burghers, you may not hear the whole truth.'

Do you remember, Pieternel, the time of the French lieutenant's wife? Thank God, they suffered less than other people. And whom do you blame? Poor Lamotius fell in love with the woman while she and her husband were billeted in the Lodge. Her company came as a wonderful relief to him after his years of loneliness, and her pretty young face kindled thoughts in him which he couldn't contain. Like others, he lost his judgement when he fell in love. He had a little parrot caught for her, for the empty birdcage she had brought from the Cape. The birdcage had been a sign of a childless woman since the world began. What awful yearnings there must have been in her? The commander gave her gifts, the loveliest flowered silk from Java, a jewellery box of sandalwood. He took her on long walks in the forest, or on a sampan to the island at Kroonenburg. In the beginning, but less and less frequently as time went by, her elderly husband accompanied them. One could see their friendship progressing, one could see in her how much she enjoyed it, and it was obvious that with Commander Lamotius she found something pleasurable, which was lacking in her own husband. They were of the same social class, the same cultural background, had the same interests, and were at least closer to the same age. One could see that she suited Lamotius better than her bad-tempered, boastful husband. Could the old man still satisfy her at his age? They all felt sorry for her, trapped here among them in the same helpless circumstances as her faded, silent parrot in the birdcage.

They knew that the old lieutenant was becoming jealous, when he started making denigrating remarks about the commander, and calling the parrot Onan, because he spilled his seed on the ground. In due course he demanded to be allowed to farm on Noordwyks Vlak. He insisted that it had been arranged at the Cape; he was supposed to support himself by farming. Lamotius could not refuse, and had a house built for them opposite the posthouse at the Vlak, just where the bridge spanned the river, so that the workers at the post could keep an eye on the troublesome exile. And of course the commander himself occasionally lodged at the posthouse on the plain when he came on inspection for one week every month. To this new house at the bridge, Dubertin lured the free burghers with an open barrel of French brandy, sowing suspicion and division. There, he also lured the workers at the post on the Vlak, and incited resistance and rebellion against their commander. And there Aletha lured the poor Lamotius, with her sweet young face and her company.

Lamotius woke up when reports came of farmers, led by Dubertin, planning an armed march against the Lodge, where the garrison would join them, and they would capture Lamotius and collect affidavits against him to forward to the Cape. So, one Easter night Lamotius dispatched four soldiers to bring Dubertin and his wife to the Lodge. And they took the lieutenant in his bed, but on the way, by the light of the full moon, Dubertin dived into the forest and disappeared so completely that for eight months he was not seen again. The next day the commander had Dubertin's house burned down and his weapons and his few livestock confiscated.

Once he had taken fright, it was too late. He avoided the woman, and during those months Aletha lived alone in an empty house at Lemoenboom Plain, where the farmers' wives visited her with food and messages of support, and fresh news of her husband. They told her that Lamotius was planning to shoot him, have him die in an accident, so that he could get her. And from there she left on a hooker of the Company, for the East. She was not an exile after all, she could leave as she wished. Do you remember, Pieternel?

The latest scandal was that Gert van Ewijk surprised his wife Esther in adultery with their only slave. She was arrested, and readily confessed everything. Their estates were separated, and she waited in prison to be sent to the Cape for trial. The slave was still a fugitive in the dark ravines of the Black River Mountain. One day the man approached Daniel, where he sat against the cliff behind his house, looking out over the farm and the sea, and reflecting. He was an Indian, a tall man with an intelligent face. He mixed Portuguese with Dutch to talk to Daniel. He wanted to surrender to be tried, he said. Would Daniel please help him to get to the Lodge? So he took the man home, gave him food and a place to sleep, and asked Pieternel: What must I do? She said: Ask Jaap's wife to come and talk, because they are of the same nation. The man told Jaap's wife that if van Ewijk were prepared to divorce, he would be happy to marry Esther. And Daniel made her tell him most emphatically: Death waits at the Lodge. He wanted the man to understand this clearly: Death waits at the Lodge. Then Daniel took him to South-East Harbour on the sampan to speak to Commander Lamotius. He said, in front of the commander, that the man admitted his transgression, so interrogation was not necessary. And in India the punishment for adultery was not death. Gert and his father-in-law, old Noordoos, would demand the slave's blood because of their disgrace, but his main worry was about *Baas* Steen. And Lamotius promised to protect the prisoner against violence.

And yet the man died. He wouldn't eat or speak in prison, nobody laid a hand on him, he just died. Why, wondered Daniel, why? Because he wasn't a Hollander, nor a Christian, and didn't have a white skin, those were the three reasons. What was the use of his interference and his intercession? Could Lamotius not see the beam in his own eye? Would he again have to carry a complaint to the Cape, or would it have to be as far as Holland this time?

This Abraham Steen, it was he who had led the four soldiers to arrest Dubertin that Easter night. One of them was Hans Pigt, from the commander's bodyguard, and Steen had sworn high and low that it had been Pigt's fault; he had deliberately allowed Dubertin to get away. Pigt was detained for weeks and interrogated, his back was beaten to a bloody mess, and while he was lying there in detention, Steen spread the word in the slave lodge: whoever wanted to bed Pigt's wife, might do so with impunity. When she was raped by a slave and fell pregnant from it, nobody troubled the rapist or Steen in any way; not a finger was raised against them, not a tongue wagged, because she was a black woman from India.

But Lamotius had to discover at any price where the French lieutenant was hiding. So he began to chastise the farmers and the garrison, he had them flogged, he had troops billeted with them, he had their houses burned, he forced people he didn't trust to move closer to the Lodge, just to persuade them to say where Dubertin was hiding. And there were those like Jan the Swede and Hans Pigt who admitted under the scourge that they had given the man food and shelter, and helped him to the next house. Others fled into the bushes at Steen's approach, even if it meant that their farms would be burned down behind them. Only at the distillery at Black River Mouth Lamotius never made enquiries, because those people had given their word to him personally. But it was in Daniel's house that the farmers schemed for eight months how they would move the lieutenant from one hiding place to another, with a slave to guide him. In Daniel's house Dubertin spent the last fourteen days eating and sleeping, and from there Daniel took him to an English ship, thankful to be rid of the vain, vociferous braggart.

Lamotius asked Daniel: 'You too, Daniel? You gave me your word. I have always been honest with you.'

'That is why, commander. So that you will not get blood on your hands.'

After that the matter cooled off. People were still fined, as it became known that they, too, had helped Dubertin, but slowly the matter subsided into silence. And poor Lamotius lost all the respect of the free burghers and his garrison in those eight months, and he became thin, and bitter. At the same time his head woodcutter Steen turned into a frustrated tyrant feared by the people, and his first clerk Jacob Ovaer did the same in a more underhand manner.

The affair of the French lieutenant lent Daniel a certain esteem on the island. It became customary, when someone wanted to undertake something, to say: 'Have you spoken to Daan Zaaijman about it?' People turned up to ask his advice. Even officials, about matters like standing surety, about lending and renting and divorcing and faring, and Batavia, and the Cape, and recalcitrant children, and livestock. He knew the island's coastline with all the gaps in the reef and the small bays behind, and he knew where in the ravines the rarer kinds of wood could be found. He was successful in agriculture, he knew about planting and harvesting manioc and pineapples, and his young palm trees flourished. Perhaps it was because of his blessings, the visible signs of his success and happiness, that people brought their problems to him.

But it took hard work, and it certainly wasn't always with all sail, full and by. Especially after that period of unrest there were other setbacks, like when the bottoms of both their stills burned through just when they were beginning to distil arrack of the finest quality. Lamotius commandeered old Noordoos's still for their use, and dispatched the broken ones to Ceylon on the first ship, which was *Spaarpot*. Noordoos didn't forgive them for that, and demanded heavy compensation, which was of course refused. From Ceylon the stills went to the Cape on *Silverstein*, and from the Cape back to Mauritius on *Westerwijk*, but at Madagascar the ship was taken by pirates and their two stills were never seen again. For more than two years they had to make do with the single old-fashioned still, and Noordoos's curses over their heads.

It was a dry time, the driest he could remember in the eleven years since Pieternel had come to the island. Mauritius was becoming parched. The cattle were thin, the Black River ran lower and lower, even their swimming hole became shallow and green with slime. Wild buck came to graze in their garden at night, and there were barely enough vegetables for their own use and next to nothing to sell to ships. In that dry period he seldom went far away from his house; there was too much that required his attention. From the hunter or the quartermaster who came to collect their arrack, he and Pieternel did receive news from beyond the mountain. For example, that the burghers of the plain were commandeered to help build a bridge with heavy ironwork just above the waterfall in the South-East River, and that Aunt Theuntje had married old Hein Karseboom, and that old Maijke had died and left nothing but a bag of rags. On her deathbed she had disinherited her children.

They also heard about the world beyond the sea. Once or twice a year there was a ship at the Molucca Anchorage with news from Europe or India. There came a long letter from Sara van Brakel, Barbara Geens's daughter. Her mother had passed away; on her deathbed she had asked her to send word to them and to inform them about the village of Stellenbosch, in case they might wish to move there. It was a pleasant climate, the soil was fertile and good for vineyards and wheat. Slaves were hard to come by, but Hottentots were prepared to work in the vineyards, or tend sheep and reap wheat for some tobacco and clothes. So life was quite cheap and people were prospering. Some thought that the Cape was paradise, all that was still missing was a devil. Her mother had left money to her slave to be manumitted, and he himself was now farming on his own. A hundred or more French refugees had been settled in the outer district, poor but hard-working people. The district had its own *landdrost* who governed in conjunction with the *heemraden*. Every October there was a fair in the village, most convivial. It coincided with the call-up of burghers for military training, and lasted for a full week; the governor came from the Cape to attend. Long Piet van der Byl got married here this year to Annie Bosch; his farm was called Babylons Toren. Both his parents were still alive. Soon after her mother's death her own youngest was born – another little redhead, it looked like a bunch of red flowers. They called her Barbara, after her grandmother.

In those days of unrest, the old inhabitants said that Mauritius was no longer the place they had come to know. Perhaps the Cape was now the better place, where one could find assistance more readily. This drought was the main cause, and then the diseases for which they had no medicine and no doctor, and no pastor to bury you, just as there was nobody to baptise you or marry you. In those two years twelve free burghers fled elsewhere on ships. Daniel believed that it was the drought that disheartened them. The people had to be patient and have faith; he remembered the Mauritius of earlier years as a wonderfully green and pleasant place.

They arranged with their neighbours to have a festive evening the last night of the old year, with a huge bonfire on the beach. The air was close, windless, hot. He and Pieternel had almost forgotten what it meant when their slave woman Anna disappeared, but later remembered the previous occasion, seven years before: there had been a hurricane brewing, and Anna had gone off into the forest without a word. He hesitated, then sent word to Jaap that the weather showed signs of a hurricane, and sent out two men to look for Anna. Then he began to batten up, hammering shutters fast, and anchoring his outbuildings and the roof of his house with ropes to tree roots and tent pegs. His new boat was dragged out on rollers to higher ground far from the river, turned over and tied to the rollers, and its mast, sail and rigging taken home. They hurried to get everything ready: storing fresh water, salted meat and rice in vats, secured linen, porcelain, salt and powder together with their few books in barrels, and covered everything with tarpaulins.

Two days after Anna's disappearance, on the last day of 1689, the sunset lay red as blood from horizon to horizon, the sea was stained red, and a lukewarm wind came whispering from the north-east. Then they brought in the last food from the yard, the fresh milk and drinking water, and a coop of poultry, called the slaves inside and let their stock out of the kraal. They all came together in the big room. While the rain thrashed down harder and harder on house and yard and thunderbolts incessantly cracked overhead, the children, their own and those of the slaves, lay on a bed under the table, with the boat's sail drawn over like a tent. By that time the wind was exceedingly strong; towards midnight it was the full hurricane. In the flickering light of oilwicks they waited, staring at one another, wide awake from worry and the great noise, and the tugging of the storm at their house. It was wreaking havoc in the jungle; in the palm forest it thundered like a waterfall, with sharp cracks where trunks snapped. At times Daniel thought he could hear cattle lowing, and wished he could go outside to tend them.

In the pre-dawn the noise began to abate, and when soon after daybreak the eye of the storm passed over the island's west coast and the sun rose in a calm sky, they went outside to look. The river had broken its banks and was rumbling past the house to the sea, filled with driftwood and mud. There were injured cattle among the fallen trees; one lay under a tree trunk with two broken forelegs. Daniel cut this one's throat on the spot and anchored the carcass to a tree to be skinned later. He told his people to eat and drink, as the quiet would not last long. Pieternel lit a fire in the hearth and boiled milk for the children. With the help of the slaves he tightened the anchors of the house, shored up a ground wall around it against the water, and dug trenches to the river. Less than three-quarters of an hour later the wind came gusting back from the opposite direction, with a deep roar; soon after it grabbed the house by its four corners with a loud scream and shook it as if to tear it from the ground, mowing away on all sides through the groaning forest. They could feel the earth underneath shudder and tremble. The wind tore shutters from their wall, opening at first only the smallest cracks in the roof, then forced them wider to strain itself inside. Through these openings rain blew in, until their floors were flooded. For six hours the wind continued to shake the house and tug at it, causing roof beams, door jambs and window frames to break from the plaster.

When the hurricane was over, their small farm was destroyed. The river looked like a muddy jumble of trunks and branches streaming rapidly past to the sea. In bright sunshine he and Jaap Baldyn met on the river bank, offered mutual help, enquired if their people were safe. Thank God they had built of stone. Around them, fragments of their outbuildings lay strewn about among broken and blown-down trees in the mud. To all sides the bare trunks of palm trees, broken or partly broken, had been torn from the ground. The whole forest had been pushed over at an angle towards the mountain, where the wind had passed, and the earth was littered with branches and leaves. They made food, and dragged animal carcasses to the river to be washed away down to the sea. They rigged up lines to dry their linen, clothes and canvas. Every piece of canvas they could find was stretched over the roofs and tied down with cable thread. Daniel had to tell Pieternel that all her milking cows had disappeared. And he went to inspect the scene at the river mouth, his musket under his arm in case he came across living animals out of reach. On either side of the mouth was a man-high pile of wood, flung ashore as if a large fleet had been stranded there, mostly old trees from the mountains among which he noticed good ebony, which could be dragged out later. Among those branches and trunks, buried in mud, were dead deer, dodos, pigeons, tortoises and some of his cattle. It would be best to stack a pyre there on the beach for the carcasses, otherwise they would be smelling for weeks. The whole inner water was dark brown from mountain soil, and over the reef the disturbed water was still foaming white, high, turbulent.

On the second day their slave woman returned, speechless, dazed with fright, but unharmed. And for weeks they worked on cleaning the yard, clearing away mud, bringing wood from the beach and chopping it up, built walls, repaired the roof, dug the garden, put coconuts in the earth, scoured the mountain for Pieternel's cattle, of which only three were found. Everything had to be started over. Do you remember, Pieternel?

Just six weeks after the hurricane warm air from the north-east unnerved them again. When Pieternella mentioned that Anna had gone off once more, without a word, Daniel went to the forest to pray. On 9 February the second hurricane moved in over the island from the north-west: once more the pitch-black night, the thunderclaps and lightning flashes, the fearsome wind stripping branches from the last palm trees; once more a day and a night of torrential rain as if it was poured down from buckets. Every indentation became a dam, every ditch a stream, and the river ran deep and brown and wide among their houses. No outbuildings, fences or kraals remained standing, even their ruins were buried under mud. Their new vegetable garden, sugar, tobacco, Pieternel's flowers and herbs, everything had been washed away with the topsoil to the sea. The distillery had been torn from the ground, the old still with head and coil lay totally shattered under a pile of bricks. The coastal plain to the south towards Pieter Both's Kop was bare, and a broad line of flotsam indicated that the sea had turned a hundred feet above its usual high-water mark. Beyond the yard, a few cattle had to be slaughtered. In six weeks everything had been destroyed which had taken them years to build; it was all gone, off to the sea. But their people were safe, except for poor Anna. He had arranged with Jaap that they would make tents from canvas and palm fronds, and gather their families and dependants and all their food together. As soon as he could get away, he would go to report at the Lodge.

The Sadelberg glistened with waterfalls as Daniel sailed through the South-Eastern Gap, but at his feet was an unknown, devastated land-scape. The whole tract from Breakers Point past the Lodge, through the small farms of Lemoenbos and round the bay to the Chalk lay in complete silence under a bright sun, and it was only when he approached to hook the head-rope of his boat around the only quay pole left in front of the Lodge, that he could see the terrible damage there. It was like a battlefield. It resembled his own place at the other end of the island.

Lamotius invited him inside, like a sailor: 'Come on board, Daniel.' It was good, it made him feel at home. Like a sailor after a shipwreck, with his cloth cap, bare feet and salt-hardened clothes, after half a night and a day at sea. The commander was obviously exhausted too; his face revealed a weariness and worry heavier than the weight of his years. It was a weariness of the spirit as much as of the body, because it was his island. 'Tell me what happened at your place. Are your people safe?'

Daniel thanked him. They were safe except for Anna who hadn't returned. What about the Lodge?

Lamotius gestured wearily. Here the west wind had driven the sea right into the Lodge, two flood tides without an ebb in between. The Company's books had been lost, washed away, carried off by mud. Everything in the warehouse was spoiled. Their gardens were gone, and what wasn't gone was ruined by the salt water. Bodies from the graveyard had been washed to the sea, and the cattle as well. The sloop *Europa* had been carried ashore by the first hurricane, battered to pieces by the second, totally wrecked. On the Noordwyks Vlak fourteen thousand vines had been washed away. All the houses at the post were down.

'As the books are also gone, Daniel, I don't know how much credit you people have. I have nothing on record about the coming and going of people or ships over the last year. I don't know what was in the shed. The directors have been planning to close down this outpost for a long time. For the sake of the sawmill I kept on pleading. Now I don't know what to tell the Lords.'

'We shall rise again, commander. We'll open a new book, at the first page. The fellows at Lemoenbos and Noordwyks Vlak, they are eager to farm.'

'I believe it, I have seen it myself. You regard Mauritius as your home, your fatherland. But I feel we should now close down and go home. I want to get away from here now. Everything I had, I've lost here. But what do you want, Daniel? I have nothing to give you.'

'There's some good ebony at our river mouth, and I suppose at other mouths on the west side too, and throughout the inner water around the island. All that needs to be done is to collect it before it sinks to the bottom. It's a few weeks' work for the woodcutters with *Vanger*. As for me, without a still I cannot distil. Jaap and I want permission to go to North-West Harbour, and try to make a living there.'

It was as if the commander wished to say: Why do you still try? But his words were: 'Even our journal has gone to sea. Now nobody will know of the trouble we have taken over this last year.'

'What about the annual return fleet which will be to the north of the island at this time of the year, commander? I thought those *oorlammers* might need us. I reckon we must be ready to help them. That is why we started this outpost at the time, after *Aernhem* and the others.'

'Permission to move I can give you. Food and clothing I do not have.'

'As much rope as possible then, commander. And a few cows and a bull.'

When Daniel came home with the news that they could move to North-West Harbour, the huge pyre on the beach was not yet burned out. Jaap's slaves had found Anna's body among the rubble in the river mouth. Daniel unpacked what he had found: sweet potatoes, pumpkin and cabbage, a bit of salt, arrack and tobacco, two barrels of old rope, a few bolts of narrow canvas for clothes, a dog. That was all, for them and his slaves. But there were fish in the sea to live on until they were settled again in the north. There was no longer any reason to exert themselves at Black River Mouth, with the still and all the palm trees gone. Baldyn and his wife were ready to move, Pieternella was looking forward to the new home. That same day they began to carry the best timber from the old houses down to the boat, to sail north with.

On the north side of the bay at North-West Harbour a small river ran down a slope into the sea. And there, well above the flood mark, they levelled the ground, made frames for houses from timber and palm leaf, built, dug gardens and irrigation ditches. The houses, on the incline above the sea, had a good view towards the reef. In the mouth of the bay was a long low island with the stumps of palm trees. The day Daniel brought his wife and children with the last of their household possessions from the old place, he drew Pieternel's attention to it.

'Here I can stock everything a sea captain may need.' He pointed out the peaks and heights of the jagged mountains forming a wall around the bay, and told her their names. 'That is the Thumb. There is the Lookout. If you climb up there, you can see Cobbler's Last in the north, far beyond Endless Bay in the sea.' In the small cove at the river mouth he said: 'Here we'll stay.' And that was how it was; they remained there to the end. Of all his abodes on the island it was the one where they lived the longest and where he enjoyed the most pleasure and success. Pieternel was happy there, even though during the last three years or so she was afraid of being there alone.

Once or twice she wanted to visit the Lodge. There were people whom she hadn't seen in years. Sometimes she would say: Why am I suddenly thinking of Aunt Theuntje, she must be talking of me now. And when Daniel brought her the commander's promise of cattle, she asked whether both of them could go, so that she could select the cows herself. She said she would enjoy bringing the cattle up from the Lodge, and he agreed: Good, let us do it. I'll choose a good day.

When the houses were up, they left their children in the care of Jaap and his wife to go to the Lodge. From North-West Harbour they sailed south inside the reef, without hurry. In the clear water below their boat were fish, coloured coral, sea turtles, sometimes a small herd of dugong. Half buried under sand in the shallow water of the Plaat giant clams lay with their shells open, waiting for food, while little fishes swam in and out of them. Pieternel already knew the shell, like two giant dishes with sharp edges locking into one another. He told her what people said: that one could lose a foot or a hand if the thing grabbed you. From Pieter Both's Kop it became late; they were already in the shadow of the mountain, and he wanted to get past Klimopsberg, so that they could spend the night at Vermaaklikheidskiel. He wanted to hear what she would say about that place, his favourite spot, and to his own mind more pleasant even than Kroonenburg. So he made sail and moved further away from land where the wind was stronger.

They were still in time, the sun was not yet down when they entered the river mouth at Vermaaklikheidskiel. There was time to spread their bedding on a groundsheet at the waterfall, catch an eel and clean it, and sit beside their fire watching the red sun sink behind the trees to their right while a golden full moon rose from the sea on the left, both in the sky at the same time. Before them, across the river, was a small yellow beach in front of the dark green forest. There was no sound from the sea on the reef, no sound from the forest, only the water cascading down the wall of rocks behind them. And while they sat there, a deer came from the forest to drink from the river.

He wanted to know what she thought of the place.

'Sven told me it was here that he'd seen the mermaid on the sand. He was already married then.'

'Poor man.'

'Why do you say that? He told me about all the beautiful places. I used to think you would show me one day. It's ten years already, perhaps I should have gone with him.'

'I'll show you myself. Come, let us swim here before it gets dark. Then I'll show you the mermaid.'

From South-East Harbour they walked home with four milking cows and a bullock. It took them four and a half days. Daniel turned aside to look at the ruin of the sawmill, to see if it could be rebuilt, but it was too dilapidated. At the Lemoenbos farms they went to greet friends they hadn't seen in years, and from there crossed the island in a north-westerly direction with the round peak of Kompasberg to guide them. At times they were drenched by showers and then got dry again. At night they tied the cattle to trees, with thongs around their horns. The footpath was well established and as the ground slowly rose towards the middle of the island, there were places from where they could look back, and looking between two hills, they could see the whole of South-East Harbour and Sadelberg far in the distance. Pieternel became more withdrawn as they went on. Tired, he thought. When they reached Kompasberg in the middle of the island, Daniel showed her the Noordwyks Vlak, and the islands of Kroonenburg to the east. Sven had told her about those too. She seemed to be haunted by Sven, ten years after he'd been buried, he thought to himself. What could the good-for-nothing have been to her?

Natte Bos was veiled in mist when they moved through it, and water was dripping from the grey moss hanging from the trees like beard. The earth was bare and rocky; she could see for herself why people came here so seldom. Once they reached the other side, Daniel tied up the cattle so that they could first climb the hill of Bokgat to look into it. The unexpected sight of the steep green well at her feet made her gasp. And when she turned round, and saw in the west the slender black spires of the Three Teats, rearing up from the empty plains, she was speechless.

'No, I don't know either how they came to be like that. The hill over there is the Guardhouse or Corps de Garde, as the soldiers call it. It guards the pass to North-West Harbour. That is where we must go through.'

After travelling for two more days they went through a narrow kloof in the ring of steep mountains which, like the broken edge of a large cauldron, formed a wall behind their bay, and then they could see the whole plain and bay of North-West Harbour below. There was only one big river to cross, an enormous gash in the earth, where it took a mighty effort to get the cattle through.

The long journey had worn Pieternel out. She slept a lot, and for a long time afterwards remained quiet and without energy. When the quartermaster arrived a few days after them, with their boat carrying all their purchases, she had hardly put a foot out of the door yet. Perhaps she had overdone it, Daniel thought, without questioning her about it. She had wanted to see their island, the things Sven had told her about, so now she'd got what she wanted. Not what Sven had impressed on her mind? He didn't ask whether she'd enjoyed it. It was the island. Now she had measured it with her feet, hopefully learning something about herself.

Berg China, one of the Company's biggest and finest, came from the sea, weather-beaten, low in the water and with only a stub of its fore-mast still upright, and fired a gun behind Cooper's Island to call for help. Since the two hurricanes they had wandered about the ocean for a full month, pumping and sinking. Its rudder was gone, and the entire, large, decorated stern piece had been broken loose and was hanging like a door from its hinges. Daniel helped them to enter, and showed them where the ship could reach the shore on a high tide, and where they could pitch their tents beside the river. The ship was beached stern first at full tide and heaved higher on rollers with multiple blocks and tackle at the next, but it was difficult as the sand was loose and the ship heavy. A large part of the cargo was offloaded there, and on the next high it was pulled up a few more yards. Afterwards Daniel took the captain and some of the passengers, among them a few ladies, to the Lodge in his boat.

For eight months it was like a town at Cooper's Island, what with the smoke going up and the banging of caulking mallets and people bustling about. A sailor with a telescope and his rations climbed up to the Lookout every morning to watch the horizon and light a stack of firewood should he notice a ship, so that they could get a message off to Batavia or the Cape. Sailing sloops with labourers, and implements and white-collared councillors came and went between the Lodge and *Berg China*. The whole crew was lodged in tents on shore; the ship's cook set up his cooking place on Cooper's Island. The cargo was removed down to the bottom boards and stowed under canvas on the island. Bales of cotton and linen that had become wet, were carried to the river, washed, and dried on lines between the trees. Bales of cinnamon were shaken out on canvas and raked open in the hot sun to dry. But the sea surrounding the island remained empty, and no signal was made from the Lookout.

Daniel and Pieternel earned well from lodging, cooperage, woodcutting, fishing, hunting, milk and butter, and he discovered exactly how remunerative the provisioning of ships could be. He bought one female and two male slaves from passengers who had intended to sell them at the Cape. With the slaves he walked to Noordwyks Vlak, returning with a few barrels of tobacco, to sell to the sailors. Captain Hoffe and his two mates lodged with Daniel, and all the other officers with Jaap Baldyn.

Someone he met there was the gentleman Samuel Elsevier, who was on his way to the Cape to become *secundus*. He stayed mostly at the Lodge, but sometimes he, or both he and Lamotius, came to see what progress was being made with the ship, and then they lodged with Daniel. The *secundus* was a pleasant gentleman, well disposed towards high and low. He questioned Pieternel about the Cape where he was going, about its agriculture and the Hottentots, because from everybody there she had lived at the Cape the longest. Lamotius became a friend of the *secundus*; they called one another by their first names. In Daniel's presence Elsevier promised that when he reached the Cape he would try to get Lamotius transferred to the East. And Daniel tried as well as he could always to present their island in a positive light, so that the Lords would think twice before closing it down.

On 10 November he piloted *Berg China* out. The previous day two prisoners had been brought from the Lodge, to be taken to the Cape for trial. One was Esther of old Noordoos, who had committed adultery with the slave. The other was Hester of Pieter van Nimwegen, who had been married to Adam Cornelisz, because she and her sister had attempted to poison her husband. And unexpectedly there was an ugly quarrel between Captain Hoffe and Commander Lamotius, because Hoffe refused to accept the box with seedlings of twenty different indigenous trees which Lamotius had hoped to send to the Cape. He had no water to waste, Hoffe said. Lamotius stood with his fists on his hips, saying: 'This is how you bastards try to ruin us here. After all the help we gave you.' And *Secundus* Elsevier could not help him, because the captain's word was law on board.

At last, two years after the hurricanes, Lamotius's successor arrived on the hooker *Duiff*. He was Roelof Diodati; who was to become Daniel's son-in-law. He stood there solemnly in his black suit on the grassy square in front of the Lodge, listening to Lamotius reading his letter of appointment in public to the garrison and the people. When Lamotius had done, Diodati brought a letter from Governor van der Stel from his pocket, and ordered the garrison to arrest Lamotius and Steen and Ovaer and send them on board as prisoners, to be tried in the East. And all of that, because of Aletha Uijtenbogaert's delicate body, that fatal woman's part which can sometimes destroy a good man. Just because her clothes had been loaded on the wrong ship years before. Do you remember, Pieternel?

In that year of Diodati's arrival their second son was born. The previous one was Pieter, named after her father. This one was Daniel, an attractive boy who clearly took after his mother, and quite dark of skin. Wouldn't the boy become a sailor one day? A skipper, perhaps. There were parts beyond the East where no one had been yet. He would feel very proud if his son were to develop a liking for the sea.

This Diodati sometimes gave Daniel the impression of being two-faced. He came to North-West Harbour on his first inspection, and Daniel didn't like the way he was looking at Catharina. On the first visit he told Daniel that the Lords were expecting two hundred cuts of the very best ebony from him per year. These cuts were in great demand in Europe. He had heard that Daniel knew the island. Well, where and how? Daniel answered: There are murderers in the forest and the boats are rotten. He trusted that the runaway slaves in the forest would be brought under control. The forty-foot boat which Borms had built was drying out without tar at the French Church, and *Vanger*, the Lodge's right hand, was also leaking, he heard. Then Diodati had second thoughts; he had not approached the old fellow in the right way. He said that he had seen lists of all the island's plants, birds, animals, fishes and things compiled by Lamotius, who also wrote that he'd had Daniel's help with the lists. There was a vacancy for a master woodcutter at the moment, and if Daniel was interested in the post, it could be arranged.

'What do I look like to you, sir?' he replied.

When there were no ships, Daniel preferred to be alone on Cooper's Island, but Diodati came to distract his attention from his work. True, he did occasionally come with an order, but he might just as well have sent a note. Then Diodati would come and sit down there, and say that he'd read wrongly, it wasn't two hundred cuts of ebony but twelve hundred. What did it matter? asked Daniel. They never sent a ship to fetch it. Somebody at the Cape was trying to sink this island, he'd been sensing it for a long time.

He couldn't tell for sure whether Diodati was coming to visit his daughter or perhaps Jaap Baldyn, but at any rate it wasn't him. Diodati and Baldyn came from the same region below the Alps. They spoke the same language, loved olive oil, loved singing in their language, and were as companionable as cousins. It was a pity that Baldyn's daughters weren't older, then Diodati could have paid court there. Pieternel had previously encouraged Catharina to invite young men to take her for walks along the beach when her father fell quiet and put away his sharp tools; she had to watch out for the signs.

Daniel disliked the idea of having a commander as a son-in-law, but

Catharina was soon infatuated with the fellow and Pieternel had approved him without much ado. As for him, this courtship of his daughter might turn him into a grandfather, and he resented any man who interfered with his life. In due course that was how he would feel about all his sons-in-law. They came here to make him old.

Then Diodati would recount, when they were still seated at table after the meal with Spanish wine he'd brought from the Lodge, that he'd been clerk of the court when Esther van Ewijk had been sentenced at the Cape to be thrown into the slave lodge for five years. The thought was, if she wished to couple with slaves, let her. And by day she could labour with the slave women in the service of the Lords.

'It may be just,' Daniel said, 'but is it prudent? She's been locked up here for so long, she may have changed her mind.'

No, it was setting an example that was important, Diodati reminded him; it was intended for others to learn from it.

Daniel thought: Dear Lord, save my poor children.

For two years no Company ship visited the island, but Daniel constantly remained in readiness for Englishmen, who stopped over twice or thrice a year at North-West Harbour. They spread his name in India, outward- and homeward-bound seamen all knew about him, and they called his place Cooper's Island in English.

For Catharina's wedding they sailed to the Lodge. The boat was bedecked with palm boughs and plaited greenery and a large prince's flag, and they were welcomed with a gunshot as they rounded the corner of Fisherman's Isle and came in sight of the Lodge. All his old friends were there, fellow free burghers, with their wives and families; people he seldom saw, some of them quite grey by now, like Hein Karseboom and Theuntje, and old Noordoos, bent and embarrassed by his daughter's disgrace. There were several young people of whom he had no idea who they belonged to. Daniel invited them all to seat themselves at the guest tables. The officials and tradesmen, the garrison and the slaves had been accorded half a Happy Day too, because their commander was getting married, and Daniel spoke to their foremen and paid for everybody to be served food and wine.

Halfway through the festivities a dilapidated yawl entered through the sea gap, strange of line with its bow curling backwards, making straight for the Lodge where the smoke of the cooking fires and the flags and banners stirred slightly in the breeze. At the quay their patched sail was lowered, and there the guard awaited the crew and brought them to the commander's table.

They approached hat in hand, seven scarecrows. They were French. Diodati spoke to them, fast and annoyed: what did they want? Daniel understood enough of the language. They were Huguenots, from Diego Rodriguez Island in the north-east. They were on their way to Île de Bourbon, and had been at sea for almost a month in the open boat. Irritable, Diodati motioned them out of the way: Go and wait at your boat until we have finished. But Daniel didn't like it; he fetched the people and brought them to the tables. 'Sit down, messieurs, or stand if you suffer from tailors' bottom. I am Daniel Zaaijman of Mauritius. My daughter Catharien is getting married today.' He had wine poured for them, raised his glass to them, and welcomed them: 'Eat and drink with us.'

The leader was François Leguat; he sat down on the bench beside Daniel and told him of their tribulations. Commander Diodati looked unhappy about it. He spoke little, and glowered at the guests. And afterwards Daniel learned that Diodati was disgruntled because he had allegedly acted as if he were in charge of the island, and that might be the reason why Diodati subsequently treated those French so scurvily. He accused them of being spies, and kept them prisoners for three years of their lives on Tobacco Island in all kinds of weather, in sight of the Lodge, as if he challenged anyone to offer them help. Daniel found it hard to remember to call Diodati by his first name, and occasionally still called him sir, as before.

But in the ten years that Diodati had the command, Daniel became used to him, and he was glad to see that his daughter was happy. No commander of Mauritius smiled readily or for long.

And in all that time it happened very rarely that a ship of the Company visited the island.

At North-West Harbour they were completely isolated, cut off from the problems of administration, and things happened at South-East

Harbour of which they had no inkling, and which later frightened them at the thought that their own daughter also lived in the Lodge. Like when fifteen of the staff died of dysentery in the drought of '94. But there was worse. Catharina was pregnant with her first, like poor Mrs Lamotius long before, when three slaves took an oath to murder all the whites on the island and set fire to the Lodge, warehouses and stables at different places, so that the houses, offices, the Company's books, the small supply of food, the sawn timber, the workshops with precious tools were once again destroyed by fire. The powder magazine exploded with a bang that swept away whatever was still standing, but by that time the people had fortunately fled. Their daughter Catharina was miraculously unscathed, and the arsonists were tortured to death in the presence of the Company's slaves. But all this they only learned at North-West Harbour eight days later.

Other experiences concerned the island as a whole, like the terrifying hurricane lasting two days in February 1695, when once again their cattle and sugar were washed away to the sea, and the last remains of Commander Lamotius's wonderful sawmill were swept along. Weeks later Daniel made exceptionally good earnings from the English ships damaged in that hurricane. In September a flute came from Batavia, carrying on it a person who brought news of the unwinding of Lamotius's trial. The fiscal there asked for the supreme penalty by decapitation for his maltreatment of the French lieutenant, of Hans Pigt, Jan the Swede and others, but the Council of Justice had mercy on him, sentencing him to scourging and six years of hard labour in chains in the Company's salt mines in Rosingain. Pieternel cried when she heard it. Poor Margarethe, she said. Had she still been alive, this would never have happened. But how could she be sure? Aletha had also been a particularly attractive woman, do you remember?

Down at Black River Mouth new families moved in to farm and possibly earn something from the ships. Gert van Ewijk was there, now without any relatives at all, and Jan Retson, or John Richardson, the Englishman who had married the late Hans Pigt's daughter, and Jan and Aaltje Lodewijks with their children. And when Daniel's third daughter, Eva, later married Herbert van Schoonhoven, they also went to live there. It didn't bother Daniel that others were also making money out of the ships; there was enough for everybody, and he was glad that more people had come to live on the western side of the island, as there were more and more murderous blacks in the forest who didn't give a damn for a human life.

Nor did the threat come only from blacks. In '97 a number of convicts were banished from the Cape, among them Sergeants Haan and Pieters, two former judicial officers of the Company who had abandoned their sacred oath and lived off crime; Jean du Seine, a consummate blasphemer and scoundrel; a Dutch deserter known as Smous; and Jantje of Batavia, a young slave of sixteen who had long slept with a Christian girl at Stellenbosch. They had barely been incarcerated in the prison behind the Lodge, when the first four broke out, stole *Vanger* from its anchor and went off to sea. Their planned destination was Île de Bourbon. They first had to steal food and weapons from the farmhouses. For that reason they entered the Black River Mouth, where they scared the people in their houses for a few days, before somebody could escape to raise the alarm. Armed and with dogs, the farmers from North-West Harbour sailed up the river mouth in Daniel's boat, tied a rope to *Vanger* and pulled it out, and then pursued the convicts on foot.

They were shrewd enough, those convicts, to disperse and meet again after a set number of days, because every time the refugees dispersed the pursuers had to do the same. It meant days and days of pursuit with dogs through the mountains, but at last news began to filter through that one had been caught at Lemoenbos, another in the smithy on the Vlak where he'd nearly severed his hand with a chisel in an attempt to cut off his manacles, while the third was shot by a farmer's wife on Noordoos's old property on the Geerlofs River. In that time Pieternel was alone at home with the children, and pregnant again, and Daniel could do no more than give her a gun in the hand and go off to the forest with his slaves and dogs. It was in times like those that the distance from the Lodge was a worry to him.

Just after the escapade with the convicts Diodati told him that he'd asked for a transfer. He had to go to the East, where an official could make a proper career. Daniel asked him whether he was now beginning to understand Lamotius's problems, but he refused to admit it. He said that he felt he was labouring against death. The island was declining, the climate was impossible, there was no longer game in the woods or fish in the sea, and runaways were becoming a danger to the settlers. Previously everything was easy and abundant. Can't you see, Daniel asked him, that it is a good and fertile island? We free burghers can make a living here, but the Company must leave the trade to us. Let us hunt the game, catch the fish, distil the arrack, cut and sell the wood for our own account. Leave it to us to haul the runaways from the forest. Let us trade with Ceylon and the Cape with our own ships. We don't need anything from the Company here. Arrange it this way. Make your Lodge close down, and save your Company the money.

'It cannot happen, because you are Dutch citizens. The Company is the only Dutch concern that has the right to trade in this ocean.'

'We needn't be Dutch. We are citizens of Mauritius and that is enough for me.'

'That is sedition, Father-in-law.'

'Yes. And here is more of the same: the Cape government is stifling our hard work, and they're making a mockery of you. Look at you: every morning you have the flag hoisted and the trumpet sounded, and you have wood cut and throw people into the sea, but the Cape thinks so little of you that there aren't even ships coming here any more. These days it's the English who keep our island going. Does the Cape still read your letters?'

'Father-in-law, I must add this, that the Cape has sent word, but I kept it a secret because I am sorry for you people: the lighter carrying your samples – you will remember, the tobacco, salted meat and cane arrack in your special barrel, your soap, sugar, butter, white sugar, brown sugar, everything you'd built your hopes on – capsized on the anchorage in Table Bay.'

Daniel could do nothing but laugh, but it really wasn't funny. 'Shall we try again, commander? There is no other way out. I know Mauritius as a good island. What it had offered Pieternel and me, it can offer my children too. Nature is merciless, but so is every sea captain. So it is on the sea.'

Daniel saw his blessings increase. Jan Bocklenberg came to visit them, the young chief surgeon who had been sent out, and a real doctor too, not a surgeon. He was the son of a German wine farmer and knew something about distilling brandy, and occasionally he would spend a few nights with them when Daniel was distilling cane arrack. He had his eye on their Magdalena. He and the girl did nothing to hide it, and he was most welcome in their home, as they liked his disposition. Daniel thought: We already have a commander, a doctor and a farmer in the family. Can it not be destined for Eva, my youngest little one, to take a sailor? It never occurred to him to think of Pieternel's hand in the education of her daughters; he believed that everything in his house was exactly as it should be. The day Magdalena and Doctor Jan were married, Daniel sat on a bench under a palm tree, trying to count his blessings on his fingers. A good wife, healthy children, progress in his work, a second daughter in the Lodge, slaves, livestock, plantation, a good boat, gardens – he did not have enough fingers on his hands.

He hadn't added his common sense, but it was a gift that many envied him. He could see a hurricane coming, from the clean, bright appearance of the summit of the Thumb the previous daybreak, and from the behaviour of insects and birds, when others had to wait for a line of scarlet clouds like a bleeding vein on the horizon, that final daybreak or sunset, before they could be sure. By that time Daniel's stock had already been taken to a kraal on high ground, his boat was hauled up and secured on open ground, his house tied to the earth and his shutters battened down. Even so, like others, he would suffer huge damage in the form of sugar cane too young to cut, and his young vegetables in the ground. There was, for instance, that four-day hurricane in '98, when he had been prepared to the utmost. On that occasion the Company's garden on Noordwyks Vlak was hit hard: the entire harvest of sweet potatoes – the next year's staple food – was washed from the ground, the long palisade of fourteen thousand stakes was blown away, the houses stood up to their window sills in water. And after the hurricane there was a month-long plague of rats in the green shoots and buds of trees and plants which had mercifully survived and started sprouting again.

But as the sailor's proverb has it: *It's an ill wind indeed that blows no good for seaman, farmer, miller or washerwoman*, and in spite of his losses on land, Daniel had also acquired a rich son-in-law, as after that terrible storm Herbert and Eva found a solid block of ambergris weighing forty pounds on the beach. On the Company's books it was worth ten thousand guilders, and the Company could resell it for seven, eight times the price in Europe. Poor, honest Herbert handed it in to Diodati, who sent it to the Cape, and he and Eva began to wait for the Company's rich reward.

The next they heard, was that a new governor had been appointed over them. It was yet another van der Stel, the old one's son. This Willem Adriaan had no regard for people's feelings; he wrote frankly to Diodati: Do not send me any more of your soap and tobacco. We receive enough of everything from Holland, and the Company will not change its existing contracts.

'Can you see, commander? Do you remember what I said? Here the two-faced lot are showing their hand. Tell me what you read in those words?'

'Even if our products were cheaper and of better quality than those from Holland, the Cape will not market it for us.'

'Exactly. Because the Cape officials get a commission on those Dutch contracts. Will they admit it? No, commander, I'm just a lout who never wore out a school desk, but here in my house *Secundus* Elsevier explained it to me with the words "unwanted interference". They want to stifle the humble efforts of our peasants to their own advantage.'

'I don't know what to say, Father-in-law.'

'Don't say anything. Let me talk. From now on it's every man for himself. Do what you have to do for your Company and your people, and I'll do the same for me and mine.'

New settlers moved in at North-West Harbour. From his workplace on Cooper's Island Daniel could see smoke curling up from cooking shelters behind as many as fifteen houses among the palm trees around the edge of the bay. To the great joy of Pieternel and the children

Theuntje and Hein Karseboom also came to live there, to grow sweet potatoes and vegetables for the neighbours, and for the English ships. It seemed at the time as if Diodati was giving up and no longer cared where his people moved in search of a living, and more and more it seemed as if free burghers preferred this western side. Down at South-East Harbour the Company pretended to cut wood, and elsewhere on the island the free burghers could send up their smoke and try to make a living. But he was prepared to live in peace with everybody as long as they granted him his.

Strange how fate can provide. Just after twelve families came to live at North-West Harbour and another four south of them at Black River Mouth, a pirate ship ran aground against Black Rock on the eastern side of the island.

Diodati sent a runner with a letter from the Lodge to ask that Daniel arm all the able-bodied men of his section, white and black, and lead them to the Lodge, because 170 pirates were stranded at Black Rock. Daniel carried the order from house to house, saying that he expected everybody between sixteen and sixty at his workplace on Cooper's Island before daybreak. There was no need for him to say anything about pirates and their habit of taking whatever they wanted without respecting age or sex; the people knew that well. Pirates were rubbish from West India, who were now making their appearance in these waters after the Spanish had gone bankrupt on the other side. East India and the Red Sea were their new hunting ground, and Hollanders, Muslims and English were their prey.

With twenty-five men, they left from Cooper's Island in two boats, and caught up with Jan Retsen's two boats with eighteen able-bodied men and a child south of Black River Mouth. And so they sailed in convoy round the underside of Pieter Both's Kop, to the Lodge, where the commander had the courtesy to welcome their flotilla with a volley. The people from Lemoenbos, and those from Noordwyks Vlak were already there, and sabres, powder and lead were distributed. Including the garrison, there were now ninety of them. In the council of war Daniel insisted that they shouldn't give the invaders any opportunity of making themselves comfortable. They'd now been there for three days, and the spies had reported that they were still struggling to move their possessions off the reef. Most of their powder would be useless. He proposed that they move against the strangers without delay and propose peace to them. If they refused, they should be exterminated, but if they were amenable, a treaty should be arranged and help given to get them away from there as soon as possible. In the meantime, they should all be alert and say their prayers. They could take a gift of arrack and tobacco; the strangers would be in need of it.

The unity among the people came as a surprise to Daniel, and he was glad to see his son-in-law buckling on a cutlass, to march out at their head, while they all knew that he was suffering from dysentery. They went inside together to take their leave of Catharina and her little boys, and there Diodati placed the Company's banner in Daniel's hand. Then they said goodbye to Magdalena, as Jan Bocklenberg, with his doctor's chest on a shoulder band, had to go with them.

At Devil's Point, as the Third Corner was called from then on, the pirates came towards them, holding empty hands outstretched. The skipper was John Bowen, his ship was *Speaking Trumpet*. They were powerless, he said, and had lost almost everything. Everybody could see that their ship was a wreck, there were no facilities to dry powder on shore and hardly a weapon in sight, and no ambush in the shrubs. Around the wreck floated a few rafts, and swimmers were working in the water with ropes. Diodati said to Bowen: pitch camp on the beach at the high-tide line, and there they might hammer a boat together, but they had to remain there. The farmers would bring meat, arrack, tobacco and fish for sale, but no vegetables or starch at all, and they had to keep away from people's homes and animals. If Bowen wanted to visit the Lodge, he had to do so on his own; should he want to bring company, he had to send a message an hour before. Everything else was a capital offence. And the man agreed to that.

So it became an opportunity for the farmers of Noordwyks Vlak and Lemoenbos to trade for three months, and earn a fair amount of hard silver and gold in their pockets, but those living on the west side made nothing out of the pirates, and moreover they had to take turns with the others, for a week at a time, to stand guard at the Lodge. In those days they turned the cannons at the Lodge round, two east and two west, and kept almost a thousand hand grenades loaded and ready.

In 1704 there were changes in Daniel's life which intimated to him that blessings were temporary and good times came to an end. He had expected it; for a long time already his grey hair had warned him about the cold breath of time in his neck, suggesting that he'd entered a more precarious passage. Their son Johannes was born at the beginning of that year, a slight, blond child with something of Sven Telleson in his looks – a pretty child who would later be the first on their side of the island to contract malaria. By the middle of the same year Diodati's release finally came, and he left with Catharina and their two sons for Batavia, where a good post awaited him. He had always been an ambitious man, and the East had ceaselessly called to him. Pieternel grieved for a long time, as Catharina was her eldest and she was uncommonly attached to the girl, but they had promised to write, every time there was an occasion. And then, in November, news came from the Lodge that Magdalena had died there of malaria. At the funeral all Jan Bocklenberg said to them was that he could not stay any longer, he had to get off Mauritius Island if he wanted their children to survive. And with the first ship he left for Batavia with their three little girls and their small son, barely one year old.

From that year, when Abraham Momber took over as commander, a searing drought came over the island. The mountains turned brown, and in due course the valleys too; old trees near the house withered and died, and drinking water for the Lodge had to be brought from the Black River by ox cart, until the tremendous twin waterfalls high in the Black River Gorges also dried up. There was barely any grazing left for their stock, and the deer came to the houses in search of food. One found them lying in the veld, dead and parched. Fish nearly disappeared from the inner water, and dugong and sea turtle were seen no more. Dead sea creatures from the reef washed up, like octopuses or shellfish. Daniel had his suspicions about the cause, for the sea of the inner water was unpleasantly warm, which reminded him of the ocean surrounding Ternate Island, the two or three months they had been anchored there before the volcano erupted. But he didn't want to tell Pieternel about it, because where could they escape to, if something like that were to happen here? Once, lying awake in the torrid night, he woke her up to tell her, but then couldn't bear to do so.

'Pieternel.'

She pressed his hand, and held it. 'What?'

'Everything.'

'I know.'

Did she perhaps have a premonition of something terrible about to happen, like the slave woman they had had, years ago?

'Our time is running out,' he said and tried to sleep.

She was frightened, her neighbours were frightened; they were infected by each other's fear as if it was a disease. In the forest were possibly a dozen runaways, all of them armed with assegais and so familiar with their surroundings that they could not be tracked down by dogs. Daniel himself had become wary of going into the forest on his own, because those slaves had sent word that whoever they found alone would be cut to ribbons. They chose their own leaders, planted tobacco in the ravines of the Black River, lived by hunting and whatever they could raid from the farmers' pens and gardens. Now, with the drought, they came down to the houses of North-West Harbour at night too.

What could he do if his poor wife thought she heard her cow breaking a halter at the manger in the night; if her children kept hiding on her lap, turning their eyes to the door all the time; if ghost crabs came scuttling in their thousands from the dark beach to the light; if rats from the cane stack jumped up against their shutters? What could have scared the rats like that? Really, in those days fear hovered on both sides of their door. And down at the black marshlands of the Chalk, they had been told, from the hot, stinking pools where the fever disease lurked, balls of pale yellow fairy fire rose at night to float along the valleys as far as Lemoenbooms Plain. All, all because of the terrible drought. If the rains were to come, they would be fine, but the rains were sure to return in the form of two or three hurricanes, and that they didn't want. They had to be patient, Daniel advised when he heard somebody complain, he had come to know this island as a good place, and the wheel would turn again.

The year after Jan Bocklenberg left for Batavia, they received a letter from him. At the supper table Pieternel read it to them, and stopped halfway, and went to their room. He was at the Cape, Jan wrote, at the new settlement of Stellenbosch. He was now a free doctor and made a living, even if patients paid him with merchandise. His children were well, but with much regret he had to inform them that Catharina Diodati had died in Batavia. She had been buried in the Reformed Church there. It was the sickness of the town. God had shaken the city, and it was dying. They should no longer expect anything from that part of the world; the Honourable Company and all its people were bleeding to death, and the symptoms could be seen everywhere. Roelof Diodati had asked him to inform them of the grievous news; he had immediately left Batavia with the two little ones, because it was sick. They had made him commander of Japan, and so they wouldn't hear from him again soon, as only one ship per year was allowed there. So Jan himself had also taken his children out of that city in search of a cooler climate. Here at the Cape they were experiencing an unpleasant rebellion of the free burghers against their government; they desperately wanted to shake off the governing regime. What a time humanity was living through, there was no peace or quiet anywhere any more.

Although the children asked him to read it aloud to them, Daniel folded the letter, said grace, and went to Pieternella. He now realised, he told her, that they, too, had their best years behind them. God had shaken their home, and from now on it would be downhill, and both of them were dying slowly, slowly but surely.

The signs of the Company's decline were visible everywhere. At the Lodge the *secundus* died after a duel with the surgeon. Could you believe such behaviour? Where did such things come from? Parts of farm wagons ordered from the Cape, and on which the carpenters had worked for so long, had still not been collected after two years, and were drying and rotting in the sun at French Church.

Then Commander Momber ordered a census to be held of all the people on the island, or at least of those his clerks could trace. And the people were worried, because they knew that a census challenged fate and brought misfortune. Children born in a census year were bound to die young. Pieternella's youngest was barely six weeks old – they hadn't even decided on a name yet – and other women were also pregnant. But the main concern was, of course, that after a census one had to expect new taxes, which was why people complained when the clerks visited your house. The officials doing the survey said that Commander Momber's instruction had come from the Cape. Daniel's personal return recorded: one man, one woman, five sons, ten slaves, thirty-seven cattle. He was curious to know how many people there were at North-West Harbour at the moment, and the clerk told him: on paper fifteen men, twelve women, thirty-two children, forty-seven slaves, and 281 cattle. In the end they called their youngest son Salomon, so that a place could be reserved for him on the eternal roll, as he appeared to be sick all the time in that terrible drought and heat, particularly from his stomach, and he did not survive that census year. They buried him, unbaptised, under the oldest palm trees in the backyard.

In the trade with foreign ships Daniel was still doing well. Under his shelters of palm mats on Cooper's Island lay everything a skipper in distress might need, from planks, knees, spars of different lengths and thickness, to a rudder the size for a hooker, which with Diodati's permission he had removed from the wreck at Black Rock. Good pieces of wreckage could also be gathered on the beach, like old English oak, which he cut into staves. His son Pieter was eighteen now, and a fellow according to Daniel's reckoning not without promise, with that straight defiant gaze his mother had learned from the van der Byls, and a solid grip in both hands. He could do arithmetic and wrote a reasonable hand, the way his mother had taught all her children. And he was skilled with axe and adze; already he could be trusted completely with a barrel or a length of ship's timber.

Daniel made his son work for his own account, so that he could see where his bread came from, and arranged for him to be given all the piloting tasks at North-West Harbour. When a ship fired a shot from beyond the reef at night, or the little ones came running from the hills with the news: 'Dad, there's a flag going up!' it was Pieter who had to put out to sea with his own serang. And before long the fellow knew some sea English, and when the hereditary enemy wished to depart, a sailor would come knocking on the door with a note and ask for Master Zaaijman, the pilot.

From those officers they learned how the English Company was flourishing in the Indian trade, how they sent out regiments of redcoats against recalcitrant kings and rajas and nawabs, stealing the land from under their feet. And here the English were swarming around Mauritius now, and sailing home, deeply laden with the treasures of India. In the year 1707, when they explained to Pieter that in future their flag would have a touch of blue in the upper left-hand corner, Daniel saw it as a sign that the English were now ruling over this ocean, which meant the end of the Dutch Company as master of the whole Orient. Its passport had been written. Did it mean that a new war between nations was looming?

At the very time of the new English maritime flag, the yacht *Jerusalem* arrived on the anchorage with letters from Batavia. For this matter Commander Momber summoned all the heads of families to the Lodge. Daniel got dressed and left, half a night and a day by sea, with his neighbours Jan Mauritz, Hendrik de Vries, Jan the Swede, Daan Onderwater, Ben Meulenbroek, Jan Carstensz, Jan Muur, Gert Romond, Freek Heijland, Kobus van Laar, Hein Karseboom, Henk van Balen, Roelf Osenberg and Adam Adamsz, together in two boats. They went like convicts summoned to the gallows. At the Lodge all the burghers from Lemoenbos, Noordwyks Vlak and Black River were gathered under the trees in their Sunday black. They agreed, yes, they believed they knew what was coming.

The commander told the gathered friends in the big hall that the Company wanted to close down and clear out. They were going to send two ships here, so they had to choose where they wished to be taken, Batavia or the Cape. He could grant no postponement, their answer had to be forwarded with *Jerusalem*. As for himself and his household, they chose the East, where chances of promotion for an official were better.

In the silence, followed by the shuffling of boots and bare feet on the floor, Daniel remarked that this was really very sudden, they would need time to reflect. The other free burghers agreed, bringing out their tobacco and pipes. But the commander quickly stopped them: No smoking indoors. Fire hazard.

'If the Company gives us its flag, commander, perhaps those of us who wish to do so, can remain behind after you have left. We can go on farming on our own and provide the Company's ships with what they need.'

'We already have the answer to that, Uncle Daniel. The Lords believe that you may well want to maintain a refreshment station here for pirates and Englishmen and others who harm the Company's interests.'

'That we shall most certainly do. You can take it from us,' they agreed.

The whole business, to a sailor, was an unfamiliar anchorage, and they needed to plumb it first. One might say that sailors readily move about, but these free burghers had taken root in the soil, and old trees cannot be transplanted. So they went outside to smoke and gaze at the white foam on the reef, while the late-afternoon sun was turning the clouds to yellow and orange. Before their feet in the shallow water the sea was lapping lazily at the land. Daniel and his two sons-in-law stood smoking, discussing what would be in the best interests of wives and children, as they waited for the guard to toll the bell for them to return inside. Should they not take up arms, and refuse to leave? What could the Lords do to them here? On the small square above the quay Daniel took the decision for Pieternel and himself. This was where he had married his Pieternel; this was where he had almost been damned into eternity by that drunken boatswain whose name he could not remember now; this was where his two darling daughters were married, married well to white-collar officials, and every time Pieternel was here with him in the land he had chosen for her. Now he had to consider her first. She had lived on islands since childhood. Grant now that she, and I, be given a country. When they were called inside, he wrote: the Cape.

Only four families chose the Cape. The other thirty-seven still heard the East, calling with that sweet, seductive voice. But did they really listen well? Daniel wondered. Suppose the real words were: *'Come and save me'*? He and his sons-in-law Hendrik de Vries and Herbert Jansz, and Michiel Romond, chose the Cape. He personally believed that Herbert should have chosen Batavia, on account of that huge block of ambergris for which the Company still owed him, even though it would mean losing Eva. But Herbert said: My treasure is at the Cape, and I'd better go there, otherwise I could easily lose everything.

All right, said the commander, then here are the instructions from the government. All the officials must go to Batavia, and no official will leave the island before the last free burgher has gone. Do not sow or plant anything, because rice and other provisions will be sent from Batavia. Slaughter as many cattle as possible, and salt the meat; the Company will buy it. The stock you keep alive, I shall buy from you at three rix-dollars a head when you leave. You are not allowed to take any dogs with you or to shoot them; leave your dogs behind so that they can catch the remaining stock and game. After you have left, officials will go round to set fire to your houses, crops, boats, remaining furniture and everything else. Nothing must remain here for the benefit of rivals like the English or the French. Keep all this secret from your slaves, to prevent their absconding into the jungle.

Those were the instructions. Among themselves they conferred about the timing: in six months they would begin slowly to slaughter the stock, starting with the oldest.

They returned to their homes with that dismaying news. When the Company's slaves heard about evacuation, the poor ignorant people had visions about a freedom which in their respective countries was as unknown as for the Dutch in theirs, and they made a plan to save themselves before they would once again be transported to foreign regions. The difference between white and black was obvious, after all, so if they were to cut the throats of all the whites, they would be of one heart. The only ones to be spared would be the young white women and Daniel Zaaijman, who should pilot them to where they wished to be, for there were some who wanted to return to Madagascar.

But this hollow plan came to light very soon. Commander Momber had three alleged ringleaders arrested, and consulted his books to find a way of making an example of them for the benefit of those who had to remain behind. They were tied to wheels and the flesh was torn from their bodies with red-hot tongs, before their murderous hands were cut off and they were sent to the Devil with a sledgehammer blow to the breastbone. Thereupon the wheels were set up downwind against trees.

On the night *Jerusalem* was offered its farewell, the reception ended under the stars, on the square outside the Lodge. All the officers were present, glass in hand, in the balmy evening; one could hear their laughter resounding far into the night, and the captain said: To every shot fired by this Lodge in honour of the laudable Company, *Jerusalem* out in the pool will reply with two. That was because during the meal he had teased the commander that his cannons had gone rusty from never greeting ships any more. Daniel heard, for the gospel truth, from one of those who had been there, that Momber himself held the lintstock while the shooting continued, to and fro, for almost half an hour. Shots in honour of the laudable Company, shots for His Excellency the governor-general, echoing against the Sadelberg in the quiet night, while the orange-red flashes from *Jerusalem* shimmered over the black water. Shots for the honourable governor at the Cape, shots for *Jerusalem*, shots for Fort Frederik Hendrik, causing fragments of smouldering wadding blasted from the barrel to fly downwind to the roof of the Lodge, causing the hand grenades suspended under the rafters to start exploding, and Lodge, warehouses, workshops, even the flag on its pole, once again to be burned to charcoal and ashes. Momber was such a quiet, pensive man. Do you remember, Pieternel?

Little Christiaan, their last, was born after Johannes showed the symptoms of the fever in his fourth year. He had been the first in their district to catch the disease. Perhaps his sickness was linked to the drought, because all their rivers were now stagnating in green pools, but all they knew was that the malaria was now raging at North-West Harbour too. Johannes suffered badly from the fever, but he survived his second and third attacks. That was the way of the East Coast fever: it took hold of you, shook you to the threshold of death, then left you until later, but it came back, year after year, until you wished you would die. And because there was no medicine against it, the best you could do was to flee with your remaining children, if you could.

Hendrik de Vries and their daughter Maria had a chance to escape with their three small sons, when *Blenheim Castle* of the English Company arrived after heavy weather at sea. They lost their carpenter when they lowered him overboard to repair the rudder. People were either happy or jealous about Hendrik's good fortune. But if one had to go, then the sooner the better, and Hendrik promised to investigate at the Cape the best ways of making a living there, without returning to the Company's service. So their Maria left with her husband Hendrik in the service of the English. Their commander had approved it, dispatching several letters for the Cape governor with him.

That was when their son Pieter had the idea to ask if he could stay behind until the ships came to fetch them, to see what he could earn from the English and the French, and leaving for Batavia later with the last officials. Pieternella and Daniel were not against it; they could see that it would be to his advantage, as that would give him the chance to be transformed into a miraculous *orang lama,* with experience of the East; but they suspected that it really had more to do with the commander's daughter, and perhaps for the same reason, Momber agreed.

On 2 November 1709, a year to the day from their gathering at the Lodge, *Carthago* dropped its anchor behind Cooper's Island, to pick up the passengers for Batavia with their slaves and property, and on the same day the galliot *Mercurius* arrived at the anchorage in South-East Harbour, for those who had chosen the Cape. On Christmas Day they set sail, and at sunset the brown peak of Pieter Both's Head had already sunk into the sea. Do you remember, Pieternel?

7

THE CLERK

. . . islands, solitary in an empty sea
So send! Send to know for whom the bell tolls.

Lectori Salutem!

YOU SEE BEFORE you the clerk Johannes Guilielmus de Grevenbroek. He writes by candlelight in an outroom on the farm Welmoed, on the Cape side of Stellenbosch. He has no wife, child or family in this country or abroad. The two people he calls friends live in a kraal of the Overberg Koina, but he has no enemies. In town people raise their hats to him, not without respect. He speaks seven languages, was Secretary of the Council of Policy, and several times elder of the church and *heemraad* of their district. He knows much about the affairs of others, but keeps his mouth shut. They know that he spends his days and large portions of the night writing, but do not know on what. Whatever he writes, remains in his bookcase. People avoid him, presumably because he is old, ugly and learned. So they raise their hats, bow in his direction, let him pass. He avoids people because they bore him; most of the people at the Cape he regards as boorish, uncouth. In one of his writings he has called them 'African monsters', and will do so again; he does not care what anyone thinks of it. He has outlived his contemporaries, and he has no illusions about life, history or his own erudition.

Tonight he has an undergraduate's gown draped around his shoulders. The robe is without warmth, moth-eaten in the seams, threadbare over the shoulders and green with age. His desk was once the dining table of a fairly large family. In his room are an unusually high and wide bookcase, which looks like a linen press and previously was one, with his table, a chair and a *katil*, everything of red ebony, and all bought at the same auction. His other clothes, on nails behind the door, are simple, old-fashioned; he mends them himself. His meals are frugal and infrequent. The farmer allows him the use of the room, of a horse and saddle and the service of his labourers at a small remuneration, as the former secretary refuses to accept it otherwise. On his wall is a small painted Madonna which is strangely reminiscent of Botticelli's models.

At the moment a thought has entered his mind, something of doubtful consequence, but he does not want to forget it. He writes it down in Latin: *Try to live in such a manner that it creates hope of an afterlife, otherwise human existence is meaningless. If there is nothing after our death, no hereafter, we should have lived in such a way that it will be an injustice.* He rereads the epigram, replaces the word *creates* with *promotes*, places a question mark beside it, dots every *i*, and thrusts the paper into the top of his gown's sleeve for later contemplation. The idea he received more than sixty years ago from a father abbot, and he is still working on the wording. He is convinced that he can improve on it. Perhaps it may turn into a useful epigraph one day. What he is already certain of, is that if there is nothing after life, no one will ever know it. He moves that thought out of the way, dips his pen and bends over his writing.

The task he is now working on is to order information he has gathered during his career in the service of the Company and afterwards to extend it into a history of the first fifty years of the Cape settlement. He is familiar with the period as well as the people who lived during it. He felt the need to write as strongly as thousands of his contemporaries felt the urge to reach the golden East, but after more than five months on more than two hundred foolscap pages, he had still not progressed beyond the years of settlement. That was when he realised that he would not finish it in his lifetime. It was too late, he had waited too long to begin. And simultaneously with this, another notion turned to certainty: that there were other stories crying to be heard, like the hand of a drowning person rising from the sea and a voice saying: Help me, for God's sake.

The information he has gathered for his *Portrait of the Cape*, as he provisionally entitled his manuscript, contains personal details of people still alive and wealthy enough to take him to court, should they believe that they can endure the distasteful experience of a court case. But that threat barely weighs up against the oath he himself took, to keep secret what he learns in the course of his service. Sound judgement is necessary. Almost the whole meaning of the title 'secretary' comes from *secretarius*, a confidential officer, which concerns careful judgement, an understanding of people's susceptibilities and receptiveness, courtesy, an ability to speak and read languages correctly, to use knowledge or remain silent about it. Consequently, no one who could not distinguish acutely between good and bad deserved the name of secretary. This is what he was, and how he wishes to remain known, J. G. de Grevenbroek, Secretary of the Council of Policy, 1686–1694, his image perfect to the end of time, his reputation untarnished.

It has been both interesting and eventful, that first half-century, which is just over. Typical of revolution born from greed, the period under his investigation has been married to death and baptised in blood. Is that phrasing it too strongly? But it certainly has been a painful birth. He knows for sure that the Reverend Valentyn in Holland is also working on a manuscript about the period, as well as the young man Kolbe, who used to work here in the *landdrost*'s office, but Kolbe's knowledge is deficient. Even though Kolbe had access to the Company's documents for six years, it is doubtful whether he understood head or tail of personal intrigue, like the jealousy between van Goens and van Reede in 1685, and how van der Stel tried to exploit it. He made a mistake lending the young man his notes, to copy freely before returning to his *lieber Heimat* in Franconia. Still, after Kolbe's departure educated company has been scarce, and the fellow's theories about the nature of comets were interesting to say the least. He remembered how a former commander on Mauritius had displayed his apprehension of this harmless phenomenon. And he himself was now most interesting company, that unfortunate Commander Lamotius.

Stellenbosch is a blind and stupid village, and there is little hope of its changing. There are three or four people living here with whom he exchanges a word from time to time, people who had the occasion to attend a university abroad, even though they hardly benefited from it. Like the Reverend Beck who visits, officially on behalf of the church, but in reality to exercise his smattering of French. After so many years the man has still not grown in wisdom or deviated from dogma. As pedestrian in his views as he was when he arrived here twenty years ago, he still plods on: colourless, vague, boring, predictable. Still, an interesting case, in that he had the courage to marry *Secundus* Elsevier's daughter, and became a source of information on Elsevier's attitude and role in the political struggle between the regime and the burghers, which was very big news in these parts some years ago, and ended in the banishment of the government and three or four of the top officials.

Then there is the farmer Tas, whom he used to like more in the past than he does now. The man's personal journal, which was used against him in court during that struggle for civil rights, was a surprise and a joy to read, even though it had been intended to be private and contained some personal remarks about him. The fellow has a primitive style, witty, with some rather coarse wordplay, and wonderfully comical, particularly where the righteous freedom fighter, important civil leader and prosperous *heemraad* secretly falls in love with his pregnant wife's sixteen-year-old sister. Tas has a natural talent, even if it tends towards the vulgar, and it is a serious loss to the Cape community that he should now be hiding it under a bushel. Hiding a talent is sinful, and sin means death. It would be a pity if Adam Tas chooses not to write again.

That struggle, or perhaps their success in the struggle, turned Tas and his comrades into boors. Because they succeeded in defeating the class of gentlemen, they came to reject the style of gentlemen. One can see them shying away from stately occasions, from dressing properly. One sees them drinking wine from the bottle without the use of glass or mug, and walking barefoot. It is becoming customary to prepare food outside and eat it there as in a military camp. Every man, if he is to be regarded as a true man, must have an outside hearth, a platform of stones like a biblical altar where meat is roasted on gridirons, on the blue embers of sawn vine stumps. Tas calls it the altar of Bacchus. There they sit behind the house on crates and barrels, invariably the men only, joking and mocking, thinking up derogatory nicknames for their neighbours, telling crude jokes and boasting loudly about guns, dogs and horses, while consuming sides of mutton, spiced sausage and whole bottles of sour peasant wine. They are people with the mentality of common soldiers.

Who else is there, wasting the blessed advantage of foreign education on this town, dulling the edge of intellect with gossip on farming, politics and the weather? Mankadan wasn't without promise, at least he was a defrocked *dominee*, but here he spent his time on the teaching of children and the much more successful seduction of a young girl. He himself married those two, without banns, as van der Stel unceremoniously stood them before his desk one afternoon. A forced marriage and cheap brandy were the end of Mankadan as an original thinker. Then there are the few *landdrosts* he has known, like Starrenburg, trapped in an impossible manner between justice and duty, duty and position, position and justice. And the painter Corneille, whose name was here vulgarised to Craaij, who visited with his young wife Barbara, the lovely girl to whom Tas had once lost his heart, with her mass of curls like a bouquet of red flowers on her head. Craaij was twice her age, an intelligent fellow and well read, also clearly out of place in this rural village. De Grevenbroek, as church elder, had noticed the young lady in church since her childhood. Her mother was the daughter of Barbara Geens.

They visited him several times here on the farm in connection with the interpretation of certain documents, and he dragged out his explanations so that he could see her again, and yet again. A wonderful power the child had. She was medicine for his weary mind, because he could truly think more clearly, and felt physically and spiritually younger, after every visit; and he would look forward to the next time, as he carried her image in his mind for days. After he had doubted for a long time, often with deep concern, whether he should ever complete his *Portrait of the Cape, the First Half-Century*, her encouragement strengthened his faith. On his table, propped against the wall, was a small painting of Barbara Craaij's golden head, the reddish gold of autumn leaves in the forest of Ardenne, which he'd demanded from her husband for the deciphering of faded title deeds to two pieces of land on the outskirts of Paris. It was like this: he felt *good* after seeing her, and even started humming old tunes and smiling to himself. In her blessed presence he was now able to bend over his writing day and night, until the end of his life. And then they moved away to the Cape. At last the only one left with whom he can exchange thoughts is Isaac Lamotius.

The scraps of paper on which he'd jotted down information, mostly scribbled hastily from minutes, letters and affidavits he had to use in an official capacity as secretary, and which over a period of ten years he'd carried home in the sleeve of his gown, obediently fell into line before him on the large dark table, presented arms for inspection, content to be drilled for a march or for an attack. Yes, he thought of them as his soldiers. It was his aim with them: they had to destroy an enemy. After he'd sorted his notes on his table and in due course, as they multiplied, on the floor of his room according to their force and weight, and as each soldier came to know his place and function and started performing, his story took shape. He strung his bits of paper on a single thread so that each would keep its place in the procession, without straying. There was no doubt about it, they worked. But then, strangely, they themselves chose a different battlefield from the one he'd planned, and their own route to reach it, and even his chosen enemies were not worth their attention. Their own narrative remained an image of the Cape, but the Cape was just the painted backdrop behind a stage on which a bitter comedy was enacted, and the van der Stels, father and son, were no longer the villains of the piece, but shrank among the *dramatis personae*, right down among the servants and foot soldiers.

Secretary de Grevenbroek had been wronged by those two gentlemen, and felt aggrieved. He was not insulted by them, he did not, after all, lose any honour or respect. There are those who are very conscious of honour, wearing it like a shield, and enjoy talking about it, citing the soldier's honour. 'I have been under arms since my thirteenth year. I assure you, upon my honour as a soldier . . .' Do not believe it, it is a tissue of fables and vanity, and a groping for imaginary status. He knew the army, the taste of its bread and salt, the mercy of its water and wine, marched on its attacks and retreats, personally read its formularies beside graves in mud and rain. He was in the very front line, the fool with the banner, that was he, and he was no longer misled by fables. The difference between the honour of the soldier and the honour of the executioner is merely illusion.

Those two van der Stels mustered their rank and status like an armed bodyguard around them. The van der Stels were governors; he had to address them as 'Your Honour', doff his hat and bow. And while they were playing the honourable gentleman, they caused people to wither and waste away, to die in their hands. While they constructed private whitewashed manors, they allowed huts and little gardens to decay on small islands. And people died there too, for people are islands.

How does one become a gentleman? On Mauritius a free burgher once said: 'Commander Hugo, now *that* was a gentleman. This Lamotius is just a *seur* of forty guilders.' This quip he did not carry home in the sleeve of his gown, Lamotius told it to him himself. How does a scoundrel become a gentleman, and a gentleman a scoundrel? In brief:

His own interest in the Cape began at the University of Leiden. Of course he'd known about the Cape since his youth. Every Dutchman who supported the great adventure in the East knew what role the Cape played in the economy of his waterlogged country. They could all recite it like a nursery rhyme: The key to the Dutch economy was the Company, the key to the Company's success was control of the Eastern trade, the key to the Eastern trade was successful shipping, the key to shipping was the Cape replenishment station. Decades later he himself discovered what was still lacking in that tottering house of cards, that the key to the Cape replenishment station was its outposts. And even that knowledge was incomplete. There was still more to know: the outposts were *living people*.

His old father was a Latinist. No, not *old father*, because the undying language had a preserving influence on the spirit, as surely as the Egyptians managed to conserve the bodies of their kings. They lived in one of the narrow houses on the Raapenburg opposite the university, where he gave private tuition in Latin to undergraduate students. At the time when the city fathers allotted a number to every building and insisted that it be displayed on the front door, he'd painted the number six for his house in Roman letters on the door. He had a letter delivered to him by a polite clerk, with the request to change it to an ordinary figure for the convenience of the night watch. And he wrote his reply in Latin: that every one of his visitors considered the figure as common, that those who did not know it, were not welcome there, and that in his life of sixty-one years no night watch had ever knocked on his door. He had his letter delivered by a lawyer. That was his father, who had his only son christened Guilielmus instead of Wilhelmus.

As for himself, he never attended school as a child, because it wasn't necessary. If a child in Leiden has to spend his day in a classroom, there must be something wrong with his parents. Every public building inside the Singels is a school. The city wall with its five gates, the medieval Keep, the Cloth Merchants Hall, the weighing house, the city hall with its *roepstoel* for the town crier, the busy little port, every canal boat, every smoking workshop in that small city is a school. In the academic quarter between Pieterskerk and the Doelen every resident is a walking school, with the world in his head and humanity in his heart. *Here you see freedom* is the city's motto, eloquently demonstrated by the misconduct of drunken students, shouting in the narrow streets at night or stumbling home along the short cut, straight through the canal.

But it is a town with a strong military history, a town that withstood the Spanish siege, so long and so bitterly that when the widows came crying to the burgomaster, begging him to surrender as they had no food, he unbuttoned his shirt: 'Here, eat me.' This is how one grows up in Leiden. If you love freedom, keep your powder dry, that is a simple truth. In his own childhood every man still had to shoot two afternoons a week with bow and arrows at the targets, in case the town were attacked on a rainy day. One could hear the dull hum of arrows like a swarm of bees as far as the Raapenburg. And the community knows what they have won with the sword of resistance, and vigorously demonstrate their appreciation of the victory won by the forefathers over the Spanish every year on the third day of October, with

pealing bells and a thanksgiving service in every church followed by
exuberant festivities in streets and houses until well after midnight.
That festival shows what resistance can achieve. The prince came to
the town and said to the city fathers: 'How can I prove my appreciation to Leiden? Would you like to be free from Dutch taxes for ever?'
They said: 'Give us a university.' Then he took the nuns' convent on
the Raapenburg, and gave it to them: 'Your university.'

That was where he grew up, in the university district. In the garden
of the old nuns' convent the *hortus botanicus* was planted and plants
from all over the world were gathered and propagated to be studied.
Perhaps the Dutch were not used to flowers because in the present
cold period there was little sign of the cycles of nature, but the *hortus*
became the pride of the university, luring enthusiasts like bees from
all over Europe. Bulbs, seed, kernels, dried flowers, root-stocks, blocks
of sawn wood were transported there by the Company's ships from
the far corners of the world, and carried on lighters up the Vliet through
Delft to Leiden's small port. There he met brown sailors handling the
boxes and barrels: homeless wanderers, *sapitahu*, dogs without a name,
which was how he called them in his youthful ignorance. In summer
he worked in the *hortus* as an assistant, a handyman equally at home in
black gown and brown overcoat. He moved the barrels and boxes
outside on trolleys, unpacked them in the sun, prepared beds for
seedlings, carried water, prepared cuttings, pollinated ripe flowers by
hand, set up samples for lectures. In late autumn the plants from tropical regions had to be brought inside again to sleep there until the
spring. In that way he earned a few guilders, for his writing paper and
ink and his share of domestic expenses.

Choose an academic career, kind people advised him. Then it would
have to be botany, because inaudible sounds, intangible shapes, invisible colours carried in seeds called out to him, like the desk from an
acorn, the draft manuscript from papyrus seed, wine from the stone
of a ripe grape, a mug of foaming beer from a grain of barley, smoking
war from the grain of assegai wood. He spent his summers in the *hortus*
in the company of gardeners and students, until his father would decide
that he was sufficiently versed in Latin to register, in order not to be

a burden but an aid to the professor. In the university library during the long winters he read, and read, and read.

In winter, when the water of the Gallows Field was frozen white and students skated by silvery moonlight with a wine bottle in one hand, he did not join them. He preferred to read, about warmer lands. Now he knows what that fateful withdrawal from his peer group predicted. It is not true that the child is father to the man, because the child *is* the man. Apart from the Latin of his father's home for university and church, he could also read French and English from an early age. Strange lands existed in libraries. The whole world was in books. Mysterious heroes, part myth and part intimation, from Persia, Rome and Greece were resurrected in his room, and the East was right there outside his doorstep. Among the knowledge of his youth were romantic fables too, which he ingested by coincidence through the reading of French chivalric tales. In his heated adolescent imagination he would then become a homeless knight without sin or blemish, clothed in white, wandering about to save damsels in distress, and dedicated to the service of the holy woman whose face he sometimes believed he could see in the clouds.

In his eighteenth year war broke out against the alliance of France and England. What he never forgot, was Leiden's history of resistance, *haec libertatis ergo*. The students marched through the town with banners and drums, behind their leaders, boisterously passing the wine bottles from hand to hand. 'To the Doelen. To the Doelen,' they shouted. Now was the time for loyal blood to stand up for freedom. His father said: Go, so that you can find peace, and then come back. So he went to war.

At the Doelen they were sworn in by two of the prince's sergeants. The first march took them from Leiden to Voorschoten, the next from Voorschoten to The Hague. There his path took a wrong turning, when he was made a clerk because he could write, and he spent nearly a year in an office, until a bag of confiscated documents arrived which in the absence of the translator, he read and translated from French and English into Dutch. After that he was sent to report to the headquarter unit, and with that itinerant camp he criss-crossed the country, never far from the battlefront and often in its very heart. They were the personal company of the prince, and in his third year he was made an ensign and regimental scribe. There was a lot of writing to be done in French and Latin, mostly instructions to army commanders in far corners of the country, proclamations to the ordinary citizens and to town councillors, new taxes, worthless receipts, sentences. He had to interrogate prisoners after each battle and communicate their information to the commanders. In every town on their way came citizens with personal petitions to the prince, and once the councillors had approved or rejected their requests, he would transcribe the prince's reply in proper court Latin.

Then he became worried. He wanted to find the meaning of life, as he called it at the time. He read the philosophies, antique and new, and wanted to know what to do with that knowledge. Once he asked his father: 'Do you agree with this concept I read on a wall at the university: *Youth is a mess, maturity a struggle, old age self-reproach?*'

'It is Ecclesiastes.'

'That I didn't realise. Do you agree with it? Why does the author find so little joy or value in life? Cynicism is only cheap pretence.'

'Wait and see.'

Now he was grown up, having marched for five years behind a banner, and he wanted to know what life looked like ahead. And the only advice he'd had was: Wait and see, then speak. The prince was his own age, there was no experience to be expected from that quarter, but the captain who signed his discharge form wished him success on the journey.

'The world is big around us, and beyond the borders other wars will try to seduce you. They are not your concern. You just stay on your course.'

Stay on course, yes. That was the easy part. Was he prepared for the journey, though, which turn-offs should he avoid, which inns pass by? With his Latin New Testament and a few pieces of clothing in his rucksack he took ship to Portugal, walked through the land from south to north and asked the abbot of a Benedictine monastery to be accepted as a lay brother. Three months later he was on his way again, to the next abbey, and then the next, and the next. Where was he going? From Redondo down to Abrante, to Beira, to Covilha, to Lamego, to Miranda. In the pre-dawn dark he was awakened: *Dominus tecum*. The Lord be with you. Every porter who saw him leave called after him: *Dominus tecum*, one after the other, until he'd crossed the border into Spain. From monastery to monastery he went, praying, eating, singing, working in their fields and stables, wearing their clothes: brown Benedictine, grey Franciscan, black Dominican, white Carmelite, barefoot Capucine, begging Servite and reasoning Jesuit. He was blessed from home to home, *Dominus tecum*, from the brother who woke them to the brother porter who let him out, all the way, the Lord be with you. And he was content as a mole in his tunnel.

Life was good to him. The world was tranquil, the monasteries quiet, with time for reading, for listening. That was his need. It suited his nature. At night his company was his books and the crucifix with the tortured Christ on the wall of his cell. In that time, like other brothers, he seldom saw a woman. The Madonna of wood or clay, and painted blue and white, was the only female image he would see for months, but she was alive and warm in their thoughts when they kneeled in the prie-dieu or lay on the bare boards at night, for a man remains a man, unless he'd had the operation of Abélard.

Who was she, that poor girl without a trace of cheerfulness on her face, whose image was displayed in all the remote corners of the civilised world? It looked as if she had something important to say, but had been ordered to be silent. Where had she grown up, who were her parents, how did her family earn their bread? Did she not have any male or female friends? Where were they? She seemed lonely, isolated. Who was there to speak on behalf of this woman?

He knew that in 1617 Pope Paul Quintus had declared the Virgin Birth as official Church doctrine, prohibiting all other opinions. Even if she herself had other information, she would henceforth have to keep silent about it. It was also announced what she should look like: *In this most merciful mystery Our Lady must be represented in the flower of her youth, twelve or thirteen years old, with loving, grave eyes, her nose and eyes perfectly formed, blushing cheeks, long, wavy hair. Her robe is white, her cloak blue. Her eyes look up at the heavens, her hands are meekly folded on her chest.* Then the papal artist went to find a mournful girl and hired her as his model. And since then she has been carved, plastered, painted like that.

And there she sits still, spread open and stuck like a butterfly behind glass. She has become their sacrifice. She dies, trapped at twelve or thirteen, tied to the corpse of her child, as an example to others.

He saw her again and again, in towns and villages and cities, or exhibited beside the road for the world to look at. Every time she was grieving, a child without guilt and without voice, without a stake or say in the fate dealt to her. Everywhere along the road she waited for him. One or two small statues had the hint of a hesitant smile, but he had the feeling that the painter would be sent back to repair it. Who was she really? He would have liked to know more about her child-hood, before she became famous, because he felt sorry for her. He himself had no sisters, and had not yet come to know female friends – the war had come between him and his youth – and in his grave, romantic heart he felt obliged to do something for the young damsel in her distress, and like monks and white knights before him, he dedicated his service to her. But there was nothing at all he could do for her.

He no longer felt at ease. He was scared of becoming, in his turn, the nameless victim of other people's ideals. Waiting and seeing was too slow, took too long. How would he know what promises life held in store for him if he could hardly see anything? He left Spain in the robes of a Benedictine, took a ship to Naples, and from there went north with a staff in his hand on a road paved two thousand years earlier by the Romans. He wanted to get to Rome, to attend a Mass offered by the Pope himself. Perhaps he would find a message for him there. But there was nothing either. In Rimini, the town of Dante's frustrated lovers, he turned his back, provisionally, he thought, on Europe. Further to the east was coarseness, deeply rooted, spread wild and wide. After four years on the road he reached Leiden again.

His father had sold the house in Raapenburg and was rector of the Latin school in Nijmegen, the town of his birth. Now Johannes Guilielmus de Grevenbroek was alone on the cold stone square in front of the Pieterskerk. He knew some foreign languages, and he was in need of money, all exactly like twelve years before. At this stage he was worried, as his entire youth, everything he had done before the war, had been designed to prepare him for an academic career. Now he was nearly thirty years old, much older than the average undergraduate student, and there was barely any time left for an academic career. Should he write off those years of his life as worthless, his first twenty years as much as the last ten? What should he do? Back to the army? Perhaps a trade? A teacher like his father?

The *hortus* flourished, still buzzing with foreign and local interest. Perhaps in there? But then he would have to enter as a hired hand, should a vacancy arise. One day he went up the massive spiral staircase into the main building of the university. Already in his childhood he had noticed how each stair had the shape of a huge keyhole, and it was like a large number of keyholes stacked on top of each other, each one turned just a fraction further, as one ascended from one to the next. Each keyhole led to a room of knowledge, he imagined, and all of them together carried one upward, upward, to that strange empty room he was on his way to now.

He entered the Sweat Room, and examined the walls. They were covered with a myriad of names scratched into the plaster. This was where a candidate had to wait after his discourse to the examiners, sweating while they discussed his thesis, live his nightmare, await his fate, here he might write his name on the wall before the porter came to call him to look his judges in the eye again. For him the writing was on the wall. Before the war had taken him away from here, before his father had said: Go, so that you can find peace, he had believed, without once doubting it, that one day he would write his name here. As a boy he had sometimes come to this small room, experiencing the stifling feeling the students had spoken about, writing his name invisibly with a fingertip in an open space. That dream was still alive, but no longer that prodigal son. His name would remain invisible for ever. He touched, in farewell, the cold wall for one last time. Were he to write now, it would be: J. G. de Grevenbroek, *causarius miles*. Casualty of war. At the Cape in later years he would occasionally append this code to his name, to van der Stel's annoyance.

In July 1864 he sailed on the ship *Maas* for chamber Rotterdam, to the East. The woman at the gate in Delftshaven, with the hump and the two white eyes like pearls, had died. People said that the little box, in which her much-feared prophecies were locked, had been opened; and all they'd found in it were a few coins, a pistol, a lottery ticket and a printed tract entitled *The Surprises of Love*. That had been the sum of her knowledge. It was the sum of foresight mankind needed. His prospects were reasonably good. In his sea chest was a copy of a recommendation to the Supreme Council in which his proficiency in languages and his military service were mentioned: six years as clerk of the Prince's Advisory Council, three of them as ensign. The original had been stowed among the Batavian letters placed in the captain's care. He was clerk of the ship, or *seur*, as Jack Tar calls that official, and was relying on a good post in the secretariat of Castle Batavia, under the eyes of the governor-general, after which promotion would soon follow. But at the Cape he lost his compass, as Jack Tar has it. In his case, he would say in later years, his ship was wrecked. Hope was lost, and as if it concerned a real ship, he would talk about this disaster as the shipwreck of the Good Hope.

It was November 1684. A month earlier Commissioner van Goens had arrived, and with him a load of despair like a dark cloud from the north. Van der Stel was commander at the time, van Goens, his guest, was a councillor of India and commissioner, and his master for the duration of his stay. After His Excellency's letter of commission had been read to the Council, he and his retinue moved into the posthouse at Rustenburg, and remained there for seven months. He was ill, he announced. He required doctors and a slave and a first-class clerk, his wife needed two slave women. He was not prepared to travel to the Castle, the Council had to meet at his lodging, to which he would summon officials as and when he required their reports. His entertainment, during his long illness, resided in meals and pleasant conversations with an old acquaintance, the lieutenant Jean-Baptiste Dubertin, who had served on his staff on Ceylon for years, and his young wife, the daughter of a friend of his youth, State Advocate Uijtenbogaert. What was more, the fair young lady gratified his eyes and revived his faded senses.

After the arrival of the ship *Maas*, when its captain met at Rustenburg for the first time with van Goens and the Council, van der Stel complained that there was no one on his staff who could write a letter in English or French, or could read or write Latin. He was sorry, he declared with a measure of satisfaction, but he did not have a single competent clerk to place at the disposal of Commissioner van Goens. That was when the captain of *Maas* demonstrated his goodwill. 'What about our *seur*, a fellow called de Grevenbroek?' he helpfully offered.

De Grevenbroek protested, explaining that he had to continue to the East, until van Goens threatened that he would have him brought ashore with force if he did not comply voluntarily; the Article letter of the Lords made provision for that. So J. G. de Grevenbroek became a clerk in the secretariat of Simon van der Stel, seconded to Commissioner van Goens for the duration of His Excellency's stay. And the ship *Maas* left for the East without him.

He hid his disappointment, he tried to make the best of it, perhaps the commissioner would reward him. But months, half a year, went past with no sign of release. He wondered: Why? Am I delivered, like Job, into the hands of the Devil, to do with me as he chooses? Is my patience and my acknowledged loyalty being tried, that such things should happen to me? I hope it has been arranged for my life to be spared. So, in desperation, did he cling to the word hope, a weary swimmer abandoned in the ocean. Later, at the end of his life, he was grateful for what had happened. Then he understood: there was a witches' kettle brewing, and those who were destined to dance around it were already on the water on their way here, each one bringing a little something for the pot. They brought it from afar, from long ago, and it was selfishness, and revenge, and self-interest, and greed, and jealousy. Pinch of this, pinch of that, for the pot. All of it to ensure that mild Lamotius would be destroyed on Mauritius.

Yet, it was an interesting period. He saw the commissioner every day. Van Goens was extremely proud of his late father, the famous governor-general. His father had straightened out this refreshment station at the Cape after it had nearly foundered. It had been set up in the Table Valley to supply the Company's ships, but for many years it was unable to do so; on the contrary, the ships had to supply the refreshment station. His late father, who had become governor-general of East India after Maetsuyker, demanded to know the reasons for the failure. The Table Valley, north of the mountain, had too much wind, too poor soil, too little water, severely limited grazing, no timber, little fuel. By contrast, everything in the Liesbeeck valley, here to the east of the mountain at Rustenburg, was exactly the opposite. Thereupon he advised van Riebeeck, the commander at the time: Expel the Hottentots from this valley, occupy it, fence it in, fortify it, till it, set up outposts and farm it. That was when supplying the ships succeeded for the first time. All of it had been his late father's doing.

What interested de Grevenbroek was the question: Those natives driven from these riverside pastures with their abundance of water, what had become of them? The more he read about them, the more he wanted to know about their fate. The answers, to him as a new arrival at the Cape, were most fascinating. It would appear that the Company had deliberately promoted their addiction to liquor and tobacco in order to obtain their cattle cheaply. The cattle were required for agriculture and transport. Valentyn, the *dominee*, had already published a few things about it. He, de Grevenbroek, would do so too; perhaps he now found himself in the most favourable position to make a contribution to human knowledge, to the record.

What he subsequently discovered about the natives in journals, letters and other documents on his desk, he scribbled in brief notes on shreds of waste paper, carrying the shreds back to his room in the spacious hollow of his gown's sleeve, for future use. By that time there was already so much official writing on his table, from both van der Stel and van Goens, that he could not deal with it all during office hours. The two seemed to be in competition: if van Goens gave him eight letters, van der Stel would give ten to trump van Goens.

In the Company's books he learned about outposts, how they fulfilled the various functions of the refreshment service. One provided thatch, another shell lime; one guarded a frontier, another provided transport, or gathered salt, chopped firewood or planted vegetables; another caught fish, yet another transmitted signals. There were a great number of them. It opened his eyes to the problems of the region's economy. They really carried the Company, because without outposts the Cape could not function, without the Cape Batavia could not function, without Batavia the Company was powerless, and so on all the way to the top, where the prince and his advisory council in Holland were carried on a shaky shield.

But the contribution of outposts was more than commercial. From Outpost Mauritius, Commander Lamotius sent seeds of the island's plants, both to the university's *hortus* and to Director Huydekoper, a lover of botany. From Outpost Hottentots-Holland, Corporal Lourens Visser provided the aloe stumps, dried flowers containing the seed pods and small bulbs for the *hortus*. On Robben Island the postkeeper collected insects and beetles for the university. This, and more, de Grevenbroek discovered from the Company's documents, in that burgeoning archive which was the biography of the colony's birth and infancy, growing in number and degree of neglect on the floor of *Secundus* de Man's office in the Castle.

Commissioner van Goens did not want to hear about plants. He had a total revulsion of botany. It was what one might call a family disease. His late father had been governor over parts of Ceylon, when he acquired the Malabar coast of India for the Company. Malabar was rich in merchandise. Van Goens won Malabar for the Company, and in 1670 the Lords appointed a young officer named van Reede over it.

It might well have been the regular requests of Doctor Cleijer, of the Company's laboratory in Batavia, that started the interest in the Malabar vegetation in the young van Reede. The hospital was battling with Oriental diseases for which Cleijer had no medication. Cleijer needed to know what the natives used, and he had letters written to all the heads of post in East India and on the Indian subcontinent to make enquiries, and to ask for examples of all the medicinal plants in each region. His request travelled even as far as the Cape outpost of

Hottentots-Holland, where Postkeeper Lourens bought honey from the Koina with tobacco for the Lords' pharmacy in Batavia.

Van Reede was charmed by the plants of Malabar, they dominated his life. In the seven years of his administration he sent a large number of specimens to Cleijer, and to Leiden. He personally went on expeditions into the bush, he was rowed along rivers by natives in sampans or carried in a hammock through the bush and over plains and mountains, to gather information from the inland herb doctors about the region's vegetation. He identified a few thousand species and described them in detail: the plant, flower, fruit, habitat and human use. Sometimes he was absent from his post for months, and at his Fort in Couchin he had a nursery and a laboratory built to promote his research.

While the grey old Governor-General Maetsuyker struggled for two years to die, van Goens, the elder, took charge in Batavia. He repeatedly criticised van Reede for employing the Company's staff, from clerks to draughtsmen, gardeners, interpreters and porters, to promote his research, misusing its buildings and gardens for it, while the commerce in his region was deteriorating rather than improving. He expressed his disapproval in open letters.

Thereupon van Reede resigned. Of his massive but still unfinished manuscript *Hortus Malabaricus* he had two complete copies made by the Company's clerks and draughtsmen, and had them dispatched home on different ships. To every one of the rajas and princes of Malabar he wrote a letter of gratitude and farewell, and had a long, thorough memorandum compiled for his successor on its administration, commercial policy and relations with the region's chiefs. Then, embittered and aggrieved, he returned home with the unfinished manuscript of *Hortus Malabaricus*.

The youngster with all this information was Hendrik Swaardecroon, who was only nineteen years old. In that year of 1685 he was, firstly, van Reede's secretary and, secondly, van Reede's nephew. De Grevenbroek and the nephew sat in the draughty anteroom of the posthouse at Rustenburg, outside the closed door behind which van Reede, with van der Stel as witness, conversed with van Goens Junior, literally under four eyes, as he wore two thick sets of glasses on his nose, one upon the other.

They could barely hear the voices behind the heavy doors and solid walls, but de Grevenbroek had a suspicion of what was being discussed, and the nephew – too young to possess the judgement of a secretary – freely dispensed information, while one hour after another went past as they waited in case they should be called in. Here van Reede was the Company's high commissioner, entrusted with a mission to discover and exterminate the neglect, self-enrichment, smuggling and other forms of misconduct at every post and office in the service. He had the right to dismiss, or even punish, even make terrifying examples of transgressors if necessary.

The innocent, of course, had nothing to fear, the nephew whispered confidentially. In Amsterdam the Lords were expecting that by this time, after so many months, van Goens would have completed his Cape inspection, but here they found him still prostrate in Rustenburg. For six months he had been lying like that. De Grevenbroek, innocent bystander, outsider, had no knowledge of these people and their troubled background before; with childlike bright eyes and obvious family pride, the nephew had informed him about it.

Van Reede and his party had landed here in April. From the first day there had been conflict, suspicion and a resumption of the feud between the two families. The nephew explained it all to de Grevenbroek. His master had bought Huis Mijdreght to gain admission to the chivalry, with the title of Lord of Mijdreght. It was only a smallish, square house next to the church, smaller than this posthouse and with almost no land around it. His master didn't even live there, but in a new house in town. Already he had made strong, very strong, new friends within the order of chivalry, like the Lord Huydekoper van Marseveen, who was one of the illustrious Lords Seventeen. His master van Reede had become a close friend of Huydekoper through their shared interest in plants, for Huydekoper was a collector, infatuated with exotic plants, and collecting from every region. In his garden grew the plants of Mauritius, of the East Indies as well as of the Cape. It was noteworthy that science was becoming a powerful new force beyond the scope of the old order. Some military men had a revulsion of the sciences, but commerce was going to put modern science to use, and take control of it. Perhaps Monsieur de Grevenbroek should take note of it.

It sounded like van Reede's parrot talking, thought de Grevenbroek. Still, interesting.

'Huydekoper is helping my master financially to complete and publish his manuscript on the plants of Malabar, as my master is not wealthy. He did not use his time in the East to amass a fortune like others. Three volumes have already been published, but there will be twelve in the end. The general public won't buy it, of course. My master is worried about the cost. And there are still years of research and writing waiting in the East. An author with an unfinished manuscript is a sick man. Always depressed, always in suspense. It's a pity that my master should have this clash with van Goens at the very beginning of his commission, but he himself says it may be better so. When they hear about this in the East, it will make his work easier.'

De Grevenbroek listened in disbelief, keeping his own mouth shut. What was the lad talking about?

'When old van Goens, this one's father, who used to be governor-general, arrived back in Amsterdam three years ago, the city welcomed him like a prince, a hero who had helped Holland to win its empire in the East. But when he died last year, Huydekoper was burgomaster, and he didn't want to have anything to do with the funeral. He arranged for the whole thing to be sent down to The Hague. That made the young van Goens very bitter.'

Simon van der Stel opened the door, and said, 'Enter.'

As on other days, van Goens lay on the couch, his legs covered with a spread. Van Reede and van der Stel sat opposite him, on either side of the desk van Goens used daily. Behind the desk stood two chairs.

Van Reede stood up, holding out his hand to de Grevenbroek. 'Hendrik van Reede.' This was the man who'd had his unfinished manuscript copied twice before taking to sea with it, and who now had to embark on a new career, after several years, because of his unfulfilled and burning need to see it finished.

The clerk took the fingers, making a bow. 'Your Honour.'

'Ha,' called van Goens from his couch. 'Why don't you lick his boots too?'

'Please keep the minutes, both secretaries. We shall have our collation after this meeting, so be ready to draw up your final copy in this room for signing. We shall have two original sets of minutes, each with five original signatures and three seals impressed in sealing wax.'

It was clear that the three gentlemen had spent the previous hours preparing the soil, sowing the seeds and ripening the fruit. Now it was time for harvesting, and they were the reapers.

'I request His Excellency Commissioner van Goens to present to me the report of his inquiry into the state of the Company's interests at the Cape.'

'My commission comes from the Lords. My report will go to them.'

'I request His Excellency to allow me to peruse his report and appendices, in order to avoid an unnecessary repetition of work done by all the relevant officials, and a waste of time.'

'I have not finished yet.'

'I put it to His Excellency that the commission entrusted to me by the Lords Masters, in consequence of its later date and my more senior rank, supersedes his and renders it null and void.'

'That I wish to hear from them.'

'I put it to His Excellency that he has already exceeded, by a wide margin, the reasonable time that was necessary for his inquiry.'

'What are you now accusing me of?'

'Please reply to the point put to you.'

'My illness prevents me from working on it any faster.'

'Does His Excellency expect an improvement in his health, which would allow the Company's service to resume in the near future?'

'That I do not know.'

'Has His Excellency recently obtained medical advice on his condition, and if so, would he kindly produce the certificate for it?'

So it continued, for half an hour, until van Reede asked van Goens whether he still had anything of consequence to add? But it was turned down, with a curious shrug and a gesture of the head as if all this did not concern him. On what last anchor could the man still be relying?

Then first the nephew and afterwards the clerk had to read out their versions of the minutes. While they compiled their final copy, the conversation among the three gentlemen continued, and in the end wax was burned, and papers, pens and ink were passed round for signature. The copy which van Reede offered van Goens when he took his leave was dropped beside the couch by van Goens. Van Reede raised a finger to de Grevenbroek.

'Please file it with Mr van Goens's documents.'

After that it was as if van Reede wanted to remove van Goens from his sight. But van Goens fought back. Van Reede dispatched a doctor to Rustenburg, but the man returned with the announcement that co-operation had been refused. Upon which de Grevenbroek and Swaardecroon were ordered to accompany the doctor, with a message that a report on His Excellency's health was required. Should van Goens not be prepared to assist the high commissioner with this, he would be dismissed from the service and carried on board. 'Will you please talk to him?' asked Swaardecroon.

The doctor's report stated that he could find no defect or weakness which might prevent the honourable gentleman from resuming his journey.

Thereupon van Reede sent de Grevenbroek out with a letter to the effect that the commissioner was granted a month to prepare for his journey to the East, otherwise he would be constrained to tender his resignation or return to Holland. And he removed de Grevenbroek from van Goens's service, replacing him with a junior clerk called Borremans.

Next, van Reede initiated the prosecution of Lieutenant Dubertin. Van der Stel had reported him, said the nephew. This French lieutenant was a rare bird, he was always looking for an audience, like an out-of-work actor. He had the reputation of being hospitable: he used to entertain the Cape councillors every week, when he would liberally ply them with liquor, to ensure their attention. In that way he bought their favour in weekly instalments. Then he would boast with his big voice and small, piercing, round eyes, telling them for example that almost single-handedly he had suppressed the rebellion of the cinnamon growers on Ceylon at the time when van Goens had been governor there, and that he'd forced open again the trade for the Company, and paid the ungrateful rebels for their treason with blood. A ludicrous scoundrel he was. He predicted to the councillors that Commander van der Stel was going to experience rough passage at the hands of his friend and patron, Commissioner van Goens. He dared even to contradict van der Stel at council meetings, where van Goens was present. Then he would position himself opposite van der Stel with all the haughtiness of a European confronting a half-blood. This caused van der Stel to turn white. And that was the man who was a favourite of van Goens.

Van Reede came to de Grevenbroek's desk in the secretariat saying: '*J'aimerais vous parler en personne.*' And when he answered, '*Certainement, monsieur, à votre service,*' the rest of the conversation ensued in French. He was ordered to accompany the fiscal to Lieutenant Dubertin's workplace, to inform him that following the high commissioner's command he was being dismissed from his position and restricted to his house with immediate effect; he was not allowed to receive visitors, but his wife was free to come and go. De Grevenbroek was to address the man in French, addressing him as monsieur even if he insisted on his rank. The fiscal would carry the warrant, for which Dubertin had to sign. What is at the heart of all these words? De Grevenbroek thought. Dubertin had to be cast out on an island, for van Reede wanted the man socially and professionally castrated, put out of action, banished, as an example to all who looked for favour with van Goens. Any island would do.

Dubertin immediately appealed to Commissioner van Goens, strutting like a cockerel, but that was something de Grevenbroek had often seen in the army; short men tended to react like that. He merely made a deep bow and left, followed by a volley of curses and oaths.

During and after van Reede's investigation, he was sent to Dubertin's house on three occasions: once to search it for stolen or smuggled wares, once to ask Dubertin to respond to accusations of people who had raised his crimes in sworn statements, a third to make an inventory of his furniture and other possessions, in case these had to be sold to pay a fine, or if there should be a divorce. Every time he was coarsely insulted by the man, and every time he was impressed by the sweetness of the beautiful woman.

Once they could see in which direction the matter was heading, the lady asked him to request an interview with van Reede. But the high commissioner replied: No, she had to put her request in writing. Her request was to return to the fatherland to arrange her affairs so that she could follow her husband to whatever fate was accorded him. This was approved by van Reede. The expectation was that the Frenchman would be carrying seashells on Robben Island for many years. And they never suspected how on that voyage his wife left the country with her husband's smuggled jewels and also a large portion of old van Goens's ill-gotten gains. No one would have expected it of such a pretty little baby face. But when her big-mouthed husband boastfully dropped the brick ('Borghorst is not the only one who carried jewels in hot spots'), he was thrown out of the country, to Mauritius. Let him go and play the fool there.

Van Reede and van Goens had not yet finished fencing. A week before his month was out, de Grevenbroek and Swaardecroon were sent to Rustenburg to remind van Goens of his date of departure, and offer their help to ease the preparations. Every time it was de Grevenbroek who had to do the talking. The day before his ship sailed, he was sent to invite the commissioner and his wife to the farewell dinner, with instructions to say that if van Goens declined it, a coach for them and another for their baggage would be waiting at Rustenburg at daybreak.

At first it seemed as if all the fight had gone out of van Goens, but once he was on board and the captain only waiting for wind, the post-keeper at Rustenburg sent notice of missing pots, pans, plates and the slave woman who had attended Mrs van Goens. Then somebody noticed that the clerk Borremans had not shown up for work that day. It was a difficult task for de Grevenbroek, because every captain was unquestionably in command on his ship. First, he had the fiscal wait in the boat alongside, and succeeded in persuading the captain to institute a second search for stowaways. Then he managed to speak to van Goens in the cabin, assuring him that the captain would not leave the anchorage before the ship had been searched; if necessary, the fiscal and his henchmen would be called on board for it. In this way he got his missing persons, but he was not inclined to hunt for pots and pans under somebody's bed. And he was satisfied that in the whole process he had never affronted either of the two parties or van der Stel.

On his trips to Rustenburg during the spring months, he managed to collect some of the rarest plants that flower only during those three weeks of the year, and offered them via Swaardecroon to van Reede. He also told him about his experience as a labourer in the Leiden *hortus*. Swaardecroon brought a note of thanks from his master van Reede, and an invitation to visit the natural science collection in the Garden House with a group of visitors. That was the government's guest lodge in the Company gardens. About twelve men and women from van Reede's company gathered before the Garden House to be escorted by the head gardener Oldenland. The language of communication was mainly French, as if Dutch had been debased by the losses of the recent war. What have we of Leiden fought for then? wondered de Grevenbroek. What is the use of all my years of service?

'The things inside here,' Oldenland told them, 'are not all of Cape origin. Here is a stuffed Cape lion, there the spotted forest ass, called *quacha* by the Hottentots. It is already getting scarce. Here is a stuffed porcupine. No, Your Honour, I honestly cannot tell you how this species copulates. Most cautiously, I should say. Here is the ostrich egg with a volume equal to that of two dozen chicken eggs, I have been told. There is the foot of the ostrich. Here we have different kinds of wood – this is closer to my own training – all sawn into discs, so that we can see the growth rings. Cape narrow-leaf yellow-wood, the wild almond, black ebony from Mauritius, red ebony, and here the fruit of coco de mer. According to Commander Lamotius it does not grow on the island, but comes floating from the west.'

As the guide and his guests move forward, talking, van Reede stopped to turn the coco de mer round and round in his hands, and under the impression that one of his friends was following him, asked: 'Is this the Venus palm?' Proceeding in English, so that the ladies would not understand: 'What a curious resemblance to the business end of wenches, don't you think?'

'A perversity of nature, My Lord,' de Grevenbroek said behind him, 'perhaps understandable, as even its marvellous diversity must have limits.'

Van Reede turned round. 'Oh, Mr de Grevenbroek. Aren't you a bachelor? You reason like a Jesuit.'

That little conversation led to the most satisfying period of his career, which he later recalled with much pleasure. There in the Garden House the high commissioner asked him about his experience, his knowledge and abilities. He was particularly pleased with his basic botany and his Latin. He was planning a *Hortus Africanus*, restricted to Cape plants really, actually a *Hortus Capensis*, once his study of Malabar's flora was completed. Did de Grevenbroek know what Professor Hermann of Leiden had to say about the Cape's spring flowers? 'Heavenly fields, heavenly fields . . .' If de Grevenbroek were willing, he would ask van der Stel's permission to let him start a *Hortus Capensis*. Oldenland had been well trained here, and van der Stel had a quite capable draughts-man in the garrison, a student of Doctor Cleijer, called Claudius. If de Grevenbroek would undertake to do the Latin descriptions, he would be remunerated for it.

Van Reede remarked: 'I see you sometimes wear the academic gown. Which university?'

'No, Your Excellency. I was literally born on the doorstep of Leiden, but I wasted my time. This gown I got from a medical student who needed a few guilders.'

'For drink, or a slut, if memory serves me.'

'Oh no. A body for anatomical examination, he assured me.'

When van Reede left for the East, he took de Grevenbroek with him, against van der Stel's wishes. For two years on that voyage he learned the art of taxonomy from van Reede, while the high commissioner travelled from office to office to examine their systems and eval-uate their results. He was grateful for opportunities those years had given him. He knew that it wasn't just because he had helped to put down van Reede's opponents, because van Reede had hardly known van Goens and Dubertin. One had been his late enemy's son, the other was van der Stel's enemy. What good could their fall do van Reede? It must have been because of the way in which he, de Grevenbroek, had executed his commission. That was what van Reede noticed, and that was what gave him the pleasure.

In due course he asked to return to the Cape. He wanted to start the *Hortus Capensis*, and a study of the Company's first fifty years at the Cape, with special reference to the West Cape Koina. His plan, about the Hottentots, had been growing inside him for a long time. He would ask to go on a land journey to visit the natives, and collect plants. He believed that van Reede would ensure that the Cape governor approved it.

One night, working on a preliminary outline for the *Hortus Capensis* in his room in the Castle, this was what he wrote in Latin: *In this country there is something like an everlasting spring because of the sunny flowers and gay colours. The mountains, hills, pastures and orchards are covered with flowering grasses and shrubs, the scents more pleasing than the incense of Saba, sweeter than the perfume of Venice. All the flowers attest to the Creator in their perfect parts, fine design, wonderful variety, brilliant appearance and sweet fragrance. They proclaim loudly: God, God, and their annual reappearance symbolises the resurrection.*

He reread the paragraph, and sat staring at it for a long time as if he could not believe it. Colourful, certainly. Full of little flowers, yes. But was this botany? Perhaps he had no gift for science. He was beginning to get to know himself. His gift was language. And his heart, he knew, had never been in botany.

From Batavia van Reede ordered that upon arrival van der Stel had to appoint him as Secretary of the Council of Policy. It was a good step forward, and for the time being it was enough reward. In future his progress would depend on his patron. But van Reede never returned. He died under suspicious circumstances; poisoned, it was said, by the rats he'd tried to drive from their holes. And van der Stel's attitude towards him and all other staff members immediately hardened, his voice grew icy, his tongue sharp and often venomous. This was the real Simon van der Stel, the man whom his foreign visitors and favoured guests at Constantia never met.

All the documents of the Council of Policy, everything that had to be written in Latin, French, German, Portuguese or English, all the secret documents, all the correspondence with the Directors, the Council of India, sea captains, keepers of Cape stations as far away as Mauritius, all the most confidential and personal documents, the analysis of surveys of stock or staff, all the draft correspondence which an administrator customarily preferred to do himself, were given to de Grevenbroek. Perhaps it was a penalty, a punishment for the trust a high commissioner had previously placed in him. In addition, van der Stel made him his private secretary, requiring an oath from him and burdening him with his personal correspondence. From this source he learned about the family relationship between Huydekoper and Simon van der Stel. They were no less than second cousins.

The higher one rose in the Company's hierarchy, the more fringe benefits became available and accessible, in quite honest and proper ways. The seventeen Lords, as prime investors in the business, had the right to buy at a reasonable tariff a part of a cargo that interested them. If, for instance, the Company bought something for ten rix-dollars in the East and handling and transport cost another forty dollars, then a lord could buy it from the ship's holds at sixty dollars. With this profitable little purchase he could do as he chose. Mr Huydekoper dealt in sugar. He could buy all the sugar in the cargo, wholesale, and either sell it in small quantities at a large profit to the city's merchants, or – it was a matter of comfort and loyalty – sell it back at a smaller profit to the Company. Mr Huydekoper had the contracts to provide the Cape with sugar and tobacco. It was important; de Grevenbroek carried the information home in the sleeve of his gown.

Van der Stel tried to intimidate people with his rowdy irascibility. That was his customary weapon; the second was summary banishment. In his report on the Cape, the high commissioner advised van der Stel to put an end to his autocratic and bombastic style of government. But it did not change. One morning, for example, he arrived at the Castle in a fit of rage. By that time he'd been away on his farm Constantia for a week. He was there so often instead of in his office in the Castle, that a foreman wanting to report a labourer had to threaten the fellow with, 'It's time I went to Constantia again', rather than 'I'm going to the Castle'. Van der Stel entered de Grevenbroek's office ranting and beating his cane on books and furniture, and demanded the title deed to the farm Witteboomen. De Grevenbroek had a fright, but remained calm and looked for it in a file in dignified silence. Van der Stel tore it from his hands, scribbled the word *Cancelled* on it between two lines, flung it down and stormed out again. The next morning de Grevenbroek read in the journal that it had been a decision of Council to remove Coenraad Visser of Witteboomen from his property and banish him to Mauritius, because he only wanted to hunt, rather than grow wheat. Two fresh lies that morning in the Honourable Company's journal, because in the first place there had never been a Council meeting, and secondly, after van der Stel had calmed down, he gave Visser permission to wait until his wheat was ripe for the sickle before he left Witteboomen. So Visser's fault came to light, it had been that the governor wanted his piece of land which bordered on Constantia, and he'd been unwilling to relinquish it in humble subjection. That was what the king had ordered Naboth to be stoned for, wasn't it? Should free Hollanders allow this covetous man to have his way?

When van der Stel came to the office again that afternoon, de Grevenbroek pointed out to him that the banishment had not been a decision of Council. Van der Stel's sallow skin went pale. He shook his finger in front of his face.

'You keep your nose out of my affairs, if you wish to remain in your post.'

'The high commissioner appointed me to this post.'

'He is dead. Stay out of my way. Keep your trap shut.'

As another example, van der Stel would summon the postkeeper at Robben Island for no other reason than to fulminate at him for a trifle. Old Sergeant Callenbach namely thought that he was doing his duty to write to the governor that there was a young cow on the island which needed to get to a bull, as it would be pity for such a fine animal to remain barren. Why was van der Stel furious at Callenbach? Not because of a cow or a calf, but because there was still an official left who dared to think for himself; a moth not paralysed by the heat of the candle. And in his disappointment Postkeeper Callenbach put a few Latin words on paper: *I take care of my enemy*, which was a very common proverb, but van der Stel applied it to himself. He ordered de Grevenbroek to translate it.

'So it says: I take care of my enemy. Is this the exact translation, or your own interpretation? What is *your* interpretation?'

He tried to protect Sergeant Callenbach, tried to explain that it was one of eighty or a hundred proverbs of Roman origin that most pupils had to learn. It could not be taken seriously; it was no more than a witty phrase. It implied that you were cautious about your opponent, as much as that you took trouble for someone who did not appreciate it.

That was the explanation van der Stel wanted. He had Callenbach with his chest removed from the island and confined him in the Castle until the next ship left for the fatherland, because of a miserable scrap of paper found in the island's posthouse by a *soebatter*, a servant trying to curry favour. In that way the Company was deprived of an experienced official, an old man who had loyally served the fatherland in its darkest hour. An able servant, with nearly forty years of experience at his various outposts, was discarded, dismissed and expelled as watermaker on a home-bound ship.

De Grevenbroek was not one to look for company. He had few possessions, and took his meals of dry bread, an onion and water in his room. For Fridays he bought a fish. Faithful as a soldier to his duty, he worked in his office from eight in the morning until ten in the evening, by candlelight, by lamplight, by torchlight, without asking an hour's sick leave. He was too busy doing his duty to realise that he was like a horse caught in a rut before the plough, each day following a single furrow. Until the bitter day when he wrote his last Council minutes and sent it round for signature, with another Latin proverb following his name: *It is a duty to work, but not in the dark*. Van der Stel wanted to know what it meant, and he told him.

'You want the Lords to read it. Stop your nonsense and leave your little messages out of it. It is for me to say what goes into the book and what not.'

Was that how a governor spoke to the secretary who handled their employer's confidential documents, after so many years of personal service? The thought became too repulsive. At the end of the month he concluded his work, signed it and wrote under it: *Prodesse orbg. nocere nemine* – To all I have done well, and harmed nobody. Thereupon he left his employer's service. Became a free burgher, as they put it in these parts.

But under the van der Stels no burgher was free. The episode with Coenraad Visser had already shown that. Free burghers, or servants like poor Callenbach and Sergeant Jerling, were like serfs, and if you were not strong enough to keep your spirit out of the master's hands, you became like an animal in his team, a dumb ox before the plough, silent under his whip. If you couldn't bear that, you had to fight for your freedom as well as you could. If the pen was your weapon, you wrote. That was why he, the clerk de Grevenbroek, made brief excerpts over many years for future use, carrying them home in his sleeve.

There was one letter from the directors which van der Stel did not let him see. He said there was nothing in it that concerned the Council of Policy. Later the letter appeared on file. A year or more ago van der Stel had confiscated a snake stone, an amulet with supposed magical powers, from an Oriental exile, and the exile had complained to Batavia about it. Their letter ordered van der Stel to return the amulet; they did not wish to have any discontent in the East. The Council raised its eyebrows: Who on earth would think that the honourable gentleman could have wanted to steal a poor exile's amulet? What did he want to do with it? Did he believe in black magic? On another occasion the Lords demanded an explanation from van der Stel for rumours that he owned a golden *kris*, a golden crown set with jewels, and a golden skull with large rubies in the eye sockets, stolen from the wreck of the Portuguese ship *Nossa Senhora*.

Once, Lords Seventeen exclaimed in disappointment and helpless rage over ten thousand miles of green seawater, in their missive to van der Stel: *We cannot comprehend how it could possibly have entered your brain to destroy in this manner a man who had been the Company's friend and had served us loyally for so many years, and we fear the consequences of your act, which will cause bitterness and hate among the Hottentots.* He, the Cape governor, had not even deigned to inform the Directors that he had attacked and annihilated Captain Dorha's Chainouqua tribe in the Overberg, the one tribe which had nourished the Company for almost forty years through its most difficult times, and had helped it to establish its refreshment system.

And the fables the man could invent to dish up to the Lords. At Outpost Klapmuts, he wrote, he had devised an apparatus to rid a patch of wheat of wheat lice. It consisted of a length of finger-thick rope, with a number of pebbles tied to it with string. Two labourers from the post carried the apparatus lightly across the wheat tops, dragging the dangling pebbles through the stalks, causing them to beat the lice from the stalks like tiny hammers, so that they fell to the ground and died there. It was a childish fable, as ridiculous as the advice he had sent to the commander on Mauritius to keep rats out of young sugar cane. He didn't say where they were supposed to find the labourers, he didn't say how they were supposed to dig into the volcanic rock, he didn't say what made him think that rats couldn't swim, all he said was that they should dig deep trenches around the plantations and fill them with water, then all the rats would fall in them and drown. De Grevenbroek had asked Lamotius: What was the reaction of your Council at the time you read it? And Lamotius replied: The members were careful about what they said around the table, but one of the leading free burghers said outright: Tell him he is dreaming.

Was it from hope or despair that rats jumped from a sinking ship into the sea? He did not know. He did not resign from the Company's service out of fear or hope, but out of resentment against a single official, in order to strike back later in revenge, or at the very least with a kind of correction, exactly as the mighty van Reede with his eternally unfinished manuscript had hoped to do in an attempt to restore balance between good and evil. A secretary with sound discrimination could never respect such a superior. One no longer expected gratitude, appreciation or promotion, only reproaches and reprimands; his very presence kindled resentment against the person and against the service. For him, there had been too many disappointments, too many complaints, too many cracks in a wall the Company had erected for its own protection.

Fortunately he had served only under the first van der Stel, and had already retired, fled and retreated to this farm four years ago to work on his *Portrait of the Cape*, by the time the son Willem Adriaan, as governor and successor to his father, turned himself into an oppressor of his subjects and an enemy of the people.

Now this was neither a new story nor a repetition of the previous one, but a troublesome continuation of a long, long tale which would drag out until the end of time, the way sea turtles crawl up sloping beaches to attempt an ancient story anew. Put Willem Adriaan aside for the time being, without compunction. He can never be forgotten, nor can he escape. He is caught, pinned down, a colourless insect with a nasty sting, trapped for ever under the magnifying glass, and people will come to look, not to learn something, but from curiosity. 'Come and look, ladies and gentlemen. For a *stuyver* you can see Willem Adriaan van der Stel.' If there is any sympathy, keep it for his wife. People will visit the green fishpond in the Castle's inner court for more money, to see where that poor person tried to drown herself. And what will they discover there? Rippling water.

Let us first go back, to Mauritius, because it is Easter night, thirty-two years ago. Church leaders decided that the third full moon of the year should be Easter night. *Fiat lux,* it is the third full moon of the year. During the day a huge ebb tide nearly sucked dry the lagoon in front of the Lodge. The pilot boat lies dry at its anchor, way in front of the end of the jetty. Before sunset the moon rises behind Tobacco Island: huge, silver, a damaged round face with the pale silence of a corpse; its light begins to form transparent shadows over the farms of Lemoenbos. Commander Lamotius has made sure that he would not be in the Lodge tonight.

At Black River Mouth Pieternel is home alone with the children. She is heavily pregnant. The sunset was sweatily hot, the children have been running about naked all day, and she feels sorry to call them inside to put on clothes, because with sunset come the mosquitoes. She goes out into the backyard to call them inside, and sees the silver of the moon, still behind the dark mountain, shining up against the twilight. She remains there to show them the first hard glimmering sliver of light. Afterwards she feeds them at the big table, washes the smallest ones and makes them lie down under their nets, gathering the bigger ones around the Bible.

She tells them about Easter night. It is the night the Jews fled from the house of bondage in Egypt. The full moon stares balefully over that even desert, like a great red eye through clouds of dust. All over the land the first-born children and the first-born of all the animals lie dead. There is a terrible weeping, people are running to and fro. Hundreds of slaves run to the sea: at this ebb tide they can get through to the desert beyond. The dogs bark after them. Soldiers on war carriages thunder past after them.

Pieternel's children look around restlessly, fidgeting about, feeling frightened. She herself is scared, and nauseous. It is the day the Jews came to take our sweet Lord from among his disciples to crucify him. A large moon hangs low behind the Olive Mountain, in the garden the dark leaves shimmer with light. No, I don't know why! They were full of arrack. Today, in Dad's land across the sea, everybody walked to church in the cold. It is late winter there now, but almost, almost springtime. At the Cape they have a church too. About this time at the Cape the March flower opens its blood-red cup, then it is time for winter to begin. No, the word is *chalice*. Now everybody who understands anything knows that the first full moon after the March flower brings the rain. Two or three days before, or two or three days later, but often enough exactly at the time of the full moon, the first rains begin. The grass turns green, rivers begin to flow, there are shiny vleis brimful of fresh water, in which little frogs sing, and the Koina can come to rest and stop their roaming in search of pasture. Already their veld food is growing, sweet wild bulbs and wild almonds, cows fill pots with their creamy milk, the sheep are fat and heavy with voluminous fat tails. There is rich fat at home. The young boys want to show the girls all manner of grown-up tricks, but the mothers rein them in. This is the very best time of the year. In the town the housewife says: How can I bake with wet wood, with wet washing, wet shoes, mud on the floor, children with colds? But in their *harubis* homes the Koina are laughing.

Pieternel invents thoughts until her children are ready to sleep. Why does she pretend that the Koina are happier than the white man? It is nonsense. She has to keep her head. It is still a few hours before midnight. She leaves their lamp burning, for the smell helps to ward off mosquitoes. Then she rolls down and buttons her sleeves and goes outside to see the moon hanging over the ridge of the mountain. It is Easter night. Why does the Lord use this one full moon to illuminate all those terrors? For the first time that day she puts on shoes and walks down to the beach. Where the darkness begins at the first trees, she meets the ghost crabs. They scuttle in all directions on their pale legs, it looks as if they're floating over the ground, so fast their legs move. The Koina talk about a ghost, *hei-nun*, the grey feet, because you cannot see him step on the ground. Tonight is the true third full moon of the year. Tonight the year turns round, the seasons change, the unborn die.

Commander Hugo told them, as they sat at his table to get their marriage certificate, that he'd experienced it every year on the coasts of this warm ocean – Somalia, he mentioned, Aden, Arabia, Persia, Malabar, Maledive and Nikobar – that on this one night of the year the turtles come to land in hundreds of thousands, on islands, islets, sandbanks, continents. All of them female, each one carrying a hundred eggs. It is their moon the Lord provides, for tonight the sea comes out higher than ever, almost up to the trees. Every female from those foam-white waves drags her heavy body up the incline of the beach, resting every now and then, slowly, it can take an hour or more, to the highest dry spot on the beach where she lays her hundred eggs in warm earth. One sits in the moon shadow under the palm trees, listening to the deep sough of their dragging over the coarse coral sand; over the illuminated sand one sees the dark bodies approaching, rowing laboriously up the incline towards one. There are hundreds upon hundreds of them, one can hear them groaning. At about midnight, when the moon is at its zenith and the sea gives its last pushes almost up to your feet, you strike fire, passing the tinderboxes from hand to hand, lighting lanterns. Then forty or fifty of you make a charge, and start turning them over, turning, turning them on their backs, throwing them upside down with a jerk and a shout, until the whole beach is covered with helpless females waving their legs in the air. That is when you fall on them with hollow-ground knives and start the butchering. In all the languages spoken on these shores, they call it the death of the unborn. All the peoples praise the Lord for this night.

Pieternel can see no star in the faintly glimmering sky, but a broad yellow band of moonlight stretches all the way to the reef. The moon is moving towards midnight. What will become of her children if she dies? She has been feeling nauseous for days. She weeps with her forehead against a tree.

Before daybreak the two boats return from Turtle Bay: Daniel and Jaap and four slaves on one sloop, and the commander with a number of sailors on *Vanger*, drunk with killing and slaughtering, oil-besmirched and bloody, the boats loaded up to the gunwales with eggs, barrels of oil, barrels of meat and fat, shells, and strings of live tortoises dragged after them on ropes, with the pale full moon still in the sky.

With her clothes on, she lies on the bed, crying. She does not want to speak to him, she will not prepare food for them. Daniel goes to Lamotius to say: 'Sorry, commander. It's her condition.' She hears it, and it makes her cry more. All morning they work under the lean-to, continuing to slaughter, salting meat and eggs, filling the jugs and barrels with oil, dividing everything properly among three parties. Then they clean the yard, scour the boats and barrels in the river, and jump into the swimming hole to wash themselves. Jaap's wife feeds white and black together under the shady trees.

It was that night that Lamotius had the French lieutenant dragged from his bed, and he himself did not want to be near the Lodge. Daniel came to ask her whether she would mind if the commander spent the night with them.

She said: 'Why do you murder the unborn animals?'

He said: 'We have to eat. One man's death is the other man's bread.'

'It's a lie,' she said to his face. 'I despise your proverbs. What right do you have to say that to me?'

Somewhat to the north of the island the north-east wind changes to a south-wester. The seasons change. The palm leaves move softly above their house.

Explanations may cover up transgressions, but they do not soften anything. Van der Stel used his temper and his power and never tried to hide it, except through silence. Oh, those were two who knew how to cover their tracks, that father and son. Had he not known from the archives about an outpost on Lourens River in the Hottentots-Holland, he would never have suspected the existence of something like that. The generation who knew about it has almost died out now; the new generation has never known. 'That is why history must repeat itself,' the farmer Tas said, 'because the stupid bastards won't listen.' And it does repeat itself, in unexpected ways.

The outposts, he read in van Reede's official report, had a variety of functions. Hottentots-Holland was responsible for cultivating wheat from the year when Groote Schuur became exclusively a transport depot. Secondly, it had to link with the Peninsular Koina for bartering stock. It was also the post closest to the Overberg region, and whenever an expedition went to the Overberg, to shipwrecks at Agulhas or bartering with the Chainouqua and Hessequa, travellers had to spend the last night there, take new teams of oxen, and with the help of the post men and slaves move the wagons and cattle to the top of the mountain. The workers at the post also had to collect specimens of the animals, plants and birds from the two regions, for the learned professors abroad. That is how it is documented in official language. That outpost existed from 1673 until 1703, when Governor Willem Adriaan arrived, looked about him carefully, and pocketed it with buildings, fields, wagons, animals, implements, postkeeper, slaves, harvests, everything. It quietly disappeared from the Company's list of outposts, reappearing in the landscape as Vergelegen, the new governor's estate.

Now, it was no longer strange to hear about the estates of highly ranked gentlemen. Locally, Simon van der Stel's Constantia was a familiar example. In the East country residences were familiar phenomena. Ever since God had shaken the city of Batavia and caused it to die, and the corpse of the city began to stink, more and more gentlemen of high rank moved away to establish small delights in the cool air of higher hills, three hours or so away from the doomed city. They were stately homes in the cool Oriental style, with large gardens, orchards, and sweet-sounding names from the fatherland, like *Uitwijk*, *Weltevreden*, *Buitenzorg*. One would not suspect anything amiss at all.

Was it coincidence then, or planned by the Almighty that at the turn of the century there should have been a massive earthquake in the mountains behind the city? The city was shaken, with a rumbling that lasted for minutes, but the damage in the centre fortunately seemed negligible. A large cloud of dust prevented them from looking outside. After a few days messengers were sent to climb tall trees from where they could survey the interior. The mountains looked unchanged. Then the rains came, and it rained and rained. The Grogol and Chiliwong came crashing down with tons upon tons of trees and mud washed right through the city, all broken loose by landslides and rockfalls in the mountains; every stream on the plains, every ditch and canal in the fine old city was clogged with mud and branches and slush. The brown flood broke through the river mouth, pushing up into the sea for miles. Suffocated fish were floating belly-up over the outer anchorage. Water traffic came to an end, lighters could no longer enter the city to unload, and within a month the first plague of gnats and mosquitoes were hatched in the stinking marsh. Dysentery was followed by the East Coast fever, malaria. The hospital was overflowing, the poor died without help in their kampong. Scores died every week, and the Dutchmen of rank, from the governor-general down, left the castle and the city, escaping with their families to the cool of the hills, to their pleasure houses above the wind.

But what was to become of commerce and administration of the Company, of the Netherlands, if warehouses were no longer guarded and their contents controlled? Who kept the books up to date? What resident remained to complain to the city administration about the stink of the canal next to his house, and to ensure that something was done about it? The gentlemen might come into their offices every third day, as there no longer was any water transport, and then leave the city again before the mosquitoes started humming at twilight. The gangrene that arose in one limb, branched devastatingly until the whole body was inflamed and recovery no longer possible. Batavia was ill, and in due course the honourable Company had to die in the fatherland. The best anyone could hope for, was to survive personally, until his contract allowed him to escape home from here.

Such was the situation in the East, and the reason why prosperous gentlemen built country residences for themselves. But at the Cape in those days, not a single reason existed for Governor Willem Adriaan to establish an estate for himself a full day's journey from the Castle, apart from greed and a desire for power, both of which he had in abundance. Nobody, free burgher or servant, would dare to mention that Governor Willem Adriaan had stolen an outpost of the Company with everything on it, moving and unmoving. He was merciless. Look at what he did to Sergeant Jerling, officer of the guard.

He arrived from his country residence after midnight at the Castle gate, which had already been locked at sunset with the elaborate ritual customary all over the world. When the coachman sounded his bugle at the gate, Jerling went out personally, as he wanted to ask the coachman for the password to show that he was doing his work properly — he would not allow a Trojan Horse to enter. What did he get for a reply? The governor alighted, struck him four blows in the face with his cane. 'There's your password.' You didn't want to oppose this man, for God's sake, you didn't want anything in the world to do with him, you just wanted to keep away from him. At the Cape, Justice, always blindfolded, had lost the ability to see. Commissioners were sent to inspect the colony. That was why Adam Tas, Piet van der Byl, Koos van der Heiden, Henning Hüsing, van Brakel and others started the conspiracy against him.

'Batavia is a pitiful sight right now,' the hired hand Lamotius said to de Grevenbroek. 'When we were young, it was the city of our dreams, the capital of our empire in the East, founded by Ysterjan Coen, the hero of Holland. There, fortunes were made, dreams realised, fame won. If I had any choice at that time, monsieur, between Batavia and heaven, I would have chosen Batavia without a moment's hesitation. We had, at least, a map and a documented history of Batavia. Certainty, you understand? Look here.' He pulled a rolled map of the city from a tube. 'I bought this from the printer in the Castle over there.' He slightly raised two crooked red fingers from his wide sleeve. 'Two guilders. Here is the date, 1689. That was soon after you yourself were there. Beautiful, isn't it? But it is all nonsense. It no longer looks like that. These three long canals – sorry, I cannot read their names – with side canals from one to the other, have been filled up. This district is now a marsh, the whole city wall from here to here has crumbled and caved in. All these avenues of small trees – they were coconut palms and *kanari*, remember? – have been drowned, rotten. In the affluent district here, you now find the hovels of beggars. Property is worth little. That is why they sell these maps for two guilders.' He let go of the map and allowed it to snap back by itself, and pushed it back into its tube with some effort.

'We were fortunate to have seen the old city.'

'One day, Monsieur de Grevenbroek, we will arrive at the golden gate, and discover that it, too, is no longer what it was.'

De Grevenbroek was on a visit as a church elder, but he did not reprimand the man. Lamotius has some strong views of his own. The first time he visited Elsenburg, was as deacon on a house visit with the Reverend Beck. The owner was at home, and had been expecting them. *Secundus* Elsevier he had known for some years now, and he had seen his wife in the Castle on a few occasions. Elsevier called in his children and labourers, to attend the scripture reading and prayer. Someone said that the hired hand had asked to be excused. Elsevier replied: 'Tell him that I order him to come,' whereupon a figure wrapped like a Bedouin in a brown robe entered. Elsevier presented him: 'Isaac Lamotius.'

They looked at one another in silence. Lamotius asked: 'More wine?'

He nodded, pushing his glass across the table. Lamotius's hand and forearm appeared from the robe, hairless, swollen, red; higher up a bandage smelling of herbal ointment protruded. He lifted the carafe with contorted fingers, tilted it over their glasses. Blood seemed to pour from his fingertips. His red eyelids, without any sign of eyelashes or brows, stared from the fold of his headpiece. De Grevenbroek nodded his thanks. When during that first meeting Elsevier mentioned his name to present him, he wondered: Is it possible that this unfortunate man, the engineer and adept of the natural sciences, the administrator of Mauritius whose horrible story he had retrieved from the archives, can be a leper too?

'You may consider it sour grapes, monsieur, but I am grateful that I shall never see Batavia again. When I was set free from Rosingain, I thought I'd try to make a living in Batavia, but everywhere you look, you see things that once were beautiful perish around you. It is depressing.'

'I understand. May I ask how old you are?'

The brown hood almost covered up his face. 'I'll be sixty this year.'

He was an interesting talker, a man with broad knowledge and strange experience, one who risked much, without showing any regret for what he had lost. This year, eleven years later, Lamotius left for Holland. He said he longed for the place of his birth. We all become like that: the body starts yearning for the dust and water from which it was formed. Nature wills it so. But it is one friend less in this awful place.

He only came to know Lamotius personally after *Secundus* Elsevier had been banished from this colony with Governor van der Stel and other officials. Lamotius managed the farm with an open mind, tended Elsenburg for eleven years, and transferred the income to the owner in Holland every year. He was good for the farm, and if such a thing were possible, one might say that the farm showed its gratitude. It was a pity that the employer would never see how the hired hand had improved the place. Lamotius was a tidy, enterprising farmer, an energetic builder, good with irrigation and the uses of water. At the end of an ornate canal he had a big mill for grinding wheat. There was one place where one would swear the water was flowing uphill, if you looked from a certain angle. The slaves suspected that he was an Arab or some other Muslim who could cast a spell on water. He was a pleasant host too, but he never left that farm for business or pleasure. Church elders, the *landdrost*'s clerk, the messenger of the court, farmers wanting to rent the mill, contractors for wine and slaughter stock, the surgeon, they all had to come to him, and he would send a slave with a letter if he wished to communicate with one of them.

As it became possible for de Grevenbroek to speak to Lamotius more often, he himself had also begun to detach himself from public life. For three terms he had been *heemraad* for Stellenbosch, and church elder for two, and he no longer wished for status in the community. What is the community these days? Rowdy, drunken apprentices and peasant youths who clamber about the town's mill wheel at night and break it from its cogs. What satisfaction is there in the respect of savages? He stayed at home, refused invitations, seriously devoted himself to the writing of his *Portrait of the Cape*, sometimes completing three or even four foolscap pages a day. He forgot about the world and was forgotten by it, as the proverb says.

When he had to speak to Lamotius, he first sent a message, and invariably the answer was: Come and visit. Later, with the addition: I'm sending a horse carriage to fetch you. Such a visit might take three days and four nights. Lamotius was getting used to him. He asked the man: What is a salt mine? The answer was a pencil sketch: Here they lower us in a box through a hole in the ground; here we are chopping away crystals with a pick, we scoop up the mounds in baskets, carry the baskets up the incline, and empty them in the boxes; here we hoist up the boxes and lower them again.

'Is it harder work than carrying seashells on Robben Island?'

'I don't know.'

'The foremen humane?'

'It varies from man to man.'

'What do you say?'

'I'd prefer death.'

'What happened to Abraham Steen?'

'Dead. The air down there is salt gas. Salt attracts water. The air remains in your lungs. You smell it on your breath and taste it in your mouth. It draws the water from your body, it pickles your skin. I saw bodies there . . . Once we opened a shaft that had fallen in fifteen months before, and the corpses down there were fresh, cured leather like that briefcase of yours. It burns your skin and kills it. Look, these wounds will never heal. Fortunately parts of my skin were already dead, from a fire many years before. Your nails die and fall out. Your hair goes white and falls out, all over.'

'You were on Rosingain for six years. How many hours per day did you work?'

'Day and night. You sleep on salt bags, among the piled-up salt. You cover yourself with a bag. In the morning you lower yourself from there on a rope, in the evening they pull you up again. The walls sparkle the torchlight back into your eyes.'

De Grevenbroek even dared to ask about Aletha Dubertin. All the voice said was that he still had something of hers, a keepsake. He wanted to ask him: Let me see your face, I want to see what Isaac Lamotius looks like? But he remembered that what was hidden here was a third face. Just as little as he could ever come to know the first or second man, he could see their faces. With his own imagination he had to create him.

Because he was no longer allowed to read the government archives, de Grevenbroek lost some of the people he was interested in. Lamotius helped him, as far as he could force his thoughts back to his island, but sometimes he had the impression that Lamotius was not willing to return to a specific date or place. He knew, for example, in which year the Lyreman had died, because he'd been at his deathbed, but he didn't know when Sailor Borms or Master Woodcutter Sven had died. And then the boy Salomon, he'd been one of the first to die of East Coast fever, but later they had become too many to remember.

Secundus Elsevier, who saw the foreign correspondence, helped him with information from before his banishment. Prince Willem, whom he'd followed as a young soldier, had been invited to become King of England in 1689. Then why, and about what, for God's sake, had that war happened, a mere twelve years earlier? But they didn't think much about him or his wife over there, now referring to him as Dutch William, as if he were a gardener, or William the Third, like a mistake being repeated, or William and Mary, like two horses.

What had become of Fiscal Deneyn? Elsevier said his scandal could also be read in the Company's documents. After his career in the East he returned to the fatherland. He'd made his fortune, and retired not without honour, as in that year he was officially appointed Fiscal of the Return Fleet, holding life and death in his hand. Now he was *orang lama*, the desired status which was a whirlpool so loaded with destructive forces that it could easily pull in a youth until he became, first, invisible, and then absolutely nothing. Pieter Deneyn was no youth, and yet he too vanished. Nineteen days after the fleet had left Batavia, Captain Ganswijk signalled to the admiral that he wished to call a meeting. They were almost halfway between Batavia and Mauritius. The fleet turned by on the bottomless ocean, and drifted down under shortened sails. What could it be? Each ship lowered its yawl, sending its captain and secretary under sail to the flagship.

Fiscal Deneyn attended that meeting of the Broad Council on the flagship as the accused. His captain demanded that he be dismissed and punished for unbridled licentiousness. His crime was being drunk daily, and in addition there were the repeated complaints from a passenger's daughter. The Council dismissed Deneyn from his post as morally incapable, he had to pay his passage for the rest of his voyage, and his wine ration was limited to one *muts*, morning, noon and night, like those of the sailors. If the young lady were to complain again, he would be locked up in the hell.

It is a pity that Deneyn never married. A good wife might temper him first, later help him to stabilise. Artists benefit by marrying above their station. Somewhere abroad, two little books were published. First *Lust-hof der Huwelijken* or *Marriage Paradise*, in which he described the matrimonial customs of Oriental nations (but bear in mind that everything south or east of the island Walcheren belongs to the East on the Company's compass) as he'd experienced them during his years of service. A few years later followed his *Vroolijke Uuren,* or *Happy Hours*, which attracted attention at the Cape for containing a poem about Robben Island and one about Gisela Mostert. Elsevier possessed a copy, which he took out to show. It was no more than a series of odes dedicated to Bacchus and Venus, common boozing-and-whoring verses, in stark contrast with the Cape realities, such as Deneyn's dour discourses in court, for example about the five young Koina permanently chained together. It was no wonder that Mary Hugo had turned to him. She had known him, and knew that he would understand.

From Lamotius's explanations came an understanding of the economy of Mauritius, and of its handful of free residents. It was really interesting. Something de Grevenbroek began to understand better from his conversations with the former commander and with *Secundus* Elsevier, was how heavily the Cape relied on its outposts, and each outpost in turn on the potential of its own available people. Happy people made a good outpost, but if the balance was disturbed, one was landed with a bad outpost. Was that true?

'Yes.'

'The Cape suffers. Is that so?'

'Yes.'

If that was the case, how would he portray poor Lamotius in his *Portrait of the Cape*? What would he say, how would he describe the man? That he had been a talented young engineer, a man with a dream, with ambition. His hope of success had been based on that dream. Yes, financially too. With regular promotion in rank and pay, Lamotius could have looked forward to a satisfactory career of thirty, forty years, followed by a happy retirement in the fatherland. And his spirit? Because of his faith in his sawmill, he had assured his wife and Lords Seventeen that his invention would achieve what no commander before him had managed to do with the rare woods on the island. Profit? What was profit if not high production at low cost? The shining circular blade of his saw had made their eyes gleam; that was why they'd given him Mauritius. In his imagination he saw a rainbow around his sawmill, with the pot of gold at its foot. What else? Why would an intelligent man carry a young noblewoman and their child to an isolated place at the back of the globe, where there was no doctor, no school for the child, no *dominee* to baptise or to bless, and no relatives to bury him and comfort the widow? Such things were the pillars of a Dutch community.

The answer is: Lamotius believed unshakeably in his invention, as implicitly as if it had been told him by an angel. That cursed sawmill must have broken his heart. Like a woman who cools early in life, it succeeded in first making him depressed and then indifferent. That only one ship per year, and later one every two years, was sent for the timber, is charged with a different meaning. Imagine it: a tropical island, according to all reports green, wet with an abundance of water, yet when it had to turn his sawmill, drought ruled for decades, dusty earth, dry river beds, young deer drinking seawater. And when it rained, it came to wash away everything he had made. That mill was an emblem of the island's decline as well as of his own failure, and there was nothing at all he could do to stop it. The sawmill was Lamotius's last anchor; if that were to fail, he would be stranded and the sea would break over them all. With his mill, his honest promises to the Lords, to Governor Bax, to his parents-in-law, to Margarethe, to Isaac Johannes Lamotius himself, fell to pieces. His raft sank under his feet; he was left alone in the water, eye to eye in the foam with every sailor, clerk and peasant. How would he survive at that level? He would have to use rank and force to be salvaged. He would be forced to step on them and get away with it, like the van der Stels and their ilk knew to do so well.

On his right hand, his master woodcutters, Lamotius relied to help him realise his dream, and when he struggled, they were expected to help him carry the boat over the reef. But Telleson, an adventurer and a sloth, saw his saviour step ashore with the magical sawblade, listened to his sweet gospel about how much labour it would save, believed and followed, and when it didn't work, tried to stab the helpless prophet in the back. First Telleson, then Steen, more of an artisan from the labour classes, but a born man of violence, who took his lead from his commander. When the Cape rejected their island, Lamotius was left totally alone, helpless, a low island under a hurricane. About the meaning of the loss of the poor man's wife and child, God alone could tell. Who else would know?

When he tried to find Lamotius's present face in the dark hollow of a monk's cowl (perhaps there was only a skull with empty eye sockets inside – a diabolical, bony, talking death's head), de Grevenbroek had another thought about the hundreds of scraps of paper he had carried home in his sleeve with dark design, like an ant carrying leaves against winter. *Portrait of the Cape* was good, but at the outposts everyday life was contained in people like Lamotius and himself, people with souls, or who once had souls. Like islands separated from the continent, a commander would try to impose order there, families would try to eke out a living, convicts and slaves crawl from day to day, soldiers toss and turn on their beds in a sweat, every one alone. Each struggled to establish something, or simply to survive; they tried with their hands, sometimes in silence, sometimes furtively, sometimes with violence.

Against all their precautions and toil and labour stood the blank unknowingness of the sea, seasons, distance, time, and the changing authorities, about whom, on their remote outposts, they were, like children, ignorant. In his mind de Grevenbroek saw a half-naked, bearded, elderly man and a slave weaving a fishing net from grass, naked brown children sleeping under a net, a woman wearing a hat of palm leaves hanging washing on a line between two trees. What dramatic mountain peaks were those towering behind? What was the meaning of that orange-red sky? Who were these people? he wondered. What did their voices sound like? If they were Hollanders, what did they know about God and the Company? These were the reasons why he pitied them. They were defenceless, in every respect, under the threatening sky.

His own bitterness against the van der Stels, the morsels of information on scraps of paper which he'd strung like a Chinese kite on a thread to send into the world, for people to learn the truth about those two demons, no longer mattered. Bitterness, he acknowledged, is a symptom of defeat. By removing them from his story he could excise his own bitterness from it. Old Simon was dead, his children banished. He had survived them, and could now cleanse himself of them. Only, it was too late. Mauritius had been vacated and lay deserted, the documents had been signed, closed and tied up with ribbon in folders, the familiar ships dismantled, the people he would have liked to know, but never met, were dead. So, the time of man will end, and darkness return to the deep.

But undoubtedly history will repeat itself, and what was, will be again. And if something like an ending is desired where no ending exists, if information is required to represent an ending, then all right. Only, one can never tell it in such a way that understanding is complete, because the listener is caught in his own dream. True understanding and a true ending there will never be, because a circle runs on without end.

The driver of the Company's post wagon that arrived on Welmoed to buy old wine barrels for staves, recounted that a fleet was being prepared and equipped, three hookers, to start a new outpost on the east coast later in the year. There was gold in the interior, behind the blue mountains in the west, but the first thing the government wanted from there was black gold: slaves. Here we go again, thought de Grevenbroek, the wheel keeps turning. A remote outpost in the heart of the fever region, and slaves. Hadn't they learned?

Four years ago an auction in Stellenbosch had been advertised, a few deceased estates of paupers whose meagre possessions had been lumped together to be auctioned on a single occasion, to save the costs of auctioneer and refreshments. He went to have a look, because he was poor himself (van der Stel had not given him a pension, and he wasn't going to *ask* for it) and needed cheap furniture, something with doors he could use as a bookcase, a table with a large surface to write on, and some other odds and ends. The possessions of the poor are usually simple, home-made, but he didn't want anything fancy. Moreover, there would be fewer bidders as the devastating country-wide smallpox epidemic was barely over and people were still apprehensive about public gatherings. In fact, there were still deaths in their district, as close as Hottentots-Holland and the French Quarter, but he wasn't afraid of it, as he'd encountered pox in the monasteries of Spain and again in Naples, both the bovine and the human kind. He hoped to acquire a few pieces of furniture at a low price.

The gathering was small, as expected. There were almost no one except for the auctioneer and the bookkeeper, one or two of those whose possessions were up for sale, and a few impoverished people who had also come to bid. The junk was spread out on the floor of the millhouse: pots and pans, harnesses, shoes, a broken sword which might still be used to top vineyards, a butter churn, a small stack of window glass, and then on one side against the wall, a table, chairs, linen press, a *katil* with a mat of thongs. On the table sat a carpenter's chest with cooperage tools, with some initials carved into the lid, but already half effaced. There were no books, which was a pity. He bought what he wanted, and then spoke to the bookkeeper to pay and arrange for delivery. The clerk paged in his book, opened it at a name, and entered the amounts. The name was Pieter Zaaijman of Mauritius.

'Is this his estate?' he asked.

'No, he sent it in. Almost all the stuff comes from the Cape, but it won't fetch a price. They are still scared of people there. And these are poor man's things, not good enough for your Cape people.'

'When you pay him, please tell him that I'm anxious to hear from him. I am de Grevenbroek, I stay with the farmer van der Heiden at Welmoed.' He saw the clerk writing down his name and put a few coins on the book for him. The furniture was a bargain.

One morning, as he was having his tea outside under the oak tree, a young barefoot man approached across the yard from the direction of the Cape. De Grevenbroek put his book down, watching him over his spectacles. He was walking with a stick, as he was slightly lame in one leg, and so thin that the dogs didn't even look up. He wore a washed-out blue canvas shirt and breeches with broad red-and-blue stripes, of what was known as ticking in these parts. Round his head a red-dotted kerchief had been tied, and a scarf of what looked like black silk was tied around his waist with a bow. So young that he scarcely had any beard, and what there was made his face look dirty and older than his years.

'Come and rest, pilgrim,' he said. 'Where are you going?'

'Is this Welmoed? They told me there were dogs at Welmoed.'

'Let them sleep. Sit down, have a bowl of tea. I am de Grevenbroek.'

'I am Daniel Zaaijman from Mauritius.'

He leaned his head over backwards to get the boy under his spectacles, examining him with some incredulity.

'So who are you?'

'Daniel Zaaijman. Brother Piet asked me to come here and present his compliments.'

'Oh,' said de Grevenbroek, rising to his feet to hold out his hand to the boy. 'I am pleased to meet you.'

'The same.'

He sat down at the other side of the table, staring intently at de Grevenbroek, suddenly raised the tea bowl to empty its contents into his throat, carefully replaced it, then stared expectantly at him again. I wonder if he is retarded, thought de Grevenbroek. 'I wonder, young man, if you can show me on which side the moon comes up?'

'Is that why you asked brother Piet to come? You could have asked one of the people in the house to look for you.'

'Ah, I understand.' Later he came to understand them even better. They were quiet people, they could spend hours in silence, while their eyes read the environment and their ears listened to insects, the wind over the sea, birds in the grass, wavelets on the beach, while the nose and the hair on their skin tested the surrounding air for temperature and scents, changes in the wind.

He learned, through a series of questions, that the boy was on his way to the farmer Roelof Steinbock, to hand over some of the auction money. Pieter had sent a letter to ask that the man have mercy on them. Pieter had work, and the poor-relief would help Daniel to work, then there would be two of them to pay what was still owed on the farm.

And gradually the boy relaxed, and no longer spoke as if he was being interviewed by a ship's officer.

De Grevenbroek poured more tea. 'Which farm, if I may ask?'

'Patryzen Valleij, over there.' He pointed to the north of the town, towards Kromme Rhee.

'When did you live there?'

'Shortly after we arrived in the country.'

'Did it remind you of Mauritius?' Because he knew exactly what the surroundings looked like, directly under Papegaaiberg. The road to Elsenburg passes through it. There are deep valleys, steep heights, pointed mountain peaks to the east.

'I was too small. Perhaps Father and Mother thought so.'

'How are your parents?'

He put his hand down flat on the bow of the black scarf on his hip. 'They both of them died of the pox.' Tears brimmed over his eyelids. De Grevenbroek stared at him.

'I'm really sorry to hear that. I found Pieter Zaaijman's name at the auction, and I wanted to question him about your father and mother, and about you children. A very interesting family, very interesting. Come and look here.'

In his room he showed him the furniture. The boy nodded towards the cupboard, nodded at the *katil*, nodded at the table. 'Did you buy Father's tools? No, what would you do with them?' He rested his two hands on the table, leaned forward, and fixed his eyes on de Grevenbroek's Madonna, turning his head sideways as if he was listening to something, but said nothing.

'How many children were you?'

With a light sigh he stood upright, pointing with his finger at the eight places around the table. 'Father, and Mother, and Pieter, and I, and Christiaan, and Johannes, and old Kaleb, and Moses from Malabar.' The last two were slaves.

'And your sisters?'

'No, they were already married. All four of them died young. If you want to find out, you must ask Pieter, he is the oldest now and he knew them.'

'Died, so young?'

'It's the island fever.'

He arranged with the farmhand for a horse to be lent to the boy. He could ride, the boy had told the hand, it was a fall from a hired horse that had hurt his hip. He would be back before sundown, and if the owner didn't mind, could he lie his head down in the forecastle?

De Grevenbroek took his leave: '*Dominus tecum.*'

'Thank you. It was nice.'

That evening they ate together at the big table in his room; the housewife sent food for two. De Grevenbroek went on asking questions until the boy started yawning at the table. They offered him a bed in the house, but he preferred to lie down in the loft.

It is a terrible tension to have an unfinished manuscript on your table for a long time. You drift in a storm, without help. You still write every day, make small changes to the manuscript. You're treading water, you must go on, you know you must save yourself, and you know you're getting weaker as time goes by. Nobody can help, nobody knows how. Your hand is writing in water. Nothing remains of it.

A summer and a winter passed while de Grevenbroek, deeply worried about his mounting years, tried to arrange for him and Pieter Zaaijman to spend a few days together, so that he could hear details from him about the last days of the family and the island under the Dutch flag. The man had a wife and child, perhaps two, he couldn't abandon his work to be interrogated here at Welmoed. He himself could not afford to pay a carpenter's daily wages. He was thinking about asking Lamotius if he could offer Zaaijman work at Elsenburg for six or seven days, but decided against it; the man was too thin-skinned. He also asked van der Heiden, who offered to give him the money. But this he wouldn't accept, he already owed the man more than he could ever repay.

For days and months he wrote at his table, once dejectedly counting the pile of foolscap paper in his cupboard. There were more than seven hundred sheets. When the *landdrost* came to the farm, de Grevenbroek asked him about work opportunities in town, and if he happened to know about a farmer who might want to hire a carpenter for a week? Later he rode to Adam Tas on horseback. The man was still jovial, with a round face, a glass and a pipe in hand like the portly fellow in the painting by Hals, but his hair and beard had turned grey.

'Old friend,' said Tas. 'You must think like a Jew. Look around you, everybody in our little group is sixty-five, seventy years old. We have just buried scores, and there is much fear and apprehension among our people. You know exactly what is on their minds. So why don't the two of us buy some pine boards and screws, then we hire your man to make us twelve and a half coffins. The kind with the little pitched roof, so that if a man jumps up at the sounding of the trumpet he doesn't break his neck. Then we sell them to the richest men in the district. I know quite a few of those. We pay the carpenter, we make a nice profit, and each of us gets a coffin. No, I'm dead serious. I shall handle the business, you just write to your man and tell him to come.'

De Grevenbroek took Tas's hand, went down on one knee, pressed

the hand to his forehead. His tears moistened Tas's hand. As Tas helped
the secretary to his feet, de Grevenbroek thought: It is as if he's lifting
a drowning man from the sea.

'I myself would like to hear what happened, Mr Secretary. So much
has been kept from us.'

Pieter set up his workshop in the pressing shed on Tas's farm. Like
his brother he had dark brown, sharp eyes, and a habit of looking one
straight in the face until after he'd spoken his last word. Tas and de
Grevenbroek sat close to his workbench, one with a carafe and glasses
at hand, the other with paper, plumes and ink. But the man couldn't
speak, he warded off their questions. He could work, or he could talk,
but not at the same time. He was working on a coffin, his client had
to be satisfied. They must understand, he wasn't working for today's
bread but for tomorrow's. Every day he worked for his name, and his
name ensured tomorrow's bread. His late father had always said, if
people came to talk at his workplace on Cooper's Island: Wait, put in
the bung first, I have to think. If he cut a tenon too narrow for its
mortise, he had to throw away the wood; if he cut too short, it was
wasted. They could ask their questions, he would listen; but they had
to understand if he said nothing, because he had the grain to watch,
and tools were merciless if one didn't watch.

So they spoke in the late afternoons, and evenings. Tas made him
stow away and sweep up early, then they could talk. Pieter wasn't shy
to talk, not intimidated either by the one's wealth nor the other's learning. Tas couldn't help offering his wine carafe again and again, until de
Grevenbroek restrained him with a hand on his arm, asking him not
to cloud Mr Zaaijman's memory. De Grevenbroek would have liked to
ask him a hundred more things: What do you think of our government?
What does the future of the Koina look like to you? Do you see a
future for your children here? They're talking about a new outpost in
Mozambique for gold and slaves. Still more slaves here, what future?
But he refrained from doing so. What did it matter what anybody
thought of the future? The future unfolded as it must, blind, indifferent. At the end, he knew, Tas would give the man a present of wine.

He had the same build as his late father, he said, that was stocky, sinewy, brown. He should think that he had his father's nature, very calm, serene, but oh heaven, if an injustice was done to him, he instantly became a devil. It was very dangerous to be like that, he prayed not to be led into temptation. Something like these chisels, this awl, this bodkin, he preferred to keep at the bottom of his toolbox when they were not in use. His mother . . . he wasn't really sure what she'd looked like, a son doesn't look at his mother, and moreover in recent years, since she'd come here, she started looking different. Here people tended to dress from head to toe, with a bonnet on the head. How would one know what one's mother looked like? She had stopped laughing, her shoulders had sagged, her footsteps were slow. Many people around here looked like that, but on the island she'd been as young as her daughters. One could hear their laughter through the house.

Perhaps she'd been pretty in her childhood, as they called it. When they'd lived outside here on the farm, they'd gone to church on foot on Sundays, a long distance, and one day his mother had just said she didn't want to go any more. But his father still took the children, and the next time at the church he'd shown them a very rich man getting out of something like a coach with his family, Mr van der Byl, and his father had told them: 'That man was your mother's beau when they were young. If she'd chosen him then, you would also have travelled in a coach today.' He sounded unhappy. They refused to believe it.

Tas pointed the stem of his pipe at the eighty-inch coffin on the trestles. 'That is for van der Byl.'

'Father thought Mother had become ashamed of him, because we're poor.'

He wasn't present when his parents and brothers arrived in the country, but he knew now that they were poor and unhappy, and they remained like that and never became used to this place or felt at home here. Kept grieving, yearning back. He himself had remained behind on the island after they'd left, and once there was a message from them: 'Don't give up, we're coming back.' But they never came home again.

How the island was vacated? Look, first there were the two ships from the Cape to collect the free burghers. *Carthago* was too big for the anchorage at the Lodge and went to wait at North-West Harbour, from where it sailed for Batavia in early December, heavily overloaded and almost without provisions. Aunt Theuntje went with them to the East; his mother grieved a lot for her old aunt. As for *Mercurius*, it sailed from South-East Harbour with its people and their slaves for the Cape on Christmas Day, and at the end of January they were in Table Bay. All that was left on the island were the commander and his garrison, and a number of very dangerous runaways in the forest, and he. And the dogs, of course. He was about twenty at the time, and preferred to be left alone with his thoughts. Not that he was a terribly deep thinker, it was just that he preferred being on his own, like his father. Wherever he went, there were fifty dogs on his heels. Later the hunter came for them, luring them with meat; he tied them up in bags, and put them in the deserted cages and pens at Black River Mouth, to be released when the garrison was lifted, so that they could clear the island of game and afterwards of the runaways.

His father had told him how, when they'd arrived here at the Cape, they had struggled to find peace for body and mind. The youngest ones immediately fell ill of flu and all kinds of measles and whooping cough and chickenpox. Their house was cold, and although it was summer, it was as if they were all suffering from cold. Time and time again Johannes was struck down by his malaria. Every morsel of food had to be bought; there was no longer a chicken run or a vegetable garden where one could fetch what was needed. When his father wanted to keep a few pigs, he was forbidden. And the prices were high, shocking. He had to sell most of his slaves to acquire a small plot of land. His father would have liked to be near the sea, as he had the idea of making a living with a boat, as they had done on the island, but there were no longer plots to be had near the sea.

They had never intended to sell the slaves; most of them had been with the family for years, and his father had wanted to use them for fishing, in which case he might be able to keep two, even three boats. In the end he had to sell them, to afford that town plot and a single little boat, a one-master.

The plot was situated above the vegetable market on the mountain side. If you stood behind the house looking towards the sea, the well on the market square was about a hundred paces distant. Looking south, the slave lodge would be a hundred paces ahead, with the Company gardens on your right, and of course the hospital and the church and everything in front, with the slave lodge. His father had said: I've been without church for forty years, now my soul can come to rest at last. He immediately had the three youngest children baptised.

But the people, the Cape people, were strange. They, coming from the island were different, their clothes poor, their language old-fashioned. On the island they had used one or two Oriental words, but here there were many more, as well as Hottentot, and French, which one seldom heard on the island. They were also too direct. 'Good day, cooper.' 'Good day, commander.' 'Good day, *baas*.' Only when white-collars came, like Monsieur Elsevier, they would say: Your Honour. These people looked askance at them, nor did they always look one in the eyes, he'd seen that himself. His mother and father became unhappy, particularly about people. Look, on the island they had been respected. Yes, they were the commander's in-laws, but it was not about that, because they were humble folk, but they were honourable in their ways and an example to others, therefore big and small respected them, and because of his work they looked up to his father. The English governor from Bombay and his wife and children ate at their table, and others too, from his mother's damask and blue porcelain. Understand this, we were held in high regard, even among foreigners. And we children felt it. We were the Zaaijmans, it made us feel good, and safe. We would always have food, even if others were struggling. That was how vain we were. And what about it if we chose to walk barefoot?

But the Cape knew nothing about it. They were too absorbed by their own importance: who sat in the front pew in church, who was at that councillor's banquet, who walked about with a parasol as in the East, who had the contract for wine, for brandy, for meat. Even the wife of the man who had the contract to remove night soil went about with her nose in the air. But it was no laughing matter, Monsieur Tas. His mother was hurt if his father knocked on a door with fish and was sent round to the back door, to find the same woman opening it. Never in his life had he experienced that, and he was a Hollander. Later he was almost afraid of appearing in the street with his work. The people laughed at their canvas clothes and bare feet, and because one day they had unwittingly nearly sat down in the third pew. Here only slaves and Hottentots walk barefoot, and a white Hottentot was quite a joke. 'Are you from the Mourisies too?' they asked him.

Remember, messieurs, he himself had only landed here two years after his parents, and when he heard for the first time that they were called *basters*, he couldn't understand it, he thought it was just another word for people from the island. That was one reason why his parents wanted to get away from the Cape to a remote farm. But here in Stellenbosch it was the same, and *that* was why his mother no longer wanted to go to church, because the woman who got out of the coach might ask her husband: What did the *baster* woman want from you? In the Cape his mother hardly ever ventured out in the streets; it was half-blood and the *baster* and the *wasmeid*.

His brother-in-law Abraham de Vries, who was married to his sister Maria – poor Maria and her son Pieter also died from the pox – plunged himself into debt for life, borrowing money to buy a quarter of the meat contract. 'If I don't trade, we will never get out of our need, Father-in-law,' he said. 'Only money will save my family from this curse. I cannot steal and I don't know how to beg. I shall have to borrow to save our lives.' So he jumped into deep water; never in his life could he get out of debt, he was too old for it, but that was all right, they left the town. The government gave him a loan-farm in the Butcher's Field, which he called Vriesefontein. It is a few hours up the coast, and there he put sheep and a few cattle to graze. His second wife cared for sister Maria's children, and Abraham was hard-working and still had his trade as ship's carpenter.

Brother-in-law Herbert Jansz had asked his father to accompany him to the Castle on account of the ambergris, with the receipt Commander Roelof, that is to say Diodati, had given him for it. And you won't believe it, messieurs, they told him: Yes, it is in order, the ambergris weighed forty-two pounds over there, but on our scales it is only thirty-five pounds.

'Somebody stole seven pounds.'

'What, what, what?' Others came into the office to listen.

'Cut off, stolen. Here is my receipt for forty-two pounds.'

'Your scales were wrong. That's all.'

'This is a receipt from the Company.'

'Go to Amsterdam if you don't want to take my word, and if you think you can afford the passage.' It was because of their clothes, and because they had Herbert on a lee shore, that the *seur* spoke like that. 'But you will find it is not worth your expense, because we have a letter from the Lords, and if you come back tomorrow, you will see for yourself that the price is down from five dollar an ounce to one dollar, and a bottle of arrack. Only, you will have to wait, as we don't have arrack in the cellar right now.'

'Come, Herbert,' his father said. 'It seems to me they don't need us here.'

His father had to sell his fish out on the anchorage, when there were ships. If there were none, he made *boucan,* or *bokking* as they call it here, or his mother made *karri* for the winter, as most of the time he had to wander up and down without selling anything. Otherwise he could give it away to one of a few honourable gentlemen for next to nothing. Father could see that it was closed shop, as he was not going to sell fish on the streets. 'No,' they would tell him at their doors, as they examined his father's fresh fish: 'I am a Cruywagen man, I buy my bread from Brand and my fish from Cruywagen.' His father could see that they were cutting us out. What was it that bound them, he wondered, were they all members of the same family? But the whole town could not be Cruywagen's family. We talked a lot about what the reason might be. We tried to make enquiries too, but they said nothing, just looked at you, closed up in your face. What has happened to freedom, monsieur? To buy and sell, for legal money at essayed weight, that's the law of the weighing house in Vlissingen, is it not? But they refused to let us in.

It was in that time that he received word: Don't give up, we may be coming back, because his father was still hoping that he and Abraham and Michiel and Herbert could get together and return home. We'd rather bear hurricanes and malaria and the runaways who cut off your head, than this place. And they wanted to get away before the flag was lowered at the other side and the occupants of the island lifted off, before they burned down the houses and turned the dogs loose into the forest.

They went to the Castle, the four of them, with their petition. After that it was a month before the Council met again, and one day they were informed of the date on which they had to appear. But the governor refused to listen.

'Didn't your Commander Momber inform you why you had to be evacuated? So that you wouldn't provide for the enemy?'

'Yes, he did. But whether we provide for the enemy, or the enemy occupies the island and does it himself, is the same thing. The island won't lie deserted for long.' When Momber had summoned the people from all over the island, the burghers should have taken their weapons with them and told Momber: Here you see the dark mouth, we refuse to go, and we challenge the Company to come and take us away. He was sure they could have succeeded. Even the runaways took a chance on freedom. The burghers discussed it, but his late father refused to take the lead. He promised his mother: I shall take you home. If it hadn't been for his late father, it would have been a different story today. But now it is too late, for all time.

'Then why did he want to take her back later?' de Grevenbroek asked.

'Mother no longer knew the Cape. She no longer knew anybody here, and came to resent the people that looked down on her.' And they were so poor, with the three small children. They would have to go out begging in the winter, when his father couldn't go to sea. His father was ready to approach the church for poor relief, but his mother pleaded in tears: 'Please don't, Daniel, otherwise everything would have been in vain.'

His father had the audacity to tell the governor that he knew why they wanted to close the island. It was because the English were becoming too strong in the East. And the Cape couldn't buy their tobacco and sugar because Huydekoper or somebody else held the contracts, but there was no reason why a few families could not continue there on their own. Why couldn't they try to make a living from provisioning for the ships?

The governor laughed at him, because the East India Company had been given a monopoly by the States-General as the only Dutch firm with the right to trade in those waters. His father was desperate, because they were in a position to help him if they wished, yet did not lift a finger. They were sitting high and dry in a boat seeing a man drifting away, but refusing to row closer. They saw him struggle, and sink, they stared, but made no sound. He was desperate. He said: Try to tell that to the English. And to the governor: You're throwing our island like bait to the English, so that they're rather take that than snatch this Cape out from under your backsides.

But it was like a shout against a storm. What could one man do against the Lords? It was all to no avail. He must have felt: this time it is no longer Daniel Zaaijman against nature, or even against the Devil, but against his fellow man, and that made him very sad and depressed. Then his father and mother put their house in the Cape on the market, and bought the farm here outside Stellenbosch for about five times as much, but they thought: as long as they could get their children away from that town. They simply had to start again, and work hard. Their beginning was a wet and cold winter, with snow white on the mountains for months; they had drifted away from other people.

He wasn't here yet. He was still on the island, and had to see Batavia first. That still lay ahead of him, and because like any young man he was looking forward to bearing the name *orang lama*, the delay made him impatient. But it dragged on for two years. The Cape sent the old ship *Overrijp* to lift the settlement and take it to Batavia, and a month later the galliot *Mercurius* arrived as well, to take the last ebony and wagon parts and the Company's twenty slaves back to the Cape. But *Overrijp* had to turn back with a damaged bow, and only by pumping day and night could it reach Table Bay again. There it was written off as totally dilapidated. Why hadn't they noticed it before, messieurs? They could have been killed, all of them. Then *Beverwaard* was sent in its place to lift off the occupation.

It must have made the Cape governor look up when *Mercurius* also returned, without slaves or wagon parts. Or perhaps not. Perhaps the honourable gentleman didn't even raise his head from his desk. The ones who did get a fright were they, on Mauritius. The galliot had been in front of the Lodge for only a few days, when the hunter came to tell Commander Momber that there were four giant French warships in North-West Harbour, looking for food, fuel and liquor. Momber didn't want the French to discover the island's weakness, for then things might turn out badly for the Honourable Company, so he dispatched *Mercurius* back home in a hurry with a letter to Governor van Assenburg. In that letter he informed the governor of the wretched situation of the outpost. They were living on half-rations, with boiled water as their only drink, and there was no rice, bread or vegetables. After all, Batavia had instructed them to stop gardening, yet had not sent them anything either. The service contracts of the garrison had all expired, they were demanding discharge and their wages, scorned discipline, refused to serve. They accused the commander of hoarding away food, they insulted the officers, lazed about on Kroonenburg, or wandered through the forest, coming and going as they wished. Everybody, even he, went about in rags. After *Mercurius* had left, Momber personally walked the distance to North-West Harbour to speak to the French.

Commissioner van Hoorn happened to be here at the Cape on inspection at the time, and he saw to it that *Mercurius* was immediately dispatched with food and clothing, and to find out whether *Beverwaard* had completed its mission to the island. Six weeks later *Mercurius* arrived in South-East Harbour. The Lodge and all the outbuildings had been burned down, the post was deserted. Only a dog barked at them from the end of the quay. After a search of two weeks, *Mercurius* turned back for the Cape.

Pieter learned from shipmates about this last visit by the Cape galliot *Mercurius*. In his turn he could tell a story that would interest seamen. The French had taken whatever they wanted at North-West Harbour. He was relieved that his parents were no longer there, for the waste of timber and meat was revolting to see. They had thrown more than eighty English prisoners of war ashore to fend for themselves, and then spent six weeks hunting, carousing, plundering, before they set sail again, and he was left standing there on the beach without a coin in his hand to show for his service to the French flag. A month later, *Beverwaard* arrived at the anchorage in the mouth of Black River, to lift off the occupation. He himself piloted the ship in, brought it to anchor, and then accompanied the captain and a boatswain to inform Momber and hand over the letters. Momber wanted *Beverwaard* to shift to South-East Harbour, to ship in everything from there, but Pieter felt uneasy as he could see that there was a hurricane brewing, for the first time in perhaps eight years, and he warned Momber and the captain about it. He had to make the commander and the captain understand: *Beverwaard* could not be loaded here in the shallows before the Lodge, they themselves would have to carry everything to North-West Harbour and go on board there, and head for the open sea before the hurricane cornered them inside the reef.

Fourteen cannon, building material, smithing implements and garden tools were buried at the Lodge. Gunpowder, nails, pots, porcelain, pistols, drums with their snares, and hundreds of other objects in perfectly good condition had to be thrown into the ditch. It was heart-breaking to see the smashing and destruction and waste. Holes were drilled into all three boats, and then they were sunk with their anchors on board before the French Church. It was all a single day's work. After sunrise on the second day, the Lodge was set on fire, and 174 people, among them the sick, the old, women and infants, with their possessions loaded on ox carts, or carried on their heads or in their hands, left South-East Harbour on foot in a single group, into the hills of Lemoenbos Plain, to walk to North-West Harbour. It was a trek of four, maybe five days.

In North-West Harbour *Beverwaard*'s officers could feel the change in the weather, the ship's head jerked down by the anchor. Its captain was at the Lodge, and the first mate had to move *Beverwaard* to the open sea. Through a runner, the first mate knew about the people on their way, and he had to choose between risking the ship in a hurri-cane on the inner anchorage, or getting out and leaving the travellers to their fate on the exposed beach. One of the two parties would not survive, he thought, but for the moment he decided to keep the ship at anchor. From one watch to the next the swell in the bay rose higher, the sky darker, the waves crashing over the reef fiercer. White and high the waves came storming in over the reef. The ship began to stagger at its anchors. On the second morning the chief mate had *Beverwaard* on three anchors, its tops struck, its rigging stripped to the bare masts, and every hatch nailed down. On the morning of the fourth day it started raining softly from the north-east.

Well, the messieurs probably know that, but the distance they had covered on foot, from one corner of the island to the other, was like the distance from the Castle to well beyond Stellenbosch. An able man could not do it in a day; it was uneasy terrain, rough, densely wooded, with deep ravines in which rivers streamed in the rainy season. And they had ox carts to push through, and the children and baggage to carry, and the old people. In the Wet Forest, at Deer Hole and Cold Pipe, their many feet churned the ground into a deep muddy mess. He remembered the relief as they arrived on the other side, on a reasonably even plain. He remembered how they could still see those weird peaks which they call the Three Teats, standing in the distance like these three fingers of his, black against a blood-red sunset. After that it was once again one hill after another, uphill, downhill, one after another, uphill, downhill, and it was also the last time they saw the sun for a week.

As they went through the kloof on the fourth afternoon into the half-circle of mountains at North-West Harbour, where they rise behind the bay like the shards of a shattered cauldron, the sky to the north-east was overcast, grey, low, dense, with the strong, warm wind at their backs. Their commander and the captain made them put down some of their baggage there, so that they could move on before the hurricane trapped them among the mountains, but some of the people were reluctant to lose their only possessions, especially the poor slaves who had so little, so the people had to be forced to open their bundles, sort through them, and discard. About a dozen people could not go on, but the commander had stretchers made from coats and sticks, four men to a stretcher, with the sick and their baggage on top. The rain started coming down heavily. He was thankful for being young, and not causing anybody any trouble, but it was the captain and the commander who helped them through. The one encouraged them, cajoled them, arranged at every resting spot for them to fold their hands and pray; the other herded them on through the mud with great oaths and blows of his cane and threats of a thrashing.

On the high plain before the mountain it was raining so hard that they could no longer see the bay, and they didn't know whether the ship was still there. Two men had to go ahead to see, and to warn the first mate from which direction they were coming. Then he had to hoist the tops and square his yards and get ready, and send rowing boats to the beach, but should the wind get too strong, he had to think of the ship only and head out to sea under foretop and mizzen. The wind shot the rain like arrows into their faces, they were drenched to the skin, water was filling all the ditches around them. They crossed the last rivers with churning foam up to their armpits, with the children tied to ropes so that they couldn't be washed away. When they reached the beach in the dark evening, the ship was gone. They tried to find shelter in the abandoned houses – there was no time to secure them – and spent three days there on the bare floors without food or water, while the houses were torn apart above and around them piece by piece by the screeching storm, and the rain and sea together washed over the foundations. He had never been so cold on the island before, down to the marrow, and some people died there.

Two days after the hurricane *Beverwaard,* its foremast snapped off short and without mizzen or maintopyard, came back from the horizon again, to the inner anchorage, and they had to break wood to make fires, the good red and black ebony of the Company.

Batavia was a bustling, sweating and stinking, stuffy little city, with a thunderstorm every afternoon. A number of canals at the back of the city were sweltering, overgrown with grass and shrubs; it would take years to be cleared. The people from *Beverwaard* were first lodged in the Castle, which was built almost on the beach, as the messieurs would know. The government provided them all with clothes on an advance, and he was given work in the timber yard at Onrust, where their ship was also careened for caulking and repairs. His friends, each with his own plans, parted there. Commander Momber, he knew, died a few months later, after a recurrence of his fever. For some time he went about with the idea of signing on as a soldier to see where it would take him, but that would mean being away from home for three more years, and he was worried about his parents who might not have transplanted well, as the proverb has it about old trees.

At the time they lived on the farm Patryzen Valleij, of which he didn't know yet, and they were suffering there. They could make a living for the family, but that first year there was no profit to pay off anything on the purchase price, and his father mortgaged the farm to keep them afloat for a year or two. The whole property had not yet been cleared or ploughed, and when his father discovered that he no longer possessed his former strength, they were stuck with the farm, as they could no longer afford slaves. Yet they were happy there, convinced that with hard work things would improve. His father sowed some wheat for bread, and bought two cows on credit, and some lambs and piglets to sell when they had grown.

The second winter was even wetter than the first, once again with snow far down into the valleys, and almost all their poultry died from cold. The other animals fell ill when the winter grass came out; a neighbour told his father that it was from eating tulips. Before their wheat was ripe, his mother and father decided to sell the farm with the remaining stock and the standing harvest to make it more attractive, and to see if they could pay off the mortgage and perhaps have something left to pay off part of the purchase price. His father said he was going back to the sea; the sea had always treated him well. So they returned to the Cape.

They could get the old cottage back, but only to rent. His mother's courage was broken by something that happened there with one of their old slaves. It had been her own slave and she'd sold him as she had no food for him. But when the farmhand at Elsenburg bought him, they were glad, because on a farm like that he would have a better life than on their impoverished plot. Unfortunately there were two slaves who soured his life with bullying and fighting and false accusations and abuse. They told the farmhand that the Mourisies slave was casting spells on them, he wouldn't stop. To put an end to the daily fighting the farmhand of Elsenburg sold him to Eksteen from the Tygerberg.

And from there he ran away one night, and threw a burning faggot on the roof of their slave lodge, so that the two liars might burn to death.

They caught him there as he stood looking how everybody ran with water to douse the flames, and beat him up and handed him over to the *landdrost*. But he made no attempt to defend himself, and merely said that he preferred death to life. His punishment was to be burned to death. A hand for a hand, an eye for an eye, as the law prescribed, and as an example to others. Pieter's mother was deeply saddened, believing that it would not have happened if she hadn't sold him. They would not allow her to speak to Moses in prison, and on the day of his execution she went in black clothes, and stood right in front against the low wall, waiting for him to be brought out. She loudly called out to him, but he didn't look up. The firewood had been stacked around the stake like a kraal, and Moses was fastened to a short chain, so that he could either run or remain standing. As the smoke and flames enveloped him, she could hear him say: '*Dio me pais.*' This was the man who had eaten with her at table. She remained there until they had scooped up the remains with shovels and flung it on a cart. A hand for a hand. His mother no longer wanted to live.

His mother scrubbed for people, on her knees to keep the three little ones at school. With her Indian cotton and her porcelain she parted piece by piece to those who kept on nagging, like the church elder, and the doctor who took care of the children when they had the measles. All she said was: We cannot eat porcelain. She took in laundry, her hands turning red from washing and ironing to keep her family. And fortunately he could help his parents a little with carpentry. At the time he was assistant to the carpenter who partitioned the church pews with small doors, to prevent others from taking your seat. The messieurs should know: '*In my father's house there are many mansions.*' But there was still a long road ahead before he would have the paper of apprenticeship. There was no longer lunch at home, and for going to sea his father had only his own *bokking* and well water drawn at the vegetable market, to last him the day. In summer his father used to go out to sea before sunrise. He could still see him walking through the door, with his large hat of plaited palm fronds, and the square rattan

basket with his hooks and lines and sinkers, and his water bottle and
bokking – always the best in the house, his mother saw to that.

In the early dawn one day in February his father went to sea and
fortunately it was full moon. The wind was north, and he effortlessly
glided downwind, behind the Lion's Rump, behind the Signal Hill,
behind the Lion's Head, until he came near the little Hottentot's
House. As he moved on, he pulled in his handlines: cob and fat black
hottentot, and lots of mackerel. He drifted right through a shoal of
mackerel, and looked south in the dawn: What mountain lies here
before me now? He looked again. What is wrong with my eyes today?
There stood the Company's entire return fleet of thirteen capital ships,
loaded to the hatches, anchored in the moonlight, directly across his
path. You already know, messieurs, about what happened; what scandal,
what misfortune came to the Cape with those ships. He nearly fell
over backwards into the water with shock. Was he imagining it, at
four o'clock in the morning? But that was what it was, those were
the home-bound ships, the entire return fleet. He rolled up his lines
and loosened and shook out his sail to move in under the flagship's
quarter. What was going on here today? Here were the good Lords'
thirteen ships a morning's sailing from their destination on a terrible
lee shore. Why didn't the admiral move into the bay, to the roadstead
in front of the gallows? Messieurs, how can you believe something
like that today, even if you can understand it?

All he can think now is: the return fleet had been set down there
in front of his father. Still and dark the fleet lay in the moonlight, and
his father moved in under the anchor cable of the flagship, but keeping
his eyes open, in case there was some design in it. He grabbed hold,
and shouted: 'Hoy, *orang lama*. What are you doing here, are you catching
fish?' The anchor guard jumped up from his sleep and shouted: 'Come
alongside, mate. The skipper wants you.'

What his father heard, from the mouths of Admiral van Steeland and
Captain Tiemermans, was that the fleet had been waiting there since
the previous sunset. Where is your signal flag on Lion's Head? The
admiral asked. There had to be a flag on the Lion's Head to show that
the Cape was under Dutch rule, everybody knew that. Since sunset

they had been studying Lion's Head in the moonlight every hour through a telescope, but there was no sign of a flag or a lookout. The skippers were called to a meeting, and decided rather to move a small distance out to sea and anchor there, ready to slip in case they had to run, while waiting for sunrise. If there still was no sign of life then, they had to continue to the fatherland, but it was a hard thing to do with disease on board. And now there was this fisherman calling to them before daybreak.

Had it still been Mauritius, his father thought, he would have been as rich as a lord by now, for life. But perhaps it was still a lucky day. He told the officers that he knew nothing about the flags on Lion's Head, it was the first time he hadn't seen a lookout up there, but that was the acting governor's business. The Cape tended to be lifeless at times. All he could offer, was to pilot them in and then take a few people to the Castle, but it would cost him his day's bread. Don't worry, the admiral said, we shall reward you, and I also know you fellows all have the name of an inn and a good washerwoman who pay you a premium. Now look, there are three thousand seamen here, and you can rely on it, your friends will be well rewarded. His father thought: this is indeed a lucky day, and he tied his little boat to the ship, sold his fresh fish to the cook, piloted the fleet in, and that afternoon went home with a basket of washing on his shoulder. All of it was ladies' things from the admiral's wife and daughters, to be washed and bleached and starched. This was a blessing from above. How happy Pieternel would be, he thought, that their family had been saved by this merciful coincidence. But you already know, messieurs, that in that basket he carried the pox ashore.

His parents were among the first to fall ill. His father asked him: Take the little ones away from here; I shall hire a servant to look after us. We can afford one now. So he left with his three brothers for his brother-in-law Abraham and his stepsister in the Butcher's Field, to his everlasting regret, because there too he brought death with him. But he could still return with two of the three to bury his parents. And he still cannot understand why the two lookouts had not been on duty that night. Even Acting Governor Helot had spent the night in his country residence when the fleet arrived, and had no inkling of it at all, with no refreshment or hospital or other services ready for the fleet. And his father, if only he'd left the fleet there for the harbour master to pilot in, then the fiscal and the surgeon would have gone on board first, they would immediately have discovered the pox and dispatched the ships to lie in quarantine behind the island until it had run its course. But what does it matter now? It has already happened.

The orphan master applied on behalf of his brother Daniel for the Company to employ him as sailor. The Company had advertised for seamen for the new outpost to be established in Mozambique, to buy slaves. The Council had made it clear: no more free burghers from the fatherland, but black slaves from Africa to do the Company's work in this country. He advised his brother rather not to go, but Daniel is a youngster who likes to do as he pleases. At the Cape an expedition leader has been appointed. It is *Seur* van Taak, recently married to the youngest daughter of this farmer with the eighty-inch coffin, van der Byl. But East Coast fever is a terrible scourge. May the Lord protect the poor people. It will be the old story from the beginning. And afterwards? Afterwards, afterwards it will again be as if it has never been. In all of this only the sea remains the same, empty and endless.

This is how history repeats itself: the first time as tragedy, the second time as farce. One circle merges into the next, nobody notices it. The great ocean moves on and never changes. A man becomes a ship, ships become people. A man becomes an island, islands turn into people. A man becomes an ark, a sanctuary in endless space.

Thus was slain the dragon Time, the damsel delivered, his errand done. There remains for the clerk only to draw up his testament. As witnesses he calls heroes of liberty: Adam Tas, van Brakel, van der Byl. For his funeral he wishes to be carried, wrapped in his blue blanket, by two slaves, after sunset, to a grave on this farm, without procession or prayer, and on his grave a plain stone with the words: *Hic exspectat resurrectionem.* J. G. de Grevenbroek.

Acknowledgements

My thanks to Helena Scheffler, cultural historian, thalassophile and friend, for her share in this long story. Also to Tafelberg Publishers, who arranged for the manuscript to pass through her hands. Where I changed her facts, it was for the sake of the reader, and I accept responsibility for it.

The possibility that Pieter van Meerhof's name may originally have been Peter Havgard, was suggested to me by the genealogist Mansell Upham.

That history repeats itself, the first time as tragedy and the second as farce, is a humorous adaptation by Marx, more than a century ago, of a statement by Hegel, another century earlier. The truth is much older. There is no history other than the analysis and interpretation of documents, a search for survivors in endless space.